**Two brand-new stories in every volume...
twice a month!**

Duets Vol. #47

Bestselling Harlequin Temptation author Lori Foster
returns this month with a dynamite Double Duets
focusing on the Sawyers siblings, Annie and Max,
and their adventures in love. "Ms. Foster's engaging
style and sharp wit are a powerful combination
that will impress readers from all genres,"
reports *Rendezvous*.

Duets Vol. #48

"Love and laughter is never more delightful
than from the clever pen of Cathie Linz," says
Romantic Times Magazine. Cathie leads off this
month's Duets with the delightfully funny
Between the Covers. Joining her in this volume is
talented Jane Sullivan with a wonderful tale in the
MAKEOVER MADNESS miniseries.

Be sure to pick up both Duets volumes today!

"What on earth are you doing here?" Guy barked

Annie frowned and shook what appeared to be a cooking spoon at him. *Dear God, please don't let her be cooking.* He could likely survive anything but that.

He shuddered as he tried to figure out what to do. There was no place to hide in the kitchen. Hobbled as he was by his crutches, trying to run would be ludicrous. The only thing worse than being caught in the raw with Annie as a spectator would be to put on a bigger show by fleeing.

She advanced on him. "Uh, Guy, do you realize you're naked?"

Guy glared at her and waved one crutch. "Of course I realize it! It'd be a little hard to miss, especially with the way you're staring!"

Annie didn't answer, and she didn't avert her gaze. "Look at my face, dammit!"

She did, but she took her sweet time about it.

For more, turn to page 9

"Why chase me?" Max asked

Maddie took another step closer to him. "Because you're not just any man, Max. You're a man of experience, a man with an awesome reputation. I've been good all my life and all it got me was a guy who preferred kinky feathers to me!"

"I hate to break it to you, but feathers aren't really all that kinky."

"You didn't see where she was tickling him!"

Max coughed. "So, you want to use me to notch your bedpost?"

She bobbed her head, her look endearingly sincere.

Max was offended. "All because your idiot fiancé fooled around on you?"

"It was so humiliating, I wish I'd just left him tied there forever."

Her grumbling tone made Max smile. "What *did* you do?"

She cleared her throat. "I went out to dinner. And a movie," she added with a wince.

For more, turn to page 197

HARLEQUIN DUETS

ISBN 0-373-44113-4

ANNIE, GET YOUR GUY
Copyright © 2001 by Lori Foster

MESSING AROUND WITH MAX
Copyright © 2001 by Lori Foster

Annie,
Get Your Guy

Lori Foster

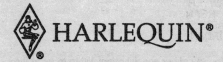

HARLEQUIN®

TORONTO • NEW YORK • LONDON
AMSTERDAM • PARIS • SYDNEY • HAMBURG
STOCKHOLM • ATHENS • TOKYO • MILAN • MADRID
PRAGUE • WARSAW • BUDAPEST • AUCKLAND

Dear Reader,

Well, readers, you wanted Annie. And you wanted her with Guy—you were all quite specific about that! Luckily that's what I planned all along! I hope you enjoy the way I got them together, even though poor Guy really had a tough time.

And Max...oh boy. *Poor Max.* He really thought he had things all figured out until a homely dog and a pushy woman took him by surprise. Max had to learn the hard way that life is best when we have others we can love.

I received so many letters requesting these two stories. Thank you for that! I hope I did the characters justice, and that you close this special Double Duets with a smile on your face, and a warm heart.

Do let me know what you think! I love hearing from readers. Contact me at P.O. Box 854, Ross, OH 45061 or lorifoster@poboxes.com

Best wishes,

Lori Foster

Books by Lori Foster

HARLEQUIN TEMPTATION®
786—SAWYER
790—MORGAN
794—GABE
798—JORDAN

To Barb Hicks, a wonderful friend
and dedicated reader. I can't thank you enough for
all your support! You give me my daily smile, Barb.
Thank you for that.

male response that had her hesitant. "I don't know
Lace. I mean, I don't think any personality traits
she sexually inspired. "

"No doubt about that. Which is why you're so-
ing to solve that. "

Annie's eyes widened. "But I've never seduced
anyone in my life. Last time I tried that with Clay
I hadn't hit on Tim in he

1

_____

ANNIE SAWYERS felt her jaw drop at the impressive
pile of magazines, articles and books her friend had
just carried in. She'd had no idea the topic could
be so...extensive. "Good grief. Are all these on
sex?"

Lace huffed as she dropped the large stack onto
the floor. "Every single one."

"But...I thought sex was...you know, pretty
clear-cut and basic."

Lace chuckled. "Variety is the spice of life. And
believe me, they make fascinating reading."

"You've read them all?"

"These, and dozens more." Lace was a well-
known sex therapist and Annie's best female friend
to boot. Just recently, she'd married Annie's older
brother—to the shock of the rest of the family. Not
because they didn't adore Lace, but because Daniel
was such a stuffed shirt. The two of them comple-
mented each other perfectly.

Lace straightened and gave Annie a smile. "If
you're not inspired after this, I give up."

Annie didn't say it, but inspiration wasn't her
problem. It was feminine confidence, and lack of

male response, that had her hesitant. "I don't know, Lace. I mean, I don't think Guy particularly wants me sexually inspired."

"No doubt about that! Which is why you're going to seduce him."

Annie's eyes widened. "But I've never seduced anyone in my life. Last time I tried that with Guy, he thought I was challenging him to arm wrestle. And he let me win! Do you know how humiliating that was?"

After three blinks, Lace asked, "How in the world did he confuse—"

"Maybe I should have taken off my clothes first? Do you think it'd help if I got—"

"No! No, don't do that." Lace gave her a wan smile. "I'll help you. Your seduction techniques will be unparalleled. Irresistible. Provocative. I promise, he won't stand a chance."

"I dunno." Annie felt the tiniest bit queasy. "What if I do this, take my best shot, give it all I got…"

"Annie."

"…and he laughs at my technique and pats me on the head? That's what he usually does, you know." Annie frowned, hating her own hesitation on this particular subject, but still very aware of her irrefutable shortcomings. She was a wonderful businesswoman, strong, independent, capable, but she wasn't beautiful and sexy like Lace. She wasn't feminine.

She had no siren's call.

For the most part, Guy thought of her as a tomboy and a little sister. She loved him beyond distraction, more so every day it seemed, while he was content to give her brotherly advice, and the occasional stern lecture on propriety. He didn't seem to realize that her efforts at looking more appealing, more womanly, weren't meant for the general male masses, but rather his very individualized notice. All he cared about was protecting her—the same as her two overbearing brothers. It was more than any mortal woman should have to bear, and was behind her request for help from Lace.

Lace gave her a patient look. "Annie, Guy might not even realize you're interested. He's been with your family for a long time, now. And with you being the only female in a household full of males, he's naturally adopted the same attitude as your brothers and father. It could be he just needs a bit of…encouragement."

Annie sighed. Guy was her very best friend, her confidant, and he knew her in ways her family didn't. She'd been in love with him forever. Still, what Lace said did make a bit of sense.

"I suppose that could be it." Guy had been living in the Sawyers household since his early high school days. He and Daniel were sophomores when Guy's father had to take an early retirement due to health problems. Guy's mother and father had moved to Florida, but Guy and Daniel had been friends forever, played sports together, hung out together. They were both popular, and they'd had their futures mapped out. It only made sense that Guy would want to finish school in his hometown. So he'd been welcomed into the Sawyers household.

Lace nodded. "Guy has pretty much adopted your family as his own. And now that I'm in the family, too, I see how they tend to put you on a very high, pastel-pink padded pedestal. They don't want to think about you leaping off the damn pedestal in search of debauched entertainments."

Lace laughed. She'd always been amused at the way Annie was pampered by the men in her family. "I imagine Guy feels no one is allowed to have sexual thoughts about you." Then, with a prissy voice, she added, "You're too pure."

"But I don't want to be pure!" To Annie, that word had almost become an insult.

"Pure is rather boring, isn't it?" Lace agreed. "But you haven't helped that image by turning interested men away, you know. You've got 'sweet and innocent' stamped all over you, and it's my guess the men in your family like it just fine that way. I know Daniel does. He's fighting the image of you as a grown, mature woman with all his might, despite my encouragement to the opposite."

Annie's groan was long and frustrated. If even Lace, whom Daniel adored beyond all reason, couldn't turn Daniel around, how could she ever reach Guy?

"Of course I turned men away," Annie mut-

tered. "The only man I want is Guy. I fell hopelessly in love with him when I was eighteen."

Lace sat down and crossed her long legs, her
expression rapt. "Details if you please."

Annie stared at Lace, debating. The memories of
that long ago day were precious to her, and she'd
never had anyone to share them with. She hadn't
dared tell any of her female friends, not when they
were all actively lusting after Guy themselves. And
she could just imagine what would have happened
if she'd tried talking to Max or Daniel about it. Her
brothers gave new meaning to the term "overprotective."

She sighed, then opened up to Lace. "Guy had
caught me crying in the backyard. It was Mother's
Day, and I was upset, though why I don't know. I
don't even remember my mother, she died when I
was so young. But it seemed so lonely that day.
Dad always took off then, during every holiday,
really, like he couldn't bear the memories after losing Mom, but I know Mother's Day was especially
hard on him. And Daniel was studying, Max was
probably off getting into trouble somewhere." She
glanced away. "And I just felt so…alone."

"I understand."

As always, Lace's tone was gentle and commis-
erating. Annie really appreciated having a sister-in-
law that she could confide in. It was a unique thing,
and very nice. "Guy started out by sitting on the
porch swing with me and patting my back in that
awkward way men have when they don't know

what to do with a female. It really bothered him whenever I cried, I guess because I didn't do it much. Being raised with all boys has a way of toughening a girl up.''

Lace made a face. ''I know they treated you more like a little brother than a sister.''

''They did their best, especially since Dad was so withdrawn. And for the most part it was fun. I got to do all the things they did, fishing, swimming in the lake, playing baseball. They always included me. Well, except that one time when I caught them playing spin the bottle with a bunch of neighborhood girls. I thought Daniel would box my ears for spying.''

''The hypocrite.''

Annie laughed. ''It made them very uneasy if I acted at all feminine. The first time I wore panty hose, or when I got my ears pierced, they harassed me for days. And I remember when I had to ask Max to go to the store for me to buy tampons. He actually said, *what for,* and when I just glared at him, his ears turned red!''

''Did he go to the store and get them?''

''Oh sure. Max would do anything for me, but he didn't like it. After that, he made Daniel do all my shopping.'' She laughed again. ''When Max first noticed I'd matured, he accused me of 'sprouting breasts' as if I'd done it on purpose just to nettle him. He went out and bought me a bunch of vests. When I refused to wear them, he got into the habit of walking in front of me, so no one would notice.''

Lace had to bite her lip to keep from laughing. "Max is a rascal."

Annie shook her head. "As if anyone would notice such an unnoticeable attribute." She stared down at her modest bustline. Puberty had come and gone a long time ago, so she supposed it was time to give up hope.

Lace made a disgusted sound at Annie's distraction, then prompted, "So you were in the backyard, crying, and Guy was trying to console you…?"

Just the memory made Annie warm inside. "He patted my shoulder, then hugged me, asking me not to cry. He kissed my cheek, like he'd done a dozen times. I turned toward him, he drew a big shaky breath, and the next thing I knew, he was holding my face and giving me this killer kiss and it was *incredible.*"

"You mean—"

"Yeah—" Annie nodded enthusiastically "—tongues and all."

Lace struggled with a smile. "I was going to ask if that was your first kiss, Annie, not the actual particulars of it."

"Oh." Annie frowned in thought before answering. "No, it wasn't my first kiss, but it was definitely my first lust."

"Ah-ha. Got to you, did it?"

"Boy did it." The kiss had been a hungry, *I-want-you-bad kiss*. It had startled her a little at the time because it was the first time she'd felt a man's tongue, the first time she'd really understood lust, or wanting a man so much. She'd been hugged up to Guy's muscled chest many times in the past, but that time it was different because he didn't feel like a friend—he felt like a man, hard and hot and so sexy.

She'd belonged to Guy ever since. She still wanted to curl up and savor the memory whenever Guy failed to see her as a grown woman. For at least that one moment, on that one day, he'd wanted her. Almost as much as she wanted him.

Lace's look was thoughtful. "What did you do when he kissed you?"

"I'm not really sure. I know I stared at him and I kind of froze. Guy started apologizing, stammering all over himself, backing away as if he thought I might leap at him. Then he suddenly just walked off and he never mentioned it again. Since then, it's almost like he's avoided me. Except when he wants to lecture me on something."

Lace snorted. "He and Daniel are a lot alike."

"Like brothers."

"So Guy's never kissed you other than that one time?"

It was difficult trying to explain the way their relationship had gone over the past few years. Annie was twenty-five now, but Guy treated her almost as if she were still eighteen and off-limits. She understood his reservations when she had been young and inexperienced.

But now? Well, she was still inexperienced, but he couldn't know that for sure. And at twenty-five, she sure wasn't too young. But whenever she got too close, he started putting up barriers and she hated it.

"Once," Annie said, dredging up the wonderful memories, "on New Year's Eve two years ago, I took him by surprise. We were in the basement looking for more folding chairs because the party got a little bigger than expected. When the clock suddenly chimed and we heard all the shouts, Guy laughed because he knew everyone was kissing. I didn't give him a chance to think about it. I…well, I sort of jumped him."

"And?"

Frustrated, Annie muttered, "And he let me kiss him for all of about thirty seconds. Then he stumbled back like I'd slugged him. He accused me of being drunk even though he knew I hadn't had a drop. He hustled me back up the steps, keeping me at arm's length—and Guy has incredibly long arms. He spent the rest of the night glued to his date while watching me like I was a molester of innocents."

"That's it?"

"No. There's been a handful of times, but it's usually only because I'm able to take him by surprise. Like when I turned twenty-one and he gave me my necklace." Instinctively, her fingers curled over the small, glossy black pearl on the delicate silver chain that she never removed. It felt warm to the touch. "I threw myself against him that time and tried kissing him. He laughed, but only until I caught his mouth. Then he kissed me back."

"Ahh. Progress."

"For about three seconds."

"Let me guess. He ran again?"

"Yep. Like someone had scorched his very sexy backside."

"Men can be so difficult."

Since Lace was not only a sex therapist, but married to Annie's brother Daniel, Annie figured she knew all about difficult men.

"He's not like that with other women, you know."

"He's thirty-five, Annie. Surely you don't expect him to be a monk."

"No. I've heard plenty of women talk! According to them, he's a fabulous lover, but I can't even get a second look out of him."

Annie picked up the book on top of the stack and flopped back onto the couch. "I'm dying here. All my sexuality is going to atrophy if Guy doesn't take notice soon."

"I have a feeling he'll come around."

"And I'll turn into an old dried-up loaf of whole wheat while I'm waiting." Annie opened the book, surveyed a few pictures, then tilted the book for a better angle. "Good grief!"

"Looks interesting, doesn't it?"

Actually, it looked more than interesting. It looked downright seductive. And enticing. "Is that even possible?" She turned the book, trying to figure out what body part belonged to which person.

"Trust me, it's possible."

"It doesn't look very comfortable."

Lace peered over her shoulder, then shrugged. "It's...creative, I agree."

"Guy will never go for it."

Lace burst out laughing. "He'll go. Trust me."

Annie desperately wanted to be convinced. Not a day went by that she didn't imagine what it would be like to be married to Guy, to sleep with him every night, to have the right to touch him however and whenever she wanted.

The thought of however and whenever had kept her awake many a night.

She wanted them to share a life, to share everything. "You're the therapist."

"Only a sex therapist, Annie. And since you haven't gotten to the sex part yet, I have to admit I can't predict people's reactions about situations. I'm only going on good old female intuition when I tell you Guy must be somewhat interested. If he really thought of you as a little sister, as he claims, none of those hot kisses ever would have happened. Even you have to realize that."

"Do you really think so?"

"Yes, but honey, wanting and loving are worlds apart. Do you think you can handle it if Guy makes love to you, but isn't *in* love with you?"

This was where it got tricky. Unlike Annie, Guy had no problem dating—frequently. He had his pick of women and most of them were more like Lace— sophisticated, sexy businesswomen with a style all

their own and lush bodies and self-confidence oozing out of every feminine pore.

Annie's body wasn't something to brag about.
She was built okay, and she wasn't ashamed of her
body, but it certainly hadn't driven Guy into a lust-
ful frenzy yet. And though her small bookstore was
a source of pride for her—something she loved
dearly—it was far from a glamorous job.

It seemed to her that if Guy was going to fall in
love with her, he'd have done it by now. But she
couldn't simply give up. And at the moment, she
only wanted to concentrate on one thing at a time.

"The truth is, Lace, when I imagine going my
whole life without ever getting to be with him, I
feel miserable. I want *something,* even if it doesn't
last. And who knows? Maybe if we do make love,
and he doesn't want me after that, I'll finally be
over him. It could be a sort of exorcism. But I have
to at least try." Then she winced. "If you really
think he'll want me, that is. I don't relish the idea
of making a complete fool of myself."

Lace lifted her brows. "Men are pretty basic in
some things, Annie. Guy's already shown a physical interest, and even though you're always denying
it, you're a real cutie. I'm guessing—but it is only
a guess—that he'll want you once you give him a
proper nudge in the right direction."

"Maybe," Annie allowed. She was used to em-
ulating the men in her life, going after what she
wanted with full force, unwilling to let incidentals
discourage her.

She said aloud, "But...*seduction*. I don't know anything about seduction." The idea tempted her, getting to explore the long length of Guy's lean body, getting to touch him and kiss him to her heart's content.

It would take forever.

But there were drawbacks. If she bumbled it and lost Guy's respect, on top of everything else, she didn't think she could bear it.

Lace reached out and patted her arm. "That's my field of expertise. So with my help, and the books, you'll ace it. I promise, most unattached, interested men are not too difficult to seduce. The only problem now is going to be picking the time and place."

Annie had her mouth open to offer a suggestion—such as the sooner the better—when the doorbell rang. She looked at Lace, her brows raised. She didn't want any interruptions now, not when they were just getting to the best part. She scowled at the door. "Sorry. Let me see who it is."

The second she opened the door, her brother Daniel burst inside in a very uncharacteristic way. "Listen up quick. Guy is right behind me. He'll be here any minute. Don't tell him I just got here, but I had to talk to you before he did. I knew he was coming here, so I raced to beat him."

Annie stared owl-eyed. "What in the world is the matter?" Daniel, her levelheaded, oldest brother was definitely in a dither about something.

He drew a deep breath. "Guy's getting married."

That blurted comment had Annie groping blindly

for a chair as the world seemed to tilt beneath her. *"What?"*

Obviously frazzled, Daniel roughly ran a hand through his hair. "He said he plans to ask Melissa to marry him." Before Annie could find a response to that, Daniel raised his hands in immense frustration. "I know. I know. She's all *wrong* for him. I tried to tell him that, but he's not listening to me. So this is where you come in, sis. You're close to Guy, in some ways more so than I am. Make him think it over, Annie. Reason with him. Try to get him to take some time…"

Daniel suddenly stopped talking, as if only then realizing how quiet she was. "What's the matter? You look ready to faint."

Annie tried to answer him, she really did. Her mouth moved, but nothing came out. Marriage? All her plans were disintegrating before she could even try them out. Her soon-to-be-learned excellent seduction skills would never find fruition?

Thank goodness for Lace, who stepped into the breach. "Your delivery needs work, Daniel."

"Lace!" He eyed his bride with ill-disguised suspicion and just a hint of lust. "I thought you were out shopping today."

"I was. I bought a couple of up-to-date books that your little sister's conservative bookstore doesn't carry." She flashed her patented wicked grin, guaranteed to make him wary.

Daniel's eyes narrowed. "Books on what?"

Annie loved her brother dearly, and she knew he

loved Lace. But to him, Lace was everything Annie wasn't, sexy and seductive and mature and totally female from the top of her platinum blond head to the bottom of her long sexy legs. When they'd first met, Lace had thrown Daniel for a loop, driven him crazy, then to Annie's relief, she'd returned Daniel's love. The two of them were perfect together, but Daniel was still skeptical about Lace assisting in Annie's transformation from tomboy to femme fatale.

He didn't want her to transform.

Lace shrugged her shoulders. "Books on sex, of course."

"What?"

With a taunting grin that had Daniel's glasses fogging, Lace said, "We're gathering modern info on seduction, sweetheart." Then she leaned close to him to whisper, "Annie's seduction as a matter of fact."

Into the quiet that followed that statement, Guy suddenly appeared in the open doorway. "Who the hell is trying to seduce Annie?"

Not a blessed soul, Annie wanted to scream, but she was temporarily sidetracked by her one true love.

The wind outside had played havoc with his ruthlessly short, light brown hair. It stuck up in odd, spiky angles, making his hair look like an animal's natural defense.

His ears and his lean cheeks were ruddy from the cold and his endlessly long, leanly muscled jean-

covered legs were slightly damp from the freezing
rain. He had the collar to his bomber jacket turned
up and Annie could see a wrinkled flannel shirt beneath. It didn't look as though he had shaved today,
and his brown eyes were red rimmed, giving the
impression he hadn't slept much the night before.

He looked tall and lanky and tired—and so sexy
she wanted to take his hand, grab a book and head
for the nearest bedroom.

Annie slowly stood while devouring him with her
hungry gaze. "No one is trying to seduce me."

Lace smiled, examined a fingernail, and announced, "Annie's going to do the seducing."

Both Guy and Daniel turned to stone. *"What?"*

Annie sent Lace a reproving glance, which she
ignored. That was the problem with having a friend
who was just a bit zany, with too much intelligence
and imagination for her own good. Annie held no
fear that Lace would actually give her away. In fact,
she probably thought she was helping by whetting
Guy's curiosity. But Guy didn't look whetted, he
looked appalled. And to mention it in front of Daniel? Her brother was not a man taken to frivolity,
despite Lace's constant assurances to the contrary.

"I'm twenty-five years old," Annie explained,
trying to calm the two men staring at her with the
same morbid fascination they might give to a train
wreck. "I think my sex life should be my own business."

Guy shoved the door shut behind him then

crossed his long arms over his chest. Somehow he managed to look even taller. "What sex life?"

A good question.

Again, Lace spoke up. "You certainly didn't expect her to remain a virgin forever, did you?"

"It was a nice thought," Guy muttered.

Daniel rounded on Lace, his face still red. "This is all your doing, isn't it?"

"I certainly didn't arouse her, if that's what you're talking about."

Daniel sputtered while Guy's eyes widened. "Annie is aroused?"

He sounded horrified, and then to her discomfort, he looked her over as if checking for signs. Annie squirmed.

Lace shrugged, her grin in place, looking a bit smug. "It's been known to happen."

Guy noticed the books and magazines then and stalked forward. "My God. You've got a literary arsenal here." He picked up the copy of *Kama Sutra* and flipped through it, his eyes growing darker by the moment. His gaze cut to Annie. "How many men were you planning on seducing? A baker's dozen?"

She could feel her face turn hot. She hadn't figured on anything as outrageous as a group confrontation, for crying out loud.

With few choices, she tried to bluster past her embarrassment. "If need be."

"Why?" Guy demanded, at the same time Daniel said, "The hell you will!"

She glared at each man in turn. "I don't need to explain myself to either one of you."

Daniel brushed past Lace and picked up *The Year's Most Popular Erotica*. He skimmed the titles inside, then gawked at Annie. "Good grief, Annie. What are you doing with this stuff?"

Since Annie wasn't quite certain what she was doing, she lifted one shoulder and grimaced a smile. Lace went on tiptoe to peer over Daniel's shoulder. "Ahh. Erotica. I brought that one so Annie could compare. You know, most women think their fantasies are odd or different or even weird. I wanted Annie to have an idea of what some of the most popular fantasies are, so she wouldn't suffer that insecurity."

Daniel scowled at Lace. Guy looked positively apoplectic.

Lace remained supremely unaffected by their silent condemnation. "She does have fantasies, you know."

Twin masculine stares turned Annie's way. She cringed, wishing she could find a hole to hide in, or else a big piece of tape to slap over her friend's uncensored mouth. "Uh, Lace..."

"I also brought the first and second issue of *The Joy of Sex*. Great text, and the illustrations are superb—and very inspiring."

Since Lace's course of action had effectively silenced both men, Annie felt a bit braver, and decided to join in. She picked up a slim volume and pretended to be familiar with it. "This one is on the male…uh, orgasm. How to make it better.'' She almost choked as she said it—then immediately imagined Guy in the throes of passion. She stared at him, unblinking.

"Actually," Lace commented, "it's how to make it better than great." She waved a hand. "Not that most men need any help in that area. But I couldn't find that many books on helping women increase their own pleasure. I brought some articles though. They ought to ensure that things go satisfactorily for you."

Guy wheezed as if he'd gotten sucker punched in the gut.

Daniel huffed and stomped over to first one wall then another. His dark gaze bounced off Lace several times while he paced. Lace just smiled her serene smile at him. She knew Daniel could never stay angry at her for long. And Annie knew, deep down, he loved Lace's free-spirited, natural way. She only wished she could be so cavalier.

Guy finally caught his breath, then looked slightly ill, but he refrained from glaring. Guy seldom got really angry, and when he did, only those who knew him well were aware of it.

He wasn't so much mad now, as confused and obviously irritated. Confused because, after all, Annie was "pure," and irritated because she didn't want to be.

Seeing Guy like this was pretty intriguing. Generally, he got along fine with everyone, even with their middle brother Max, who had a hard time getting along with himself, much less anyone else. But Max liked Guy. Everyone liked Guy. He was an unofficial member of their family. Except to Annie.

She wanted more, so very much more.

Unlike her family, she wanted to thoroughly debauch Guy, and have him debauch her in return.

In a lethal, almost predatory tone she'd seldom heard from him, Guy asked, "Who are you planning to seduce, Annie?"

Lace chuckled and leaned toward Guy with a wicked gleam in her eyes and a conspiratorial stage whisper. "The guy's a real dope. Can you believe he hasn't even noticed her, and she's sending out all the signals? Annie's getting desperate." Then Lace's gaze settled on Annie, and she said, "I have a feeling the guy's getting desperate, too, if you know what I mean. He's thinking of taking some pretty desperate measures himself."

Annie felt her heartbeat pick up. Surely Lace wasn't suggesting Guy would marry another woman just to set himself apart from her? That seemed to be stretching it just a bit. Or was it? *Oh please, don't let him be in love with another woman.*

"It's not that Perry fellow, is it?" Guy growled. "He's not at all right for you, Annie. We talked about that, remember?"

Perry Baines was a nice enough person. He worked with Guy at the company as an advertising executive, and he had been persistent in his pursuit. But Annie wasn't interested. She'd only gone out with him as a friend. *And to make Guy jealous,* a small voice prompted. But since it hadn't worked, since Guy had only warned Annie that Perry was a wimp, without a single sign of jealousy, she ignored the small voice.

"Perry is...nice," she said, unwilling to admit she had no prospects at all.

Guy whirled around and said to Lace, "You know I love you to death, Lace, and I think you're the best thing that ever happened to Daniel—"

"Gee, thanks, Guy." Daniel's tone was wry.

"—but is it really necessary for you to encourage Annie in this ridiculous business?"

It was Daniel who answered. "Lace finds it impossible to keep her nose out of anything. She's been working on fixing Max up, too."

Annie winced. Now that was a dead-end endeavor. Max would never settle down with one woman. He had wanderlust in the worst way.

Annie made the attempt to regain control. "Both of you just leave Lace alone. She's certainly being more helpful than you two would have been."

There was a general enthusiastic grunting of concordance from the men on that point, since their idea of help would have been to dissuade her—or lock her in a closet.

Suddenly Guy frowned at Daniel. "What are you doing here?"

"Ahh..."

"He was just leaving with me," Lace said, saving Daniel from a lie. "He promised me a ride

home.'' She latched onto Daniel's arm, hugging it
to her breasts, and at the same time scooped up her
black wool cape. Everything Lace wore was dark.

Since Daniel was caught, he didn't refute Lace's
claim, but neither did he look happy about it. He
pulled Annie close for a hug with his free arm, then
whispered, ''Talk some sense into him, sis. Make
him think about what he's doing.''

Annie nodded. ''I'll try.'' *Boy, would she try.*

Daniel resisted as Lace attempted to drag him out
the door. He caught Annie's hand. ''And for Pete's
sake, don't seduce anyone!''

Lace gave a theatrical groan. ''Big brothers are
surely a nuisance. I'm glad now I didn't have any.''
And with that, she led Daniel away, leaving Annie
and Guy alone. Annie bit her lip.

Silence filled the small apartment after the door
closed, then Annie turned to face Guy. He watched
her closely, which sent her heart into a tailspin. She
tried to swallow her nervousness.

Damn, why hadn't Lace given her a few basic
instructions before taking off? She didn't think
there was any way she could wing it on her own.

His eyes narrowed speculatively, and in a low
voice, he asked, ''Well, Annie? You want to tell
me what this—'' His hand swept the pile of books,
''—is really all about?''

2

NOT ON A BET, Annie thought, wary of the way Guy watched her now. She stiffened her shoulders and refused to look away from his probing gaze. He probably thought he was intimidating her.

In truth, she was getting a little turned on.

Having all of Guy's undivided attention made her warm inside, and a little giddy.

"What I do, and who I do it with," she said with what she hoped was a decisive tone, "is my own business, Guy Donovan."

As she spoke, she began gathering up the books. He was right, there was enough reading material to keep her busy for a month.

One thin book fell open to a particularly graphic image of a couple intimately, happily entwined. The woman, positioned mostly on the top, wore a lecherous grin and little else. Somehow Annie couldn't quite picture herself propped up on Guy that way.

But the lecherous grin, oh, she could easily give in to that right now!

Annie quickly scooped the book into the stack. She peeked at Guy, and knew that he had seen the picture, too. A strained expression replaced his frown.

Annie cleared her throat. "Why are you here?"

Guy shook his head as if to clear it. "We can talk about that later."

"We can talk about it now. All other discussions are over." Planning to be a seducer was difficult enough. Talking about it with the seducee would be impossible. She needed time to formulate her plans without Guy's verbal assistance.

Guy tilted his head, then closed his large hands over her shoulders as she started past. Her knees almost turned to pudding.

He was so big her head barely reached his chin, but she loved every single inch of him. All her life, she'd known she was loved by her family. But her father had always either hidden away, too overcome with his grief from losing his wife, or too involved with his skiing equipment business, to pay much attention to his children.

Daniel had filled in as best as he could, so he was as much a parent figure as a big brother, which gave him a double-whammy impact. But Daniel had always been studious and very serious about his education. He'd seemed a bit overwhelming to a little sister who made B's with an effort and was shy to boot. And Max...well, her brother, who also happened to be the epitome of a middle child, was just plain difficult and always had been. She never doubted his love, but he was more likely to tease her than hug her. That's when he was even around. Max was traveling more often than he was at home.

Guy gently shook her out of her reverie. "Promise me something, honey. Before you actually decide to do anything, talk to me about it. Okay?"

Since she suspected at least a little discussion would be necessary before she could seduce him, Annie nodded agreement. Anything to put this subject to an end. Then she remembered that Guy was supposedly marrying Melissa, and there wouldn't be a chance for her to do any seducing at all.

Her heart punched against her ribs with the heavy throb of panic. Damn him, why was he so blind and stubborn where she was concerned?

Guy watched her with a concerned expression. "You okay, honey? You want to talk about it?"

Guy was almost always there for her when she needed him—just not in the way she needed him now.

"Sometimes talking doesn't do any good."

He obviously didn't like hearing that. "You know I'll help you out any way I can."

"Really?" Maybe if she just told him she wanted to sate herself on his body...but no. She wanted so much more than that. She wanted sexual satisfaction, but she also wanted his love.

She wanted everything.

Sadly, she shook her head. Guy stepped forward and hugged her close and Annie found her nose pressed to the lower portion of his hard chest. She drew a deep breath and sighed. Man oh man, he smelled so good.

"I have needs," she said, her words muffled by his flannel.

Guy froze. She could feel the accelerated thumping of his heartbeat. "Uh...money?" he asked hopefully. "Business advice? Because you know I'd gladly—"

"Personal needs." Then she said more boldly, *"Intimate needs."*

Guy turned her loose like she'd caught on fire. "What the hell do you mean, talking like that?"

Innocently, she asked, "Like what?"

His big hands flapping in the air, Guy said, "About...*needs* and all that."

Annie realized she was botching it in a big way, but darn it all, she was tired of pretending she wasn't a woman. In the past, Guy had always just seemed to know when she felt alone or lonely or sad. Even before he'd come to live with them, he never appeared to mind when she hung around, which meant a great deal to a young girl who didn't make friends easily.

Being with Daniel Sawyers and Guy Donovan had given her instant popularity in school, especially with the girls who vied for the older boys' attention. Both Daniel and Guy had always been well known in the community, and sought after as eligible bachelors from the time they'd graduated high school. But they each had planned their futures, so while they dated, they didn't get serious with any one female. And they had always allowed her to tag along.

Through it all, Annie had fallen hopelessly, irrevocably in love.

This was the first instance that she could remember where Guy wanted distance between them. She hated it. Summoning up a skimpy smile, she asked, "Don't we always discuss things, Guy?"

His gaze moved over her face, as if searching, then he spoke very slowly. "Yeah. Most times we do. I wouldn't have it any other way, Annie."

"Then you should know that, despite how you see me, I'm a woman. I'm not sexless."

His face colored and he sputtered, "I never said—"

"And I *do* have fantasies."

"Good God!" He took the books from her hands and set them aside. "Listen to me—"

"Do you want to hear my fantasies, Guy?"

He swallowed hard. He cleared his throat. "Okay. Yeah. We can...uh, we can talk about that." He led her to the couch and dragged her into a seat. "Now the thing is, fantasies are fine. I just don't think you're ready to actually seduce anyone. Definitely not that ass, Perry. See what I mean?"

Annie's eyes narrowed. "You don't think I can do it."

"I never said that, dammit!"

"You think I don't have what it takes. You think I'm not sexy enough."

"I think you're plenty sexy!"

"Really?" Annie scooted a little closer to him, beyond pleased that he'd made such an admission. Progress, she thought, whether he realized it or not.

Guy stared into her eyes, then at her mouth, before he growled and leaped away from the couch. He stalked around her small living room, grousing as he stepped over and around the variety of sex books, and finally stopped in front of her with his hands on his hips. Looking far too resigned and determined, he said, "Not to change the subject—"

"Ha!"

"But I came here to tell you something."

"This sounds serious." She felt herself shaking inside, with dread and heartache.

"I suppose it is. Not bad, really. But...well, I'm going to ask Melissa to marry me."

Even though she already knew it, Annie flinched. Hearing it from his own mouth was worse than when Daniel had said it. "Is that so?"

"I know it's kind of unexpected, but she'll be the perfect wife for me. Even your father thinks so."

"Dad?" Now how did her father get into this? It was true he valued Guy very highly. After all, neither of his sons had followed in his footsteps to help run the prized family business. Only Guy had done that, and done it very well, so well that Dan Sawyers seldom set foot in the offices anymore.

Guy had also taken over the family home, given that they'd each gotten apartments. Guy's presence there had changed Annie's memories of the house, and made them all pleasant. He'd insisted that their family home should be preserved, and if Annie ever wanted it, it would be waiting for her.

She wanted to share it with Guy, but now he was talking about marriage to Melissa.

Annie considered the possibility of hitting him over the head with one of the sex books, since that might be the only use the book got. But he was so much taller than her, that would be difficult.

"Your father let me know," Guy said, "in very blatant terms, that it was time I had a wife. He's changed a lot since Daniel's marriage. He looks at things differently now."

Her father *had* changed. Used to be, she seldom saw him at all. His grief had sealed him away to the point he avoided most reminders of the love he'd lost, including his family. His feelings for his wife had been so all encompassing, nothing else had mattered. Only very special events had warranted her father's attention.

When her mother died, Annie had only been two years old. She didn't really remember her mother, but years later she'd overheard Daniel saying to Guy that he'd lost both parents on that awful day. Now that Annie was older, she realized what a godsend Guy had been for Daniel. Guy had been there for him as he tried to bear the brunt of the familial burdens.

Guy interrupted her melancholy thoughts. "Your father suggested she be someone smart, savvy, independent, a woman who could make a man comfortable—''

Standing to face him, Annie said, "There you go. He obviously wasn't talking about *Melissa*."

He gave her a familiar chastising look. "Don't be sarcastic, Annie. Melissa understands the business. And she's the only woman I've been seeing lately, so of course that's who Dan meant. I doubt he expected me to grab some stranger off the street."

She swallowed hard, trying to get the melon-sized lump out of her throat. "But *Melissa?*"

Guy stifled a laugh and reached out to yank on her hair. "Listen up, brat. Just because you don't like her doesn't mean she's bereft of qualities that appeal to a man."

No no no! Annie did *not* want to hear this. She slapped a hand over Guy's mouth. He very gently pulled it away, then held on, rubbing her fingers between his own.

"It's not the end of the world, Annie, despite what your big brother thinks."

Annie chewed on her lips a moment, trying to gain composure. It wasn't easy with Guy touching her. "And what does Daniel think?"

"He says I'm allowing myself to be seduced by the idea of marriage, not by the bride. Marriage isn't something to enter into lightly. There should, at the very least, be strong emotions involved."

Guy sounded just like Daniel as he said it, even to the point of mimicking Daniel's somber voice.

"Well, he's right," Annie said, quick to defend her brother. Especially since they seemed to be on the same side for a change. "Daniel should know, what with just getting married and everything."

"The way he floundered with Lace hardly makes him an expert. He almost lost her before he realized he was madly in love."

"Do you...that is..." Annie couldn't quite force the words out of her mouth, not at all certain she wanted to know.

"Are you trying to ask me if I love her?"

Annie could have guessed, given the way he said those words, that Daniel had already been over this question many times, too. Though they had ended up in vastly different careers, Daniel and Guy were still very close.

Annie looked up at him, and her heart squeezed painfully tight. "Do you, Guy?"

He looked so incredibly, impossibly masculine standing there staring down at her with such intensity. It didn't matter that Guy had originated the "grunge" look long before it became popular. It didn't matter that his short hair was always going in odd directions, or that he often skipped shaving in the mornings, which left him with a faintly appealing beard shadow.

Guy was kind and generous, strong and proud. He worked hard for her father, and had nearly doubled the company since assuming the position as the "heir to the throne." He valued his friendships and was loyal to those he loved. He never tolerated injustice or bullies and he went out of his way to help others.

He was tall. He was gorgeous.

And he smelled so good.

She loved him.

Guy jerked off his coat and tossed it to the couch. His well-worn jeans hugged his thighs and his faded flannel shirt hung loose over a snug gray T-shirt that clung to his flat abdomen. His very large, booted feet were braced apart, and his frown was fierce enough to make most people quail in apprehension.

People who didn't know him well.

"Do you?" Annie asked again.

"No." He sounded disgusted, with himself and with her for asking. "Not the romantic, mushy heartsick love that you're talking about. But I suppose I respect her—"

"You suppose?"

"Dammit, Annie. You're as stubborn as your brother."

And doubly motivated.

"I think we'll make a good marriage, all right? I'm almost thirty-five, and it's time I started a family. The last thing I want to do is wait until I'm old, then end up with an only child, like my parents did."

Annie knew how much he had resented being alone all his life, and how much he had gravitated to her busy family. Guy's father had been somewhat ill for a long time before he retired, and between work and the restrictions of his illness, he hadn't been able to do the things with his son that most men did. Her father had filled a huge void in Guy's life, at least some of the time.

Annie softened. "That was difficult for you, wasn't it?" She wanted to understand why a man like Guy would want to marry a woman he didn't love.

"It wasn't that big of a deal," Guy denied. Then he continued, "But it's time I settled down, and since I haven't found any one particular *perfect* woman, it might as well be Melissa. We get along well. And God knows, she fawns all over me."

"She fawns over the business." Melissa had made no secret of the fact that she wanted to work with Guy.

Guy grinned. "She's not immune to my physique either, brat."

Annie considered hitting him.

"But you're right. Since she's involved with her own company, I can talk to her about the business without confusing her. We have similar interests—"

At that little bit of idiocy, Annie promptly choked. Everyone knew Melissa was a woman out to make the most of her life, be it fun, men, or money. Guy was just the opposite. He genuinely cared for people, and would give a man the shirt off his back if he needed it.

Guy gave her a mocking glare. "I should think you would be happy for me."

"I should be happy that you're planning to—"
Marry the wrong woman. "—make the biggest
mistake of your life?"

"Actually, I'm trying to avoid a few mistakes."

Annie had no idea what that meant, and Guy
didn't look willing to explain. She drew a deep
breath. "What you need, Guy, is some isolated,
quiet time to think things over, to really decide
what it is you want."

"That's Daniel's speed, Annie. Not mine. I'm
the mover and shaker. Remember?"

Annie tossed up her hands. "Those are Dad's
words, and you know how ridiculous they are. It's
insane that Dad's still disappointed just because his
son refused the family business and became a very
respected doctor instead. Good grief, you'd think
Daniel was a derelict the way Dad goes on."

Guy laughed. That was one of the things Annie
loved most about him. He always had a ready smile
or a friendly laugh, even when he was frustrated.
"Dan's as proud as any father could be, even of
Max, and heaven knows that proves he's a proud
papa for certain since Max *is* a derelict."

Annie shook her head, trying to conceal her own
smile. "Max is just trying to find himself." At
least, that was what Lace had claimed.

"In the wilds of Canada? All alone?"

Annie shrugged. "So Max is a little different.
That's no reason for Dad to complain."

"Your dad enjoys complaining and you know it.
That's why he grumbled so much when you bought

the bookstore and went into business for yourself. He likes to grouse.'' Guy glanced around her newest selection of reading material and shook his head. ''Heaven knows he'd have a conniption if he saw what you've gotten into now.''

''Evidently,'' Annie said, ignoring his reference to her seduction plans, ''he enjoys playing matchmaker too.''

''He only made the suggestion, Annie. But he was right.''

Annie was of the opinion he couldn't be more wrong. She desperately needed to convince Guy of that. ''You know my dad isn't the most astute of men. That's why you're running his business for him.''

Guy shrugged. ''He needed help. Daniel wanted to be a doctor, you wanted to be independent of the family, and we're still trying to figure out what the hell Max wants to be, other than a pain in the ass. Dan needed someone.''

''So you felt obligated to be there for him?''

''Not obligated,'' Guy quickly denied, but Annie could see the lie in his expression. ''Dan would never put pressure on me, you know that.''

''He's pressuring you to get married!''

''No he's not. He just…suggested it.''

''And you feel obligated to do as he asks.''

''Will you stop putting words in my mouth? The fact is, I respect Dan. A lot. He made it possible for my father to retire early. And he did take me in and treat me like one of the family.''

Which, since Dan tended to hide from life, wasn't really saying that much, at least in Annie's opinion. She wished Guy's mom and dad were here now. They were wonderful people who had worked for her father for years. They were friends as much as employees, and Annie knew her dad wanted only what was best for them.

They were also very reasonable, and would probably be able to talk some sense into their only son. "Have you told them about Melissa yet?"

Guy shook his head. "After I propose and Melissa says yes, I'll call them. Or maybe fly down to see them." Then he added with a touch of enthusiasm, "You could go with me. Mom would love to see you again."

And Annie would love to see her. Mary Donovan had done her best to mother Annie until they'd moved to Florida. "Just me, you and Melissa on a honeymoon trip, huh? Yeah, I can see what a fun trio we'd be."

Guy frowned, then turned away. "Yeah. Maybe not."

Annie reached out and touched his forearm, bared below his rolled-up sleeves. The warm, smooth muscles bunched beneath her fingers and turned rock-hard. The impersonal touch she'd intended was forgotten as she got lost in the feel of him. Guy looked at her over his shoulder, one brow raised in question.

Annie dropped her hand and cleared her throat.

"You haven't mentioned marriage to Melissa, yet?"

"I was waiting for the right moment. I will soon, though."

Annie felt renewed hope. There was still a chance to steer him around. Melissa would never make him happy. Guy might not be willing to admit it, but she knew he wanted a family of his own. Melissa wanted to get ahead without any encumbrances, especially encumbrances that required diapers and midnight feedings. She'd never love him, never make him and their marriage a priority.

In a way, Annie would be saving Guy by forcing him to see the huge mistake he'd be making.

She could save him by seducing him.

Annie pondered her own forced justification of what she planned, but found no real drawbacks. Feeling lighthearted again, and just a bit anxious, Annie asked, "You feel like pizza? I'll treat, sort of a we-hope-you-come-to-your-senses celebration."

With a wry smile, Guy said, "That can go both ways, you know. Maybe with a little time you'll get over this dumb idea of jumping some guy's bones."

"Well," Annie said, looking at him through her lashes, "I had hoped to be a little more subtle than that, but if you think jumping his bones might be more successful—"

"No!"

Annie grinned and he added, "Bone jumping is not the way to go."

Advice from Guy? It'd be a perfect addition to her plan. "Okay, so why don't you stick around and you can give me some pointers on what is—or isn't—the way to go?"

His face once again a mottled red, Guy snarled, "Now how could I refuse such a wonderful opportunity?"

She wouldn't try to make a move on him tonight, she decided. After all, she hadn't even read the books yet. And since Guy was the only man she could ever remember wanting, she knew nil about turning a man on. But she could test the waters, so to speak. And if she could get him to open up just a little, maybe she'd be able to find out specifically what it was *he* liked—and then she could use it to her advantage.

A few months ago, when she'd confided in Lace that she wanted Guy, Lace had given her several suggestions on how to find out if Guy was indeed interested in her or not. And true to Lace's predictions, he hated it if she flirted with other men, if she went to a singles' bar, even when she dressed in clothes that showed her more feminine side.

But then, so did both her brothers, so that really hadn't told her a thing.

Maybe now was as good a time as any to try another experiment. Her heart raced with nervousness—and anticipation.

She gave Guy a fat grin. "Call and order the pizza, then make yourself comfortable. I have a few quick things I have to do."

He nodded, his gaze wary now as he focused on her bright smile. Annie wondered just how he'd look at her when she finished getting ready. One thing was certain. Before he tied himself permanently to someone else, he would see her, actually *see* her, as a woman, and not just the younger sister he never had.

And then he could make his choice.

3

GUY LET OUT the breath he'd been holding as the
bedroom door closed behind Annie. He felt tense
from his toes to the roots of his hair, and that was
saying something since his hair was so short, roots
were about all he had.

His present mood had nothing to do with this
wedding business, though he was half-dreading that
already, too. No, it had to do with Annie. It was all
her fault.

Seduction? What the hell did his sweet little Annie know about carnal seduction? Guy snorted to
himself. Nothing. She knew absolutely nothing
about it, he was sure of that. Why, she'd seldom
even dated, and never seriously! Not that she
couldn't if she chose to.

Most times she seemed unaware of it, but Annie
was a real looker. Though she might be a petite
little thing, her gentle curves were in all the right
places, perfectly symmetrical, perfectly balanced.
Perfect.

Good God, now she had him thinking about her
curves.

He swiped a hand over his face and paced to the

couch. The phone sat on an end table and he called the familiar number of their favorite pizza place. After he replaced the receiver, he looked around, trying to find something to occupy his mind other than Annie's body.

Or her plans for seduction.

Or her selection of reading material.

The books were impossible to ignore, given that they were scattered everywhere, the titles fairly screaming up at him. Sex, sex, sex. In Annie's apartment, where sex didn't belong.

He didn't want to, but he picked up *The Joy of Sex* and skimmed through it. He got hot under the collar and hot in his pants, at the same time. His brain felt confused and bruised as he imagined Annie looking through the same book, planning on incorporating what she saw with some faceless, nameless man. *Dammit.*

Guy paced some more. Whoever the guy was, he wasn't good enough for her. Not if Annie had to resort to seducing him. Was the guy a blind fool?

Women like Annie were rare. She was kind and gentle and smart and she knew how to take care of herself, though her brothers spent the better part of their lives trying to do that for her. Guy supposed he was guilty as well, only to a lesser degree. But she was such a tiny thing, with such an enormous capacity for compassion, it would be easy for someone to take advantage of her.

The thought of someone breaking her heart filled him with a killing—and jealous—rage.

He knew what he had to do then. Once he resigned himself to his fate, he actually felt a bit better. Guy sprawled on the couch and put his feet up on the square glass coffee table. While he formulated his plans to save Annie from her own curiosity, he idly flipped through the books. They weren't without their appeal, he had to admit. In fact, they were downright sexy as sin. And Lace had been right; the pictures were exquisite.

Annie definitely needed his protection. A sweet little thing like her could easily be swept away by the sexual promises the books described. It would be a great injustice for Annie to waste her innocence on a jerk who didn't really want her, who might not appreciate her. *A guy she had to seduce.*

An image of that damned Perry fellow came to mind, the way he looked at Annie, with the familiar sign of lust in his eyes. Guy's palms started to sweat. He definitely would not let Perry touch her.

He wiped his hands on his jeans, then decided he'd just have to help her, whether she realized she needed help or not.

It wouldn't even be that difficult. There was an easy camaraderie between them. Guy had felt it from the first time he'd met Annie, when she'd been no more than elbow high to him. With ten years separating them, he'd always considered her something of a baby. She'd been all big blue eyes and wild dark hair then, with skinny little legs and a shy smile. But she'd trusted him. And he'd liked her. Whenever Daniel had been too busy studying, or Dan had been working, or Max had been harassing, she'd come to him. Her faith in him, her friendship, was something he'd always hold dear, something he valued more than anything else in life.

Their relationship had been strained on occasion as Annie matured; there were times when his riotous hormones possessed his mind and his body, blocking out all rational thought. He'd forgotten that she was his best friend's baby sister, and done things then he shouldn't have done.

Like kiss her.

And touch her.

And want her.

But for the most part, he suppressed those urges. *For the most part.*

There were still nights when his subconscious took over and he woke up from a dream of loving her and suffered immense disappointment. What he needed, he'd decided—thanks to Dan's less than subtle hinting—was his own woman. Then he wouldn't use Annie to fill all the gaps in his life. It wasn't fair to her to make her a surrogate mate just because he couldn't find a woman he wanted to get serious with. It was a lamentable breech of friendship to use her that way.

And maintaining his friendship with Annie was definitely a priority. He was close to Daniel, but the male-based friendship had restrictions, rules that couldn't be ignored. With Annie, he didn't have to worry about being one of the guys, about maintain-

ing his macho image. He loved Daniel—and even
Max—like brothers. But it was Annie he was totally
at ease with.

Because they were so damn close, it was easy to
let his thoughts go wandering into taboo directions.
But it shouldn't be that way. And as soon as he
married, it wouldn't be. There would be someone
else to fill the void.

Before he got engaged, though, and everything
changed between them, he'd take care of this one
small problem for her. That's what friends were for,
and Annie was still his best friend. She always
would be. She deserved a guy who'd chase her, not
the other way around.

After coming up with a course of action, Guy
immediately felt more relaxed. Hell, if he was home
and in his own bed now, he might even be able to
sleep. God knew he hadn't gotten a wink of rest
last night, he'd been so keyed up with thoughts of
his future.

He was busy reading a small book on sensitive
parts of the female body, nodding in recognition of
most and raising a brow over those he doubted,
when Annie walked in. He looked up, and the book
fell from his hand, landing with a thump on the
carpeted floor.

Every male-inspired cell in his body sprang into
full alert, shooting his relaxed state straight to hell.

He gulped twice, tried to speak, and decided the
effort was beyond him. He shook his head instead,
trying to gather his frayed senses. Annie gave him

a slow, sleepy smile, and glided—*he'd never seen her glide before*—on bare feet over to the couch.

"I thought about what you said, Guy." Her voice was low, throaty. Seductive! Guy gripped the sides of the couch to keep himself from joining the damn book on the floor. "And I decided I should talk to you. Who better to tell me what I'm doing wrong around the...uh, man I want to seduce?"

Guy eyed the slinky little outfit she had on with grave misgivings. This was definitely not a good thing. Oh, it looked good enough. Real good. Perfect in fact. And that was the crux of the problem.

Very, very slowly, he came to his feet. "Uh, Annie..."

"Do you think this dress would turn him on? I have high heels to wear when I'm actually going to seduce him. That way, we'll be on more even ground." She gave him a sly look. "He's a lot taller than me."

His eye sockets felt singed. "Everybody's a lot taller than you." He spoke deliberately, trying to give his mind time to catch up with his tongue, which suddenly felt clumsy. And that was probably because his tongue had thought of much better things to do than talk.

The dress, a beige, sweater-type material, literally clung to her small body, outlining her soft breasts, displaying her flat belly and rounded thighs. The damn thing landed well above her knees and perfectly matched the color of her pale, smooth skin.

When he finally managed to lift his gaze to her face, he saw she was blushing and watching him very intently. She was probably waiting for a compliment—damned if he'd give her one! He'd take no part in encouraging her to wear such a provocative dress out in public.

He'd take no part in her seduction.

He felt his brows pull down in a vicious frown. He jutted his chin toward her, knowing he was about to hurt her feelings, but not seeing any other way. "You look more naked than not."

She didn't even blink an eye at his harsh tone. "You've never seen me naked, so how would you know?"

His blood seemed to pump hotly through his veins. Moving closer so that he towered over her, he said in a low, drawl, "I've seen you. Don't tell me you've forgotten?"

He hoped to embarrass her just a bit, and then she'd go and change back into her requisite jeans and loose top.

Only she didn't do that.

Annie immediately averted her gaze while scuffing her bare pink toes on the carpet. "I was only seventeen then—and a very late bloomer. It wasn't like there was much to look at."

Tenderness swelled inside him, almost obliterating his shock at seeing her appear so sexy. He could remember that day as if it had just happened. Hell, he'd go to his grave remembering.

"The way you carried on," he said, his tone low

and gruff, "I was afraid the whole neighborhood would know what had happened."

"I was mortified," she admitted with a shrug. "When Marcy and Kim convinced me we could skinny-dip without getting caught, I stupidly believed them. But of all the people to catch us..."

He couldn't help but smile at the memory of their combined high-pitched girlish wails. He'd had a headache for an hour afterward. "I'm not sure who was stunned more. Me or you three girls."

"Marcy and Kim both swore they were in love with you after that."

He'd barely noticed them that day. All his attention had been on Annie. "Marcy and Kim were both trouble. I should have told their parents instead of just walking away."

"Walking?" She peeked at him, then quickly away again. "As I remember it, you stomped off cursing and even your ears were bright red. *After* you gawked for a good five seconds or so."

Chuckling now, he touched her chin to tip her face up. "I was set to strangle you when you got home. Here you were, all ready to hide for the rest of your life, and I wanted to wring your neck. Neither of those two girls would leave me alone after that. They both thought I'd be overcome with lust for their adolescent bodies after seeing them in the raw."

"Actually," she said, now smiling too, "I believe they were counting on it."

Embarrassed as he'd been, Guy had known he

had to talk to Annie right away, or she'd be avoiding him forever. He was older, mature, a grown man despite how the sight of her had affected him, so he knew it was up to him to relieve her embarrassment.

He'd pretended outrage, both to help her through the awkwardness of it, and to hide his own unaccountable discomfort with the situation.

She might not have considered herself physically ripe, but his reaction to her was staggering. He'd felt like a lecher because he'd even noticed her, much less that he couldn't get the image out of his mind. It was the first time he'd ever really thought of Annie being female, of being someone other than Daniel's little sister, or a cute kid who he liked as a friend. She'd stood shivering in the shallow water, one hand over her very small breasts, the other splayed over the notch of her thin thighs, and his knees had damn near buckled. He'd had to limp away like a man with two broken legs.

He still felt guilty when he remembered it—and he remembered it more often than he should.

At ten years her senior, he was far too old then, and too trusted by the Sawyers' clan, to be thinking the things he'd thought. At the time, he hadn't even known there were such vivid, carnal things to think about. He certainly never had in the past. Not that he was a prude. Hell no. But females had come and gone in his life without a lot of notice from him. He'd taken pleasure in them, enjoyed them, and then gotten on with his plans.

Annie, well, she had inspired him to new depths of lust.

And he'd been fighting himself ever since because no matter what he told himself, no matter how much he loved her as a friend, his gonads insisted she was uncommonly sexual and appealing. He and his gonads had been on very bad terms ever since then.

Guy groaned and walked away from her. He'd felt so damned disgusted with himself then, as if he'd done something obscene to her when, in fact, he hadn't even looked for more than the few seconds it took for her nudity to register. And as much as he hated himself, he'd carried that picture in his mind ever since as a teasing reminder of Annie's shy, innocent femininity.

She wasn't acting so shy now.

"Guy?"

Her tone made his spine stiffen. He kept his back to her, thinking that might be safer than actually looking at her, so soft and sweet and curious. "You can't really be thinking of wearing that thing in public?" he grumbled.

"Of course not."

His knees turned to butter. *Thank goodness!* He was just managing to regulate his heart rate when she said, "It's for private viewing only. Maybe at his apartment. Or mine."

Before he could think better of it, Guy whirled to face her again. "Who the hell is this jerk you want so badly? If it is Perry, I swear I'll—"

Annie crossed her arms under her breasts and he realized she wasn't wearing a bra. He started to shake.

"Oh, no you don't," she said, sounding annoyed, oblivious to his struggle for control. "You'll try to intimidate him into staying away from me, won't you?"

That was exactly what he intended to do. He was beginning to feel just a bit desperate. "Honey, any guy who doesn't want you, isn't worth all this trouble."

As she turned to pace away, Guy got a tempting view of her backside in the dress.

To hell with the pizza. He had to leave.

He started to reach for his jacket, but Annie forestalled him.

In a very small voice, she asked, "What if he has good reason for staying away from me? What then?"

"Don't be ridiculous." He didn't mean to sound so harsh, but she was torturing him by slow degrees. "What possible reason could he have? No, the guy's just an idiot, and you don't really want to bed down with an idiot, now do you?"

Staring at him in what appeared to be humble exasperation, she muttered, "Unfortunately, I believe I do."

He drew a long breath. "Annie, honey, let me explain something to you about sex."

Her brows lifted, her expression intense and fixed.

Guy faltered, then forced himself to go on. "Sex isn't all romantic."

"It isn't?"

He shook his head. "No, it's hot and sweaty and sometimes crude and..."

Her eyes darkened, her lips parted, her cheeks flushed. "You make it sound wonderful," she breathed.

Guy had absolutely no idea how to reply to that. The doorbell rang.

Annie took a deep, shuddering breath, then started toward it.

Guy grabbed her arm. *"Don't even think it."* He knew he sounded panicked, but there was no way in the world he'd let her go to the door in that dress.

"What's the matter with you?" she asked, and damn if she didn't sound amused.

Guy pulled her toward the hallway and out of sight. "The poor pizza kid would likely have a heart attack. He's young and vulnerable, and probably horny enough as it is without you flaunting yourself in front of him. Here, stay out of sight while I get rid of him."

Annie grinned, but thankfully, she didn't fight him.

After he'd accepted and paid for the pizza, then closed the door, Annie came up to stand very close to him. "So you think my dress looks good enough to turn on the pizza deliverer?"

"He's nineteen. A strong wind would turn him on."

Surprise replaced her expression of anticipation. "Really?"

Guy moved away from her, needing the distance from her barely veiled body. "I think your body looks good. The dress isn't even noticeable."

"You mean it?" Annie skipped next to him to keep up with his long-legged, agitated stride. She stared up at him anxiously with those big blue eyes. "You honestly think I have an adequate body?"

Adequate? Guy thunked the pizza onto the counter in the kitchen and turned to glare down at her. Was she yanking his chain, or did she really have no notion of how sexy she was? Right now, in her bare feet, she probably stood five-two. Her hair, a rich shiny shade very close to black, but softer in color, fell past the middle of her back and made a man wonder what it would feel like drifting over his chest, his abdomen.

Other places.

Her blue eyes were huge, thickly lashed, staring up at him while she awaited his reply.

He didn't want to, but his gaze dropped down her body again. Everything suddenly seemed warmer, slower, closer. He could hear her small unsteady breaths, smell her soft, clean scent—a fragrance unique to Annie and guaranteed to drive him crazy.

His stomach muscles clenched when he saw that her nipples were tight against the soft fabric of the dress. She had her hands laced together over her middle, her knees pressed close together, her toes curled.

Evidently he was no stronger than the pizza kid.

He gave up with a groan, leaning down in slow motion, giving her plenty of time to move away, even hoping she would because he felt beyond control.

Instead, she moved into him, lifting her face, her lips parted, her breath now coming faster. He was a fool, an idiot... *Oh damn, she tasted good.*

His mouth ate at hers, carefully, thoroughly. Every time he kissed her, it was better than the time before. He gave a small suction and captured her soft tongue, then gave her his own. He heard her weak moan. Her lips were damp and clinging and tasted incredibly hot and sweet.

But he didn't touch her otherwise. He kept his hands resolutely at his sides, though it almost killed him, especially with her pressing so close, letting him feel her rounded breasts against his rib cage, her stiff little nipples burning him. He wanted to lift her to the counter, to part her slim thighs, to...

Her small hot hand opened on the left side of his butt, and she copped a feel.

Guy jerked back, panting, disillusioned, turned on.

Eyes dreamy, Annie sighed. Her smile was content—her hand squeezing. The world shifted a little, then righted itself and everything became clear.

She was practicing on him!

The first curse word out of his mouth made her

jump. The second had her scowling darkly and removing her hand from his backside. The third...well, he didn't know what the third did because he didn't wait around to see.

It was time to leave. Past time to leave. Damned if he'd let her hone her skills on him while planning to seduce some other fool.

Halfway out of the room, he realized he couldn't leave things this way, not with the plans she had in mind. He'd never get to sleep wondering if and when she was following through on those damned idiotic plans.

He turned back—and Annie, rapidly dogging his heels, slammed into him. He clutched her shoulders to keep her from falling, then gave her a slight shake. "Don't seduce anyone! Do you hear me?"

"Everyone on the block likely heard you!"

He gave her another small shake. "If the man needs to be persuaded, then there's something wrong with him. Trust me on this, Annie."

"No." She still looked a bit dreamy, her eyes softened and her mouth swollen. The hand that had clutched his bum was now cradled protectively to her chest. "There's nothing wrong with him. He's perfect."

Guy roared in frustration. "You," he said, lifting her to her tiptoes, "obviously don't know a thing about men. I'm telling you, the guy's dense."

With a placating tone, she said, "Okay, okay. He's dense." She struggled to catch her breath, staring up at him with round, hopeful eyes.

"So...what you're saying is that I'm enticement enough? He'll actually want me *without* this planned seduction?"

Guy's eyes widened; he didn't know what he was saying, but it sure as hell wouldn't be an admission like that!

He gently shook her again—it seemed his safest course. "You told me to think about proposing. All right. I'll make you a deal. You think about this seduction business, and I'll think about proposing. We'll both give it a lot of thought. All right?"

To his surprise, she immediately agreed. She stuck out the hand she'd used to grope him and said, "Done."

Cautiously, Guy enclosed her slender fingers in his own. "Annie...?"

"You can't back out now, Guy." She pumped his hand hard twice, then released it. With her fists on her hips and her chin tilted up so she could stare at him eye to eye, she said, "Before either of us makes a move on our new intentions, we'll discuss it. We'll hash it out completely. We'll make totally certain we know exactly what we're doing, what we're letting ourselves in for. We'll have no doubts before we—"

Guy put a finger over her lips. "Enough, Annie." He moved his hand quickly enough when he felt how damp and swollen her mouth still felt from his kiss. *He had to leave.* "I'll call you tomorrow. And in the meantime, try to think about why you'd even want to sleep with this jerk."

She smiled at him and then sighed. "I already know why."

Her voice was so soft, so heated, he felt it lick right down to his abdomen. And it hurt, a kind of hurt he didn't even want to acknowledge, much less think about. Stepping back, he cleared his throat and tried to come up with a logical reason for leaving so soon.

Annie didn't give him a chance. She flapped her hand in the air. "I know, I know. You're leaving." Then she grinned. "Do you know, you do that every time you kiss me."

He carefully inched his way toward the couch where he'd thrown his coat. "What?"

"Kiss me and run. Why is that?"

How could she stand there in that lethal dress and question him so innocently? It was a mystery set for greater minds than his own. Especially when he could barely concentrate on what she was saying. "I, ah, didn't mean to kiss you."

She sighed again, more dramatically this time. "Oh, Guy. It sure felt like you meant it."

"Annie," he said, feeling desperate, "you know I think of you as—"

"I am not your little sister, Guy!"

Didn't he know it. He cleared his throat. "Maybe not, not literally anyway. But I've watched you grow up, seen you turn independent. And you are Daniel's little sister. He trusts me. Dan trusts me. Hell, even Max trusts me, and that's saying a lot because from what I can tell, Max doesn't trust any-one.''

She looked confused. ''What does trust have to do with this?''

Everything, he wanted to shout. Her family de-pended on him to look after her just as they did. They depended on him to view her in the same light.

Her father had said plenty of times that Annie needed someone special, someone who was just right for her. And Daniel often worried that she'd get taken in by a man playing on her sensitivity, her vulnerability. Max wanted to wrap her in cotton and tuck her away someplace safe. He'd gladly pound anyone who hurt his sister—they all would. Annie was so sweet, she just didn't have what it took to shield herself from the many users of the world.

Because he was male, Guy knew exactly how base men could be. He knew what they had upper-most on their minds. From a pizza delivery boy to a corporate wheeler-dealer—they all wanted the same things. Annie just hadn't realized it yet.

He owed the Sawyers family, more than Daniel or Annie or Max knew. Hell, even he hadn't known the extent of Dan Sawyers' generosity until a few years ago. It had been more than enough that Dan had let him move in, that he'd forced himself out of his self-imposed isolation to attend some of Guy's high school awards ceremonies, that he'd at-tended his college graduation. He'd treated Guy like a son, and taken great pride in his educational accomplishments.

But Dan had gone one further. He'd paid for that damn education while letting everyone think a scholarship had been provided. He'd known there was no way Guy's own parents could foot the bill, and rather than make it difficult on Guy, he'd silently, and very privately, taken care of everything.

Somehow, someway, Guy vowed he'd manage to pay the man back, not only the money, but all the support. The Sawyers clan had accepted him, made him one of their own. They believed in him even when he didn't believe in himself. He owed them all a lot, whether they knew it or not.

He couldn't very well repay them by getting involved with Annie. Not when all the men in her family were so overprotective. They wanted the best for her, and as a hanger-on, an outsider, a damn charity case, Guy was far from the best.

His chest hurt with the reality of that, but he refused to dwell on it too long.

When he didn't reply, Annie gave him a challenging look. "I'm not wearing any underwear, Guy Donnovan. None at all."

All the breath in his lungs wheezed out of him in a loud gasp, as if he'd just taken a sucker punch. At the same time, his body tightened in acute arousal. *"What?"*

She dared to laugh, the little witch, shaking her head and sending her hair drifting over her shoulders so that one long curl fell forward to frame a tight nipple. She smacked his shoulder, gave him a brief distracted caress, then said, "I was just making certain you were still with me. You took so long to answer my question."

What question? It was difficult to remember after her little bombshell.

He sternly instructed his eyes to stay on her face, not to go wandering down that luscious little body again, trying to see things that he'd be better off not seeing. His eyes nearly crossed with the effort.

"Guy, I was only teasing. I have my panties on."

Even hearing her say the word "panties," making a reference to her intimate apparel, had him in a frenzy of lust. He was pathetic, beyond the ragged edge. He considered gagging her before she killed him.

Annie laughed again at his blank-brained expression. "Relax, Guy. I only said that because Lace told me it was a big turn-on for men. You know, telling them you were naked beneath your dress." She waited two heartbeats, then asked, "Is it?"

"Is it what?" He felt like an idiot, but he wanted very much to see if she was telling the truth. For some reason, every male hormone in his body screamed that she really was naked beneath that not-quite-there dress. He had to curl his hand into a fist to keep it from sliding up her thigh, seeking warm feminine parts, discovering the truth on his own. If she wasn't wearing panties, he'd feel her soft, silky skin, her damp flesh, her...

His body reacted accordingly to the mental provocation. He closed his eyes and said a quick prayer she wouldn't notice his blatant erection.

"Is it a turn on," she patiently repeated, "for men to think a lady is naked beneath her clothes?"

He snatched up his coat and pulled it on with more force than grace. Within seconds, he was on his way out the door, his pace determined, his head down in concentration.

"Guy?" She hung half out the door, watching his hurried and desperate retreat.

"Yes," he shouted back, "it is. And stop listening to Lace."

"Why?"

Now that there were a few feet separating them, he slowed and walked backward, watching her watch him, and he said, "Because young ladies shouldn't do or say things like that. And," he added when she started to take umbrage, "it's very bad for my general health."

Annie laughed in undiluted delight. "Too much stress?"

Too much temptation. "Get back inside your apartment before someone sees you." After that frowning order, he gave a quick wave of his hand, then raced down the steps and headed outside.

Thank God it was still raining. He could use the freezing shower to cool off his mind and his body. He had to get a grip. Annie was not for him and she never would be, despite the fact she seemed to want to experiment with him—probably because she did trust him so much, which was all the more reason to resist. She was a friend, a valuable friend that he didn't want to lose.

And if he lost Annie, he'd lose Daniel and Dan and Max, too. They were family to him. Very close family. He loved his mom and dad, but he'd been an only child, born late in life, and they were so far away now. He saw them three or four times a year at best, and spoke to them only monthly.

Dan had been able to do all the things with him that his own father couldn't do. He'd taught Guy things, took him under his wing and showed him how to run the family business. And Guy and Daniel were every bit as close as brothers could be. *They were his family.*

So what the hell was wrong with him?

His hair was soaked by the time he got into his car, and his hands were shaking, as much from his turbulent thoughts as from the cold. He was still slightly unsure about marrying Melissa, but he was dead certain he had to do something. He couldn't screw everything up by doing things with Annie he had no business doing.

And oh, the things he wanted to do.

Erotic things. Carnal things. Hot, wonderfully debauched things. Her brothers would kill him if they could read his thoughts right now.

He'd noticed the small, black pearl necklace he gave her years ago, nestling between her breasts still. The necklace had been a gift of friendship then; tonight it had turned him on painfully to see it against her skin, to know she wore it always.

Even when she slept, or showered. When she was naked.

He didn't want to lose her. He didn't want to lose her family. He felt nearly overwhelmed with conflicting emotions when he pulled out into the early evening traffic. His mind churned over several possible ways to solve his dilemma, but his thoughts kept coming back to her damned seduction, and how *he'd* like to teach her anything and everything she ever wanted to know.

He was busy cursing the fates that had thrown two female problems in his lap at once, when a traffic light turned green and he started forward. Unfortunately, the oncoming semi tried to stop for the light, but when he put on his brakes, the icy rain made the task impossible.

Guy watched, seeing it all in slow motion as the truck skidded and slid sideways, and then, with a horrifying crunch, rammed into the side of his car.

He barely had time to think, much less react. And then it didn't matter. His car crumbled in around him, and his head hit something solid. Everything went black.

4

WHEN THE PHONE rang, Annie jumped a good foot. She'd been lying in the bed for hours, perusing one of the many magazine articles Lace had given her and daydreaming about seduction techniques and how to apply them to Guy Donovan. He'd been on the ragged edge tonight, of that she was certain. He wanted her.

At least in that dress, he did.

She felt guilty for the wicked thoughts she'd been conjuring, almost as if the caller could read her mind. She actually blushed as she answered the phone on the third ring. She tried to sound sleepy, rather than excited. After all, it was past midnight.

"Hello?"

"Are you awake, Annie?"

Daniel. Something must be wrong for him to call so late. "What is it? What's happened?" At first, she feared Guy had done something stupid like elope, and her stomach knotted in dread.

But it was even worse.

"He's okay now. Really. But Guy had an accident after he left your place. He's here at the hospital."

The words barely registered before she was out of the bed, the phone caught between her shoulder and ear, and she was scurrying to find jeans to pull on. "What happened? What's wrong with him?"

She could hear the panic in her own tone, but didn't think Daniel noticed. "He damaged his knee a bit, enough to keep him from jogging for a while. And he's got some pretty ugly contusions, especially around his ribs."

Her vision blurred. "Oh God. *Contusions.*"

"Bruises, Annie. Just very colorful bruises. He also hurt his head."

His beautiful head! She began shaking, feeling as if she might split apart. "How..." She had to gulp. "How bad?"

"He's awake, and he's going to be okay. But he's a bit antsy and unmanageable." There was a pause, then, "Honey, can you come to the hospital?"

As if she'd stay home? "I'll be there in just a few minutes."

"No! You'll be here in about an hour. It's a long drive for you and the roads are a mess. The freezing rain turned to snow and plows are out everywhere. Just take it easy and drive careful, all right? I don't want both of you in here with me."

"I'll be careful," she promised, then hung up before he could caution her more. It was just like Daniel to be overly concerned with her driving at a time like this. He would hurry, but he didn't trust her to do so.

She was out the door in two minutes flat, her hair still ratty and uncombed, her clothes hastily donned, her shoes pulled on without socks. Daniel was right, she soon discovered. The roads were awful, and recognizing that fact only made her more anxious. How badly had Guy been hurt in this horrid weather? Daniel's reassurances didn't relieve her one bit. He was capable of softening the truth, to keep her from rushing. Guilt swelled inside her until she thought she'd choke on it.

Her awesome seduction technique had driven him away! He'd literally raced from her apartment and it was all her fault.

It took her half the time Daniel had predicted to reach the hospital, despite the road conditions. She rushed through the emergency room door and then skidded to a halt when Lace came forward to meet her.

"Lace? What in the world are you doing here? Did Daniel call you too?" Had he called the whole family? Was Guy even worse off than she'd first suspected?

Lace gave her a generous smile. "I was here visiting Daniel when they brought Guy in. Come on, I'll show you where they're keeping him."

Though she hurried forward, Annie felt her own misgivings. "Is he really okay, Lace?"

Lace gave Annie's hand a squeeze. "He's going to be fine, but he's a little dopey at the moment. Ah, here's Daniel, and Annie, you know what an excellent doctor your brother is."

Annie did know; Daniel was one of the very best. But at the moment that fact didn't ease her anxiety one bit.

"Daniel? Tell me what's wrong with Guy. Why is he still here if he's okay? And where is he? I want to see him." She would only feel secure that he was truly okay after she'd scanned the length of his magnificent body herself.

Daniel clasped her shoulders to stop her from pushing forward and gave her a brotherly squeeze. "Just hold on, sis. I need to talk to you before you go in."

"Oh God."

"Now, Annie, you have to get a grip. It's not as bad as it looks. Guy has a lot of colorful contusions, but we've cleared his cervical spine. There were no neck injuries, no trauma to his head."

"You promise?"

"Honey, you know what a hard head Guy has." Daniel smiled at her.

"But he doesn't have much hair to cushion it."

"I promise, other than a few bruises, his head is fine." Daniel patted her back in his brotherly manner. "He does have some pretty severe, and I'm sure painful, scrapes and bruises to his right shoulder and ribs, and his right knee might need some orthopedic care. Right now we can't determine the extent of the injury to his knee because of the swelling. In a few days he can go to a specialist and see about the possibility of surgery, though I doubt it will be necessary. For the time being we've put an external, removable knee immobilizer on him, and he'll need pain medication for a spell. He'll have to use crutches to get around, and I'd recommend as much bed rest, with his knee elevated, as possible for the next few days.''

Annie covered her mouth with a hand while tears welled in her eyes. And Daniel claimed it wasn't too bad? It sounded worse than awful.

It sounded like her attempts at seduction had almost killed him!

''Now Annie,'' Lace said, coming to stand by Daniel, then leaning against his side. Daniel slipped his arm around her, taking comfort from her nearness. ''You can't go in and talk to Guy if you're falling apart. He really is going to be okay, you know. Your brother wouldn't lie to you.''

''Of course not,'' Daniel said, doing his best to soothe Annie, but looking relieved to have Lace's help. ''Nothing is broken or seriously injured, but bruises can hurt almost as bad as a break, so he's going to need some care.''

''I'll do it,'' Annie blurted before she could temper her reaction.

Daniel sighed. ''That's what I assumed. You two were always closer than most brothers and sisters.''

Lace rolled her eyes, but at Annie's pleading look, said nothing.

''Can I see him now?''

''All right.'' Daniel reluctantly eased away from Lace, then took Annie's hand to lead the way. ''The thing is, honey, he's a little screwy and disoriented at the moment. Considering his body size and his injuries, I gave him a whopper of a painkiller. But I think I may have overdone it." Daniel laughed. "At least now I know why he never drinks."

Just as they rounded a corner of the emergency room, Annie could hear someone singing. It was an old *Mary Poppins* tune, shouted out in a flat, wavering baritone that had all the nurses holding their ears.

Daniel merely chuckled. "He's right through there. You can just follow the noise. But watch yourself. He tried to hug me—and nearly tossed me to the ground."

"I had to save him," Lace said with a grin, sidling up to Daniel again. "We all three almost toppled."

Annie wavered forward, her steps tentative.

Guy rested on his back in a narrow metal bed, a thin blanket pulled up to his waist. His hard, hairy chest was bare and decorated with numerous bruises. His short hair jutted out every which way, his eyes were squeezed closed, but his mouth was wide open.

He started in wailing, "Ohhhh, su-per-cal-la-frag—"

And Annie whispered, "Guy?"

He grew instantly silent, then cocked one eye open. "Ahh, another little lady friend. Come to inflict more torture on my poor male person, have you?"

He was grinning, but she flinched at his words. "Of course not. How do you feel?"

"Like I fought with a semi and lost. And yourself?"

A semi? Thank God he wasn't killed. She approached his side slowly, her feet dragging, her heart pounding. "You look like you lost. You've got bruises on top of your bruises."

"You look like you're ready to cry." He studied her face with blurry, pain-filled eyes, then said softly, "I'd really rather you didn't."

"I won't."

"Did you like *Mary Poppins* when you were little?" Before she could answer, he laughed. "What am I saying? You're still little. I meant when you were younger."

She nodded, pulling a chair up to the bed and sitting beside him before her knees gave out.

Very carefully, she reached through the bed railing and closed her cold fingers around his large hand. "You used to watch it with me when no one else would."

"Impossible. I hated that damn movie. Still do. Maybe not the first dozen times I saw it, but after that…"

She felt her bottom lip begin to quiver. Even though he'd hated it, he'd still watched it with her? "Guy, I lo—"

"Are you wearing your panties?"

Her declaration died in her throat. *"What?"*

"Tell me the truth now, Annie. And no more of

your teasing.'' He eyed her body from head to toe, but since she wore her usual of jeans and a sweatshirt, he couldn't see a thing. ''Well? Are you or not?''

His brow was puckered with a suspicious frown, and Annie had to draw a deep breath to calm herself. Good grief, she'd almost blurted out that she loved him. Not that he would have thought that much of it. Her family was loving, and it wasn't uncommon to show it, to say it, to make it known. But she wouldn't have meant it the way he'd want to take it.

She was trying to find an answer for him when Daniel walked in. ''So, how are we doing?''

''Daniel.'' Guy suddenly had a sappy grin on his face. ''Do you know you're the best doctor in the whole damn world? I mean it, man. You saved me.'' Then to prove Annie's earlier point, he said, ''I love you like a brother, Daniel.''

Daniel shook his head. ''I love you, too, Guy.'' To Annie, he said, ''That's about the twelfth declaration of undying love I've gotten from him since the pain medication kicked in.''

Annie stifled a watery grin.

''And I mean it, too. It was my only spot of luck this dark night, that you were on duty.'' Guy groaned, his eyes squeezing shut again. ''Damn but I wish my head didn't hurt so bad.''

''As long as you insist on yodeling, your head is going to continue to hurt like hell. You need to rest *quietly*.'' Daniel grinned as he said it, apparently amused despite his suggestions. "Annie, why don't you step out here a minute. The nurse needs to check Guy's vitals again and I want to talk to you."

Guy jerked his eyes open and his gaze landed on Annie. "Are you leaving?"

He sounded almost desperate, and the dreaded tears threatened again. She pitched her voice low in a soothing tone, in deference to his aching head. "No, of course not. I'll be right back."

"Promise?"

"I promise."

Guy grimaced, then shouted loud enough for the fourth floor to hear, "Daniel, make damn sure she's got all her underwear on!"

Daniel started in surprise. "For crying out loud, Guy!"

"She's a tricky one, I tell you." He winced as he lifted his arm to point an accusing finger in her direction. "You best keep an eye on her."

Daniel pursed his mouth shut, and Annie gasped. She quickly escaped out the door, towing Daniel behind her. Two nurses began to chuckle.

The second they were out the door, Daniel laughed out loud. "I told you he was juiced. Never seen anyone quite so high on legitimate pain medicine before. So far he's confessed to loving me, the X-ray technician, and the nurse who took his blood."

"Has he mentioned me?"

"Nope, sorry honey, but he hasn't said a word

about you. He may be upset with you about this foolish scheme of yours to experiment.''

Annie stiffened. "It's not foolishness.''

"Yeah, well, whatever nonsense it is, do you think you can put it on hold awhile?''

"Why?''

"Because I've thought of a way to save Guy from himself.''

Lace sauntered up in time to say, "This ought to be good.''

Daniel looked over the rim of his glasses at her. "I'm glad you're still here, sweetheart. I think we can use your help.''

"Oh goody.''

Daniel had to force his gaze away from his wife, then he stated, "I want you to kidnap Guy.''

It took a moment for Annie to realize that he was done. He wasn't going to expound on that small instruction. She cleared her throat, tried to erase the sound of her burgeoning excitement, and inquired with a feigned calm, "Oh?''

Lace looked at the ceiling and whistled. Daniel ignored her.

"If you nurse him, and keep everyone else away from him, he'll have nothing to do but think about how asinine it is to propose to Melissa. He'll probably be laid up for a few days, maybe even a week before he starts feeling whole again. I could give you complete instructions to follow on how to care for him, how to medicate him—''

"How to soothe his savage breast?" Lace asked innocently.

Daniel shrugged. "If need be. It would be the perfect time for him to reflect on what he's doing and why he shouldn't do it."

"How, exactly," Annie asked, intrigued despite her worries, "do you propose I do this? Guy is actually a whole lot bigger than me, so it's not like I can bully him."

"He's not up to a fight right now," Daniel explained. "And with the medication, I think he'll be more agreeable than not."

"He'll want to check in at work, you know that."

"He can't get around well enough for that. It's important that he stays off his feet."

"By phone then."

"I don't mind phone calls," Daniel told her, "but he'll need to take it easy, relaxing and recuperating until the swelling in his knee goes down. If anyone attempts to visit him—"

"Like Melissa?"

"Especially Melissa," Daniel agreed. "But all things considered, she should understand that he's not up to visitors."

Annie was beginning to take to the idea. Alone and isolated with Guy? It had possibilities. If he couldn't run off, if he was grounded, mostly in bed—*a perfect position*—then his life wouldn't be threatened by her seduction techniques, now would it?

"That's it?" she asked carefully, wanting to make sure she understood. "You want me to keep Melissa away from him?"

"It's a start."

Annie certainly loved the idea, but it had its drawbacks. "I'm not sure I can bar people from his apartment, Daniel. I mean, bedridden or not, Guy will have something to say about that, I'm sure."

Daniel cleared his throat. "I wasn't exactly talking about his apartment. I think you should take him away from here."

"Take him away?"

"From this area. Annie, you know he could use the time to reflect on this marriage business and to take a break from work. I'll talk to Dad. He can certainly fill in, or find a replacement for Guy for awhile."

Annie blinked at Daniel. "But...where would I take him?"

Daniel removed his glasses and began polishing them on the hem of his white coat. "Well, now I had an idea about that. We have this, ah, cabin of sorts."

"A cabin?" Annie eyed the smile on Lace's face and the way Daniel wouldn't look at her. "You and Lace bought a cabin? When?"

"Well...actually..." Daniel slanted a look at Lace, then stiffened his spine. "I bought the cabin before I met Lace."

"You did?" Her brother seemed very edgy all

of a sudden, making Annie frown in contemplation. "How long have you had it?"

"For a while now. It's a nice place, but a little rustic." He tried to distract her by changing the subject. "I'd take Guy there myself and force him to listen to reason, but I can't manage time away from the hospital right now."

Annie was amazed—and not the least bit diverted. "You own a cabin and you've never told me? Do Dad and Max know?"

Daniel wasn't one to lie, but Annie could see he was considering doing just that. Then he nodded and looked resigned. "Dad and Max, and even Guy have all been there. It's a bachelor's cabin, Annie, and that's why you didn't know."

Lace hooted with laughter. "Now that really hurt, didn't it? I mean, admitting to your sweet little innocent sister that you're a normal man." She turned to Annie, still grinning. "Since our marriage, however, Daniel has only been to the cabin with me."

"Actually," Daniel said, his expression stern, "Lace and I were there *before* we were married."

Rather than being embarrassed by this divulgence, Lace seemed more amused.

In a conspiratorial tone, she whispered to Annie, "All macho men need a place to indulge their baser instincts, a place to be human, without tarnishing their poor little innocent sisters with the lusty knowledge of it." She leaned against Daniel's shoulder and grinned widely. "That's right, isn't it, doctor?"

Fascinated, Annie watched Daniel turn his very stiff back on Lace, almost causing her to fall. "Everything you need can be delivered there before you arrive. I'll call first thing in the morning and have a couple loads of wood dropped off so you'll be able to stay nice and warm. The fireplace has a blower, so it pretty much heats the whole cabin. And I'll have some food put in the fridge. The freezer is already stocked."

"You have electricity for appliances, but no heat?" Annie had a hard time taking it all in.

It was Lace who explained. "Think about it, Annie. Isn't a warm, cozy fireplace more of an inducement to romance than a furnace? There's even a store of wine and soft music aplenty, isn't there, doc?"

Daniel didn't answer her, but he did flex his fingers. Annie wondered if he was thinking of strangling his wife. "I wouldn't suggest giving Guy any wine. Between his low tolerance and the pain medicine, who knows how he'd react to it."

Annie shook her head, still dumbfounded. "Max has been there. And Guy? And *Dad?*" It was bad enough imagining Guy taking a woman to a secluded cabin in the woods for sensual purposes. But her father?

Again, Lace answered. "It's as I keep telling you, Annie. No normal, healthy person lives as a monk. Responsible, mature sex is a vital part of life.''

Daniel turned on her. ''That's enough out of you.''

In a gentle tone, Lace asked, ''What's the matter, Daniel? Afraid little sister might find out how human you are? Or are you afraid she might find out how human *she* is?''

Daniel seethed in silence for a moment, and Annie thought what a ferocious sight he was. It was the first time she'd ever thought of her oldest brother that way, he was generally so...so...*placid*.

Daniel visibly calmed himself. ''I'm not as dense as you think I am, sweetheart.''

Lace lifted both brows. ''No?''

''No.'' Then Daniel took Annie's arm and dragged her three feet away from Lace.

''I seriously doubt Guy would give up work and go to the cabin willingly. You know how devoted he is to the job. So we're going to have to outmaneuver him.''

Lace rejoined them as if she'd been invited. ''You know, I'm all for Annie doing this. But tell me, what did this Melissa do that was really so bad?''

''Nothing. She's just not right for Guy.''

''Why?'' Now Lace sounded suspicious. ''You aren't intimately acquainted with her, are you?''

Daniel gave Lace the most evil grin Annie had ever seen on his handsome face. ''Jealous, sweetheart?''

Lace's eyes narrowed and she started to turn away, but Daniel caught her arm and whipped her back around to face him. Before Annie could blink, or give them a moment's privacy—not that she really would have—Daniel treated Lace to a scorching kiss. Annie felt her cheeks heat.

Who needed books when her own brother carried on so right in front of her? And contrary to Guy's reaction, Lace seemed to wallow in Daniel's technique. It was beyond fascinating.

"I love you, Lace."

"Hmm. I know." She patted his chest and smiled. "But that doesn't answer my question."

"Melissa is a businesswoman through and through. She isn't the type to inspire thoughts of hearth and home. At least, I didn't think she was. But now with Guy... I just can't believe such a mess. The whole idea of marriage is ludicrous." He tilted his head. "Does that answer your question?"

"Fortunately for you—yes."

Daniel went back to the business of the cabin, keeping one arm possessively over Lace's shoulders. "You'll be isolated enough, so Guy will have nothing to do but recuperate and think on how ridiculous this marriage plan is."

Annie nodded.

"And you," he added, "can think about this crazy seduction farce."

Lace smiled widely. "Oh, I'm sure she will. After all—" she winked at Annie "—the cabin is set up for seduction. How could she *not* think about it?"

And better yet, Annie thought, how could Guy not think about it? The setting would give her the perfect opportunity to try her hand again, only this time Guy would be at her mercy. He wouldn't be able to run away from her.

"But what if something happens to him?" Annie glanced toward the room Guy was in. She could still hear him singing, and a gaggle of nurses hovered, peeking in at him, giggling and flirting.

Shameless hussies.

What good woman took advantage of a downed man?

Annie frowned, realizing she intended to do just that! "What if he starts hurting worse, or he needs a different medicine?"

"I can make sure you have all his prescriptions before you leave, which should be sometime tomorrow morning. I want him to stay tonight just so we can keep an eye on him, but he'll be fit enough to go tomorrow—with the right care. In fact, if I know Guy, he'll probably be insisting on leaving."

"You make this sound pretty easy."

Daniel nodded. "It will be. I'll write out all the instructions for you. But to be on the safe side, you can take my cell phone with you. Just be sure to hide it from him. If Guy knows you have it, he'll call for a cab and race on home to propose." Daniel gave Annie an understanding look. "And we don't want that to happen, do we?"

"No." She most definitely didn't want him offering himself up to Melissa.

Another nurse started into Guy's room, and Annie heard Guy greet her with a whistle. The painkillers had put him in a strange mood, and she wasn't willing to let another woman—not even a nurse—take advantage of his sudden vulnerability. "I'm spending the night with him," she announced, then waited for someone to argue.

Instead, Daniel merely nodded and Lace said, "Do you want me to run home and get anything for you?"

"Thanks, Lace, but I'll be fine." She just wanted to get back to Guy, to see him and be with him— and keep other women away.

Lace held out her hand. "Give me your keys. I'm willing to bet you didn't park your car for the night."

"No, it's in the emergency zone." She dug in her pocket and extracted her bulky set of apartment and car keys. "Thanks."

"You're very welcome." Lace decided to call it a night after she moved Annie's car, and kissed both Annie and Daniel goodbye. Daniel promised to be home soon. His shift had ended hours ago, just as Guy had been brought in. Annie knew he had to be exhausted.

Daniel turned at a loud growl from Guy's room. He muttered a curse. "I think our patient is acting up just a bit. It shouldn't surprise me, I suppose.

Men generally make the worst sort of patients. Come on, the nurse can probably use our help.''

Annie followed quickly, anxious over the cursing complaints that echoed out of Guy's room. When they stepped through the doorway, Guy was struggling with a flustered nurse while she tried to remove his blanket.

''Get your hands off me, woman!''

''I need to check your ribs, Mr. Donovan.''

''You're not getting me buck naked!''

Daniel rushed forward with a sigh. ''That's okay, Ms. Dryer. I'll take care of it.''

Guy focused on Daniel's face, his own expression indignant. ''I've been harassed by pushy women one too many times today.''

Though Annie felt the heat pulse in her cheeks at the charge, Daniel didn't seem to notice. And he certainly didn't understand Guy's meaning.

Daniel tried to placate Guy. ''I do understand. But the fact is, if you want to be released in the morning, I have to make a final check on your hulking body. Big as you are, you aren't invincible. Especially up against a semi. So shut your trap and let me do my job.''

''You're a damn good friend to me, Daniel, you know that? Damn good.''

Daniel slanted a look at Annie that clearly said, here we go again. Daniel lowered the sheet, barely maintaining Guy's modesty, and Annie got an eye-opening view of his solid midsection. His abdomen was ridged with muscle, even in his relaxed state.

And lower down, his hipbones appeared lighter than the rest of his skin, dipping in toward delectable male territory.

The same hair that lightly furred his chest ran in a silky trail down to circle his navel, then further down to...

Guy looked up and caught sight of Annie watching with rapt interest. He snatched the sheet back up to his stubbled chin while looking at her as if she were a pervert.

Daniel glanced over his shoulder at Annie, and his face softened in an understanding smile. He tipped his head toward the door. Gently, he said, "Give us a minute, sis, will you? Guy's feeling unduly shy all of a sudden."

She didn't want to leave.

She wanted to stay and see more of Guy's powerful body. She wanted to pull that sheet just a tad lower. Maybe more than a tad—to his knees would be nice.

She wanted to inspect every single bruise and scrape and hurt on his entire body, and she wanted to kiss them all better. It didn't matter that he was badly battered, he still had the most beautiful male body she'd ever seen, all long muscles and hair-dusted skin. She loved him.

Hopefully, once she had him at her mercy, she'd be able to view a bit more of him. Like maybe, all of him. In great detail. She smiled with the thought, then left the room reluctantly.

She busied herself by arranging for her assistant

at the bookstore to work full shifts until further notice. She gave the woman both Daniel's and Lace's numbers, and received a promise that everything would be looked after properly.

It was another fifteen minutes before Daniel came out again. He went directly to where Annie anxiously waited. "He's fallen asleep. I figured the medicine would take him out sooner or later. Come on. I'll get you something to eat and we can talk about the cabin."

"I don't want to leave him."

"He's out cold, Annie. He won't know if you're there or not and I've given instructions for the nurses to page me if he wakes."

"I'm not hungry, Daniel. Can't I just sit beside him?"

Daniel gave her a speculative look, then finally nodded. "All right. I'll have an orderly bring you up a more comfortable chair. Would you like a pillow, too, just in case you get a chance to doze?"

"Thank you." Annie would have agreed to anything just to get it settled. More than anything, she simply wanted to be by Guy's side, holding his hand and assuring herself he was truly okay.

Above her guilt, which was extreme, she felt the driving determination to give a relationship with Guy every opportunity. If that meant throwing herself at him, taking advantage of him, acting like a trollop, then she would.

And if her heart got broken in the bargain, she'd just deal with it.

Daniel gave her one more lengthy look, then drew her close for a hug. "I have to get out of here. Guy should pretty much sleep through the night, but if there's any problem, you can call me at home. Dr. Morton will be here the rest of the night, and he's good, but I'd still want to know—"

"I understand. I love him, too." Annie smiled up at her brother, fighting off her tears. "And I promise to call you if there's any reason."

Daniel kissed her on the forehead. "Don't wear yourself out. Try to get some sleep. Guy's going to need a lot of attention in the next couple of days, and you'll have to be up to par. Especially given how he reacts to those painkillers."

After Daniel left to order the reclining chair and pillow, Annie slipped into Guy's room. Standing by the bed, she lifted his large hand and cradled it between her own. She watched his chest rise and fall as he breathed deeply in sleep. She inspected the swelling bruise on his temple, the ugly scrape on his shoulder. She didn't realize she was crying until a tear landed on their entwined hands.

She *would* do what was best for him. If that meant whisking him away to someplace private where he'd have to listen to her reasonable arguments, then so be it.

She'd do whatever was necessary to keep Guy from marrying the wrong woman. And if while they were at the cabin, he convinced her he truly only loved her as a sister, that Melissa was the right woman for him, then she'd give him up without a hassle. She wanted him to be happy.

But first he'd have a choice. He'd know how much she loved him, that everything could be wonderful between them if he'd only give them a chance. And then he could decide.

The chair was delivered and situated close to Guy's bed. Annie sank into it, but she didn't sleep. Instead, she stayed awake all night and planned Guy's seduction. She intended to give this her very best shot. Guy was more than worth the effort.

5

"HE WOKE UP off and on all night," Annie told Daniel first thing the following morning. "Part of the time he wanted to sing, and part of the time he was groaning. The nurse gave him pain medicine twice, though he didn't really come right out and ask for it."

"He wouldn't. He's a stubborn ass, and you know it."

Calling Guy stubborn was a gross understatement. Throughout the night, Guy had been downright impossible. He'd hurt, but he resisted admitting it. "He still looks exhausted."

"Don't fret, Annie. I think his exhaustion has more to do with what was on his mind before the accident than the accident itself. My guess is, he's suffering conflicting feelings about his intention to propose to Melissa."

"You don't think he really wants to get married?"

Daniel lifted a brow. "I think he wants marriage a lot. It's Melissa I'm not really sure he wants. He likes her fine, and she's a very attractive woman, not to mention smart."

Lace poked him in the ribs. "You're on thin ice."

"Lace! When did you get here?"

"I left the house shortly after you did."

"I thought you had to be at the radio station this morning."

"Not for a couple more hours." She turned to Annie. "I hope you don't mind, but since I had your keys, I went by your apartment and packed a bag for you. This way you can stay here with Guy until it's time to leave for the cabin."

Annie hadn't even thought about packing a bag. "Thanks. How did I ever get along without you?"

Daniel, with a gentle smile, said, "I've often wondered the same thing."

Lace grinned at both of them. "It's too early for drama, so both of you can just knock it off." She leaned into her husband, who put his arm around her. "Annie, I put the bag in the back of your car already. And don't worry, I packed everything you could possibly need."

"Uh...thanks." Annie briefly wondered at the impish gleam in her friend's eyes, but she figured that could be as much from the fact her husband was caressing her hip as anything else.

Annie had been given a toothbrush from the hospital staff and she'd washed up in a private bathroom. Her clothes were a wrinkled mess, but she didn't care enough to change them. Her hair—she'd almost groaned when she'd seen how ratty it was. She untangled it the best she could, then put it in a long braid. Lace had once told her she had beautiful, sexy hair so she should wear it loose.

There was nothing sexy about it now. It was such a hassle keeping it tangle free.

They were on their way back from the cafeteria where Daniel had insisted that she eat some fruit with her coffee. The food sat like a lump in her belly. In minutes, she'd be stealing away her one true love and with any luck, she might get the chance to apply some of her new lascivious lessons to his person.

Daniel thought she was going to nurse Guy back to health.

Instead, she intended to molest him.

She knew, were Guy not loopy from the drugs, he'd never agree to letting her steal him away.

Daniel handed her a couple of pieces of paper. "Here, I've written out directions on how to get to the cabin. You shouldn't have any problems, but keep my cell phone handy just in case. And here's a list of things you'll need to know, like who to call if you need more supplies or anything. There's a local woman who keeps the place clean and does the linens and keeps the cabinets stocked. And there's instructions on how to work the controls on the hot tub—"

Annie drew to a halt. "The hot tub?"

Daniel kept walking, ignoring her interruption and not looking at her as he said, "Soaking in the hot tub might be the perfect therapy for Guy if he's up to it. But he'll definitely need help getting in and out."

Guy wet and warm from frothing water...

Daniel hid a smile and nodded to the list. "Everything is pretty easy, but I don't want you to have any trouble getting settled."

"What if the ride makes Guy uncomfortable?"

Daniel checked his watch. "Given the timing on his last pain pill, he shouldn't feel a thing for a few more hours. But often the next day after an accident is the worst. You're more aware of all your aches and pains then. If he's resistant to the pain pills, you might try—" Daniel coughed "—giving him a, er, massage. That ought to...set him straight."

Annie wanted to rub her hands together in glee. "I'll take care of him, Daniel. Don't worry."

Daniel nodded, and Annie realized just how tired he looked. "When was the last time you slept?"

He gave her a crooked smile. "I was on my way home when Guy came in last night. All things considered, I didn't rest easy when I did finally get in bed."

Lace made a sound of mock outrage. "That was your fault! I was nearly asleep when you started—"

Daniel again covered her mouth. Grinning, he pulled her close and kissed her. "Why don't you go out and start Annie's car so it can warm up while we get Guy ready to go."

Lace looked a little dazed and disgruntled. Finally, she just agreed and went out. Daniel watched her go, that silly little grin still on his mouth.

Annie said, "I had no idea you were so insatiable."

Rather than looking embarrassed this time, he shrugged. "I didn't, either. But Lace...well, she distracts me mightily. And last night I needed a distraction."

Annie hoped Guy would feel the same. She was ready and able—eager—to distract him in any way necessary. Most especially in the way she assumed Lace had distracted Daniel. "You know, marriage appears to agree with you."

"Having Lace close, loving her—that's what agrees with me. I'd recommend it to anyone. Including you." Daniel flicked the end of her nose. "When you find someone who's good enough for you, that is."

"And just who would be good enough, Daniel? Answer me that, will you?"

Daniel drew up blank, his expression bemused. Just then a nurse interrupted to tell Daniel that she'd found some newer scrubs for Guy to wear home.

Lace pulled the car right up to the emergency room entrance. Daniel helped maneuver Guy into a wheelchair for his ride outside and even supplied him with a few blankets. Guy's long body overflowed the chair in every direction, and his injured leg, jutting out straight with the support apparatus around his knee, preceded them out the door. Daniel carried a pair of brand new crutches for him, then stowed them in the back seat.

They barely managed to get him situated in the front passenger seat of her small car with a seat belt around him before Guy started snoring again, his head dropped back against the seat. Annie tried to smooth his hair, which immediately popped back up into small spikes. She covered his legs to keep them warm, then put the car in gear. Daniel stood to the side, Lace beside him, both of them waving her on.

Guy toppled over, his breath leaving him in a whoosh as the impact caused him renewed pain. Annie waited for him to awaken, but he didn't. She adjusted her position so that his head was in her lap, and when Guy looped an arm around her thigh one broad palm beneath his head, it took all her concentration to keep them safely on the road. His fingers were so close to where she'd often imagined them being. Of course, now, he was all but unconscious. And still it gave her a thrill.

She was a pervert, she decided, and didn't care. An hour long ride?

With Guy so close, it would probably seem twice as long, but she thought of the possibilities when they finally arrived, and she started to hum. Fate was on her side this time. She would read her books, she'd study hard and Guy, bless his wounded heart, wouldn't stand a chance.

The next time she had him this close, he'd be

wide awake and fully aware. With any luck at all, he'd even be willing.

ANNIE TURNED OFF the engine and gently shook Guy's shoulder. Other than wincing every now and then, he hadn't moved during the entire ride. The last sleepless night, and those before it, were taking their toll. She knew he had to be sore, so she was careful when she tried to wake him.

He slept on.

"Guy?" She shook him a little harder this time and he stirred the tiniest bit. His large hand squeezed her thigh more firmly and he turned his face inward, nuzzling against her in a most scandalizing way.

In a most thrilling way.

Annie froze. *"Ohmigosh."* Surely it was depraved to enjoy the attentions of a sleeping man.

"Shh." Guy, evidently not quite sound asleep, yet not quite awake, kissed her leg, his fingers now cuddling. "Not so loud, sweetheart."

Never in her life had she heard that tone of voice from Guy.

His fingers...good grief. They were sliding higher and he was so hot she felt burned. She could barely breathe. "Uh..."

"Just relax," he murmured in a low, sleepy, persuasive tone. A seductive tone.

Did he even know who he was touching? If he called her by another name, she'd...

Annie gripped his shoulder again. "Guy Donovan! You wake up this instant!'' If they were going to do this, Annie was just scrupulous enough to insist the man at least be fully conscious.

Guy went still, then yawned hugely and started to stretch. He ended that quickly with a grimace.

Bleary-eyed and not quite focused, he struggled into a more or less upright position and looked around. He saw the cabin, tilted his head, and yawned again. Without a word, he started to leave the car.

"Guy wait!'' Annie hustled out and around the car. Guy cursed and groaned as he managed to crawl out of the car. He swayed on his feet when Annie handed him the crutches and grabbed his side. Luckily, someone had salted the gravel drive so there were no apparent slick spots, but it was still uneven and rocky.

"Don't move,'' Annie told him, aware of the cold cutting through her, the wind whistling, "until I get the door unlocked. Do you understand me?'' He was still entirely too dopey for Annie to trust him. But he seemed to be holding himself steady, and she knew she had to get him inside.

Guy propped himself against the car and gave her a cocky grin.

Annie had no idea what to make of that. She watched him closely, constantly looking back at him with a frown as she made her way to the front door. There were two locks, and she'd gotten them both open and had started to turn when Guy muttered a low complaint right behind her.

She whipped around and nearly ran into him. Luckily she stopped herself in time because she really didn't think there was any way she could control his weight if he started to topple. "I told you to stay put!"

He used only one crutch, letting it take some of the weight off his right leg as he hobbled past her. "I need to lie down."

Annie hovered. She wasn't quite sure what to do. He seemed to be managing okay, so she hated to touch him and maybe put him off balance. But Guy still seemed more asleep than awake, moving by rote toward the bedroom.

She followed along behind him like a shadow. She'd never seen the cabin before, and wasn't getting much of a chance to look at it now as she rushed behind Guy, so she figured he knew where he was going better than she did.

She noticed a warm fire crackling in the fireplace behind a glass screen, a huge entertainment center, and a lot of open space as Guy led her along. An enormous seating arrangement—she thought it might be called a pit—was strategically positioned in front of the fireplace.

When Guy safely reached the bed and sat down on the edge, she breathed a sigh of relief.

Cold air blew in through the open front door, and Annie was just about to go close it when Guy started struggling with his coat. Annie rushed to help him. He kept giving her sappy grins and thanking her as she tugged the bomber jacket off his wide shoulders. Annie smiled at him. He was so silly with the effects of the drugs.

Then he pulled his shirt off over his head, and her smile fell away. Even with the bruises, he looked too gorgeous for words. She was standing there watching him in appreciation, his coat clutched to her chest, when he stood, balanced on one leg, and untied the drawstring at the waistband of the scrubs.

Before she could draw a deep breath, the loose bottoms dropped to his ankles.

He had nothing on underneath.

Without so much as a blush of modesty, Guy sat back down on the bed and clumsily worked his shoes and socks off. Annie didn't think to help him. The man was naked; looking at him was a delight. Getting close to him would have been too much temptation to resist.

She just knew she'd want to touch something. Maybe everything, but a few things specifically...

Once his shoes and socks were off, he gingerly lifted his injured leg onto the mattress, then fell back with a long hearty sigh.

Annie was so enraptured by the up close and personal view of his nude body, it took her a couple of minutes to realize he was snoring again. He was on top of the quilts, stretched out in beautiful bruised perfection, wearing nothing more than a stabilizer on his injured knee.

Annie licked her lips. Well, well, well.

Who'd have thought the man would be *this* accommodating!

She realized he apparently associated the cabin with nakedness, and that took away her smile. As she continued to survey him from collarbone to knees, she wondered at the myriad of things he'd done with the women he brought here. Just how lascivious and lewd were the cabin interludes?

Wind carried a dusting of snow in through the open front door and drew Annie out of her voyeurism. She forced herself to back away from Guy.

When she reached the warm fireplace she turned and hurried outside. The sooner she got the car unloaded, the sooner she could go back and feast her eyes on him some more. Who cared if it was unethical? An opportunity like this might never come along again.

Annie grinned as she thought of his reaction when his head finally cleared. Guy obviously had no idea what he was doing, and that gave her an absolutely splendid idea.

She could barely wait.

GUY WINCED AS he got one eye open and tried to focus on the source of his irritation. The setting sun, in vivid shades of orange and crimson, sent a slanted beam of light through the narrow opening in the drapes directly into his eyes. His mouth tasted like cat litter and his body ached from one end to the other. When he started to sit up, a flash of intense pain radiated from his knee to every other muscle in his body.

He groaned out a quiet curse.

It dawned on him slowly that he wasn't at the hospital anymore, nor was he at home. However, the room, even the bed, were familiar. *The cabin.*

Guy looked around at the nightstand and saw by the hand-set clock that it was nearly six-thirty. The last thing he remembered clearly was Daniel waking him at the hospital, shoving him into scrubs and telling him it was time to go. That damn medicine the nurse kept forcing on him made him groggy. When he took it, he felt like he was dreaming and awake at the same time.

And in those odd dreams, Annie was always there. Touching him. Smiling at him.

Letting him touch her.

He looked down at his throbbing leg and saw it was stiff as a morning erection, sticking straight out thanks to the wraparound brace cushioning his knee.

Besides desperately needing a drink of water, a shower, and something to eat, Mother Nature called. Rather loudly.

Guy threw off the quilt and carefully scooted to the edge of the mattress. Crutches were propped by the padded swivel chair and he reached for them, using them to haul himself to his feet.

Thank goodness the cabin wasn't large, so the bathroom wasn't too far away. Otherwise, he doubted his ability to make it.

The bedroom was right next to the bathroom. Naked, he hobbled the short distance, awkwardly using the crutches to try to take the pressure off his knee. His shoulder hurt like the devil too, but he ignored it. When he stubbed his toe, he swore crudely.

"What in the world are you doing out of bed?"

Guy jumped and almost fell off his crutches.

Annie!

She stood there before him, looking like the woman he'd always known, and the woman he couldn't help dreaming about.

He quickly scanned the cabin, but he didn't see anyone else. All he noticed were dozens of opened books and magazines, scattered around everywhere.

Good God, she'd been studying!

Undeniably alarmed, Guy stared at her. Her dark hair fell loose to her waist. She had brushed it into soft waves and it reflected the crimson and gold glow from the crackling fireplace. She wore some type of lust-inducing skintight leggings that fit her like a second skin, and his own flannel shirt, unbuttoned far too low.

She looked tempting as hell to his foggy brain and abused body.

Guy shuddered as he tried to figure out what to do. He was naked, after all, and there was no place to hide. Hobbled as he was by the crutches and the knee wrap, trying to run would be ludicrous. Not that he intended to do so anyway. The only thing worse than being caught in the raw with Annie as a spectator, would be to put on a bigger show by fleeing.

With no other options left, he crisscrossed the crutches in front of his lap—hardly adequate coverage, but it was the best he could do under the circumstances—while balancing on one leg. "What the hell are you doing here?" he barked.

Annie wasn't the least bit hurt by his tone. She frowned and shook what appeared to be a cooking spoon at him. Dear God, please don't let her be cooking. He could likely survive anything but that.

She advanced despite his frantic warnings for her to stay away. "You should be in bed."

He answered that by asking, "Where's Daniel?"

"At home, I suppose." She shrugged one narrow shoulder, causing his shirt to shift lower on one side. He could see the swell of her right breast. "He was heading that way right after he saw us off."

Guy squeezed his eyes shut and concentrated on not shouting. No. It couldn't be. Daniel wouldn't leave him here alone with Annie.

"Uh, Guy, do you realize you're naked?"

Guy stared at her like she'd suddenly gone blond. "Of course I realize it! It'd be a little hard to miss, especially with the way you're staring!"

Annie didn't answer, and she didn't avert her gaze. He felt her appreciation like a hot stroke smoothing his chilled skin. "Look at my face, dammit!"

She did, but she took her time about doing so. "Well how was I to know?"

"How were you to know what?"

"That you realized you were naked? You didn't realize it earlier. Or at least if you did realize it, you sure didn't care. Not that I'm complaining, you understand."

Guy shook his head, trying to make sense of what she said. He was naked, he was unsteady on his feet, and though he hated to admit it, he was mortified. Plenty of women had seen him naked. Plenty of women weren't Annie.

"What do you mean—"

She lifted her dark brows high and smiled at him. "I mean you stripped naked right there before me, grinning the whole time. You pretty much flaunted yourself, and I found it very…educational."

Horrified, he shook his head and said, "I didn't."

Annie nodded. "You did."

She looked pleased with that fact, and waved her spoon at his abdomen and the crossed crutches, which only managed to hide the really essential stuff. "All this belated modesty…well, you might as well not bother. I've seen everything you own. In fact, I studied it real close, too."

Worse and worse. "You didn't."

She nodded again, vigorously. "I did. And I don't mind telling you, it's all rather strange."

Guy choked and she took another step closer. "Oh, I didn't mean *you* looked strange! No. Of course not. In fact just the opposite! You're so…well…"

She'd gotten breathless, and her gaze ventured south once again.

"Annie."

"Okay, never mind that." A slight blush colored her cheeks, but Guy had no idea if it was embarrassment or excitement. "I was talking about how it'd work. For sex. You didn't really seem... *capable*—"

Masculine outrage washed over him. "I was asleep! And drugged!" He was beginning to sound hysterical. Not good. He definitely needed to remain in control.

Guy cleared his throat. He couldn't deny that he felt affronted at her criticism of his male parts. But he shouldn't. It didn't matter...

"Dammit, Annie, this is ridiculous. Now please turn your head. Or better yet. Leave the room completely."

"Why?"

"Because," Guy said, gritting his teeth, "I have to use the bathroom and the situation is getting critical."

"Oh!" Annie took another step toward him. At this close range, the crutches did him no good at all. "I can help."

"Not in this lifetime!"

With the spoon clutched in one fist, she propped her hands on her hips and scowled. "Daniel said I was to help you."

Pain, embarrassment and annoyance caused his

eyes to narrow. "Daniel won't be able to say anything else when I get through with him."

"Now don't be like that. You're the one who asked to come here."

"I did not!"

"Sure you did." She sounded positive on that point. "You said you needed time to think and to recuperate, and so you wanted me to bring you here. Daniel agreed and told me all about the cabin." She gave him a severe look. "I can't believe you all kept this from me."

He had no idea how to defend their deception on the cabin. In truth, having Annie here was a specific fantasy for him, one he'd never thought to find in reality.

He gave up trying to think of excuses and explanations when Annie reached for his crutches. She was so determined to help, she left him the option of either falling on his face—which he had no intention of doing, especially not bare-assed—or letting her have her way.

She had her way.

Annie repositioned the crutches under his arms and then rushed into the bathroom ahead of him. "I took up the throw rug from the floor so you wouldn't slip. Do you want me to stay and help?"

She sounded far too hopeful. *"Hell no."*

"Spoilsport." She started backing out, her gaze cataloguing every small part of his physique. He couldn't recall ever feeling quite so vulnerable. He didn't like it.

"Let me know when you're done," she said, once again sounding breathless, "so I can help you back to bed."

Using his crutch, Guy shoved the door closed behind her. He squeezed his eyes shut and tried to convince himself this was only a dream. A bad dream. A damn nightmare.

But when he opened his eyes again, the tile floor still felt cold beneath his feet and his knee still throbbed in discomfort.

How the hell did he end up in this situation? He'd just have to put an end to it immediately. As soon as he cleaned up a bit, he'd have Annie take him home where he could suffer in silence. And he would suffer, but not because of his injuries. His home was Annie's home.

The house she'd grown up in, the house that had sheltered all three Sawyers siblings and one hanger-on, would have been sold long ago if Guy hadn't taken it, preserving it, waiting for Annie to want it for herself. So far she'd refused the house with all its less-than-perfect memories. To Guy, the memories were wonderful.

Daniel, now that he was married, was starting to come around. He even talked about his mother more, and he and his dad were beginning a new relationship.

Annie would come around, too, eventually. He'd always figured that some day she would marry and want the house. He'd accepted that as a fact. But he'd never thought about her getting sexual with a man. Now she wanted to experiment and it was eating him up inside.

He couldn't stay here alone with her.

After he splashed his face and brushed his teeth, he was done for. He hurt in places he hadn't even known about. Just getting back to bed would be a triumph, much less facing the cold and the long drive home. But he'd find the energy somewhere.

Guy limped to the door and opened it a crack. He peeked out, and caught Annie peeking in.

They both jumped.

"Are you okay?" Annie asked, at the same time Guy demanded, "What are you doing?"

Annie sighed. "You're awfully surly. Do you need another pain pill?"

His entire body throbbed, his shoulder almost more so than his knee, with his ribs running a close third. He did his best to ignore it all. "No, I don't want any more pills."

"Afraid you'll do something even more outrageous than stripping down to your sexy hide?"

Guy ground his teeth together. The last thing he wanted was for Annie to think his hide was sexy. *Liar.* "No."

"No what?"

It was his turn to sigh. Through the closed door, he yelled, "No, I'm not afraid I'll do something else outrageous." What could be more outrageous than flaunting himself to her? *Don't even think it.* "And no I don't want any damn pain pills. What I do want is something to wear."

Guy waited, but when Annie didn't answer, he peeked out the door again. She was still there. And she was still peeking. "Well?" he asked.

"I'm thinking about it."

He grumbled, and she quickly said, "If you get dressed, it might make you more uncomfortable. I mean, you're only going to be in bed under the quilts anyway. At least, I hope this time you get under the quilts. Last time you flopped—" She hesitated, then said, "Well, flopped isn't a very pretty word is it?"

Heat rushed up his neck. "Annie," he growled with very real menace.

"What I meant was," she rushed to explain, "you *sprawled* on top of the quilts and I had to work for almost twenty minutes to get one free from under you." And in an undertone she added, "You weigh a ton."

"I weigh two twenty-five and you should have left the room, not played around with the quilts!"

"It wasn't the quilts I wanted to play with."

"Annie!"

"As to that, I couldn't quite make myself leave the room, either. Everything of interest was in there." In a softer voice, she added, "I love the differences in your skin texture. Did you know the skin on your hips is smooth and you're so hard and—"

Guy tried for a measure of patience. "Go—get me—something—to put on. *Right now.*"

"You are so stubborn!"

He could hear her moving away and gave a sigh of relief. The paneled wall felt icy against his bare back as he leaned against it, keeping his injured leg straight out. He'd noticed in the mirror that he had so many bruises, he looked like a beat-up tomcat. At the moment, he felt more like something the cat had dragged in.

"Here you go."

Annie started to come in, but Guy held the door firm, only letting it open enough to get his hand out. "I can manage."

"I wouldn't mind helping."

He'd never survive her help; the conversation alone was about to kill him. "I've been dressing myself since I was two. I think I can get along without your assistance."

"But now you're injured."

"This conversation is hurting me a lot more than any damn injury! Go...cook something."

Dear God, he couldn't believe he said that. It was a true indication of his discomfort that he'd make such a horrid suggestion.

For good measure, he not only closed the door firmly, he locked it. Annie was in a very strange mood, and though his head was now finally clearer, he still felt very confused about some of the things she'd said.

In no way did he recall asking her to bring him to the cabin. Hell, he didn't even remember the drive or climbing into bed. And he sure as certain had no memory of strutting his nakedness—or *flop-*

ping—in front of her. Just the thought nearly sent him into spasms.

But she had looked.

The image formed in his mind: Annie looming over his bared body, studying him in minute detail. Her long hair had probably touched him in ways he'd only dreamed about.

She'd said his hide was sexy.

Guy shook off that damning fact. Annie was in a curious frame of mind these days, and so he assumed a certain amount of that curiosity extended to him. He supposed it was natural, even if it did make things a little sticky for him. She was now interested in the more sexual side of men, and he was a man she trusted.

He'd treat this incident just as he had the one at the pond, when she'd been so young. He'd ignore her embarrassment—even though she hadn't really exhibited any.

6

GETTING THE SCRUB bottoms on were harder than he'd figured. Thankfully they were soft and loose, and that helped, but the bathroom wasn't exactly spacious. He sat on the edge of the wide square Jacuzzi tub, which took up the majority of the room, and sort of bent sideways at the waist until he could hook the pants around his foot on his injured leg. After he'd gotten them pulled halfway up, he stuck his other foot in. Hopping around on one leg, which jarred his aching head and made his ribs and shoulder hurt worse, he managed to get the pants to his waist.

That was all she'd brought him. No shirt. Not that he should care. Annie had seen him without a shirt before, but now that she'd seen him without his pants too... It just seemed different. More intimate.

He opened the door and Annie, who'd been leaning on it, nearly fell inside. Guy managed to hold on to his crutch with one hand and catch her with the other. Given the fact that she was so slight, it wasn't difficult.

She smiled up him and her hot little hands flattened on his pecs. He noticed right off that her nipples were hard.

Now his were, too.

Forcing his gaze to her face, he gave her a stern look then stepped around her. "Where are the rest of my clothes?"

Annie hustled along behind him as if waiting to catch him in case he fell. Ha! He'd flatten her if he did. He was way taller and over a hundred pounds heavier.

"Why do you want more clothes?" she asked.

"Because we're leaving."

"Leave! But we can't."

"We most certainly can."

"No."

"Yes." Why the hell was she being so difficult? She probably had no idea what torture it was to be this close to her, but determined not to touch her.

"I've hid the keys to my car."

Little witch. He wouldn't look at her. "I have no idea why you're doing this...."

"I'm trying to force you to think about a few things."

"I can think better at home."

"You're not going home."

He'd almost reached the bedroom. "You don't want to drive me, fine. I'll call a cab."

"We don't have a phone."

He glared at her over his shoulder. "Try again, Annie. There's no way Daniel sent you up here without a phone. I know him too well for that."

She looked deflated. "If you go home, Melissa will just convince you to marry her."

He took another awkward step toward the bedroom. "Is that what this is all about?"

"No." A moment of silence, and then, "You promised to tutor me."

Guy halted in mid hobbling step. Very slowly, he pivoted on his one good leg to face her. "I did what?"

Annie crossed her arms under her breasts. It was blatantly obvious she wasn't wearing a bra, which led his beleaguered brain to wonder if she'd foregone her panties, too.

He concentrated hard on keeping his gaze on her face, trying to sound unaffected. Failing, he asked, "Have you forgotten your underwear again?"

She shrugged. "Lace packed for me, but she didn't include any underthings. In fact, she didn't really pack me too much in the way of clothes at all."

His breath caught in his lungs. "Lace needs a good swat on her backside."

Annie's eyes widened, darkened. She stared at him intently. "I read about that. Some men like it." Her gaze studied him, searching. "Some women, too."

Damn, he was putting ideas in her head. *He was putting ideas in his own head.*

"Do you?"

Guy sucked in a long breath. "We're not going to discuss this."

"You do!" She looked equal parts scandalized and excited. "It's okay," she rushed to assure him. "I thought it sounded...interesting." Then she frowned. "I prefer that you don't think about Lace's bottom, though."

Guy flexed his fingers on the rail of the crutch. "I don't—"

"You promised," she smoothly interrupted, "to tutor me. You said you wanted to come here so you'd have time to think and heal and because you didn't want me seducing someone else. When I argued with you, you promised me that you'd teach me everything I needed to know."

Guy stared. His body was as still as he could make it, but he felt himself thickening, extending. In the loose cotton pants, there'd be no way to hide his erection.

Tutor Annie? The thought was almost too erotic to bear. Had he really made such a promise?

His brain actively tried to recall even a smidgen of what she claimed. Finally he shook his head in denial, even while his heart pounded with need.

Annie grinned. "You said I could ask you anything and you'd answer it honestly."

His lungs deflated. She meant tutor her, as in verbal explanations.

Disappointment warred with relief.

"I can do that," he said, quick to reassure her that words were fine, while trying to make sure he didn't accidentally promise anything more. "We can talk about anything, you know that."

"You also told me you'd explain things. Everything." Her lashes lowered, her cheeks warmed. "And that if I was so curious you'd even be willing to demonstrate—"

Annie stopped in the middle of her sentence. "Guy? Are you all right?"

His knees were back to feeling like butter, even the hurt one which only moments before had been vying with other male parts to be the stiffest. His leg had been losing.

"C'mon," Annie said, grabbing his arm and practically dragging him to the bed. "You look feverish. I think you need to lie down. Daniel said you should stay off your leg as much as possible for a few days."

Guy gratefully dropped to the side of the mattress, glad for the excuse to collapse.

Annie placed her wooden spoon on the nightstand, then put her small hands on his bare shoulders and gently pushed him flat. Her soft breasts moved beneath the flannel, teasing him, cramping his muscles. The black pearl rested in her cleavage, and he knew it would be warm to the touch, just as Annie was warm to the touch.

It was bad enough that she was so near, so determined. But then she crawled right into the king-size bed with him to fluff the pillow behind his head and put another pillow beneath his leg.

She didn't cover him.

Guy snatched the quilt over his lap, and it too

tented over his erection. He doubted a layer of lead could hide his present state of arousal.

Annie didn't appear to have noticed. Yet. "Are you comfortable now?"

He was in bed with her, never mind that he was all but incapacitated—his imagination was working just fine. Of course he wasn't comfortable.

He firmed his resolve and grumbled, "I have a damn headache." He hoped she'd take the hint and leave him alone in his misery.

Her small cool palm cupped his jaw. "Would you like a pain pill?"

"No!" If he did anything at all to blunt the edge of his control, he'd end up with Annie naked in the bed with him. He groaned at the image.

She gave him a coy look. "You don't trust my motives, do you?"

He didn't trust his own, especially when he was drugged.

Her smile told him she knew exactly what he was thinking. "You know what would help?"

She continued to stroke his face until he caught her wrist and pulled her hand down. "Some aspirin," he suggested, anxious to give her something to do besides taunting him. "They're in the medicine cabinet in the bathroom."

Annie shook her head. "I was reading some of the things Lace packed for me—"

"Not those damn sex manuals?"

"Well, yeah. Some of them." She looked at his mouth. "The best ones actually. I guess that's why she couldn't pack me more clothes. The books took up a lot of room."

"Lace has no business—"

"She's being more helpful than you!"

"I doubt she would be if you were coming on to her!"

Choked laughter filled the bedroom. Annie wiped her eyes as she tried to subdue her humor. "Bet that'd even take Lace off guard, huh?"

"Nothing takes Lace off guard."

"Do you really think I'm coming on to you?"

Guy refused to answer.

"Is it working?"

He pinched his mouth shut.

"You know, myths and jokes aside, an orgasm gets rid of headaches."

Guy strangled on an indrawn breath. While he wheezed and sputtered, Annie patted his chest and continued her discourse. "According to what I've read, an orgasm helps to dilate the blood vessels in your brain, which relieves a headache."

Was she offering him an alternative to the aspirin? He finally caught his breath enough to utter, "That's pure nonsense."

"It's documented data, in a book."

"You shouldn't be reading those books."

"We could try an experiment." As she said it, she looked at his lap, then blinked.

Guy groaned, knowing exactly what she'd seen. Though his reaction was all too common to being in bed with a beautiful woman, Annie wasn't just any woman. She was his best friend. She was Daniel's little sister.

His body didn't seem to care. And there was nothing he could do about it now except brazen it out.

"You have an erection."

She said that with the same enthusiasm as if he'd just solved world peace. She looked overjoyed. "Is that for me?"

It took all his control not to cover himself with his hands. He'd never before been embarrassed about his body's reactions in front of a woman. But then, he'd never had to fight this hard to resist a woman.

"Annie, this conversation has gotten way out of hand. In case it's escaped your notice, I'm kind of banged up."

"That's why I'm trying to help! Did you know sexual fantasies can increase your tolerance to pain?" At his skeptical look, she said, "It's true! In a study, people who indulged sexual fantasies were able to tolerate discomfort three times longer."

"Good grief."

She touched his leg, low on his thigh. "You're not wincing anymore."

Bemused, Guy realized she was right. Not only had his leg stopped throbbing, he'd forgotten he even had legs. All his awareness was centered on what was between them.

Now, with her hand petting his thigh through the

quilts, he was only too aware of his body parts. All of them. Sexual fantasies suddenly dominated his mind.

"And another thing. An orgasm can—"

"I know, I know." Even hearing her say it made his skin heat. It was the strangest, most arousing conversational topic he'd ever indulged in. "It supposedly gets rid of a headache." Guy wondered why no one had ever told him that before. He wondered if Daniel and Max knew. Max probably did. Max knew everything about women inside and out. He was such a Romeo.

And Max would probably kill Guy if he knew he was in bed with his sister thinking things he shouldn't think.

"Yes," Annie agreed, "but it can also relieve muscle strain and help you sleep, and—"

"Cure the common cold?" Maybe he could joke his way out of this. Maybe Annie wouldn't notice how rough his voice had gotten, or how his hands shook.

"Actually," she said, her own voice a little raspy, "it does help to relieve the symptoms of a cold. It can clear up your sinuses and temporarily get rid of your stuffy head."

Guy covered his face with an arm, wishing for oblivion. Annie began to massage his leg.

"Stop that!"

"I want to make you feel better." She stretched out next to him on the bed, keeping her head propped on one hand. In a sexy whisper, she said, "Let me help you, Guy."

His leg didn't ache, but everything else on him did. "Annie, this is insane." She was so close he could smell her and it made him want her even closer. It made him want to nuzzle between her breasts, between her legs.

Of its own volition, his arm circled her, his hand opening on her waist.

"Because we're friends?"

"Of course." His words were low and rough and he struggled to regulate his breathing. "And besides that, I'm in no shape to...to..."

"Have an orgasm?"

His stomach clenched. "I was going to say have sex."

She licked her lips and it was all Guy could do not to lick them, too. Annie had one of the sexiest mouths going. Full, pink.

"In one of the books," she whispered, "there's this whole chapter on handwork. I could—"

Guy covered her delectable mouth. If he didn't shut her up, he was likely to explode. "Don't even say it, dammit."

She tried to nod and speak at the same time, but her words were muffled under his hand.

"Annie, you want your first time to be special, don't you?"

Her blue eyes looked very soft, almost caressing his face as she nodded.

He gulped, refusing to interpret that look. "Then you need to wait."

Her eyes darkened and her brows drew down, indicating she had something to say. Cautiously, Guy uncovered her mouth.

"You're a hypocrite."

Guy sighed. "I'm just trying to protect you."

"Ha. How many women have you been here with?" As she spoke, she sat up and Guy could see that his rejection had hurt her feelings.

"Annie." He tried to catch her hand, but she bounded off the bed.

"You come here for your lascivious little rendezvous with other women, then tell me I need to wait."

"I come here for privacy, that's all." He scowled at her—until the left side of the over-large flannel dropped down her shoulder and she didn't bother to pull it back up. She was too busy pacing, but Guy was on pins and needles thinking it might dip further any second and then he'd see her breast.

And her nipple.

He held his breath and tried not to stare.

"I guess that's what I'll do, too."

Guy reared up in the bed. He'd totally lost track of the topic, what with her teasing him with the possibility of a peek show. "What the hell does that mean?"

"It means since this is a family cabin, I can have my own sordid little affairs here. I'm sure Perry won't be as unwilling as you are."

Before he could respond to that she marched out of the room.

"Annie!" Guy was just about to climb out of the bed and go after her when she returned with a glass of water and the aspirin bottle.

"Here's your miserable pills." They hit his chest with a plip, plip. The water sloshed over the side when she shoved the glass into his hand. "I doubt they're half as much fun as what I suggested. Of course I can't say for sure since you refuse to co-operate."

Guy sputtered at her audacity. "You make it sound like I turned you down for a loan! Sex is more intimate than that. It's not something you can jump into lightly."

She leaned down until she was nearly nose to nose with him. The neckline of the flannel gaped, testing his honor not to peek. The necklace swung free, glinting in the lamplight.

In a growl that spoke of frustration and anger, she said, "I don't intend to jump lightly. When I jump, it's going to be whole hog, hot and sweaty and with no holds barred."

Guy scowled at her as he tried to ignore the throbbing in his groin. "You don't know what you're saying."

"Shocked you, huh?"

Actually she was turning him on. "Yes."

"Well aren't you the discerning one?"

His eyes narrowed. She was verbally doing him in and he didn't like it. "I try."

She stuck her nose in the air. "For the record, I didn't even ask you for sex. I offered to service you."

"Oh, for the love of..." He sounded horrified, but he couldn't help that. The image was now firmly rooted in his brain and his gonads more than liked the idea. Every nerve in his body, especially those in his more sensitized regions, screamed for him to say yes.

He shook his head no.

Annie snatched up her spoon, shook it at him, then turned on her heel to storm out again. Guy shouted, "Where are you going?"

She looked at him over her shoulder. "Now I have a headache, too, but I'll be damned if I'll settle for aspirin."

She closed the door behind her.

Guy sat there in the bed, utterly speechless. His body pulsed, his mind ached. He had a raging hard-on.

Surely she didn't mean to insinuate she was... that she'd... *Did she have that chapter on hand-work with her?*

He held his breath and listened as hard as he could, but he didn't hear a sound. Of course, he had no idea how much noise she might make. All women were different and...

Every pain on his body had magically disappeared, overwhelmed by sensual awareness. It dawned on him that Annie was right, that his fantasies had obliterated the hurt from his injuries.

Even a semi couldn't compete with Annie bent on seduction.

Hell, she'd yelled him into arousal.

But now he had a new pain, the ache of acute sexual frustration. He'd take a throbbing knee any day.

ANNIE STIRRED THE contents of the pot as it came to a boil, then turned it on low and stuck a lid on top.

What was Guy thinking right now? She was caught between amusement at the last alarmed look on his face, and righteous indignation that he had turned down her offer flat. Lace had been wrong; Guy needed more than a little encouragement.

Annie had just settled onto the couch with another book, hoping to find a way past his defenses, when the bedroom door opened.

Guy stood there, his face flushed darkly, his chest straining with interesting muscles as he used the crutches to support himself. He filled the doorway.

Annie closed the book and came to her feet. "You should stay in bed!"

He looked her over slowly, as if checking for signs of sexual satisfaction. Annie flushed. Had he really thought she'd be out here cavorting all alone? The image that came to mind, what *he* must have been imagining, scalded her cheeks.

Tentatively, trying to cover her new embarrassment, she said, "You must be getting hungry. I'll have food ready soon."

Guy didn't answer her, and her nervousness increased. "Did the aspirins help?"

His eyes narrowed. He looked...hotly aroused. Annie checked the book in her hand to reaffirm her suspicions. *Straining muscles, flushed skin, dilated eyes.* Yep, Guy had all that. And as she looked at his chest she saw his small brown nipples were drawn tight, visible beneath his springy chest hair. Her breath caught.

"What have you been doing, Annie?"

The gravelly edge to his tone made her experience every single one of the symptoms she'd just catalogued on Guy. She cleared her throat. "Making soup?"

He looked toward the kitchen, as if he didn't quite believe her.

"It's just chicken noodle. You know I'm not a very good cook. But it should be ready soon. I know how often you usually eat, and so I thought..."

She knew she was rambling and drew to a halt. Oh, he looked hungry all right. "Would...would you like to rest here on the couch instead of in the bed? Maybe we could watch a movie."

His nostrils flared, and without a word he made his way to the couch. Annie shoved aside her pile of books.

The seating arrangement was actually as wide as a bed and formed an open square. "Careful now. Let me go get you a couple of pillows."

Guy groaned as he lowered himself, but the

sound was quickly cut off. Annie knew he wanted to hide his discomfort from her.

She also knew she'd added to that discomfort.

Shame at being so self-centered in her goals bit into her determination.

But he had been hard, she reminded herself. So she knew he wasn't totally immune.

She rushed into the bedroom and grabbed the pillows off the bed. She also saw the aspirin still sitting on the nightstand and got caught with a grin.

Guy had his eyes closed when she approached him. Softly, she touched his shoulder. "Lean forward for me."

He did as she asked and Annie slipped the pillow behind him, then carefully lifted his leg to wedge another pillow under there. "Daniel said to keep your leg elevated. Here." She handed him the aspirin and the water, then admonished, "Take them this time."

He didn't argue. After he'd swallowed the pills, he asked, "Did you oversalt the soup?"

"Nope, not this time."

"Did you throw in any weird ingredients?" He kept his eyes closed, holding himself away from her.

"I didn't season it at all because I was afraid I'd ruin it."

Annie sat on a cushion beside him. It was very difficult, but she managed to keep her hands to herself. "In fact, I'm not sure I'd even call it soup, really. I just boiled some chicken until it was tender, then threw in noodles. I was going to make a salad to go with it.''

"How much longer do you think?''

He was being cautiously polite, and that broke Annie's heart. Since he'd slept the better part of the day away, she knew he had to be hungry. Now for food as well as satisfaction.

"I can get you some now if you like.'' She stood, but before she could walk away, Guy caught her hand.

"Annie.''

She squeezed his fingers. "It's okay. I shouldn't have pushed you like that.'' She pulled away, not wanting him to say more, unwilling to hear his explanations and excuses for turning her down.

From the kitchen, she asked, "Do you want milk or water or tea?''

"Milk. Thank you.'' He hesitated before saying, "It doesn't feel right to just sit here and be waited on.''

"I want to do this, Guy. You'd do the same for me.''

"Damn right I would. But that's different.''

"Why?'' Annie loaded up a plate.

"Because you're female. And small.''

"And you care about me?''

A slight hesitation, then: "Yes.''

She could feel him watching her, the heat of his gaze. "I care about you, too, even though you're big and male.'' *Especially because you're big and male.*

"And you trust me?"

I love you. "Yes."

"That's good. Because I want to talk to you."

Outside, the wind rustled branches against the roof and ice pellets drubbed the windows. It seemed a new storm was brewing, though inside they were warm and cozy. The fireplace burned hotly, and there was plenty of dry wood on the hearth and on the covered porch. She'd called Daniel while Guy slept earlier. Everything was set. He could talk all he wanted, but she wouldn't take him home.

Guy appeared content enough sitting up on the seating group with his leg cushioned. Annie placed a tray in his lap with the chicken and noodles, a small salad, milk and the salt and pepper shakers. She got her own plate of food and sat across from him.

After Guy had salted and peppered his food, he tasted it, then gave a nod of approval. "Good."

Annie grinned. "Had you worried, didn't I? But there's no need. Daniel knows I'm not the best cook around so he made sure there was simple stuff to fix. We won't starve."

His brown eyes smiled at her. "I remember those chocolate cookies you baked for us." Gradually, Annie could see him relaxing. "You'd used unsweetened chocolate."

"I didn't know there was a difference."

"Max ate them with his beer. Said they were better than salted nuts."

They both chuckled, and for the next hour they

joked and teased and generally carried on in their normal mode of camaraderie.

When Guy was done eating, after three refills, he patted his flat abdomen and sighed. "Delicious. I probably just put on a few pounds, but it was worth it."

Annie carried the dishes to the kitchen. She wished she'd thought of some kind of indulgent dessert, but she hadn't. Cautiously, she said, "You know a good way to lose weight?"

His groan turned into a laugh. "Don't tell me. Sex."

"You already knew that one?" She resettled herself in the seating area with him.

"Annie, honey, you've got sex on the brain."

It was more than her brain clamoring for attention right now.

"It's a fact!" she assured him. "Why, you can burn off a lot of calories in vigorous sexual activity. Not that I really know the difference between the vigorous and the lazy stuff, but I thought it was interesting."

Guy twisted to face her. His expression was still somewhat strained, but also accepting. "Sweetheart, sex is not a cure-all for everything that ails you."

Annie stretched to reach a specific book, and then flipped to a dog-eared page. "Sex," she said, reading out loud, "can lower your cholesterol and tip the good cholesterol/bad cholesterol ratio. It kicks your respiratory system into overdrive which makes you breathe deep and adds oxygen to your blood, which nourishes all your organs and tissues. And sex releases endorphins, which are effective pain-killers.''

Guy rolled his shoulders, as if easing tense muscles.

Annie flipped to another page. "Accelerated blood flow to the…uh—" she nodded at his lap "—that area, takes pressure off the brain which helps you relax and eases tension in your neck and back.''

She frowned at him. "Guy, you *do* look tense.''

He burst out laughing, which wasn't quite the reaction she'd been going for, but at least he wasn't pushing her away again. Deliberately, Annie shrugged one shoulder and let the flannel droop again. She'd noticed his preoccupation with the shirt earlier, how it had affected him each time the material had slipped down her shoulder.

This time was no different.

His laughter stopped abruptly.

"I'm surprised," she said, adding an edge to her tone on purpose, "that you don't already know this stuff. I mean, here you have this little love nest and you don't even know what you're doing.''

His jaw firmed. "I know exactly what I'm doing.''

"You couldn't prove it by me.''

"Honey, I don't want to prove it to you.''

"Okay, so you don't want me. Tell me what you

do with other—'' she nearly choked, but managed to finish ''—women.''

Guy came up on one elbow to frown down on her. His brown eyes were intense, as hot as the flames in the fireplace. ''I have sex. Is that what you want to know?''

Her heart thundered in jealousy, but she tamped it down. ''I want details. Do you strip for them like you stripped for me? Do you let them examine you?''

The look on his face was comical. ''I feel violated.''

Annie snorted. ''I'm not buying that for a minute. I'll tell you it surprises me, though. Being that this is a little love nest, I figured I'd find some neat stuff. You know, like mirrors on the ceiling, or sex toys hidden away. I guess the Jacuzzi tub counts, but I'm not quite sure how it'd work.''

Guy groaned.

''You could at least take this seriously,'' she said, watching him closely to catch his reaction, ''so when I approach Perry I won't embarrass myself with my ignorance.''

His short hair stood on end. ''You really want to get involved with Perry?'' His voice rose to a near shout.

''Not involved. I mean, I don't want a relationship with him.'' She shuddered even as she assured him of that fact. Perry didn't turn her on. No man turned her on, except Guy. ''But so far he's the only one willing. You're certainly not.''

Guy dropped flat to the couch and covered his face with his arm. He muttered, but Annie couldn't hear what he said, except for the key words of "torture" and "intolerable" and "witch."

"As I just pointed out, Guy, sex is necessary for my general health and well-being." She saw his chest rising and falling with labored breaths. "You do want me to stay healthy, don't you?"

Guy didn't respond to that, except to give another groan. Annie said, "I guess you don't need all the props, huh? That, or else you don't know what to do with them. Is that it? No experience with the kinky stuff?"

"I'm not discussing my personal...experiences with you, Annie."

She shrugged, and the flannel slipped just a little bit more. She waited and when he finally looked at her, she shrugged again for good measure.

Guy's hands curled into fists, held at his sides on the couch. "I don't want you going to Perry."

Her heart pounded, making her breathless, making her body tremble. "You don't want me, period."

He looked away and Annie could practically hear his turbulent thoughts.

Finally, very softly as if the words were forced out, he said, "Yes I do."

Annie's mouth opened, then snapped closed. Cautiously, hope building to the boiling point, she asked, "You do?"

Guy scooted up on the couch until he was sitting

upright with his leg stretched out before him. He took up a lot of room, and looked sexy doing so.

His eyes glittered at her, unwavering. "My erection is for you."

"It is?" She felt like a damn parrot, but he'd done such a quick turnaround, she wasn't sure what to think.

She hadn't known brown eyes could look so burning. Guy reached for her, caught her arm, and pulled her up to his chest. "It is. And now I'm going to start your instruction."

7

GUY HELD HER close, feeling her nervousness and glad of it. "You're too brazen, sweetheart. You need to learn some subtlety."

"Do I scare you?"

What she was really asking, was would she scare that other man, the man she wanted to seduce. It enraged him. "No. But you can push a guy right over the edge, when what you want is a man who's in control."

Her dark lashes swept down to hide her eyes. He wasn't fooled for a second.

"Look at me, Annie."

She did, and her expression was so hungry, so anxious, he almost lost it.

"What are you going to do?" she asked. She looked at his mouth, his throat, then met his gaze.

Control, Guy reminded himself. He had to stay in control. "Anything you want me to."

Her indrawn breath was sexy and sweet at the same time. "I want you to...have sex with me."

She had started to say make love, he was sure of it. But she didn't want him to love her. She just wanted sex. She wanted to experiment.

Guy understood that, but everything in him rebelled against it. Annie was a healthy, attractive, energetic woman, and it was only natural that she wanted to experience more of the sensual side of things. The wonder of it was that she'd stayed innocent so long. Of course, she'd been so protected by her brothers when she was younger, any male would have had a hard time inching close. And then she'd stayed busy getting her bookstore opened up and off to a good start. For the most part, she had never seemed all that interested in sex.

Now he knew better.

Because he understood, and because he cared about her, he'd show her a few things, and still hold on to what honor he could. Anything would be preferable to her going to Perry; the mere thought made him nuts.

"Lie down here beside me."

Annie bit her lip. "Should...should I take my clothes off first?"

Muzzling her became a real possibility. It might be necessary to save his sanity.

"No. Quit pushing. From here on out, let me tell you what you need to do, okay?"

Her lips parted. "Is this a fetish of yours?" Obviously that idea appealed to her. "I mean, you being dominant and everything? Because I've read a whole chapter on fetishes and..."

His hand covered her mouth. "I'm not...dammit, Annie, will you just do as I tell you?" His control was nearly nonexistent.

She laid down. Stiffly. Staring up at the ceiling. The audacious woman demanding satisfaction was now hidden behind a mask of uncertainty.

Guy rested his hand on her belly. He felt the heat of her and his own body burned. She was so soft, so slight.

She was holding her breath.

"Annie, are you nervous?" Gently, he caressed her and watched her face color with desire. That, or she was suffocating.

She gasped for air. "I'm...worried."

Guy leaned down and kissed her temple, a featherlight touch, teasing, brushing. In her ear, he whispered, "About what?" In the back of his mind he thought perhaps now that he'd called her bluff, she'd back off.

In his heart, he prayed she wouldn't.

"Orgasm face."

His hand, his heartbeat, stilled. "What?"

"I'm worried about orgasm face. I read this article that said some people look really dumb when they climax. They make funny sounds and jerk and jump and roll their eyes and I'm afraid I'm going to look really bad because I've had very little practice."

Every pulse beat of his heart made him more rigid. He couldn't quite seem to form a coherent sentence.

Annie, still stiff beside him, turned her head to see his face. "You could go first." She sounded inordinately enthusiastic about that idea. In her new eagerness, she forgot she was nervous and reared up over him, bracing one hand on his bare, bruised shoulder, the other tucked close to his side. He could feel her breath on his nose. "If you went first, I could see how you look and then I wouldn't be so worried how I'd look."

"No."

Her eyes crossed, trying to see him so closely. She frowned. "Why not?"

Guy didn't tell her he had no intention of taking his own release.

He felt pressured into assuring her first experience was a good one—a good one not with Perry—and that was his plan. But he wouldn't actually make love to her. He wouldn't share intercourse because that would cross too many boundaries.

And once he crossed them, he wasn't sure he'd ever be able to find his way back.

When he didn't answer her right away, her face softened into lines of understanding. "You're a grunter, aren't you? Do you scrunch all up, too? I won't mind, I promise. If we both look dumb, then I guess we could just close our eyes, right?"

Ignoring her ridiculous words, especially since he had no idea what the hell he looked like when he came, Guy caught the back of her head and pulled her down until he could kiss her throat. Another series of light, tempting kisses.

Annie groaned. "I like that."

He kissed her collarbone.

"And that."

He opened his mouth against her skin.

"And that!"

He sighed. "Annie, I don't need a blow-by-blow report."

Her chest heaved and her fingers dug into his shoulder. The pain was nothing compared to the pressure building in his groin.

Panting, she said, "I read in one book that you should tell your partner what pleases you."

"I know what pleases you."

"You do?" She pushed back to see his face again. "How?"

Guy turned the smallest bit and kissed her wrist. Her fingernails had left small indentations in his bruised skin. "By this. By the way you react."

"Ohmigod! Am I hurting you?" She looked appalled by her own actions and would have pulled away if he hadn't caught her to him. Her squirming not only hurt his aching body, but it further incited his lust.

Muscles clenched, Guy asked, "Do you feel how close you are to me? You're pushed up against my hip. I can feel your heat there. And where our chests touch, I can feel your heartbeat pounding." He smoothed his hand over her back. "Why don't you just forget the damn books, okay?"

She tucked her face into his throat. "I don't want to hurt you."

He smiled—until she reared up and said sincerely, "I'll be gentle with you, I promise."

The laugh took him by surprise, and annoyed Annie.

"I don't want you to laugh at me, either."

"I'm sorry." He smoothed her thick, silky hair. "But I think you're adorable."

She peered down at him, considering his words, before nudging her face into his throat again. "What if I have a silly orgasm face?"

As she spoke, her lips brushed his skin, burning him, driving him nuts. "All women look different—"

Her arms stiffened, lifting her away. "How many female orgasm faces have you seen?"

Ferociously, she stared down at him. Guy bit back his grin. He hadn't expected this, hadn't expected to laugh with her, to have fun with her now. He'd been all set to be a martyr, but Annie wasn't letting him.

"Every orgasm face I've seen has been female. I sure as hell haven't been watching any men."

"That's not what I mean and you know it." Then she blinked. "Have you...you know. Ever seen yourself?"

Despite her resistance, Guy pulled her down to rest against his chest. "Rule number one. You never discuss other partners when in bed."

She tried to stiffen her arms again. "But—"

"Rule number two." He crushed her close so she couldn't wiggle. "You don't ask the guy you're with embarrassing questions."

"Why should you be embarrassed? I bet you look great when you're straining and groaning—"

"Rule number three," he said, deliberately drowning out her words. "Never argue with a man who's trying to give you pleasure."

She slumped against him. One second she was docile, limp, the next she clung to him so tightly his shoulder and ribs screamed in protest. "I don't mean to argue with you. I'm sorry."

"Shh." He could feel the tremors in her body and knew she was excited. Just because he had to suffer unrequited lust, didn't mean she should. Hopefully, what he intended would be enough. She couldn't go to Perry. She deserved so much more than that slobbering fool could offer her.

Since he couldn't think of a single alternate to Perry, he had to sacrifice himself. *Sacrifice! Ha!*

"I'm going to kiss you, Annie." At least that would give her mouth something to do beside bombard him with outrageous comments.

"Hallelujah."

"Don't be a smartass," he warned. "Now just relax, okay?"

"I have been kissed before, you know."

A growl rumbled in his chest. "I don't want to know."

"Why?"

Guy covered her mouth with his own. It was a simple kiss, easy, as teasing as the kisses he'd put on her throat. Annie pressed closer; her lips parted.

Lightly, he slipped his tongue in, then back out again.

She gasped. Their lips were still touching when she said, "Can you do that again?"

He did. And again and again.

She tried to follow him, tried to deepen the kiss, but that would have interfered with his plans.

Her small fist connecting with the center of his chest took him by surprise.

"Stop teasing me!"

Guy smothered a laugh while he rubbed away the new ache. "And you accused me of trying to be dominant."

Before the words had finished leaving his mouth, Annie had clamped her hands on either side of his head and held him immobile for a killer kiss. What she lacked in finesse she made up for with verve.

He wanted her. More than he'd ever wanted any woman. He struggled to distance himself from the effect of her warm damp mouth on his, her slim body along his side, her hands, gentle and warm and so damn small and female. He knew he'd lose his head entirely if he didn't break the kiss.

He did that by the expedient manner of grasping her behind.

Annie lurched up with a moan. Her eyes, heavy and soft, stared at his face in wonder. "Do I look like you?" she asked on a husky whisper.

Her thick lashes were at half mast, her blue eyes vivid with heat, her rounded cheeks flushed to a rosy glow. She was beautiful. "Hell no."

She touched his jaw. "Your face is flushed," she murmured low, "and your eyes look…hungry."

His abdomen pulled tight; his erection throbbed. "Then yes, in that way you look like me."

"Is it always like this?"

He cuddled her behind a little closer, wanting to distract her, wishing she wouldn't keep analyzing things. "No. Usually the woman is too involved to be so chatty."

"Oh."

"Kiss me again. I like it."

"I thought you weren't supposed to tell me what you liked—"

Guy took control. He kissed her, stroking his tongue deep, slanting his mouth over hers, amazed by the perfect fit.

"Give me your tongue, too, sweetheart."

She did, shyly at first, then hungrily. Her hands coasted over his chest and stopped at his nipples.

"Annie." She gasped as he took her wrists and tried to move her hands away. "Don't do that."

"Why?"

He shifted to the side to face her more fully. His knee smarted and he winced until he'd gotten it properly situated. He kissed her palm and said, "There are better places to touch me." Like on his back, where it didn't matter as much.

"I read that men are as sensitive there as women."

"Let's find out." He covered her breast through the flannel. Soft and delicate. He wanted her naked, but wasn't sure he could take the sight of her nudity.

Her heartbeat slammed against his palm. Her eyes closed, her back arched.

"Such a reaction," he whispered, using his thumb to taunt her nipple into a stiff peak.

"I—"

"I know. You like this."

With her eyes squeezed shut, she bobbed her head.

He didn't mean to, but he heard himself ask, "Have you ever lain like this with another man?"

"No."

He watched her face, gauging her reaction to his touch. "Has any other man touched you here?"

"*No.*"

His blood rushed through his veins. "Then no other man has done this either." He caught her nipple between his finger and thumb and tugged gently.

Her moan was loud and very satisfying.

Guy kissed her chin, the bridge of her nose, her closed eyelids while he continued to tug and tease and roll. Her breaths turned loud and harsh.

"Guy!"

"What about this?" Easily lifting her slight weight, he levered her upward until he could reach her breast. He took her flannel covered nipple into his mouth.

His teeth nipped, causing her to jump. His lips plucked, and she moaned in response. He suckled, and her entire body stiffened, bowed. The shirt, once his but now scented by her body, grew quickly damp.

Annie's hands tunneled through his hair and held him tight. Her leg came over his, bumping his knee but barely noticeable other than the fact her body was perfectly aligned with his, the notch of her thighs pressed tight to his groin. He covered her bottom and drew her closer still. His hands were large enough to completely cover her rounded tush.

Suddenly she pushed him away and before he could ask, she started fumbling with the buttons on the flannel.

"Annie, wait." He caught her hands and tried to still them.

If she stripped, he'd lose his fragile grasp on control. "Let's go slowly here, honey."

"No." Buttons went flying when she gave the shirt a frustrated jerk. Eyes wide, she looked at him, chagrined.

"Well." Guy cocked a brow and tried to ignore the sight of her partially bared breasts, her cleavage, the edge of one firm nipple. He cleared his throat. "That's the first time a woman's ever ripped her own clothes off for me."

Annie's chin lifted. "You're hurt. I was trying to give you a hand." Then she looked uncertain. "Would you rather I rip your pants off?"

Tenderness overwhelmed him. He'd known this woman since she was a shy little girl. He'd watched her grow up in the shadow of her older brothers, one a serious, somber overachiever, and one so charismatic, everyone loved him, male and female alike.

Her father had ignored her, her brothers only wanted to protect her. And Guy...he just wanted to love her.

He did love her.

Curving his hand around her thigh, he urged her to lift her leg completely over his waist.

"Guy?"

"I want to get a good look at you, Annie. You're so damn beautiful." He nudged and shifted until he had her sitting on his abdomen.

Her face was pink, her gaze wary. "I'm not beautiful," she said, trying to scoff. But at his scorching look, she asked, "You think I'm beautiful?"

Slowly, Guy parted the shirt until it slipped down her arms. He had a hard time swallowing past the lump of affection and lust and love choking him.

"I think," he rasped, cuddling each small breast in his large hands, "that you're sexy and sweet and undeniably beautiful."

"Oh Guy."

"Lean down here."

Her thighs tightened on his hips. "Lean...?"

"Down here." He glanced up and caught her breathless anticipation. "I want to kiss you some more."

Her chest rose and fell. "My mouth?"

"Your nipples."

"Ohmigod."

Guy paused. She was aroused, but also wary. And he knew without a doubt that she was a virgin. The last thing he should do was to rush her. "You're shaking."

"It's...well, we're..." She frowned at him, gloriously naked from the waist up, her hair steaming down to her behind. "Shouldn't we be in the bed?"

Guy wondered if she was changing her mind, if she was stalling. "Why does it matter?"

"Because I want you naked, too, and it'd be easier to work these bottoms off you in the bed. There's really not enough room here."

Now he was shaking. "Here is fine."

Annie gave him a speculative look for a good five seconds, then slipped off his body before he could stop her. A nice bounce in her breasts distracted him as she stood beside him by the couch.

"I want my first time to be in a bed." She made it a demanding statement.

"Honey, it doesn't matter." Except in his mind. Getting in bed with her would definitely be a mistake. He just knew it.

"I want us both naked and ready, not just me."

He leaned up to look at his lap. His erection tented the scrub bottoms. "Uh, Annie, I'm as ready as I'm going to get." Beyond ready. Desperate actually. Not that he needed to be ready for what he planned.

"But it's getting late," she pointed out. "I didn't sleep much last night."

The way her mind worked never failed to amaze him. "Why not?"

"Because I watched you sleep." She seemed unaware or unconcerned with his scrutiny of her breasts. "Those damn nurses kept creeping in and trying to look you over. They're shameless."

Guy ignored her comments on the nurses. There was a husky catch to his voice when he asked, "You stayed all night at the hospital with me?"

"Of course."

She was so matter-of-fact, as if any other choice would have been incomprehensible. His heart softened even more.

"And since I know we're both tired," she added, "and already well fed, I figured we'd do…*this*, now that you're being more reasonable. Then we'd turn in."

He desperately tried to put her off. "You make *this* sound like baking bread."

"Oh, no." She looked down the length of his body. "I expect this to be loads of fun and very exciting."

"Not that you want to put any pressure on me, huh?"

Annie scowled at his dry tone. "I'm willing to make allowances for your injury." She glanced at his leg. "Will you be able to do this with your injured knee? We can refer back to the books for some different positions if it'll help to keep from hurting you."

He didn't want her nose back in those damn

books. "You're not going to cause me any pain," he assured her. *No more than the pain of a terminal hard-on.*

"Still, it'll be better on the bed where we can maneuver. I realize sex requires some mobility."

"For the love of...we're not going to be doing acrobatics." At least he didn't think so. Perhaps she'd read a chapter on *that* too! And ridiculously, the thought of Annie being "mobile" made his stomach clench and his muscles tighten with sexual expectation.

Annie shrugged. "I read that men just want to sleep afterward. So we might as well be in the bed so you won't have to move again."

With every breath, she managed to insult him. "Only a total pig falls asleep right afterward!"

"A pig, huh?"

She looked so skeptical, he figured the books had convinced her otherwise. Then he added, "Perry would probably fall asleep."

"You think so?" With her upper body naked, she sauntered to the fireplace and banked the fire until only mellow glowing embers remained. She closed the glass screen securely.

Guy watched in appreciation, every small turn and twist of her slender body. The shadows in the room emphasized all the curves and hollows of her perfect body.

With a smile, she returned to him and picked up his crutch, then began tugging on his arm. "C'mon.

I'll help you to the bed. Then you can just doze off afterward.''

Gritting his teeth, Guy insisted, "I will *not* doze off."

Determination shone in every line of her face. Giving up, Guy hauled himself painfully to his feet. He didn't tell her that he knew he wouldn't fall asleep because for him, there'd be no afterward. Just Annie's pleasure, her response, her awakening.

He swallowed hard.

He'd ease her into things. He was the experienced one, the one in control. He'd overwhelm her sexually and she wouldn't even realize that he wasn't completely involved, that he'd held himself back.

He'd use his hands, his mouth and his tongue, to make certain she enjoyed herself. Once he'd given her a climax—and he fully intended to watch every nuance of her orgasm face—he'd cuddle her close and, given what she'd just told him about being up all night, *she'd* be the one falling fast asleep.

In *his* arms.

It would have to be enough for him.

Guy stopped by the side of the bed and propped the crutches against the footboard. The air was chilled, the bed wide and comfortable. The small lamp on the nightstand was on, lending dim illumination to the room.

He drew a slow, deep breath and tried to gentle his voice, to stop the trembling in his hands. He'd be careful with her. He'd be tender and understanding.

He'd go very, very slow.

Before he could turn and face her, Annie reached around him and pulled open the drawstring on his bottoms. They dropped to his knees.

"Annie."

"Indulge me," she whispered, unrepentant. "I really do like looking at you."

He gasped, but then her arms were around him, both her small warm palms cuddling his painful erection, her soft breasts pressing into his back, and all he could do was feel.

His moan was a harsh sound in the otherwise silent room.

Against his shoulder blade, he felt Annie's open mouth, damp and delicate. "Does this bruise hurt?"

"No." His voice was a croak.

"This one?"

He shook his head. Her inquisitive hands measured his length, his width.

"It's amazing how you feel," she said with awe. "Silky soft over such rigid hardness."

"Oh God."

"I wanted so badly to touch you this afternoon. I should be sainted for resisting your irresistible body. I hope you appreciate my consideration." Her hand squeezed with just the right amount of force. "Another woman wouldn't have shown you such regard, you know. But I respect you."

He wondered what the hell that was all about.

"No other woman," he rasped, pointing out an irrefutable fact, "has taken advantage of me in a drugged state."

"No other woman has *had* you when you were drugged. I think, under the circumstances, I've shown exemplary behavior."

With her small hands stroking, cuddling him, he could barely follow her words, much less offer up an argument. "Annie." He tried to reach down for the scrubs, intending to cover himself before it was too late.

"Don't be shy, Guy. I'll be careful with you."

He growled. Their hands did battle for control of the bottoms, and Annie won. But then, his heart wasn't in the struggle. Not really.

"You feel wonderful," she breathed. "But you have so many bruises. I'm so, so sorry you were hurt."

She began kissing him every place that he was marked and it was the most exotic, the most erotic thing he'd ever experienced.

Thank God she stayed on his back. If she'd moved to the front with her hot little mouth, he'd be a goner.

Just thinking it nearly did him in.

Guy clenched his fists, hoping to regain his sanity, knowing it was futile.

Her hand squeezed. "I read about this in the books, too. How a man likes to be held tightly, more roughly than a woman."

She'd read about it, Guy thought, in anticipation of doing this to Perry.

That dark thought infuriated him and he jerked around to face her. The abrupt movement caused pain to shoot up his leg, and he didn't quite manage to hide his wince or his low grunt.

"Lie down."

Annie, breasts flushed and rosy nipples tight, pressed against his shoulders even as her eyes drank him in. The way she looked at him was better than how most women touched. And it made lying down a necessity.

After shoving a pillow beneath his knee and admonishing him not to move, Annie stretched out beside him. But she didn't stay there. Her hands were everywhere, stroking, exploring, exciting.

Guy attempted to slow her down, but she kissed him, his shoulder first then his collarbone, then his ribs.

Her southerly path had his mind rioting with ideas. "Annie," he gasped, "stop."

"Shh. I want to make you feel better." She squirreled around until her delectable backside faced him, and she could give all her attention to his groin.

And she showed no reservations at all.

He was supposed to be initiating *her!*

Guy started to tell her so, but her tongue touched a bruise on his upper thigh and stole his voice. His body lurched.

"Easy," she whispered, seducing him, setting

him on fire, stealing away all his hesitation. He was
beginning to feel like a virgin on prom night.

"I studied up on this all day while you were
sleeping," Annie told him. "I'm pretty sure I know
what I'm doing."

"You're not supposed to be doing anything," he
reasoned. "You're a damn virgin."

She peered over her shoulder at him, and gave
him a pitying look. "Virginity and stupidity are not
synonymous."

"Virginity and timidity should be!"

"Oh good grief." She climbed off the side of the
bed and started shucking off her leggings. Guy
could only gape.

And breathe hard in anticipation.

And feel his body react.

Too late to close his eyes now.

"I know I'm not perfect," Annie explained, "but
Lace assures me it won't matter."

She straightened slowly, her bottoms on the floor,
her face bright red but her gaze direct.

She hadn't worn panties.

Guy thought he might come from just looking at
her.

Not perfect? She was the most perfect woman
he'd ever seen. Her body, her smile, her blush. The
brazen way she'd seduced him so thoroughly, her
strength and her determination. Her caring. They all
combined to make her irresistible to him.

Guy took a deep breath and held out his hand.
"C'mere."

Two seconds later Annie was in the bed with him, her skin silky and hot against his own, and he knew he was a goner.

The battle had just been won.

8

"IT'S KIND OF cold in here, isn't it? Are you chilled? I don't want you to get sick on top of everything else."

Guy could hear the concern—and the slight nervousness—in Annie's tone as he pulled her on top of him. She tried to keep her legs closed, and he clasped her thighs and opened them over his. His injured knee got bumped, but the pain was a dull ache compared to his pounding lust.

Annie tucked her face in close to his throat and her fingers bit into his upper arms. Now that they were all situated, now that he'd quit fighting her, her bravado had melted away.

He hadn't done a very good job of seducing her, overwhelming her, making her forget herself. She was all too aware of the uniqueness of being with him, and that wouldn't do.

He wanted her mindless with wanting, and set about getting her there.

"It's hot as hell," he told her, stroking her shoulder, the small of her back, over her firm, silky bottom. "You make me hot."

"That's—" She gasped as his hand slid between her thighs from behind. "—*good.*"

She'd nearly screeched, in mingled surprise and excitement. He didn't need to ask if any other man had touched her this way. Her reaction was telling enough for him to know this was a new experience.

Stroking his fingers over her, he found her wet, ready, despite her nervousness. He touched her gently, opened her, then carefully pushed one finger inside.

Her muscles clenched, her body tightened, and he whispered, "Shh. Easy now."

She was deathly silent.

Guy kissed her shoulder, her throat, loving the taste of her warm flesh, inhaling her scent. With his free hand he rubbed her nape, then brought her mouth to his.

He took her gasping breath and gave her his own as he continued to stroke deep inside her.

His mouth still against hers, their lips wet, he whispered, "You're so tight."

"I'm sorry." She wiggled, trying to accommodate his finger, the unfamiliar intimacy, and the movement tantalized his swollen erection.

"Don't be sorry. I love it." *I love you.* The words burned in his throat, but Annie didn't deserve his emotional trap. He'd give her what she wanted, but he refused to burden her with the rest.

"I...I want to touch you, too."

He couldn't give her that. "Not right now."

"Guy—"

"I'd lose it, sweetheart. I'm too close to the edge already." An understatement if ever there was one. In truth, he'd fallen off the cliff the second she'd popped the buttons on her flannel shirt. He'd been teetering there for months anyway. Maybe even years.

Marrying Melissa was out of the question.

Hell, he couldn't marry anyone, not when it was Annie he loved.

Yet she was just experimenting, and this was only one step in all the new experiences she wanted, *deserved,* to have.

"Do you know how soft you feel, Annie?"

Gasping, her narrow back arched, she asked, "Am as I soft as you are hard?"

"Yes." He kissed her again. He wanted to imprint himself on her, to force the same memories on her that he knew would stay with him forever.

With one arm tight around her waist, he brought her higher so that the warm notch of her thighs rested on his bare abdomen and he could attend to her breasts.

Annie helped by stiffening her arms, raising her breasts over his mouth. To his distraction, the movement also caused her mound to press more firmly against him, making him nearly incoherent with need.

Keeping his hips still, holding back the savage urge to take her, was the hardest thing he'd ever done.

She made no sound as he drew one taut nipple

into his mouth. Other than the grasp of her feminine muscles, she was immobile. He drew on her for long minutes, stroked her with his fingers until they were both shaking and on the verge of coming.

"Annie?" She didn't answer and when he looked at her, he saw her face was utterly still, drawn tight, her eyes squeezed shut, her teeth sunk into her bottom lip.

Guy smoothed her backside as he studied her. "Sweetheart, I need to know if you like what I'm doing."

Her head bobbed, sending her hair to play over his chest, his shoulders.

"Tell me."

Her eyes snapped open; her breath left her in a loud rush. "You told me not to," she rasped, accusing. "You told me to be quiet."

Her nipples were wet, stiff. He plucked at them with his fingertips. "I told you I didn't need a blow-by-blow report. I never told you to hold your breath, to be so quiet I wasn't sure if you were still alive."

Her lashes lifted until her eyes were round. He could practically feel the groan bubbling up inside her before it burst out, loud, heartfelt.

"I *love* what you're doing to me! I feel like I'm melting on the inside and coming apart on the outside and I never want it to end, but I want to find the end if that makes any sense and—"

Guy kissed her, smiling, damned pleased with her enthusiasm. "And this?" he asked, still teasing her mouth with his as he moved his fingers out of her, higher, finding a spot that made her entire body shudder.

"Yes!"

Watching her face while he carefully stroked her, he judged her response, and he saw the moment she was near climax. He wanted it with her. He wanted to see her scream, to see her face contort. Orgasm face. He smiled painfully, biting back his own cresting need to come.

Annie lurched off him. Panting, she moved out of reach before he could stop her.

"What is it?" Was she afraid of what she felt? Ha. Not his Annie.

"I want you with me." Her breasts rose and fell rapidly, shimmering, her nipples flushed dark and pointed. She swallowed hard, still breathing in pants. "I want you inside me my first time."

The words alone were almost enough to send him into oblivion. Summoning herculean control, he lied, "I don't have any protection."

"I do."

His conscience slumped in regret while his body did a robust cheer.

Then all he could do was gaze in mute surprise as Annie pulled a shoebox out from beneath the bed. It overflowed with a variety of rubbers in every color of the rainbow, every size, some French ticklers, some haltingly plain.

"Where in the world...?"

"Lace sent them. She included a note telling me

not to show them to you until the right time, because some of them might intimidate you."

Annie climbed over him, the box in hand and settled herself at his side. She stared at his erection, the box, then asked, "Large?"

Guy dropped his head back on the pillow and stared at the ceiling. He wasn't a saint. And no mere man was set up to resist the irresistible.

With a distinct lack of enthusiasm, he said, "Average will do."

"You're kidding?" Her voice rang with disbelief. "They come larger than *that?*"

He didn't open his eyes; he wasn't prepared for her speculation on the size of male parts, especially not his male part.

Actually, he wasn't prepared for any of this.

"Are you okay, Guy?"

"Yeah." Why not? Why not do this for her, and then suffer silently while she carried her newfound knowledge to that other lucky bastard?

This, he was certain, was one of those times when a man's two heads debated over the ideas of wisdom. And in this case, bigger was not better— not when the smaller of the two was winning.

"Blue? Red?"

His hands fisted in the sheet. Her voice was breathy, anxious, awed. He couldn't answer, then realized he didn't need to when he heard the rustling of plastic, and felt Annie's warm fingers fold around him.

"It's all right, Guy. I know you're probably nervous. I promise I'll be very, very careful. You'll barely notice me.''

Barely notice her? She was naked and sitting beside him and had his average male part held securely in her hand! Every fiber of his being was noticing her in a big way.

Annie expertly slid the condom—plain, thank goodness—onto his erection. He ground his teeth together, some small part of his honor still warring with his decision, and still losing.

''You did that awfully well,'' he half complained, thinking that a little fumbling on her part might have helped him to regain his senses.

''I've been practicing.''

Guy lurched as damning pictures ran through his mind. His sudden tensing caused her hand to tighten on his erection.

When their gazes clashed, Annie soothed him by saying, ''Not on men, at least not before now. The book said to practice on a broomstick. I nearly went through an entire box before I got it right.''

He fell back in relief, right before her thighs encased his hips and her hands braced on his chest.

''I can't know why they suggested a broomstick, though. As far as I can tell, there's absolutely no resemblance.''

''Annie.'' Guy stared at her, amazed by her initiative, her determination.

''Shh,'' she said, stroking one pectoral muscle which he'd just noticed was incredibly sensitive to her touch. ''I'm not going to hurt you.''

If he hadn't been so turned-on, he might have laughed at her cocky, clichéd assurances which, under normal circumstances, she should have been receiving, not giving.

Instead he gave up. Annie on the make was a heady experience. Too heady to temper.

"Scoot up a little."

She anxiously did as he asked.

"Just relax, Annie." His fingers were large, rough against her soft flesh, and she made a crooning sound as he opened her, his touch as gentle as he could make it.

He held himself ready for her, and with the other hand cupped her bottom as she carefully prepared to slide down his length. "Easy now."

She flinched as his erection began to stretch her. It tore at his heart, and at the same time made him feel like doing the tarzan yell.

Sweat broke out on his brow.

Not to be deterred, Annie continued her descent despite her discomfort. In a rasp, she asked, "Are you sure you're just average?"

Her innocence filled him with warmth. "I promise."

Using the tip of one callused finger, Guy stroked her slick female flesh, up and around her most sensitive nerve endings. Her stifled groan broke the silence.

Clamped against his sides, her thighs tightened even more. He stroked her soothingly, insistently, watching her lips part, her eyes close. She was wet, but still a virgin, and she needed his careful care, his restraint.

"Go as slow as you like—"

His words died on a shout as she abruptly forced herself down in one hard, fast movement, taking him deep inside her, enclosing him in snug wet heat.

Sweet hell! Her nails bit into his chest, her muscles grasped him tight, and she yelled, "Guy!"

Amazingly, he felt her contractions begin. His back arched, his body pulsed. Pain radiated from his knee, his shoulder, but he didn't care. Pleasure overrode the pain. The pleasure of Annie coming, her scent, her gasps, her hands clinging to him.

His body alternately went into spasms of intense sensation, explosive release, then blessed numbness. It was by far the most pleasure he'd ever had, more than he'd ever expected.

He sank into the bedding, Annie draped over him, her soft mouth touching his throat as she gulped for air. Her limbs were still shaking, her heartbeat still thumping in counter time to his.

Long minutes passed while he refused to think. And then he heard Annie whisper, her voice still shaky but soft, "See, that wasn't so bad."

His every nerve ending was still tingling and she thought it wasn't *so bad?* He got his eyes open. She watched him, her elbows propped on his chest, one hand stroking his jaw.

Weariness dragged at him. He felt too lethargic, too sated, to stay alert.

"I love your orgasm face," she said, and he realized that rather than watching her, she'd watched him!

"Annie." Damn, choking back the words was near impossible. He'd done what he shouldn't have done, and gotten more than he'd ever counted on. Regret weighed him down; regret that they couldn't stay here forever, regret that he couldn't claim her as his own.

Regret that she intended this as the first experience of many—with another man, a man who didn't deserve her.

Knowing he shouldn't, but too tired to stop himself, he touched her face, her lips, and whispered, "I'm sorry, Annie. So damn sorry. This never should have happened."

Her face paled, but she didn't say anything, just lowered her head. Guy thought she was going to kiss him again, and he closed his eyes, waiting. But the kiss didn't come, and then it didn't matter—because like a pig, he fell asleep.

GUY CAME AWAKE with a start at an unfamiliar noise. He looked around the room, but he was alone. He didn't know what had disturbed him, but now that he was awake, he discovered that every bruise on his body held new complaints.

Annie had loved him thoroughly, that was for sure. And then, without any pillow talk, without any reassurances, he'd passed out.

Damn, he was worse than Perry!

He closed his eyes while considering what he'd done.

Making love with Annie had been the sweetest, most emotionally devastating thing he'd ever experienced. She was good. Better than good.

Maybe he should read a few of her books.

Guy smiled. He felt so replete, he almost chuckled. *Annie had made love to him.*

"Look at him!" a familiar voice said, intruding into his thoughts. "He's banged up from one end to the other and he's smiling like a sap even in his sleep."

Guy lurched half out of the bed and his eyes snapped open so fast that his head throbbed. Silhouetted by the sunlight streaming through the large front window, Daniel stood there in the bedroom doorway. He looked like an avenging angel, highlighted as he was.

Then the significance of his appearance registered.

Daniel!

Obviously, Daniel was responsible for disturbing his sleep, but his appearance at this precise moment didn't make any sense. "Uh…"

Daniel frowned. He looked over his shoulder at someone and asked, "Is he still drugged? No? Then I'd like to know what he's so happy about, all things considered."

He turned to Guy again, waiting.

"Uh…" What the hell could he say?

And where was Annie? Guy hated to think of her being a witness to her big brother's disapproval.

Although Daniel didn't look disapproving so much as curious.

With a guilty start, Guy realized that the sheet barely maintained his modesty. And it was obvious he'd been sleeping naked. It was an effort, but he forced himself into a sitting position and covered himself more thoroughly.

In an affected tone that he hoped sounded calm and reassuring, Guy asked, "What are you doing here, Daniel?"

"Melissa knows where you are," Daniel said without hesitation. "And she's on her way."

"What?" The very last thing he needed was for Melissa to show up. Having Daniel as an observer was more than enough to have to deal with.

"Dad told her you were here. With Annie. I can't believe he did, but he did." Daniel shrugged.

"But...where is Annie?" He tried to see around Daniel and couldn't. It dawned on him that the cabin suddenly felt...empty.

And so did his heart.

He moved to the edge of the bed to stand.

Daniel rushed to his side. "Hey, you should take it easy. Here, let me help you."

Panic edged away Guy's guilt and any pain he felt. "Where the hell is Annie?"

Daniel, looking faintly satisfied, said, "She said she was getting ready to leave."

"Leave?"

"Yeah." Daniel clasped Guy's arm and helped him to stand, then grinned when he saw Guy was naked. "You think you should get dressed before you start chasing my baby sister?"

Guy's face went blank. What the hell was he doing? *What was Annie doing?* He shook his head and hurriedly looked around for something to put on. Daniel again came to his rescue and produced the scrubs from where they'd been half kicked beneath the bed.

Guy felt color race back up his neck when he remembered the way Annie had stripped him. And now her brother was standing before him.

Raising one brow, Daniel asked, "Undressed in a hurry last night, did you?"

With a lot of groaning and wincing, Guy sat on the side of the bed and worked the bottoms on over the knee immobilizer. He ignored Daniel's question to ask one of his own. "Why is Annie leaving?"

After adjusting his glasses, Daniel said philosophically, "I guess she figured that with Melissa here, she might as well take off."

"*Is* Melissa here?"

"She should be any minute."

Seconds later Daniel's younger brother, Max Sawyers, daredevil, world wanderer and admitted woman addict, stuck his head around the door. "The virago has arrived."

Guy felt stunned at Max's appearance. The last he'd heard, Max was still in the wilds of Canada, wrestling bears and personal demons.

Daniel nodded at Guy and answered unasked questions. "Yep, he's back. And no worse for the wear of roughing it in total seclusion."

"I had a relaxing time," Max claimed, and as usual he omitted any details. "That is, until your lady friend insisted that I give her a ride here." Max made a face. "She's not a happy woman."

Melissa pushed her way past Max. "What," she demanded in a shrill yet cultured voice, "is going on here?"

Guy, still shocked at seeing Max after so long, had just gotten to his feet. At the sight of Melissa, he dropped back down to the bed.

The enormity of what he'd planned, how idiotic it had been, slapped him upside his head.

He'd already decided he wouldn't marry Melissa, but now he realized he had never really wanted her.

Certainly not in the uncontrollable way he wanted Annie.

She stood there in a calculated pose, her rose-colored sweater, trim skirt and knee high boots designed to look outdoorsy chic and ultimately feminine. Her hair, an enhanced blond, was twisted on top of her head in a becomingly loose swirl.

The sight of her left Guy cold.

His mind was filled with the image of Annie's face as she'd stood before him in his enormous flannel shirt, wielding a spoon and ogling his body.

From that moment, when acceptance of their isolated circumstances had invaded his brain, he'd known he would make love to her. He'd fought it, but not hard enough.

Max sauntered the rest of the way into the room, ignoring Melissa—which made her fume—and concentrated on Guy.

Looking Guy over, Max took in every bruise and scrape and bandage. "Damn, what did you do to yourself?"

Daniel lounged in the doorway. "He tangled with a semi. And lost." Then, his gaze directed at Melissa, he added, "Annie has been nursing him."

Max straightened abruptly at that. "That's what she was doing here? But I thought she'd just found us out."

"No." Daniel gave an unaffected shrug. "I told her."

Melissa arched a brow. "She's been alone here with Guy in this cabin?"

Daniel smiled. "Yep."

Max, his eyes darkening to near black, asked, "Just what the hell is going on here, anyway?"

When no one answered him, Max looked at his smiling brother, then at Guy's guilty expression. He whistled. "I see. Well, if Annie was here to *take care of you,* then why did she just hightail it out of here so fast?"

Guy shot off the bed, hobbling and limping and cursing. The others darted out of his way, but he made it only as far as the living room when he realized Annie was gone. And despite the crowd gathered behind him, the cabin was empty without her.

Through the front window, Guy could see the spot where Annie's small car had been parked, now empty, the snow crushed in the wake of her departing tires.

Nearly numb with self-disgust, he stumbled, then allowed Daniel to help him to the couch.

Frustration exploded inside his pounding head. He could still feel her, her heated, brazen touch, and he could hear her scream when she came, her ragged panting breaths. He felt again the way she'd squeezed him during her climax.

Annie turned him on, made him laugh, delighted him and amused him and made him whole. He loved her so much—but not as a sister. There was nothing familial in his feelings.

"Damn it all," he said, venting before he exploded, "you people have rotten timing!"

Melissa took umbrage at that. "You and I had some business to discuss, and then suddenly you left and no one—" here she glared at Daniel "—would tell me where you'd gone. What did you expect me to do? Just wait around for you to make a deal with someone else?"

Guy groaned. The very last thing he wanted to discuss with Melissa was business, of either a personal or professional nature. He wanted to go after Annie. He wanted to explain...*what?*

There was nothing to explain.

Nothing had changed.

He looked at Melissa, his eyes red. "What we have to talk about can wait."

"Oh no you don't. We either have a deal or we don't."

Daniel threw up his hands. "Marriage is not a damn business deal!"

"Who said anything about marriage?" she asked.

The men all quieted. Guy waved a hand at her, weary to his very bones, hurting all over, especially in his heart. "I was going to ask you to marry me. But I've changed my mind."

Melissa looked astounded when he mentioned marriage, then insulted that he wouldn't propose to her after all. "What do you mean you've changed your mind?"

The entire situation was so bizarre, Guy laughed. "Can you honestly say you wanted to marry me?"

She examined a nail, pursed her mouth, shrugged. "I don't know. I'd have to think about it."

Sizing up the situation in a heartbeat, Max said low, "It'd be a damn shame if you married him."

Eyes wide, Melissa looked at the brother they all called a Lothario. He hadn't gotten his reputation by mistake. "Why?"

Guy watched in fascination as Max transformed from weary traveler to man-on-the-make. His eyes grew darker, his smile taunting. He no longer looked tired, so much as fit and strong. *And able.*

"If you married Guy," Max explained, "then you'd be unavailable."

Equally amazing as Max's mood switch, was the blush on Melissa's face. It made her look younger, and far more vulnerable than Guy had ever witnessed. She actually dithered.

"I...well, I'm not marrying him, now am I?"

Max took a step closer to her. From every pore, he exuded raw masculinity and sexual appeal. Guy and Daniel shared a look of awe.

"Do you love him?"

Mute, Melissa shook her head.

"Do you particularly want to marry anyone?"

"Not for a long, long time."

Max grinned. "Why don't you go wait in my car for me? I'll be right out."

Melissa may have been susceptible to Max's charm, but she was still a businesswoman. "Not so fast." She rounded on Guy. "We discussed a joint venture that would benefit both our businesses. Is that still on?"

Guy closed his eyes and leaned his head back. Every ache he hadn't felt last night now roared for attention. He felt like someone had used the semi to pound him into the ground. "We can discuss the particulars on Monday."

Melissa brightened. "I'll hold you to that." She glanced at Max. "Don't keep me waiting."

"I wouldn't dream of it."

After Melissa had left, Daniel shook his head at his brother. "You're dangerous."

Max shrugged. "I could see Guy needed some help. Poor beat-up bastard. She'd have made mince-meat of him."

Guy didn't bother to open his eyes. "True."

"So." Max carefully stepped over Guy's injured leg and sat beside him. "You want to tell me what's happening here?"

Guy had no intention of telling him a damn thing.

Unfortunately Daniel didn't suffer the same reserve.

"Annie wants to seduce someone."

Max shot to his feet again. *"What?"*

Guy groaned and covered his face. From bad to worse.

Without an ounce of sympathy, Daniel explained, "Annie told me she was going to have sex, and that was that. Lace was helping her."

There was a long hesitation, then Max said, "Yeah. That's the part I want to hear."

Daniel slugged him in the arm. "Lace gave her all these damn idiotic books on sex. Annie was all revved up to give it a try and Goofus here was planning on asking Melissa to marry him, so I sent the two of them here together to work it all out."

"Work it out, how?"

Guy dropped his arms. "I'm waiting with bated breath for this little explanation myself."

With credible unconcern, Daniel lifted off his glasses, polished them on a sleeve, and admitted, "I thought maybe you'd have sex with her."

Guy's jaw should have dislocated, it dropped so

hard and fast. Max nodded slowly, as if thinking it over—and deciding it made sense.

Not knowing if the look on his face would give him away, Guy wheezed, "You wanted me to... to...?"

Max plopped back down beside him. "Better you than some other yo-yo. At least we like you, and we know you're one of the good guys. Hell, I always kinda hoped you and Annie would tie the knot. Come to that, maybe this is a good step in that direction."

Daniel crossed his arms over his chest. "So how about it?"

Guy slowly sat upright. He felt defensive and hopeful and angry enough to take on both brothers, even with his body more battered than not. "How about what?"

"Did you and Annie—"

"That's none of your damn business!"

Max and Daniel shared a look, then broke out in enormous grins. "They did," Max guessed, and Daniel said, "Looks like."

Guy started to jerk to his feet, but Max caught his arm. His smile was gone. "So what are you planning now, Guy?"

"I'm not planning a damn thing." How could he make plans when Annie wanted to take what he'd shown her and apply it to some other nameless, faceless guy? The thought made him crazed. Was that why she'd lit out of the cabin the second someone else had shown up to take him home? Was she that anxious to try out her new knowledge?

His hands fisted until his arms trembled from the strain.

Max held up both hands. "Hey, don't bludgeon me. It was a simple question. I mean, considering Annie was near tears when she left here—"

Guy grabbed him by his shirt collar. "Annie was *crying?*"

"Close enough."

"Why?" Why would Annie run out on him and then get weepy over it? Or had Daniel yelled at her? But no, he hadn't heard any yelling. Besides, Annie could hold her own against her brothers.

Daniel patted Guy's shoulder. "Turn him loose, Guy. Or have you forgotten that Melissa's waiting out in the car for him? If you mess him up, you'll have to deal with her."

Disgruntled, confused, Guy let Max go with a shake of his head. "I wasn't going to hurt him."

Max laughed. "Damn, but you remind me of Daniel when Lace was tormenting him."

"She still torments me," Daniel clarified, "I just like it more now than I did then."

"You look haunted," Max told Guy. "But Daniel survived this love business, so I suppose you will, too."

This love business sucked, but Guy didn't bother denying how he felt. He was too busy thinking about Annie crying, and it made his insides twist. "You know I love her?"

Max snorted. "What am I? Blind?"

"Lace hinted," Daniel told him, "although she wouldn't give me any names."

"That's why she sent all the condoms," Guy said with sudden understanding, then wanted to bite his tongue off when both Max and Daniel scowled at him. "Uh, I mean…"

Daniel shoved his glasses back on. "I'm going to put that woman over my knee."

Chuckling, Max asked, "Want any pointers?"

Guy decided he'd had enough. He pushed painfully to his feet and faced both brothers. "I want her to marry me."

Daniel sighed in relief. "Good."

Max nodded. "You better."

"You're okay with that?" Guy felt like he'd had the wind knocked out of him. "I mean, you've always said how no one was good enough for Annie and—"

"We've said the same about you," Daniel told him.

"You have?"

Max laughed and headed for the door. "You and Annie will be perfect together. Now if you'll excuse me? I'm off to be the sacrificial lamb."

It seemed Max's departure galvanized Guy into action. He gimped his way into the bedroom to finish dressing, and regardless of how Daniel cajoled, he refused a pain pill. For what he had ahead of him, he needed his mind to be crystal clear.

He had to get to Annie.

Her days of experimenting were at an end.

But first he had to settle things with her father.

9

DAN SAWYERS, the founder and owner of the company that Guy ran, looked right at home behind the desk he seldom used anymore. At that moment, Guy wondered if he'd been an enabler, making it too easy for Dan to shy away from the world and live in self-imposed isolation with the memories of his wife's death.

Since Guy was making such a huge change in his life by admitting his love for Annie, he decided to go for broke, and also force Dan to start taking a more active role in his own company, and with his family. Daniel couldn't do it, because as Dan's son, the hierarchy had already been decided. Max didn't appear to care enough to try, and Annie was too kindhearted to force the issue.

Guy was the only one close enough, yet also detached enough, to see the situation from all angles.

"I have something serious to discuss with you, Dan."

"Guy!" At Guy's entrance, Dan laid aside his pen, closed a folder and came to his feet. After one good look at Guy, however, he drew up short. "Good God! You look even worse than Daniel led me to believe. Shouldn't you still be in bed or something?''

Guy felt worse than he looked. But he was also determined. Against the dragging weight of physical bruises, regret that he'd inadvertently hurt Annie and concern that Dan might not understand, Guy straightened his shoulders.

"I love Annie."

Dan blinked at him. He circled his desk to lean one hip on the edge. With an undue amount of caution, he asked, "You do?"

"Yes." In an even firmer tone, Guy added, "I'm going to ask her to marry me."

A slow smile spread over Dan's face. He rubbed his hands together. "Was it Melissa showing up that did the trick? I worried about that, you know. If maybe I was sending her too early. But you understand, I couldn't let you dither around about my daughter any longer."

The words swirled around Guy, confusing him further before they started to make sense. "You knew I was in love with Annie?"

Dan started to clap him on the shoulder, saw the precarious way Guy balanced himself on his crutches, and changed his mind. "Are you kidding? You watch her the same way I used to watch her mother." A familiar, accepted sadness invaded Dan's eyes, and he shook his head. "That kind of love doesn't come along every day."

"But…you suggested I should marry Melissa."

Dan snapped to attention, shedding his melan-

choly as if it hadn't existed. "I did no such thing!"
He went so far as to shudder. "She's a nice woman
and all, and very astute when it comes to business.
However, I don't think she's right for you."

Drowning in confusion once again, Guy asked,
"When you were talking about marriage—"

"Why, I was talking about Annie, of course!"

Guy found it hard to believe he'd been so dense.
But evidently everyone had known what he felt, in
spite of his attempts to hide it.

Still… "There's another problem."

Dan smiled as he once again rested against the
edge of the desk. "Besides getting Annie to say
yes, you mean?"

Guy didn't want to think of that. Annie had to
say yes. He'd find a way to convince her. Drawing
a deep breath, Guy blurted, "I'm not going to run
the company anymore."

Dan straightened. "But of course you are! You'll
marry Annie, the company will become yours, and
that way it'll stay in the family!"

Guy resolutely shook his head. "No. I'm already
living in your house. I don't regret that," he added
quickly, seeing Dan ready to interrupt again, "because now, Annie will live there, too."

"If you convince her to marry you."

Through his teeth, Guy said, "I'll convince her."

"All right, all right. I'll take your word on it."

"But there's also the money I owe you…."

Like a fresh-baked pasty, Dan puffed up. "Now

you can stop right there! You don't owe me a thing, dammit!''

"You paid for my education."

"And got a hell of a lot in return!" Dan's face turned red with umbrage. "So don't even start on that."

Rubbing his aching head, Guy said, "I can't just let the money go. I want to pay it back."

"Fine. Pay it back by staying on in the company."

Surprised that Dan had misunderstood, Guy explained, "I wasn't going to leave the company. But I don't want to run it anymore, either. You should be running it. I saw you there behind the desk, and you can deny it all you want, Dan, but you were happy."

"True. But I've been out of the loop too long, and if you think it'll make me happy to step in full-time and blunder and possibly make us lose money, well you're wrong." He began pacing around the office. "Here's what we'll do. We'll be partners, running it together." He speared Guy with a look. "*You* can't deny that running the company makes you happy, too. You're a natural."

Guy shrugged. He loved the business and always had. "I won't work sixty-hour weeks anymore."

"Neither will I. We'll split up the load. With the company growing, maybe there's a chance I'll even be able to talk Max into getting serious and joining us."

Guy snorted at that. Max wasn't settling down

for anyone. Plenty of women had tried to get him to do just that. "We'll see."

Suddenly Dan looked at his watch. "Now that we've got all that settled—"

"Nothing is settled. I owe you—"

"Don't argue with me!"

Guy raised a brow at that tone. He'd never heard it from Dan before. In a way, it was nice to see him being passionate about something besides his grief.

Dan was still scowling as he said, "You're like a son to me. I care a great deal about you, and I owe you more than money could ever repay. So forget that nonsense."

"You have it backwards." Guy knew if anyone should be grateful, it was him. But when he started to say so, Dan interrupted him.

"If you want to catch Annie, you better be on your way."

"Catch her? Isn't she at the bookstore?"

"Nope." With great relish, Dan said, "She came in to see Perry. I believe they're in his office."

Guy staggered back two steps. Damn, but she was moving fast! She'd only left the cabin that morning, and lunchtime had barely come and gone. If she was orchestrating a little office rendezvous already, Guy would...what? He had to tell her how he felt first, then see about the rest before he started doing the caveman routine.

He turned around so quickly he almost fell off his crutches. Dan hurried to open the office door for him. "I'd welcome you to the family," Dan said, restraining Guy with a hand on his arm, "but I've *always* thought of you as a son."

Guy softened in the midst of his turmoil. "Thanks, Dan."

A shaky smile in place, Dan said, "Go convince my daughter. And Guy, I'd lose that evil look in your eyes first."

ANNIE WAS JUST handing Perry the book on bird-watching that he'd ordered from her shop when the office door flew open and bounced against the wall. Startled, she jerked around to see Guy filling the doorway. Heaving.

He hadn't shaved yet.

The stubble on his chin was now almost as long as the hair on his head. Combined with his dark eyes and the grim set to his mouth, he looked enraged.

Gorgeous and sexy, but enraged.

"Guy." She turned to stare at him. "What in the world are you doing up and about?"

Even as Annie said it, she thanked her lucky stars that she'd thought to wear sunglasses. The last thing she wanted was for Guy to see that she'd been crying. She knew he'd feel responsible and start more of his brotherly nonsense. At the moment, she didn't think she could take it.

Perry took his book from her numb hand and backed up three steps until he was behind his desk.

Guy stared at Perry as he growled, "You ran out on me this morning."

Annie forced a shrug, but her heart was in her throat, choking her. How dare he force her to relive this now. "Melissa was there."

"I didn't want Melissa there." He glanced at her briefly, and that one quick look carried the impact of a heated embrace. "I wanted you there."

"Really?" But she wouldn't get suckered in again. He probably meant as a little sister. He probably wanted her there so he could lecture her some more on propriety and explain to her that what had happened couldn't ever happen again.

She made a face and looked at him over the rim of her sunglasses. "Why?"

"I had...questions, for you."

He was still staring at Perry and that infuriated her. She stepped into his line of vision. "Stop trying to intimidate my friend."

Oozing menace, Guy asked, "Is Perry a *friend?*"

Perry edged out from behind his desk and held up the book. With more bravery than she'd ever given him credit for, he frowned and said, "She brought me this. That's all. Annie told me weeks ago that she didn't want to be more than friends, and I've respected that decision."

Just that quickly, Guy deflated. "Weeks ago?"

"Yes. And since it's obvious the two of you have things to discuss, I think I'll give you some privacy."

Annie didn't try to change his mind, and Guy said only, "Close the door on your way out, Perry."

Giving Guy a wide berth, Perry made a hasty and not too dignified exit.

Once they were alone, Annie asked, "So what questions did you have for me?"

"Do you think I'm a pig?"

"What?" That wasn't at all what she'd been expecting.

Guy shrugged, then limped toward her and put his crutches against the desk. "I did fall asleep," he explained while gently lifting her sunglasses away. He looked at her red-rimmed eyes and sighed. "You've been crying. Why?"

Annie folded her arms across her middle and fought the new rush of tears. "I don't think you're a pig. I told you, the books say that a lot of men fall asleep—"

"I'm not a lot of men," Guy interrupted to say. "And if I hadn't just been run over, there's no way in hell I would have left you like that."

She searched his face. His eyes were darker than usual, hot. "You wouldn't have?"

"No." Very, very gently, he kissed the bridge of her nose. "So why were you crying?"

No longer so certain of herself, Annie looked down at her feet and lied, "I just felt foolish, that's all."

There was a heavy moment of silence, then: "Making love to me makes you feel foolish?"

Her face heated. "No, I didn't mean that."

Guy cupped her cheeks. "I love you, Annie."

Smiling wistfully, she met his gaze. "I know. I love you, too."

Guy paused, then shook his head. "No, I mean I love you, and I love making love with you, and I want to continue making love to you, only after I'm able to get around without the crutches."

Her pulse started racing. She wasn't a coward, but she was terrified of believing him, of having her heart ripped out again. "Why the sudden change?"

"It's not sudden."

Annie licked her lips. "Right...right afterward, you told me it was a mistake, that it shouldn't happen again."

His thumbs smoothed the corners of her mouth before he bent and kissed her. Against her lips, he said, "Have you ever seen Daniel looking for his glasses, and they're right there on top of his head? Or in his pocket?"

"Yes. So?"

"They're so familiar to him, so much a part of him, that he overlooks their presence sometimes. That's what I did with you."

"I've never sat on top of your head."

"No, but you've been curled up in my heart for a long, long time. So long that I've just gotten used to you being there. I like having you there. Losing you would leave me with an empty heart."

The tears trickled down without her consent. "Then why did you keep pushing me away?"

Guy closed his eyes and rested his forehead on

hers. "Please don't cry. I'd rather be run over again than see you cry."

She sniffed, and managed to get her tears slightly under control.

"Annie, I was so afraid of changing things, of messing up, of maybe losing you and your family."

"You can't lose family, Guy, unless you walk away."

He smiled. "I know that now." He kissed her again, this time with more intensity. "So what do you say, sweetheart? Will you put me out of my misery?"

Annie gulped down a laugh. It felt like happiness exploded inside her, making even her fingertips tingle. Shyly, she circled her arms around him and rested his palms on her hard backside. "Do...do we really have to wait until the crutches are gone?"

Guy stared at her, them slowly broke out in an enormous smile. "I'd like to take care of you next time."

"I didn't mind." Annie nuzzled against his chest. "Even getting rid of the condom was educational."

He groaned. "Damn, I hadn't even thought of that."

"Will you marry me, Guy?"

Laughing out loud, he asked, "Will you ever let me be the aggressor?"

Annie cuddled herself up to him, carefully hugging him close and laying her cheek against his hard chest. "That sounds like chapter four in my newest book. We'll need some ties, only you never wear any, so I don't know—''

Guy tipped up her chin and kissed her. ''Yes, I'll marry you,'' he whispered against her lips, and in his mind, he made a mental note to be wearing a tie the next time he saw her.

Play **LUCKY HEARTS** for this...

exciting FREE gift!
**This surprise mystery gift
could be yours free**

when you play **LUCKY HEARTS**
...then continue your lucky streak
with a sweetheart of a deal!

1. Play Lucky Hearts as instructed on the opposite page.

2. Send back this card and you'll receive 2 brand-new Harlequin Duets™ novels. These books have a cover price of $5.99 each in the U.S. and $6.99 each in Canada, but they are yours to keep absolutely free.

3. There's no catch! You're under no obligation to buy anything. We charge nothing—ZERO—for your first shipment. And you don't have to make any minimum number of purchases—not even one!

4. The fact is thousands of readers enjoy receiving their books by mail from the Harlequin Reader Service®. They enjoy the convenience of home delivery...they like getting the best new novels at discount prices, BEFORE they're available in stores...and they love their *Heart to Heart* subscriber newsletter featuring author news, horoscopes, recipes, book reviews and much more!

5. We hope that after receiving your free books you'll want to remain a subscriber. But the choice is yours—to continue or cancel, any time at all! So why not take us up on our invitation, with no risk of any kind. You'll be glad you did!

Visit us online at
www.eHarlequin.com

- **Exciting Harlequin® romance novels—FREE!**
- **Plus an exciting mystery gift—FREE!**
- **No cost! No obligation to buy!**

◀ DETACH AND MAIL CARD TODAY! ▶

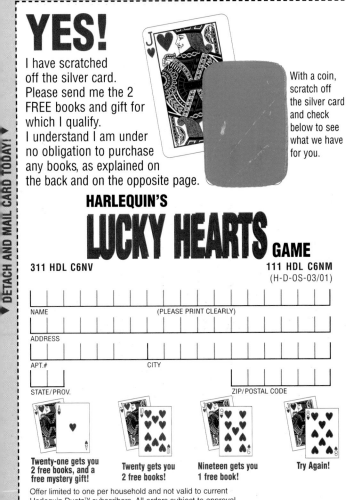

YES!

I have scratched off the silver card. Please send me the 2 FREE books and gift for which I qualify. I understand I am under no obligation to purchase any books, as explained on the back and on the opposite page.

With a coin, scratch off the silver card and check below to see what we have for you.

HARLEQUIN'S

LUCKY HEARTS GAME

311 HDL C6NV

111 HDL C6NM
(H-D-OS-03/01)

NAME   (PLEASE PRINT CLEARLY)

ADDRESS

APT.#   CITY

STATE/PROV.   ZIP/POSTAL CODE

Twenty-one gets you 2 free books, and a free mystery gift!

Twenty gets you 2 free books!

Nineteen gets you 1 free book!

Try Again!

The Harlequin Reader Service®—Here's how it works:

Accepting your 2 free books and gift places you under no obligation to buy anything. You may keep the books and gift and return the shipping statement marked "cancel." If you do not cancel, about a month later we'll send you 2 additional novels and bill you just $5.14 each in the U.S., or $6.14 each in Canada, plus 50¢ shipping & handling per book and applicable taxes if any.* That's the complete price and — compared to cover prices of $5.99 each in the U.S. and $6.99 each in Canada — it's quite a bargain! You may cancel at any time, but if you choose to continue, every month we'll send you 2 more books, which you may either purchase at the discount price or return to us and cancel your subscription.

*Terms and prices subject to change without notice. Sales tax applicable in N.Y. Canadian residents will be charged applicable provincial taxes and GST.

If offer card is missing write to: Harlequin Reader Service, 3010 Walden Ave., P.O. Box 1867, Buffalo, NY 14240-1867

BUSINESS REPLY MAIL
FIRST-CLASS MAIL   PERMIT NO. 717   BUFFALO, NY

POSTAGE WILL BE PAID BY ADDRESSEE

HARLEQUIN READER SERVICE
3010 WALDEN AVE
PO BOX 1867
BUFFALO NY 14240-9952

NO POSTAGE
NECESSARY
IF MAILED
IN THE
UNITED STATES

Messing Around
With Max

Lori Foster

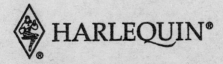

TORONTO • NEW YORK • LONDON
AMSTERDAM • PARIS • SYDNEY • HAMBURG
STOCKHOLM • ATHENS • TOKYO • MILAN • MADRID
PRAGUE • WARSAW • BUDAPEST • AUCKLAND

To Barbara O'Neill, an awesome online comrade. Thank you for always sharing your thoughts on my books, especially the wonderful Amazon reviews! I appreciate it more than I can say.

1

RAIN AND HAIL hitting the door was one thing. A woman was another.

She ran into it at full speed, and Max stared, seeing long blond hair stick wetly to the glass panel, a small nose smooshed up hard, red and looking miserably cold. The rain came down in a curtain, muffling her grunt but not obliterating it entirely.

Cleo took an instant dislike to the intruder.

Hurrying around the counter of his sister's bookstore, Max opened the door. The small feminine bundle tumbled limply inside. At first Max thought she'd been shot or bludgeoned on the back of the head. In a fury he stepped over her and peered through the downpour, looking for another body, for any type of threat. There wasn't anyone there. Just the miserable rain.

Cleo continued to complain and snarl and as Max knelt down by the felled body, which now moaned loudly, he said, "Pipe down, you mean-tempered bitch."

The woman on the floor gasped, rolled over onto her back, and started to open her eyes. She moaned again instead.

"I'm wounded," she snarled, every bit as ferocious as Cleo. "I could certainly do without your abuse!"

"I wasn't..." Max stopped when she got one eye peeped open. It was a startling, dark blue eye, fringed by dark brown lashes. It was just the one eye, not even both, but he felt the impact of her gaze like a kick.

Cleo snuffled closer, poking her wet nose against the woman's face while emitting a low growl.

"Where are you wounded," Max asked, still not sure why she'd thrown herself against the door, or why she was still on the floor.

"All over." That one eye regarded him steadily. "Even my teeth are rattled, so the least you can do is not insult me while I'm still down."

Max wondered if that meant he could insult her when she got up. *If* she got up. She didn't seem to be in any rush to do so.

"Cleo," he explained, more quietly this time, "is my dog. And she is mean-tempered, but not really ferocious. She won't hurt you."

"I'm not afraid of dogs." Even in her less than auspicious position, she managed to appear affronted by the very idea, then she turned her disgruntled one-eyed frown on Cleo, who whimpered in surprise. "I just don't want snout tracks on my cheek."

Max hid a grin. "C'mere, Cleo. Leave the lady alone." Cleo obeyed—a first as far as Max could recall. She came immediately to his side, but continued to grumble out of one side of her mouth, making her doggy lips vibrate, while keeping her watchful attention on the downed female.

A puddle had formed around the woman and since she continued to recline there on the tile floor, apparently at her leisure, Max looked for injuries. He found instead a rather attractive if petite bosom covered in a white T-shirt that read I Give Good Peach.

His brows rose. What the hell did that mean?

The shirt, now soaked through, was practically transparent and put on display a lacy pink bra beneath. Not that he was looking. Nope. He'd made a deal with Cleo, and he intended to keep to his word. He stroked his fingers through Cleo's ruff, just to reassure her.

The damn dog looked beyond dubious.

Maybe she knew him better than he knew himself.

"Are you okay?" Max asked the woman, in lieu of what he was really thinking, which had to do generally with her wet shirt and specifically with what it was molded to. He *would* distract himself. But it'd be easier if she'd just get up.

With what appeared to be a lot of undue effort, she got both eyes opened and stared at him. "I'm seeing two of you," she muttered in surprise, "and surely that's a fantasy, not reality."

"A fantasy, huh?" Maybe she was delirious. Maybe she was drunk.

Maybe she was fodder for his next advice column. No sooner than he thought it, Max discarded the idea. It was just a tad too far-fetched to be believed. Even for his eclectic audience, who so far seemed to believe anything he told them.

One small hand lifted to flap in his face, the gesture making Cleo positively livid. The female human ignored the female dog.

"Well, you *know* what you look like, I assume. Two of you would be…never mind." As if just realizing what she'd said, she cleared her throat. "Yes, I think I'm okay."

Max had never met a woman like her, and that was saying something since he'd known a lot of women. He was so knowledgeable on the subject of females, in fact, that his column was a rousing success—written anonymously, of course. Even his family had no idea that he wrote it.

They all thought he was jobless.

This woman was most definitely different. She was flirting, then withdrawing—all while stretched out in sodden disarray on the tile floor. "You're sure?"

"My pride is permanently damaged," she admitted, "but beyond that I believe I'll live." She pushed herself into a sitting position, long legs stretched out before her. Cleo again tried to sniff her, but when the woman turned that blue-eyed stare on her, Cleo whimpered, backed away, and from a safe distance, started snarling again.

Max could understand that. Her eyes were incredible. Not the color, the shape or the size. But the intensity.

"Where's Annie?" the woman asked, looking around the bookstore with an air of familiarity.

"You know my sister?"

"I've bought tons of books here," she explained, "to use in my work. Annie and I've gotten to know each other pretty well over the past year. Now we're friends." Then she asked, "Why was the door latched?"

Cleo, suddenly acting brave, inched one paw closer and the woman absently petted her. Outraged, Cleo yapped and howled, and the woman ignored her bluster while continuing to stroke the dog's too-small head.

Amazed, Max could do no more than stare. No one other than he had ever ignored Cleo's hostile swagger to give her affection. Max looked the woman over again, this time with a different type of interest. His heart beat just a little too fast.

He was on a bride hunt, and since his bride absolutely had to get along with his dog—he was marrying for the dog, after all, to give Cleo a stable home and the love and acceptance she'd never had—he couldn't help taking note of the somewhat tenuous friendship forming right before his eyes. It amazed him.

It warmed his cynical heart.

In a way, it even made him horny. But then, the rain had made him horny, too. Hell, he'd been so long without, a smack in the head would have turned him on. The only action he'd seen lately had been in the damn newspaper column, and that sure as hell wasn't enough to appease a man of his appetites.

The woman snapped her fingers in front of his face. "Where'd you go, big guy?"

Max laughed. "Sorry. My mind wandered."

"I could see that." She looked him over slowly, brazenly, then asked, "Why are you in here with the door latched?"

Max remembered that his sister had the habit of leaving the door cocked open, something both he and Daniel had grumbled about endlessly, which was probably why Annie continued to do it. She lived to irritate her brothers.

"Annie isn't here, and the storm kept whistling through the door, so I closed it. I hadn't figured on many people shopping today anyway. And of course, I hadn't counted on a woman throwing herself against it." More softly, because she had that effect on him, he said, "That must have hurt."

She sluiced water off her arms, and wrung out her hair. "I nearly knocked myself silly, but I'll survive."

Cleo, still looking ferocious so no one would realize her real intent, nudged the female's hand for another pet. Max nearly gawked. "What are you doing out in this storm?"

"I needed a book. I was running to keep from getting soaked, but obviously I hadn't planned on hitting a closed door." Suddenly she grinned, and it made her face go crooked, made her eyes squinch up. She looked adorable, even with her smeared makeup and rain dripping from the end of her red nose.

And she was still petting his dog.

And Cleo was still allowing it.

Max settled himself more comfortably on the floor, where it appeared their conversation would take place. The woman showed no signs of rising any time soon.

Doing his best to ignore her clinging T-shirt and the equally enticing long legs displayed by her tight rain-soaked jeans, Max asked, "Do you need a doctor?"

"Oh, no. Really, I'm fine." She continued to grin, then added, "I'm Maddie Montgomery." To Cleo's dismay, she stuck out a slim wet hand, now slightly coated with dog hair.

Max took it, felt how cold her fingers were and held on. "Max Sawyers. You're freezing."

"And you're Annie's most disreputable brother."

"Her brother, yes, the rest is debatable." Especially lately, Max added to himself. His life as a monk was not an acceptable one.

Maddie pulled her hand away and struggled to her feet. "You know, I've heard tales about you that could curl a woman's hair. You look different from how I'd imagined."

She'd imagined him? Max walked toward the back room where he could find a towel, deliberately removing himself from temptation. Sexual excitement, the thrill of the chase, the discovery, had already begun a heady beat in his heart. After so many years of indulging his basic nature, his actions were often instinctual. He'd find himself seducing a woman without even realizing it, as if he went on automatic pilot or something.

A woman commenting on his reputation just naturally left herself open to a firsthand display of that reputation. Only now he needed a bride, not merely a temporary bedmate. Which meant he had to move slower than he preferred.

But he couldn't stop himself from asking over his shoulder, "How did you expect me to look?" *And,* he added silently, needing the information if he hoped to succeed in his new altruistic plans, *whom did you hear it from?*

"I dunno." She followed on his heels, the squishing and squeaking of her sneakers echoed by the tapping of Cleo's nails. "I thought maybe you'd have long hair, like the guys who model for the women's magazines. Maybe gold necklaces. Something along the lines of the gigolo look."

Finding her description absurd, Max shook his head. He picked up a towel and turned to face her. "Here you go."

She swiped at her face and throat. "You're not offended, are you?"

"More like amused. And curious." No woman he'd ever been with would have described him as anything less than macho, virile...but never a gigolo.

Intrigued, he asked, "Who's been talking about me?"

"Your sister, mostly."

Max almost tripped over his own two feet. "Annie?" Well, hell, that wasn't in the least exciting.

"Yes. Your sister loves you dearly, and she's very proud of you. But she claims you're a reprobate."

"Annie told you I wear gold chains?"

Maddie laughed. It was a nice laugh—natural, warm. Cleo stared at her as if confused, her doggy lips rolling and shuddering as she gave a low growl. "No, that part I imagined all on my own. Annie just told me what a romancer you are, how women seem to find you irresistible."

Max nodded. As many women as men read his column. And they sent him letters of appreciation. He knew women, inside and out, body and soul.

Which was why his weekly column was so successful. He liked it that no one knew he wrote the thing. Anonymity was his friend, otherwise he could just imagine the women who'd be chasing him. It was bad enough that his reputation was so well known, but if women found out he was the weekly love expert...

"I've heard about you from some other women, too."

Her statement drew Max out of his reverie. "Is that right?"

Maddie blotted at her hair as she spoke, oblivious to the sexy display of her breasts beneath the transparent tee. For the most part, Max kept his gaze fixedly on her face. But he was human and male and that combination made it impossible to ignore her tightened nipples completely. He couldn't *not* look every now and then.

"You're the world traveler," Maddie claimed

with fanfare, "the lover extraordinaire, the prize every woman wants to win."

Her candid banter charmed Max. He couldn't quite decide if she was coming on to him, or poking fun at him, but she did it in such a way that either was okay. It was a unique approach, one he was unfamiliar with.

He leaned in the doorway, Cleo by his side. "Every woman?"

That crooked grin appeared again. "Certainly. I feel ready to faint just being in your presence. The sexual vibes are all but knocking me over. Why do you think I spent so long on the floor?"

Biting back a grin, Max asked, "Because you'd nearly knocked yourself out?"

"*Au contraire.* Because I opened my eyes—"

"One eye."

"—and saw you and the world tilted. I was far too dizzy to sit up straight."

Those beautiful eyes—both of them for double the impact—twinkled at Max, keeping him from knowing how serious she might be.

She started to dry her shirt, looked down and gasped. "Good grief!" She shielded her breasts with the towel and glared at Max. "You could have said something!"

Purposely being obtuse, Max asked, "About what?"

"About...about... I'm showing through!"

He shrugged. "It didn't bother me."

Grumbling under her breath, Maddie turned her back on him and tied the towel around her upper body, knotting it at the side like a sarong. Cleo barked, the sound far from playful.

"There, you see?" Maddie said over her shoulder. "The dog agrees that despite your reputation, you should have been gentleman enough to let me know that more was showing than should have been."

"Actually," Max explained, "Cleo just hates people to turn their backs on her. She distrusts anyone who does."

"Oh." Maddie shifted slightly toward Cleo, tilted her head, and said with real sincerity, "Sorry girl. But Max was rude for not saying anything."

Apologizing to his dog?

Cleo snarled.

"Aha!" Maddie said. "She obviously agrees that you're lacking in manners."

"Because I didn't tell you that your breasts were showing?" Max watched her closely, waiting for her to blush. She was far too cocky to suit him.

Maddie nodded at him instead. "Exactly."

Her lack of embarrassment disappointed him.

"You should have told me. A gentleman always lets a lady know when her modesty is threatened. And being a gentleman doesn't detract from your reputation, I promise."

"Okay." Glancing down at her plump bottom in the snug jeans, Max said, "You've got a rip."

She blinked at him over her shoulder, not understanding. "I've got a...?"

"Rip. In the seat of your jeans. Your panties,

which match your bra and are really quite pretty, by the way, are showing.''

Max watched as she slapped her hands over her behind. It was a generous, well-rounded behind and her hands weren't adequate. He added, ''Just being a gentleman.''

Maddie back-stepped to a chair in the seating area of the bookstore and plopped down. ''I don't suppose you have another towel?''

''Nope. Best I can do is offer my shirt.''

She flashed that silly, endearing grin. ''Now, I certainly couldn't turn that down. But not yet please. I need to keep my wits about me for a bit longer, at least until I've gotten what I came for.''

''Which is?'' Max pulled out his own chair and straddled it to face her. The storm still raged, rain lashing the front windows and lightning splitting the dark afternoon sky. Thunder belched and rolled.

The lights in the bookstore flickered once, and all three occupants looked up to see if they'd go out. When they stayed on, Cleo settled herself nervously at Max's side, her head on his foot.

Max absently patted the dog while watching Maddie. She really was cute, though he hadn't thought so at first. And he enjoyed chatting with her. The things she said took him by surprise—not that he'd ever admit it to her.

It was a cozy scene, comfortable, until Maddie said, ''Annie told me about *Satisfying Alternatives to Intercourse*.''

Max almost fell off his chair. He did jerk to his feet to tower over Maddie, disbelieving what she'd said, not about to hear this concerning his baby sister, never mind that Annie was getting married soon. His reaction startled Cleo who howled like a hungry wolf.

"Now I see where she gets it," Maddie muttered, eyeing Max's antagonistic stance.

Startled, Max wondered if she was right, but he didn't relax one bit.

Shaking her head, Maddie gave an aggrieved sigh. "Well. It's obvious you know nothing about it."

Max choked. "Ha! I know a great deal as a matter of fact!" If he hadn't sworn off casual sex, Max thought, he'd show her just how much he knew.

"No." Maddie shook her head, looking somewhat pitying and utterly positive over her conclusions. "You're clueless."

Heat rose up Max's neck. He felt his male consequence pricked, challenged. In a tone caught between menace and sultry promise, he said, "I can name any number of alternatives. As to how satisfying they are, I suppose that'd depend—"

She actually laughed at him. "Down boy."

Cleo sat.

Maddie laughed again. "At least the dog obeys."

Ready to strangle her, Max shook his head. "Only when she wants to, which isn't often." Then he added, "And never for women. Cleo hates women."

"She doesn't appear to hate me."

"I know. Strange."

Maddie leaned forward, teasing glints in her blue eyes and whispered, "It's a book, Max."

"What's a book?"

Her eyelashes were spiked from the rain, her collarbone still dewy, and she smelled nice. Like the fresh air outside and a sexy woman inside. His muscles tightened. She was teasing and bold and funny...and she liked Cleo.

He wanted her, dammit, but he had made that ridiculous vow to his contrary dog.

"I work at the women's shelter," Maddie said, "teaching classes and counseling various groups. One of our biggest problems used to be unplanned pregnancy, but with one of the groups I have now, there's more to it. I mentioned this to Annie, and she ordered me a book that she'd heard about."

So she was a counselor, Max thought with admiration, and decided her extra empathy and area of expertise had a lot to do with why she'd so easily understood Cleo, and gotten past the dog's bluster. An amazing woman.

And an amazing reaction for him. He could never recall having such an instant liking and respect for a female.

On the heels of that thought, comprehension dawned. Max resumed his seat. *Satisfying Alternatives to Intercourse.*

"Yes, that's the title." Maddie bit her lips, and Max thought she was trying to keep from laughing at him again. He appreciated her restraint. Of course, he also enjoyed the sound of her laughter.

"Annie left me a message last week saying the

book was in, but I haven't had a chance to pick it up until now."

Max continued to watch her, a variety of thoughts winging through his mind—most of them now centered around why an attractive, intelligent woman would need a damn book to tell her such things. She had to be, oh, maybe twenty-six or so. Old enough to have learned plenty of alternatives by now. Heck, he'd even invented a few, and that was while he was still a teen.

"So you're going to use this book for... research?"

"More as a reference. It's nice to be able to state documented facts to back me up when I give information or make recommendations. Also, what I learn in the book will help make me more credible in some situations. Despite my four-year degree, two years specialized and two years in the field, I still get teased for being a newbie."

Fascinated, Max asked, "Wouldn't women accept what is said more readily if it came from... experience?"

Max hoped she'd give a clue as to whether or not her brazenness was derived from experience or just plain old cockiness. With women you could never tell, and he'd long ago learned never to make an assumption about a lady.

But his question backfired on him in a big way.

"That's an excellent idea! It's so nice of you to volunteer!"

"But I never..." Max faltered. "Volunteer for what, exactly?"

"Why, to talk to the women, of course." Leaning forward, her damn towel gaping a bit, she elbowed him in a show of conspiracy. "I can imagine you'd hold their attention, at least."

Max leaned back in his chair in appalled denial. "Absolutely not."

"You're refusing?"

"Yes!"

Scrunching up her face with a dark frown, Maddie grumbled, "Then it was worthless advice."

Max glanced down at Cleo and they shared a look. Strangely enough, the dog was silent. Her tongue lolled out one side of her mouth, and there was a look of confusion on her furry face that mirrored Max's. He cleared his throat. "Uh, *you* could tell them."

She seemed to give that a lot of thought. "After you tell me?"

He supposed that answered his question about experience. Maybe. With this one he couldn't be certain. But his curiosity grew by leaps and bounds with every word she uttered. "I'll be glad to…discuss things with you."

"Hmm. I'll think on that. Now—" Maddie tilted her head. "—do you happen to know where Annie might have put it?"

"It?"

She made a sound of exasperation. "You do have trouble following along, don't you?"

"Not usually, no." In fact, he was generally the one guiding the conversation. He wasn't sure if he liked this new development.

Maddie drummed her fingers on the chair arm. "The book? The reason I'm out in this miserable storm in the first place?"

"I'll look." In fact, he'd be glad of the opportunity to gather his wits and get his thoughts back in order. But just as he said it, another rumbling boom split the air with deafening force. The lights flickered and went out.

Max, slowly sinking back into his seat, said, "Then again, maybe I won't."

They weren't in total darkness. Though the sky was gray and threatening, it was still midafternoon and some light penetrated the thick, ominous clouds. Added to that was the continuous flash of lightning, strobing across the sky. But the sudden obliteration of every noise—no humming light fixtures, no air-conditioning, no buzz from the small refrigerator in the back room—left them in a cocoon of silence.

Cleo yowled and launched her rotund body into Max's lap. Since she wasn't exactly a small dog, and in fact bordered on fat, she was an armful. Fur went up his nose, into his eyes, and a wet snout snuggled frantically into his neck.

Max caught her close, but couldn't prevent his chair from tipping sideways and both man and dog went sprawling flat.

Over Cleo's panicked rumble, Max explained, "She's jittery in storms anyway, which is why I have her with me today, but she's especially afraid of the dark."

Max expected some criticism from the woman.

But as he attempted to soothe Cleo, crooning to her and rubbing her ears, Maddie left her chair and knelt beside them. Her knee bumped Max's chin.

"Poor doggy. It's okay." Cleo whimpered and barked and snarled, but still Maddie stroked her.

Her understanding was seductive. And Max could smell her again, that fresh sexy smell of woman and rain. He cleared his throat, afraid he was fighting a losing battle.

Maddie straightened. "I'm going to go lock the door. It's never a good idea to leave your shop open in a blackout."

Since she'd evidently forgotten about the tear in her jeans, Max got to glimpse those satiny pink panties again as she rushed across the room to the door. She should have looked ridiculous, he thought, what with her hair wet and a towel tied around her breasts.

Instead, she looked oddly enticing. At her ease, obviously very familiar with the shop and his sister, with soothing fractious creatures, human and animal alike. Maddie flipped the many locks and turned the Closed sign around.

When she faced Max again, there was a funny expression on her shadowed face. A look of mixed anticipation, wariness, and greed. Yes, it was definitely greed. *Strange.*

"I suppose," she whispered, her eyes never leaving his face, "we should both be heading out."

Max nodded and sat up, Cleo's quivering, lumpy body held protectively in his lap. "Yeah. I need to get her home. She'll be more comfortable there."

Maddie bit her bottom lip. "The thing is, I took the bus here. And now—"

"You don't relish sitting at the bus stop in this storm and with no lights."

She nodded. "And wearing a towel and with a rip in my pants. I don't suppose I could impose on you for a ride?"

That look was still in her eyes, driving Max beyond curiosity. No matter what he told himself, he simply couldn't let her walk away. Not yet. "I can take you home. No problem."

And maybe by taking her home he could learn a little more about her. If she'd be suitable as a wife, well then, he owed it to himself to find out.

Her smile was blinding in the dim room. "Thank you."

"About your book..."

"It'd be hard to find in this darkness, I'm sure. Unless you know exactly where Annie put it?"

"Nope. Afraid not." Doggy slobber ran down his neck and into his collar. Did Cleo have to drool when she was nervous? But then again, she was always nervous. Which was why Max felt compelled to give her a stable home, to show her the good side of life.

Max hugged her closer to his heart—and he saw a very discerning, sympathetic smile on Maddie's face.

"I can come back tomorrow and get it from Annie," she said in a soft voice that made his muscles clench.

"Annie may not be here." Readjusting his bundle, Max stood and faced her, trying to ignore the rushing of his pulse. "I'm minding the shop for her while she and Guy make wedding plans."

Maddie's frown reappeared before she forced a smile. "That's right, she's getting married, isn't she? That's, um, wonderful." In a stage whisper, she added, "Guy *is* a hunk."

Max scowled both at the compliment to another man, and the attitude she couldn't hide. "Annie's marrying him because they love each other."

"Of course."

Max glared at her. "You sound skeptical and you aren't even hiding it well."

Maddie lifted one shoulder in a negligent shrug and brightened her smile another watt. "I'm sure they'll be blissfully happy. I just don't happen to believe in matrimony."

Cursing under his breath, Max asked, "Care to tell me why?"

"Sure, why not? But let's do this on the ride to my house." She turned away, again forgetting about the rip in her jeans. But Max noticed big time. He hoped she wasn't serious about not believing in marriage, because if she were, he'd have to stop noticing.

And he'd definitely have to put his lust on hold.

2

HE HAS A DOG, Maddie thought with a wistful sigh.
A fat, ugly, needy dog that he treated like a queen.
Her heart thumped with unnamed emotions; suddenly, Max Sawyers no longer seemed like just a
sexy body, but also a very compassionate and sensitive man. Those extra qualities only added to his
appeal—but they also made him something of a
risk. She didn't want to be drawn to him in any
way but sexually!

Annie should have told her more about him.
She'd said Max was good-looking, but she hadn't
explained that he was devastatingly gorgeous. And
she'd said he was cavalier about life, but cavalier
men did not commit themselves to mutts.

Annie had claimed Max would be perfect—in
that she was correct. Except that he was *too* perfect.

Maddie looked at his profile as he drove. The
wipers worked double time clearing the windshield,
but still the rain was blinding. Thunder rocked the
truck.

Maddie felt oblivious to it all.

The man was too attractive for words. Just thinking of the things he knew, the things he could do
to her, teach her... Her skin tingled into goose

bumps that had nothing to do with the cold and everything to do with Max. She had expected to be attracted to him; she hadn't expected to like him so much right off the bat.

Despite her innate timidity, Maddie would have brazenly sat close to Max, and had intended to do just that. But when they'd dashed through the rain to his truck, Max had left her to fend for herself while he strapped Cleo into a doggy seat, located right between them. And anytime she tried to lean closer, to see him better, Cleo snarled. The dog was already so upset by the turbulent storm, Maddie couldn't bring herself to cause the poor creature more distress.

She understood Cleo on a gut level. The dog's defensive attitude was similar to those of the women she dealt with in her job, and her heart just naturally went out to the canine. Not that Cleo needed Maddie's understanding when she had Max fawning all over her.

Cleo watched her with a jaundiced eye, curling her lips every so often in what might have been a silent threat, though Maddie thought that was just the dog's way of mumbling, since she hadn't actually done anything vicious.

Cleo was about the ugliest dog Maddie had ever seen.

Yellowish fur with streaks of white and gray, a head far too small for such a corpulent body, and squat legs, made her look like some botched scientific experiment—something between a dog and a pigmy sow, maybe a furry ball with a head and feet.

The whiter fur circled the dog's tiny head, making it appear that her head had been morphed on in the wrong spot. Maddie thought the dog's tail was long, but because it stayed curled up between her hind legs and glued to her belly, it was impossible to tell for sure.

"Why is your dog so mean-tempered?" she asked cautiously, and watched Cleo show a few more pointed teeth.

Max glanced at her, but gave most of his attention to the road, which now resembled a large puddle with the rain water pooling on it. "Whoever had her before me didn't treat her well."

Maddie nodded in understanding. The dog tried to fend off all friendly overtures, rather than trust anyone and risk more hurt, just as Max traveled the world, searching for meanings he couldn't find at home. When Annie had told her of Max's penchant for traveling, especially during the holidays, she'd naturally begun ruminating on his psyche.

Her specialized education and work experience made it easier for her to understand others.

Understanding herself hadn't been quite so easy. It had taken her friends to point out the obvious to her, that she was now determined to arm herself with specialized knowledge so no man could ever humiliate her or take advantage of her again, due to her naiveté.

Looking at Max now, seeing the tender way he smiled at Cleo, her heart thumped. Though she knew she was getting in over her head, she still insisted to herself that it was a good plan. "How long have you had her?"

"I found her in the middle of the road about a month ago. She was just lying there and I thought she was..." He dropped his voice to a whisper, and spelled, "D-E-A-D."

Horrified as she was by the picture he painted, Maddie bit back a smile. "I gather your dog doesn't spell?"

In all seriousness, Max said, "Just a little. There are some words I can't say, hint at, or spell without her going nuts on me."

"Like what?"

"Like another word for inoculation, if you get my drift. Or the professional who might give her that inoculation."

"Ah. She hates medical personnel?"

Cleo howled. Obviously, Maddie had used words she recognized.

"That's about it," Max confirmed.

"So how do you get her there?"

"I speak to her in French." He sent Maddie a devilish grin, and added, "All females are partial to having French softly crooned to them. Makes them mellow."

Maddie snorted. "I don't understand French, and if a guy was going to croon to me, I'd darn sure want to understand what he was saying."

Why that made Max laugh, Maddie wasn't sure. His reactions left her confused as to whether he found her to be laughably odd, or appealing.

"She used to hate baths, too," Max said around his chuckles, "but I changed all that."

At the word bath, the dog's pointed ears lifted off her skull and she barked. Max laughed and rubbed her head.

"Should I ask?"

His grin was pure wickedness, but all he said was, "She especially loves bubbles."

Another bark.

Maddie found herself grinning, too, charmed by Max and his eccentric dog. So what that things weren't working out quite as she had meticulously planned? Annie had said nothing about a dog being at the shop, but then maybe she hadn't known. Perhaps Max only brought the dog along, as he'd said, because of the storm.

The unplanned rip in her jeans and the unfortunate transparency of her T-shirt had certainly gotten his attention.

She cleared her throat as they neared her street and said, "I'd like to repay you by cooking you dinner."

Max skipped another look her way. His eyes were so dark, so intense, they made her shiver.

"Not tonight." He answered slowly, as if coming up with an excuse—or because he didn't really want to say no. Maddie wasn't sure which but she hoped it was the latter. "I need to get Cleo home and out of the storm so she can settle down."

"Exactly. My apartment is close and quiet," Maddie urged. "Why make Cleo ride farther when you can come in for a spell and relax, eat a little, and maybe by then the rain will have stopped.''

Max looked undecided, so Maddie worked on Cleo. Leaning close to the dog, she asked, ''Would you like to come in, girl?''

Cleo snarled at the invasion of her personal space. Her lips rolled and undulated, her teeth dripping as growled threats escaped.

''There, you see,'' Maddie said, not the least put off by the surly dog. Cleo's reaction this time was based on jealousy, Maddie was sure. She had things all worked out and there was no way a possessive pooch would thwart her. ''She likes the idea.''

Max chuckled. ''You really aren't afraid of her, are you?''

Maddie shrugged. ''I think I understand her. She doesn't dislike me so much as she's afraid to like me.''

''It took me two weeks,'' Max admitted, ''just to get her to trust me enough to let me pet her.''

Hearing that, Maddie felt tears at the back of her throat. No wonder Cleo was possessive! On impulse Maddie threw her arms around the dog and hugged her tight. Both Max and Cleo looked stunned.

''Well,'' Maddie said in a slightly choked voice, ignoring them both as she pressed her nose into Cleo's soft, clean fur, ''she certainly loves you now.''

Had Cleo been abandoned and ignored, Maddie wondered, much like the ladies she worked with?

Max interrupted her thoughts. ''So why are you set against marriage?''

Startled, Maddie blinked at him. "That was a quick change of topic."

"You looked ready to cry," he explained with a shrug. "I can't abide whimpering women."

"I never whimper." Maddie sniffed, wiped her eyes, and said, "I'm not exactly against marriage, not really. It's only that I'm in no rush to get tied down any time soon. I tried that and it was humiliating in the extreme."

Max perked up. "Humiliating? How so?"

"You really want to hear this?" She no sooner asked the question than she had to instruct him to turn onto her street. Within minutes she'd be in front of her apartment building. It was either gain his interest now, or possibly lose the opportunity.

Max turned the truck, then said, "Yeah, I want to hear it."

Drawing a deep breath and doing her best not to blush, Maddie confessed, "I came home early one day and found my fiancé tied spread-eagle and naked to my bed while a woman I'd never met tickled him with a feather."

Choking, Max said, "You're kidding?"

"Turn here. This is my apartment building." Maddie felt the heat in her face, the remembrance of deep humiliation, and lifted her chin. "Nope, I'm afraid there's no joke. The feather was a huge lemon-yellow one."

"So what did you do?"

Maddie smiled. If he was curious enough, perhaps she could use that against him. She'd already sensed that his male pride was a good lever as well.

When she'd teased him about being clueless on the book, he'd all but vibrated with sensual menace. It had made her heart pound.

"Come inside," she offered slyly, "and I'll tell you."

"Said the spider to the fly?"

Maddie gave him a cocky grin. "Afraid of getting eaten?"

His eyes heated, grew even more intense. "A double entendre if ever I heard one."

"I'm surprised you realized it, after all your admitted confusion about things sexual."

His teeth locked with a snap. "That sounds like a challenge."

"So it is." Annie had sworn to Maddie that forced seduction worked quite well on men. It certainly had worked for Annie! Guy had been resisting her for years, but once Annie got him alone and she could have her way with him...

Maddie grinned at the thought of having her way with Max. After she got him in the door, she'd make her move.

Max pulled into her parking garage and turned off his truck. Cleo was none too happy with the situation at all, and her menace was aimed at Maddie. The thick fur around her miniscule head bristled and stood on end. Maddie patted it back down, knowing good and well how important styled hair was to a female, even a mean female dog.

Through the impromptu grooming, Maddie continued to grin. Or was a grin considered a leer when one had lascivious thoughts on her mind? And how could her thoughts be any other way when Max was sitting beside her? He smelled good, his hot scent detectable even over the heavier smell of wet dog. And he looked good, his dark hair clinging to the back of his neck, his damp shirt showing off an impressive array of chest and shoulder muscles.

He was surprisingly kind for a Lothario, strong and gentle and understanding with Cleo, patient with Maddie herself.

Max smiled at how silly Cleo looked with her fur parted in the middle and brushed to the sides. Then he sighed in resignation. "So tell me, Maddie. What are we having for dinner?"

Maddie thought about saying *beefcake,* but curbed herself in time. Her mind moving a mile a minute, she climbed out of the truck while Max unlatched the dog and hooked Cleo's leash onto her collar. "How about chicken? I can cook that pretty quick." And then they could get onto better things.

"Chicken is fine."

Cleo woofed, for once in agreement. Her vocabulary, Maddie thought, was surprisingly varied. "We'll have to debone yours, girl. I wouldn't want you to strangle on a bone."

Max paused with Cleo held high in his arms. "You intend to feed Cleo, too?"

Appalled that he would suggest otherwise, Maddie said, "I certainly wouldn't eat in front of her!"

"And you'll even debone her meat?"

Maddie shuddered. "Can you imagine how she'd look gagging on a chicken bone?" She shuddered. "Please Max, it's not a pretty picture."

Max smiled. Then his smile spread and the next thing Maddie knew he was laughing.

"What?" His laughter had a curious effect on her, warming her from the inside out, making her toes curl. She led the way through the parking garage to the building entrance, while Max continued to carry Cleo rather than let her walk. Cleo looked as if it were perfectly natural for him to cart her around in such a grand style.

"Maddie."

His voice was so soft, so compelling, Maddie froze, then shivered. If he could do so much with just a word, she could only imagine what he'd do with his hands, his mouth.

"Are you sure you're against marriage?"

Looking at Max over her shoulder, Maddie saw his teasing smile, the sexy twinkle in his dark eyes, and she waved off his comment. Everything his sister had told her proved Max was a confirmed bachelor who intended to remain that way.

According to Annie, women chased Max daily, beautiful women, young women, mature women, wealthy women and women of lesser means. He'd traveled the world and everywhere he went, women wanted him.

Yet Max was still single.

That said a lot. And it told her that if she wished to gain her education, she'd have to keep things casual.

"Oh, I imagine I'll make a fine wife *someday*. But not for a long, long time."

"So if you don't want marriage, what *do* you want?"

Keeping her back to him, Maddie said, "To understand the attraction of a feather. To understand the lure of sex." She took a deep breath. "To notch my bedpost."

There was a pause behind her, no footsteps, no breathing. Even Cleo was silent. In a rush, Max again caught up. He didn't say another word.

She reached her door on the second floor, well aware of the fact that Max had carried fat Cleo up the stairs and still he wasn't breathing hard. He was in such superb shape.

She could barely wait to get a bird's-eye view of his body.

"Here we are," she said, trying to sound cheerful instead of triumphant. She stepped inside and waited, ready to pounce the moment she had the door closed behind him, barring his escape.

But Max hesitated on her doorstep.

"It just occurred to me," he said, looking down at Cleo who stared back in unblinking worship. "I should let her take care of business first. I wouldn't want her messing your apartment."

Maddie nearly panicked. Was he trying to escape already? And she hadn't even tried anything yet! Maybe she had come on too strong, maybe she shouldn't have mentioned that part about notching...

But then Max said, "You should change out of those wet clothes. We'll be back in five minutes or so."

Some of the tension eased from her muscles. He sounded sincere enough. "All right. I'll leave the door unlocked for you."

His eyes narrowed. "As soon as I get back, you can start explaining."

He made it sound like a threat, but Maddie was just glad he'd promised to come back.

The second he was down the stairs, she ran into her bedroom and shuffled through her closet, wondering what to change into. Not another pair of ultra tight jeans, she decided, unwilling to take the risk of a new rip. Tearing her clothes had *not* been part of the plan.

Of course, slamming into a closed door hadn't been on the agenda either. Still, she was working with what she had.

For late April it could still get cool, so she decided against a sundress, and instead pulled out a snug, long sleeved dress of beige cotton. It fell to midcalf, but hugged her bottom and her breasts. Across the bodice was a colorful mauve rose and the words In Full Bloom. And on the back, Freshly Plucked.

She rushed to the mirror, then gasped at her bedraggled appearance. It was a toss up who looked worse—her or Cleo. She grabbed a comb and attempted to get the tangles out of her hair in record time.

She heard the front door open and close. "Maddie?"

"Be right there." Quickly, she creamed off her ruined makeup and opted not to bother with more.

She'd heard sex, when done right, was a hot, sweaty business. Surely Max would do it right, so perhaps makeup would be useless anyway.

Trying to look sexy and tempting, she floated out of the bedroom toward where Max stood at her picture window overlooking the main street. Both he and the dog were now more wet than ever. Cleo saw her first and got so outraged at the sight of her that she began bouncing as well as barking.

Max turned and attempted to calm the dog. *"Cleo."* Then he caught sight of Maddie and whatever else he'd intended to say never came out. She was sure she saw him gulp.

Cleo subsided, but not without a lot of grumbling. Almost defiantly, she went to Maddie's old, floral couch and climbed up—with a lot of effort—to spread out full length on the cushions. Even as her eyes closed, she continued to snarl.

Max cleared his throat. "I'm sorry. I'll get her down..."

"She's fine."

"She's wet."

Maddie shrugged. "The cushion covers are washable." Maddie looked at the dog, so worn out from all her nastiness and her fright of the storm. Even in her exhaustion, with her eyes closed and her round body looking like a boneless pile of scruffy fur with a head, her teeth showed in a low warning growl.

Maddie's heart softened. Speaking softly so as not to disturb Cleo, Maddie asked, "Do you think she's cold? I could get her an old blanket."

Looking a little bemused, Max walked toward Maddie. "She's got plenty of fur to keep her warm." Max stopped about a foot in front of her, well within range, she decided. Doing her best to repress all her old inhibitions, Maddie thought of what she might learn tonight. Never again would a man take her by surprise with his sexual preferences—like yellow feathers. She looked at Max's mouth for added courage, took a couple of deep breaths, then launched herself at him.

Taken off guard, Max fell back a step with the impact of her body. "What the—"

Maddie clasped his face, held on tight and found his mouth with her own.

Not bad at all, Maddie thought, and scoffed at her initial hesitation. He tasted even better than she expected. He tasted of experience, of sin incarnate, of a man who knew what he was about. A man who loved women and his dog.

He tasted hot.

Maddie waited for raging lust to take control of Max's body. She waited for his sexual instincts to kick in. Her ex had always told her that men could only take so much provocation, which was why he'd been driven to cheat.

So she waited.

Then she felt Max's smile against her mouth.

Well heck! Maddie opened her eyes to look at him. Not only wasn't he overcome with lust, it appeared he was about to laugh.

MAX'S FIRST thought was that she knew next to nothing about kissing, and his second was how soft she felt. His third thought was that if Cleo woke up, there'd be hell to pay.

Cleo didn't like other females to touch him.

Of course, the fact that she had gone to sleep in a stranger's place showed she was somewhat at ease with the newly introduced woman, and that shocked the hell out of Max.

If only Maddie wasn't against marriage.

Max held still, a little surprised, a little amused, a little turned on. He didn't kiss Maddie back as she smooshed her mouth against his, but neither did he push her away. He smiled, thinking how determined she seemed.

Around panting breaths, Maddie asked, "What's wrong?"

The words brushed his lips, heated with excitement, touched with anxiety. It was a potent combination. Max clasped her shoulders and held her back enough that he could breathe. "Oh, did you require my participation?"

"Well..." She looked uncertain. "Yeah."

He couldn't stop himself from caressing her, feeling the smallness of her bones, her softness. For such a gutsy, outspoken woman she was amazingly lacking in knowledge. "I take it my sister has been filling your head with her astounding seduction tactics?"

Maddie nodded.

It was almost laughable, only he couldn't quite seem to get so much as a chuckle past the lump of lust in his throat. It was like the blind leading the blind. "Why, Maddie?"

"Why what?"

"Why are you attacking... I mean *seducing* me?"

She blinked uncertainly. "Because I want you?"

"You aren't sure?" Max struggled to ignore the feel of her soft body against his while he tried to figure out what was going on. Even as brazen as she behaved, Maddie didn't strike him as the type of woman to jump into bed with men she barely knew. Not that he knew her well. But he knew enough. She said she'd been engaged, and he'd already witnessed what a giving, understanding woman she was. She treated Cleo as gently as he did.

Max narrowed his eyes. He was beginning to think he'd been set up from the start.

"I'm positive." She nodded again for good measure. "I want you."

He felt compelled to tell her the obvious. "I know women really well, Maddie."

Her lips parted. "I'm counting on it."

She looked so damn ready, Max shook her. "I mean, you little schemer, that I know when they're conspiring. You, Maddie Montgomery, are up to something."

If a man had written to him in the column with this exact situation, his advice would be to run like hell. But then, Max was only good at giving advice; he'd never been any good at taking it.

Maddie shrugged. "As you said, seduction."

Max was still skeptical. "And that's all?"

She took him completely by surprise when she

said, "Why else would I have been out on such a miserable day like today? I planned the whole thing. Well, not the *whole* thing. I hadn't figured on hitting a closed door and ending up at your feet, or having my clothes play peekaboo. I just thought, what with the rain and all, I'd be stranded and you could offer me a ride home...."

"And we'd end up exactly where we are?"

"Sorta. I had figured on having you naked and in my bed by now."

Max forced himself to laugh. A nice, hearty male laugh of superiority that hid his surge of lust. "Your plans went a tad awry, didn't they?"

"I wanted to meet you face to face. After all the wonderful stories Annie's told me about you, I already felt like I knew you. I definitely knew I wanted you. So I suppose I can't complain."

She just kept knocking him off guard, Max thought, disgruntled. "So you didn't really want the book at all?" He was almost relieved. The thought of any woman reading such a ridiculous text made him shudder.

"Of course I want the book. It sounds fascinating and I'm looking forward to every word."

Max groaned.

Hearing the sound of his frustration, Maddie leaned forward and touched his shoulder, her eyes earnest. "But I wanted to meet you more than I want the book."

Max rubbed a hand across his forehead. "So you could seduce me?"

"Yeah."

Plenty of women had come on to him, but none had thrown themselves against a door, gotten drenched in the rain or cozied up to his dog.

It was the last that was getting to him more than anything else.

It ate him up to see how loving she could be; she was just what Cleo needed—another person to care about her, to make her feel loved. Yet Maddie said she didn't want marriage. What a situation. A suitable woman was close at hand, begging for sex, loving his dog, and Max felt forced to reject her because she didn't want a lasting relationship. Talk about the vagaries of fate!

"It occurs to me," Max pointed out, "that you could have just about any man. You're attractive—"

"Why thank you."

"And nicely built."

She beamed at him.

"So why chase me?"

Maddie took another step closer to him. "Because you're not just any man, Max. You're a man of experience, a man with an awesome reputation. I've been good all my life and look what it got me. A guy who preferred kinky feathers to me. Now I want to know about feathers! I want to know... *everything*."

"I hate to break it to you, but feathers aren't really all that kinky."

"You didn't see where she was tickling him!"

Max coughed, then decided to let that one go. "So, you want to use me to notch your bedpost, huh?"

She bobbed her head, her look endearingly sincere.

The idea should have been appealing to just about any red-blooded male, so why did Max feel so offended?

"All because your idiot fiancé fooled around on you?"

"It was so humiliating. I just didn't have the experience to deal with it, so I stammered and stuttered and made an idiot of myself." She shuddered with the memory. "I wish I had just left him tied there."

Her grumbling tone made Max smile. "What *did* you do?"

She snorted. "I'm ashamed to say I just stood there, staring. I couldn't think of a single word to say, and then the woman screeched and grabbed her coat and ran off."

"Just like that?"

Maddie nodded. "She left the feather behind. Troy was, as I'm sure you'll understand, in a rather awkward position."

Now that was a picture Max could enjoy. It was no less than the dishonorable blockhead deserved. "How long did you make him suffer?"

Maddie blushed.

"Maddie?" Max bent to see her averted face. True, he hadn't known her long. But he had a gut feeling that despite her declaimed lack of experience with such situations, Maddie would have found a way of getting even. "C'mon. Give."

She cleared her throat. "I went out to dinner."

Max grinned, pleased by her creativity.

"And a movie," she added with a wince.

Laughing, Max asked, "What'd you see?"

"I don't remember. I barely paid any attention. I was just trying to decide how to get Troy out of my apartment." She peeked up at him, all big blue eyes and innocence. "I thought about calling a friend to untie him, but then I didn't think Guy would appreciate it if I asked Annie to get that close—"

"No! That would have been a bad idea."

"I know. You're protective of your sister. I think that's nice." She patted his chest absently in approval, then said, "I finally just decided that I had to be adult enough to deal with it. So I went back. Troy started cursing me and threatening me the second I walked in, so I went to the kitchen and got a big butcher knife."

"You didn't...?" Max saw her wicked smile and relaxed.

"Scare him to death? Sure. It was no more than he deserved. He went from cursing to pleading. But then when I cut his right hand free and he realized he was safe enough, he went right back to being obnoxious."

Max saw something in her eyes, something wounded. Of course her vanity had been crushed.

Gently, he touched her chin. "What did he say to you?"

"Typical drivel coming from a man who's had to hold his bladder for four and a half hours. He blamed me for everything." She shrugged. "Not woman enough, not sexy enough, too naive, too prim, blah, blah, blah."

Max flexed his fists, wishing he could get alone with the jerk for just a few minutes. It was no wonder Maddie was out to prove her sexuality. "I hope you didn't give his words a second thought."

She shook her head. "He was scum and I told him so. It took a lot of nerve for him to try to fob the guilt off on me." Her face red, Maddie started to raise her voice, and Cleo yawned. She cast an affectionate glance at the dog and began whispering again. "I decided to look at the nasty scene—and the nasty man—as an omen."

Max was touched by her feminine strength. No doubt about it, Maddie Montgomery was one helluva woman. "An omen, huh? How so?"

"Troy's faux pas was nature's way of telling me that I need to expand my horizons before I think about settling down. Without experience, it's no wonder I made such a bad mate choice. I mean, it takes practice to figure out what you really want. And with more experience, I'll be better able to empathize on the job with the women I talk to, and better equipped to handle the men I might see in the future."

"I see." He didn't see at all, and he didn't like

the idea of her with other men. "You want to start practicing with me?"

Looking pleased that he understood, Maddie smiled. "Yes! You'll be the first of my wild oats!"

A thought occurred to Max. "Will you tell your fiancé what you're doing?"

"No, why?" She appeared puzzled by the question. "And Troy's not my fiancé anymore. He's an ex. What I do or don't do isn't any of his business."

"Are you sure you aren't planning to make him jealous?" Not that he'd blame her, Max thought, but he hoped she was well and truly over the fool.

"Well, I'd certainly accomplish that! I mean, look at you." Her gaze drifted over Max from sternum to knees, like a sensuous lick. She took a deep breath that mirrored his own. "You'd sure make any guy jealous."

"Uh, thank you."

Maddie shook herself. "But that's not what I'm going to do. Why should I? I'm not an idiot. Troy can indulge in all the feather tickling he wants, so long as he does it away from me. He's of no concern to me at all any more."

Max accepted her sincerity.

"But," she added, "if you're worried about getting into a hostile confrontation with him, you don't need to be. I would never let him bother you, I promise."

Max immediately rebelled. "I wasn't worried about a confrontation and I certainly don't need you to protect me." He probably weighed a hundred pounds more than Maddie, and he sure as hell wasn't concerned about some idiot who indulged a feather fetish.

Maddie patted his chest again, then caressed him, then sighed. "I understand. You're a lover, not a fighter." Her patting hand was now stroking, driving him to distraction. "But that's all I want you for anyway, so it's not a problem."

That was *all* she wanted him for? How insulting! He was good for more than just sex, dammit. Feeling more like his dog by the second, Max growled, "I am *not* afraid of a fight."

"Shh." She attempted to soothe him, her small hands gliding over his chest, lower...

Max caught her wrists. He was breathing hard, his muscles aching. She stirred him, aroused him and annoyed him. "Dammit, Maddie." How the hell did she affect him so easily?

There was no easy way to break it to her, except to be brutally honest. The sooner the better, before he lost his thin hold on control. "I'm sorry, sweetheart, but the simple fact of the matter is, I'm not interested."

She snorted. "Yeah right. Annie says you're always interested."

He would strangle Annie when next he saw her. "Maybe a month ago I would have been. But things have changed."

Maddie's face fell. "You don't want me."

He cupped her cheek, let his thumb brush the soft fullness of her lower lip. "Oh, I want you all right. You can be sure of that." Max felt her uncertainty all the way to his bones. Here he was, shaking with lust, and she doubted her allure.

She stared at him, not comprehending for a long moment, and then suddenly she smacked her head. "I understand now!"

He almost hated to ask. Her assumptions had been so far off the mark all along, he wasn't sure he wanted to hear her newest revelation concerning his character. Resigned, he asked, "What is it you think you understand this time?"

"When we were discussing the book! You were totally confused about the whole thing."

"I was not."

"Don't look so indignant." She gave him a pitying look. "I know how reputations can get blown all out of proportion. I should have realized that no man could be so awesomely adept. It's almost absurd."

Max was ready to defend his awesome adeptness, but Maddie wasn't done explaining things to him.

"You don't have to worry about my expectations, Max. If you don't know everything, that's okay. It's not like I'm going to keep a scorecard. Heck, I don't know much, either, so I doubt I'd even notice if you screw up."

For the first time in years, embarrassed heat ran up the back of his neck. "Why, you little—"

She waved away his umbrage. "I'm sure we'll muddle through." Then, as if getting a brainstorm, she added, "The book could probably help! Besides, I just want to experiment and you're gorgeous and there must be at least a little truth to your reputation, right? So I know I'll be inspired.''

Max saw her through a red haze. He squeezed the words out of his tight throat. ''You expect us to…muddle through?''

''If need be, you can just lie there. I won't expect you to perform.''

Max stared at the ceiling while he counted to ten. And then to twenty. Oh, it was *so* damn tempting to show her everything he knew, methods of seduction he'd learned in foreign countries and at home, all the different ways he could make her body sing.

And all the ways he could make her beg.

Men who read his column wrote to him for advice, and got the very best. Then women sent him letters of gratitude.

And this woman expected him to *muddle through?*

He met her gaze again, outwardly calm while inside he seethed. ''You're not even close, honey.''

''Uh-huh.''

His temper cracked, then crumbled. ''Stop sounding so damn skeptical!''

She pursed her lips in a wasted attempt at obedience. Max wasn't sure if he wanted to kiss her or throttle her. Both choices seemed equally appealing. ''I have valid reasons,'' he managed to say with a semblance of calm, ''for not wanting to get into another purely sexual relationship, and not one of them has to do with lack of expertise or fear of a physical confrontation.''

"Is that right?"

"Damn right."

"And those reasons are?"

Max opened his mouth twice, but nothing came out. What could he possibly tell her? That he wanted to settle down for his dog? That one mangy beat-up mutt—a mutt now snuffling and snoring loudly on the couch—had accomplished what no woman could?

Even to his own mind, it sounded ludicrous.

He stalled for time until his brain started functioning again, then said with laudable nonchalance, "I don't travel anymore."

That took the wind out of her sails. "Why ever not?"

"I've been just about everywhere, seen just about everything."

She looked fascinated, a sentiment that reflected his own when it came to exploring the world. "Annie says you sometimes stayed gone for months. How did you support yourself?"

Such a personal question, although he appreciated her candor, her honest interest. "I worked."

"In foreign countries?"

"And in the States." He shrugged as he explained, "There's always something to be done, new building efforts in war-torn or natural disaster areas, odd jobs here and there. I've signed on to fishing vessels and cargo ships and done excursions for tourist kayaking in Alaska. And I've been an interpreter at the Olympic Games in Japan."

Her eyes were so huge, so impressed, Max felt

himself puffing up. The only thing he'd ever missed in all his traveling was someone to share it with. He wondered if Maddie knew how much money he'd saved over the years, that he thrived on traveling without luxuries, living off the land instead. It was a cheap way to go, and because of that, he had quite a healthy savings account.

"Recently I decided it was time to settle down. And," Max said, expounding on his explanation though he wasn't certain why, "I have new responsibilities that keep me closer to home."

Her mouth formed an O. "Annie said something about Guy needing you to take your rightful place in the family company, but she didn't think you ever would. I'm glad she was wrong. She said it really hurt your father that you didn't want any part of the business."

Poleaxed, Max went speechless. It was true that Guy had asked him to come to work in the company, but he'd repeatedly refused. What could he contribute that his father and Guy hadn't already given? Max would only be another warm body, and there were plenty of those to go around. He had nothing unique, nothing special that the company *needed* from him. In fact, he'd never felt needed there, and he refused to feel needed now just because Guy was marrying.

"Actually," he said, slightly annoyed, "it's not that I have no interest in the company. It's just that I already have a job."

"Doing what?"

Max ignored her. His column was personal, and

anonymous. And it took up very little of his time, so it wouldn't be a good example anyway. "With each new development comes another. I'm no longer traveling, and I'm no longer looking for meaningless relationships."

She drew herself up. "I don't think I like being referred to as meaningless."

"I didn't mean..." Max knew if he lived to be a hundred, he'd never be this frustrated again. "Maddie, getting together just to notch bedposts would be meaningless."

"A relationship based on devastating sex would be very meaningful to me!"

Exasperated, Max said, "So now I'm supposed to make the sex devastating when seconds ago you promised me I could just lie there?"

She blinked in surprise, then shrugged. "So I lied. I was trying to convince you. Truth is, I want you mobile and participating."

"You want me to be devastating?"

"Could you?"

Max almost smiled at the sweet, polite way she asked that. Droll, now that he felt in better control, he said, "It'd be a tall order—not that I'm not up to it, you understand."

"I'm not sure what to understand! One minute you claim all this great prowess, and the next you're running shy and saying you're not interested in a sexy affair."

"To a man who's had his fill of them," Max explained with ruthless and entirely false candor, "it sounds boring." She started to speak again, so he reiterated, "I-am-not-interested."

"I don't believe you."

Stubbornness made her eyes darken to midnight blue. Max cursed because he found her expression oddly appealing. Would her eyes go that dark when she was in the throes of a climax? When he was buried deep inside her?

Would she be this talkative, this argumentative, in bed? Or would she be sweetly submissive when he gave her the awesome sex she'd requested?

Those thoughts caused him to overstep himself, to admit more than he'd intended. "Look, it's not like I said I was becoming a monk or something. It's just that I want to settle down, to find a wife—"

She slapped her hand over his mouth. "That's not funny!"

Max pried her hand away, noticing how slim and cool her fingers felt in his. "Not funny, but true. I want a wife."

"Then why aren't you married already? According to Annie, women throw themselves at you."

"I have very precise requirements."

"Oh."

She looked crestfallen, but he had no idea why. "I'm sorry to disappoint you, sweetheart. I really am."

He started to tell her she'd have no problem finding someone else to play with, but the words stuck in his craw. She shouldn't be playing with anyone. She should be a man's wife so she could share all that fire, all that caring, for a lifetime, not just for the duration of an affair.

Maddie turned around and paced away. Max watched the slight sway and bounce of her rounded behind, the way her hips moved seductively, and called himself ten times a fool. The woman was delectable, no doubt about it.

He also reread the decorative letters on her back. *Freshly Plucked.*

Just what the hell did that mean?

"If you want to get married," she said, sounding strangled, "that's fine with me. Hey, more power to you. But why not have fun until you've found your paragon to wed? Unless of course—" She didn't turn to face him while she made her gibe "—I managed to scare you off?"

She waited, not looking at him, and even though Max knew it was a tactic meant to make him relent, he couldn't stand the challenge. She'd struck at the core of his manhood one time too many.

It was past time he got control not only of his raging libido, but little Maddie Montgomery as well.

3

MAX CREPT UP behind her, determined to set her straight, to make her learn the error of taunting his testicularity, which he had in spades. Hell, he *oozed* testicularity, blast her—and the loyal followers of his column could swear to it.

She was still unaware of his approach when Max whispered near her ear, "You could hardly scare me off when you kiss like a nervous schoolgirl."

Maddie gasped, her shoulders stiffening.

It was his own form of attack, and though he'd only known her a few short hours, he already knew she had pride and gumption—which was why she was determined to win with him. Her fiancé had wounded her, and she wanted to reassure herself the only way she knew how.

It was a contradiction of sorts, but he was glad she'd chosen him rather than some other man. The thing to do now was to reel her in for more than a quick tussel.

"I never claimed to be overly experienced," she stated, then asked worriedly, "Was I really that bad?"

"You showed no subtlety, sweetheart. No finesse.'' Determined to hide the tenderness he felt, Max added, ''I felt mauled.''

She started to turn to face him, but Max caught her shoulders and held her still. ''Don't berate me. You claimed I was running scared, but you know that's not true. In fact, I'd say you're the overly nervous one, given the awkward, rushed way you jumped my bones.''

''They're such nice bones, Max, I couldn't resist.''

With comments like that, *she* was the one who was hard to resist!

Hesitation lacing her voice, she said, ''I promise I'll control myself in the future.''

Max didn't really want her to control herself. No, he wanted to get to know her better, to talk to her— and *then* she could jump his bones.

He needed to find a way to make her feel as intrigued as he did. He needed her to want more from him than just his sexual techniques—stellar as he knew those to be.

Close to her ear, he whispered, ''I'm not afraid of any woman putting her hands on me. That's not it at all. In fact, I already told you the reason—lack of interest in a brief fling.'' He could feel her tension, her excitement, vibrating all along his nerve endings.

He stroked her arm. ''But now I feel challenged to set you straight on your assumptions.''

He heard her swallow. Good. ''Should I demonstrate my lack of reserve, Maddie?''

Expecting outrage at his taunt, she surprised him by saying, "Yes."

Laughing softly at her wholehearted agreement, anticipating his little lesson more than he should have, Max bent to press his mouth to the side of her throat in a barely there kiss. He was starting to realize that Maddie would always manage to take him by surprise. It wasn't an unpleasant realization.

"Always go slow," Max whispered. "It helps to heighten the expectation."

He kissed her again, this time letting his tongue slip over her madly racing pulse. Her need to reassert herself, to prove her appeal, was mixed with the sweetest vulnerability he'd ever witnessed. She was audacious but caring, honest and earthy. Her skin was warm and getting warmer by the second, and she tasted nice.

Maddie braced her hands, fingers spread wide, on the wall in front of her. Max saw that she was trembling and more than anything he wanted to simply hug her, to tell her that there was no real rush. But he gave her just a little of what she'd asked for instead. With any luck, she'd realize on her own that a little more time would only make things better.

He skimmed her ear, his tongue briefly touching just inside, teasing. He heard her breath catch.

"You put your tongue in my ear!"

Max hesitated. "Yes."

Her sigh was long and heartfelt. "That was… nice. I hadn't realized…"

Shaking his head at her ex-fiancé's apparent stupidity, Max licked her ear again. Goose bumps raised on her skin. "A smart man always knows to take his time. The more frenzied stuff," he breathed, "can come later."

"More frenzied stuff?"

Her voice was hopeful. Max peeked at her face and saw that her eyes were squeezed shut. He smiled, and loosened her right hand from the wall. Lacing his fingers with hers, he brought her hand up to his mouth. "Sexual tension should build and build, and yes, it often ends up frenzied. Didn't you and your fiancé...?"

"Ex-fiancé. Yes, we did, but it wasn't *frenzied.* More like..." She searched for a word, then settled on, "Mundane." Her voice was low, breathy. "I guess I liked it okay."

Max vowed she wouldn't be left in his bed *liking it okay.*

Her hand tightened on his. "The thing is, Annie swears to me—"

"Forget about my sister and whatever hare-brained things she told you. Annie likely has even less experience than you." Under his breath, Max muttered, "Or at least she did before Guy succumbed."

"She's read a lot of books," Maddie pointed out.

"And has been suggesting them to you?"

"Yes, but I like the idea of firsthand experience much better."

I just bet you do, Max thought, then got started on his instruction again. "Never neglect the less obvious places."

"Okay, right." She looked at him over her shoulder. "What less obvious places?"

Biting back a chuckle, Max cuddled her closer to his body. He drifted his free hand up to cup just below the soft weight of her left breast. "Everyone knows that women's breasts are sensitive, right?"

"Yes."

Max could feel her heartbeat thumping, knew she was nervous because despite her bravado, she wasn't accustomed to throwing herself at men. If her fiancé hadn't done her wrong, she wouldn't be here now.

Slowly, tantalizingly, he coasted his fingers down to her belly. "And here." Damn, she felt wonderful. Soft and firm and her musky female scent was beginning to get to him. Her hair, still slightly damp, felt cool and silky against his jaw. Max was aware of her stomach muscles clenching, of her suspended breathing.

"And lower?" she rasped hopefully, bringing him out of his fog of sexual need.

"Definitely lower." His voice was too rough, too affected by her nearness. "But that comes much, much later." Like in a week or more, he thought, if he could last that long! "There are other places to visit first, places that can really excite, too."

"But not like lower." She tried to sound insistent and even went so far as to squirm against him.

She sorely tested his resolve. But Max could hear Cleo snoring in the background, which helped to keep his purpose at the forefront of his mind. Cleo needed a stable home, and Maddie seemed perfect to assist in that. She was the only woman he'd ever met who'd understood the dog right off. She'd make a perfect mother for Cleo.

Max wanted to move slowly enough that Maddie would insist on seeing him again. And again, until she got over her determination to be footloose and fancy-free. Until she was ready to go one further and really get to know him.

Max smiled. "Let me show you something." He lifted her arm and slowly kissed her wrist, deliberately leaving it damp from his tongue.

"Okay," she gasped, "that's great. But—"

Before she could continue, he kissed her palm, gently stroking with the very tip of his tongue, again leaving her heated skin damp, letting his warm breath fan the spot.

She gave a humming response.

He wanted to show her how nice going slow could be, but he didn't want to get overly intimate doing it. Cautiously, deliciously, Max sucked her middle finger into his mouth.

Maddie nearly jumped out of his arms. *"Oh my."*

He wrapped his tongue around her finger and tugged. Kissing her, experiencing her unrehearsed response, was a distinct joy. He wanted more, of her body, her time. Her affection for his dog.

And he always got what he wanted, one way or another.

Shifting restlessly, Maddie pressed her bottom into his growing erection. "Max," she breathed.

Realizing he'd gone a little too far, that she'd

been more susceptible to his brief seduction than he'd expected, Max released her and stepped back. He had to catch her so she wouldn't fall.

Stumbling around, Maddie faced him. "You *have* read the book," she accused. Her eyes were heavy, her face flushed. "You know exactly what you're doing."

Max caught her gaze and held it. "I don't need to read the damn book."

She didn't look convinced. "Whatever. It doesn't matter to me, as long as you agree to a fling with me."

One side of his mouth kicked up into a regretful grin. She was so persistent and so entertaining. And so sweet. He wanted to say yes. "I already explained that I can't."

Shoulders stiff, lips tight, she said, "You're a tease, Max Sawyers!" Her face flushed darkly and her eyes glittered. "They surely have a name for men like you."

"Yeah," Max said. "It's 'experienced.'" He refused to take all the blame when she'd more or less dared him. And besides, it had only been her finger he kissed, not all the places where he really wanted to put his mouth.

His heart kick-started with that thought.

While Max watched, that calculating look came into her eyes and they narrowed, the blue getting brighter, hotter. She was so easy to read.

Sort of.

"I believe you're more than up to it."

Max bowed his head, a man accepting female

accolades. "Of course." Now all he needed was for her to agree to his terms.

"And it's obvious you're not immune to me as a woman." Her gaze dropped to his lap, a look that was nearly tactile and as hot as a live flame. "I mean, I don't think you're carrying a roll of dimes in your pocket, are you?"

Forget his terms! Max's growl of outrage sounded in the room. "A *roll of dimes?*"

She shrugged.

"More like a flashlight!"

"Size, I assume," she said with a sniff, "is in the eye of the beholder."

"And you haven't beheld a damn thing yet, so don't go calling a man's business 'small.'" With a low growl, Max considered showing her just how impressive his... No, bad thought. He was struggling to resist her, not give in to her.

Maddie stared at him hard, knowing she'd almost won. "Small, large, it doesn't matter when you continue to refuse my very nice offer."

It *was* a nice offer, Max conceded, and just a few months ago he'd have accepted without hesitation. "Why such a rush, Maddie?" he asked, buying himself time to think.

That endearing vulnerability flashed into her gaze again before she squelched it with a come-hither look. "I'm twenty-six. I've been good all my life and now all I've got to show for it is a broken engagement that I'd rather forget and a lot of time on my hands."

"So why pick me?" Max hoped to hear something complimentary, something meaningful.

He was doomed to disappointment.

"I know all about you! Annie has told me so much. Ever since I met her, I've been enthralled with the stories about you. You're everything I'm not."

That surprised him. "Like what?"

"Exciting, experienced, daring. I've lived my whole life being a Goody Two-Shoes, and in my profession, that isn't really a plus. Evidently it wasn't a plus in my personal life, either."

"Your broken engagement," Max said gently, "is a blessing, I'd say."

"And I agree! But now that I'm free, it only makes sense to gain my own experiences. As you suggested, I'll have a better perspective for the job, and I'll have fun, too." She lowered her lashes, her look now timid when she added, "Besides, I sort of feel like I know you, because of Annie. Being with you feels...safe."

Max suddenly realized he was taking the wrong tact with Maddie. She was reacting on the rebound, doing what she could to counteract the embarrassing feather episode. Her haste was probably due in part to the fact that she might chicken out if she didn't rush through things.

Perhaps Maddie would forget about the *brief* part of the fling if he showed her how sexually satisfying a real relationship would be.

That idea appealed a whole lot more than walking away did. He didn't want to walk away; he *did* want to make love to her.

Why not? Maddie suited his criteria. She did her best to nurture his dog, she wanted lots of sex, and she was cute to boot.

He'd be holding up his promise to Cleo, and satisfying himself in the bargain. What more could a guy ask for?

He needed more time to consider the possibility of roping Maddie into marriage, but he had a gut feeling that once she was roped, she'd be incredibly loyal and giving. And she'd love Cleo. Maybe she'd even learn to love him.

That thought was far too heavy for his peace of mind, so Max decided to just enjoy dinner, and see what happened. For sure, Maddie wouldn't bore him.

Then his gaze again drifted to Maddie's breasts, and he got blessedly distracted. "You know, I'm just dying for you to tell me what all these suggestive slogans mean. *In Full Bloom, Freshly Plucked.* And earlier, your shirt said *I Give Good Peach.*"

Since Max was already thinking in possessive terms, jealousy nudged him and he asked darkly, "Do you want to have an affair with *me*, or are you hoping to turn on the entire male population?"

MADDIE ATTEMPTED to calm the mad gallop of her heartbeat. But it wasn't easy because Max was staring at her breasts and even though he sounded unaccountably annoyed, his rough voice stroked over her sensitized nerve endings like a slow kiss.

The way he'd touched her... Her finger would never feel the same. Even now, she realized she was holding it out apart from the rest of her hand. It was still damp, still tingling.

It was just a damn finger.

Maddie cleared her throat, determined to be as cavalier as Max. "Bea, one of the women I work with at the clinic, creates slogans for clothes." Talking normally was difficult, but Maddie thought she managed credibly.

"This was one for a florist, and a big hit, I might add. It was used as a giveaway when you ordered a certain amount of flowers and it drew in a lot of the younger crowd. Wedding orders came in like crazy."

Dryly, Max said, "I can imagine."

"The other one was for an independent company that created specialty jams."

"Specialty, as in peach jam?"

"That's right. And passion fruit—the slogan for that one is awesome—and kiwi, and wild blackberry, too." Maddie looked down at the dress that she knew complimented her figure but hadn't been enough to win Max over. "I think the slogans are nice."

"I think they sound downright nasty."

Maddie laughed at that, then dredged up another taunt. With any luck, he'd decide to prove himself to her again. "To a man who's afraid to submit to his baser side, it makes sense that the slogans would intimidate you."

Far from appearing amorous, Max looked ready to strangle her. "I am not intimidated!"

Maddie sighed. She knew he wasn't. He also wasn't the unconscionable playboy she'd imagined. No, Max Sawyers was a gentle man who loved his dog and had an innate honor that caused him to turn her down repeatedly.

He wanted to go slow, but going slow meant getting to know him, and already she liked him far too much. The more time she spent with him, the more risk to her heart.

She didn't want to care about another man. Glancing at Cleo snoring on the couch, Maddie decided it was bad enough to care about a man's dog. If she let it go any further than that, she could end up with her pride butchered beyond repair.

No, she wouldn't allow herself to get roped in like that again. If Troy with his limited experience had played with feathers, there was no telling what a man like Max played with—other than women's hearts. Getting overly involved with him would be like jumping from the frying pan into a raging inferno.

She was just about to let Max off the hook, to concede defeat, when he asked belligerently, "Were you just kidding about dinner, or do you intend to feed me?"

Her spirits lifted. "Can you be bribed with food?"

"No."

Despite her disappointment, she laughed. His honesty delighted her; she knew without a doubt that Max would always be truthful with her; his sister was right about that. He might be a confirmed bachelor, but he was an honorable one. "I'll feed you. Would you like to help me in the kitchen?"

"Will you behave?"

"Heavens, no!" Maddie winked at him, enjoying the banter between them. Never had she carried on so before, and it was fun. Not as much fun as she was sure an affair would be, but still very enjoyable. "I had no idea that becoming a vamp would be so enjoyable."

"You're not a vamp yet, Maddie," Max said with a growl reminiscent of Cleo in a malcontent mood. Not that Cleo appeared to *have* any other moods.

Maddie patted his shoulder. "Come on. You can tell me about your travels while I cook, and we'll both, unfortunately, behave."

An hour later Maddie had dinner ready to be served. Max had surprised her by being more help than she'd expected. Not only wasn't he a shallow playboy with only personal gratification on his mind, but the man knew his way around a kitchen. One more thing to like about him, she thought, and frowned at the idea. Liking him was *not* part of the plan.

As she set the food on the table, Maddie heard a noise from the couch and saw Cleo's nose move first. Then her front left paw. Her stubby legs started jerking as if she were trying to run to the table, but her eyes were still closed.

Maddie laughed out loud. "She's so fat, and still so attuned to the smell of food."

Max grinned, too. Softly, so softly Maddie barely heard, he said, "Cleo," and the dog's small head jerked up, her too large ears rising to attention. "Food," was his only other word, and Cleo instantly lumbered off the couch and to Max's side, to sit next to his chair.

Rubbing the dog's scruff, Max explained, "She was near starved when I found her. Since then, she eats like a glutton."

Hearing that brought a glitter of tears to Maddie's eyes. With a wavering smile, she reprimanded Max. "She's like a little kid with too many treats. Sometimes overindulgence isn't the best way to prove love. Look at her. She needs more exercise and less food. Or at least buy her food that won't make her any heftier."

So saying, Maddie began cutting up some skinless chicken into bite-size pieces. Max watched her with a curious little grin on his face. "You should have a dog of your own, Maddie."

"I would if I could afford one," she assured him. For the longest time she'd wanted a dog and a cat and a house—and a husband and children of her own. Maddie shook her head—that plan had come and gone. She said negligently, hiding the remnant of longing, "My salary doesn't allow for a lot of extras. And I'd never get a dog if I couldn't take care of her properly."

Max said nothing to that, but he had a strange look on his face.

"C'mere girl," Maddie called, then set the plate on the floor. When Cleo growled and snarled her way over to her, Maddie smoothed down her fur. "I think the local pet shop sells special food for overweight dogs."

Max shook his head. "She doesn't like dog food."

"Then disguise it with some chicken or something she does like for a while. You know it's best for her."

His gaze locked on hers, Max said quietly, "I can't believe you're really worried about her."

"Who knows," Maddie said around a laugh, "maybe her disposition will improve when she feels healthier. Do you walk her every day?"

"In the park."

Giving her attention to her plate so Max wouldn't see her yearning, Maddie said offhandedly, "Maybe I could join you both sometime."

"Maybe."

Jerking her head up, Maddie stared at him. "You mean it?"

"Sure, why not? You, Maddie Montgomery, just keep amazing me."

Why that made her blush, Maddie didn't know. It probably had something to do with the way he said it, with a hint of admiration and a look of lust in his eyes. At least to her it looked like lust. Not that she was an expert, just very, very hopeful.

She also wasn't used to praise, and certainly not that kind of praise. So she amazed him, hmm? "Enough to give in? Enough to put me out of my misery, to want to be the first notch on my bed-post?''

To her amazement, he didn't immediately refuse. Instead, Max thoughtfully chewed a bite of chicken, then swallowed a drink of milk before finally saying, ''It's possible.''

Maddie's eyes widened until she thought they'd drop out of her head. *It's possible* was a whole lot more encouraging than *I'm not interested*. Progress, she decided, and throughout the rest of the meal, she barely tasted her food.

Once Cleo realized the food was all gone and the humans wouldn't be handing her any more scraps, she slunk off to sleep on the couch again. Maddie watched her go, noticing that she moved even slower now than she had before being fed. When she lay down, her body looked twice as wide, spread out on Maddie's couch. Cleo was one lazy dog.

''What are you thinking, Maddie?''

Red with guilt, Maddie turned to Max and admitted, ''I was thinking of conniving a way to get Cleo on a diet.''

Rather than being angry or insulted, he nodded. ''Good luck. If you can find a way to get her to eat the good stuff, I'd be indebted. My vet mentioned a diet last time we were in—''

At the word ''vet,'' Cleo jerked awake, then fell off the couch during a vehement snarling jag. She looked surprised and embarrassed to find herself sprawled on the floor.

Max just shook his head, but Maddie leaped from

the table and ran to the distraught dog. Despite Cleo's furious barking, Maddie cuddled her close and hugged her. "Shh. It's all right."

Cleo, going quiet in a heartbeat, looked as flummoxed as Max. Maddie ignored them both. She hated to see anyone or anything afraid.

She pressed her face against Cleo's scruffy neck and said again, "It's all right."

Very slowly, as if half afraid to move, Cleo began crawling toward Max with her belly scraping the floor. She kept casting worried, suspicious glances at Maddie, and Maddie kept pace with her, scooting along on her knees until they were both at Max's feet.

Maddie released the dog and saw that Cleo was staring up at Max, her expression a request for aid. It was obvious Cleo had no idea how to deal with Maddie's affection, which reminded Maddie of the women she worked with, how they'd first behaved when meeting her.

Many of them had moved on with their lives, happier, more content. The few that Maddie still saw now loved her, as she loved them. She hoped the same outcome was possible with Cleo.

Max laughed out loud and Maddie sat back on her haunches, shaking her head at both dog and man. "She still doesn't trust me."

"I beg to differ. She doesn't know what to make of you at all." Max patted one knee. Maddie started to move, but Cleo beat her to it, and lumbered up onto his lap.

She sighed. Max's lap looked very comfortable. But there wasn't room for both of them.

Cleo gave Max one grateful lick on the chin, then looked back at Maddie with a worried frown. Her furry brows were pinched together, her teeth were showing, but for once, not in a snarl.

"You're covered in dog hair," Max pointed out as his gaze slipped over Maddie's breasts.

"Oh." Maddie looked down and attempted to brush herself off, but the last thing she was concerned with was a few dog hairs.

Setting Cleo aside, Max said, "Go lie down."

Maddie assumed he was speaking to the dog.

Cleo gladly retreated to the couch and again settled herself there, yawning and stretching and sighing in relaxation.

Maddie smiled. "Let's be very careful not to mention that 'v' word again. I don't like seeing her upset."

Without warning, Max caught her beneath her arms and pulled her upward until she was on her knees between his open thighs. It was a very nice place to be. Her face tilted up to his, her hands clasped his shoulders for balance.

Max stared at her mouth, and said huskily, "You've convinced me."

Maddie's heart leapt. She was half-afraid to believe what she hoped he meant by that. "Convinced you...of what?"

"That a sexual fling between us wouldn't be meaningless."

Her fingertips dug into his shoulders—nice solid

shoulders—and she held on in case he suddenly changed his mind. "This means you're now willing?"

"Willing, able and anxious."

Ohmigod, ohmigod, ohmigod. "Tonight? Right now?"

Max glanced toward Cleo, heard her snoring, and smiled. "All right," he said gently, and his eyes seemed to be peering into her soul. "If you're certain that's what you want to do."

Maddie was more than certain. She was insistent. Fanatical even. "Yes."

Lifting her, Max brought her face up even with his. The new position caused Maddie's belly to flatten against his groin and she had to swallow back a groan. He was hard again! Or was it that he was hard *still?*

That thought made heat curl through her in dizzying intensity.

Max caught her gaze, refusing to let her look away until the very last second when his mouth touched hers. Her eyes drifted shut. The damp heat of his mouth, the sultry scent of his hard masculine body, the feel of his large rough hands, all consumed her.

Maddie's last thought was: *Finally!* And then she couldn't think at all.

4

MAX TASTED HER deeply, ready and willing to fall off the deep end. Damn, he'd had no idea that watching a woman coddle his dog could be such an aphrodisiac. He loved Cleo, had loved her from the second she'd tried to bite him while he carried her off the road. Seeing someone else love her was a heady thing.

He hadn't known anything was missing from his life until he'd brought Cleo home.

He hadn't known anything was *still* missing from his life, until he'd seen Maddie press her face into Cleo's yellow fur and squeeze her so tight that the dog had no breath left to growl.

Cleo had looked helpless against the emotional onslaught. Her feelings had mirrored his own.

Something insidious and sweet and warm expanded in his chest the second Maddie went to her knees by the dog, making Max's heart feel full to bursting.

The more emotional feelings blended with the sharp sexual desire he'd been trying so hard to ignore, leaving him with no way to resist her.

Max's hands trembled as he held Maddie a tiny bit away from him. Her eyes were heavy, sexy, the blue heated to a midnight hue. Damn but he wanted her.

And he knew in his gut that it wasn't just physical desire, though physically he was so aroused his bragging about a lead pipe earlier was coming back to haunt him. He felt so heavy, his jeans were now painfully tight. But it was more than that; Maddie had nurtured his dog when no other woman even wanted to look at her, much less touch her.

Max had felt the dog's loneliness, her need for love behind her bristled warnings, and Maddie had seen it, too. She was a special woman, too special to let get away. He was already convinced that she'd be perfect to mother his dog. He had a feeling she'd be perfect for him, too. One way or another, he'd convince her to marry him.

What better way to start than by making her body need him?

Max brushed the corner of her mouth with the edge of his rough thumb. "Why don't you go get ready while I put our dishes away? I'll join you in five minutes."

Eyes wide, Maddie asked, "Umm... Get ready?"

She sounded scandalized, and Max couldn't help but grin. "You don't have to put on risqué lingerie or break out the oil. Just get rid of the excess dog hair clinging to your clothes. Maybe turn down the bed. That's all I meant." He added, "Most women like a few seconds alone to themselves."

She stared at him blankly and Max sighed. "You

do have some sort of birth control on hand, don't you?"

"Uh…"

Max felt the urge to laugh with disbelief, or shout with frustration. "I gather by your long face that you don't?"

Maddie licked her lips. "I figured you carried condoms."

"Often I do. But not this time." Mostly because he knew the lack of protection would go a long way in deterring him from giving in. He was scrupulous about birth control, and didn't take chances. Period.

But now… "I could run to the drugstore."

Maddie's eyes were hungry as she stared at him. "How long will that take?"

"Half an hour, tops. Why? You have someplace to be?" The thought that another man might be waiting in the wings tonight did not sit well with Max.

Maddie shook her head so hard her long blond hair whipped against his leg. "No! I'm just…" She shrugged, then gave him a wavering smile. "Impatient."

Max touched her cheek again. He couldn't seem to stop touching her. Her honesty was another turn on, nearly driving him over the edge. "I'll be quick." *As quick as humanly possible!* "I still have your key so I'll let myself back in. Go ahead and get ready and if Cleo wakes up, tell her I'll be right back."

Still she hesitated, and Max asked, "What is it?"

"You won't change your mind while you're gone?"

Tenderness exploded inside Max, mixing with the lust and the other swirl of emotions with combustible force until it was all he could do to force himself to his feet. He needed to join with her, and it was tempting to say to hell with protection. At the moment, lowering her to the floor and taking her right beside the table seemed like a grand idea.

"I won't change my mind," he promised.

The rain poured down in buckets soaking Max to the skin as he dashed to his truck. He drove faster than he should have, but for once it wasn't just Cleo waiting for him. No, now there was an adorable woman who displayed her brazen sexuality as often as she did her naiveté. He could barely wait to take her, to show her what her idiot fiancé obviously hadn't.

The lights from the all-night drugstore barely penetrated the constant rain. By the time Max was back in his truck with the paper bag on the seat beside him, every inch of him was dripping wet. Not that it mattered because he expected to be out of his clothes very soon. He was so hot, it was a wonder he wasn't steaming.

The apartment, as he let himself back inside, was quiet except for Cleo's snoring. Her back paws went through spasmodic jerks and her lips curled in a soundless howl as she dreamed of chasing some hapless critter. Max smiled affectionately.

In some ways, Cleo reminded him of Maddie.

She was pushy and insistent one minute, in the next so sweet he wanted simply to hold her all night.

He couldn't hold Maddie all night. He'd have to leave so that Cleo was in her own home come morning. The dog had a problem that he doubted Maddie would care to experience.

If it wasn't for the doggy door Max had installed after the first two days of bringing Cleo home, all the carpets in his house would have been ruined. It wasn't Cleo's fault, so he'd never scolded her. She woke disoriented and nervous, and would run in circles trying to find her way out. Anytime she'd had an accident, she had looked heartsick about it, and strangely enough, embarrassed. So Max had ended up comforting her rather than scolding her.

As soon as Cleo had figured out the doggy door, she'd learned to hold on until she got outside. She'd still run around, baffled for awhile, but eventually she'd hit the door and find herself in the backyard where trees and shrubs beckoned.

Max smoothed his hand over the dog, settling her back into a deep sleep without pesky rabbits or birds to provoke her, then he looked toward Maddie's bedroom. A bright light shone from around the partially open door. Max's stomach tightened in anticipation.

There was only one bedroom in her apartment. It was a nice place, though very small. The kitchenette led into the tiny dining room that led into a sitting area with a small television and a stereo system. Her bookshelves were filled with books, rather than photos or bric-a-brac. Her reading material displayed her intelligence, and as he imagined *Satisfying Alternatives to Intercourse* joining her other more academic texts, he winced. Perhaps after a few days of play, she wouldn't need the book at all.

Everything was decorated in floral patterns—cream-colored flowers, soft greens, hints of mauve. He liked it, and decided the small no-nonsense apartment suited her personality just right.

Dripping rain and gripping the paper bag, Max started toward that bedroom door and Miss Maddie Montgomery. He pictured her naked, in a sexy pose on the bed, her fair hair spread out over the pillow.

He pictured the smile on her face, the welcome in her dark blue eyes.

Holding his breath, Max pushed the door open—and jumped when Maddie let out a small shriek of surprise.

Clutching her heart, she said, "Ohmigod, you startled me, Max."

Max lounged in the doorway. "You were expecting someone else?"

Maddie wasn't naked, and she wasn't posed.

She wore a thin teal blue robe that fell to her knees and left the bottom half of her shapely legs bare to his view. Nice knees. And sexy calves. Small feet...

"No, of course not." She stepped away from the window where she'd been watching the storm. Nervously, she folded her hands over her flat stomach and shifted her bare feet. "You got here quicker than I thought and I didn't hear you come in."

He didn't tell her how much he'd hurried. "I was quiet so I wouldn't wake Cleo."

"She's still sleeping?"

"Like a baby."

Maddie's smile was all too obviously forced. Max knew he couldn't rush her, despite his clawing need and all her bravado. Every time she met his gaze, she blushed, so he looked toward the bed instead. She really did have a four-poster, he was amused to see. Would she actually carve a notch in the thick, smooth oak?

"I expected to find you in the bed."

The silky robe shimmered as she lifted one shoulder. "I wasn't sure you'd want me there."

Her reply surprised him, since she'd all but roped and dragged him to the ground. "So," he said, flashing her a smile, "now my wants matter?"

"I thought you might prefer us standing against the wall, or perhaps bent over the chair."

Max couldn't hide his surprise.

"I'm not looking for the conventional wham-bam here, Max." Maddie took another step closer to him. "I was thinking along the lines of adventure." She shrugged.

She gestured toward the overstuffed flowered seat that held her dress. "It has padded arms on it, and a nice soft seat."

His tongue stuck to the roof of his mouth. As outrageous as her words were, they brought with them pictures of Maddie bent at the waist, her bottom in the air for him to cuddle and pet and kiss.

He could almost see her, and that wasn't good for his libido.

Maintain control, maintain control, he told himself, repeating the advice that often graced his column. After a deep breath that didn't do a damn thing to slow the racing of his pulse, Max asked, "So you're looking to get kinky, huh?"

Maddie bobbed her head enthusiastically. "The way I see it, if I'm going to do this, I might as well go all out."

She was making him feel cheap, Max realized with astonishment, quickly followed by annoyance. He wanted their first time together to be romantic, not merely sexual. He'd never cared overly about being romantic before, but now he did, dammit. And romance wasn't likely if she insisted on getting risqué right off the bat.

He'd always thought there was a lot to be said for good old-fashioned missionary sex.

Keeping his expression and tone level, Max said, "Kinky it is. What would you like to try first?"

"I dunno. You're the supposed expert."

Supposed, ha! Going for the one thing Max knew for a fact would turn most women off, he said, "What about a ménage à trois?"

Her eyes widened. "You'd do that for me?"

Max nearly swallowed his damn tongue; her willingness threw him. He was beginning to think he'd made a huge mistake, and would have to walk out on her after all.

Then she took the final step that brought her body close to his and severely weakened his resolve.

With the most innocent expression he'd ever seen on a woman, she asked, "Do you know a guy who's willing, or do I get to pick him?"

Max jerked back a step. "A guy! I meant another woman."

Maddie gave him a mock frown. "No way! This is my show." Her smile proved she'd been teasing all along. "Why would I want to share you?"

Shaking his head, Max started to laugh. Maddie came close again to cover his mouth. "Shh. You'll wake up Cleo."

"I can't help it. You're so funny." Max pulled her against his chest, which effectively soaked her robe since his clothes were still dripping wet, and kissed her hard and fast. Maddie didn't complain. If anything, she hugged him tighter.

"How about," Max whispered against her smiling lips, "we get naked and climb into bed."

"To do things the conventional way?"

"It's a nice easy way to start, honey, I promise."

That seemed to appease her. Without missing a beat, she dropped the damp robe and turned her back on Max to climb into the large bed. *What a view!*

Heat roiled and welled beneath his skin. His control slipped a little, but he reined it in, determined to make this the best *notching* Miss Maddie Montgomery would ever experience.

As Max peeled off his clinging wet shirt, he couldn't stop himself from growling, "You have a gorgeous bottom, Maddie."

"Really?" Her face bright pink from her brazen

display, Maddie scurried under the covers, then gave him a beatific smile.

Toeing off his shoes, Max added, "Really."

Her cheeks remained heated, but she watched as he dropped his pants, leaving his clothes and shoes in a sodden pile on the floor. He started for the bed.

"Turn around."

Max paused by the footboard. "Why?"

"I want to see if you have a nice backside, too."

Feeling a little self-conscious, Max obediently turned, and was startled by the sound of Maddie's low wolf whistle.

"Very nice," she said. "Now bring your hunky self to bed." She threw back the covers and patted the mattress beside her hip.

Chuckling at the uniqueness that was Maddie, Max settled himself beside her. He didn't have time to reach for her.

No sooner was he laid out flat than Maddie launched herself on top of him. Soft flesh moving against hard, silky hair against rough. Max barely had time to grab for a breath before her mouth covered his and her hands began mauling him again.

Max struggled to the surface of his turbulent lust. It wasn't easy because while his mind rebelled at a rushed, frenzied mating, his body was all for the idea.

A mauling had never felt so good.

"Maddie," he said, trying to hold her off. It wasn't easy. Maddie might be slender and delicate, but she was stronger than she looked.

She bit his neck, panting. "You're a tease, Max Sawyers. Stop teasing me and give it up."

Forcefully, Max held her back then flipped over to pin her to the mattress. "You want to wrestle, sweetheart? I'm game."

"There's no wrestling involved, you big ape, when you just hold me down."

Max knew there was a big goofy grin on his mug, but dammit, it felt good to be wanted so much.

"Why don't we talk a bit first," Max suggested, needing a distraction to regain some control.

Maddie shook her head. "I didn't get you into bed to *talk.*"

He was starting to feel used again.

Being desired physically was great. Hell yes, it was wonderful.

But Max wanted to feel that she had picked him specifically, not just because of his body or his reputation. He needed to be reassured.

How lame for a macho stud! he thought in disgust.

Maddie had made it clear that she didn't want to get to know him, she just wanted "it."

Max seethed, wanting to tell her that he could give her more than sex, more than a warm male body in bed. But it sounded foolish. And unaccountably female. Gad. He wanted sex, for crying out loud! And up until a short time ago, sex without commitment was right up his alley.

But everything had changed.

Max rallied forth and said, "Okay, then let's decide on what type of kinky stuff you want to do."

"Everything." Maddie tried to get her arms free but couldn't. She finally subsided, staring up at Max with wide eyes shadowed by long lashes. Her hair was in an appealing tangle around her head, her cheeks were pink, her lips parted.

Max sighed. He was so hard he hurt, and he was getting harder by the second. "Spanking?"

Maddie's eyes widened even more. Good, at least *that* shocked her.

Then she said, "I doubt I could ever get you over my knees. You're too big."

That was one taunt too many.

Growling, Max abruptly sat up, making Maddie squeal as she realized she'd gone too far. But she didn't escape even halfway across the bed. With no effort at all, Max caught her by the waist and expertly flipped her across his naked thighs. Her long legs kicked and her soft white behind beckoned his hands. He couldn't resist palming her, squeezing gently.

At the touch of his hand on her behind, Maddie stiffened. "Don't you dare, Max Sawyers!"

The squirming bundle draped across his lap no longer sounded so derisive.

"Don't dare what?" Max asked. "This?"

"Max!"

His palm landed with a barely there thwack. Still she gasped and redoubled her efforts to get free.

"Max Sawyers! You stop it right now!"

Max easily controlled her. "You look mighty sexy like this, Maddie." He thwacked her again and she quit struggling to twist around and look at him.

"You think I look sexy?"

"You're naked," he explained reasonably. "Of course I think you look sexy."

She licked her lips. "You wouldn't hurt me, would you, Max?"

He turned her over and cradled her protectively in his arms. She was flushed, nervous and inflamed. Max absorbed it all, and felt that twisting inside his heart again. "Not even if you asked me to."

No longer fighting him, Maddie drew her left hand slowly over his shoulders. She tested his muscles, tangled her fingers in his chest hair, and when she looked at him, pure lust shone from her eyes.

Max bit back a groan. "Maddie…"

Leaning forward, she kissed his throat. "Please, no more teasing. I can't take it. I've been thinking about this forever, and now I want you too much."

"All right." At the moment, teasing was well beyond him. Hell, breathing took an effort.

"I love how you smell, Max."

Max tightened his hold on her. Finally, they were moving at a normal pace toward a proper goal. He dipped down to rub his cheek over the crown of her head. "I like how you smell, too, sweetheart. Sweet and soft and so very female."

"Female isn't a smell."

"Mmm. Female is most definitely a smell, a scent unique to every woman."

Her thumb brushed his nipple, stretching his control to the breaking point. "You know what I said about a small pistol?"

Max spread one hand over her behind, weighing

the soft fullness in his palm. He nuzzled her cleavage. "You wounded me to my masculine core. I doubt I'll ever forget."

"I was teasing. There's nothing small about you at all, is there?"

Max met her gaze, and promptly lost the battle. Dropping backward onto the mattress, he allowed Maddie to settle herself on top of him. He gave himself up to her, relishing the kisses she rained over his face and throat and chest, wallowing in her tentative touch, the way she wiggled her pelvis against his straining erection.

He gave up trying to slow her down, and just went with his senses.

"Shh," Max told her when she cried out in surprise at the intimate touch of his fingers down her elegant spine, her generous bottom, and further. He traced around her most sensitive flesh with gentle fingertips.

Maddie reared up, stiffening her arms. "That... that feels good, Max."

"It should. If anything doesn't feel good, Maddie, I want you to tell me."

Eyes squeezed tight, teeth biting into her bottom lip, she nodded agreement.

"You're nice and wet." Max was so hot, his voice sounded disembodied, vague.

A groan broke past the restriction of Maddie's teeth as he continued to explore her, skimming over her delicate, swollen tissues.

Her rigid posture had brought her plump breasts right above his face and Max took swift advantage.

Her nipples were dark pink, puckered and too enticing to resist. Max licked first, lazily stroking with the rough wet heat of his tongue, letting her know his intent. She trembled, her breathing now audible as she leaned forward, making it clear what she wanted.

Max drew her deep.

Maddie's hips jerked, causing his fingertips to slide over slick flesh.

"Relax for me, Maddie."

"*Impossible.*"

Smiling, Max insisted, "It's very possible. And you don't want to wake Cleo."

"Okay. Okay. Okay..."

Max pushed one finger slowly, deeply inside her. Her feminine muscles gripped him in a tight silky vice.

"*Okay!*"

Using the only way he could think of to quiet her, Max kissed her hard. Maddie fell into the kiss, taking his tongue and giving back her own, consuming him, making him crazed with lust. He'd never had a kiss like this, inexperienced but so hungry, so generous and hot.

The gentle thrust of her pointed nipples on his chest was a seductive lure. Combined with her scent, stronger now that she was so excited, and the softness of her hair and skin licking over his heated flesh in dark sensual places, Max gave up. He knew she was ready, knew he was beyond ready, and decided it was time.

Getting Maddie to turn him loose took some doing though.

"Just let me get the condom," he urged.

Her fingernails bit into his shoulders, firing his lust further. "Don't leave me, Max."

"I'm not going anywhere except to the nightstand." He put her to the side and then got distracted looking at her body. She was slim but shapely, her breasts rosy now with need, her stomach tightened, trying to hold in the sweet ache of desire. Her long legs shifted restlessly on the bed.

And her blond curls…they were damp and inviting.

Max bent and pressed a kiss low on her belly.

"Max!"

He rested his chin on her thigh. "You need to stop shouting, honey. Think of Cleo as a baby. If you wake her, she's not going to want to go back to sleep. Putting her outside the door won't help. She'll howl loud enough to wake the dead."

With dawning fury, Maddie said, "You've locked her out when you were with other women?"

A woman like Maddie could quickly grab a man's heart. She was aroused, wet and ready. Her breasts rose and fell with her deep heavy breathing and her skin was warmed to a rosy glow.

Yet she had the sensitivity to consider his dog's feelings.

Max gently stroked her thigh, high near her hipbones, and then very lightly, between.

"No," he whispered, bending to kiss her again. He hadn't been with many women since getting

Cleo, mostly because Cleo hated them all and wasn't shy about letting Max know it. He'd tried, but having an hysterical dog on his hands wasn't his idea of fun. And the women had complained mightily when he'd chosen to calm Cleo over bedding them.

Selfish women.

Women unlike Maddie Montgomery.

"I tried shutting her out a few times," Max explained, letting his breath fan her skin. "so she wouldn't shed in my bed. She…ah, didn't like it. She really has this thing about closed doors, especially when she's on the wrong side of them."

Mollified, Maddie pulled a pillow over her face. When she spoke, her voice was muffled. "This will help. You can proceed now with what you…started to do."

Never before had Max suffered the combination of humor and lust and tenderness. It kept him off guard with no way to protect his heart. Max gently urged her legs wider apart, then paused.

"What are you doing?" she mumbled from beneath the pillow.

With his heart in his throat and blood pulsing hotly through his veins, Max said, "Just looking at you."

The pillow lifted and Maddie's gaze met his. "Why?"

Touching her lightly with his fingertips, Max said, "Because you're so pretty and pink and ready for me."

The pillow slapped back over her face. "Oh."

Savoring the moment, Max kissed her softly, then as his hunger raged, not so softly.

Maddie's legs stiffened.

He teased her, teased himself, using his tongue, his teeth, and when she was sobbing beneath the pillow, her hands clenched in the pillowcase, Max drew her into his mouth and suckled her right over the edge.

The pillow proved inadequate to properly stifle her wild cries, but it helped enough. Thank goodness for small favors, Max thought to himself as he moved in a rush to the nightstand and ripped open a condom package. He couldn't have waited a minute more. Not a second more.

Maddie, her pillow now limp beside her equally limp body, got her eyes open enough to watch him sleepily as he slid on the protection and moved between her thighs.

Her hand lifted tiredly and stroked his shoulder. "That was...indescribable."

"Better than okay, huh?"

"Definitely—*oh!*"

Max tried to hold back as her body softened to accept him, as his erection slid deep inside her to be squeezed by hot, moist flesh. He growled low in intense pleasure. "Oh, yeah."

"Max?"

"Easy now, Maddie. Just a little more. Damn, you feel good."

She took two gasping breaths. "So...do you."

He pulled out, felt her hands grip his shoulders,

her legs curl around his hips trying to keep him close, and he drove forward again.

Maddie tipped her head back on the pillow. "This is better than any damn feather!"

"You better believe it." Max gave up the fight and began a rhythm that supplied just the right amount of pressure, just the right friction. "Squeeze me, Maddie," he rasped. "It'll make it better for you. Tighter." He moaned. "That's it."

Holding him with arms, legs and hidden muscles, Maddie began to feel a part of him, a very necessary part.

Max meant to make the pleasure last, meant to give her a half-dozen orgasms so that she'd never be able to forget him, never be able to move on to the next man.

But it was already too late for him.

With a roar worthy of a wild beast, he came and Maddie joined him.

Unfortunately, their combined yells woke Cleo, who was highly affronted by their unseemly behavior.

And just as Max had predicted, she refused to leave the room.

Their night of debauchery was over.

5

"WHERE'S THE BOOK?"

Maddie drew up short, staring back at the three women eyeing her so suspiciously. Darn, she'd forgotten all about the book!

Tossing her backpack—what she carried instead of a bothersome purse—into a seat, Maddie slumped onto the cracked leather couch. "I don't have it."

Bea snorted, making her white hair wobble precariously. Bea spent more time on securing her big hairdos than she did on anything else. "You mean it doesn't exist."

"Does too," Maddie returned petulantly, then grimaced as Mavis and Carmilla shared a look. "I'll get the book. It's just that…well…" A big grin broke over her face and she leaned forward in excitement. "You guys were right!"

Catching Maddie's enthusiasm, all three women leaned forward. Silver hair blended with white blended with glaring red. Hands wrinkled from time and a working woman's life reached for Maddie.

Carmilla spoke first, her tone hushed with scandalized delight. *"You didn't."*

Bea laughed. "I'll bet she did! Just look at her. She's *glowing*."

"Only one thing gives a woman a glow like that," Mavis agreed, and she was grinning like a loon. "'Bout damn time, if you ask me."

"No one asked you," the other two replied, always too contrary to agree with Mavis's constant predictions.

Maddie let all three of them hold her hands, her wrists, her shoulder. "He's positively dreamy," she said. "A stud, just as you told me he should be."

"Give."

"Yes, every single detail, honey. I wait with bated breath."

Carmilla chuckled. "Mavis, there ain't a damn thing she can tell you that you haven't done a million times yourself, so forget the 'swooning young girl' act."

Mavis slanted Carmilla a venomous look that didn't mean a darn thing. Maddie knew they just loved to twit each other.

"Carmilla, darling, at sixty-eight, I *am* a girl compared to you."

Bea slapped her knee. As the oldest at seventy-five, she often played the peacekeeper. "She's got you there, old girl."

Maddie cleared her throat. "Do you three want to hear this or not?"

Mavis waved a hand. "Tell all."

"I did everything you said—well most of what you said. And he took me home just as you told me he would. It was a little rocky, but I finally won.''

Carmilla blinked dark brown eyes. Her face was wrinkled and worn, but in a nice way, like a favorite pair of house slippers that only became more comfortable and appealing the longer you had them. ''Whatd'ya mean, it got rocky? He didn't jump your bones?''

''Uh, no. I jumped his.''

Mavis harrumphed indignantly. Her eyes spit green fire, which went well with her bright red hair. She resembled a beacon in the night, able to pull in any wayward male souls—which had been the point back when all her work was done at night. She kept the bright hair out of sentiment, and because the senior men still tended to flock to her like flies to honey. She had that special ''oomph'' or charisma—whatever you called it—that men never seemed to outgrow.

According to Mavis, she sometimes missed working the corner. Holding hands and behaving like a lady didn't suit her at all.

''What kind of man,'' Mavis demanded, ''would have to be jumped?''

''He's a very good man.''

''Honey, there ain't no such thing.''

Bea swatted at Carmilla. ''Don't tell her such a thing! Of course there are good men.''

''Good for certain things, but she's not ready for love everlasting again so soon.''

''For pity's sake, Carmilla, no one mentioned love everlasting!''

"Look at her eyes, Bea. That girl is smitten."

Everyone turned to stare deeply into Maddie's eyes. She squirmed and immediately felt defensive. "It's not like that at all! You know I've given up on that."

"After what your scumbait fiancé did? Hell yeah, you gave up. I still think you should let us contact a few old friends. I'm tellin' ya, Tiny would love to give your old beau a good goin' over."

Bea shook her head in exasperation. "You are so bloodthirsty, Carmilla."

Mavis snorted. "I agree with her. We should all rough him up, the miserable bastard."

Laughing, Maddie took turns giving each of them a hug. She always felt comforted by their fragile, warm embraces, given from the heart.

She'd been working as a counselor for several years now, and she'd made some friends along the way. She'd started with troubled teens, and gradually been shifted to older women. A lot of those women were now in homes with families and jobs, or doing volunteer work. But Mavis, Carmilla and Bee were aging rebels, women who refused to conform to society's strictures. They were fun loving and adventurous despite their fragile bones, and energetic in a way that belied their years.

They no longer needed her counsel, but they still liked to meet. And being with them helped temper the more stressful sessions Maddie had with abused women, or recovering alcoholics.

Maddie loved Carmilla, Bea and Mavis dearly. For her, they served as surrogate mothers, aunts, best friends and confidants all rolled into one. She admired them for what they'd survived, worried about them endlessly, and counted on them much more than they counted on her, though not a one of them would ever admit it.

She smiled at them. "Max is a good man, I promise. He's a hound dog, no doubt about that—which makes him perfect for my coming-out. But he's also honorable."

"All men," Carmilla said, "are hound dogs, some are just better at it than others."

Mavis raised a slim, drawn-on red brow. "So is this young man good?"

Maddie bobbed her head, making the women laugh. "Yeah." In a whisper, she confided, "He said I was sexy." Then, even lower, "And he seems to know all kinds of kinky stuff."

Carmilla gulped. "Kinky sexual stuff?"

Bea shook her head. "Of course she means kinky sexual stuff. What'd you think? That he wears his shoes backward?" Then to Maddie, "So what'd you do?"

"Nothing kinky," she rushed to reassure them. "He sort of lost control. But the good old conventional stuff was…well, *incredible*."

"Well then," Bee said, setting aside her round glasses. "It's no wonder you're running a little late this morning."

Mavis signed. "I remember those mornings."

Carmilla nudged her hard enough to almost knock her off her chair. "Baloney. What you remember is the money on the nightstand, not a warm body in the bed.''

Mavis grinned. ''That, too.''

It never ceased to amaze Maddie how open and...cavalier the women were about their hardships. To hear them tell it, life as a hooker had been a lark. But she'd talked with each of them enough to know that was simply their way of burying the past.

It sometimes broke her heart.

This time, as always, she hid her reaction with a smile. ''Max didn't spend the night.''

''What?''

''That cad!''

''I say we get hold of Tiny,'' Carmilla growled, ''and let him teach old Max a few manners.''

''It's not like that,'' Maddie hurried to explain. ''You see, he has this dog.''

Blank stares were the only response.

''The dog is adorable. Well, not physically. But she's very sweet. When she's not growling.''

Mavis chortled. ''Sounds like Carmilla.''

''Ha ha.''

Biting back her own laugh, Maddie said, ''The dog has a...well, a bladder problem.''

Bea leaned toward Mavis and said low, ''I can certainly relate.''

''Oh, for goodness sake, be quiet Bea!''

Maddie raised her voice to forestall the start of a new quarrel. ''Max didn't want the dog to soil my carpet, so he went home.''

''Afterward?'' Mavis asked suspiciously.

Smiling, Maddie confirmed, "Yes, afterward." And in dreamy tones, "Way afterward."

"She's got that look again."

"Well," Maddie explained, "it was more wonderful than I'd ever imagined."

"Hurray!"

"'Bout damn time."

"Your damn ex-fiancé should be shot."

Maddie laughed out loud with the joy of it. She'd never imagined, never guessed, that sex could be so wonderful. Max had scandalized her with a few of the wonderful, incredible, sizzling hot things he'd done to her and with her.

But she wouldn't have had him stop a single one.

"So when are you seeing him again?"

At Bea's question, the other two got quiet, all of them waiting for her reply. Maddie forced a negligent shrug.

"I don't know."

"What the hell does that mean?"

"I'm sorry, Carmilla, but it's the truth. I'm not sure what to do now. Max is a confirmed bachelor, and I'm afraid if I get too clingy, it'll spook him."

"You assured him," Mavis asked, "that all you wanted was some good one-on-one experiences to store away for a rainy day?"

"Yes, I told him all that. I don't understand him. He seemed to really resist me, but then once things got going, he was..."

"Into it?"

"Yes."

"Typical man. Fickle, all of them." Mavis shook her head. "Why, I knew a guy once—"

Bea threw up her hands. "You knew lots of guys in lots of ways, Mavis. For cryin' out loud, let's don't go tromping down memory's bumpy lane right now. We need to figure this out for Maddie."

Carmilla crossed her arms beneath her massive bosom and said three words. "Let's call Tiny."

"I have a better idea," Mavis said, ignoring Bea because she had obviously *wanted* to go down memory lane. "Forget about him."

Maddie bit her bottom lip. Though she knew it was probably best, and it *had* been her original plan, she didn't want to forget about Max. Not yet, maybe not for a long, long time.

Maybe not ever. *No,* she would *not* think that!

Bea patted her arm. "Now look what you've done, Mavis! You're going to make her cry."

"I'm not crying!" Maddie had no intention of getting maudlin over Max Sawyers. This was an adventure, an experience, a way to add lascivious excitement to her PG-rated life. She wouldn't let herself get hurt over it.

"Get rid of that long face, Maddie," Mavis said with a laugh. "I didn't mean forget about him forever. Just long enough to whet his appetite. If this Max fellow is anything like you say, he'll expect you to be after him now, wanting more of his sexy body and all the well-oiled parts. Well, throw 'em for a loop, I always say! Don't give him what he wants."

Carmilla gasped with glee. "Exactly! That's brilliant, Mavis!"

Mavis pretended to have a heart attack over the praise and wouldn't quit until Bea threatened to give her mouth-to-mouth resuscitation.

"Men always want what they can't have." Carmilla rubbed her hands together. "As long as you don't give it to him, he'll keep coming back."

"I already gave it to him."

"He'll want it again, and more."

"But..." Maddie wondered how to phrase her worry. Then she decided that with these three, delicacy wasn't needed. "I *want* to give him more."

"Music to my ears." Bea patted her hand and said, "You're a healthy woman, honey. Just tell him that. Sex—but nothing else," she warned. "It's the 'nothing else' that'll get his goat. I promise, it'll drive him plumb crazy and before you know it, he'll be the one chasing you."

"But wait at least a week," Mavis advised. "After a week, he won't know what to think! He'll be gnawing on his own insecurity. Oh, it'll be so sweet."

"I want to meet him," Bea suddenly declared. "Bring him around. I want to judge for myself if he's worth all this bother."

Maddie knew firsthand that Max was more than worth it, but she wanted to show him off to the ladies. She wanted them to see him and experience his charm.

"I could go to him in a week to get the book—"

Carmilla's rough laugh interrupted Maddie's plan. "A book that claims to have *Satisfying Alternatives to Intercourse* has to be drivel."

"Or an outright lie." Bea watched Maddie with a calculating eye as she delivered that insult.

Trying not to laugh, Maddie assured them, "It exists, and I have it on good authority that it's excellent."

"Bring it, and the young man. We'll check them both out."

"Yes, Mavis," Maddie agreed. "And then all three of you will owe me an apology."

There was a general round of grumbling over that prospect, then a snort of contempt, proving that not one of them planned to apologize at all. No, they just intended to meddle, but Maddie didn't mind. She could barely wait to see Max's reaction to them.

She figured if she could be cordial to his dog, dealing with Mavis, Carmilla and Bea ought to be a piece of cake.

SHE DIDN'T CALL, she didn't write...

Max paced the small confines of the bookstore, his temper high, his mood black.

His manly ego thoroughly damaged.

He'd written three columns on the evils of women-on-the-make, then had to destroy them. Truth was so often stranger than fiction, and no one would have believed that he was actually *complaining* about the situation.

In fact, he could barely believe it himself. But

dammit, he'd bought a box of condoms just for her! He had three of the little silver packets in his wallet right now.

Yet she hadn't so much as blinked when he'd told her he couldn't spend the night a week ago. She hadn't offered him her phone number, hadn't invited him back, hadn't done anything but thank him.

And now he knew why.

Maddie truly had just been using him. One time. One lousy damn time and she was through with him. She had the number for the bookstore, and she knew Annie. She could have gotten his home number. But no. She'd ignored him without hesitation.

The hair on the back of Max's neck bristled. *How dare she?* He was no lady's conquest! He wasn't a man to be trifled with!

He had a good mind to storm over to her apartment and see for himself if she'd reduced him to a nick in the bedpost. Only...what if she was with another man when he showed up?

What if she took his visit as a sign of jealousy?

Max cursed and started pacing again. If he found a man there, he just knew he'd get rip-roaring mad and probably do something foolish—like punch the guy out.

And he sure as hell didn't want it to look like he was chasing her. Ha! The very idea was absurd. Women chased *him,* not the other way around.

Max sighed as he stalked the perimeter of the bookstore once again. It was bad enough to be in such a foul mood without having to deal with Annie's shop as well. But his little sister and Guy were off wallowing in premarital ecstasy, on a wedding planning venture that seemed to have no end in sight.

Guy insisted that Annie have the biggest and best wedding around. And his father agreed. They didn't know he had a job writing for the paper, so they probably thought they were doing him a favor, keeping him employed. Ha.

Curse them all.

Cleo whined, tilted her small head and gave Max a quizzical look. If he didn't know better—but he damn well did—he'd think Cleo missed Maddie, too. Impossible. The woman was too pushy to be missed by man or beast.

So why had Cleo been moping so much? Why had she been so maudlin? He loved Cleo, he really did, but it was almost repulsive to see her dragging her chubby little short-legged body around in a depression. He preferred her grumbling and snapping to the worried, unhappy look she'd worn since Maddie left.

Now he knew where the term "hangdog expression" had come from, because Cleo wore it all over her furry face.

"I'm fine, Cleo," Max bit out, "so quit frowning at me."

Cleo looked unconvinced. She whined again and laid her head on the floor, resting it on her front paws and staring up at Max with wrinkled brows and quivering whiskers.

"Stop fretting!" he demanded, unable to bear it

a second more. "It doesn't suit you at all. Besides, I'm just stewing in my own juices."

"And what juices would those be?"

Max jumped at the soft, teasing female voice. Maddie stood there in the doorway looking sweet and sexy and happy to see him, as if a damn week hadn't gone by, as if she hadn't been ignoring him completely after taking him like a convenient body with no soul.

No, Max admitted to himself, that wasn't quite the way it had happened. She'd taken his body, yes—most thoroughly in fact—but she'd also grabbed his heart and soul with both fists.

It was unbearable.

Just looking at her hurt.

Cleo, the traitor, took one peek at Maddie and began leaping about in near maniacal excitement. Her snarls and growls actually mingled with happy woofs. Max glared at her.

Then her tail—a tail seldom seen since it spent most of its time curled safely against her belly— gave a one-thump wag of delight.

"Well, I'll be damned."

Maddie went straight to the dog, not even slightly put off by Cleo's mixed display of joy and wrath, and hugged her tightly. "Did you miss me, sweetie?"

Yellow fur clung to Maddie's hot-pink T-shirt, a T-shirt that read *Made In The Sun*. Cleo went so far as to lick Maddie's ear.

Oh yeah, Maddie with her long blond hair hanging free, her blue eyes smiling, would look very sweet under the hot sun. Naked. Open for him.

Max cleared his throat, angry at himself for responding to her. Sure, she loved all over his damn dog, but she'd barely said two words to him.

It was as if she hadn't missed him at all.

"Well, well," he murmured in his most sarcastic tone, "look what the cat dragged in."

At the word "cat" Cleo's ears lifted, her portly body trembled and she went bonkers. She snapped at the air and raced around the small bookstore, bumping into shelves and sticking her snarling nose into every small space, searching for the heinous feline creature.

Maddie frowned at Max. "Now look what you've done!" She rushed after Cleo, her white sandals clicking on the tile floor as she ran through a haphazard game of tag that had Maddie, too, bumping into bookcases before she finally got both hands anchored in Cleo's collar. "Shh. Shh. It's all right, Cleo. I promise, there aren't any other creatures here except us."

Cleo wasn't about to trust anyone and so the game continued. Maddie got dragged several feet before she gave up and released Cleo's collar, only to rush after the dog, explaining all the while.

Max sauntered off to the back room to get himself a cola. He was being ignored, so he figured no one would miss him. Let the two ladies have their fun. He'd ignore them right back.

He'd finished half the bottle of soda before Maddie again appeared in the doorway. The tight tee outlined her breasts and her long legs were displayed under an itty-bitty white cotton miniskirt.

She looked good enough to eat, he thought. Then in the next second, he got hard.

"What are you doing?"

Max shrugged, the epitome of a man without a care. He ruined the pose, though, by grumbling, "Not a damn thing, why?"

"My, my," she said with raised eyebrows. "Surly this morning, aren't we?"

Surly? *Surly!* Max paused, thinking, Did real men act surly? Good grief, he didn't think so.

He mentally shook himself and gathered together his lauded control.

"Sorry," he uttered, once again sounding like himself, a man without a care, a man who excelled in deception. "I had a...late night."

There, Miss Montgomery, he thought, work that over in your conniving little brain.

Yawning hugely, Maddie said, "Me, too."

Max jerked to attention and demanded, "A late night doing *what?*"

"Working."

"Oh."

She gave him an impish grin. "What did you think I was doing?"

"Notching more bedposts?"

"And that would have bothered you?"

"Not in the least."

Her smile was smug and he wanted to kiss it right off her face. No sooner did the thought enter his mind than he decided, why not?

Max stalked her, his intent gaze letting her know exactly what he wanted, and Maddie began backing up as she chuckled.

"Cleo finally settled down." She giggled as she said it, and stopped abruptly when her back came up against the small cool refrigerator.

Max caged her in, flattening his hands on either side of her head. "She ran out of gas, that's all. Cleo can raise a racket for hours until she literally flops down exhausted."

"That exactly what she did! One second she was running around—"

Her words were swallowed up by his kiss. Damn, she tasted good. Too good. Even better than he'd remembered.

Max had almost forgotten how wonderful her soft mouth felt under his, how teasing her tongue could be, her delicious taste. "Mmm."

He lifted his mouth from hers and pressed soft, biting kisses down her throat. "You like hickeys?"

Maddie, breathing roughly, rasped, "Hickeys?"

"Love bites." He licked her throat. "Do you like them?"

"I...I don't know." Her hands clenched in his shirt, her hips pressed into his. "I don't think I've ever had one."

Max opened his mouth on her neck, right over her thrumming pulse, and sucked her skin gently against his teeth.

Maddie responded with a long, hungry groan.

Max made sure the mark would be low enough that she could cover it easily with her clothing, but she tasted so good he didn't want to let her go. He kissed her throat again and again, then moved on to her jaw, her ear.

Maddie panted. "This is wonderful."

She made him crazy. Max took her mouth hard in a voracious kiss, all the while his mind was churning. He knew he should hold back, knew he should set things straight with her. He couldn't. Not right now.

"Ever had a nooner?"

Maddie slowly blinked open her heavy eyes. "A nooner?"

Max cupped her cheek and smoothed her skin with his thumb. She was so soft. "It's afternoon. A great time to play."

Her eyes widened. "Play, as in...?"

"Make whoopee. Here. *Now*." He wanted her so badly, just getting the words out was an effort.

Maddie glanced around the tiny back room where unopened boxes crowded the floors and file cabinets were squeezed into the corners. One small square table held a coffeemaker and was surrounded by three mismatched chairs. The miniscule refrigerator hummed against her backside. Max could feel the teasing vibration through Maddie, their bodies were pressed so closely together.

Most importantly, though, was the open door leading into the rest of the bookstore. Any customer coming in might be able to see them if they got close to the door. Max saw the confusion, the scandalized excitement that darkened Maddie's eyes.

She bit her lip. "Here?"

In one deft move, Max flattened her more securely to the refrigerator and pushed himself between her thighs. With a tilt of his head, he could see the front door, but no one coming in could see him unless they rounded the corner. Max knew she felt his erection, as well as the way his hands shook. But he didn't care. All he cared about was hearing her soft enticing groans again as she came.

"Here," he growled.

"Standing?"

"Standing. You offered this last time, remember? The only difference is that the fridge is nice and cool, and I swear, you'll appreciate that in a minute."

"Why?"

"Because I'm going to make you burn up."

"Oh." She touched his chest, looked around the room again. "I'm...I'm kind of wobbly," she said worriedly.

Max smiled. "I won't let you fall." Hell, his muscles were so tense, so tight, he was more likely to break than bend.

Maddie licked her lips slowly while her eyes searched his. "What if someone catches us?"

Kissing the corner of her sweet mouth, Max whispered, "It's an exciting thought, isn't it? Doing the forbidden? Taking a risk? But the door has a bell, remember? We'll know if anyone comes in." With a touch of demand, he added, "Trust me."

Her fingers gripped his upper arms, squeezing, caressing. "All right."

Breathing hard, Max held her gaze as he caught

the hem of her miniskirt and slowly raised it. Maddie moaned.

"We need to get rid of your panties," he told her, knowing his words would work as foreplay, "so that I can touch you."

Maddie closed her eyes.

"You want me to touch you, don't you, Maddie? That's why you're here again." He'd have rather believed she'd missed him, but he was a realist. Fingers on her thigh, he asked, "You missed *this*, didn't you?"

She nodded, her chest heaving, her thighs trembling as Max ran his fingertips up and over her legs to her hips.

With no warning at all, he cupped her through the silky triangle of underwear.

"Why, Maddie Montgomery," he said softly, "you're already hot and wet." Max moved his fingers over the damp silk, outlining her swollen folds, then higher, stroking her through the material. Maddie gasped.

"Mmm," he said. "Right there, huh?"

She didn't answer, so he paused, keeping one finger pressed teasingly to the ultrasensitive spot.

Maddie's eyes opened and she stared at him, looking somewhat dazed. "Max?"

He loved hearing her say his name. "I want you to answer my question, Maddie."

She swallowed, drew a steadying breath. "What question?"

Her rasping voice shook; Max liked that. "Is this where you want me to touch you?"

He flicked gently, then deeply, and Maddie's hips jerked against him.

"Yes!"

"I want to see your breasts, Maddie."

She stared at him.

"Show them to me." This was Max's favorite game, taking charge, making specific sexual demands. And after the week he'd been through, waiting for her, hoping she'd call, thinking she never would, he especially liked it.

And she especially deserved it.

Looking undecided about what to do, Maddie again bit her lip. It was an innocently sexual expression that turned him on even more.

Max quit stroking her, making his demand. "Show me your breasts, Maddie."

She swallowed hard, then began inching up her shirt. She had on a barely there bra of matching hot pink, transparent and sexy as hell. Max bent toward her. "Keep the shirt out of my way."

Her nipples were hard points against the thin material and Max closed his mouth around her hotly.

"Max!"

He tasted her other breast, leaving both nipples covered with damp clingy fabric. Leaning back to enjoy his handiwork, Max said, "Nice. Pretty."

He didn't want to take a chance on being interrupted, so he decided not to stall any longer. Maddie's skirt was bunched around her waist, her T-shirt up under her chin. He slowly took a step back, and cautioned her, "Don't move."

She barely even breathed.

Nodding in approval, Max knelt down and pulled her panties to her knees.

The door chimed.

Maddie started to jerk away, but Max quickly rose and held her still. He covered her mouth with two fingers scented by her body. Against her ear, he said, "Don't you move a single muscle, sweetheart. Do you understand me?"

Panicked, her eyes huge, Maddie mumbled against his fingers.

"Shh. Trust me."

A heartbeat of silence passed while they stared at each other and the interruption he'd wanted to avoid became a real risk. Finally she nodded.

Just that quickly Max left the backroom, closing the door behind him. There was nothing he could do about his noticeable hard-on except hope the two female customers wouldn't look at him closely until he got behind the counter.

They didn't. They were too busy picking up their favorite romance novels. They discussed authors and new releases and made faces at the goofy clinch covers. In the short time he'd been filling in for Annie, Max had noticed that their biggest sellers were romances.

Luckily the customers didn't wake Cleo, but they did give her horrified stares. She was stretched out on the floor beneath a table, snoring.

Max ignored the ladies' aghast expressions and waited on them patiently. Maddie, he was certain, would have thought Cleo looked cute. She wouldn't have regarded the dog with distaste, but rather with that small, endearing smile of hers.

Max could just picture her still standing against the old refrigerator, her legs open, her hands fisted in her shirt, breasts bare, panties around her knees. She looked so sexy, so sweet. So impatient.

He had to shake those thoughts away or he'd embarrass himself.

It was a good ten minutes before the store was once again empty. Max took a deep breath, flexed his hands and rolled his head to rid himself of the worst of his tension. In the corner, Cleo lay sprawled in boneless languor, the most relaxed she'd been since she'd slept at Maddie's apartment. Since then, she'd been watching the doors, the windows, and Max knew she'd been waiting for Maddie.

Just as he had.

That sudden insight annoyed him enough that he quickly opened the back-room door and walked in.

Maddie was standing just as he'd left her.

Her tiny pink panties were still twisted around her knees and her nipples were still erect little points, telling Max that her thoughts hadn't veered from the sexual at all. She may not have missed him, but she'd missed what he could do for her. And she had come back to him. He'd build on that. For Cleo's sake.

Without a word, he knelt in front of her again. As if they hadn't been interrupted at all, Max traced a path up her thigh and asked, "You ready for me, Maddie?"

Her stomach clenched. "Yes."

Slowly, enthralled by the contrast of her moist pink flesh against his dark hand, Max inserted one finger inside her. Maddie didn't look away. Her legs parted as far as the panties would allow, straining against the bonds.

"Do you want me to kiss you?"

"Yes." Then, almost as an afterthought, "Please."

She no longer hesitated at all in her answers. Max's heart pounded hard, and his control was a thing of the past. Still with his finger inside her, gently probing, Max breathed in her musky scent, then opened his mouth over her in a voracious, consuming kiss meant to bring her desire to an acute edge.

Maddie's breath left her in a harsh groan. Her hands settled on his head, her fingers inadvertently pulling at his hair.

He didn't mind. He liked her unrestrained show of excitement.

Max brought her right to the edge, teasing, nibbling, kissing softly, then not so softly. He used his tongue in a never-ending, rasping stroke—then left her.

Quickly stripping her panties the rest of the way off, Max tucked them into his back pocket.

Max stroked her bare bottom as he explained, "Quickies are sometimes an elusive thing for women," Max explained as he stroked her bare bottom. "They need more...preparation. More stimulation."

How the hell he was stringing so many words together when all he could hear was the roar of his own racing heartbeat, Max wasn't sure. Maddie neither wanted nor required explanations. But he wanted her enjoyment to be a foregone conclusion, and talking not only aroused her further, it helped to calm him so that he could see to her pleasure. He refused to take a chance on leaving her unsatisfied.

"You talk too much, Max."

Max smiled at the crackle in her voice, the way she held herself so still and ready. Her back was pressed hard against the door of the fridge, her hips tilted outward, legs spread. Her little belly was so cute, so inviting.

He unzipped his jeans in a rush, then pushed them below his hips. "When I come into you now, the friction will be just right."

He felt the heat of Maddie's intense gaze, watching him as he rolled on the condom. She reached for him when he stepped between her widely spread thighs.

She held him tight when Max instructed, "Put your right leg around my waist. That's it, a little higher. Now just... Umm. That's right." She was so wet, he sank easily into her. "Tilt your pelvis toward me more."

Maddie anxiously followed his instructions. "This is fairly kinky, isn't it?" she panted.

"Yeah." He'd win her over yet, he thought. He'd make her insane with lust, make her understand that there was a special chemistry between them. Max kissed her again, and intent on making her hotter with words, he whispered, "What did you think about while I was with the customers, sweetheart?"

"You," she whispered. "What you just did to me?"

"Yes?" Max could already feel his triumph. She'd wanted him to kiss her, to pleasure her. "What about it?"

"I thought about...doing that to you."

Max froze. His vision clouded.

Unconcerned with his reaction, Maddie persisted with her arousing admission. Her breath pumped in and out, making the words stilted, as she moved against him, pleasuring herself on his rigid body.

"I thought about being on my knees in front of you, of taking you into my mouth, tasting you and sucking on you the same way you—"

With a muffled shout, Max drove into her. He was a goner, coming even as he heard Maddie's soft chuckle of success. He let her laugh, because seconds later she was climaxing, her nails biting into his butt, his arms the only things keeping her upright.

It seemed as though they stood there for hours, propped against each other, both of them gasping for breath. And then the damn door chimed again and with a dark oath, Max pulled away from her.

Would nothing ever go as he planned with Maddie? Every time he intended to overwhelm her with sex, she managed to turn the tables on him. And now, instead of being able to discuss things with her, the store had suddenly become as busy as a bus station, repeatedly drawing him away. Max disposed of the condom, pulled up his jeans, and staggered on wobbling legs out to the counter.

Unfortunately, this customer was much more observant than the others had been. She took in his disheveled state, the heaviness of his eyes, and said with characteristic cheerfulness, "Why Max Sawyers, you reprobate. You've been fooling around in Annie's bookstore!"

Lace McGee Sawyers, his sister-in-law, knew sexual satisfaction when she saw it. As a sex therapist, she was well acquainted with the subject.

Max looked at her, frowned, then said over his shoulder, "You might as well come on out, Maddie. It's just Lace, and I know without asking that she's not going anywhere without an introduction."

"At least I got here *after*," Lace said with a grin.

Max gave her his laziest look. "You're good Lace, but not good enough to be sure of that."

"Oh, I'm positive." She laughed, then hugged him tight. "Because otherwise you'd be throwing me out!"

Getting Around to You

holding him so tightly that she didn't even feel she just leaned.

"Just what the hell have you been here?"

Max was her every nightmare on Lacy, plucking his bad head from her lips. Maddie's fastening their mouths wasn't ... He gave her a hot kiss, which Cleo away from Max.

6

MADDIE WANTED to be a coward and hide, but more than that, she wanted to meet Lace McGee Sawyers. Lace was married to Annie's oldest brother, Daniel, the doctor. She'd never met Daniel, but Annie assured her that he was every bit as hunky as Max, just in a different, more somber way.

She straightened her clothes the best she could, considering her panties were still in Max's pocket. She could hardly believe what she'd just done; as far as memories went, that one was a keeper! But it was more than the sex, because Max was more. She would have enjoyed talking with him, asking how Cleo had been. She wanted to try to find out if he'd missed her at all because she'd definitely missed him.

But as per her original instructions, he'd shown her a good time. She knew that was for the best, but she still wished they'd had time to…cuddle.

Shoulders back, Maddie walked out of the room. She was prepared to be adult, to be cavalier about the experience. But then she drew up short.

Lace was wrapped around Max! And he didn't seem to mind! The cur.

It made Maddie so angry to see another woman

holding him so closely, that she didn't even think, she just reacted.

"Just what the hell is going on here?"

Max eyed her over the top of Lace's platinum-blond head. At first his look was questioning, then quietly satisfied. He even grinned before setting Lace away from him.

"Cursing, Maddie? My, my."

He looked mighty pleased about something, but Maddie was more interested in Lace. The woman was drop-dead beautiful. A real knockout.

Maddie felt instantly deflated.

She had no idea what to say, how to defuse the situation so she could make a hasty escape. Cleo came to her rescue.

Slowly getting to her feet, Cleo started snarling and sniping and making vague threats at Lace.

Maddie smiled.

Cleo came to Maddie, sat on her foot, and growled at the other woman. Maddie, feeling somewhat vindicated, patted Cleo's head.

"I have no idea what that dog has against me." Lace looked at Max. "She still hates women?"

Maddie answered before Max could. "She doesn't hate *me*. She *likes* me."

Lace grinned. "So I see. I suppose, considering the fact that Max seems rather partial to you as well, it's a good thing."

Maddie, surprised at how nice and reasonable the other woman was being, said, "Uh…"

Lace stepped forward, keeping a wary eye on

Cleo, and offered her hand. "Hi. I'm Max's sister-in-law, Lace."

Maddie had no choice but to accept the woman's hand. "Maddie Montgomery."

"So you're Maddie! Annie has told me all about you. I understand we have a lot in common."

Maddie looked at Lace's gorgeous, perfect figure decked out in a striking black silk dress that showed off her incredibly beautiful blond hair in stark contrast and said again, "Uh..."

"I'm a sex therapist," Lace explained, "and Annie said you work with social services for planned parenthood and troubled teens on sexual issues?"

Max piped in, saying, "And I love sex. We all have something in common."

To Maddie's chagrin, Lace merely poked Max in the side, treating him like a little brother. "You're outrageous, Max. Don't embarrass your lady friend."

Max snorted. "As if that's even possible. In fact, it's generally Maddie who's embarrassing me. She's so...candid."

Maddie thought about kicking him. Cleo must have picked up on her thoughts, because she gave Max a disapproving whine.

Lace shrugged. "In our business you need to be candid. Maddie would hardly be effective at what she does if she sat around blushing and stammering."

Damn, Maddie thought. The woman was beautiful and intelligent and likeable.

Max threw his arm around Lace, making Maddie

narrow her eyes. But then he said, "Maddie, did you know Lace has always treated me like I'm twelve? I swear, I'd try to flirt with her and she'd pat my head."

Lace rolled her eyes. "Don't let it bother you, Max. I was in love with your brother, remember?"

"But you didn't know it at the time."

A feline smile enhanced Lace's already perfect features. "No, but I did know that I wasn't in love with you."

"Heartless wench."

Maddie grinned. They carried on just like siblings. "It's very nice to meet you, Lace. I listen to your radio show all the time. It's wonderful."

"Thanks. Maybe we could have lunch today and get to know each other better? Are you free?"

Maddie wanted to, she really did. But she had a few things she'd already committed herself to. "Could we make it another time? I have...plans for today."

Max took a step forward, no longer looking amused. "Plans to do what?"

She couldn't tell him without ruining the surprise. Maddie peeked at Cleo, saw that the dog was on alert, and shrugged. "Just...some things."

Max ignored Lace, who stood there looking beautifully spellbound by the sudden tension in the air, and he growled, "Things involving *debauchery?*"

Maddie gasped. How dare he try to embarrass her in front of his sister-in-law. She raised her chin and lied convincingly, "Yes."

Max started to reach for her, but Maddie stepped away. "In fact," she said airily, her anger a near tangible thing, "I should be going."

It was the perfect exit line, but Maddie hesitated.

Max had her panties in his pocket. She was more than a little aware of being naked beneath her skirt. When she looked at Max, she knew he was aware of it, too. His look dared her to leave without them, and dared her to request he give them back.

Maddie lifted her chin. "Thanks for the…"

Max smirked at her, and even then he looked so handsome she wanted to drag him back into the other room.

"The what?" he taunted.

Maddie ground her teeth together. Lace silently watched them both, her gaze moving from one to the other. "Why, for the entertainment this afternoon, what else? I'd have been bored to tears otherwise."

Lace choked on a laugh.

Maddie turned to her. "How about lunch on Friday, Lace? Are you free then?"

With a beaming smile, Lace said, "That'd be wonderful. Shall I meet you here at eleven-thirty?"

Maddie nodded. "Sounds perfect. I'll look forward to it."

She waggled her fingers at Max. "See ya later, Max." Then she went to her knees—carefully so that her skirt kept her naked behind well covered—and hugged Cleo. "I'll visit again soon, Cleo! And maybe next time you'll be able to stay awake."

Cleo's growl turned into a begrudging woof.

Maddie walked out without another word to anyone.

MAX WAITED until Maddie had rounded the corner outside the shop, then said in a rush to Lace, "Do me a favor, sweetheart. Watch the shop for a few minutes."

"Max! Where are you going?"

Max reached in his pocket for his keys, felt Maddie's silky panties still tucked in there, and smiled. "I'm going to follow her, of course."

Cleo ran to Max's side and growled her approval as Max trotted out the door.

Lace hurried behind them. "But...she looked ready to kill you, Max! Maybe you should give her a little time to cool down, after provoking her that way."

"Ha!" Max headed for his truck in the parking lot. "You should get to know Maddie better if you want to see the definition of provoking. Besides, if Maddie plans to do any more debauching, I plan to stop her."

"*More* debauching?"

He grinned despite his urgency to catch up to Maddie. "She's a wonderful debaucher."

Lace caught his arm. "Then why stop her?"

"Because she should be doing all her debauching with *me!*" Max reached his truck and jerked the door open. Cleo sprang inside and Max quickly buckled her into her doggy seat. He could just see the back of Maddie as she walked toward a small white compact parked on the opposite side of the street.

He turned to Lace, who leaned in his open door window. "I promise I'll only be a minute."

"This is my lunchtime, Max."

"I'll bring you back something Mexican."

Her eyes lit up. "Deal. But I only have an hour."

"Gotta go, sweets. I'll be back on time, I promise." Max gunned the truck and pulled out several lengths behind Maddie.

They didn't have far to go. In fact, they were still on the same street, but Max couldn't believe it when she pulled the little car into a parking space in front of a well-known fetish shop. Eyes agog, he said to himself, "No way."

Cleo whimpered.

"Can you believe this? What the hell is she up to?"

Cleo had no answer, only a worried frown.

"You stay put girl, and I'll go check it out. I'll only be a minute." Max adjusted both windows to let in enough breeze for Cleo to be comfortable, then slipped out of the truck. Maddie had indeed gone into the fetish shop, bold as you please.

Dashing across the street, Max sidled up to the enormous front window that was draped with a dark blue curtain, hiding all the scandalous material for sale. He could just barely see inside where the curtains didn't quite close all the way.

Maddie had gone down a long aisle, so Max opened the door and followed her in.

He heard her talking to a salesperson.

"I want it to be red leather. With colored gems and silver studs."

Red leather! Studs?

"I have just what you need," the salesman said. "Follow me."

Ha! Max thought to himself. He was the man who had what she needed, not some salesman. He slunk along, feeling like a very determined fool. When he peeked around the corner of a tall shelf holding a variety of adult magazines and books, he saw Maddie testing the strength of a thick red leather collar.

His stomach dropped to his knees.

He was outraged, scandalized—and horny as hell.

The salesman said, "Would you like to see the ankle and wrist cuffs as well?"

In her oh-so-innocent voice, Maddie asked, "Ankle and wrist cuffs? Really?"

The salesman—a young fellow with an array of earrings—gave her a smarmy grin. "They're padded with sheepskin so as not to abrade."

Maddie's beautiful blue eyes widened in fascination. "Show me."

Growling under his breath, Max made his way back up to the front of the store and skulked behind a display of soft velvet whips. Just what did Maddie think she was going to do with that paraphernalia? Max wondered. Then such an interesting parade of ideas flashed through his mind, he almost didn't notice when Maddie came to the counter to pay.

He was shaking too badly.

She had her back to him, so Max couldn't see her final purchases, but the bag she walked out with was enormous. Almost as enormous as the smile on her face.

Max stewed as he followed her, keeping a safe distance away so as not to be observed. She was actually humming. He could hear the happy, devil-may-care sound easily over the noise of the street.

He narrowed his eyes as he watched her get into her car. Oh, Maddie may have been making some fantasy-based plans in her creative little mind, but Max decided right then and there that her plans were about to change.

She'd just started the car when Max leaned into the window.

"Maddie."

She squealed and jumped a good foot. With a hand over her heart, she said, "Good grief, Max! What are you doing here?"

Max smiled. *I've got you now, sweetheart.* "I was just picking up some lunch for Lace."

He saw Maddie's smile turn into a frown. "She's having lunch with you?"

"Yes."

"What," she demanded, "does her husband think of that?"

"My brother's not an ogre who chains a woman to his side." Then he admitted, "Besides, he knows he can trust Lace."

That gave her pause, and rightfully so, because it was apparent she didn't trust Max at all.

All she said was, "Oh."

"What are you doing here?"

Her face turned beet red. "Max." She looked around, as if someone might hear her, then said, "Actually, nosy, it's a surprise."

"A surprise for who?" That was the part that was getting to him. If she wanted to play sex games, Max was willing. As long as he was the only other player, and they played by his rules.

"For you, who else?"

Now that pleased him. Who else, indeed.

"Here, I have something for you." Max pulled her panties out of his back pocket and offered them to her.

With a horrified gasp, Maddie snatched the underwear from his hand and shoved them under the car seat. "You, Max Sawyers, are the most annoying, the most—"

Max cut off her diatribe with a smoldering kiss. When he finally pulled away, Maddie was soft and warm and smiling at him.

Amazing.

"I thought about keeping them," he murmured. "Sort of as a trophy."

Rather than taking offense, Maddie asked, "Like a notch on the bedpost?"

It was hard to smile. "Yeah. But then I kept thinking about you running around bare-assed all day and I knew it'd make me crazy."

Maddie looked at him through her lashes. "Crazy...how?"

"Crazy with lust. Crazy with wanting you again. The thing about nooners, they're the equivalent of an appetizer.'' He trailed one rough fingertip down the line of her throat to her shoulder, then to the swell of her right breast. ''I want the full course.''

Sighing, Maddie said, ''Mmm. Me, too.'' But she added, ''Not that this afternoon wasn't nice. Exceptional in fact.'' And with a small smile, ''I loved it. Thank you.''

Damn, she was about to bring him to his knees right there in the middle of the street. Max cleared his throat.

''I gotta go, babe,'' he said regretfully. ''Lace only has so long for lunch.''

As if only then realizing what he'd done to her, arousing her again then saying goodbye, Maddie scowled. ''Cad. But I'm glad you're here. I meant to ask you two things before you made me mad enough to leave.''

Max didn't want her dredging up her pique, so he said quickly, ''Ask away.''

Now, Max thought, he'd find out about the bondage stuff. She'd ask him how he felt about it, if he'd be willing. And of course, Max would be understanding, and cooperative and—

''Will you come to work with me tonight?''

Vivid sexual images faded away to nothingness. ''Uh...to work?''

''Yes, I have meetings several times a week with different groups, and tonight's the night I get together with some really special women. I'd like you to meet them, and as we discussed, you could share some firsthand experiences.''

"Uh, Maddie..." Max was positively horrified by the idea.

"Please Max." She blinked those sexy big blue eyes at him and Max felt himself melting. He'd have to remember to write a column warning men about the effects of big blue eyes.

"I already told them about you. And about the book. I'd appreciate it if you could bring it along, too, since you...distracted me when I was there and I forgot to get it."

Max grinned. "Is that what the women are calling it these days? A distraction?"

Maddie returned his humor. "A very pleasant distraction, to be sure."

"Pleasant?" He snorted at her and pretended to be insulted. "I thought it was more like mind-blowing, climactic—"

Maddie purred, "Definitely climactic."

Her tone made his nerve endings riot. Max eyed the tiny back seat of her car and wondered if they'd fit...but no. Cleo was waiting in his truck. Damn.

If talking with young women who were complete strangers about sexual variety was what it took to see her again, Max figured he could handle it. After all, he had altruistic motives. Cleo needed Maddie. Today was proof of that.

But he wouldn't like it.

Grousing, he asked, "Where and when?"

"Thank you, Max!" Maddie shuffled through the glove box then handed him a business card with the address of the clinic printed on it. "Five o'clock, okay?"

Still uncertain of the whole idea, Max hesitantly nodded his agreement and took the card. Maddie reached out and caught his hand. She lifted it to her mouth and kissed his palm.

"And Max?" she whispered. "Would you want to come over to my apartment afterward?"

Desire snaked through him, nearly curling his toes.

That had never happened to him before. If one of his male readers had written to Max about curling toes, Max would have called him a weenie.

Now he had to reevaluate, because his toes were indeed curled.

And Max Sawyers was definitely not a weenie.

"No." The seductive teasing left Maddie's gaze, until Max leaned close and murmured, "I want you in my bed this time, little tease."

Her lips parted.

Max kissed her gently, sealing their agreement. If Maddie wanted to try her dominatrix tricks, it'd be on his turf.

"We'll have dinner," Max told her, stroking her sun-warmed cheek, "then I'll drive you to my house." And he'd damn well keep her there all night, he decided. Maybe even for a week. Possibly for the rest of her life.

It was the least he could do for Cleo.

When Max got back to his truck, tapping the clinic's business card against his thigh, Cleo gave him a sullen look.

"I'm sorry, girl, did you miss me?"

Grudgingly, Cleo licked his chin.

"Thanks, Cleo. I needed that."

Max found out how true that sentiment was the second he stepped back into the bookstore. Lace practically pounced on him.

"Okay, what's going on?"

In no hurry to bare his soul, Max carried the Mexican food into the back room and placed it on the table. Cleo, smelling the food, stayed hot on his heels. So did Lace.

"What's going on with what?"

When Lace didn't answer, Max looked up to see her staring at the small refrigerator. It sat out of alignment, crooked instead of flush against the wall. He grinned.

Shaking her head, Lace said, "You're such a rogue. And quit smiling. I refuse to ask you anything about it."

"Great. Then let's eat." Cleo barked in agreement, making Lace jump. The two females kept a good deal of space between them.

Max knew if Maddie had been there, Cleo would have still been sitting on her foot.

Lace had only eaten two bites of her burrito before she said, "Why are you dodging Dan and Daniel?"

Oh hell, Max thought. He didn't need this today. "Lace..."

"No, don't start with your excuses. You're needed at the business and you know it. I've been patient with all this middle-child moping, but Max, it's time to move on."

Max glared at her, wondering how in the world

he'd run head on into two such bullheaded women in one day. Through his teeth, he said, "I do not mope." And his damn toes didn't curl either. "The simple fact of the matter is, there's nothing for me to do at the business."

"There's all kinds of things for you to do!"

"Okay, let me rephrase that. There's nothing that I'm needed to do. You know I'd go crazy sitting in an office, crunching numbers or sitting in on board meetings. That's not my speed, Lace. I'd be like a fish out of water."

After glancing at her watch, Lace gobbled down the last of her food and stood. She crossed her arms and gave Max a calculating stare.

"What?" he asked, feeling uneasy about the way she seemed to dissect him with her gaze.

"Guy wants to spend more time with Annie now. You know he worked extra long and hard trying to keep himself occupied so he wouldn't think of her."

"Yeah, so? I gather it worked, given how long it took him to wise up and admit he loved her."

Lace nodded. "And you know Daniel has no spare time with the hours he puts in at the hospital."

"You're not going to guilt me into anything here, sweetheart, so you might as well give it up."

Lace ignored his interruption. "A lot of the workload that Guy's looking to get rid of involves travel."

Max couldn't quite hide his sudden interest. Damn, he missed traveling. He'd been born with a heavy case of wanderlust and missed being on the road. Even the simplest trip was a pleasure for him.

But since bringing Cleo home, he'd curbed all those tendencies. Cleo needed him. He rubbed her ears as he said, "You know I can't leave my dog. And there's no one she'd be comfortable staying with."

They both heard the ding of the front door and knew a customer had come in. Max stood, ready to wrap up their conversation. And Lace needed to get back to the radio station.

"Maddie could watch her," Lace suggested as she gathered up her purse.

Max put his arm around Lace and headed her toward the door. "What makes you think I want to leave Maddie behind either?"

Suddenly a big male body, taking up the entire doorframe blocked them. A low voice said, "Then take her with you. Take the dog with you, too. I'll pay for arrangements that'll accommodate all three of you. But Max, I want you in my company."

Max stared at Dan Sawyers, his mostly absentee father, a man who until very recently had retreated from life. Annie's engagement had given him new purpose and forced him out of his self-imposed exile. Max was glad; he wanted his father happy.

Things had just gotten very complicated.

Distracted, Max watched Lace slip out of the shop in a hurry. Dan stood there, looking determined and somewhat uncertain.

Cleo, the traitor, abandoned him to chew on a rawhide bone.

Never before in his entire life could Max remember his father asking him for anything. His brother Daniel had been the father figure, filling in when their mother died and Dan retreated from everyone, including his children. He'd provided for them and seen that their physical, medical and monetary needs had been taken care of. But every holiday he'd sought isolation, leaving their emotional care to Daniel.

Max respected his brother more than any man he'd ever known. For most of his life, he'd resented his father.

"Can I get you anything, Dad? I think there's some coffee left."

Dan appeared to let out a breath he'd been holding. "Coffee would be great. A little conversation would be even better."

"Strange. I didn't think you cared for conversation." Max wanted to hold on to his resentment, to nurture it. But his thoughts were softened by Maddie, and he was in too mellow a mood to be angry.

They each pulled out chairs at the table Max and Lace had just abandoned. Max poured the strong, stale coffee.

"I owe you a lot of explanations."

"No. You owe Daniel, not me. And you owe him more than lip service."

"I know." Dan turned his coffee cup this way and that, took a sip and then winced at the bitterness. "Daniel and I are working things out. It was grossly unfair the way I abandoned him to deal with everything.'' In a softer voice he added, ''He's an exceptional man. I'm so damn proud of him...''

Max gulped down his own coffee. All his life he'd been known as the difficult one. Daniel was the oldest, the most mature, the patriarch of the family from the time he was a kid. Annie was a sweetheart, the only girl, the most loving. But Max...he'd indulged in mischief for as long as he could remember and as soon as he'd gotten old enough, he'd taken to traveling.

As if reading his mind, his father said, ''I'd always thought you'd outgrow your love of travel, but Lace tells me it's a part of you.''

Max shrugged. ''I enjoy it, but I've given it up.''

''You don't need to give it up. I meant what I said. Guy has never liked traveling or dealing with the chore of buying from our manufacturers. In fact, he threatened to leave the company unless I took an equal share of the responsibility.''

''I see.'' It figured that his father would find a way around accepting that agreement. ''So you want me to fill in for you now?''

''Not at all.''

Max held his cup a little more tightly. That wasn't what he'd been expecting to hear.

Smiling, Dan said, ''Given the way I've behaved in the past, you have every right to your assumptions. But the fact is, I'm enjoying being involved again. I'm enjoying life again.''

Heart softening, Max returned his smile. ''I'm glad.'' Then he asked, ''What brought about this drastic change?''

A small smile on his face, Dan said, "I got some good advice."

"That right?" Max sipped his coffee. "What kind of advice?"

Dan tugged on his ear. "Sexual advice." Before Max could quite assimilate that, he added, "I was assured that a little sex would improve my disposition greatly. I've decided it's worth a try."

Max choked on a swallow and was forced to spend several minutes regaining his breath. When he was finally able to wheeze again, he said, "Sex!" and with a rumble of blustering menace, "Did Lace fill your head with nonsense?"

"Nope." Dan grinned. "Got the advice straight out of the newspaper. From that guy who writes the column on sex."

Max promptly choked again. Dan stood to thwack him on the back several times, but it didn't help. Good God, he'd advised his own father to make whoopie!

The vague memory of an unsigned letter, which he'd answered in the column, slipped through Max's brain. It had been good advice, he thought. But not for his *Dad!*

"The thing is," Dan continued, as if his youngest son wasn't turning red and strangling to death, "I've been out of the loop too long, both personally and professionally. The personal end I can work on myself."

"Glad to hear it," Max managed. He knew for a fact he couldn't offer any more suggestions, so it was a good thing his father didn't want any.

"But I'm too old to start dealing with the entire

workload all at once. You have a way with people, Max. Everyone respects you and likes you."

The praise not only distracted Max from his father's first bomb, but it also warmed him from the inside out. That didn't sit well with him. At his age, he shouldn't want or need a father's approval.

But it felt good to get it just the same.

Dan watched Max a moment, then continued. "Guy hates to travel, I'm not up to it, and you like it. Also, because of all your traveling, you're up on which supplies are quality, and what's needed where. You've hiked, skied, trekked through Africa, spent weeks alone in the wilds of Canada... You'd be the perfect one to make purchase recommendations."

Max glanced at his watch. The shop would close in an hour, then he'd head home and shower, make sure Cleo was fed and comfortable—and be with Maddie again. He could hardly wait.

Curiosity got the better of him and he asked, "How much travel are we talking?"

"In the States, pretty regularly. But as I said, the company can afford to accommodate you in whatever way you want."

"I won't have Cleo closed up in a damn storage area. She wouldn't understand and it would upset her."

Dan looked at Cleo, who was now snoring loudly. He grinned. "We have a small private plane. She can ride with you."

Damn but the idea was appealing. The need to be on the move had been eating at him for weeks. And Maddie had claimed she wanted to travel...

Of course, she'd also claimed to want him only to notch her bedpost. He'd have to work on her.

Tonight, he'd wrap her in such a hot, sensual spell, she'd become addicted and gladly follow him around the country.

Ha, and Cleo would learn to fly.

Max cursed low.

"What does that mean, Max? Are you considering it?"

"I don't know. I was actually thinking of something else."

"The foreign travel?" Dan asked anxiously. "Because there won't be much of that. Just one or two trips a year to Mexico, perhaps Taiwan or China."

If Maddie stuck around, Cleo could stay with her. It'd be nice to have them both to come home to.

Max flattened his hands on the tabletop. "Actually, I was thinking of a woman I've met recently. I'm not too keen on the idea of running off and leaving her unsupervised. She's…well, she's enticing as hell. Without me around, there'll be a line of guys trying to take my place."

Dan blinked at Max, then threw his head back and laughed.

Max couldn't remember the last time he'd seen his father laugh. "Care to share the joke?"

Dan wiped his eyes, still chuckling, and managed to say, "You're in love! By God, that's wonderful. And Max, don't misunderstand, I'm thrilled!"

Love? Max shook his head. "I don't know her that well."

"So? I met your mother and within minutes knew she was my life."

"Maddie makes me crazy."

"That's a good sign. When I first met your mother, I couldn't decide if I wanted to kiss her or throttle her."

"I guess kissing won out, huh?" Max found himself smiling, too.

"Absolutely. And she was worth all the effort it cost me to win her over." Dan looked at Max, his face again solemn. "There've been a lot of lost years, son. I hope you can forgive me, but I can understand if you can't."

Without a single hesitation, Max said, "I forgive you." In many ways, he was beginning to realize the loss was more his father's than his own. He'd had Daniel and Annie and Guy...but his father had had no one and nothing but his grief.

"Thank you." Dan smiled in relief, then released Max and stood. "You do love her, son. I can see it in your face."

Also coming to his feet, Max said, "I don't know. It's not that easy."

"Love never is! But you're a good catch, so I'm positive she feels the same." Dan clapped him on the shoulder. "Think about the job. We really do need you there."

Grinning, Max said, "I'll talk it over with Maddie." Who knows, he thought, Maddie said she wanted to travel. Maybe the job would be a lure to help get her to commit.

At this point, Max was willing to try anything.

7

MADDIE WAITED outside the clinic for Max. She couldn't stop thinking about what he'd done to her, what they'd done together! It was so wonderful.

And she couldn't stop thinking about Cleo.

Darn it all, she missed the dog almost as much as she missed the man. They were both so special! How many young, handsome, virile, world-traveled men would have settled down to take care of a dog? A very needy dog.

Not many.

No two ways about it, Max was special.

And she was sunk.

Maddie collapsed back against the brick wall of the clinic. How much longer would she have with Max? A few days, a week? Admitting to herself that she'd gotten emotionally involved wasn't easy. She'd meant to keep things superficial, to gather up some memories without commitment, the same as so many others did. Her ex had accused her of being too prim, and she'd wanted to prove him wrong. But now, what he thought didn't matter.

Deep down where it really counted, which was in her own heart, Maddie had always known that she wasn't the type of woman for sexual flings.

Oh, flinging with Max was great. Superb in fact. But she also wanted him to hold her. She wanted to talk to him and ask about his travels. Most of what she knew of Max she'd learned from Annie. And it wasn't enough.

Bea and Carmilla and Mavis swore she needed to hold out on him. Not sex, because Max could get that anywhere and from just about any woman. She needed to hold out on all those things she so wanted to give to him; affection and caring and... *love*.

Maddie groaned, knowing she was already too deeply involved to hold back on anything.

A bright yellow dandelion grew up through a crack in the sidewalk in front of the clinic and Maddie ruthlessly brought her sandal down onto it.

She could not love Max Sawyers!

A long, low whistle brought her head up. Max stood there, grinning like the devil, his dark eyes full of teasing good humor. "You got a thing about weeds, I gather?"

Maddie stared at him blankly. "What?"

"You looked like you had murder on your mind."

Maddie devoured the sight of him. He looked scrumptious in a casual white shirt and khaki slacks. His dark hair was windblown, his teeth white in his tanned face. Her heart did a flip-flop, and was followed by her stomach.

She couldn't give him love, but she could give him female appreciation.

Maddie threw herself at him. Max looked startled

for just a second before Maddie got hold of his head and brought it down for her kiss. "I missed you, Max."

He gave a murmuring reply against her lips. "Hmm. I like this welcome."

"Everything we did this afternoon... I haven't been able to stop thinking about...it." She'd almost said *you* but that would have given too much away.

Max lifted his head, looked up and down the street and smiled at her. "We're being watched by about a dozen people."

"Oh!" Maddie quickly straightened. Good grief, she worked here. The last thing she wanted to do was put on a show.

"Did you put your panties back on?"

"Of course!"

"Spoilsport."

Oh, the way he said that. He could make her want him with just a whispered word. "Max, behave. You'll get me all flustered and then I won't be able to concentrate on the meeting."

When she started to turn away, he caught her hand. "Tonight, how do you want it? Conventional or kinky?"

"Max..."

"Hey, a man needs to make plans. So which is it to be, sweetheart?"

He obviously liked to fluster her, Maddie thought. She looked up at him, touched his bottom lip, and said, "How about both?"

Maddie felt his indrawn breath both from her touch and her reply.

"You little witch," Max said with something that bordered on admiration. "Both it is."

"I was just teasing!"

"I'm not." Max handed her the slim book she'd requested. "Have you read this thing?"

"Not yet. Why? Did you?"

"Bits and pieces. It was...interesting, but not always accurate."

"There you see! I knew your perspective would add a lot." She smiled at him.

Max groaned. "Let's go get this over with before I change my mind."

Catching his arm, Maddie led him into the old building and down the tiled hallways. "You're not nervous are you?"

"Nervous about speaking to a bunch of young women on sexual dos and don'ts? Why ever would I be nervous?"

His sarcasm was plain to hear.

"Um, Max, about the women..." Maddie started to explain to him that the women weren't exactly young, but as she pushed open the door to the conference room, Max froze. Her friends were already inside.

Mavis, dressed in a long flowing dress of bright cherry red that nearly matched her hair, sat with her feet propped up on another chair. She wiggled her foot in time to whatever music was coming through a set of headphones plugged into a portable CD player.

Bea, wearing jeans and a white ruffled blouse, paced, obviously deep in thought. And Carmilla was secluded in the corner talking to someone who sat behind her. Maddie couldn't see who it was.

Maddie cleared her throat and drew everyone's attention.

Max looked around the room, then at Maddie. Bending close to her ear, he whispered, "These are not young women, Maddie."

"Uh, no."

Bea gave Max a thorough once-over, then let loose with a wolf whistle.

Nodding in agreement, Mavis said, "Ho, baby. He's a hottie."

Bea added, "Our girl knows how to pick 'em, doesn't she?"

"Neither," Max said, his face bright red, "do any of these women look the least bit confused about anything sexual."

Bea said, "Ha!"

Mavis added, "You got that right, sweet cheeks." And she gave him a cocky grin.

"They're very nice ladies, Max." Maddie tried glaring at Mavis and Bea so they'd back off just a little. Max looked ready to make a run for it. "I promise."

Carmilla finally stepped out of the corner and a man rose up from behind her. He rose and rose and rose some more.

Easily six feet six inches, the man was enormously built and bald as an ostrich egg. He wore a black Harley-Davidson T-shirt with the sleeves cut off to show massive biceps. His right forearm sported an intricate tattoo of a naked lady. When he moved his arm—which he was doing now by flexing his knuckles—the naked lady danced.

Maddie gulped.

Max said with certainty, "That is no lady."

The big man started forward.

Mustering up her courage, Maddie tentatively tried to offer her hand, and instead found herself tossed behind Max's back.

Carmilla burst loose with a robust laugh. "Honey, your heart's in the right place, but you sure ain't up to taking on Tiny."

Maddie peeked around Max. "Tiny? That's really you?"

Eyes narrowed, Max turned to face her suspiciously. "Is this another one of your jokes, Maddie? Like that 'small pistol' business. Because there's nothing tiny about that guy. He's *huge.*"

Maddie giggled nervously. "You mean just like your roll of dimes?"

Max gave her a belligerent look and growled, *"Flashlight."* Then he jutted his chin and added, "Industrial size."

"Oh, yeah." She giggled again. "I remember now."

"I know him," Carmilla interjected, "and I can guarantee you he would never hurt Maddie." Then, just because Carmilla was so dang bloodthirsty, she added, "But I make no guarantees where you're concerned, young fellow."

Max snorted.

Scooting out from behind her erstwhile protector, Maddie said, "Tiny, it's so nice to finally meet you!'' There had been times in the past year that she'd wondered if Tiny was real, or a romanticized figment of Carmilla's imagination.

The man was very real. Imposingly real.

And though he took Maddie's hand and kissed her knuckles in a curiously old-world gesture, he kept looking at Carmilla with adoring eyes.

Well, well, Maddie thought. She glanced at Bea, who winked, and then to Mavis, who was still eyeing Max's more interesting parts.

''*Down,* Mavis,'' Bea suddenly said. ''Apparently our Maddie is the jealous sort. Just look at her, her eyes are turning red.''

Mavis looked and said, ''I'll be damned. Even her nostrils are flared.'' Then to Carmilla, ''Quit playing touchy-feely with your boyfriend and come look at Maddie.''

It wasn't just her eyes that were red after that comment. Especially when Max, wearing a huge grin, peered directly into her gaze.

''Are you jealous, sweetheart? And here I didn't say a word when Tiny kissed your hand.''

''So,'' Mavis said, sauntering forward. ''You're the young stud Maddie has been telling us all about.''

Max stiffened, then glared at Maddie.

Shrugging, she whispered, ''I didn't tell them *everything*. I just…''

''She bragged on you, is what she did. And after that worthless creep she almost married, we were more than glad to hear it.''

Max gave a parody of a smile. "What exactly did she tell you?"

Bea stepped forward and gave Mavis a warning frown. Then she turned her smile to Max. "Why, she told us you'd made her happy." Her smile lit up just a bit more. "And Maddie definitely deserves some happiness."

Things were out of control, Maddie decided. "Are we having a meeting today or not?"

"Not," Carmilla said. "We want to get to know Max better. That's more important."

"And it's for certain he can't tell us anything about sex that we don't already know," Bea added.

"After all," Mavis said with a sniff, "we got paid for our expertise."

Maddie whipped around to face Max, giving the women and Tiny her back. In a pleading voice, she said, "I'm sorry!"

Surprising her, Max touched her cheek and said, "For what?"

"I..." She felt confused and lost her train of thought. "I meant to tell you about this, about my friends..."

"They are friends, aren't they?" She nodded and he said, "I think that shows what a special woman you are, that friendship has grown from counsel meetings."

"Damn right," Carmilla said, and Bea added, "Best friends. She's like a daughter to us, and you should remember that."

Mavis laughed. "Calm down, Maddie. He's not

afraid of three little old ladies. Are you, young man?''

Max looked over Maddie's head at the others. His eyes were lit with challenge. ''Why don't we all sit down?'' He threw his arm around Maddie, almost making her drop the book. ''I'll wager there's a few things I can still enlighten you on.''

Tiny smiled.

Carmilla snorted.

Bea and Mavis said in unison, ''You're dreamin'!''

Maddie wished she could just crawl away. But Max had hold of her hand and his grip was unbreakable.

Oh, dear. This wasn't at all what she'd planned.

MAX WANTED TO laugh at the silly little sick look on Maddie's face.

Prostitutes! Who'd have thought she was counseling retired ladies of the night? He shook his head. One thing about Maddie, she never ceased to surprise him.

''You know,'' he said to Mavis, who seemed to be the most brazen, ''I thought I was here to talk to young innocent girls who were either caught in an unexpected pregnancy or had troubled home lives.''

''You didn't expect a bunch of old biddies, did you?''

''I didn't expect mature women, no.''

''Maddie does counseling with women of all

ages. The poor young girls you're talking about meet with her on Tuesdays.''

''And they're lucky to have her,'' Carmilla told him. ''They don't come any more compassionate than Maddie.''

''Not to mention how smart she is, and such a good listener.'' Bea smiled fondly at Maddie.

Maddie had slipped down in her chair until her face was almost hidden behind the fall of her hair. She looked miserable by the turn of events.

But her long legs, thrust out in front of her looked incredibly nice. Max wanted to start kissing her slim ankles and work his way up. All the way up.

Until she was panting and moaning and... He cleared his throat.

''How many nights a week does she do this?''

Bea, catching his distraction with Maddie's legs, raised a brow and asked, ''This?''

Max shook his head. ''Have these meetings.''

Carmilla perched herself on Tiny's lap. Tiny didn't seem to mind, if his big grin was any indication. ''Two to three times a week,'' she said, ''depending. Truth is, we should have quit bugging her years ago, but she's so much fun to talk to. Like the daughter none of us ever had.''

Maddie was a nurturer, Max thought, seeing it in the older women's eyes. She didn't pass judgment on people, and she looked beyond the obvious. He knew that much about her because of how she'd so readily accepted Cleo.

''Did you know,'' Max asked, more than willing

to work to meet the women's standards, "that men can literally become addicted to a certain woman's smell?"

Maddie's head lifted, her eyes filled with fascination.

Bea scoffed.

Carmilla looked at Tiny, who delicately sniffed her shoulder.

Mavis shrugged. "Where'd you hear such a thing?"

"I've read about it in medical studies. My brother is a doctor and my sister-in-law is a sex therapist."

That got a few raised brows. Max hid his smile. "Every woman's skin has a unique scent. A man's body can get used to that scent, and if the woman leaves him—" or dies, Max thought, as his mother had, and suddenly he understood his father much, much better "—then the man will suffer withdrawal. It's probably where the term heartsick came from. You *do* feel like you have a broken heart. And it really does hurt."

Max looked at Maddie. How would he feel if he could never hold her again, never kiss her again? In such a short time he'd become very addicted to her, her laugh, her smile, her compassion. And her scent.

What exactly had his poor father gone through, knowing the woman he loved had been taken from him forever?

The women were quiet, watching Max with new respect. Max knew they'd expected him to orate on sexual positions or some such nonsense. But he was smarter than that.

"Did you know," he asked, watching them all closely, "that sex is a natural pain reliever?"

They all straightened up to listen.

"It's true. Sex releases endorphins that relieve pain."

"Fascinating," Maddie said. "Annie told me a little about this."

"Annie manipulated the facts so she could seduce poor Guy." Before that, Max thought, he'd never known how creatively sneaky his baby sister could be, or how determined she was to have Guy as her own.

"My knee *has* been botherin' me," Tiny rumbled, and everyone laughed as Carmilla swatted at him.

"Both men and women," Max continued, pleased that he had their rapt attention, "have testosterone. And testosterone is the only proven true aphrodisiac."

"All right," Bea said, "you win. I didn't know any of that."

Carmilla bobbed her slim eyebrows. "Want us to tell you some of what we know?"

Lounging back in his chair, his arms spread wide, Max said, "Sorry girls. I already know it all."

Maddie threw the book at him, which he handily caught, while the others all hooted and made lewd observations. Max blew a kiss at Maddie and said, "I'm having fun, doll. You should have introduced me to your friends earlier."

While Maddie sat there looking openly pleased with him, Max passed the book over to Tiny. "You should check that out. Especially chapter six."

Tiny looked at the book. Max hoped like hell the guy could read! Then Tiny flipped through a few pages and grinned. "Interesting stuff, huh?"

"Real interesting."

Carmilla tried to grab the book, but Tiny held it out of her reach. "If you want to know what it says, you'll have to let me read it to you."

"Is that a dare?" Carmilla asked.

Tiny looked at Maddie. "Would you mind if Carmilla and I took off a little early? Now that I'm finally with her again, I'd like to get her to myself just a bit."

Maddie looked at the couple with dreamy, romantic eyes. "Of course I don't mind!" She sighed. "I think it's very sweet of you."

Carmilla had silver hair and faded brown eyes, but in that moment, she looked like an excited young girl. Max wanted to imitate Tiny and pull Maddie into his lap, but she stayed out of reach for the next ten minutes.

It wasn't until after Carmilla had gone and Bea and Mavis and Maddie had shared speculation on what might come of the relationship, that Max was able to really get her attention again.

He caught her close and kissed her. The older women chuckled and urged Max with ribald suggestions.

Maddie hid her face in his chest once he released her.

"So," Max asked, "which of you lovely ladies does the incredible slogans?"

Bea, looking flattered, primped with her white hair. "That would be me."

"Care to talk business for a moment?"

Bea glanced at Mavis and Maddie and then, blushing like a schoolgirl, said, "Sure. That'd be fine," and with just a touch more hesitation, "right now?"

"It's a simple proposition."

"I know all about *those*, honey!"

Max smiled. "Not that kind." He really enjoyed the women's ease and comfort with their pasts. They were obviously no longer in the flesh business, and just as obviously not about to make apologies. They were strong, blunt women, and he respected that.

"I just agreed to do some work for my father," Max said. "It'll involve traveling and purchasing." Out of the corner of his eye, Max watched Maddie make a sudden jerky move. He glanced at her, and saw that her eyes had flared, her cheeks had gone pale. He started to ask her what was wrong, but then she lowered her head to stare at her hands.

Max cleared his throat. "Once I agreed to the job, I got to thinking about other parts of the business. We deal in sporting goods and outdoor recreations like rock climbing and kayaking and such. A lot of the equipment we advertise is geared toward a younger crowd. I'm thinking your slogans may be the perfect way to draw attention to them."

"Oh, this could be fun," Bea said, and her blue eyes were alight with excitement.

"Why don't you think on it, maybe come up with a couple of samples, and we'll present them to my father to see what he thinks."

"I'll get right on it!" Bea sauntered away, murmuring to herself, already working on thinking up ideas. Watching her, Max noticed that she was slim despite her age, and had a rather stately walk. It dawned on him that Carmilla and Mavis were the same, though Carmilla had a very lush figure and Mavis was bordering on petite. They each had to be in or near their early seventies, but they had the attitudes and personalities of women much younger.

He wondered what his dad would think of them. He could hardly wait to introduce him to Bea. Now that his father was reentering the world, he could use a little shock therapy.

Mavis held up her hands. "I guess this makes me the third wheel."

"Not at all!" Maddie tried to stop her from leaving, but Mavis waved her off.

"I have a date anyway, honey, so don't worry about me."

Max cocked a brow. "A date?"

Maddie gave him a look. "Mavis is very popular among the retirees."

"Mmm-hmm," Mavis agreed. "Tonight I'm doing up the town with a very handsome widower." She leaned forward and confided, "He's six years younger than me! Only sixty-two. Isn't that delicious?"

Max held his humor in check and gave Mavis a hug. She was an easily likeable woman and he wished her a good time. He imagined the widower would have his hands full this night.

Once they were alone, Max asked Maddie, "You all right?" She was still too quiet and far too distracted. If she was thinking of the coming night and what she'd do with the stuff she'd bought at the fetish store, he'd gladly enlighten her to new plans.

"Yes, I'm fine."

He didn't believe her. Something was making her clam up, and Max decided he'd find out exactly what it was once he had her safely ensconced at his house. He took her hand and started her toward the door.

"You ever frolicked in a hot tub, Maddie, honey?"

Her steps faltered. "A hot tub?"

"In my backyard."

"But...it's too cool for that."

"Oh ye of little faith. I promise to keep you plenty warm enough. Hot even." Max leaned down to her ear and nipped her earlobe. "Burning up, in fact," he rasped.

They walked outside and Max started to lead her to his truck. Maddie held back. "I'll drive myself and meet you there."

No way. Max intended to keep her until he returned her to her home himself. If she was without a car, his odds were a lot better of succeeding. "Why bother," he asked. "Your car will be safe enough here."

"But..." She hesitated, then said, "Okay, just a second." Jogging over to her car, she unlocked the trunk and got out the bag he'd seen her purchase at the fetish shop. He thought of that damn collar and wanted to howl.

"Whatcha got there?" Max asked as she approached him again, the bag clutched tightly in her little fist.

Maddie grinned. "It's a surprise, remember? I promise to show you later tonight."

Oh, she'd show him all right. Max could hardly wait.

Once she was seated inside, the bag on the floor at her feet, Maddie looked at him. "Max?"

"Yes?" He hoped she'd ask for details on the hot tub, and then he intended to tantalize her with a blow-by-blow description of what he'd do to her, how he'd do it. The fun they'd both have.

"Do you taste the same as I do?"

The truck lurched hard as he pulled out into traffic. "Do I *what?*"

"Taste the same?" Maddie smoothed her skirt and settled herself comfortably in the seat. "I've been thinking about it all day. I don't mind if we play in the hot tub for a while, but when I taste you, I think we should be inside." As if sharing a confidence, she said, "I don't want to take a chance on a neighbor seeing us or something."

Max said, "Uh..." his mind still way back there on the tasting business.

She peeked at him. "I'm shy."

Max almost missed the turn onto the main street.

"You intend to—" the words were so arousing, they would barely leave his tight throat "—*taste* me?" He hoped like hell she meant what he thought she meant.

Leaning slightly closer, Maddie put her small hand on his thigh. "Yes. Just like you tasted me." And then her hand tightened, squeezing his leg perilously close to a now very noticeable hard-on, and she added in a whisper, "Everywhere."

Max pushed down on the gas pedal.

"Slowly, Max, just as you've shown me." Her fingers drifted up his thigh, and he held his breath. Then they moved down to his knee. He groaned in disappointment and relief.

"Faster at the end though." Her fingers drifted upward again. "That's the right way, isn't it?"

Max locked his jaw to keep from panting with sensual pain. He could almost feel her mouth on him, her small pink tongue playful. He gulped.

Okay, so she wanted to play with bondage. No big deal. He could handle that, especially if it got her this enthusiastic.

She wanted to taste him.

Max felt like a Victorian maiden, ready to swoon. He concentrated hard on keeping the truck on the road so they didn't end up in a ditch.

Other women had riled him, aroused him, made him burn. What Maddie proposed had been done to him before. Hell, he'd done just about everything a man could do with a woman, and always enjoyed himself. So why was he shaking now? Why was he going alternately hot and cold with the excitement of it, the utter lust?

And dammit, his toes had just curled again.

Admittedly, he was in deep—and worse, he loved every minute of it.

8

THEY SNUCK into his house like thieves. Cleo, proving herself to be a miserable guard dog, was snoring too loudly to hear them. One small light shone from the kitchen, and the glow filtered into the living room where the dog sprawled across an enormous beige leather couch. Her tongue lolled out one side of her mouth, with spittle running down the couch cushion.

"She gets nervous in the dark," Max said. "So I always leave a light on for her."

Maddie's heart again performed that strange little softening for this man and his beast. "She's not much good at protecting you."

Max gave her a solemn nod. "I'd rather protect her anyway."

He was such an incredible man. And she wanted him so much.

She was also falling in love with him. Damn. Double damn.

It had just about killed her when Max claimed he'd be traveling again. She wanted to travel, too, and see the whole world. But she'd gladly have stayed in Ohio the rest of her life with Max. At first that idea hadn't appealed at all. When he'd said he'd given up traveling, she'd wanted to bemoan his decision. She didn't understand how anyone could not want to see the world, especially a man known for his wanderlust. Now she hated it that he'd leave her.

Maybe his life wasn't as settled as he'd claimed. Soon he wouldn't have time for her anymore.

Maddie held close to the waistband of his slacks and followed him down the darkened hallway. She was here with him now, and the night was still young. Rather than regret the coming future, she should take advantage of the moment to get the most out of every second she could.

Max's house was beautiful on the outside. A mixture of Mediterranean tiles and stucco and lush landscaping. It wasn't enormous, but it was isolated, on a cul-de-sac, apart from the other houses and far more private.

The inside was too dark to distinguish precise colors, but the rooms were open, flowing into one another. The furnishings were sparse and everything appeared to be spotless. Max pulled her into his bedroom and softly closed the door.

Maddie thought of what she wanted to do to him, and how he'd react. Her stomach knotted with excitement and she licked her lips.

In the very next instant, she found herself pinned to a wall being kissed silly.

Max closed both hands over her breasts, moaned sharply, then parted her legs with his knee. He was hard, pulsing against her belly. Maddie tore her mouth away. "Max!"

Ruthlessly, he recaptured her lips. "I need you, Maddie. Right now."

She dodged him again. "I have plans!"

He groaned and pressed his face into her neck. "Your plans are what have me coming apart. Maddie, I don't know if I could bear it."

Smoothing his back, smiling quietly to herself, Maddie said, "Now Max. You're a stud, remember? Surely there's nothing I can do to you that you can't handle."

He bit her shoulder, making her yelp, then he straightened. "All right. If you're going to challenge me then I suppose I have to prove myself." He stepped away from her for a second to flip on a bedside lamp. The light was gentle, soft, just barely touching a king-size bed that was unmade and looked very comfortable.

She met Max's gaze and said, "Oh good. Now I can see you better."

His eyes nearly crossed. He took a deep breath, flexed his fingers, and then said, "Okay I think I'm ready." But as she reached for his belt he said, "No wait! It'd be better if you got undressed first."

Maddie blinked at him. "Why?"

Voice dropping an octave to where the guttural sounds stroked up and down her nerve endings, Max said, "I'll be distracted by your gorgeous bod and might be able to control myself better."

Might be able to control himself? Did that mean he was losing his control? Maddie smiled. She really liked the idea that she could push his buttons. "All right."

With Max watching her closely, his gaze a hot caress, she stripped off her clothes. She loved how he looked at her, how his muscles tensed and his high cheekbones colored with arousal.

She'd never experienced a man looking at her with so much intensity. Her fiancé never had, and she was very glad that she'd found out about him before she'd foolishly gotten married. Otherwise she wouldn't be here with Max now, and just the thought of that left her empty.

When she was completely naked she slowly stepped up to Max and undid his belt buckle. "You promise you're going to behave now, right?"

"Yes." Then he groaned as her hand slipped inside his open fly. "I'm such a liar," he gasped. "Hell no, I'm not going to behave. You're naked. You're talking about doing lecherous things to my body!"

"I'm not just talking Max. I'm going to do them."

He nodded, resigned and anxious. "Right now, I'm just concentrating on my legs."

Maddie slowly stroked him through his briefs. He was hard, throbbing and impossibly large. "Your legs?"

"Yes," he croaked. "I have to remember that I have them so I don't fall down."

Maddie chuckled. "Let's get rid of your shirt."

Before she could reach for it, Max had already whisked it over his head. It went sailing across the room to a darkened corner. Without her instruction, he kicked his shoes off and they thumped some-where behind her.

Knowing she'd make him crazier, Maddie went to her knees in front of him. She removed his socks, teasing him by taking her time. Lastly, her hands curled around the waistband of his khaki slacks. She pulled both his pants and his underwear down, then ordered, "Step out."

He did, and Maddie looked up the tall, hard length of his body. Her nipples pulled tight and her belly tingled. He was so gorgeous, all male, rigid and strong and his scent…she leaned forward and kissed his abdomen, then drew his smell deeply in-side her lungs.

Max's fingers settled into her hair, gently cra-dling her head. "Maddie." His voice was hoarse with strain.

Her fingers could barely circle him, holding him close at the base of his erection. She could feel his heartbeat there, matching her own. With her other hand she explored his firm backside, the iron hard muscles of his thighs, the soft tender weight below his shaft.

Max shook, his breath a gasping sound in the otherwise quiet room.

She kissed his right thigh, the smooth taut skin of his hipbone. His fingers tightened, inexorably guiding her to where he wanted to feel her mouth.

Suddenly overwhelmed with a need to please him and herself, Maddie obliged and without warning, without so much as a single peck to warn of her intent, she drew him deep. As deep as she could.

His taste was incredible, hot and salty and alive. She swirled her tongue around him, amazed at how seducing him was seducing her as well.

Max jerked hard, his head back, his fingers now tight, holding her close. He moved, once, twice, then cursed low. "I can't, Maddie."

She withdrew a bit, licked the very tip of him, and said, "Yes, you can."

He howled, sounding much like a wounded wolf. "You don't get it, baby." She could barely understand him, his words were so raw. "I'm about to—"

Thrilled with her success, Maddie said, "Please do," and enclosed him in her mouth once again.

A heavy beat of stillness enveloped them, not a sound, not a heartbeat. And then Max broke. Maddie nearly cried out with the excitement of it. She hadn't known a man could be so untamed in his pleasure, so hot and free.

Maddie continued tantalizing him until his legs went limp and he dropped to his knees in front of her. He sat back, still panting, then met her anxious gaze and gave her a breathy laugh.

"You're dangerous," he whispered, and pulled her close. There on the floor he held her, giving her all the cuddling she'd wanted, until the trembling had left his body and he could breathe again.

And then he got even.

MAX WATCHED Maddie sleeping the next day. It was early afternoon, but she showed no signs of waking. Her blond hair was twisted onto his pillow, and her bottom was beautifully bare. He smiled. He wanted to touch her, but more than that he knew he needed to let her sleep. After the stunt she'd pulled last night, he'd kept her awake till well past dawn.

And even then he hadn't been appeased.

Maddie was simply different. Better. More. Deeper and sweeter and more consuming. He'd never tire of her. He knew that now.

What to do? Having her around would provide the perfect home life for Cleo. And for him. He needed her to commit to him, but she claimed to be against marriage.

All night long, she'd reveled in their intimacy, but not once had she hinted at an emotional connection.

Quietly, Max slipped from the bed and went to the kitchen to get juice. He'd wake her, they'd talk, and hopefully he could find some chink in her armor, some way to make her stop distrusting marriage, and to give him a chance to bind her to him.

MADDIE AWOKE to the shifting of the bed and warm breath drifting over her bare hip. She smiled even before she got her eyes open. "Mmm," she mumbled with a languid stretch that found plenty of sore muscles from the newest night of debauchery. Max was just so damn good at debauching. A master.

"Not again, Max," she moaned, knowing she needed a warm shower before she could even think of going another round.

She twisted to face him, then jumped a foot when

Cleo met her with a loud bark. She was naked in front of the dog!

Dreadfully embarrassed, Maddie jerked the sheet up off the floor to cover herself. The bed was destroyed, the sheets pulled loose, the spread totally gone. Both pillows were in the middle of the bed and Maddie blushed when she remembered why. Max had propped her up like a pagan offering, then made her feel pagan with the carnal way he'd enjoyed her body.

Cleo came the rest of the way into the bed, a little hesitant, keeping her head low, her tail well hidden, and Maddie felt emotions rise to choke her.

Scooting so that she was more or less sitting in the bed with the sheet around her sarong-style, she opened her arms to Cleo and the dog lumbered onto her lap.

It was the first time Cleo had come to her so openly, and it broke Maddie's heart. Maddie squeezed the dog tight as tears seeped from her eyes. She loved the ugly beast as much as she loved the magnificent master.

She wanted them both. She wanted them forever.

Yet she'd argued with Max, insisting on no more than a notch on the bedpost.

"Oh Cleo," Maddie wailed softly, "what am I going to do?" Last night had been the stuff dreams were made of, and Max thought it was all a lark, a way for her to gain sexual experience.

She certainly didn't disdain what she was learning sexually. No way. Max was a remarkable lover, natural and intense and so clever. Very clever.

But she cared about more than their physical relationship. She cared about all of him, his humor and his honor and the way he loved. He gave Cleo his whole heart, and he hadn't hesitated at all to befriend Carmilla, Bea and Mavis.

He was so easy to love, darn it.

More tears trickled down her cheeks, and Cleo whined. She licked Maddie's face, then began to wail.

The dog had the worst morning breath Maddie had ever smelled, but it didn't matter. They comforted each other, and it broke Maddie's heart to admit she had played a dumb game and lost. She'd thought she could cavort in sexual frivolity with Max and just walk away more experienced. She should have known after seeing Max with Cleo that he wasn't a man who could be played with.

And he wasn't a man who women willingly walked away from.

Maddie rocked the dog, holding her pudgy body tight. Cleo shifted around anxiously, throwing her head back and really getting into the maudlin mood of it. The more Cleo whimpered, the more tears ran down Maddie's face to mat in the dog's scruffy fur. The more Maddie hugged and cuddled the dog, the more Cleo moaned and yowled.

Max came running into the room. He carried a tray with two glasses of orange juice on it and a look of befuddlement on his face. He stopped in the doorway and glared when he saw the two females huddled on the bed making enough racket to wake the entire street.

"What the hell is going on?"

MAX LOOKED AT Maddie's tear-streaked face with alarm. Good God, she didn't cry well. Her nose was red and swollen, her eyes puffy. Her cheeks were blotchy.

He wanted to hold her in his lap and beg her not to cry. First she'd curled his toes, and now she was ripping his guts out.

More softly, he asked, "What's all the caterwauling about?" He set the tray down on the nightstand. "Maddie? Are you hurt?"

She hid her face in the dog's fur. When he started to touch her, Cleo issued a low growl of warning, then snuffled her nose into Maddie's neck.

"Well, I'll be." His damn dog had switched loyalties. Max shook his head. Good thing he loved Maddie, too. *Love.* What a tricky thing to happen to a guy.

From now on, when he wrote his column, he'd be a lot more understanding with the poor saps who got themselves tangled up in the emotion. It was damn hard to deal with, setting his heart on fire and turning his brain to mush. Everything he'd always thought he knew about women now seemed insignificant, all because he hadn't yet known Maddie. Which meant he hadn't known much at all.

Oh sure, he could make little Maddie scream with pleasure, but could he make her say, "I do"? He hadn't believed in love at first sight. He hadn't been all that sure that love existed at all, at least not the type of love that had stolen his father from him, the type of love that had turned his sedate older brother into a caveman and their friend, Guy, into a ball of distraction.

Max had honestly believed that if love existed, it needed time to grow, to stew and ferment and get real sticky. But hell, almost from the second he'd seen Maddie, his heart had known she was different. He tried to claim it was just his body talking—because she was one sexy little number—but no. It had been his heart attempting to warn his head, and now he had a wailing woman in bed with his dog and a bad case of uncertainty.

When Maddie lifted her face again, Max stared in horror. She had dog hairs stuck to the tear tracks on her cheeks. She looked to be in the throes of a transition from woman to werewolf.

She sniffed loudly. And wetly. "I'm sorry, Max."

Feeling his way, Max ventured, "For what exactly?"

"For—" She sniffed again and Cleo whined in sympathy "—for carrying on so."

Max sat on the edge of the bed and ignored Cleo's protective bluster to scratch her ear. "Care to tell me what you're carrying on about?"

Maddie nodded, but then said, "You'll hate me."

"Oh, hon." He picked off a few of the dog hairs clinging to her cheeks. "I could never hate you."

"I love you."

Max drew back, nonplussed. "What?"

"See! It's awful!" Her face went back into Cleo's fur and Cleo glared at him.

Max got his mouth to close while wondering if he'd heard right. He felt mired in confusion. Cleo continued to give him dirty looks.

Max needed to take this slowly. If Maddie really was confessing to what he thought she might be confessing to, she sure as hell wasn't happy about it.

"Here, sweetheart. Drink a little juice." A totally inane thing to suggest, but at the moment nothing more brilliant came to him.

Maddie wrinkled her red nose up and turned away. "I can't drink cold in the morning. I need coffee. Hot black coffee."

"Oh." Max frowned at her. "The caffeine is bad for you."

Maddie blinked spiked wet lashes and then her face crumbled again. "What does it matter," she wailed. "Everything is ruined now anyway and I love Cleo so much."

So now she loved Cleo, too? Max looked around his room for inspiration. There was none to be found.

Making a sudden decision, he said to Cleo, "You gotta go out, girl?"

The dog abandoned Maddie's secure hold in the blink of an eye and began anxiously circling Max's feet. Max threw the sheet off the bed, lifted Maddie in his arms, and started out of the room.

"Max! What are you doing?"

He didn't slow down. Cleo danced along beside

him, her tubby body jiggling as he headed for the back door. "You look like hell in the morning, Maddie, did you know that?"

She pressed her face into his shoulder, sharing some of the tear-soaked dog hairs. "Yes. But it doesn't matter."

"Caffeine doesn't matter, how you look doesn't matter. What does matter, sweetheart?"

She started to answer, then gasped loudly as he slid the patio doors open and stepped outside. Cool April air washed over their naked bodies. Cleo shot past, running into the yard beyond the privacy fence and barking with the sheer joy of going outside. She found her deflated plastic ball in the yard and trotted it back to Max.

"Just a second, girl. I have my hands full."

Maddie clutched at him. Her red-rimmed eyes were huge and her face was pale. "What are you doing?"

She sounded squeaky, all aghast at being outside in the buff.

"I promised you the hot tub. But then you distracted me with that incredible mouth of yours." Color rushed back into her cheeks, making Max smile. "The water's warm, so prepare yourself."

Maddie tried to keep a death grip on his neck, but Max lowered her into the frothing water of the hot tub. She looked around, and when she realized they were hidden completely by tall trees and the fence, she relaxed. Her gaze was still anxious as she watched him throw the ball for Cleo.

Max climbed into the tub and joined her. "I forgot about this," he said as he lifted her into his lap and positioned her to recline back against his chest. "And didn't you forget about something, too?"

Maybe if he could distract her from her tears, Maddie would tell him she loved him again. More calmly this time, so that he could believe it.

Maddie held still as Max cupped her breasts beneath the churning water. She caught his wrists and pressed his hands closer still. "What did I forget?"

"You said you had a surprise for me," Max reminded her.

"Oh!" She twisted around to face him. "I forgot after...well, after you did what you did."

"What I did?" Max teased, glad to see she'd stopped crying for the moment. "What about what you did."

Her ravaged face softened. "I loved what I did. You taste so good, Max, and it was so extraordinary to watch you—"

Max clapped his hand over her mouth. "Shh," he warned. "I always wake up horny, and having you here makes it especially bad because I've been wanting you since before I even opened my eyes. Don't torture me now, okay?"

Maddie nodded and when he lifted his hand she asked, "Always?"

He grinned. "Yeah."

She bit her lip, and her gaze tried to see him below the water, but the bubbles made that impossible. Finally she sighed. "Okay. Can I go get my surprise now?"

Max stalled. "Uh, now?" He looked around. The

yard was secluded, but he wasn't sure he wanted to get into anything too frisky out in the open that way. "What about waiting until we—"

Before he could finish, she'd scrambled out of the hot tub—giving Max a delectable glimpse of her pale round bottom—then darted for the door. She was back in less than half a minute with her bag.

Max stiffened, anxious and turned on and curious.

To his surprise she called Cleo to her and the dog came running, her tooth-punctured ball clamped in her mouth. Cleo growled and grumbled and groused as she approached Maddie, but her tail was out and wagging. Max leaned back into the water and felt contentment swell inside him.

Life was good with his dog happy and his woman making him crazy with lust.

All he had to do was figure out this love business.

"Come here, Cleo," Maddie was saying and she seemed oblivious to her nakedness now. Max was far from unaware. The chill of being wet and in the cool air had Maddie's nipples drawn tight. He could almost taste her.

Reaching into the bag, Maddie lifted out the ornate collar. Red leather, with colorful studs, just as she'd ordered.

"Isn't it beautiful?" she asked Max. "I couldn't find anything pretty enough for Cleo at the pet store, but I'd noticed her collar was looking a little old."

Max stared at the decorative, gaudy fetish collar

and wanted to roar in hilarity at his own misconceptions.

He also wanted to moan out his disappointment. Though at first he hadn't been too keen on getting kinky, he'd kind of gotten used to it.

"She didn't like for me to mess with it," Max explained, nearly choking on his suppressed laughter.

Maddie nodded. "This one is pretty. I found it at a...specialty shop. She'll like it. It looks fit for a queen."

A queen indeed, Max thought.

Cleo held perfectly still as Maddie removed the old leather collar and replaced it with the new. Once Maddie was done, the dog cast a nervous, uncertain glance at Max, which made him wonder if she knew where it had come from.

He not only had a kinky woman, but now his dog looked a bit risqué as well.

Max was grinning too much to reassure Cleo, so she looked away and shook her head. The collar was butter-soft red leather and sparkled with multihued faux gems and shining studs.

Cleo's rough yellow fur stuck out in clumps around it.

Still clutching her bag and looking at the dog, Maddie backed up next to where Max lounged in the tub. She sighed dreamily. "Doesn't she look wonderful?"

Max looked at Maddie, his heart feeling as swollen as his male parts always did when she was around. The combination was explosive. "Yes, she does."

Cleo again shook her head to get a feel for the collar, woofed in acceptance, then grabbed up the hapless ball. With a snarl, she ran off to do battle, slinging the ball away then snatching it back again for more punishment.

Max reached out of the tub to hook his arm around Maddie's hips. "You'll never guess what I thought you had in that bag."

When he recalled his heated visions of bondage and dominance games, Max's pulse raced. There would still be time to play those games, he decided. He'd find the time.

Maddie's eyes were hot when she looked at him again. Of course, they were still swollen and red, too, and dog hair clung tenaciously to her cheeks and forehead. "You won't guess," she purred, "what I *do* have."

Lust surged upward, nearly obliterating everything else. Max sat up on the bench in the tub, retaining his hold on Maddie, and said, "Tell me."

Smiling wickedly, she pulled out a large white feather and whisked it around in the air. "I found this when I bought the collar and couldn't resist. I've decided I want to try it."

Max eyed the feather. "On what?"

"On *you*."

His stomach clenched hard and he met her gaze. "Because that's what your ex-fiancé was doing?"

"No." She leaned down and kissed the end of his nose, then whispered, "Because the idea of having you tied up and at my mercy is very appealing.''

Max tried to peek into the bag. ''What else do you have in there?'' No way would he let her use the damn feather on him, but using it on her might be fun.

Maddie held the bag away, then lifted out a velvet mitt. ''This is for stroking.''

''Ah.'' He knew just where he'd use it on her, too. ''Anything else?''

Not quite meeting his gaze, Maddie mumbled something, and Max said, ''What's that?''

She mumbled again, scuffing her bare toe along the edge of the hot tub.

Max tipped up her chin, curiosity humming thickly through his veins. ''What else did you buy, honey?''

Maddie hesitated, then reached defiantly into the bag and withdrew a sexy little barely there camisole of cream lace. It had interesting cutouts where her nipples would be, and ended at about her hipbones. Max shuddered, just imagining Maddie decorated with that bit of fluff.

''Nice,'' he rasped.

Maddie clutched the camisole to her chest. ''Really?''

''Oh yeah.'' Forcing his gaze to her face, he said, ''You'll look great.'' Then he added, ''But no better than you do standing here right now, buck naked with dog hairs sticking to your skin and your hair all mussed.''

She frowned.

He meant it.

Max reached for her. "Come here, sweetheart. I want to talk to you."

She dropped the feather and the lingerie onto a lawn chair and climbed back into the tub with a splash. When she started to sit beside him, Max again brought her onto his lap—facing him this time.

Max cupped the water in his palms and rinsed her cheeks, her chest, until the dog hairs were gone and all that was left was the effects of her tears. He supposed Maddie was one of those women whose eyes stayed puffy for hours after crying. He didn't mind.

He kissed her chin, her nose, her soft mouth. "Why were you crying, honey?"

Maddie played with his chest hair. "I already told you."

"Because you love me?" Max had never felt vulnerable before, but he felt totally exposed saying the words to Maddie now. If he had heard her wrong, if she denied them, he wasn't sure what he'd do. His heart rapped sharply, clapping against his ribs.

She bobbed her head. "Yes."

"And that's a bad thing?" He wanted her to look at him, but she kept averting her face.

"It hurts." She peeked at him, then pressed herself hard against him with a bear hug. "I don't want to put any other notches on my bedpost."

"Thank God." Max returned her hug.

"I don't want you to leave me, either, but I

promise I won't be a pain about it. If you...if you want to see me occasionally still, I think I'd like that.''

"Maddie, where is it you think I'm going?"

"You took the job with your father." She squeezed him so hard she nearly choked him. "You're going to be traveling again."

"A little." Max stroked her back, then her soft bottom. "And only if you and Cleo can come with me most of the time."

Maddie bolted back so hard she lost her balance and toppled off Max's lap. Her head went underwater then she reappeared with a sputter. Max caught her beneath the arms and lifted her.

"For crying out loud, Maddie! What are you doing? Trying to drown yourself?" He wasn't sure he liked such a volatile reaction to his suggestion.

Maddie spit out chlorinated water and wheezed, "You want us to travel with you? Really?"

The tension that had been squeezing his heart started to ease. Max grinned. "Yeah, really. Cleo needs me too much to be left behind very often. And I'd only leave her with you, anyway. No one else."

Her smile was beautiful, brighter than the afternoon sun lighting the yard. "You trust me that much?"

Max nodded. "When I go places too far for Cleo to go along, I'll have to leave her behind. I'd feel better knowing she's with you, because she loves you."

Maddie looked toward the yard where Cleo was

performing the strange act of dragging herself forward with just her front legs, scratching her behind on the ground. Maddie chuckled. "I love her, too, and I'd be happy to watch her for you."

"Here?" Max ventured, pushing just a little. "Because she'd be most comfortable in her own house."

With a wary stillness, Maddie looked at Max. "Okay, if that's what you want."

Max shoved aside his uncertainty—as any manly man would do—and stated, "You know, if you're going to be staying here sometimes, you really ought to get over this silly aversion you have to marriage and give the idea some thought. I mean, you said you love me, and you said you love my dog. Right?"

Maddie's bottom lip quivered. Oh hell, Max thought. If she started crying again he didn't know what he'd do. Her eyes would end up swollen shut.

Maddie gulped. "You...you'd want to marry me?"

He never hesitated. "Yes. I told you all along that I was through with short-term affairs. But I swear, baby, I'd never cheat on you. Not like your ex did. So if that's what's worrying you—"

"Do you care about me, Max?"

She looked so uncertain, Max grabbed her up close and kissed her breathless.

"Care about you? I'm crazy nuts for you."

"You are? It's not just sex?"

"I've loved you," Max growled against her mouth, "almost from the moment you threw yourself against the bookstore's door. And by the time you fell inside on the floor, I was a goner.''

Maddie made a small sound of surprise and he kissed her hard again. Damn, he didn't ever want to stop kissing her.

"I love how you taste, how you laugh, the crazy clothes you wear and the incredible things you do to my body. Hell, yes, I love the sex. And so much more. I especially love the way you take all the bluster away from Cleo and how you accept your friends and give so much of yourself. I kept telling myself that you'd be perfect for Cleo, but the fact is, you're perfect for me.''

"Oh Max.'' She sniffled loudly.

"I need you, Maddie. I already told my father that I didn't want to travel and leave you behind. Not even for a few days. Not when I don't have to.''

She pushed against his chest and sat up to face him. Being that she was on his lap, there was no way she could miss his erection.

She smiled. "I don't want you to put off a great job with your family just because of me. As long as I know you're coming back, I'll be happy.''

Max cupped her cheek. "As long as I know you're here waiting for me, I'll be coming back.''

Maddie reached beneath the water and encircled his erection. "Too bad I don't want to get the velvet glove wet.''

Max groaned. But he caught himself before succumbing. That thought amused him enough that he could fight off the lust. For just a moment. "I have another job you should probably know about."

Dismayed, she paused in her attention to his body and said, "More travel?"

"No, writing." He explained about the column he did for the magazine and to his surprise, Maddie glared at him.

"I read that column! You're always so cynical!"

"I was uneducated."

"Ha! You know more about women—"

"Their bodies, yes. But you've taught me about my own heart."

Her frown melted away. "Oh, Max." She kissed him, then asked hesitantly, "No one knows you write that column?"

"No, and I'd like to keep it that way."

Maddie grinned in relief. "Me, too. I'm finding I'm the jealous sort—which is new for me—and I just know if anyone found out that you write—"

A familiar female voice intruded. "Well, well. Someone go get my shotgun." Mavis sounded highly amused.

Max looked up and saw two of Maddie's friends standing just inside the gate to the privacy fence.

Bea caught his eye and added, her own voice heavy with humor, "Is it legal to carry on out in the open like this?"

Maddie screeched and slipped neck deep into the water. Unfortunately, she went between Max's legs and used his left thigh as an added shield. There was no way he could duck. A quick survey showed that his modesty was intact, thanks to the bubbling water and Maddie's shoulders.

"Bea, Mavis," Max said, trying not to lose his cool at the sudden turn of events. "What are you two doing here?"

Bea held out her arms in a grand gesture. "We came to tell Maddie that Carmilla is eloping! She and Tiny are heading to Las Vegas tonight and Carmilla expects a party when she returns."

Maddie jostled around with joy, almost forgetting her state of undress. "That's wonderful!"

Mavis laughed. "Yeah, she always talked about Tiny, but she figured he'd forgotten about her. Not so. She used your young fellow here as an excuse to get in touch with him again, and nature took care of the rest."

Bea tipped her head at Max. "Looks like nature has been working on the both of you, too. So tell me, when's the wedding?"

"Just as soon as I can arrange it," Max said, and then his father stepped out of the house.

"Wedding! Why Max, that's wonderful." Dan didn't look the least bit surprised to see his youngest son making merry in a hot tub with a naked young lady. He stepped out of the open patio doors and then caught sight of Mavis and Bea. He stopped stock-still, looking spellbound and tongue-tied. "Uh, hello."

A very slow smile spread over Bea's face as she looked him over. She winked, then said in an aside to Mavis, "Dibs."

Cleo suddenly noticed the crowd and began barking. Deciding she needed to protect her master she not only charged the newcomers, she put herself between them and her human family.

She leaped right into the hot tub.

MADDIE KNEW her face was still red. Red and swollen. But she was so happy, it didn't matter. Max loved her. He wanted to marry her. Life couldn't get much better.

She and Cleo were both drier now, except for their hair. Maddie had already combed her own and she sat on the floor, Cleo lying in front of her, while she untangled the dog's fur. Everyone else was gathered at Max's kitchen table. Dan had insisted on coffee and Mavis and Bea had seconded his vote. They all sipped a fresh cup, except for Max.

Dan, who could barely keep his eyes off Bea—which she obviously loved—said, "I came by to see if you'd be ready to travel as early as next weekend." Sheepishly he admitted, "Now that I've finally gotten your agreement to join me in the business, I don't want to take any chances on you backing out."

Max, wearing only a pair of jeans and looking sexy enough to kill, leaned against the counter drinking juice. "Where to?"

"Minnesota. You'd have this whole week to get acquainted with the product and the price list." Dan added hurriedly, "And of course your young lady and the dog are more than welcome to go along."

Cleo snarled at Dan. She wasn't the least bit

happy having the house full, but Maddie was keeping her calm.

Max glanced at Maddie and she smiled. "I'm free."

Max smiled, too, his look intimate enough that Bea and Mavis raised their brows and snickered. Dan gave both women another quick glance, then shared a small grin with Bea.

Max clapped his father on the back, drawing his attention away from Bea. "That'd be fine, then. I'll be there bright and early tomorrow."

Dan sent Maddie a look of gratitude. "I can't tell you how wonderful it is to meet you, young lady. And I'm thrilled you'll be joining our family. Annie speaks very highly of you, and Lace has been singing your praises, too."

Maddie felt ready to burst with happiness. Then Mavis stood. "All this lovey-dovey stuff is killing me. I wish you all well, but I'm much happier playing the field."

Max grinned at her. "Another hot date tonight?"

"Every night, sweetie."

Bea clasped Dan's arm. "Why don't you let me take you to lunch, sugar? Your son suggested I show you some of my slogans."

Dan glanced at Max, his brow raised in question.

"She's good, Dad. Very good."

Bea gave a feline smile. "And I write great slogans, too."

Dan choked, but quickly recovered. "Why, yes, lunch sounds very nice."

Max shook his head. It seemed his whole world

had gotten turned upside down in a relatively short time.

His brother had married, his sister had married—which included a long-time family friend getting hitched, too. Maddie had burst into his life and practically stolen his dog from him.

He glanced at her to see Cleo sprawled over her lap in bliss while Maddie bent to the task of combing out the tangles in the dog's seldom seen tail. Maddie's brows were drawn in concentration, her eyes still swollen, her nose still red.

Damn he loved her.

And now his father was actually smitten with a woman.

Max waited impatiently until everyone had left the house. Cleo whined at the back door and Maddie let her back out to fight with her ball. Dog hairs were all over Maddie's fresh clothes, but thankfully there were none on her face. She went directly to Max and held him.

Max said, "Will you marry me soon?"

"As soon as you like."

He grinned. "An agreeable woman. What a lucky cuss I am." Then he added, "Now, about that bag of goodies you brought..."

Maddie looked up at him and smiled. "Thank you, Max."

"For what, sweetheart?"

"For being a reprobate. For being a kinky, macho, adorable, loveable man." She kissed him gently. "And mostly for being all mine."

Max lifted her in his arms. "Being all yours is

my pleasure. In fact, I insist on it.'' He started toward the bedroom. ''As for the rest, I think we need to explore the kinky part just a bit more.''

He bobbed his eyebrows at Maddie and she laughed, saying, ''Now where did I leave my feather?''

His life was complete.

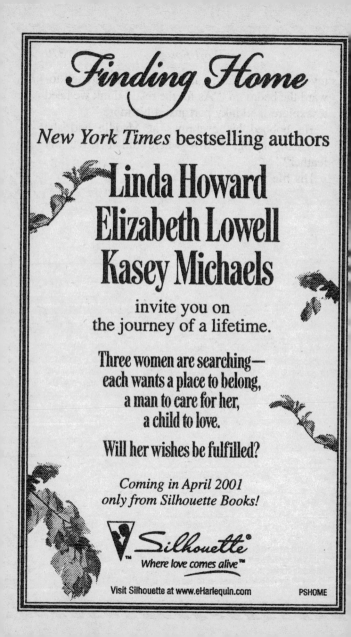

If you enjoyed what you just read,
then we've got an offer you can't resist!

Take 2 bestselling love stories FREE!

Plus get a FREE surprise gift!

Clip this page and mail it to Harlequin Reader Service®

IN U.S.A.	**IN CANADA**
3010 Walden Ave.	P.O. Box 609
P.O. Box 1867	Fort Erie, Ontario
Buffalo, N.Y. 14240-1867	L2A 5X3

YES! Please send me 2 free Harlequin Duets™ novels and my free surprise gift. Then send me 2 brand-new novels every month, which I will receive months before they're available in stores. In the U.S.A., bill me at the bargain price of $5.14 plus 50¢ delivery per book and applicable sales tax, if any*. In Canada, bill me at the bargain price of $6.14 plus 50¢ delivery per book and applicable taxes**. That's the complete price—what a great deal! I understand that accepting the 2 free books and gift places me under no obligation ever to buy any books. I can always return a shipment and cancel at any time. Even if I never buy another book from Harlequin, the 2 free books and gift are mine to keep forever.

So why not take us up on our invitation. You'll be glad you did!

111 HEN C24W
311 HEN C24X

Name	(PLEASE PRINT)	
Address	Apt.#	
City	State/Prov.	Zip/Postal Code

* Terms and prices subject to change without notice. Sales tax applicable in N.Y.
** Canadian residents will be charged applicable provincial taxes and GST.
  All orders subject to approval. Offer limited to one per household.
  ® and ™ are registered trademarks of Harlequin Enterprises Limited.

DUETS00

From bestselling
Harlequin American Romance author

CATHY GILLEN THACKER

comes

TEXAS VOWS

A McCABE FAMILY SAGA

Sam McCabe had vowed to always
do right by his five boys—but after
the loss of his wife, he needed the small-town security
of his hometown, Laramie, Texas, to live up to that
commitment. Except, coming home would bring him
back to a woman he'd sworn to stay away from.
It will be one vow that Sam can't keep....

On sale March 2001

Available at your favorite retail outlet.

HARLEQUIN®
Makes any time special ™

THE
ROAD
BEST
TRAVELED

THE
ROAD
BEST
TRAVELED

Stuart McAlpine

Thomas Nelson Publishers
Nashville

Copyright © 1991 by Stuart C. McAlpine.

All rights reserved. Written permission must be secured from
the publisher to use or reproduce any part of this book,
except for brief quotations in critical reviews or articles.

Published in Nashville, Tennessee, by Thomas Nelson, Inc.,
and distributed in Canada by Lawson Falle, Ltd., Cambridge,
Ontario.

Scripture quotations are from the NEW KING JAMES
VERSION of the Bible. Copyright © 1979, 1980, 1982,
Thomas Nelson, Inc., Publishers.

Library of Congress Cataloging-in-Publication Data

McAlpine, Stuart.
    The road best traveled / Stuart McAlpine.
        p.   cm.
    ISBN 0-8407-3184-1
    1. Jesus Christ—Biography—Devotional literature   I. Title.
BT306.5.M393   1991
232.9′01—dc20
[B]   91–7633
                                                        CIP

Printed in the United States of America
1 2 3 4 5 6 7 — 96 95 94 93 92 91

TO MY WIFE CELIA,
and to my children,
Charis, Ewen, Gavin,
Christa, and Brendan,
who are my dearest
fellow-travelers;
to my parents,
Campbell and Shelagh,
who helped me find
the road best traveled;
and to my hiking companions at
Christ Our Shepherd Church.

FATHER,
They say that penmanship reveals the man.
We scribe, and others read the hidden heart.
They say that once you wrote a single word;
That swaddled vellum fast-bound all your life.
Please dip your quill into my inked heart's well,
And grace-stroke once again that word in me . . .
Jesus.

Stuart McAlpine

CONTENTS

ACKNOWLEDGMENTS

We are not self-starters. Consequently, how we progress and what we produce is nurtured and nourished by the encouragement of others. Through Celia, my wife, divinity has ghost-written indelible truths and graces into my life, and her affirmation and discernment kept me between the lines whenever I wanted to fall off the page. I would like to express my appreciation to Kin Millen who watered the seeds of desire to communicate in written form; to Ron Haynes whose shepherding got me into the fold of an excellent publisher; to Bill Watkins who midwives infant projects and nurses fledgling writers with care and enthusiasm. I am also grateful to the family members of Christ Our Shepherd Church in Washington, D.C., who have given me more evidence of the love of Jesus on the road best traveled.

FOREWORD

WE'RE IN TROUBLE. Do not be fooled by those who say that we are the measure of all things; that evolution will make optimists of us all; that reason's voice will be heard above the clamor of anarchy; that democracy will eliminate the dictatorial spirit. Though every well-meaning voter and every well-intentioned government should be mutually encouraged by each other's respective citizenship and statecraft, the most that governor and governed can hope for is that legislation will curb evil—it cannot cure it.

We may be better educated and better off, but we are not better. The genocide and martyrdom of our century are unrivaled in history. The cries of the persecuted, the violated, the famished, the impoverished, the disenfranchised, the abused, and the seduced—together with the cries of a polluted environment and a hollow culture—combine to drown the self-congratulatory applause of old dogs and fat cats.

Jesus said that things would get worse and worse and that trouble would hallmark our life, but that there is a way to survive it, overcome it, and ultimately escape it.

WE'RE IN TRAINING. Do not be fooled by final grades and degrees, by certificates of proficiency and professionalism. Though they speak well of excellence and endeavor and should be valued as badges of honor, their framed elegance cannot disguise the fact that they are dated and that knowledge increases. We may no longer be students and apprentices, but we must humbly concede that we are forever unqualified, forever updating at endless in-service seminars and refresher courses. However, the crucial training of this life has less to do with provision for the here-and-now than it has to do with preparation for the hereafter.

It is a tragedy to be trained only to make a temporary

xii   THE ROAD BEST TRAVELED

income and untutored in what makes for eternal outcomes. We can choose our classrooms and also our teachers, but Jesus said that a common test will be applied to all trainees and that we can prepare ourselves for it in a manner that will assure us of a successful graduation from time to eternity.

WE'RE IN TRANSIT. Do not be fooled by towering city-scapes and marbled shopping malls, glass cathedrals and manicured planned communities. Though planned for infinite quality of life and designed to withstand earthquakes, their boast of permanence is only temporary. With our ingenuity and know-how, we just happen to be able to build better transit camps that last longer and are more conducive to a pleasant sojourn. Our brass revolving doors are but tent flaps.

Of course, pretensions of permanence dupe us into believing that everything is settled, worked out, taken care of . . . until earth's nature erupts or human nature corrupts. Managua and Beirut no longer host tourist cocktail parties with clinking toasts to "this time next year." Transitoriness is understood in Belfast and Calcutta.

Jesus taught that both heavens and earth are transitory and that this life is a prelude, not a conclusion, but that we could be sure about where we would be settling once we left this transit stop.

The simple and eloquent words of a familiar Negro spiritual sum it all up. In the face of trouble, the singer knew that this life was a training school for another and that he was a man in transit.

> This world is not my home;
> I'm just a-passin' through.

But some pass through faster than others.

"I AM THE WAY."
(JESUS)

Blessed are those whose strength is in you; who have set their hearts on pilgrimage. . . . They go from strength to strength till each appears before God in Zion.
(PSALMIST)

This book will make a Traveller of
    thee,
If by its counsel thou wilt ruled be;
It will direct thee to the Holy Land,
If thou wilt its directions understand.
(JOHN BUNYAN)

PART 1

HITTING THE ROAD

HUSTLERS

Some people long-stride their way up the road and mad-dash downtown; they long-hop and overnight-express from coast to coast and business-shuttle and red-eye from city to city. Sure, sometimes they get to Sunday-drive, slow dance, and sleep late, but generally, their tender life is strapped like a tough, leathery fanbelt to an ambitious engine that has to take off, move out, and get along. Like well-seasoned travelers, they touch down in a variety of places, and some of their landings and leavings are bumpier and scarier than others—though they never admit it. They enter the down-to-earth world of family, friends, and work through various arrival gates but never stay long enough to establish relationships before the next departure. They sweat through occasional emotional customs checks that ask them to examine the contents of their hearts and declare the purpose of their travel, and somehow they manage to smooth-talk their way through.

Sure, there are some perks. Frequent-flight bonuses secure the designer life-style, which is inevitably accompanied by other designs—for sexual conquest and financial gain. Once in a while, circumstances may condemn them to ride a slow train, and they get a little more time to think about where they're going, to view the scenery, to talk to a fellow passenger, but to their relief such distractions don't last too long.

Sadly—overtaken by the midair collisions of fortuitous disaster, the tangled wreckage of head-on suffering, the terrorism of time-bombed malevolence—some don't hustle as far as they would like to. But hustlers put the stopover down to bad luck and get back on track with the help of the Daytimer and the Filofax. Overreaching goals, overshooting destinations, overpowering competition, overriding objections, overtaking the plodders and the pilgrims, they travel through life at five hundred miles per hour and thirty-five thousand feet, having planned for everything except heaven. Though they travel far, and with purpose, they are not pilgrims.

HOLIDAY-MAKERS

More intent on life as vacation than vocation, the holiday-makers choose to live as tourists rather than pilgrims. In the same way that some visitors "do" Washington, D.C., where I live, they "do" life. They accept a condensed-for-convenience public-opinion guide to the main points of interest, like family, religion, politics, education, sex, marriage, work, retirement. They collect a few photo albums and videos to prove they were here; spend a lot of money for the privilege of the tour; eat a great deal; miss a few connections; but generally leave life as they found it—suddenly.

The holiday-maker is content with snap-shot generalities, but has no time for close-up details. He wants a potted history of the world in no more than three sentences and has no patience with questions and answers that threaten to delay the planned pleasure schedule.

Whereas the pilgrim is concerned about becoming someone regardless of the discomfort, the holiday-maker is happy just to be somewhere, preferably as comfortably as possible. The purposes of a lifetime are sacrificed for the pleasures of a summertime. Life is a beach, and the sand is a great place to build a house. It is more desirable to look out for "five stars" than look at the night stars. Why be challenged by the vast brilliance of the universe when you can sleep in a hotel haze?

It is more important to be one of the crowd than one of a kind. The private quest for meaning is abandoned for the bland gossip of group travel. The tabloids of wanderlust woo them to enter a world of city boulevards at night, surf and sun at high noon; to dabble in low-life escapades and fantasize in high-brow company. Sure, you get to see a lot and meet a lot and do a lot in Camelot. However, no number of cheap souvenirs and mementos will suffice when it comes to giving an account of life's journey. When the questions are finally asked, it will not do to show postcards. Though they travel far and with pleasure, the holiday-makers are not pilgrims.

HOBOES

"I was born under a wandering star." Lee Marvin's hymn for vagrants and vagabonds makes a public virtue of a lifestyle that began for many as the result of private vice. True, for some it represents an escape from responsibility or even difficulty; for others it is an unjust sentence imposed by poverty and penury.

At first glance, the tramp appears to have some things in common with the pilgrim. Neither is overly concerned with appearance or about how he is regarded by others. Both seem to hang loose from this world's value systems, and both travel light.

There is a fundamental difference, however. Though he appears to be nomadic, the pilgrim is not an aimless wanderer. The travel itinerary of his heart is goal oriented, for he looks forward to and seeks his true and permanent home. The tramp does not believe in home and has chosen to roam and meander, to live like a bedouin from one watering hole to another, to accept impermanence as a way of life. For him there is no ultimate destination—the journey alone is the thing.

There are many well-heeled and well-housed folk whose fixed abode belies the fact that they are spiritual hoboes. Led by no specific conviction, they wander from this experience to that explanation, from one ancient philosophy to another modern fad, but not so mystical that they've forgotten how to survive and satisfy basic needs.

They make a god of improvisation; they are open to everything in general and closed to nothing in particular. They are worldly wise and street smart. They are to be admired for their local knowledge and the range of their interests, for their appreciation of the environment and for their street wisdom (or savvy). However, though they form many interesting relationships on the road and enjoy shooting the breeze, they never once dare confess that they are wandering because they are lost. Though they travel far and light, they are not pilgrims.

HOMESTEADERS

All homesteaders are pioneers, and many begin as true pilgrims, in that they choose to leave something behind. It may not have been a very secure past, but anything that we know, regardless of how undesirable it is, seems more certain than an unpredictable and potentially dangerous future.

The impulse to find a place of settlement is a good one. We are creatures of space and time, and we need a sense of place.

Perhaps the greatest danger lies farther down the road, beyond the success of settlement. It has less to do with being a homesteader than it has to do with what homesteaders become. Historians and sociologists have well observed that homesteaders become entrenched settlers, and settlers become landed gentry. What began as a legitimate desire to stake a claim becomes an all-consuming passion for residency, occupancy, fixity, security. The grand irony is that in finding their present dream, they lose their future direction. The home becomes the castle, whose walls speak of security, but whose moat and drawbridge speak of uncertainty.

Spiritual homesteaders mean well in the early days. They genuinely explore what makes for peace but sadly mistake settlement in this life as the security for which they longed. The physical comforts of home fool them into believing that they have found solace for the soul. Homesteaders are tempted to stop searching and to cease longing; to put up fences and adopt definitions of life that conveniently defend and describe their present holdings; to accumulate sufficient acquisitions and attachments to deter the contemplation of a fresh start or a new move, simply because there is too much to leave behind now. Territorial rights and boundaries require vigilant guardianship, and the homesteader's mind cannot leave home for too long, to think about another country. The boldness that risks all possessions and that researches other possibilities becomes an increasingly costly and rare commodity. Life is plumb-lined to perfection, and while pools and patios, Jaguars and Jacuzzis are added, the square footage of the soul quietly erodes and shrinks.

In my wallet I carry an important card that bears two

words: RESIDENT ALIEN. Yes, I believe in residency, but only so long as we do not mistake our property for the only land we are called to seek and find. We are aliens whose eternal home is elsewhere. Resident aliens too easily become resident aristocrats, and worldly security and success too effortlessly become the only measures of our worth and progress. The most established homestead is but temporary residence for bodies that house a spirit that will not die when breaths expire and homes are pulled down. Though they may begin well, not all homesteaders remain pilgrims.

HIKERS

Perhaps if John Bunyan were writing today, he'd produce a book entitled *Hitchhiker's Hope,* for it is the image of the hiker that comes closest to the idea of the pilgrim. The hiker is not a hustler in pursuit of self, though he takes the duties of work seriously. He enjoys getting away from it all but, unlike the holiday-maker, does not believe the pleasure principle is the basis for life. Like the hobo, he loves to wander in the great outdoors, but his hikes are conducted with purpose and preparation. He always intends to return home for, like the homesteader, he believes in domicile. However, he does not allow his front gates to imprison him on his concrete driveway when there are unchartered dirt trails to explore. Unsatisfied with glossy pictures of the world and with celluloid and journalistic presentations of reality, he wants to find out about things firsthand as much as possible. Regardless of age or position, he is not ashamed or afraid to hit the road. He appears in the literature and folklore of every culture—the solitary wanderer, pursuing a quest. Once upon a time there was a knight . . . a pilgrim . . . a hitchhiker.

Whether you are more like the hustler, the holiday-maker, the hobo, or the homesteader, you have a chance to become a hiker for a short while and follow in the footsteps of someone who spent his entire public life just walking the roads. We're going to trek down some of them and hopefully track down who Jesus is and what he came to do. Are you prepared to hit the road and learn to whistle a new tune?

This world is not my home
I'm just a-passin' through.

TRAVEL PREPARATIONS

Stop talking; start walking! Agreed, but before we hit the road we need to recognize that successful, long-term pilgrimage is dependent on some good short-term preparation. The fact is that a little forethought can mean the difference between life and death on some journeys, so how we plan and what we pack are very important. Before we set out, let's have a pre-hike prep talk.

KIT LIST

If you've ever been hiking or read a hiker's manual, then you'll know that there is general agreement on the "ten essentials"—though these do not date back to Moses! They are extra clothing, extra food, sunglasses, knife, firestarter, matches, first-aid kit, flashlight, map, and compass. On our journey we're going to be more in need of certain personal attributes and attitudes than physical apparatus (though it would help to have a New Testament handy), but interestingly enough, we will require our "kit" for similar purposes. If you examine the list of essentials you will find that it is designed to satisfy the need for:

- PROVISION—We must allow for the demands of the hike and have sufficient reserves to maintain our strength and stamina when the rigors of the journey impoverish our resources;
- PROTECTION—Unforeseen conditions occur on hikes, so we must ensure that we are protected in the face of arbitrary circumstances that will impair our endurance;
- PREVENTION—We need to be forewarned about predictable problems and equipped to forestall them in the face of pressures that will impede our progress.

There's nothing worse than having to drop out or being forced out prematurely. Of course I hope that you will follow Jesus to the end of the road, but I realize that to do so, you will have to stimulate your appetite to find out more about him; you will need to fortify your mind against disinterest, doubt, and the kinds of temptations that leave you side-swiped and sidelined; you will have to be alert to those pressures that are likely to get you off track.

MAP-READING

All of our map references are taken from the gospels: Matthew, Mark, Luke, and John. They represent the hiker's travel guide, telling us where and why Jesus traveled; describing things that happened and folks he met; detailing what he said and did. To follow in his footsteps, we need to read these maps carefully. This happens to be a book about the map of Jesus' hiking, but if you've ever been anywhere, you'll know that you want to look at the map yourself before you accept what someone else has to say about it.

> STOP! If you have never done so before, read Mark's Gospel immediately. That's right! Put this book down now and pick up Mark's map. Check it out for yourself and get your bearings. Come back to this travel guide when you've done so. We won't go anywhere without you. Meet you back here, then!

There are some simple points that we need to note about these spiritual maps. Our cartographers were concerned to do certain things.

TO PRESERVE . . .

Jesus did not leave a written record, nor did he take steps to ensure that his teachings were kept for posterity, so these documents are the main sources that preserve the eyewitness accounts of those who knew Jesus and:

1. heard him *teaching* people through parables, sayings, and conversations;
2. saw him *touching* people's lives through miracles of healing and personal relationships.

These details of Jesus' words and works were not gathered like a set of "In Memoriam" essays to remember a great teacher, but collected as essential, hands-on resource material to help people to learn about a risen Christ and to preserve his truth in their own lives, in their churches, and in their society and culture.

TO PRESENT . . .

The writers present a vivid and vital picture of Jesus that is both historical and personal:

Historical. Though they are not writing exhaustive histories (there are significant gaps in Jesus' early life for example), they are concerned about historical accuracy (including material unflattering to the disciples);

Personal. Though they are dealing with common material, the differences in their own circumstances and concerns, personalities and purposes, emphases and audiences, serve to produce distinctive, though noncontradictory, portraits of Jesus.

Matthew is formal and well organized into distinct discourses. The strategic use of the Old Testament relates to his concern to convince a Jewish readership that Jesus is the Son of David, the promised messianic King. Mark is probably the oldest Gospel, certainly the most compact, vivid and punchy. He captures the immediacy of Jesus' impact and influence but tempers the action with a clear presentation of Jesus as a servant who, through humility, compassion, and suffering, demonstrated unprecedented power. The emphasis in this Gospel on Jesus' miraculous might and his command over evil was particularly appropriate for the Roman audience that was being addressed.

Luke was an impeccable historian, and his scrupulous research is arranged with chronological care. Recognizing that the Christian faith was birthed in Judaism, he uses this fact as a springboard to catapult his readers into the world of fulfilled prophecy, from which vantage point it is understood that Jesus has brought salvation to the entire world, no exclusions. Jesus is the Savior of all humankind. As a Gentile, Luke directs his account to his fellows, particularly noting the breadth of Jesus' ministry to women and children, the poor and the outcasts, and also to foreigners. His Greek readership, given their philosophic love affair with the ideal, would have been especially drawn to Luke's presentation of Jesus' perfect humanity. We call these three gospels the synoptics (common view) because they share so much common material and so many similarities in perspective.

John's Gospel, however, has a unique style and approach. He is conversant with Jewish customs and belief but presents Jesus to those who are unfamiliar with the original setting and circumstances of Jesus' life. With depth and accuracy, understanding and poignancy, he concentrates on Jesus' ministry in the south, rather than in Galilee, and engages the Greek mind with intent to convince it that Jesus is the Christ who can bring them into the same communion that he shared with Father God. Exploring the depth and intimacy of Jesus' relationship with his Father, John gives us a tender insight into the meaning of Jesus' words and works at the same time that he graphically presents the conflict between the responses of unbelief and faith. His purpose is explicitly stated and emphasized by the number of occasions that he uses the word *witness*. It is his consuming concern to promote and provoke belief in Jesus Christ as the Son of God "and that believing you might have life in his name."

TO PROCLAIM . . .

These writings were not referred to as Gospels until the second century, but it is easy to understand why this description stuck. The term is legitimately suggested by its explicit appearance in the text: "The beginning of the gospel of Jesus Christ" (Mark 1:1). Given the fact that gospel means good news, it is an appropriately bold and brief designation for the scripts that claim to communicate precisely that. It's impossible to tell good news in a nonchalant, "take it or leave it" fashion. Not surprisingly, the Gospel writers do not give us a vague proposal, but a vivid proclamation; they do not offer passing suggestions but pointed sermons. They intend their words to be heard by and supplied to specific people in particular circumstances.

Furthermore, their personal convictions about who Jesus is add another dimension to their records, for they become the means for God to speak good news personally to men and women. The word *proclaim* conveys the idea of going public with something in an official capacity. These writers are clearly doing more than scripting a factual news brief for private circulation. They are combining the facts of the case in a manner that interprets the meaning of it all and are proceeding to proclaim their findings in an authoritative and vigorous fashion.

TO PERSUADE . . .

Written by Christians, the Gospels present Jesus in a way that seeks to persuade the one who does not believe, as well as to encourage and nurture the one who does. Though containing biographical details, they are not biographies. Though historical, they are not archives. With conviction, confidence, and cogency, they give witness to Jesus, testimonials to the veracity of his communication, the integrity of his character, and the authenticity of his claims. The material is chosen and arranged to persuade all readers that in the person of Jesus, God did something unique and radical, final and comprehensive, that demands attention and commands a response.

THUMBS OUT

When we hit the road, it's important to have the right attitudes: otherwise our initial intentions will evaporate when the sun gets too hot on our backs; our resolve will be washed away when the rainstorm drenches us. Here are some things to bear in mind on this particular hike:

ENJOY THE OUTDOORS

You may not be sure about all the outcomes of a pursuit of Christ, but approach the adventure with wholeheartedness and with an expectation that you are going to learn and benefit from it.

Attitude: *Enthusiasm*

PACE YOURSELF

You cannot cover every mile at the same rate, so slow down to take in those parts of the hike with Jesus that seem more difficult than others. Don't drive yourself to take in more than you are able.

Attitude: *Patience*

TRAVEL LIGHT

You need an open mind on the open road, so try not to weigh yourself down with too many presuppositions and predispositions that will prevent you from seeing Jesus in new ways.

Attitude: *Openness*

LEARN TO ADAPT

You may discover that the hike with Jesus challenges some established norms of behavior and patterns of thinking, so be ready to adjust your priorities in order to consider other perspectives.

Attitude: *Humility*

ACCEPT ALL WEATHERS

You will inevitably experience adverse conditions that will tempt you to abandon the journey, so decide to survive the storm and persist in your quest of Jesus.

Attitude: *Endurance*

BE PREPARED TO GO IT ALONE

You may find that not everyone is sympathetic with your interest in Jesus' itinerary so don't be surprised if you have to follow Jesus without their company.

Attitude: *Determination*

Thumbs up for good attitudes and thumbs out on the road!

ROAD SKILLS

In the same way that learning skills make for effective education, road skills make for effective hiking. It's important to be street wise for long-term safety and satisfaction. Here are a few suggestions from Jesus himself, all taken from Matthew's Gospel.

WATCH THE BIRDS AND CONSIDER THE WILD FLOWERS

Pay attention to the details of the roadside, for sometimes the implications of your observations will contain more theology than many sermons you have heard, and hopefully you will conclude that you too are as worthy a recipient of divine care and as likely a product of loving purpose as any other example of creation.

DO NOT WORRY ABOUT TOMORROW

Make the most of this hike, this temporary suspension from the cares and concerns of a materialistic society and cooperate with the invitation to follow Christ and trust what he is saying.

ASK AND IT WILL BE GIVEN TO YOU

Do not be afraid to seek help when you need clearer understanding, and be sure to ask for further directions and information.

BEWARE WIDE FREEWAYS

Although some routes seem appealing with a variety of lanes and ease of travel, their appearance is deceptive, and it is necessary to exercise discernment and make right choices if the hike is to be completed successfully.

TAKE OFF YOUR BACKPACK

Jesus was a great advocate of wise rest, and he specifically advised hikers to unburden their loads and recover from spiritual weariness, so learn to relax and share your concerns.

AVOID BLIND GUIDES

There are plenty of self-appointed gurus on the trail, who talk as if they have been there and back but who are really just tapping out their own progress with the white stick of blind hearsay and blind intuition.

INTERPRET THE SIGNS

By all means, read the sky at night and forecast the weather conditions for tomorrow's trek, but let that remind you not to neglect the signs on this road that both warn and instruct about the way to secure safe passage in this life and the next.

DENY YOURSELF

No excess baggage can be taken on this hike, so it is necessary to understand that personal sacrifices will be required.

KEEP YOUR EYES AND EARS OPEN

Be alert because there are dangers and hindrances that can interfere with your progress.

All these skills (observing, studying, evaluating, listening, reading, inquiring, sacrificing) will make for a successful hike.

But did someone mention problems?

ROAD HOGS

All journeys present potential problems, so let's be forewarned about three basic kinds that can ruin a good hike, especially one in Jesus' footsteps.

DANGERS

You will run the risk of being bombarded with the falling rocks of other people's dissuasion, as well as those of your own previous persuasions. You'll be offered tempting rides that avoid the necessity of dealing personally with Christ, that skip the potential challenge of watching him in action, close up. You may twist the ankle of your rationalism and pull the muscles of your self-sufficiency. Possibly you may stumble and fall over the irregular and unfamiliar terrain of faith and trust. If you resist the refreshment offered, you may experience spiritual dehydration.

DETOURS

All manner of false detours will appear in your path. There is a constant array of do-it-yourself signs and hand-painted arrows to lure the follower of Jesus down cultic bypaths, sleazy alleys, and six-lane freeways into inns of the nth degree happiness, brothels of self-gratification, suburbs of mindless mediocrity, and classrooms of esoteric knowledge. There is no shortage of invitations to leave the way, give up the pilgrimage, abandon hope.

DISTRACTIONS

Even if we manage to stay on the road, all kinds of potential distractions can effectively deflect our vision, deviate our purpose, demoralize our hopes. You do not have to look far for possible attention-grabbers that dominate desire, that encourage daydreaming and delay. People, possessions, ideas, worries, lusts, fears, regrets—all have that power to distract us from the goal that is to track down Jesus, once and for all.

Well, how about trying to do just that without any more distractions? Check the next section as you would the highway code, for it will explain the road signs that are going to guide you down each road we travel.

ROAD SIGNS

Throughout this book, instead of chapter subdivisions, you will find some road signs that will mark different sections of each chapter. They are as follows:

Getting the Picture:

The camera lets you know that this section will help you get the general picture, either setting the scene or introducing new subject matter.

Getting the Particulars:

The binoculars indicate that this section will take a closer look at what is happening, giving more information, giving an overview maybe, and making some general observations.

Getting the Point:

The telescope indicates that there is going to be even more focus on the issues involved. This section will usually include some specific teaching and suggestions about what we can learn from the incident under discussion.

Getting Personal:

The sign of the magnifying glass marks the chapter conclusion and encourages the traveler to apply the implications of what has been seen and heard, to his own life, and look beyond present horizons and current perspectives to what lies ahead.

PART 2

FOLLOWING THE ROAD

*Finding
out
who
Jesus is . . .*

ROUTE ONE

Checking out some things about his background . . .

BETHLEHEM ROAD

MAP REFERENCE

*N*ow the birth of Jesus Christ was as follows: After His mother Mary was betrothed to Joseph, before they came together, she was found with child of the Holy Spirit. Then Joseph her husband, being a just man, and not wanting to make her a public example, was minded to put her away secretly. But while he thought about these things, behold, an angel of the Lord appeared to him in a dream, saying, "Joseph, son of David, do not be afraid to take to you Mary your wife, for that which is conceived in her is of the Holy Spirit. And she will bring forth a Son, and you shall call His name JESUS, for He will save His people from their sins." Now all this was done that it might be fulfilled which was spoken by the Lord through the prophet, saying: "Behold, a virgin shall be with child, and bear a Son, and they shall call His name Immanuel," which is translated, "God with us." Then Joseph, being aroused from sleep, did as the angel of the Lord commanded him and took to him his wife.

Now after Jesus was born in Bethlehem of Judea in the days of Herod the king, behold, wise men from the East came to Jerusalem, saying, "Where is He who has been born King of the Jews? For we have seen His star in the East and have come to worship Him." And when they had come into the house, they saw the young Child with Mary His mother, and fell down and worshiped Him. And when they had opened their treasures, they presented gifts to Him: gold, frankincense, and myrrh. Then, being divinely warned in a dream that they should not return to Herod, they departed for their own country another way.

Matthew 1:18–24; 2:1–2, 11–12

They slipped into the "Diplomats Only" parking zone in the forecourt of Herod's residence, their bold innocence fortified with seasoned *savoir faire*. They were wheezing with delight at the prospect of a great find. "Well, lads, where is he?"

The guards could see from their out-of-state bridles and their up-market safari gear that the strangers were not locals, but their evident class was at odds with their apparent lack of respect for royal privacy. The strobe-light brightness of their joy and mischievous excitement served to dispel the darkness of the previous scene's hard pilgrimage with all its grit and grind. Their unabashed merriment in this palace of man's pretensions and their unself-conscious ease in these corridors of egotistical power sufficiently represented the freedom and laughter of all the fools of this world who have become wise men simply because they took the facts about the birth of Christ at face value. "Where is he?" the strangers asked again.

Of course the guards assumed that, since this was Herod's palace, it was Herod they were after. But they were looking for an owner-occupier whose acreage and sphere of influence were somewhat greater! No doubt the chief of staff was informed, and it was deemed politically shrewd to make time for an unscheduled appointment with possible implications for foreign affairs. How global these implications would be, the guards could never have guessed! "Herod, is it?" said the strangers. "How nice to meet you! Where is he?" Their joyful anticipation showed and their mounting impatience was obvious.

When there's a newborn ruler to find, there's no time to waste in bowing and scraping to minor tetrarchs. Herod's practiced political etiquette was definitely challenged. The resident theologians, as godless ones so often do, tried to restore the smile of good intentions to the evil face.

"Where is he, indeed?" echoed Herod.

The search to adore Christ and the search to assassinate him met that day on the Bethlehem Road as they would continue to meet on thoroughfares throughout the ages.

The journey of the Magi was not a planned vacation. This excursion would reorder their private world forever. They had committed themselves to a venture that their reasonable peers warned them would bar them from respectable intellectual circles. Why sacrifice an established academic reputation, the esteem of friends, the love of family, and the respect of the community at large? As has been the case ever since, the pursuit of Christ has been viewed by many as antisense, antisocial and antiself. With hopes pinned on a star, the Magi's arduous hike must have strained every fiber of their judgment and self-respect. Yet so great was their unembarrassed desire to discover, they chose to ignore the discomfort of it all.

Fortunately, Herod's palace was not the end of their pilgrimage. While the smart guys had their heads buried in old law books doing some emergency research and proof-texting, the wise guys pulled out onto the highway, their eyes longingly raised to a constellation that seemed to move ahead of them drawing them on and on and on. Ever in their minds was the question, "Where is he?"

"It stopped."

Two simple words usher in the relief of a new dispensation. The star had opened their eyes, but a child opened their hearts. The world-proof doors that guarded the strongholds of their souls swung wide on their hinges, as they offered their treasures and their worship. The smell of that myrrh would linger in Mary's memory for many years after it had been lost on the night air, for it intimated sorrow and death and prophecies to be fulfilled.

Who knows how long they spent in this communion, but the time came to leave. Herod had invited them to drop in for a cocktail on the way home, for old time's sake and for a further exchange of information to "advance diplomatic relations with the new king." The Herods of this world have never happily espoused the interests of that other kingdom. And so it was that, like millions who would later retrace their steps, the Magi found it impossible to return by the same route, having once discovered Christ. The pained intensity of their search was forgotten as they meandered home another way and savored the scenery of a new country.

 The Gospels do not present us with a theological treatise on the incarnation, and they do not insist that the traveler understand all the details of supernatural obstetrics before he is allowed to continue his journey. They report the facts of a birth and record various responses to the new arrival. As in a good mystery, things are said that cannot be fully understood at the time; things happen that at first appear to be random, though they seem less disconnected as different players find themselves appearing on the same stage, in what seems to be a single plot.

SCENE ONE

A name was pulled out of the hat. A priest called Zechariah had at last landed the ultimate, once-in-a-lifetime honor—to offer incense in the holy place alone while Jewish worshipers waited in the outer court. Sure, it was special, but there was no reason to expect any surprises that would make him drop the incense pot. After all, national religion had been in a quiet phase for four hundred years. If God had been dumb so long, there was no fear of his speaking this year. If he was deaf, then why should he expect an answer to yet another rendition of the priestly prayer that cried for the redemption of Israel?

If the national issues dominated Zechariah's public prayer as a priest, his wife's barrenness burdened his private supplications as a husband. Elizabeth was as childless as God was wordless. What was the use? Like the nation, they had learned to live with no expectation of change.

Even so, he began to offer the prayer on behalf of others. Someone else said "Amen!" It was an angelic visitor, who told him that his prayer was heard. Which prayer? The one for the redemption of . . . "You'll have a son!" . . . or the one that Elizabeth and I . . . "and he'll be great in the sight of the Lord."

"But I'm old."

"And he'll make ready a people prepared for the Lord."

"And what's worse, so is the wife, but thanks for the thought."

Meanwhile, like all congregations, the folk were getting restless and wondering why the priest was going on so long, so inconsiderate of their business-as-usual schedules. Through the angel Gabriel God had spoken clearly and kindly, and Zechariah emerged, waving his hands all over the place. Because he refused to believe, chronic silence would continue in his mouth.

SCENE TWO

As usual, Elizabeth irradiated peace and poise. It's unlikely that her mute husband signed, "You're going to have a baby," upon his return from his tour of duty. Mind you, he seemed more amorous than usual. And sure enough, she got pregnant. Elizabeth's response was the antithesis of her husband's. "The Lord has done this for me!" No doubt Zechariah was hoping for a little credit. This miracle was not an academic theological problem for her. She saw the fact that something was moving in her body as a forecast of all that is to come: God had shown favor and had removed disgrace. (Because children were regarded as a blessing from the Lord for faithfulness, childlessness was perceived as a punishment.) If her barrenness had been symbolic of the times, what could this mean?

The greatest expectation was for a fertilization in the soil of history. Seeds of prophecy had been sown and watered by ceaseless intercession, but no Messiah had appeared. "Your prayer is heard," the angel had said. But didn't Israel need a Messiah more than this woman needed a baby?

SCENE THREE

Six months later, northwards in Galilee, Mary woke up to another day of rounds and routines. There were no strange portents in the sky the night before, nor was there a spectacular sunrise that morning that heightened her sense of expectation for a special day. She was altogether ordinary to others, but somehow of very particular interest to God. "Greetings . . . highly favored . . . the Lord is with you. . . ."

Well might she be "greatly troubled" by this unforced entry. She needed that assurance that she was in the grasp of grace because she was more conscious of the grip of fear. Like Zechariah, she felt obliged to point out something that omniscience seemed to have overlooked or underplayed—her virginity. However, a pattern seemed to be emerging, namely, that divine intervention ignored the exclusive clauses of impossibility. "This is not possible for me!" is gently transmuted to, "Nothing is impossible for God!" The message was alarmingly direct: the Holy Spirit will come upon you, you will conceive, and the result will be Jesus. No helpful instructions came with the explanation. In her response, we see external evidence of the interior life that God saw: "I am the Lord's servant."

This is hardly the best news she's ever had. This pregnancy was potentially the most destructive and obstructive event of her life. Short-term physical limitations were easy to endure compared to the long-term ignominy of bearing a child outside marriage. "How will this be?" is quickly replaced by, "May this be according to your word!" The simplicity of her obedience and trust transformed a question mark into an exclamation mark. Confusion was dispelled by confession. The outcome would not depend upon her faith or her experience or her spirituality or her worthiness or her efforts, but upon a communication that alone could sustain what it had started. Submissive despite the implications and consequences, she trusted the grace of God more than she feared the disgrace of men.

SCENE FOUR

Mary had been told that the impossible had happened to her relative, Elizabeth, so she hurried off to visit her. Little did the older "new Mom" know that she was going to be a sign for the mother of the Messiah and that the years of practicing holiness and prayer were the preparation for her present assignment—the spiritual and physical nurture of the teenage mother-to-be of her Lord during the first three months of her pregnancy.

This scene is one of the most endearing cameos in the birth narratives. Elizabeth's excitement about Mary's baby bespeaks her humility and grace. There is no jealousy, no threat, no demand for the rights of her child. Instead, we are told that John the Baptist did his first diving somersault in utero, and we are invited to meditate on the picture of a mother and fetus worshiping together.

As a mother, Elizabeth modeled the "forerunning" role that her son would soon have. Long before John said, "I must decrease. . . . He must increase," his mother had made that decision.

SCENE FIVE

Although the emphasis was on Mary, in the background was one of the most righteous men that the Bible depicts. Joseph, facing shame and disappointment, his love and life shattered by evidence of betrayal, decided upon a quiet divorce. (Engagement was regarded as binding.) However, having considered this as his best option, he too received a divine communication confirming Mary's account.

Like his new wife, he learned that if something is truly of God, it cannot subvert you, only save you. He took Mary home and had no sexual relations with her until Jesus was born. His qualifications for the role he was to play are demonstrated by his integrity: honest reflection, obedient response, and pure relationship. He didn't have a handle on everything, but in holding Mary he embraced the will of God beyond his understanding. And guess who named the child?

SCENE SIX

A major motif in the play continued to be developed. Grace is all-inclusive. It keeps putting onto the field of action those who have never made the team, those who have voluntarily benched themselves, those who have been expelled from the ballpark. Shepherds, for instance, were under-ordinary, considered untrustworthy, and generally treated as social outcasts. These guys who could not afford a standing-room-only ticket were given front seats at a cosmic concert. The angel who sang lead was something else, but they were in awe of the backup group. The birth of Christ was just another census statistic, unheralded by those who lived in society's limelight, but trumpeted to those who worked the world's night shift.

This good news was first shared with the disenfranchised. That which remained hidden to the wise was spelled out clearly to those considered fools: "He is Christ, the Lord!"

It turned out the shepherds were perfectly trustworthy. They did not build a shrine after they had seen the child but simply passed the good news on, thus becoming the first evangelists of the New Testament.

SCENE SEVEN

Two poor parents took their son to the temple to present him to the Lord, according to custom. They met an old man called Simeon who had been "waiting" and an old woman called Anna who had been "worshiping." Their longing for the Messiah was that of the ages past, and they were both drawn into the gravitational field of this child. Simeon proclaimed that the child would be a revelation to the Gentiles, and Anna perceived that he would be the redemption of Israel. However, it is said that there will be shadows as well as light, a falling as well as a rising, a sword as well as a salvation. The old and the new met on this flagstone in the temple courts where, in the not too distant future, hands would be stretched toward this being, not with intent to bless, but to bloody.

And there you have it! Sages from the ends of the earth, outcasts from the hills, old folks from the retirement home, a childless couple, an unmarried pregnant teenager, and an unknown Jew, featured in the most brilliantly directed and the most creatively produced visual presentation of the love of God.

The mystery of the incarnation has inevitably generated intense study and debate throughout church history, and we should not dismiss any attempt to understand it better. However, we should be warned that it is a great temptation to reduce Jesus to an object for our perusal, instead of elevating him to be the subject of our praise. The formulation of clearly articulated doctrine has never been a pastime for men with time to kill, but has been the passion of apostles and apologists vigorously defending the truth of who Jesus really is, in the face of heresy and heterodoxy.

The Gospels present Jesus in his basic humanity and his essential deity. He lived as his contemporaries did, a man in his own right, without any dilution of Godhead or diminution of personhood. He was not a ghost, nor was he a good guy whom God adopted as Messiah after the fact. He is presented as God in person, but subject to the limitations of humanity. This is the way God chose to achieve his purposes of revelation, redemption, and reconciliation.

The fact that the story begins with a baby is sufficient to illustrate the risk, the vulnerability, the powerlessness that was willingly accepted in order to reveal what God was really like. Dangerous? Daring? Shocking? Staggering? Yes, all of these. In Christ, God did not choose to outstrip human strength, but to strip down to human weakness. We are not allowed to forget this humble, fragile birth. For Jesus the notion of becoming a child is the key to understanding how we enter the kingdom of God and how we respond to God.

Of course, many caught between skepticism and atheism have rigorously attacked the incarnation. In *The Truth of God Incarnate,* Michael Green highlights three assumptions behind skepticism about the incarnation:[1]

1. there is no divinity in the writing of Scriptures;
2. there is no possibility of miracles;
3. there is no finality about Jesus.

The church saw fit to defend two truths. First, Jesus was both God and man. Second, he was one person, not two. The concern about error in the early church is behind the basic requirements that the apostle John specifies: a confirmation that Jesus came in the flesh and an accompanying confession that Jesus is the Christ. There have been many famous creedal attempts to articulate these truths. Important as these are, it is equally crucial that our approach to this subject be more than abstract and philosophical. Martin Luther described his approach as experiential and devotional, and this is an apt characterization of the way that the Gospels present Jesus. They invite us to walk the road, listen to the talk, and come to a conclusion. "The Scriptures begin very gently and lead us on to Christ as to a man and then to one who is lord over all creatures and, after that, to one who is God. So do I enter delightfully and learn to know God. But the philosophers and doctors have insisted on beginning from above; and so they have become fools. We must begin from below and after that come upwards." The Bethlehem Road begins that gentle pursuit.

The divine needle has been continually at work in embroidering the tapestry of history. When we only look at this part of the pattern—or that—we see its local beauty and significance and admire its gracious lines. But when we stand far enough back and take in the bigger picture, we can make connections. We can relate those prophets to these fulfillments, those laws to these graces, those explanations to these experiences. Especially, we can relate the foreshadowings and fulfillments of the birth narratives to the manifestations of Christ's later ministry. Luther warns about the danger of becoming fools, which brings us back to the need to be wise people who pursue Christ regardless of personal cost and prejudice, who respond to his own injunction to find out and test if these things that are said about him, especially at his birth, are true or not. This particular guidebook travels on the highway laid by the historic creeds, and it denies as subversive those who seek to break up this road by denying the uniqueness of Christ. Make up your own mind as you travel it for yourself.

"Silent night . . . all is calm, all is bright." Bright, maybe, but hardly silent or calm! As you read the birth narratives, you are aware of the hurried movement of people responding to directives. There is an air of uncertainty and restlessness. All is not peace and light. The frequency of "Do not be afraid" indicates shocked systems and jangled nerves. It is a troubled time. Herod tries to deceive the wise men and is then responsible for the murder of infants. Joseph and Mary have to flee to Egypt. Like a newspaper headline that appears one day and is relegated to the back page the next, the significance of this birth seems to blow over. However, long after the Magi have returned home and Herod's stooges have forgotten their late-night research about some upstart ruler, snatches of Mary's song can still be heard: "My spirit rejoices in God my Savior. . . . His mercy extends to those who fear him. . . . He has performed mighty deeds. . . . He has scattered those who are proud. . . . He has filled the hungry with good things. . . ." Like a duet, the refrains of mercy and favor mingle and mesh into a single theme—salvation. Mary's lyric sings the universal authority of Christ and anticipates the total renewal that his saving work will achieve. We haven't heard from a single professional theologian yet! Just bleating sheep, camels' hooves, scurrying footsteps, and a pure voice singing to the wind.

 The invitation to step inside a barn near the Bethlehem Road is equally an invitation to begin a journey pursuing this child through the years and observing his baptism, listening to his teaching, staring at his cross, and shouting into an empty tomb. The manger states a fact: he came. It also raises a question: why? To celebrate the fact is pointless unless the question is invoked and unless a memory is provoked, so powerful and subversive that it shatters stable sentiment and recovers the meaning of that cross and that tomb. Of course, many people will look at the manger as some folk look through the glass on the maternity ward at the newly born baby of a friend. To visit is kind and courteous; to express best wishes is sincere and thoughtful; but fortunately the baby demands nothing and the next appointment can be kept. The baby does not threaten the schedule. It seems that society has a vested interest in ensuring that when Christ does go public in a big way, at Christmas, that he does so as a baby only. Let us not bother with the fact that the child became a man, learned to speak, and addressed his words to me. The babbling Christ fits nicely into the arms of Santa Claus. The Christ who said, "I am the way, the truth and the life" must have picked up some serious mental problems on the way, and the Christ who said, "All power is given to me" had clearly developed a megalomania inconsistent with the manger. Christ in swaddling clothes is memorable, but controllable. The Jesus of Galilee and the risen Christ will not so easily be rocked to sleep.

Zechariah's priestly prayer in the temple for the redemption of Israel, way back at the beginning of the story, seemed mere form and formality in an age of spiritual barrenness and fruitlessness. And yet an old messianic prophecy said a shoot would come up from the stump of Jesse. The stump was a good image for a hope that had been stripped down. The greenery of good times had long since withered, and the trunk of personal and national stability had long since been felled. Simply put, in Bethlehem a shoot came up from the stump, and it has continued to shoot forth in other seemingly lifeless stumps in the forest of God's husbandry.

JORDAN TRAIL

MAP REFERENCE

*T*hen Jesus came from Galilee to John at the Jordan to be baptized by him. And John tried to prevent Him, saying, "I have need to be baptized by You, and are You coming to me?" But Jesus answered and said to him, "Permit it to be so now, for thus it is fitting for us to fulfill all righteousness." Then he allowed Him. Then Jesus, when He had been baptized, came up immediately from the water; and behold, the heavens were opened to Him, and He saw the Spirit of God descending like a dove and alighting upon Him. And suddenly a voice came from heaven, saying "This is My beloved Son, in whom I am well pleased."

Matthew 3:13–17

You couldn't expect a Jewish family to get excited about a permanent home in the land of the Pharaohs. Joseph and Mary were relieved to return to Israel after their time of refuge in Egypt. They settled in Nazareth, where they raised Jesus, who no doubt tested the child-proofing of the carpenter's workshop by chewing on wood shavings and collecting splinters. It's significant that the Gospels have little to report about his early life, presumably because he was utterly normal. There are no ecstatic school reports predicting a meteoric career, no accounts of his healing pets or performing amazing feats of strength. He didn't glow in the dark at bedtime or write theological books before other kids had learned to speak.

There was one occasion that suggested unusual abilities. His parents took him to Jerusalem for the official outing that marked his initiation into the observance of Jewish ordinances. His parents lost him for three days and eventually found him in the temple where he was having the time of his life with the law teachers. He was a small-town boy with big-time questions, and it seems that the convictions and conclusions of his adolescent mind created quite a stir amongst the old boys. Mary wasn't particularly impressed with the academics of it all, saving her astonishment for the fact that he could have caused her such anxiety. He said something enigmatic about being in his father's house, which struck Mary as precisely the place he should be, and the sooner they got back to it in Nazareth the better.

Without dissent, he returned with his parents to the village where he dutifully and obediently matured into adulthood. There is no hint that he viewed himself or was regarded by others as a prophetic protégé. He was clearly gifted, extremely well liked, and remarkably astute for his years, but he was not a *prima donna* and definitely not as strange or intense as his cousin John.

Eighteen silent and secluded years passed before the two of them crossed paths in public. On a bank of the Jordan River the old world met the new and that prophetic promise caught sight of its fulfillment as John looked at Jesus.

John was certainly not everyone's idea of a good time. He would ravage our gentle lead-ins to services with their finely tuned choirs and warm-up humor. After years in the wilderness, he burst onto the scene with all the social graces and poise of a caveman who had gate-crashed a high-society tea party. Most of us know what it's like when we think the pain-killing injection has done its work and we're just getting into the piped music in the dentist's surgery when, suddenly and excruciatingly, the drill hits a nerve. Prophetic ministry had the knack of exposing those methods and messages that tried to get the job done by immunizing men and women to the cost, the shame, and the pain that have to be faced when truth breaks in upon the soul.

John was a divine drill without the novocaine. Nerves screamed and social manners squirmed as he proclaimed his message of repentance. He erupted in the consciousness of his audience as uncomfortably as the strong, warm desert wind, that *ruach,* that heavenly breath that let a man know he was being acted upon. His voice was raw and penetrating, and the words tumbled out like poured gravel. His approach was not the touch of silk but the rub of rough sandpaper. His dress and diet set him apart as an outdoorsman, wild and woolly. He was considered to be a prophet of the old school—all guts and glory—and it was not without cause that he was often compared to Elijah. Since not even the oldest in his audience had any experience with a real live prophet, it is not surprising that John's ministry provoked such interest and curiosity. The Old Testament had suddenly come alive again after an extended period of holding its breath.

 John did not look for an audience. His congregation came to him. His messages were not laced with pleasantries or anecdotes, and he did not seem the least bit concerned with the crowd's comfort. He did not give invitations— he issued demands. He was direct and confrontational and did not preach with a view to being invited to itinerate around suburban synagogues. He had no theological certification or ministerial connections, but he did have the most necessary and least common credential: he was "a man sent from God." There was no waffle with John, no "skyscraper preaching" (story after story), no attempt to be liked or accepted, save by God. He spoke of impending danger and the need to be right with both God and man.

He called people to repentance from their sin and declared that their liturgical confessions were a waste of breath if unaccompanied by evidences of change. He denounced those whose spiritual security rested on their relationship to Abraham. Neither religious pedigree nor religious performance would be sufficient insurance policies on the day of judgment. His actions reinforced his full frontal verbal assault on descent and indecency. Baptism was understood as a rite of passage for Gentiles who were converting to Judaism. Logically, to baptize Jews was to declare that without repentance from sin and a right relationship with God, the chosen race was no different from the unconverted Gentile. John proclaimed both God's mercy and the need for social justice. He warned that those who lived a pretense would feel the chainsaw of judgment felling them to the dirt. Clearly, he did not deliver an "Anti-stress and Pro-success" seminar package, but he did provoke a response—both anger and conviction. Such was his impact that he was actually mentioned as a possible candidate for the vacant messiah seat. His directness therefore brought him the temptation to think of himself as other than who he was.

However, his response to such suggestions was adamant, almost harsh. "No way. . . . I'm not even qualified to be the slave of the coming Messiah and take his shoes off. . . . I am not the Christ. . . . If you think my message is hot, then be warned that it's like water compared to his fire. . . . If you think I'm heavy-duty then wait till you hear him. . . ."

Given his role as preparer of the way, John's presentation of Jesus would be a determining factor in the people's expectations. We find that John made no attempt to launch Jesus' ministry with a sparkling pen portrait that would encourage the crowds to feel that the ideal place for future family picnic plans would have to be wherever Jesus happened to be located. In fact, we find the very opposite. The image conjured by John is vivid: "He will baptize you with the Holy Ghost and fire. . . . His winnowing fork is in his hand to clear his threshing floor and to gather the wheat into the barn, but he will burn up the chaff with unquenchable fire. . . . Behold the Lamb of God, who takes away the sin of the world. . . . One more powerful than I will come. . . ."

Anyone who came into contact with John would have been aware of his power. When people perceived the courageous passion and bold intensity with which he spoke and when they took stock of the fact that he emerged from the desert where all those violent guerrillas and revolutionaries hatched their plans, when they observed the bitter reaction of the religious leaders to his preaching, what did they imagine the one "more powerful" than he would be like? Wilder than John? More forceful? Louder? More controversial? Was it possible?

Meanwhile, it seems that God did nothing to tone John down. No, Jesus was not going to be a desert revolutionary. Yes, he would perfectly manifest the love of God. However, the point here is that John is revealing something of the true nature of spiritual forcefulness in the Son of God, that could not be confused with political control on the one hand or religious rule on the other. The power would be neither of the sword nor of the temple.

We should be relieved that God determined the strategies for Jesus' preparation for ministry; consequently, John must have been the perfect foretaste, as well as the ideal forerunner. Certainly, there are important and distinctive differences between John and Jesus, but we should not ignore the consummate continuity between them. If we do, then we will fail to understand the full impact of Christ's radical and spiritually violent assault on the powers of evil.

If, after the hurricane of John's prophetic proclamation, after the laserlike pointedness of his witness to the light, we think that Jesus was going to be a popular teacher who eased into ministry and secured a following with velvet speech and social grace, then we have made a big mistake. If John got people agitated, then Jesus would more so. If John was an offense to accepted taste, then Jesus would be more so. If John struck people as too strong, too indecently explicit, then Jesus would be more so.

It was during one of John's prophetic discourses that Jesus edged his way forward, walked into the water, and firmly yet quietly asked John to baptize him.

You could have forgiven the bystanders their annoyance. John was just getting into his graphic, apocalyptic stride when this stranger put a damper on it all by requesting baptism. Admittedly, that's exactly what John was there for, but their imaginations had been shaped, fired, glazed, and kilned by John's preaching, and their expectations of the one who was to come were in sharp contrast to this silent, almost demure figure who had interrupted the epic messianic movie that was rolling in their heads. They'd just have to wait for the next scene, when this newcomer got out of the water. Little did they know they were in for a live preview showing!

Baptists are not easily blown out of the water! However, on this occasion, there was every reason for John to be perplexed. What's the deal here? The ripples in the water that marked Jesus' entry into the river might as well have been a tidal wave that was about to flush John's theology down river. He'd been happy to pronounce that this person was the Lamb of God, who would take away the sin of the world, for thankfully that meant that there was one person who did not need to be baptized. No sin here, no baptism needed. Next, please. Others were watching, so this was no time for public debate, but speaking under his breath, he did need to get straight to the point. "What on earth are you thinking of? You want me to baptize you? We've got this thing completely the wrong way round." John's earnest, almost agitated whisper was answered by an authoritative yet gentle insistence that allayed John's objections. "Just let it be this way because this is the right thing for me to do."

John's humility had dissented, but now that same virtue consented. For John to baptize Jesus was a major event by any standard, but it is not presented by the Gospel writers as the climax of the incident. The main act was still to come.

John's voice was something. The new voice that was heard as Jesus came out of the water was something else. From the very beginning of his account, Luke is concerned not only to describe human responses to various events, but also to report heavenly revelation regarding what those events signified. The angelic explanation to the shepherds of what had happened in Bethlehem is twice as long as the actual description of the nativity. Without the meaning, the event was dumb. Time and time again, above the chattering and questioning of human voices, another voice is heard—by Zechariah, by Mary, by Joseph. Through the prophetic communication of Simeon and Anna, the revelation continues to amplify the original message: Jesus is unique, and what he is going to do will have universal application.

Just as spoken revelation heralded his physical arrival in public as a baby, so it accompanied his vocational arrival in public as an adult. What that voice said was not primarily for a crowd—if in fact they heard anything at all—nor was it for John. The most needy recipient of that message was Jesus himself. "This is my beloved son, in whom I am well pleased."

This message is not a polite and relieved vote of thanks after a well-executed religious ceremony. ("Splendid chap and jolly good show!") It is not like a vague, schoolmasterly, end-of-year progress report that affirms the student but leaves the recipient wondering if the pupil could or should do better. ("Nice lad—pleased with progress.") On the contrary, it is a heart-pounding, breath-stopping volley of affection that cannot be contained within heaven and explodes on to earth.

There's a marvelous moment in à "Tom and Jerry" sequence when the senior mastiff beams with pride at junior's efforts to keep the cat at bay, and he exclaims, "That's ma boy!" Sure, it seems a big leap from Christ's baptism to a cartoon canine, but to miss the personal, generous, thrilled, and fatherly affirmation of Jesus here is to miss a lot.

 Many things are being established in this baptismal event that will be developed more fully later on. Among others, let's note what we learn about Jesus' relationship with people and with God.

1. JESUS' RELATIONSHIP WITH PEOPLE

At the outset of his public ministry, Jesus humbly identified with the world that John addressed which included both the Jewish pharisee and the Gentile Roman soldier, later co-venturers in his removal from public life, albeit temporarily. Voluntarily, he put himself in the same place as those who were being told that they needed to repent of their sin and be baptized.

John had been right to balk at his request, for what possible logic was there in a sinless one pretending that he needed to repent? John was in order to point out that this was neither appropriate nor advisable. For Jesus it was clearly not a matter of pretense, but of obedience. He made the choice to be "numbered with transgressors" long before a kangaroo court insisted upon it. Despite his separation from sin, he was in solidarity with the sinner.

2. JESUS' RELATIONSHIP WITH GOD

Long before we see what Jesus can mean to people, we see what Jesus means to Father God. The first recorded words of Jesus in the Gospels had intimated an early understanding of a unique relationship with God: "Did you not know that I must be in my Father's house?" It was this sensitive and discerning commitment to the will of the Father that had brought Jesus to this baptism and that would become the sole criterion for his decisions and the sole motivation for his actions. From the beginning, he is not presented as a solo artist whose self-sufficient giftedness is going to guarantee one miraculous exhibition after another. He is portrayed as a son whose security and sufficiency rests not on his successful performance but on his father's provision and personality. Although this relationship with Father God emphasizes the nature of his divinity, it also serves to illustrate the needs of his humanity. He did not need a divine voice to give him some good advertising to launch a charismatic crusade. What he needed was what he got and what any son requires: acceptance, approval, and a sense of achievement. He was not an insecure entrepreneur who needed an endorsement from a famous figure, but a secure son who needed endearment from a trusted father.

Jesus' baptism is thus an overture that brings together the chords of the great themes of the Gospel: his identification with people in their sin and suffering and his intimacy with his father. His relationship with his father and his redemption of people are the cause and effect of the Gospel. He is the Savior because he is the Son.

All of us need affirmation, appreciation, authentication. We seek for such solace and succor in many ways and many places. We naturally prefer the wateringholes of social intercourse, the springs of human ingenuity, and the fountains of aesthetic pleasure to the ragged banks of the dirty Jordan river, where we are reminded that the only sure basis for vocation and fulfillment is an agreement with God's will for our lives. The voice of John that speaks of our responsibility for our actions and our accountability to God does not sit well on the ears of those who make a virtue of independence and an idol of self-determination. The voice of God that identifies Jesus as the one to watch is distracting to those whose eyes are set on prevailing cultural models of success. Baptism that represents a turning from sin and a turning to God is not what most people have in mind when they express their desire to "make a splash."

Like Jesus, we must be convinced that a relationship with Father God is the only sure basis of determining our relationships in this world and navigating our way through its contrary currents. We need to be assured of his acceptance of us, which means we need to know his unconditional love and forgiveness. We need to be secure in his approval, which means we need to know what he invites and equips us to be. We need to have a sense of achievement and significance, which means we need to know what he wants us to do with our lives. But how can this be? Well, stick around and watch how Jesus demonstrated exactly who the Father is and what he wants to give and how we can know Him.

Jesus and John went their separate ways. Later, while he was in prison, John wondered momentarily why there wasn't more strong-arm, Old-Testament-style confrontation coming from Jesus. John's life was on the line, and he needed evidence that his labors had not been in vain. Like the prophets before him, he paid the full price, as the seductive voices of adultery and dance at one of Herod's parties demanded his death as a floor prize. The Gospels leave us in no doubt about the violence that assaults those who dare to challenge the world's status quo with the truth of another kingdom, and we cannot hide the fact by quickly replacing the lid on the platter that served the head of John the Baptist.

Later, when John's disciples went and told Jesus about the murder of John, something about the ultimate cost of obedience to the Father, something about the greatest sacrifice that would ever be made, must have passed through the mind of the one who was "more powerful" than John.

DESERT TRACK

MAP REFERENCE

*T*hen Jesus, being filled with the Holy Spirit, returned from the Jordan and was led by the Spirit into the wilderness, being tempted for forty days by the devil. And in those days He ate nothing, and afterward, when they had ended, He was hungry. And the devil said to Him, "If you are the Son of God, command this stone to become bread." But Jesus answered him, saying "It is written, 'Man shall not live by bread alone, but by every word of God.'" Then the devil, taking Him up on a high mountain, showed Him all the kingdoms of the world in a moment of time. And the devil said to Him, "All this authority I will give You, and their glory; for this has been delivered to me, and I give it to whomever I wish. Therefore, if You will worship before me, all will be Yours." And Jesus answered and said to him, "Get behind Me, Satan! For it is written, 'You shall worship the Lord your God, and Him only you shall serve.'" Then he brought Him to Jerusalem, set Him on the pinnacle of the temple, and said to Him, "If You are the Son of God, throw Yourself down from here. For it is written: 'He shall give His angels charge over You, To keep You,' and, 'In their hands they shall bear You up, lest You dash Your foot against a stone.'"

And Jesus answered and said to him, "It has been said, 'You shall not tempt the Lord your God.'" Now when the devil had ended every temptation, he departed from Him until an opportune time.

Luke 4:1–13

Much more than water had been displaced in the Jordan. With the echo of that voice still resonating in his head, Jesus sensed that the historic river had now become a watershed in his life. It was of no less significance than it had been for the Israelites centuries before when they had crossed it and entered the land of promise. Yes, it had been a necessary rite of passage for him, and he felt a strong urge to get away for a few days to pray and ponder and let the boom of that incredible communication die down.

Later that evening, as he tracked into the stillness of the desert mountains, he realized that he was moving less out of personal desire than out of an instinctive response to a familiar impulse. He had learned to recognize the promptings of this palpable presence. What may have begun as a personal need to retreat, mentally recollect, and spiritually reorient had now become the firm conviction that he was about to enter a critical boot camp before he engaged in the battle. In a few days he would wonder if the comparison with the Israelites was relevant. They went from the wilderness to "wonderful." The baptism had been "wonderful." Was not the wilderness therefore a regression?

It was many things, including the place where satyrs were said to dwell, where nights were coldest and shadows were longest; it was certainly a far cry from Nazareth. As he gathered his outer coat about him before he attempted to sleep on that first night in the wilds, he must have recalled the sensation of security that he felt back home—the warmth of human touch and household comfort, as well as that strange but heady mix of smells: baked bread, warm wine, and resinous timber.

A sharp chill shuddering through his frame would have been sufficient to fragment the memory. Perhaps it occurred to him that this coldness had an unusual quality. The more tightly he pulled his coat around him, the less he felt its protective pressure. The more he sought to blanket himself with evening meditations, the more he felt that the covers of his soul were being stripped away. He not only felt exposed and vulnerable, but almost weightless. It would have been the ideal moment for that voice to speak again, but the skies were dumb and dark.

The temptations of Jesus are presented as the necessary initiation into his ministry. Before he engaged his public, he faced his protagonist. In this wilderness barracks, something basic had to be settled about the nature of the campaign, the strategy for combat, the deployment of resources. That he was a unique person with a unique power was not in question. But how he presented himself and how he performed his mission were the subjects of examination.

It would have been Jesus himself who gave this account of his own private dealings with these issues. When he actually described it to the disciples is a matter of conjecture, but it makes sense to think that it was after his resurrection, by which time his followers would have had a retrospective understanding of the reasons he had chosen to veil his identity in some ways and manifest it in others. If this is the case, then the instructive purposes of this testimony take on a particular significance in that they prepare for the reception of the Holy Spirit at Pentecost with the consequent concerns about the nature and exercise of spiritual power.

Regardless of when he shared this experience, it is clear that it expresses and explains Jesus' foundational convictions about his relationship *with* God, *to* the world, and *against* the devil. Attested by the divine, he would now be tested by the demonic. He had not been lured to that place but led, and it is reasonable to suppose that the foe hardly anticipated the inevitable confrontation with much relish. It is not an imaginary debate or a dramatized soliloquy. Jesus' account is realistic, vivid, and utterly consistent with the biblical portrayal of the devil as distinctively personal and deceptively powerful. Jesus would have been familiar with the devil's voice as recorded in Genesis, where God was slandered in man's hearing, and in Job, where man was slandered before God. There were clues about the devil's origin, character, and fate for those like Jesus who had read such great prophets as Isaiah and Ezekiel, both of whom give insights into an angelic being of beauty and brilliance, whose tragic corruption and violent fall are graphically presented. Later in his ministry Jesus would momentarily draw back the curtain to reveal his pre-existence when he said, "I watched Satan fall from heaven like a flash of lightning."

Lucifer, a being of high position, was beyond reproach until he traded in the closed market of divine authority and worship. Instead of releasing delegated authority, he retained it for himself, and instead of directing worship to God, he desired it for himself. History is the handbook that illustrates the demonic necessity to take authority and thus demand worship. Power cannot maintain itself without respect. In seeking worship, Lucifer challenged authority and by taking authority in his own name, he demanded worship. In Augustine's terms, the sin of pride is simply the wish "to exist as one's own." Unsatisfied with being glorious on God's terms, Lucifer intended to be magnificent on his own account.

The choice to revolt is not presented as being prompted by any outside temptation, for as one hiker has put it, "He revolted from himself outwards." In *Paradise Lost,* Milton perceives that a grievance against God is the inevitable offspring of the cohabitation of self-indulgent pity and self-exalting pride. Another hiker has commented, "In the midst of a world of light and love, of song, feast and dance, he could find nothing to think about more interesting than his own prestige."[2]

The cult of self-esteem had a treacherous beginning and the forceful eviction of the rebel and his supporters from heaven is evidence that it will meet a treacherous end and will forever be barred. Satan's pride flaunts itself in the face of God's goodness and love. To rebel against your creator is to rebel against the very source of your power, to bite the hand that feeds you. Thus sin is folly, and thus the proverb, "In the mouth of the foolish is a rod of pride." It is the folly of the moon trying to outshine the sun, the source of its light, or "it is like the scent of a flower trying to destroy the flower." It is always the fool who establishes his independence by declaring that there is no God—but one, of course.

At the heart of demonic defiance is the error as expressed by Isaiah, "I will make myself like the Most High." The demonic delusion that Satan has power to create, "to make himself," rests on the idea that he is a self-existent being, denying that he is created and consequently subordinate. The anatomy of violence and sin in the Scriptures that Jesus knew was not in a blow-by-blow account of a bloody warfare in heaven, but in the precise delineation of pride that the book of Proverbs says will precede disgrace and destruction. Jesus would have read the description of the fate of "the son of the morning" in Isaiah ("fallen from heaven . . . cast down to the earth . . . brought down to the grave. . . .") and in Ezekiel ("I drove you in disgrace from the mount of God. . . . I expelled you O guardian cherub . . . I threw you to the earth . . ."). The fact of this expulsion is sufficient proof that the sum of Satan's violence was powerless against God's might, but clearly a would-be usurper will resort to any measure, no matter how violent, to maintain the appearance of power. In the words of one busker,

> And so the Great Pretender must continue to pretend
> That he didn't fall like lightning from the sky. . . .[3]

The goal of the ultimate narcissist and nihilist, eroticist and apostate, is "to transform humanity into God," to convince every person of the offer made to Eve: "You will be like God!" As with Eve in the Garden and Jesus in the wilderness, he does not come as a disembodied spirit, offering ethereal rewards. Instead, he specializes in using material media, whether people, places, or possessions, to embody his principles and practices. Of course, he also operates through a host of spiritual forces that assail and afflict, possess and plunder at the dictates of his presidency over unified evil. It is against this background and with this ruler that Jesus now wages war.

An astute observer on our hike has commented: "Satan is condemned to an eternity of rationalizing Satan into God, and God into Satan."[4] At the same time that he wishes to be as God, he seeks to demean and defame the character and actions of God so that, in Baudelaire's words, "If there is a God, then he is the devil." The object of all Satan's attacks, on whomever or whatever, is God himself. His destruction of humankind is but the defacing of the image of God. Job may well be devastated by the successive blitzkriegs on his stuff, his skin, and finally his spirit, but the main point of it all is not to destroy Job, so much as to induce Job "to curse God and die."

The temptations presented to Jesus are bad enough for his sake, but the ultimate concern is to cause Jesus to do something that will score against God by denying his will and the trustworthiness of his love. With subtlety and subterfuge, and of course, with sensitivity and style, Satan approaches Jesus with his most seductive and suggestive lines.

The devil can waltz with you and contribute to your charity ball while his cohorts are burglarizing your home in your absence. Jesus is in no doubt about the reality of the devil's power or the extent of his influence.

 In his account, Luke prefaces the temptation scene with a genealogy, the last words of which are "son of Adam, son of God." It is Luke's concern to clearly present Jesus as Adam "Mark II." This is important because Jesus is confronting Satan as a man, not as a superman. The devil tempts Jesus to become a superman and put on his red cape and pull off all manner of sensational capers.[5] This would kill two birds with one stone. By becoming a superman:

1. Jesus would surrender his *identification with people* by becoming someone that they could not be;
2. Jesus would surrender his *intimacy with his Father* by doing something his Father had not told him to do.

By accepting the temptation to become a superman, Jesus would cease to be both Savior and Son. The point behind Jesus' use of Scripture to resist and repudiate the temptations is that all the verses he quoted were from the book of Deuteronomy—instructions *given to man*. Jesus is not representing the angels but men, so he puts himself under the law, standing where Adam once stood. Just as the outcome of Adam's failure affected all people for evil, so the outcome of this head-to-head would affect all people for good.

Jesus was not ignorant about the devil's stratagems. Later

in his teaching he would say, "It was not this way from the beginning," so he was cognizant not only of God's original plan for purity but also of Satan's original plot to pollute. Jesus knew that the first Adam was not left in Eden to come up with a theory about God as a result of his deductions from available evidence. God was there to be known intimately, not inferentially. The very nature of that relationship between Adam and God had been a sufficient goad for Satan's hatred, without the added fact that dominion had been entrusted to these "new kids on the block."

The opening words of Satan's welcome message to them from the local reptile house are, "Did God really say . . . ?" Couched in this apparent interest is the very strategy of evil. As with Jesus in the wilderness, the communications to Eve are a distortion and come as stimuli, not as statements. They force a response at the same time that they suggest an alternative way of looking at things and doing things. Satan's characteristic method of attack is to sow doubt and then secure denial, and in the book of Genesis, with a minimum of maneuvers, he directly challenges three fundamentals:

1. *God's Word:* It is the Word of God that creates, governs, and cares for what is created. Therefore, to destroy the bonds of love between God and man, the trustworthiness of that communication must be discredited.
2. *God's Judgment:* This is denied by suggesting that the threat is not only imaginary, but also impossible to execute. To deny judgment is to make light of sin, which can then be planned without fear and performed with impunity.
3. *God's Goodness:* This is subverted by the suggestion that God has set unwarranted limitations on his creation and furthermore has threatened them with judgment.

Typically, Satan persuades the one being tempted to disobey by guaranteeing them:

safety—because there is no threat of punishment;
satisfaction—because what is being obtained is desirable;

success—because we have the power to achieve
whatever we want to do.

The temptations that Jesus faced came with all these guarantees, but they also bore the telltale signs of malevolence, dressed up in good manners and suitably disguised with rented evening wear and patent shoes. What took place was a power play. The devil sought to change Christ's power of love into a love of power, tempting him to use legitimate power in ways that are pragmatically justifiable, humanitarian, and effective, but inconsistent with prior and proven convictions and calling. Satan was a "grasper" but fundamental to our understanding of Jesus' incarnation is his willingness to release legitimate rights to inviolable divinity, to refuse to "grasp" legitimate position and power, and instead, to embrace the "no-guarantee clauses" of humanity. The temptation to "grasp" was before him again in the desert. There were three distinctive assaults that challenged Jesus physically, spiritually, and vocationally.

1. THE SUGGESTION

Turn stones into bread!
Weak after extensive fasting, Jesus is encouraged to turn rock into roll. What could be more humanitarian? Why jeopardize the future with unscheduled starvation? What could be more legitimate than using one's power to provide for oneself and protect one's ministry? It is fine to help yourself if that helps you to serve God better. Furthermore, what better way to serve people than to eliminate hunger by turning gravel into grain?
The command: Man does not live by bread alone but by every word that comes from the mouth of God.

2. THE SUGGESTION

Throw yourself from the pinnacle of the temple!
A picture is worth a thousand words. The visual impact of a miraculous hang-glide without the equipment would achieve more than a thousand sermons on as many mounts. The message is important, but time is too short to get it to

everyone personally. A miracle is a much better way to advertise and a surer way of proving one's power. People are more likely to believe what they see than what they hear. The event could be restaged at other venues, and the large crowds that would attend could only benefit from the experience. Who knows? It could be performed off the Coliseum in Rome or off an Athenian column. What possible objection could there be to using one's power to introduce oneself to a mass audience and secure their attention? Angels would be lining up to be on both the security detail and the crowd-control unit of such a successful rally.

The command: Do not put the Lord your God to the test!

3. THE SUGGESTION

Worship me and you'll get all the kingdoms of the world that you're after. Instead of establishing Christendom person by person, what could be more effective than securing an immediate global control, thus ensuring unity of fellowship and uniformity of faith. Such a conquest would surely be ethical, for it would avoid needless pain and suffering, as well as securing the greatest good for the greatest number in the least time and with the least effort. Was it not the mission to reach the world? Yes, it comes with a personal price tag for Jesus, but cannot this submission to Satan be justified on the basis that his sacrifice is for everyone else's gain? Is this not what being the Messiah is all about?

The command: Worship the Lord your God and serve only him!

In every case, Jesus lets the Word of God confront and confound the word of the devil. It is the written word that protects from entrapment, that preserves integrity, that prevents enticement, and that promotes truth. Notice that Jesus does not speak in his own name, or in his own defense. Nowhere does he personalize the attack, but in every instance, he perceives it for what it is—an attempt to challenge the validity of God's control and the veracity of God's communication. At no point would Jesus concede that God could be glorified through premature or presumptuous action. The end did not justify the means. The temptation to use power to provide for oneself or to prove oneself to others, even in God's name, was rejected as not even worthy of prayerful consideration. What he needed and what people wanted were not necessarily what God willed. At the outset of his ministry, Jesus personally proves the strength of three key convictions that will become the traits of his life and teaching and the basis for his continuing triumph over Satan.

> Jesus knew that he was . . .
>   fathered by God,
>   founded on Scripture,
>   filled with the Holy Spirit.

I remember driving into Paris with an evangelistic team many years ago and passing a van that was encrusted with dirt and grime. The vehicle was worn, aging, and clearly on its last legs. It bore the scars of long journeys and quests. In the filth and dust on the back window, an unknown person had written these words: *"Vive l'alternative!"* Long live the alternative! I have never forgotten it. In a nutshell, those words represent the heart of Satan's attack on Jesus and Everyman. If he cannot destroy the ways and words of God through flagrant rebuttal, he will suggest an alternative route to blessing. He will not necessarily deny that there is a heaven, but he will suggest another means of access—the way of nirvana rather than the way of the cross or the way of man's righteous deeds rather than the way of Christ's redeeming death. Simply by obeying, trusting, and fearing God, Jesus overcame the temptation to accept any alternative to God's will. Where the first Adam was overcome, Jesus overcame.

In Eden, demonic suggestions enticed Eve into dialogue, and thus Satan's insights were treated as if they were on a par with God's truth and worthy of due and reasoned consideration. The only answer to the question, "Has God really said?" is "Thus says the Lord!" Jesus showed that our communication in the face of lies should be prophetic, not dialectic—declaration, not dialogue. Aided only by our experience, our intuitions, our rationality, we cannot discuss and debate with error or explain truth. The explanation of God's Word does have dominion over Satan's questions; God's commands hold authority over specious questions.

 Jesus was like a junction box for the human race. To overcome him would be to have unstoppable access to and control over all other power lines. Satan's attempt to plug Jesus into his grid failed, and in the process of trying, Satan got badly burned. There would be no other efforts to recruit Christ, but every opportunity would be taken to destroy him. The bitter aftertaste was not in the mouth of the one tempted this time, but in the mouth of the tempter. There was no fall through disobedience, but rather a descent of obedience from that mountain into the world. The result of that first fall-out had been the settling of the dust of death and spiritual drought and barrenness. Jesus' triumph would be marked by the gift of the water of life, quenching thirst and irrigating fertile hearts. Those who had hidden from God in the bushes of guilt could now hide from condemnation in Christ's grace. Way back at the beginning, despite the rubble of Eden's fallen possibilities, the great contractor had promised a reconstruction. He said that the seed of the woman would crush the serpent's head. In the wilderness, the serpent had surely been stunned, but the crucial engagement was yet to come. However, it was clear that the reign of a stronger kingdom than the kingdom of darkness had emerged from the desert, albeit weary, weak, and hungry.

In *After the Fall*, Arthur Miller spoke for all hikers who have wandered like Cain, apart from the governance of God's word: "I am consigned to an endless argument with myself. . . ." To argue with yourself is the only alternative when you have ceased to talk with God. The good news that Jesus brought has to do with the reopening of communications with heaven, and the defeat of temptation in the wilderness was the first of many successful destructions of Satan's jamming devices. Emboldened and empowered, Jesus left the desert for more familiar places, where usually one has less reason to be threatened, but as he would find out, there would be more reason to be alert.

NAZARETH ROAD

MAP REFERENCE

*T*hen Jesus returned in the power of the Spirit to Galilee, and news of Him went out through all the surrounding region. And He taught in their synagogues, being glorified by all. So He came to Nazareth, where He had been brought up. And as His custom was, He went into the synagogue on the Sabbath day, and stood up to read. And He was handed the book of the prophet Isaiah. And when He had opened the book, He found the place where it was written:

> "The spirit of the Lord is upon Me,
> Because He has anointed Me to preach the gospel
>   to the poor.
> He has sent Me to heal the brokenhearted,
> To preach deliverance to the captives
> And recovery of sight to the blind,
> To set at liberty those who are oppressed,
> To preach the acceptable year of the Lord."

Then He closed the book, and gave it back to the attendant and sat down. And the eyes of all who were in the synagogue were fixed on Him. And He began to say to them, "Today this Scripture is fulfilled in your hearing." So all bore witness to Him, and marveled at the gracious words which proceeded out of His mouth.

Luke 4:14–22

In that wilderness encounter, it was the devil's expense account that had been loaded to the hilt, despite the fact that Jesus didn't eat a thing. Had he succumbed to his competitor's buy-out offer, Jesus would have picked up the tab, but it would have been a very different kind of price tag from the one that he would eventually pay. He had left that business meeting uncompromised by false assertions and unfingered by false aspirations. He had rejected the opportunity to establish an instant worldwide corporation that would control nations and appeal to the brightest and the best. Instead, he had opted for going door to door amongst the poor. Luke records that the devil departed "until an opportune time." His slithering retreat is contrasted with the surefooted emergence of Jesus in power and authority, confidence and joy. Clearly, he did not leave that place with his mind dominated by caution or self-preservation. On the contrary, he launched himself with apparent abandon and fearlessness into the public marketplace. However, the "opportune time" was going to be sooner rather than later.

Nazareth was not some backwoods, bumpkin village. It is reckoned to have a population approaching twenty thousand people. Nestled in a hollow on the lower slopes of Galilee, it was within easy reach of arterial highways that took soldiers from Rome to the eastern empire, traders from Alexandria to Damascus, and pilgrims from Iturea in the north to Judea in the south. Jesus had already taught in several synagogues in the surrounding country by the time he returned there so, when he arrived at Sabbath worship, his praise had already gone before him.

It would not be the first time people had turned up for their weekly religious service as usual, pleased to have Jesus there, assured that he would contribute to things atmospheric and liturgical, but completely unprepared for him to say or do anything that would make claims for himself or demands of them. Christ as fellow-congregant or fellow-participant was one thing, but Christ as someone who had a claim to be more than just an equal, more than just a temporary spiritual influence—that was something else. Nor would it be the first time that worshipers were tempted to catnap as the reading of the law followed prayers. However, on this occasion, no one made it to sleep.

There were no professional ministers in the synagogues, and it was common for a noteworthy visitor to be invited to read and preach. The service was going quite well when the president of the assembly accorded Jesus the honor of reading from the scroll of Isaiah that was handed to him. Unrolling it until he found the place that he was looking for, Jesus then stood to deliver it, as was the respectful custom.

The Spirit of the Lord is on me, because he has anointed me to preach good news to the poor. He has sent me to proclaim the freedom for the prisoners and recovery of sight for the blind, to release the oppressed, to proclaim the year of the Lord's favor.

Even the dullest ear could not miss the fact that what they had just heard was at least a very dramatic rendering. There was a tension in the air, like an invisibly stretched cord that had everyone strung out between expectation and marvel at one end and embarrassment and disturbance at the other. Of course, the ability to identify with a scripted characterization is the consummate art of the actor. However, there was nothing about Jesus that gave any hint that he was into theatrics. It would not have been disquieting if he had been intoning Isaiah, the author, but it was the way that his voice captured the personal pronouncement of the subject of the piece that resulted in a momentary awkwardness.

The matronly smiles and cross-congregational knowing glances that had exuded pride in "our fine young man" abruptly ceased, and not an eye was diverted from him as he returned the scroll to the attendant and sat down, the acceptable posture for teaching.

Every communicator studies for that opening sentence. None more explosive, more shocking, more worldview wrenching has been given with such poise and purpose. "To-day this scripture is fulfilled in your hearing." It turned out that it was less like a bombshell that had an immediate impact, than like a planted landmine that would detonate with full force when the implications of his message had sunk in and when the hearers wandered back to this spot. If they had come to hear a pleasant rabbinic tune, they were out of luck. What they got was nothing less than a deafening blast of a ram's horn, which stifled conviviality and startled conscience. The congregation was "astonished" at his communication. There was something about the rhythm that was utterly absorbing, but the lyrics were less accessible.

 The incident in Nazareth is a remarkable introductory summary to the main themes of Jesus' ministry. Succinctly, Jesus is presenting the concerns of his mission and the content of his message. It is more than a manifesto—it is a declaration of war directed to the enemy, to potential volunteer troops, and to prisoners of war. In the words of one hiker, "The emergent picture of the chief figure in the campaign, so far from being a high-souled preacher patiently indoctrinating the multitude with truths of timeless wisdom, is rather that of the strong Son of God, armed with his Father's power, spearheading the attack against the devil and all his works, and calling men to decide on whose side of the battle they will be."[6] His message in Nazareth was not what the campaign promoters and organizers ordered. Jesus is not kissing babies, giving flowers to children and chitchatting with potential voters. Three themes are emphasized that will characterize his ministry.

1. FULFILLMENT

"Today, this scripture is fulfilled in your hearing."

There had been no prophetic inspiration for hundreds of years. John the Baptist had been like the freak eruption of what was considered a dormant volcano. In the meantime, compensating for the lack of prophets, an army of teachers had arisen, and the rabbinic schools flourished, keeping alive the hope that Israel's fortunes would be restored, that the Romans would be purged from Jerusalem, and that all the world would come to the Holy City. This year, next year, sometime . . . never.

Then out of the blue, some unknown Nazarene says . . . *Now!* Jesus invaded his hearers' view of history and holiness with the bold announcement that everything that had been predicted, for which generations had suffered and longed and prayed, had arrived. No longer was it a matter of hoping—it was happening. No longer was it only about future promise—it was about a present fulfillment. He was not giving yet another prophecy that encouraged people to hang on to the frayed rope of Jewish expectation, but making a proclamation that it was time for the hands that for so long had reached out to God for deliverance, to receive that deliverance from God right now.

Of course, there was a problem. Everyone had been puzzled by the fact that Jesus omitted reading the final part of that passage. Instead of finishing with "to proclaim the year of the Lord's favor" he should have gone on to read, "and the day of vengeance of our God." No less than John the Baptist shared the consternation. If the kingdom had come in Jesus and if he was the Messiah, then where was the evidence of judgment? Jesus' answer to John's question was simply to draw attention to the effectiveness of his preaching and healing, as signs that the power of the kingdom was working here and now and overcoming the control of Satan. However, he made it quite clear that although God's rule was actively invasive, it was not yet pervasive. God's rule was evident even though his global realm did not yet appear to be established. In the words of one hiker, the world was enemy-occupied territory, and with the arrival of Jesus, the rightful king had landed and begun a campaign of sabotage.

The present communication of the kingdom's power was serving notice that its sovereignty would continue to be revealed wherever there was submission to its loving, liberating rule. There would be a final and future completion and consummation, when the defeated Satan would be finally destroyed. Meanwhile, all thoughts of the never-never were over *Today* the future had been made present in Jesus.

2. FAVOR

"He has sent me . . . to proclaim the year of the Lord's favor. . . ." Jesus declared his mission in the evocative terms of Old Testament Jubilee. This was a prescribed time for a redistribution of capital, a repossession of property, a release of slaves, a cancellation of debts. It was based on the truths that God was the Creator and ultimate possessor of all land and that just as he had freed his people from Egypt, even so they should practice the remittance of debts and bondages.

At the heart of the understanding of social justice was the character of God, and in particular, his grace. The inexhaustible, undeserved, unfathomable grace of God would be the heart of Jesus' message. It would script his stories and fuel his deeds. He would show that the grace of God knew no exclusive clauses. There was no "too late" or "too bad," "too far gone" or "too far out"; there was no acknowledgment of the differences between race or culture or pre-existing creed. There was no hierarchy of merit, no special recognition based on social standing or financial solvency. Grace would give invitations to the best party in town to the street people; it would welcome home a spendthrift dropout kid, it would pay full daily wages to those who had only worked one hour. Jesus beams and broadcasts the favor of God to the forgotten and the fearful, the disillusioned and the disenfranchised. Grace would "count in" those who had either counted themselves out or been eliminated by others. It would specialize in reaching the irregulars, the irreverent, the irredeemable, the irreligious, the irrelevant.

God's favor destroys all systems of human favoritism and calls into question any explanation of the world that denies his right to bless all men equally with the experience of his salvation and the knowledge of his will. Later, John's first and foremost description of Jesus would be that he was "full of grace" and his summary of what Jesus had given them all was simply "grace upon grace." Even cynical Nazareth admitted that his words were filled with divine grace.

3. FREEDOM

"He has sent me . . . to proclaim freedom to the prisoners. . . ." The preaching of grace always results in the doing of justice, which includes the freeing of those who have been wrongly or unwittingly imprisoned. The grace of God does not just shine a little light into the cells of moral, emotional, intellectual, spiritual, and physical bondage to do a head count. Where the light breaks in, the prisoners break out. Had not the prophets foretold it? "Those who lived in a land of deep darkness—on them the light has shined. . . . For the yoke of their burden, and the bar across their shoulders, the rod of their oppressor, you have broken . . ." In his reading of the Pentateuch, Jesus must have pondered God's words to Moses about his people: "I have heard them crying out. . . . I am concerned about their suffering. . . . I have come down to rescue them. . . ." The captive would be freed from the bonds of sin in order to become a communicant in the blessings of salvation.

 It was impossible to come out of the synagogue at Nazareth and say "Neato!" or "Cool, dude!" Jesus never set out to make people feel good about themselves or feel good about him. This message was hardly designed to impress the public and improve his ratings. Without embarrassment or arrogance, he had claimed to be greater than the prophets. Whereas most rabbis were concerned to establish the credibility of what they said by proof-texting everything in a way that demonstrated the genealogy of tradition behind their thoughts, Jesus spoke directly, authoritatively, and powerfully. More than a political manifesto, his prophetic message was a thumbnail sketch of what was to come in his ministry.

But what was intended as a shower of blessing was received like a hail of bullets. To be frog-marched out of town by a mob intent on killing you is hardly a great start in the ministry. Why did their admiration turn to anger? To be a "local boy made good" was one thing, but to be a "local boy made God" was something else. "Lad of Nazareth" was natural, but "Lord of the nations"? Jesus as a rabbi for holy Jews was great, but as a redeemer for heathen Gentiles? Like thousands after them, they would discover that he could not be employed as a butler to serve their thirsty private interests at the ring of a church bell, nor could they use him as an ecclesiastical clerk to rubber-stamp their customized doctrines, or as a waiter to take their drive-in orders for a ready-to-go religion.

Good news was first bad news. To proclaim freedom implied that there were bondages. To call people to accept his lordship, Jesus confronted their idols. His words scandalized and offended his hearers. Their amazement at his authority and articulateness soon turned to anger at his audacity.

Their oppressive parochialism was suffocating, so Jesus punctured their hermetically sealed insulation tent with a couple of illustrations that definitely let in more than fresh air. Of all the widows in Israel, why was Elijah sent to help a Gentile one? Of all the lepers in Israel, why was Elisha sent to heal a Gentile one? Jesus was giving attested examples of what he had just referred to—the grace of God in action, helping and healing those who could claim no right to be recipients of divine mercy. These were the very people on whom God was meant to take vengeance!

Jesus had dared to challenge the "sole rights" Jewish mentality, and as a result he raised the devil. He had championed Jubilee and threatened their material stability, and he had challenged Jewishness and thus threatened their spiritual security. Jesus seemed to have forgotten that you cannot build a career in the ministry by telling the truth.

He had walked wide-eyed onto the bayonets of pride that guarded the citadels of their material prosperity and religious purity. They responded by demanding:

1. PEDIGREE

"Isn't this Joseph's son?" (Where was that voice from heaven to settle matters?) At first, self-congratulatory applause confirmed the locals' pride in this homegrown product. His chances of making it all the way to the Big League looked pretty good, until he claimed to have more influence than the chief commissioner.

Some were less generous and less credulous. "Is not this the son of Mary?" The memories of her premarital pregnancy and his "illegitimate" origins were not soon forgotten. The crowd had domesticated Jesus to the confines of their own narrow living space. They were blinded by their familiarity and deafened by their gossip to the possibility that when he said he was there at the creation of the planet on which their domiciles existed, he was speaking the truth. On the basis of his pedigree they reduced him to a pathetic upstart at best, a pernicious liar at worst.

2. PROOF

There were some old rival jealousies between Nazareth and Capernaum, and everyone had heard the rumors and stories about some of the miraculous things that Jesus had done among "the enemy." The least he could do was oblige their curiosity and competitiveness by performing some miracles in their service. The miraculous seemed to have been reduced to a party trick. There is no record of Jesus ever resorting to miracles as propaganda to convince the skeptic or cynic, and consequently Mark records that he "could not do any miracles there."

Jesus fearlessly confronted the issue: "Surely you will quote this proverb to me—'Physician, heal thyself!'" He was amazed at their unbelief.

The combination of too much familiarity and too little faith was like a match to dry tinder. Jesus' good news had challenged their exclusiveness and their acquisitiveness. From the outset, Jesus was prescribing the spectacles of grace for their myopic vision, and in a single message he had completely redefined the kingdom of God.

    a) It was for everyone. . . .
    b) It was for everyone as a free gift. . . .
    c) It was for everyone as a free gift right now. . . .

Resentment became rejection. Violated pride spawned violence. Just as his words had been prophetic, so were their actions a foreshadowing of the reaction that would characterize the response of unbelief—hatred and assassination. It had been on the brow of a hill, only a little while ago, that Jesus had rejected the temptation to achieve his mission easily and painlessly. Now, on the brow of another hill, the crowd was threatening to hurl him from the summit. Yet again, he triumphed over an "opportune time" and walked through the crowd and back out onto the open road.

There are all sorts of reasons why we will be tempted to resist the regenerative changes of the Holy Spirit that Jesus outlined as characteristic of his power. The fact is that he continues to call our bluff and anatomize our sorrow and our sin. He identifies the experience of inward poverty, of spiritual bondage, of moral and intellectual blindness, of brokenness. The action agenda that he outlined in Nazareth placed him in active, antagonistic opposition to Satan's rule in the lives of men and women.

However, his mission has never simply been to stop Satan, but to save people. It is significant that Luke immediately gives practical evidences of Jesus' Nazareth declaration. He taught and people's minds were riveted; his words rebuked a fever and exorcised a demon. When he told an experienced fisherman where and how to fish, there was a successful catch. When he shook hands with the untouchable lepers, the renewal of contact brought physical healing and the reintegration of their outcast lives into society. When he forgave sins, people's lives, including their physical ailments, were sorted out. When he invited people to follow him, his word wooed allegiance. He restored relationships, redeemed souls, and redirected lives. To the sick he was a doctor who brought recovery. To the solitary he was a bridegroom who brought rejoicing. To you and me, he still says, "The Spirit of the Lord is upon me to . . ."

Like those from Nazareth, our pride wants to pick at his genealogical tree and argue about the nature of the miraculous. It will even be tempted to ground him for good by throwing him from our highbrow parapets of science and philosophy, sociology and psychology, but despite centuries of our attempts to silence him, nothing less than the grace of God has ensured that he continues to walk through our animosities and our argumentations and to invite us yet again to follow him beyond the next hill.

ROUTE
TWO

*Checking
out some
things
he did . . .*

MAP REFERENCE

On the third day there was a wedding in Cana of Galilee, and the mother of Jesus was there. Now both Jesus and His disciples were invited to the wedding. And when they ran out of wine, the mother of Jesus said to Him, "They have no wine." Jesus said to her, "Woman, what does your concern have to do with me? My hour has not yet come." His mother said to the servants, "Whatever He says to you, do it." Now there were set there six waterpots of stone, according to the manner of purification of the Jews, containing twenty or thirty gallons apiece. Jesus said to them, "Fill the waterpots with water." And they filled them up to the brim. And He said to them, "Draw some out now, and take it to the master of the feast." And they took it. When the master of the feast had tasted the water that was made wine, and did not know where it came from (but the servants who had drawn the water knew), the master of the feast called the bridegroom. And he said to him, "Every man at the beginning sets out the good wine, and when the guests have well drunk, then that which is inferior; but you have kept the good wine until now." This beginning of signs Jesus did in Cana of Galilee, and manifested His glory; and His disciples believed in Him.

John 2:1–11

There was nothing quite like a good feast to get a wedding off to a great start. Food has always had a way of giving meaning to life! Later, the wedding ceremony itself would be celebrated, followed by the torchlit procession of the couple to their new home. The festivities at Cana were typical of those enjoyed by villagers who were thankful for a respite from the laborious effort to scratch out an existence.

Who knows how Jesus was added to the guest list? It appears that Mary was in with the family, maybe even related, and was instrumental in getting Jesus an invitation. Unlike the Essenes who disdained marriage, Jesus was more than happy to participate, even at the risk of appearing insufficiently "serious" or "holy."

Of course, having Jesus attend was not a simple deal anymore, for it was understood that wherever he went, he had some disciples in tow, eager for the chance to enjoy a civilized, not to say free, meal. No doubt Jesus jokingly chided them to eat with mannerly consideration and not make it too obvious that they were "living by faith" and unaccustomed to a limitless supply of finger food. Judging from the way that things happened, it seems that they all behaved themselves pretty well, quietly minding their own business in a corner, as one tends to do at a reception where you are unfamiliar to others.

It was an old rabbinic saying that where there was no wine, there was no joy. To cut a long story short, this party ran out of joy! The laughter and gossip of the guests who still had something in their glass, conveniently drowned the anxious whispers and controlled panic that was taking place backstage. In a culture that esteemed generous hospitality, it would have been a shameful humiliation for the hosts to run out of anything, but especially the liquid refreshment.

Maybe Mary was involved in the catering; maybe she was concerned to defend the honor of her friends. Whatever the reason, she made a beeline for Jesus and agitatedly whispered, "They've no more wine!"

"Well," said Jesus respectfully, "what do you expect me to do about it?" Maybe he suddenly wondered if they were about to run out of bread too, and with that thought, shuddered as he recalled a recent temptation that he had confronted. The fact is that he had every reason to be predisposed against any "party trick" here.

In any case, instant wine production for a local wedding bash was hardly in the serious cosmic order of things. His response to Mary was not dismissive, but it was arguably disengaging. For almost twenty silent years he had grappled with the need to do what he called his "Father's business," and it was perfectly clear that carpentry had not been on his mind—or winemaking for that matter. It was necessary for him to resist lovingly, but firmly, the unconscious pressure of parental prerogative. He must avoid an unwitting insensitivity to the imperative of his Father's will and a need greater than that of the thirsty guests.

Meanwhile, not to be deterred, Mary managed one more strategic whisper, this time to the servants, who were equally upset that there would be nothing to "wet their whistles" out back. I fancy that Jesus had watched her every move and noted the way that her body language drew the servants' attention to where he was standing. Having flicked her head in his direction, she now lowered it, like a well-drilled quarterback, into the conspiratorial huddle. As it turned out, she didn't have any magic moves to share that could advance the cause, but she did say, "If by any chance he . . . you know, the one I showed you . . . happens to say anything to you . . . suggest something . . . whatever he says, do it. . . . And, guys, I mean whatever!"

If there was going to be a touchdown, it would have to come from his coaching. It's a delightful touch. I'm sure that she left them as concerned as she had been before, but I have a sneaky feeling that she was less agitated and was even having to contend with a few milliliters of mischievous hope.

If there was one thing that was utterly irresistible to Jesus it was faith. It was not merely need or crisis that motivated him, but childlike faith. The nature of the mother-son relationship had to function in a new context, and it seems that

Mary's understanding informed and facilitated that adjustment as much as that of Jesus. There was something more than maternal meddling going on at that wedding. As he watched her covering the bases, it could be that Jesus perceived a woman who knew that he was able to do more than organize his disciples for a furtive but frantic trip to the local vintner for some emergency supplies. When she left that huddle, could he have noted the calm with which she walked away, and did she throw him a submissive but knowing smile over her fragile shoulder as she merged with the other guests? In days to come, there would be a woman whose faith would find healing in the hem of his garment and another whose daughter would recover because she believed that a crumb of his love was as good as the whole loaf.

It was not the potential failure of the marriage party that Jesus responded to, so much as the faith of Mary, with all its possible vagueness and whimsy. She models two basic responses that should not only be present at every wedding, but foundational to every relationship and every life.

1. She *turned to* Jesus.
2. She *trusted* Jesus.

These two simple actions form the basis of all prospective joy. Without them, the future is potentially as tasteless and colorless as the insipid water that was the only alternative source of refreshment at that wedding.

 Do you think that Mary put the whole thing from her mind and carried on chatting with her friends? Did she see him out the corner of her eye as he sidled around the room and approached the servants, who tried to look normal and natural as they responded to his greeting? Did he ask them for a top-up, in order to elicit the embarrassing information about the wine shortage? After what Mary had said to them, did they think that he must be a well-heeled local who would send them to get a few cases from his connoisseur's cellar? Or was he a Galilean mafiosi, together with his bodyguards, who knew where there was a stash that had fallen off the back of a cart? That lady had said "whatever," and did he ever oblige with a strange one!

Puzzled but compliant, they proceeded to fill the six huge ceremonial stone jars with water. Done! Take out a jugful of the water? Right . . . he was going to do a little experiment in the kitchen. . . . Maybe he was one of those guys who knew all about herbs and potions, dyes and powders, who could doctor things to make them look real. This would be something to see . . . something exciting to tell the lads about!

No doubt a servant was already heading out back with the jug when Jesus said, "Now take the jug to the headwaiter over there. . . . That's right . . . your boss . . . and ask him if it's good enough to pour." There has never been any doubt that Jesus made big withdrawals from an individual's trust account. We are aware of some of the big heroes of faith, but what about this little guy whose livelihood is on the line and who is going to take a jug of water to an overwrought and worried headwaiter who is desperate for some wine to serve. "Is this good enough to pour, sir?" This was not a joke that would be well received, and yet he did exactly as Jesus said because that's what that lady had told him to do. This was blind obedience.

Everyone knew the vinegar that got slopped out towards the end of such a celebration, so the servant was desperately hoping that only a tiny sip would be taken and that the boss would say yes to anything that was wet, regardless. With eyes as big as brandy glasses, he watched the relieved *maitre d'hotel* take an enormously nervous gulp, close his eyes, open them, look at the jug, lick his lips, and breathe deeply as the warmth of that elixir suffused his cheeks. Meanwhile, his tastebuds were zinging and his throat was on tiptoe for more.

The collectors and experts of vintage wine may know the good years, but they will never know this best year, compared to which, the most valuable Chateau de Rothschild is mere Hawaiian Punch. Actually, like most of God's miracles of grace, this incident brings laughter. The toastmaster fell over himself as he brought the party to a halt. Of course, the poor servant had his eyes shut by then. He had seen that deep breath, clearly the sign of anger, and was now awaiting public humiliation and dismissal. It never came. Instead of an outburst of anger, there was a eulogy of praise, as the toastmaster lauded and applauded the surprised groom, who had not only kept the best wine to the last (a brilliant and novel challenge to tradition!), but had actually served the *best* wine that he, in his humble but expert opinion, had ever tasted.

In the excitement, with the guests reaching for their glasses and their most imaginative superlatives to describe the bouquet and hue of this precocious, full-bodied red, the story suddenly ends. No doubt the servants, who knew what had taken place in the improvised vats, were too busy serving the guests and drinking from the jugs themselves to consider what had happened. Did the bridegroom bemusedly play along with the adulation? What stories did he tell about where he got it, and how did he explain the fact that it was in those stone jars? We'll never know, but we do know that there was no mention of recognition for Jesus.

John tells us that this was Jesus' first miracle. Is this really the one we would have expected as the opener for an illustrious career? Of course not! Turning water into wine at a wedding? Certainly, Jesus saved the hosts from major embarrassment but that's all he saved. Is that a sufficient reason for doing a miracle? The devil's suggestion that he launch his career with a literal launching from the temple parapet was looking attractive, even wise, compared to this cute assist to a small-time caterer in a minor-league town. And don't forget that he didn't even get any credit for it! Admittedly, John does say that he revealed his glory through it, but surely that was a retrospective thing.

So much more could have been made of it. If the truth had been told, people would have traveled from miles around for a free glass of miracle-cabernet, and tasting would have been believing. Perhaps they would have tasted, but would they have seen that the Lord was good . . . or just the wine?

John's Gospel was written later than the others, which perhaps explains why most of the miracles he relates are unique to his account. He avoided repetition. However, he was not trying to entertain us with amazing stories or to go one better than Matthew,

Mark, and Luke; he was encouraging us to ponder the evidence and believe that Jesus was who he said he was, "the Christ, the Son of God." John is after more than intellectual assent. He longs for his readers to respond with all of their being, to all of Christ. For John, the events he describes are more than just take-it-or-leave-it miracles.

1. John said that Jesus did "many other miraculous signs in the presence of his disciples" which he had not recorded. In order to strengthen his self-confessed evangelistic intent, John has made a careful *selection* from the enormous number of things that Jesus did.
2. The importance of the miracle for John is not simply in the event itself, amazing and convincing as it is, but in the way that each incident functions as a *sign* that points to something beyond itself.
3. John often links the miracles to particular teachings of Jesus, using what Jesus did to draw attention to who Jesus was. By showing the *significance* of the miracles, John turns them into vital illustrative material of the nature of Jesus' personhood and power.

John captures the glory of Christ, reflective of the glory of God in his narrative.

Jesus did not blind everyone with a conclusive light show at the very beginning of his ministry. He resisted that temptation, as we have seen in the wilderness, in favor of a slower, but nonetheless sure, unveiling of his identity. In a way, it would be hard to imagine a more appropriate first miracle than the one at Cana. The source for the story was probably Mary herself, who was later cared for by John.

It happens in a down-home, real-life, this-world context, far away from large crowds and their mass demands for action. True, time would be in short supply for Jesus, and yet he is seen effortlessly and unhurriedly relating to ordinary people and circumstances. He always seemed to have time for a situation. You never get the impression that he is thinking of what he could be doing somewhere else. There is no attempt to get any messianic mileage out of this miracle. Nor was the miracle arbitrary or thoughtless. It was never an open-and-shut case, for it shows Jesus having to resolve whether or not, and for what reasons, he will perform a miracle. If faith was a prerequisite, then we learn that faith was also a product, for "his disciples put their faith in him." This miracle was hidden from public knowledge, but strategically used to teach and strengthen his close followers.

However, having said that, it was not a planned lab experiment for the purposes of illustrating an obscure theory. It happened amongst people; it needed human cooperation, and it responded to the faith and obedience that certain people expressed. Only when it was all over, and many miles and years down the road, did the full significance of the sign begin to emerge and be understood. Jesus was humble and patient enough not to interfere with the process of revelation.

Those large ceremonial jars stick out like a sore thumb. They were important vessels because they held the water that was used to wash the feet and hands according to Jewish purification rites. The stricter the Jew, the more the water that was needed. John's Jewish readers would also note that there were six of them, the number that represented incompletion. Symbolic of the law and its demands, we see that without the work of Christ, the law cannot fulfill human need. The water could remove the dirt, but it could not bring delight. Only the truth of grace could bring to completion what the law had begun to signify. Only the touch of grace could bring out the full taste and flavor of the blessings that God wanted to lavish on people.

But didn't John have Greek readers in mind, too? Certainly, and for them the reality and image of wine had particular significance. It was associated with the gods, and in fact they had a legend that one of their gods turned water into wine once. But it was only a story. In the words of one hiker who visited this town of Cana, Jesus demonstrated here that he could "do the things you only dreamed the gods could do."

This miracle is also an appropriate "first" in that it takes place at a wedding feast, which in Scripture is the great symbol of the excitement and effectiveness of God's reign as it is expressed through relationship. Only Jesus can make for the ultimate success of that wedding feast, and when he wrote the book of Revelation, John must have derived particular satisfaction from this miracle at Cana. As time went on, the significance of the image of wine would gather momentum and weight as it represented the life of this new kingdom that Jesus had declared. At the last, after a final supper with his friends, it would become the symbol of Jesus' ultimate expression of his sacrificial love for all the partygoers of this world whose joy had gone: "This is my blood of the covenant. . . ."

But that is another hike.

The significance of this first miracle continues to resonate and pulsate today. It is not surprising that it confirms that something brand new has come in Jesus.

A NEW EXCHANGE

Images of exchange abound in the Bible, representing the attempt to describe the radical difference that God can make in a situation. We read of weeping turned into dancing, of sackcloth turned into garments of praise, of ashes turned into beauty, of deserts turned into streams of water. In our story, it is about water turned into wine.

We are presented with a new state of affairs, something quite different in nature from what was experienced before. The water of the law has become the wine of grace. The water of human effort has become the wine of divine enabling. The water of ritual has become the wine of spontaneity. The water of natural resources has become the wine of supernatural supply. Jesus continues to touch the dilutions of hope and longing and exchange them for his full-bodied joy.

A NEW EXTRAVAGANCE

Some people may have a problem with this "luxury miracle," for you can hardly argue that it alleviates human misery and distress. It is easy to fall into the trap of seeing miracles only as events that function for human benefit. The fundamental lesson established at Cana is that it was God's glory, more than human need, that was satisfied and that must always be satisfied.

The great thing about this miracle at Cana is its sheer volume. Each jar contained about thirty gallons and there were six jars. One hundred eighty gallons of wine will fill an awful lot of glasses, especially at the end of the party! It is impossible to miss the point. We can apply our legalistic, fussy accountant mentality to the problem and tell God that it was bad timing and that he has to bear the blame for the inevitable waste that is going to occur. Legalism has a way of appearing more efficient than grace sometimes, though of course it's never as much fun. The fact is that God's grace and provision is given to us beyond measure. We can argue that our thirst does not need it or that there are not enough mouths to drink it, but the supply of grace will always exceed our estimated requirements. That is just the nature of grace and just the nature of our inability to assess our need correctly.

Many are going to be the needs of our life in the future, many our prayers for miraculous sustenance and empowerment, many our desires for an increase in joy. Jesus does not merely moisten lips with a relieving glassful for now. He delivers caseloads of the stuff with an abandon that would almost tempt you to think it must be a poor vintage to be so abundant and so available. When you taste it, to your delighted horror, you realize it's the best imaginable.

Jesus left no one in any doubt at Cana that there was no need for anyone to live with a spiritually parched throat. It was the extravagance of his love that ultimately caused him to drink from another full cup, which the Bible describes as a cup of God's wrath. By drinking it to the dregs, he ensured that the wine of grace would continue to flow freely and extravagantly to all who were prepared to admit their thirst and mourn over their dryness.

A NEW EXPECTATION

I have referred to the way Mary seems strangely comforted and assured that there was a potential for something wonderful to happen as long as Jesus was present. She was right. With one hundred eighty gallons of the best wine in the world, Jesus quenched every monotonous, business-as-usual thought. It's amazing how we are often tempted to think that the best is behind us, that we can never recover those times recorded in our private diaries as the "vintage" years. All Mary knew was that the best had gone. She had no idea what Jesus would do, but she did know that he would do the right thing and it would be great. Even she was shocked, not by a good substitute or a tolerable standby, but by the best. The presence of Christ always brings a new estimation of our needs, but a new expectation of his ability to meet them.

It is interesting that there is no discussion or analysis of the mechanics of this miracle. The wine was simply offered to friends, family, and gate-crashers. The proof of this new exchange, new extravagance, and new expectation was in the tasting. It was the headwaiter who unconsciously toasted heaven and raised his glass to Jesus. So he praised the wrong bridegroom! No matter, he spoke for all who have discovered the power of God that has broken the traditional ways of doing things. I'm sure that Jesus was back with the disciples in a far corner, and I'm also sure that no one enjoyed that miracle wine more than he did. Whenever he tastes the fruit of our response to his word and direction, he enjoys it. It would be a long hike now until he arrived in an upper room with his disciples and reminded them that he was the vine and they were the branches. The lesson is clear. As long as we remain in the vine, we will be in the wine business, and every year will be a vintage one.

Most of the guests continued to enjoy the party without a clue of his intervention, in the way that many people are enjoying the kindness and mercy of a gracious and longsuffering God, ignorant of what he has done for them through Jesus. But the fact is that if you know that Jesus is the one who has made the difference, then like the disciples you are going to believe in him and increase in your faith.

As the jugs continued to dip into those stone jars, did Mary catch his eye across the room, and when she did, was that a cup that she saw Jesus raise, and did she imagine a wink behind that crease of laughter?

CAPERNAUM CRESCENT

MAP REFERENCE

*A*nd again He entered Capernaum after some days, and it was heard that He was in the house. Immediately many gathered together, so that there was no longer room to receive them, not even near the door. And He preached the word to them. Then they came to Him, bringing a paralytic who was carried by four men. And when they could not come near Him because of the crowd, they uncovered the roof where He was. And when they had broken through, they let down the bed on which the paralytic was lying. When Jesus saw their faith, He said to the paralytic, "Son, your sins are forgiven you." But some of the scribes were sitting there and reasoning in their hearts, "Why does this Man speak blasphemies like this? Who can forgive sins but God alone?" And immediately, when Jesus perceived in His spirit that they reasoned thus within themselves, He said to them, "Why do you reason about these things in your hearts? Which is easier, to say to the paralytic, 'Your sins are forgiven you,' or to say, 'Arise, take up your bed and walk'? But that you may know that the Son of Man has power on earth to forgive sins"—He said to the paralytic, "I say to you, arise, take up your bed, and go your way to your house." And immediately he arose, took up the bed, and went out in the presence of them all, so that all were amazed and glorified God, saying, "We never saw anything like this!"

Mark 2:1–12

T alk about bringing the house down! Jesus had returned to Capernaum where he had set up his HQ after his time alone in the desert. It was a smart move because it offered a broader base for his ministry than Nazareth. Not only did it have a significant number of Gentiles in its population, but it also served as a junction for major trade routes that linked the Mediterranean with Mesopotamia and Egypt.

It's a surety that news about Jesus was carried great distances in his own lifetime by those who picked up the local gossip on their way through, not to mention those who would have seen him in action. Maybe one or two out-of-towners were in the crowd that gathered as soon as he turned up at the house of Simon's in-laws. By the time this day was over, people would think twice before inviting Jesus round for lunch. If you didn't have a homeowner's policy, then it would probably be a good idea to know a good local builder. When Jesus spoke and acted, you had to be prepared for the roof to be raised.

They had come to hear him teach. So big was the crowd that it spilled way out into the street, and so transfixed were the people by Jesus' stories that they did not notice the guerrilla operation that landed four guys and a stretcher on the roof. If you couldn't get to Jesus with the infantry approach, there was always the airborne division. As Jesus spoke, it was clear that the noises about him were not the brush of angels' wings! As the digging from above broke through the ceiling, Jesus got as liberally dusted with debris as anyone else. He must have loved every minute of that mess, though who knows what was going on in the mind of Simon's mom-in-law, who probably felt like many parents who have had their homes torn apart by the irresponsible friends of their kids. Simon seemed to be holding onto her as if keeping her back.

That ragged hole in the roof through which the paralyzed

man was lowered spoke of a rough-edged but determined faith, which blitzed all obstacles in order to gain an audience. When faith breaks through, sometimes things of less consequence get broken. Some saw the rubble and the damaged floor; others saw the paralytic presented as an unavoidable and unbelievable challenge. As for Jesus, he simply "saw their faith." He got such a kick out of it that by the time that the pallet arrived at ground-floor level, he was more than ready to minister. There is not a single expression of inconvenience. The fact is that suffering and the consequences of sin are messy. Ministering in a three-piece suit on a thick pile carpet, removed from the reality of human life, was not an option that Jesus ever had. The rearrangement of the living room was nothing compared to the rearrangement that was about to take place in the minds of some of those there, particularly the teachers of the law. So far this day, their notations of all his "heresies" had been few and point-stretching at that. The hole in the roof was about to have a metaphoric counterpart in their heads. "Son, your sins are forgiven you!"

"Hey? You what?" Immediately Jesus read the teachers' thoughts as if they were coming off a teleprinter tape out of their ears. "Why are you thinking that I am a blasphemer? Of course, you're right. Only God can forgive sins. Which is easier: to tell this man his sins are forgiven, or to tell him to get up and walk? Well, while you're thinking about that let me show you that the Son of Man does have the authority to forgive sins. . . . Hey, guy, get up, don't forget to take your mat and go home and surprise the folks." And he did.

The crowd parted to let him through and, as it dawned on them what had just happened, they partied, and none were praising louder than the four guys who were dancing on the roof, threatening to complete with delight the demolition job they had begun in desperation. Jesus enjoyed the second shower of dust and plaster as much as the first. He had spoken to the crowd earlier about faith as a mustard seed. It could also be as small as a particle of plaster dust. The combination of all that dust was every bit as good a cloud of glory as you would ever see. While the crowd was still gaping in wonder, Jesus was rolling up his sleeves. The man had picked up his mat. Now it was time to pick up this mess.

Jesus did miracles to remake persons. What Jesus did for people's physical needs can only be understood if it is related to what he said about their spiritual needs. In this incident Jesus discerned that there was a hidden spiritual root to this paralytic's problem. It was the direct result of personal sin, though Jesus did not equate all sickness with sin. When Jesus healed a blind man and the disciples asked him whose sin had been responsible, he said that no one was to blame. However, there were clearly some incidences when the connection was causal.

Whatever the case, it is important to recognize that the desired result in all Jesus' healings was that the person would repent of sin and live a new life. To get the man out of bed was not the main problem. No doubt if you had asked the man what he wanted more than anything else, to be a fulfilled person, he would have expressed his deepest desire to walk. As important as it is to be a physically healthy and well-adapted member of the community, Jesus indicated that there was something much more fundamental to man's experience of fulfillment. To be fully human, there had to be full forgiveness. For Jesus this implied some things:

- that we have sinned and do need to be forgiven
- that God is both willing and able to forgive and heal sin's aftereffects
- that the acknowledgment of the need for forgiveness and the acceptance of it results in a new relationship with God and in a lot of good things happening
- that God's concern is for all our needs, not just the ones that are most obvious or urgent to us.

Jesus' healings have significance insofar as they are understood as an evidence of his power to save from sin, for that is principally why he came. Jesus was not simply interested in physical health but in the wholeness and holiness of a person. There was no point in having a leg healed to run better to do evil, anymore than there was virtue in receiving your sight in order to get a better view down at the local strip joint. Yes, it is easier to speak a word of forgiveness than to heal the sick, but Jesus demonstrated that by doing what was considered harder, he had authority to forgive, and that forgiveness was in fact the greater evidence of his power. Whether forgiveness preceded or followed healing, it was inseparable from the ultimate intent of the miracle.

Jesus' power is also demonstrated by the way that he did not express a desire for change, but declared that the change had taken place. While some were still praying, Jesus pronounced what would be. There was no magic or hocus-pocus, but simply a word. He didn't stroke the head or rub the back with a unique technique. He spoke calmly, authoritatively, compassionately, and expectantly, and in so doing demonstrated his power over sin.

You couldn't walk too far in Capernaum without being near some place or other where something utterly extraordinary had happened. In fact, one of his first miracles there was in the synagogue itself, and by the way, that was no respectable physical healing followed by socially acceptable antiphonal worship. A raw, raucous disturbance by a screaming demoniac interrupted Jesus in mid-sentence, not in a brothel or a bar, but in a haven for true believers. It was typical of Jesus' ministry and authority that by simply being himself, evil that had lurked in secret places, especially in religious settings, would manifest itself, suddenly stripped of the power to conceal itself. Interestingly enough, the evil spirits recognized two things: that Jesus was God, and that he had come to destroy their power. Again, there is no esoteric incantation, but only the command to be quiet and to come out of the man. The evil that is exposed is expelled. This miracle demonstrated to people Jesus' direct power over Satan himself.

One of the incredible miracles that Jesus performed in this town did involve a "resident alien," a centurion who displayed more grace and wisdom, humility and belief than a whole synagogue of scribes and Pharisees. Mindful of Jewish tradition, he submitted his request of Jesus to the Jewish elders who gave him a glowing testimonial, pointing out his love for their nation as well as his generosity in building a local synagogue. Because of these virtues, they argued that he deserved the miracle he desired, which was not for himself, but for a servant who was greatly cared for, and at death's door. Jesus was getting this briefing as he made his way to the Roman's house, much like a doctor being prepped by the hospital nurses on his way to a bedside consultation.

Friends of the centurion met them before they reached the house and explained that the master felt too unworthy to ask Jesus to come in. If Jesus simply said the word, that would be enough, for as a soldier, he understood that because he represented a higher authority, when he ordered one of his men to do something, in monosyllables unaccompanied by explanation, they jumped to it.

This is the only recorded example of Jesus expressing surprise at the depth of someone's faith—and a Gentile, too. The outsider understood the indivisible relationship between faith and authority. Jesus' authority inspired his faith, and his faith invited Jesus' authority.

 Without argument, this town had more evidence of Jesus' power over sin, Satan, and sickness than possibly any other community that Jesus visited. It was also in Capernaum that Jesus gave some of his clearest exposition about who he was and why he came. After one of the most amazing miracles they had ever witnessed, the feeding of five thousand people out of a single lunchbox, the locals sought Jesus out with the questions that had been raised in their minds. They were staggered to find him because they couldn't work out how he'd got there. He didn't tell them that he'd taken the shortcut—he had walked across the water. (Now that's another road by itself!)

The people asked Jesus what they had to do to achieve the works that God required of them. Jesus could not have put it more clearly: "The work of God is this: to believe in the one he has sent." In other words, without belief in Jesus there is no meaning in the miracle. They had eaten miracle bread on the other side of the lake and it had kept the wolf of hunger at bay. Well, he was the bread of life—the real miracle bread, and if he was their diet then the dragons of death and spiritual hunger would never terrorize them. If there was any lesson to be learned from all these exciting healings and happenings, it was that he was the source of miracle. Salvation was not in the acceptance of the miraculous, but in the acceptance of the one who performed the miracles. Without a belief in the source of the miracle, it was just another sensation.

It was in their synagogue that he declared himself to be the bread of life, and explicitly told them that he was the mediator of eternal life, the one who had come from heaven. This was heavy duty for those who only recognized him as Joe's boy. Here, despite his miracles he lost many followers because of his teaching. Like people down through the centuries they were perfectly happy with a television show of miracles, but not so happy with a truthful sermon that questioned whether or not they understood the meaning of what they had seen. Jesus did not give a seminar on physical healing, but rather he related the miracles to the gospel and its demands. Jesus knew that the miraculous, though it may give compelling grounds for belief, is not sufficient of itself to generate saving faith. The folks at Capernaum loved the miracles, but they could not swallow his talk about his blood or body, about death and resurrection.

To observe is not to understand. To hear is not to obey. The enemies of religiosity and rationalism, skepticism and cynicism were always ready to supply or deny an explanation. Scientific and historical objections have continued to attack the miraculous without coming clean on the presuppositions and assumptions that prop up the paper walls of their cause-and-effect explanations. Historians as well as theologians have tried to separate the Jesus of history from the Christ of faith, and in particular, to relegate the miracles to a world of poetic license. The miracles are not performed by Jesus or presented in the gospels as either treats or tricks, pulled out of a cosmic bag at random. They are undoubtedly powerful events, but they are scrupulously purposeful. The big headline, "LEPERS HEALED," is followed by the small print of "Why, and what for?"

Together, three distinctive designations used to describe the miraculous give a full picture.

1. They are *mighty*—they are the result of God's supernatural power.
2. They are *marvelous*—they appeal to the imagination and arouse wonder.

3. They are *meaningful*—as signs they have a significance beyond themselves.

To those who are blind to the truth of who Jesus is, miracles are merely wonders. They are dazzled by the spectacle but remain dense as to its significance. But the purpose of the wonder is to convince the beholder of who God is and therefore convict them of his reality and the need to relate to him on his terms, which inevitably includes repentance. Thus:

RECOGNITION of the wonder should lead to . . .
REVELATION about Jesus, which should lead to . . .
REPENTANCE from sin, which should lead to . . .
RELATIONSHIP with Jesus.

Miracles were not incidental to Jesus' ministry but fundamental. Their purpose can be understood in relation to:

GOD

Jesus presents the miracles as examples of God's initiative and involvement, as illustrations of his care and concern for his creation. He did not perform miracles to improve his ratings or his influence in local politics. In fact, the minute people responded to them as evidences of his ability alone, they tried to make Jesus a king, and he was out of there before you could say "Your Highness!" No, his predominant concern was to reveal what God was like and bring God glory.

Jesus needed no persuasion to help someone who was exercising trust in his Father. Jesus was not into self-authentication. Miracles weren't his personal calling card, as is evidenced by the fact that he shared this power with others. He commanded silence after many miracles because he had no interest in propaganda that drew attention to him and detracted from his mission to testify about God.

JESUS

Miracles were not advertising gimmicks to Jesus to get attention, but demonstrations of the power of the kingdom of God, proofs that God was invading the world—challenging and changing needy people, confronting and confounding the power of evil, establishing a new order and equipping a new humanity. Jesus was not unaffected by miracles. He was moved by human suffering, so much so that on one occasion his emotions are described as being mangled. When he saw people in need, he did not see another exhibit for his display of power but sheep without a shepherd. To Jesus the miracles had the potential to:

> *Reintegrate* a fragmented personhood, mind, soul, and
>   body and . . .
> *Relate* the one healed to God.

The pressure of human anguish was a cause of agony to Jesus and a foretaste, no doubt, of the weight that he would willingly take on himself when he died and refused a miracle for himself as a way out. Every miracle cost Jesus something, not least his life because of the opposition and jealousy the miracles stirred up.

SCRIPTURE

These acts of power rang prophetic bells, fulfilling the hopes for a Messiah who would heal bodies as well as save souls.

PEOPLE

Obviously their purpose was related to people, because they got healed! From the very beginning of his ministry, Jesus had resisted the temptation to win people's approval and allegiance based on his performance of sensational miracles. He had already refused to throw himself from the pinnacle of the temple! The anti-Christ was going to perform sensational miracles.

The issue had to do with the motivation behind the miracle, and in Jesus' case it was to lead people to faith in God's saving power. Because the Pharisees did not discern the spirit behind them, they attributed them to Beelzebub. The importance of the miraculous to people has nothing to do with their short-term testimony value, so much as it has to do with the long-term change of direction and heart in the one who is blessed, facilitating a continuing witness about Jesus to the world.

 As for Capernaum, it saw it all. Mental disturbances, physical diseases, emotional distresses were all healed. The possessed and the paralyzed, Jew and Gentile, rich and poor, pious and pagan, were all recipients of his love and mercy. And yet, Jesus predicted the day would come when his deeds in Capernaum would be a cause for ridicule, not reverence: "Surely you will quote this proverb to me: 'Physician, heal yourself!' Do here in your hometown what we have heard that you did in Capernaum." It became the accepted standard for Jesus' miracles. They were the city to beat—more miracles per capita than any other town. You know how the tourist advertising works.

One day Jesus turned such smugness upside down and inside out. He began to denounce the cities in which most of his miracles had been performed "because they did not repent." Then came the bombshell: "And you Capernaum, will you be lifted up to the skies? No, you will go down to the depths. If the miracles that were performed in you had been performed in Sodom, it would have remained to this day. But I tell you that it will be more bearable for Sodom on the day of judgment than for you." Capernaum is described in the same terms as the Old Testament prophet Isaiah used to portray Satan's arrogance. Maybe familiarity bred contempt. Perhaps their pride was rooted in the fact that Jesus lived there and they were all right, Jack. To be deemed more damnable than Sodom was the pits, for together with Gomorrah, it represented the most graphic judgment of sin and presented hell as an immanent experience.

The moral is chillingly clear. Any generation that is blessed with evidence of the miraculous is more accountable for the evidence of its repentance. The true nature of change wrought by miracle has less to do with eyes that see or ears that hear, legs that run or tongues that speak, than with a life that is committed to follow Christ, in the way that a healed Bartimaeus joined Jesus' retinue.

Yes, Capernaum Crescent curved through a prosperous

town, and it was a good road to travel. Sure, as on all roads there were possible dangers, but the potential for blessing was greater. Some who traveled it never left it once they met Jesus. Take Simon's mother-in-law for example, who was last seen sweeping up the floor and organizing a roofing party. Now I can tell you for sure what was going through her mind as her roof caved in. Sure, there was initial shock, but once she realized what was happening, she agreed that it was the only solution in the circumstances. You see, what I didn't tell you was that she was probably one of the first recipients of a miracle in Capernaum. The explosive synagogue service when Jesus healed the demoniac had at last ended, and Simon had invited Jesus and the guys back for some food. Unfortunately, Simon's mom was in bed with a severe fever. When Jesus learned of this, he went to her and took her by the hand; immediately the fever left her. Fortunately, she was so excited and full of energy, all she wanted to do was entertain them all and feed them. The purpose of the miracle made perfect sense to everyone, including a hungry Jesus.

That night, the whole town plus a crowd of sick folk and noisy demon-possessed characters from neighboring villages, assembled outside her front door. Jesus, fortified by a well-served meal, ministered to all of them. Thus it was that this house became a focal point for Jesus' activity in Capernaum. So when that ceiling caved in, there was no problem. If you have once been touched by Jesus, you can understand every means employed by others to get to him, whom to find is life and love. Now you know why Simon Peter was holding her back. If he had let her go, she would have torn her own house down just to make it easier for them to get closer to Jesus.

Miracles always did violate the bondages of materialist acquisitiveness and explanation. If you welcome Jesus to your life and home, don't bother insulating the roof. If news gets out about what he's done for you, you'll need to order new tiles too!

GADARENE HEIGHTS

*T*hen they came to the other side of the sea, to the country of the Gadarenes. And when He had come out of the boat, immediately there met Him out of the tombs a man with an unclean spirit, who had his dwelling among the tombs; and no one could bind him, not even with chains, because he had often been bound with shackles and chains. And the chains had been pulled apart by him, and the shackles broken in pieces; neither could anyone tame him. And always, night and day, he was in the mountains and in the tombs, crying out and cutting himself with stones. But when he saw Jesus from afar, he ran and worshiped Him. And he cried out with a loud voice and said, "What have I to do with You, Jesus, Son of the Most High God? I implore You by God that You do not torment me." For He said to him, "Come out of the man, unclean spirit!" Then He asked him, "What is your name?" And he answered, saying, "My name is Legion; for we are many." And he begged Him earnestly that He would not send them out of the country. Now a large herd of swine was feeding there near the mountains. And all the demons begged Him, saying, "Send us to the swine, that we may enter them." And at once Jesus gave them permission. Then the unclean spirits went out and entered the swine (there were about two thousand); and the herd ran violently down the steep place into the sea, and drowned in the sea. Now those who fed the swine fled, and they told it in the city and in the country. And they went out to see what it was that had happened. Then they came to Jesus, and saw the one who had been demon-possessed and had the legion, sitting and clothed and in his right mind. And they were afraid.

Mark 5:1–15

It had been his idea to cross the lake, and it seemed like a good one at the time. He was extremely exhausted after long sessions with the crowd, and he needed some space. When the violent squall first hit, more than one of them muttered that he'd better have a good reason for the trip, for it was not proving to be a joyride. What was more, Jesus was so physically exhausted that he remained asleep on a cushion in the stern while waves were swamping the boat. Some smart aleck suggested that they should arouse Jonah before the sea monster appeared. While Jesus was dreaming they were drowning. They may have been annoyed at yet another example of the difference between him and them. They were falling apart (again) and he had fallen asleep. It was not a gentle wake-up call that they gave him. As one does when awakened suddenly, he sat bolt upright, wide-eyed, oblivious to their whining, and as if sleep-talking said, "Quiet! Be still!" They thought he was speaking to them, so they held their tongues under considerable duress until a few seconds later, when the wind had died down and the lake was as calm as a millpond, they realized that it was not their turbulence that he was primarily muzzling. His head was already back on the cushion when he quietly asked, "Why are you so afraid? Do you still have no faith?"

Right! No insurance policy, no backup boat, no life-jacket . . . no faith, if that's what you call it. While he drifted back to sleep, their brains were equally becalmed, numbed by the fact that even the winds and waves obeyed him.

"Who is this?" Answers on a piece of driftwood to . . .

Frankly, they were still in shock when they hit the shore and were relieved to feel that familiar gravelly, grinding noise as the hull scraped into the shore before listing to starboard and to rest. Any thoughts that they were going to get in a few hours' siesta and sunbathing with Jesus were rudely banished. It turned out that they were not going to have the beach to themselves. It was not your normal welcome party. In fact, it started out looking more like a full-speed "Go home, Jesus!" rebuttal. The disciples who were still down at the boat had decided to stay there, while those who were caught in no-man's land between the boat and Jesus considered it wisest to freeze and see how the matter would fall. They were close enough to Jesus to help if needed and close enough to the boat if escape proved necessary. No one could accuse Jesus of avoiding trouble.

The figure that was bounding toward them seemed to have leaped out of the world of legend with its tales of creatures that were half-human, half-beast. As this form lunged down the bank from the tombs higher up the hill, its screams mimicked the night cries of wild carnivores. As he came nearer to the unflinching Jesus, his facial disfigurement, filth, and blood-matted hair on his head and upper body all told the same story of demonic self-abuse. Jagged scars from the rough edges of rocks and stones formed lines that zigzagged across his torso as if scribbled with a demented frenzy. Like some uncouth warrior, he swung the chain that was attached to his wrist with a violence that added to his momentum as he hurtled towards them.

The agitation of the disciples turned to downright fear, for they realized that Jesus was going to be severely steamrollered if he did not take evasive action quickly. They'd seen demoniacs before, but this was the Goliath of them all. To their astonishment and relief, this barbaric monstrosity crumpled in the dirt at the last possible moment before impact, in a kneeling position. That had to be a fluke . . . or was it? In a voice they could only just hear, the disciples listened to those now familiar words: "Come out of this man, you evil spirit!"

What always amazed them was the way that Jesus was able to deal with such violence and dementia in a tone that commanded the demons with awesome authority, and yet somehow simultaneously communicated compassion and gentleness to the vessel that was filled with such vileness. At the moment that he was most engaged with the demonic persona, he seemed to be most conscious of the uniqueness of the personality before him. When he was most involved in identifying the nature and number of demonic influences, he appeared most cognizant of the particular identity of the victim. He had the astounding ability to serve an imperative eviction notice with his tongue, while he was already refurnishing the sufferer with his touch.

At full throttle, the crazed giant bellowed, "What do you want with me Jesus, Son of the Most High God? Swear to God that you won't torture me!" The disciples were staggered. First, they couldn't remember Jesus doing anything that expressed a desire to "want" anything of this character, and secondly it seemed that the nasty guy was terrified of the nice guy.

 Everything happened very quickly and they were still wondering if they could believe their eyes when the locals showed up. That was no welcome party either. Jesus had asked, "What is your name?" "Legion," was the reply, "for we are many." Suddenly, there was a frantic garbling of what seemed to be many voices scrambling for attention at the same time, all begging Jesus not to send them out of the area. So mesmerized had they been by the demonic that they had not noticed the herd of pigs. As they later recalled with some humor, though it wasn't funny at the time, it's impossible not to notice two thousand stampeding porkers making a headlong dash that took them over the edge of the steep embankment, and thence into a watery grave in the lake below. The disciples nervously looked up to the top of the hill as if they were bracing themselves for something else to come charging down at breakneck speed, with blood-curdling screams. At least the pig-herders ran in the opposite direction. Presumably they were sane.

Meanwhile, Jesus had not taken his eyes off the man and had already covered his naked body with his cloak and was sitting on the ground with him, deep in earnest conversation.

Back in the town, the story about what Jesus did with the wild man was spreading like wildfire. Some wanted to go and see, though others were happier to stay. However, when they were told about the vanishing pigs, they didn't think twice about going to investigate. They found Jesus and a remarkably sane man having a chat, but there wasn't a pig in sight. Once they failed to find the pigs, they failed to see the miracle.

Instead of seeing Jesus as the one who delivered men, they chose to see him as the one who destroyed the pigs. What people valued would always determine their response to Jesus. Either they would open their hands and put everything up for grabs, or they would grab everything they could put their clenched hands on. The Gadarene folk had always been scared spitless of the terror in the tombs for self-preserving reasons, but now they were afraid of what was going on for self-serving ones. Two thousand pigs for one man seemed like a lousy trade to them. His life wasn't worth their livelihood. What was a soul worth? Maybe a few rashers of bacon but not an entire farm-load of prime ham.

Jesus thought differently. What could be given in exchange for a soul? According to Jesus, what would it profit a man if he gained control of pork bellies worldwide and lost his soul? Twisted values like these could destroy a local economy and undermine all that had gone into making the area a pig heaven. So they pleaded with Jesus to leave, and he did. If only he could have done it differently. Like so many who have dealt with Jesus since, they would have had him stay if only he'd left their pigs intact. The price of a soul was not negotiable to Jesus, though every man has to decide what he is prepared to sacrifice to experience Jesus' radical deliverance from the power of Satan. At least one man who was bound was set free. The numbers of those who remained in the grip of demonic, materialistic power were legion. The real pigs may have gone, but having rejected the change of life and the freedom from this world's dependencies that Jesus offered, they returned to their respectable community, like pigs returning to their sties.

There is probably one thing scarier than the undesirable presence of a demoniac, and that is the desired absence of Jesus. They had sought to bind the demoniac's power with chains and failed. Now they sought to limit Jesus' power with their rejection, and they succeeded. What could be more terrifying than a temporary freedom from Jesus' demanding influence, which turned out to be an eternal bondage to Satan's damning control.

If there is one thing that the disciples were learning from being with Jesus, it was that evil was a force that was real not imagined, personal not conceptual. They were also discovering that it was impossible to keep company with Jesus and avoid confrontation with the aggressive, abrasive, arrogant, and adversarial power of the demonic. It is clear from the Gospels that healing the sick and delivering the demon-possessed were the fundamental activities of Jesus' practical ministry. "When evening came, many who were demon-possessed were brought to him, and he drove out the spirits with a word and healed all the sick." On every occasion that he commissioned his disciples, "he gave them power and authority to drive out all demons and to cure diseases." It has been rightly observed that every true theology has a demonology. The deliverance of Legion is one of only two exorcisms recorded in all three synoptic Gospels, so it therefore has an importance as a case study and as a clue to some characteristics of what it is to be *demonized* as well as *delivered*.

 The facts are these. Jesus acknowledged and taught that there was a malign and malevolent controlling personality that ruled and directed the forces of evil. Apart from other reasons for seriously considering this possibility, ranging from the private experience of temptation to the public manifestations of the occult in all cultures, the most conclusive reason for belief in a personal, intelligent devil is the conviction of Jesus himself. Neither the church's proclamation nor its practice should acknowledge the reality of the devil or of demon-possession any less than Christ did. To do so is to fudge the message and deny one of the most basic evidences for the power of the kingdom of God, namely the visible demonstration of deliverance in lives, in events, in institutions, in geo-political entities, in tribes and nations.

Jesus told his disciples that he had seen Satan fall like lightning from heaven, which tells us that this was an angelic being that once lived in God's presence, but now was exiled and on the loose. The disciples heard Jesus say this after they had returned from a missions trip during which they had encountered significant manifestations of the demonic. They therefore knew that Satan and his spiritual cohorts were directly involved in people's lives with intent to disfigure and destroy all evidence and hope of God's purposes for his creatures.

Like the dragon of legend, the real Satan was concerned to do everything possible to stop people from enjoying the treasure that he was denied. Satan is not presented as a kind of extra-evil human personality, but as an incredibly powerful spirit that impersonated human personality in order to achieve his deceptive and destructive deeds.

Jesus described him as "the prince of this world," though in doing so, he was quick to point out that although this ruler was coming against him personally in a decisive battle, he was condemned and would be cast out. In the Gospels, this much is clear:

1. Despite the range of its activity, there is a unified force of evil.
2. Despite its random and arbitrary violence, it is directed and purposeful.
3. Despite many strong demonic personalities, Satan is its commander.
4. Satan intends to imprison people in his jurisdiction and maintains his influence through personal sin and sickness (physical and mental), through human power structures, through disturbances in nature, through systems of religion and a vast curriculum of counterfeit faiths and doctrines, and, of course, through death.
5. When confronted by Jesus, the devil and demons were overcome—exposed, rebuked, silenced and expelled. This fulfilled the messianic expectation that Jesus was very familiar with from his reading of the prophets, Isaiah in particular: "Captives will be taken from warriors and plunder retrieved from the fierce."
6. Jesus explicitly taught that his death and resurrection were the death blows to Satan's power. Everything else he did was serving notice that Satan's pretense to absolute power was going to be unmasked, most dramatically in his resurrection, which demonstrated that death and its power did not have the last word. The hole in the rock revealed by the stone that was rolled away represents the escape hatch through which men and women can escape the mausoleums of satanic dominion.

7. Jesus gave his followers the authority and power to oppose, confront, and expel the demonic, and encouraged them to believe that, just as he did, they would raise a "Stop" sign to the onward rush of evil wherever they traveled, and their presence in a situation would spiritually call into question the activity of Satan, be it hidden or blatant. The conflict would continue, but "I have given you authority . . . to overcome all the power of the enemy."

8. Jesus' ministry was radical in that he attacked the roots of evil, recognizing that it was both a cosmic problem as well as one that was very close to home—even within every human heart.

It is absolutely impossible to understand the message and ministry of Jesus if it is not recognized that he saw the purpose of his coming, of his ministry, and of his death, not merely as establishing that which was good, but destroying that which was evil. Direct conflict with Satan was the central engagement of his mission. His was definitely an anti-Satan revolution. Although Judaism acknowledged the feeling of bondage to forces that were suprahuman and taught that the one God was sovereign over all powers, whether good or evil, it was confronted, through Jesus' ministry, with more than a cosmic, abstract theory. Jesus could at least appeal to this background, for if God was all-powerful and if demons were seen to be exorcised, then it had to be by the power of God and therefore an evidence that Jesus was legitimately and justifiably making the claims that he did. Listening to Christ meant hearing what he had to say about the demonic. Following Christ meant experiencing freedom from the demonic and exercising authority over it, in Jesus' name. The Gadarene hillside was another crucial laboratory class that established these convictions in the disciples through firsthand observation and experience.

FEATURES OF THE DEMONIC

- When Legion got to Jesus, there was evidence that the demons could communicate.
- They had knowledge because they could identify Jesus.
- They had strong emotions, not only evident in the way

they were violently expressed through the man in irrational and compulsive behavior, but also in the manner in which they appealed to Jesus to be spared torture.

- They are filled with arrogance as manifested in their belligerent, mocking address to Jesus.
- They had a determinative will and great physical power and strength.
- They destroyed both life and limb, robbing the man of all sense of decency and dignity, subjecting him to bestial conditions.
- They possessed him with the effect that they fragmented his identity, and the result of their invasion was a zoo of multiple personalities and insanity.
- They isolated him from community and condemned him to depressive solitude.
- They confined him to the tombs, as was typical of their obsessive morbidity.
- Their grip on the man was chronic, for he had been this way for a long time, and there was no improving of his condition, nor was there anything anyone could do to either cure him or contain him.
- Despite their power, they were subject to fear and therefore inevitably manifested the same insecurities and weaknesses in the face of Jesus' power that their master Satan did.
- They were exposed by Jesus' presence and, despite every physical effort to use the man to assault Jesus, they had to bow the knee to him.
- Although they had a will, it was subject to Jesus' command as shown by the fact that they had to leave the man when ordered to do so.

FEATURES OF DELIVERANCE

- Jesus had discernment, spiritual insider information, that prepared him for the fact that there was something significant for him to do on the other side of the lake.
- Jesus did not go hunting for demoniacs; they were either brought to him or came to him as happened in this case.
- Jesus distinguished between the man and the possessing spirits and directly addressed the latter.

- Although the spirits responded to Jesus' initial command with an uncontrolled outburst, Jesus took authoritative control of the tone and tempo of the exchange (such a conversation is the exception to the rule in the recorded incidents in the Gospels).
- He first commanded silence, before final exorcism, perhaps in line with his teaching about the need to bind the strong man before spoiling his goods.
- Jesus asked the spirits to identify themselves by name, thus underlining the specific nature of deliverance.
- Jesus delivered demoniacs with his word, not by touch.
- There is no mumbo jumbo or esoteric technique—but authority and power.
- We do not have any details, but it is clear that Jesus immediately engaged in purposeful follow-up with the man, responding not only to his physical needs but also to his need for direction.
- The commitment of the man to follow Jesus as "Lord" and tell others about him is an expected and necessary consequence of deliverance here, for only continuing relationship was a guarantee of continued release.

You can understand why the demon-possessed man had one leg over the side of the boat. Jesus had a better strategy, keen to inflict maximum damage against the power of Satan. This man had become a legend in his own right, and now his notoriety was going to give him a large audience for his newfound faith. He had been confined to tombs, and Jesus was now going to send him to the major towns of Decapolis, a Gentile area that would hear the good news. Fundamental to the expectation of the Messiah was not only the conviction that he would exercise power over evil, but also that all nations would be blessed through him. (The Jews would not be able to control God's free mercy and turn it into a local franchising operation.) Who would ever have guessed a few moments before that this demoniac would be used to spread the gospel to the Gentiles and thus give Jesus an unbelievable foretaste of what was yet to come through his obedience to his Father, to the whole Gentile world too? Unbelievable, but he had the ideal resumé! Instead of being a captive, this man was going to become a captor, reproducing his own miracle in Jesus' name.

The disciples did not make the connection immediately, but later on they started to piece things together, particularly the relationship between the things he taught and the things he did. Wasn't this precisely what he meant by that strange conversation with the angry Pharisees who publicly accused him of being demon possessed himself and of having evil powers over people? Satan didn't receive many compliments as good as that one. (One of the reasons they said this was simply that Jesus was so different from the Messiah they expected that the only alternative, if he was not that Messiah, was that he was the devil incarnate.) Of course, Jesus took their argument to the cleaners, and by the time he had laundered their logic, his enemies were more entrenched in their alliance with the demonic than they'd accused Jesus of being.

Jesus argued that Satan could not drive out Satan, or oppose himself, without dividing his own kingdom and inviting ruin. Satan didn't know everything, but he was not that stupid. Satan was a great fan of death, but that did not include plans for his own suicide. However, if for one moment there was the possibility that Jesus was delivering these demonics by the power of God's Spirit, then the logical conclusion to draw was that he was who he said he was, and these miracles were incontrovertible evidence that the kingdom of God was established among them, extending its reign and influence and showing itself to be greater than the kingdom of Satan. The choice was truly black and white . . . Satan or God?

The disciples later remembered the story he had told to clinch the point. "When a strong man, fully armed, guards his own house, his possessions are safe. But when someone stronger attacks and overpowers him, he takes away the armor in which the man trusted and divides up the spoils." That was it, exactly. If ever they'd seen the strong man, it was Legion. The demonic power had been supremely confident in its control over him until Jesus showed up. Ignoring all the satanic security alarms that were screaming and drawing attention to the unwanted intrusion, Jesus proceeded to break through every defense system and head straight for the strongbox. He needed no elaborate mechanism to get the safe open, no paraphernalia, no messy dynamite methods. He simply released the entire contents with a simple sentence that recovered all stolen property from Satan's larceny of the soul.

There were up to six thousand men in a Roman legion. In a word, this man's problems were many, certainly too numerous for the philosophies of self-help, too entrenched for the searching questions of well-meaning counselors, too violent for the controls of civilized restraints. The very opinions and theories that increasingly purported to have banished the demonic to the nursery of undeveloped, unsophisticated, uneducated humanity, were themselves the products of devil's disciples, doctrines of demons that pretended to bring understanding but have had to confess that they could bring no cure. A common man's doggerel says it all:

> If the devil is voted not to be,
> Is the verdict therefore true?
> Someone is surely doing the work
> The devil was thought to do.
>
> They may say the devil has never lived,
> They may say the devil is gone,
> But simple people would like to know
> Who carries the business on?

The next time the word *legion* arises in the Gospels it is on the lips of Jesus, in another situation when he was being confronted by a man who was possessed—Judas. When it came to the final confrontation with his adversary, Jesus said that he chose not to call for the legions of angels that were at his disposal to deliver him. Yes, he delivered Legion, so why not allow his own legions to deliver him? His answer was clear. "How then would the scriptures be fulfilled?" Jesus was not overpowered by evil but chose to hand himself over to its murderous power. To overcome its force he had to submit to its unleashed fury and revenge so that it could be seen that he had endured its ultimate punishment and had appeared to be utterly vanquished, and left certifiably dead.

Was there life after the presence of a demonic legion? Ask the Gadarene guy. Was there life after the absence of an angelic legion? Ask the man from Galilee, or anyone who has recently spoken to him.

BETHESDA STEPS

MAP REFERENCE

Now there is in Jerusalem by the Sheep Gate a pool, which is called in Hebrew, Bethesda, having five porches. In these lay a great multitude of sick people, blind, lame, paralyzed, waiting for the moving of the water. For an angel went down at a certain time into the pool and stirred up the water; then whoever stepped in first, after the stirring of the water, was made well of whatever disease he had. Now a certain man was there who had an infirmity thirty-eight years. When Jesus saw him lying there, and knew that he already had been in that condition a long time, He said to him, "Do you want to be made well?" The sick man answered Him, "Sir, I have no man to put me into the pool when the water is stirred up; but while I am coming, another steps down before me." Jesus said to him, "Rise, take up your bed and walk." And immediately the man was made well, took up his bed, and walked. And that day was the Sabbath. The Jews therefore said to him who was cured, "It is the Sabbath; it is not lawful for you to carry your bed." He answered them, "He who made me well said to me, 'Take up your bed and walk.'" Then they asked him, "Who is the Man who said to you, 'Take up your bed and walk'?" But the one who was healed did not know who it was, for Jesus had withdrawn, a multitude being in that place. Afterward Jesus found him in the temple, and said to him, "See, you have been made well. Sin no more, lest a worse thing come upon you." The man departed and told the Jews that it was Jesus who had made him well.

John 5:2–15

It was during one of the feasts in Jerusalem that Jesus walked the road just to the north of the temple that led him to the Pool of Bethesda, a watering hole with a difference. This was not a spa for the jet set but a place where the bed-bound gathered, drawn by the legendary belief that the waters were disturbed by an angel from time to time and that the first person to enter the pool would be miraculously healed.

The five covered colonnades that surrounded the pool enhanced its physical beauty but could not camouflage the human brokenness that littered the feet of its columns. The best of man's attempts to architect his environs cannot remove the reality of sin and suffering. Nice settings do harbor nasty problems, and glitzy packagings do conceal degenerating products. The gleaming columns of Bethesda vaulted skyward in sharp contrast to the earthbound disability that met Jesus as he arrived. All around him were people longing for something to happen, dreaming that one day their prince would come, their luck would change, their boat would come home. If only a friend happened to be there at the right time, when those waters were stirred by the underground spring, then there was a chance. As they took encouragement from the apocryphal stories of magic and miracles at this very spot, they were able to transmute their outside long shot into an odds-on favorite . . . for a while. They believed that special cases needed special places. They had to believe in the power of the water.

Into this world of maybe's, don't know's, what if's, and if only's, came Jesus, with poise and purpose, presence and precision. No one really knew for sure what was in the water, but there was definitely something in the air. As he began to move through the colonnades, the pool ceased to be the focus of attention for some, but not all. It is hard to take one's eyes from a pool that has been the wellspring of one's hope for years, and it is equally painful to grapple with the gnawing awareness that this pool may turn out to be nothing but a sinkhole, a watery grave for the deepest longings and the fondest dreams.

The first thing Jesus did was simply to look. As always on these occasions, he could feel the weight of all this physical desperation and emotional debris pressing in on his chest, causing him to breathe deeply and exhale in what sounded like a subterranean sigh. Next, he learned something. The cripple was grateful when the stranger broke the monotony of his blank thoughts by asking him how long he had been there. By the looks of it, he'd been there before this visitor had been born. He was right. Thirty-eight years was a very long time to be waiting for a lucky break. Jesus' next question did not register at first, any more than any statement of the obvious causes us to pin our ears back. It dropped to the ground, and its fuse fizzled for a while before exploding with full force in the man's consciousness.

"DO YOU WANT TO GET WELL?"

Was this a bad joke or just an ill-considered choice for an opener? This man had awakened every morning, for the last fourteen thousand sunrises, to the paralyzed facts of his disability. Wasn't the answer as plain as the pallets that blanketed the ground? To everyone else, perhaps, but not to Jesus.

Luck may come as a stroke, but love arrives on the scene, probing and searching, challenging the obvious before it turns its attention to the hidden world of the heart. While our eye is riveted by the specter of the disability of the man's body, Jesus is penetrating the disposition of his mind. Does he really want what he says he needs? Though change is demanded, is it really desired? Humankind possesses the uncanny ability to adjust to confinement and accommodate disability, to rationalize, improvise, and minimize. We can resign ourselves to a despairing condition and lower our expectations. We can come to favor our dependencies and fear the thought of change with its challenges and responsibilities. The crutches and the props of our atrophied hopes can become preferred to the freedoms of the walk of faith. "Do you want to be healed? . . . Saved? . . . Delivered?"

Technically speaking, there's no contest, but how about truly speaking? Jesus never did ask pointless questions when the future of a life was at stake. He knew there would be demanding consequences for anyone who chose to break out of a spiritual prison, and he knew that freedom had a price.

It's interesting but the question did not get a straight answer. The man said enough to indicate that he had a severe problem, but he implied that his present state had more to do with a lack of opportunity than with a lack of determination on his part. With incredulity in his raised voice, he exclaimed, "Sir! I have no one to help me into the pool when the water is stirred. While I am trying to get in, someone else gets in ahead of me!" Unwittingly, he confessed to two main areas of human dependency:

on himself—"while I am trying"
on others—"I have no one to help me"

Tragically, the sum total of human dependency was powerless to help him. It was well motivated and well intentioned but ill equipped. It was probably beginning to dawn on him that his lucky day had just arrived. Here at last was someone who could possibly be cajoled into helping him jockey for position in the next poolside miracle. He was not the first one, nor would he be the last, who presumed on the kind of help that Jesus specialized in. One thing is for certain. Jesus was certainly not known for the time he spent carrying stretchers. He much preferred sick people to carry their own.

Who knows what singled this man out? It was certainly not his faith that recommended him, for he had no expectation and made no request for help. Nor was it his familiarity with Jesus that gave him a leg up in the salvation stakes, for he didn't have a clue who Jesus was. Why him? Why anyone?

The inability to commend oneself and command attention on the basis of curriculum vitae is a common symptom of the condition of all who are disabled by the fallout of sin. The man, for all his needs, did not even know what to ask for. Without the compassionate initiative and involvement of Jesus, there would have been no conversation. Without any evidence of a miracle from heaven, he would have continued to believe in the magic of the earth. Without any expectation of specific help, he would have continued to waste his life on vague hopes. Without any experience of the immediate move of the Spirit of God, he would have waited in vain for a possible move of the waters. He could have continued to justify his condition. He had gained some expertise over the thirty-eight years in explaining and justifying his debilitation. There was always someone else who was luckier, who had got in it, got out of it, and got away with it. He was about to discover that being lucky was no substitute for being loved.

"GET UP! PICK UP YOUR MAT AND WALK!"

And that was that. He did get up, he did pick up his mat, and he did walk right out of there. The process was disarmingly simple:

> *respond* to Jesus' word immediately and
>   unquestioningly.
> *remove* the basis for your disabled life.

 So far, so good, but there always seems to be someone around the next corner to tell you that what Jesus has just done either cannot be done or should not be done. Of course, they can prove their case from some textbook or other, be it philosophic, scientific, or comic. Imagine the scene. The ex-cripple went charging through the colonnades as happy as Larry (bone dry, too!) with his mat over his shoulder. Turning the corner, his mat almost decapitated a gaggle of Jews, who were quick to point out that it was the Sabbath, and it was forbidden to carry a mat on that sacred day. You've either got to laugh or cry. The law itemized thirty-nine categories of work (one for every year of his disability!), and would you believe it? The thirty-ninth was about carrying loads. He didn't even know it was the Sabbath, let alone know there was a ban on mats!

Why is it that there was always a lawyer or a professional theologian around when Jesus did a miracle? Their contributions to rejoicing and laughter were rules and litigation. The man explained that the man who made him well had told him to do it. In fact, picking up his mat was an integral part of the total cure he'd just experienced, so how could he avoid it?

In any case, wasn't it logical to suppose that the person who had authority to do miracles was probably in a position to decide what was or was not important when it came to mats? Why stand around and argue a technical point about mats with the guy who has just given you back your legs and livelihood?

Here's the twist. According to the law, a mat could carry a sick man, but an ex-sick man could not carry his mat. The logic of that is that it is better to be sick than healed, for decency's sake, and to this day, such civilized legalities account for the fact that more people are on mats than there are mats on people. The law gave you mobility, but only by putting wheels on your sickbed.

Meanwhile, with a miracle staring them in the face, the Jews could think of nothing more important to discuss than what makes for a righteous rug. Maybe if the man had unfurled his mat at that point and sat on it, it would have turned into a flying carpet!

No wonder they were interested in who had told him to carry his mat. Whoever he was, he was a Sabbath breaker. Jesus must have lingered behind one of the columns and observed this confrontation. From the street you would have seen his silhouette.

The fact was that the poor guy who had been healed could give no details about his benefactor. Jesus had not given him a card or shown him before-and-after pictures of others whom he had healed. He had simply given him the greatest gift of his life, gratis, no strings attached, no money down, no sign-on-the-dotted-line, no check-the-small-print. As the crowd gathered, the silhouette disappeared.

In Judaism, the Sabbath laws were a defense against the intrusion and perversion of paganism. Unfortunately, in their zeal to keep the infidel out, they had also kept God out. In a single command—"Get up!"—Jesus dismantled the flimsy scaffolding of mechanistic, legalistic holiness.

What is the point of a structure of righteousness that obscures the mercy and love of God and retains the pain of disability? The Pharisees viewed the Sabbath negatively, as a kind of religious pause or time out. Jesus is reestablishing a positive understanding of Sabbath rest, as in restitution and restoration. Basically, Jesus was permitting what they were prohibiting, a scenario that needs to be reenacted whenever the community of faith ossifies into a cadre of legalists. As he explained later, he and his Father were always at work, if by work we mean the recovery of the peace and purpose of God in people's lives. If it was agreed that God remained active on the Sabbath, then Jesus was free, also, to initiate and imitate what he saw the Father doing.

Now Jesus was really in trouble. Not only had he challenged Sabbath law, but by virtue of his defense, he compounded his crime by claiming equality with God. As John records, "For this reason the Jews tried all the harder to kill him."

A minor miracle had displaced a major scandal. Jesus presented a clear choice. Either receive him or resist him. So evident were the facts of his power that they inevitably provoked a strong counterreaction.

"YOU ARE WELL AGAIN! STOP SINNING.

The fact that the man did not even know who healed him has less to do with his ignorance than with Jesus' humility. Some time later, following the angry disturbance out on the street, Jesus found this man again in the temple, no doubt sincerely worshiping and giving thanks for his healing. It was more than chance that Jesus bumped into him. It is quite possible that Jesus deliberately searched him out because there was some unfinished business that was vital to this man's future health. Obtaining a miracle is one thing, but maintaining the purposes for which the miracle was given is quite another. There is no virtue in the healing of a cripple who is now going to run into hell. Jesus knew not only how to initiate ministry but how important it was to do some follow-up. This consisted of two important elements that remain common to his aftercare:

1. *He confirms:* He assures the man of the reality of what has happened. There is no relation between his miracle and the temporary, mind-over-matter cures that came out of those waters. What he has experienced is of another order from that of legend and luck, of visualization and positive thinking.

Assurance about what Jesus has done is crucial to ongoing health.

2. *He cautions:* Although Jesus did not attribute all sickness to personal sin, it is clear that he knew something about this man's condition that could be traced directly to his sin. Jesus warned him that because there was a spiritual root to his physical condition, there was a necessary relationship between his healing and his forgiveness. The reception of salvation's blessings brings with it the responsibility to renounce and repent of those sins that disabled both body and soul. Walking free cannot be separated from staying clean. Our lust can wreck what his love has recovered.

Talking of recovery, the Pool of Bethesda recovered the true meaning of its name—house of mercy. It is not without significance that it stood close to one of the old gates of the city, known as the Sheep Gate. It was the first gate to be rebuilt under Nehemiah's restoration. Through this entrance, the sheep were taken to the temple to be sacrificed for the sin of the people. In the shadow of that gate, a miracle was performed by one who had earlier been described as the "Lamb of God." Similarly, the shadow of a cross would forever fall over every miraculous blessing that would ever be experienced as a result of an encounter with Jesus.

This particular miracle launched an eighteen-month campaign to destroy him. It is axiomatic to the gospel that the place of renewal is the place of redemption. There are no cut-price miracles. Blessings cannot be obtained cheaply at a believer's bazaar. Every act of grace cost Christ dearly before it demanded anything from anyone.

The conversation among the colonnades continues to echo in its simplicity and directness.

- Do you really want to be changed, regardless of the cost?
- Leave the discomfort of your disability right now before it becomes a place of permanent imprisonment.
- Do not go back to life as it was before, and don't repeat the sin that has been forgiven.

In a word, leave the pallets that make your life reasonably tolerable in the circumstances but bring no relief to your soul. Leave the pools of false hopes and counterfeit theories, that offer so much but come with sufficient exclusive clauses to keep you from ever being changed. Leave the lawyers to argue about technicalities in order to destroy your convictions about the truth of who Jesus is and who he wants to be to you. It is better to share the grime and grind of the road with Jesus than to sunbathe at a pool called Bethesda.

ROUTE
THREE

*Checking
out some
things
he said . . .*

COUNTRY ROAD

MAP REFERENCE

Then He taught them many things by parables, and said to them in His teaching:

"Listen! Behold, a sower went out to sow. And it happened, as he sowed, that some seed fell by the wayside; and the birds of the air came and devoured it. Some fell on stony ground, where it did not have much earth; and immediately it sprang up because it had no depth of earth. But when the sun was up it was scorched, and because it had no root it withered away. And some seed fell among thorns; and the thorns grew up and choked it, and it yielded no crop. But other seed fell on good ground and yielded a crop that sprang up, increased and produced: some thirtyfold, and some sixty, and some a hundred. . . ."

And He said, "The kingdom of God is as if a man should scatter seed on the ground, and should sleep by night and rise by day, and the seed should sprout and grow, he himself does not know how. For the earth yields crops by itself: first the blade, then the head, after that the full grain in the head. But when the grain ripens, immediately he puts in the sickle, because the harvest has come."

And He said, "To what shall we liken the kingdom of God? Or with what parable shall we picture it? It is like a mustard seed which, when it is sown on the ground, is smaller than all the seeds on earth; but when it is sown, it grows up and becomes greater than all herbs, and shoots out large branches, so that the birds of the air may nest under its shade."

Mark 4:2–8, 26–32

How did he manage to think so quickly on his feet, take the slightest observation, and turn it into such a memorable picture of some truth that you always wanted to understand but until now just never had the right mental hanger to put it on? His wardrobe of stories and sayings was a bit like a one-of-a-kind clothes shop. It contained the garments of years gone by, once crumpled and disused in some previous generation's attic, but now expertly renewed and restored to their designer's original intention. It also housed his own unique collection, distinctively the product of his perception of what people were meant to look like and how they were meant to live.

Such was his understanding of the shape and form of human life that he could design clothing for men, women, and children with equal skill and sensitivity. Even more stunning was his ability to blend the past with the present and yet dress you for the future. When you looked at the older clothes, fine in their own right, you could see the basic pattern that had influenced his design; and when you looked at the new, you could see how his style fulfilled and completed the work of those earlier pioneers.

The fact was that his inventory was so vast that he had something tailored to fit everyone, and he was always looking for models to present his designs to others. When his imagination was unreined, you got the feeling that he had been in the creative arts and design business for a very long time.

His mind was never more fertile than when he walked the country road. Mind you, so attentive was he to conversation and the questions of his followers that they could never work out how he noticed what was going on in the fields and mentally lathe it into an illustration that just happened to explain whatever was uppermost in their minds at the time. Of course, he used his observations and stories to teach things that had either never entered their minds or had got past the front door of their hearing, but not yet found a seat in the living room of their understanding.

Take for example the many conversations the disciples had about providing the basic necessities for themselves and their families. They had no fixed income, and judging by the rate that their potential support base was ceasing to follow Jesus, they were staring the prospect of no income fully in the skeletal face. While they were watching the bucks, Jesus was watching the birds, and with a timely interruption he pointed out the ravens circling above the adjoining field. "Take a look at that, guys. They don't sow anything in that field or have anything to reap and store in a barn. Yet your heavenly Father feeds them." (If they couldn't spot birds, how would they spot the key pronoun that he had just spoken?) "Aren't you more valuable? What do you say?" They were getting frantic and he was talking about feathered friends. "And talking of clothes . . . you were talking about clothes weren't you? . . . Take a look at those lilies . . . no, not a quick squint . . . let's all sit down and stare at them. . . . Look closely now . . . and think about what you see. Think, lads, think! Tell me what you see."

According to Jesus, faith and trust were not simply a matter of hit and miss. You could no more work up faith to produce a windfall than you could worry yourself to grow another inch. Jesus taught one of his major lessons on faith, not by whipping them into a mind-over-matter, think-positive-think-prosperous frenzy but by making them squat in front of some roadside flowers. You can have a great Faith Conference in a country wildflower patch, or if that's not quite posh enough or not thinking big enough, in a botanic garden!

Jesus knew that if people did not use their God-given eyes and their God-given brains, they were going to spend most of their lives sinking in feelings when they should be thinking about facts. The acknowledgment of what God has already done is a sufficient basis for the one most addicted to faith-lessness to compute that we stand at least as good a chance as the ravens or the lilies when it comes to being noticed by God and, what's more, being provided for. And if the lily is too much, too grand, too lucky, too special, too pretty, too out-of-my-class, too privileged—too basically "beyond my ability to identify with because they have not experienced what I have"—then Jesus graciously accedes to our protestations of commonness and the "it's all right for them lilies but it 'ain't gonna work for me" routine, by saying, "If the lilies are too threatening, too overdressed, consider the grass, so common that it's here today and burned tomorrow. Yet despite every reason why God should not spend time on these little blades, he does, and he clothes them with the same care and appropriateness as he does the bloomers."

Jesus always cut through the faithless drivel that argued it had no reason to hope, that whined past the flower shop and the bird table. Worry met its match in a local field, and the spiritual ecological lesson that Jesus wanted them to take along the road with them was that the failure of faith is not so much an inability to imagine the invisible as a failure to think rightly about the visible. Consternation is always in big supply when consideration is in small demand.

 It never ceased to amaze his friends that he could defuse their strongest fears with the most fragile of images. One day, they had reason to fear, for not only had they heard the Pharisees giving Jesus a vicious public roasting, but they had almost been trampled into the country dirt by an overzealous crowd. Much as they loved the fields from which Jesus drew his parables, they had no desire to be buried there prematurely. Frankly, they were in fear for their lives, extremely nervous and tense, and probably not sure if they could sit through the next sermon. Instinctively, perceptively, Jesus got them into a huddle before he addressed the crowd again. They certainly needed some good quarterbacking, but he surprised them once again with his call. "Hey, dear friends! What's the going rate for five sparrows?" You what? He'd been watching those country birds again. They were too numb to answer, so he continued, "Two pennies, right. Don't be afraid of those who kill the body and then can do nothing else to you. If you're going to fear, spend it on those who will destroy body and soul. You know those sparrows that you can get two-and-a-half a penny? Not one of them is forgotten by God. Things are getting dangerous, I agree, but don't be afraid. You're worth more than many sparrows!"

Of course, insecurity and fear, faithlessness and cowardice want to shout, "But how many exactly?" Fear wants a big bodyguard, and all it is offered is a little bird. And talking of birds, the man who needed to be challenged one day about the real-life consequences of following Jesus did not get a one-hour lecture on all the things he would have to sacrifice. Jesus simply said, "The birds have roosts, but the Son of Man doesn't have anywhere to lay his head." You didn't have to know a lot about country birds to learn a lot about faith and fear and following. Of course, when the birds flew away, that was not the end of the teaching!

There was more than one trek along a country road that seemed like a mile too far, but they knew that if they complained, someone holier than themselves would quote the one about going the extra mile, or was it doubling the mileage? There was a big difference! On this particular day, as so often in their pilgrimage, they needed some help with their perspective on things. What about the fantastic job they were doing, the great support they were providing, and the brilliant crowd control they were administering, not to mention their commitment to prayer or their perseverance in the face of all the abuse they had to put up with from those who were less than fans of their group? When the mind begins to do the accounting on all the great things that are being done for others and for God, it is one fine pencil away from wondering "what is in this for me?" which is how books come to be fiddled and friends get defrauded. Many times when their feet were dragging in the early evening, the disciples had watched farmhands leaving the ploughs or securing the penned sheep, and it was such a scene that Jesus now described.

Suppose that farmhand were their servant. When he got in from the field, would they fuss over him and express deep indebtedness for all he had done, or would they tell him to wash up, get the dinner, and serve it? Would they thank the servant for doing what he'd been told to do? The disciples had to admit that there was no reason at all why the master should show the servant any favor because he had performed the task he was ordered to do. Nor could the servant plead a special case when he was asked to do more of the same. The master owed him nothing because he had merely done his duty. If the servant received anything, it was a gift of grace, not a payment for services rendered. Even so, those who serve God should do so out of loyal obedience, concerned to fulfill their duty, without ever thinking that they have some claim on God. And that settled that, so it was back to the fields, to plough, sow, and, hopefully, to reap. It was this process that dominated Jesus' imagination and communication on the country road.

John the Baptist was not the only one who was having doubts about Jesus as the Messiah. If he really was the new sheriff, inaugurating a new era for the county, how come the bad guys were still in town, and how come he did not have a gunbelt on, weighed down by six-shooters, studded with rounds of ammunition?

 Those who hoped that Jesus would shoot bullets had a hard time working out why he was more interested in sowing seeds. Because all three Gospel writers record the story about the farmer sowing seeds on different types of ground, on paths and rocky places, among thorns and in good soil, it is a fair indication that this story is important for our understanding of Jesus' ministry. Without the explanation that Jesus gave to his disciples, it would be difficult for anyone to work it out. The fact that we know the story so well blinds us to this fact and blinds us to the impact of the meaning we think we have mastered. Those who expected God to drop a bomb needed to know that he was planting a seed. The seed was Jesus himself, the physical shape of God's word. Like the seed:

- He did not appear as if he was going to achieve much, in too much of a hurry
- He seemed to be more intent on disappearing from public view, working underground
- His life was presented to a wide range of human geography with a variety in both reception and result

- His message was rendered immediately ineffective when it was denied entrance by rejection or subversion; when it was ditched when the situation changed and the conditions were no longer conducive to growth; when it died because it was throttled by other competing interests
- His purposes were fruitful when his message was planted in receptive hearts

The fact is that the seed of Jesus' life and message is broadcast by God with apparent abandon (some would say waste) upon the field of the world, which included more than the obviously prepared soils like Judaism that turned out to be not as ready for the Messiah as would have been presumed. There is no deficiency in the message of Jesus, any more than in the seed. The tragedy is that certain responses will condemn people to continued hardness and barrenness, and they will have denied themselves the experience for which the soil of their spirit was intended, namely to be seeded with God's truth and covered with the harvest of his joy and peace.

Telling a story about a seed was Jesus' way of planting truth about the kingdom of God. The seed was the kingdom. Those who were looking for flares and flags, rhetoric and rallies, and other such demonstrations of power needed to know that the seed was a power capsule and that the kingdom of God, even though perceived as insignificant by many, was nonetheless a living, dynamic, presently powerful organism. This was what was so difficult for people to understand, people who were looking for an army or a charismatic political leader or a populist hero. A local country boy? A tiny seed? What is kingly or divine, powerful or commanding about this?

Maybe the story about the seed on resistant types of ground left the disciples mistakenly thinking that there was a problem with the seed and that the success of this kingdom was as tenuous as that of a farmer's harvest in arbitrary weather conditions. Well, the short parable that compared the kingdom to seeds that were scattered in exactly the same way, that sprouted and grew, gave another piece of the picture. Jesus said that the farmer could get on with his life after sowing because the soil produced grain all by itself, and there was no point in his trying to figure out how the mystery of growth actually worked. He didn't have a clue. What he did know was that the time would come when the field was covered with grain and needed to be harvested.

Jesus does not present any threats to growth here, save maybe the implied one that if the farmer got too curious about the process of germination he could mess it all up by interfering. He's better off playing horseshoes, and the seed is certainly safer! The kingdom of God does not need any help to reproduce itself powerfully and exert an influence that is one day seen to cover the field. In a way, Jesus is celebrating the inevitability of a fantastic finish, but the main joy has to do with the splendor of an insignificant, almost haphazard beginning that fools everyone into thinking that it must have petered out.

On the contrary, it is quietly pottering along with unremitting intent, and before you know it, more seed pods are bending in the breeze and propagating to places that are not even reachable by the postal service.

Does the process sometimes seem perplexing and slow? Sure, but hold on to your sickle because you are going to need it. Better still, start saving up for a combine harvester because you won't believe how big the crop is going to be. Jesus said there was one thing that could be done while the seed was growing—we could pray for all the harvesters that would be needed. He was right. It was a bit like a mustard seed. All the power-brokers and politicos may well laugh at the claims of the tiny seed, but their amusement and unbelief are later silenced by the dawn chorus of birds in the branches of the mature plant and also by the fact that the roots of this miracle tree can undermine the brick and mortar of their securities without so much as breaking sweat.

If patience is required in the seed-sowing business, so also is perception, for not everything that looks like wheat necessarily is so. How are you meant to deal with mixed crops or the desires of those who want all evil cleaned up right now and forever? Jesus' answer is given in the story about the farmer who was the victim of agricultural sabotage when an enemy planted a weed in his field, which looked just like grain but was poisonous. Is a moral crusade needed that pulls out every offending plant? Wait a minute! Why the hurry? Sure, there's a problem, and it seems that the disciples viewed it that way. They asked Jesus to explain his story of "the weeds." They never really saw any meaning in the wheat. What they should have noted was that evil can't do anything about the presence of God's kingdom. It is there and throughout the world, and all evil can do is counterfeit it. Furthermore, the roots of the nasty stuff have entwined around the roots of the all-wheat team, so if the bad is pulled indiscriminately, the good will suffer. Jesus taught that the power of good would be demonstrated in two ways:

Now . . . he advised that the fake wheat be left alone lest it become the all-consuming concern. It should be "suffered" or literally forgiven. The ability to forgive the effects of evil's presence and influence is crucial in the immediate circumstances of our lives.

Later . . . there would be a decisive and distinctive intervention that would separate the wheat from the darnel once and for all, proving ultimately the triumph of the sons of the kingdom and the Son of Man.

Anything that was not planted personally by God would be uprooted.

This was not the only illustration of judgment that Jesus plucked from the farm. He said that two men would be sowing in a field and one would be taken and the other left. He said that when he returned, not everyone would be prepared. It would be similar to the days of Noah before the flood and of Lot before the destruction of Sodom and Gomorrah—just another typical day on the ranch with no expectation of the cataclysmic. Guys would be planting out in the field, whistling their country music; and women would be grinding the grain, sharing the local gossip. Farming as they knew it would never be the same again. It would be a final roundup, and good and evil would be separated as sheep are divided from goats.

The images of the countryside continue to bear Jesus' message. He described the relationship of those who followed him as that of sheep to a good shepherd, who would leave ninety-nine just to recover one that had slipped away. He warned that there would be false shepherds who would look at sheep but not look after them, and that there would be threats to the sheep's lives in the form of thieves as well as wolves. When he saw a farmyard hen gathering her chickens, he was mindful of his own concern to gather people under his protection. One day when he passed a vineyard, he described himself as the vine and all who loved him as branches. It was his way of saying that without a vital relationship with him, his followers would have no spiritual sap in their lives and therefore no fruit.

Toward the end of his life, it was the vineyard that became the setting for his revelation about his impending death. When he told the story of the tenants in the vineyard who killed all the owner's servants and finally killed the son and heir, he hit the raw nerves of his enemies and let them know he had their number and knew their plans against him. His tale about the workers in the vineyard was one of his most explicit portrayals of the grace of God who gives the same blessings to the guy who just scraped into the work force at the last minute as to the one who has been slaving away all day. When he watched grapes being crushed, he must have shivered and wondered about a particular cup of wine that he would be called upon to drink to the dregs.

 No country journey was complete without the roadside fig trees, and many were the times that he stopped by one of them to teach a small lesson with a big truth. Did Jesus' disciples ever pass a fig tree without remembering what he had warned them would be the signs of the end of the age? Had he not told them that just as the fig tree's twigs get tender and its leaves come out, indicating the coming of summer, even so, the portents that he had described would indicate that his return was imminent? When he spoke about fig trees, it was usually serious business, like the time that he told a story about a barren fig tree on what turned out to be his last trip down a country road when he made his way to Jerusalem for the last time. It still retained a power and poignancy in the disciples' memory.

A man had a fig tree planted in his vineyard, and he went to look for fruit on it, but did not find any. So he said to the man who took care of the vineyard, "For three years now I've been coming to look for fruit on this fig tree and haven't found any. Cut it down! Why should it use up the soil?" The man replied, "Sir, leave it alone for one more year and I'll dig around it and fertilize it. If it bears fruit next year, fine! If not, then cut it down."

It is understandable if first impressions of this story assume that it is about judgment. The very repetition of "Cut it down!" reverberates in the mind. However, it is not exactly a cut-and-dried case. First of all, this fig tree was planted in a vineyard. The owner was primarily interested in grapes, not figs. The point here is that the tree was for personal pleasure. Therefore, before the judgment of the tree, there had been grace in allowing it to be there. If grace had not come first, there would have been no ground for the mercy that was shown. Clearly, the absence of fruit was a source of deep disappointment to the master, and because he was committed to productivity, he did not want to see the soil it occupied going to waste. Jesus loved to make country folk think, and he threw in a bit of a curve ball by adding another character to the story line, namely the vinedresser, who not only pleaded for grace but pledged himself to do whatever it took to give this fruitless fig tree an opportunity to live on the other side of judgment. Two characters equally represent divinity, rigorous in judgment but gracious in mercy. It is a moving picture of the Son's intercession and the Father's patience and forbearance.

At this juncture in the story Jesus deftly, yet indelibly, brushstrokes redemption's bottom line. The word used here for the idea of "leaving it alone" is the same word that Jesus pronounced later from the cross when he asked the Father to "forgive." Although this invocation of release wipes the slate clean, it is not a carte blanche for it is an invitation to a new responsibility.

The true experience of forgiveness will produce the true evidence of forgiveness. Only the fruit of repentance will save the tree from uprooting. Being a fruit tree is not the issue—bearing fruit is!

And that brings us to the fertilizer. Something else was needed to revive this tree other than the waters drawn from the springs of good intentions; other than the pesticides of protectiveness; other than the provincial wisdom of past generations' farming philosophies. A compost like no other in the world was needed.

Little did the disciples realize at the time that in the crucifixion that would soon take place near Jerusalem's garbage dump outside the city wall, Jesus, in becoming sin for them, would literally become that compost. A shocking image? Yes, but in his death was their life and the life of the world. He was going to be hailed briefly as the Messiah, but he would first choose to present himself as the mulch that lays itself down at the root of the lifeless and fruitless, in order that there would be a redemption from judgment and a renewal of the sap.

There are many aspects of compost that we would rather not engage. None of us likes the smell of death or decay, nor do we like to be confronted by the stench of our sin. And yet if we will only allow that death, that compost to be applied to us, we will discover the warmth of its nurture and the first blooms of our salvation. The fertilizer of his body, blood, and bone is alone the answer for the faithless and fruitless—in a word, the figless. Christ saw his work as the restoration of the Father's pleasure in us. It seems preposterous that a vinedresser would give his life for a tree. Even so, he did not consider equality with the vineyard owner something to be grasped, but made himself compost, taking the very nature of plants, becoming obedient to decomposition and death, even the death of a compost heap.

This country story raises questions. Are your roots dry? Are your branches unbowed by fruit? Are you failing to avail yourself of the nutrients in the soil of truth? This simple parable was told as Jesus approached the palms of acclamation in Jerusalem. Its truth is quieter than the shouts of "Hosanna!" and its triumph is less obvious than the applause of the crowd. But while the eye is attracted by the garments laid down at the feet of the donkey, the mind should consider the fertilizer that must be laid at the foot of dead trees. Messianic glitz was no substitute for the mulch of atonement, and the green foliage of shallow acceptance was no substitute for the compost of redemption.

At the heart of all his understanding of the country road was a keen awareness about the process of winter death before spring resurrection. Did he not say that unless a seed fell into the ground and died, it would remain alone, but that if it died, it would bear much fruit? Thus it is that at farmhouse tables all over the world the grainy bread is broken and the fruity wine is sipped in praise of birds and lilies, of sheep and shepherds, of ploughmen and planters, of vineyards and fig trees, but especially of seed-time and harvest.

UPPER ROOM LANE

MAP REFERENCE

I am the true vine, and My Father is the vinedresser. Every branch in Me that does not bear fruit He takes away; and every branch that bears fruit He prunes, that it may bear more fruit. You are already clean because of the word which I have spoken to you. Abide in Me, and I in you. As the branch cannot bear fruit of itself, unless it abides in the vine, neither can you, unless you abide in Me. I am the vine, you are the branches. He who abides in Me, and I in him, bears much fruit; for without Me you can do nothing. If anyone does not abide in Me, he is cast out as a branch and is withered; and they gather them and throw them into the fire, and they are burned. If you abide in Me, and My words abide in you, you will ask what you desire, and it shall be done for you. By this My Father is glorified, that you bear much fruit; so you will be My disciples. As the Father loved Me, I also have loved you; abide in My love. If you keep My commandments, you will abide in My love, just as I have kept My Father's commandments and abide in His love. These things I have spoken to you, that My joy may remain in you, and that your joy may be full. This is My commandment, that you love one another as I have loved you. Greater love has no more than this, than to lay down one's life for his friends. You are My friends if you do whatever I command you. No longer do I call you servants, for a servant does not know what his master is doing; but I have called you friends, for all things that I heard from My Father I have made known to you. You did not choose me, but I chose you and appointed you that you should go and bear fruit, and that your fruit should remain, that whatever you ask the Father in My name He may give you. These things I command you, that you love one another."

John 15:1–17

The disciples were feeling bruised and battered by the recent onslaught of verbal attacks from Jesus' enemies, and the atmosphere in the city was distinctly brittle. They felt as if they were sitting on a fault line that at any moment could give way and engulf them in chaos. Jesus had been unusually quiet and thoughtful, and anyone would have thought it was a wake they were preparing for, not the Passover Feast. Later, they would realize why he was so meditative, for after three years of continuous public teaching, he was about to distill his life message for them, in private, at what would turn out to be the end of his teaching ministry. If ever there was a barracks, the Upper Room was it. If ever there was a battle, the events that followed would be it.

If there was anyone who could have done with some attention that evening, it was Jesus. More than his disciples, he had reason to say, "I need to receive tonight rather than give."

Within his intimate group was a traitor, and the weight of that anticipated "kiss" must have burdened his mind and sapped his physical strength. His perspective could have been dominated by suffering and disappointment, and yet we read, "Jesus knew that the Father had put all things under his power, and that he had come from God, and was returning to God." At the time that he was most assaulted, he was, in fact, most assured. His awareness was not of physical pain but of spiritual power. He hung on to the basics. He knew who he was, whose he was, and what he was called to do. Such security is foundational to servanthood.

Before his disciples could even react, he had left his place, stripped off his outer cloak, and wrapped a towel around his waist. The only sound in the room was the splash of the water that he was pouring into the basin. He was about to tell them a lot of things, but no teaching would be as memorable, as shocking, as life-changing as the example they were going to witness that necessarily preceded his exhortation. He had already blown every traditional expectation of the Messiah. This was the ultimate, for whoever would have believed that God would appear in a loincloth and on his knees at your feet too! In silence, the discourse began.

TENDING (John 13)

 Every man is acutely aware of his own needs and more than happy for someone to attend to them. However, Jesus had consistently taught that it was more blessed to give than to receive, so it was logical that he would be the one who tended others, more than being the one who was attended to. Nowhere is this principle of discipleship more clearly taught than here. When Peter forbade Jesus to wash his feet, his offended reaction was understandable. He was objecting on behalf of a humanity that cannot afford to have its hierarchical structures and pecking orders of seniority and subservience challenged without so much as a democratic vote. Basins are not standard desk items for bosses. The management infrastructure of the world was about to be subverted without a voice being raised or a memo from on high being written. Peter's submission to Jesus' action represents the cooperation necessary from all who would follow Christ, in their acceptance of his style of humble leadership in the face of the world's methods of dictatorial governance. Jesus' call to everyone who chooses to follow him is mirrored in his action.

1. GET UP . . . . from feeding yourself
2. LAY ASIDE . . . . your position and propriety
3. TAKE . . . . the tools of service
4. GIRD . . . . appropriate them for practical use
5. POUR . . . . get wet with involvement
6. WASH . . . . get dirty with specific identification

There have been many fights for the throne in relationships and institutions, but not so many for the towel. It is worth remembering that Judas' feet were washed with equal care and thoroughness. Every drop of water and every dab of the towel was a touch of grace, and it was still not too late for his clean feet to be saved from running to do dirty business. To the very end, Jesus was going to put himself on the line for the betrayers as much as for the believers. When he had finished and taken his place again, he forever sealed the brassplated door that beckons to pride, position, and power, by saying, "Now that I, your Lord and teacher, have washed your feet, you also should wash one another's feet. I have set you an example that you should do what I have done for you." If he'd asked them to wash his feet he would have reintroduced the league of personal merit that he had just demolished. No one was fitter than anyone else to be the Christ-washer, but all were able to minister selflessly to each other. Jesus wanted them to see that the demand to get more for themselves should be transformed into the desire to give more to others. "A new command I give you: love one another. . . . By this all men will know that you are my disciples, if you love one another." It should never be forgotten that the beauties of Jesus' utterances about the many mansions in his Father's house or about the relationship between the vine and the branches were prefaced by the ugliness of calloused, dusty feet.

INTENDING (John 14)

As important as their commitment to one another was, Jesus did not want them to be content with a continual footwash of the same feet. If he had other sheep that were not of this fold, then he also had other toes that were not of this basin. The intimacy the disciples had just experienced was comforting, but they had reason to be tentative and fearful. Their nice fellowship was about to be challenged. They had been privileged to be close to Jesus for three years, but if they were to make a successful transition to a more demanding sphere of service, then they would need to be jostled out of their present pattern of life, out of the security of their present company. They would be challenged in two ways: they would lose some, and they would gain some.

Jesus, after giving them his attention, wants them to understand some of the intentions behind his imminent departure for both them and himself. "Lord, where are you going?" asked Peter. "Do not let your hearts be troubled. Trust in God; trust also in me.... I am going... to prepare a place for you."

Thomas asked, "Lord, we don't know where you are going, so how can we know the way?" Jesus answered, "I am the way...." They wanted to know the destination, but Jesus would only give them the direction. They wanted to know exactly where they were going while Jesus wanted them to know how they were getting there. They wanted to focus on the goal of the trip while Jesus wanted them to concentrate on the guide. True, the road they had been walking with Jesus seemed to have decidedly ended. What they did not understand was that Jesus, having taken the road as far as he could by his life, was going to lay the rest of it through his death.

Although Jesus begins by giving them words of comfort, he does not want them to get comfortable. The gift of his comfort is the preface to his commands: "If you love me you will obey what I command." Intending is all about purpose and convictions. Jesus had intentions for his followers beyond them forming an alumni association. Basic and indispensable to the fulfillment of these intentions is his promise of the Holy Spirit, who will help them to:

1. Teach people his truth
2. Touch people with his love

The work of the Holy Spirit would ensure:

1. The preservation in their minds of Jesus' words
2. The power in their lives to do Jesus' works

It is Jesus' teaching about the work of the Holy Spirit that makes most sense to him about his going. Without the Holy Spirit, God would always be only "there," but with him, God would always be "here." If Jesus came to make the Father real, then the work of the Holy Spirit would be to continue to make Jesus real to all who chose to believe in him. At the moment of departure from them, it was important to Jesus to let his followers know that this did not mean an absence of his presence. The promise that he would be Emmanuel, God with us, was not going to be withdrawn. He would yet say, "I am with you always!"

Throughout the Gospels, the activity of the Holy Spirit is present and proclaimed. At Jesus' conception, baptism, and temptations, the powerful work of the Holy Spirit was identified. According to Jesus, all spiritual renewal, all new birth was premised on the work of the Spirit that came like a wind and could not be tamed by human power or wisdom. It was only through the Spirit that Jesus said he spoke God's words and performed God's deeds; that worship was truly spiritual; that spiritual thirst could be quenched. Now, at the end of his ministry, Jesus was reminding them that as long as they understood the role of the Holy Spirit, God's intentions would continue to be accomplished through them. Jesus simplified the process so that a child could understand it, removing all the mystical mumbo jumbo.

1. The Son prays for the Holy Spirit for his followers.
2. The Father answers the Son's prayer and gives the Holy Spirit.
3. The Holy Spirit comes to them.

In this conversation with them, Jesus identified five important things that the Holy Spirit would do.

Help them by coming alongside twenty-four hours a day. Although they were feeling bereaved right then, they would never feel like orphans with the Spirit's presence.

Teach them what they needed to know, especially by reminding them of Jesus' words. As teacher, he would interpret truth to them so that they would clearly understand their relationship to Jesus and the Father.

Witness about Jesus, more than anyone or anything else. The witness of the Spirit has less to do with a confirmation of who I am than with an affirmation of who Jesus is. The Spirit would enable the disciples to bear witness too.

Convict people of their sin, of the need to change and live according to God's standards, and of their accountability for what they had done with their lives, which are a gift from God.

Reveal more insights into Jesus' words and works so that they would be able to communicate effectively with others, in all cultures and throughout all generations.

And lest the disciples wrongly assumed that the Holy Spirit was some kind of extra-strong tonic to help them keep their chins up, Jesus referred to the "world" over forty times. In other words, his intentions were not that they become an exclusive club that built a memorial to the founding member but that they hit every road that led anywhere with the message that he taught them. It is in the power of the Spirit that Jesus would send them out, sustain them on the job, and speak through them. Really? Well, if he said so, it would come to pass, despite their present perplexity.

EXTENDING (John 15)

Not surprisingly, if they fulfilled Jesus' intentions, then there would be an extension of his ministry and his kingdom. Typically, he came up with a simple image that summarized all they would need to remember about what makes for effective growth: "I am the vine; you are the branches." The image was a familiar one to students of the Scriptures, and the disciples would have recalled the prophets who likened Israel to a vine. They would also have known that the vine was regarded as the most useless of all the trees. It was neither ornamental nor functional. Without fruit, it had no meaning. The extension of the church would have nothing to do with its own plans or programs. If that was the basis for its growth, then it would just become a bigger pile of dead wood. The only true growth was rooted personally in Christ.

Jesus was letting them know that they could give life to nothing. They were branches that could only reproduce the life of the vine. "Apart from me you can do nothing. . . . No branch can bear fruit by itself. . . ." The secret of abundant fruit was an abiding life. Jesus is not giving a cute, cozy picture here because there are some serious implications.

There will be two possible experiences for every branch. It will either be cut off because there is no evidence of fruit or cut down because pruning will result in even more fruit. There was no doubt in Jesus' mind that the entire purpose for their mission was to "bear fruit" and the main task of the Holy Spirit was to "testify about me." Anything else was a reduction of his intentions and a rationalization of failure.

CONTENDING (John 16)

If you extend it is likely to be at someone else's expense, so Jesus logically went on to warn them that they would be stirring up a hornet's nest and contending with some powerful adversaries. Having taught them about their relationship to him and to each other, he inevitably would teach them something about their relationship to the world. As long as they were associated with the rejected Christ, they would experience alienation and hostility: "If the world hates you, keep in mind that it hated me first. . . . A time is coming when anyone who kills you will think he is offering a service to God. . . . In this world you will have tribulation. . . . They will treat you this way because of my name. . . ."

Jesus had always been more than "up front" with them when it came to spelling out the cost of being his disciples. Like a good commander, he had told them what to expect when they were sent into action, and he always equipped them appropriately. The disciples would never forget the barracks talk he gave them before they went out into battle on their own for the first time. It was enough to make their hair stand on end. Maybe some would have said that it was bad psychology, but on reflection they agreed that once they were forewarned, they were definitely forearmed.

Jesus warned them that they would be subject to disease and to rejection by friends and family, to violent opposition from men and demons, to brutality and betrayal, hatred and murder. At least they knew now, so the removal of the surprise factor would help to eliminate some of the fear.

But he did encourage them, too, by telling them that if they felt like vulnerable sheep, that should remind them that they had a shepherd looking out for them. He assured them that they could not only endure but also evade trouble by fleeing to the next town. He promised that since the Holy Spirit would speak through them, they shouldn't delay their mission because they were not sure what they would communicate. He urged them not to be threatened by members of their own households, for at the end of the day, when they felt that no one cared and they were in danger of losing everything, the hairs on their heads were numbered and their souls were indestructible. If their suffering proved nothing else, at least it proved that they were like Jesus.

 Though unaware of all of the dynamics of that small group gathering in the Upper Room, they would understand in retrospect that time to be the foundation and model for their thinking and practice in their home meetings in the days ahead. Hearing the words of Jesus, asking lots of questions, offering prayers, developing relationships, serving others, and reaching the world became the constituent elements of community life.

Of course, they would have a better handle on things then than they did now. Little did they know that within a few hours they would be standing at the foot of a Roman gibbet, stunned and stupefied by the whirlwind of hate that had swept through their community, lifting their master off the ground and nailing him unceremonially to a crossbeam.

There was a single link between this awful scene and the moments of peace they enjoyed together at the supper table. That link was the loincloth. Earlier, he had divested himself of his cloak to appear that way to serve them. Now, he was stripped by the world, but still wearing the loincloth of the humble and obedient servant. In the years to come, when they gathered with their friends to reenact that Last Supper, they would always acknowledge that it was God in a loincloth who had served the meal by saving their souls, as we do when we take the bread and the wine.

MOUNTAIN VIEW

MAP REFERENCE

*A*nd when you pray, you shall not be like the hypocrites. For they love to pray standing in the synagogues and on the corners of the streets, that they may be seen by men. Assuredly, I say to you, they have their reward. But you, when you pray, go into your room, and when you have shut your door, pray to your Father who is in the secret place; and your Father who sees in secret will reward you openly. But when you pray, do not use vain repetitions as the heathen do. For they think that they will be heard for their many words. Therefore do not be like them. For your Father knows the things you have need of before you ask Him."

Matthew 6:5–8

And it came to pass, as He was praying in a certain place, when He ceased, that one of His disciples said to Him, "Lord, teach us to pray, as John also taught his disciples." So He said to them, "When you pray, say:

> Our Father in heaven,
> Hallowed by Your name
> Your kingdom come.
> Your will be done
> On earth as it is in heaven.
> Give us day by day our daily bread.
> And forgive us our sins,
> For we also forgive everyone who is indebted
> to us.
> And do not lead us into temptation,
> But deliver us from the evil one."

Luke 11:1–4

They knew better than to ask questions whenever he said that he was going mountain climbing. Given all the "time-outs" that he took, it was amazing how much he still managed to accomplish, with such an unhurried, unflustered poise. It only occurred to them later that there was a relationship between the time he had alone and the time he spent so effectively with people. Later he made it quite clear that his ability to communicate with people was the product of his availability to commune with his Father.

You'd have thought that after thirty years' preparation he'd be ready to spend all his time on the street and get as much done as possible. Not so. It would not have been a surprise to discover that one of his favorite passages of Scripture was the description of Moses going up Mount Sinai to meet with God. That really got him excited, though he seemed to identify with the heartache of the prophet when he came back down only to find the golden-calf party in full swing. Finding a refuge of silence and solitude was a top priority. His pace in public was never so fast that it kept him from that place in private. He'd always return from those climbs looking as if he'd just had a few months in a Roman spa.

As for the disciples, they reluctantly admitted that the time that passed so quickly for him while he was away, crawled and dallied for them. They were curious to know what went on in that higher altitude. One day, one of them was brave enough to find out.

They'd been on the road and Jesus had just taken one of his routine prayer stops. While he was refueling, the disciples were discussing a recent exchange they'd had with John the Baptist's gang. Frankly, they'd been embarrassed. You know how it goes, when one local congregation brags about their rabbi to the congregants of another synagogue or one bunch of devotees seeks to convince the world that their master is where it's at.

John had just completed an in-depth discipleship training

school with his entourage on prayer and, of course, they were keen to compare notes with Jesus' class. To put it bluntly, John had given them more three-ring binders' worth of material than Jesus' disciples had main ideas. Their *esprit de corps* was a little bruised, and they were more than a little frustrated. It wasn't that they knew nothing about prayer—they lived with someone who prayed all the time. They felt as inarticulate trying to relate what they knew as when it came to praying itself. Not surprising, really. They said, "Lord, teach us to pray . . . just like John has taught his disciples."

That would have rattled the phylacteries of just about everyone except Jesus. Had he failed his disciples? Was John a better teacher? How could he have made such a glaring omission in his curriculum? Couldn't he have prayed less in order to teach them so that they could pray more? How embarrassing to overlook such a fundamental issue. Would the disciples' confidence in him be shaken? Would they think John had a better handle on things?

Jesus didn't apologize or say it slipped his memory or appear defensive or excuse the apparent neglect and oversight. He taught them to pray. Regardless of the disciples' motives, at least, not to say at last, they had raised the question and Jesus was more than happy to oblige. It wasn't that they'd never heard him speak about prayer before, it was just that they required it to be put in a form that helped them bridge the gap between the general guidelines and the personal application.

How could they forget the time that he reduced their Jewish word-mountain on prayer to a couple of sentences? There were a lot of foot-shuffling, tassel-swinging Pharisees in the crowd that day. The fact was that any Pharisee who wanted a bad day, or wanted to feel even more self-righteous by sundown than he was at sunup, or wanted a reason to check on the current health of his jot-and-tittle knowledge of the law could simply go and listen to Jesus for a few minutes and leave a satisfied, dissatisfied customer. The disciples knew the teaching of the rabbis. "Great is prayer, greater than all good works." They knew all about the daily Shema and the incantations and all the set times for prayer.

There were prayers for just about every occasion you could think of, and although the original intent was good, to show God's involvement in all aspects of life, these had degenerated into formulaic utterances, dull and dogged, their devotional worth seriously devalued. Some of the forms of repetition were almost self-hypnotic, and it doesn't take great spiritual insight to guess the result of the rabbinic encouragement, "Whoever is long in prayer is heard."

You could not accuse Jesus of being long-winded. "When you pray, go into your room, close the door and pray to your Father, who is unseen. Then your Father, who sees what is done in secret, will reward you. And when you pray, do not keep on babbling like pagans, for they think they will be heard for their many words. Do not be like them, for your Father knows what you need before you ask him." And that was that.

However, each sentence was like a hand grenade thrown into a pharisaic prayer meeting. Jesus opposed public posture and promoted the need for private practice. If most of your prayers were the ones uttered in public meetings, then you were in trouble. Common to all Jesus' teaching on the basic constituents of personal devotion (prayer, fasting, and giving) were a couple of prohibitions:

- don't do these for the sake of appearance
- don't do them for the sake of applause

According to Jesus the choice was between doing it in secret or doing it to be seen. It was a matter of

- recognition—by men or by God
- reward—now or later
- reality—conceptualizing or conversing

Why did he spend so much of his time warning against hypocrisy? Presumably because he thought it was the *numero uno* area of temptation and sin for most people, especially the "spiritual" ones. In fact, there was no one who gave a better teaching on how to be a good Pharisee than Jesus, especially when it came to prayer:

- Choose a public *place.*
- Use an impressive *phrase.*
- Work on your *face.*

How would Jesus have reviewed a book entitled *Great Prayers I Have Prayed?* The answer was in one of the disciples' favorite stories, the one about the Pharisee and the tax man. They had to admit Jesus was a superb storyteller! His timing, his modulation of tone, and the movement of his eyes all combined to keep you straining for every twist of the tale. He knew how to tell a joke and keep you in suspense until the last critical moment before the punchline was unleashed, like a jack-in-the-box that knocked you off your feet and rearranged your funny bones. "Two men went up to the temple to pray, one a Pharisee. . . ."

The local yokels were already sniffing the perspiring, evaporating *eau de cologne* of the portly Pharisees who formed a convenient windbreak at the edge of the crowd. "The other was a tax collector. . . ."

It was going to be another good day for the underdog. The story was simple enough. The Pharisee "prayed about himself" so was not short of anything to discuss with Deity. After an opening time of worship in which he had an awful lot of good things to say about "the wonder of me," he reminded Omniscience, who already knew by virtue of this communication what a gifted pray-er he was, that fasting and giving were meeting budgeted targets to the last crumb of self-denial and the last cent of charity. The tax man, on the other hand, didn't even know where to sit or stand and certainly was not going any farther than the back row. Getting into the building was miracle enough. He could not even raise his head, so helpless did he feel about his right to expect God's attention, let alone permission to speak. He said, "God have mercy on me, a sinner."

According to Jesus, much more was needed than just "more prayer." He was always concerned about the motive for prayer and the manner in which prayer was offered, but he also had some real concerns about content. His story brilliantly summarizes two distinct approaches to prayer, one characterized by a man who strutted in confidence, the other by someone who stumbled in contrition. One looked up; the other looked down. One was proud; the other was penitent. One was consumed by his own holiness; the other by his hopelessness. One delighted in his independence; the other despaired about his insufficiency. One was grateful for his moral character; the other was mortified by his corruption.

In human terms this contest was a shutout in favor of the Pharisees. Jesus called the plays rather differently. One left the place of prayer "just the same." The other left "justified." He who thought he had it together was allowed to think that was so. He who knew he did not have it together was put together and left knowing so. Confidence in prayer was inversely proportional to confidence in oneself.

Our hindsight and access to the post-Jesus communicators has given us plenty of time to analyze and anatomize, but although we sound as if we have more to say about prayer than Jesus, do we? While we are identifying another fifty-three steps to the throne, Jesus is having fun telling another story. The fact that some of these tales, presented without embellishment or commentary, would insult the intelligence and spirituality of many charismatic conferees at the latest concert of prayer should not surprise us. These stories are designed to winnow out any attitude that even slightly whiffs of a "we are into deeper things" incense. Take the one about the widow who kept bringing her plea to a judge who was known to be indifferent to both God and man. In the end he yielded to her bothersome tactics just to get her out of his wig. If a judge who can be bought will respond like this, how much more quickly and willingly will God respond to the pleas of his children?

It was the Pharisees who had lost the main point of it all with all their spiritual techniques and insider talk. While they were quibbling over a vein in the little finger, Jesus went for the jugular.

If your circumstances are so bad that you lose a handle on everything, you may forget all you know, but whatever you do, persist in prayer. Jesus knew the human resistance to persistence. He taught that the more we bleed, the more we should plead. At the moment that we are tempted to collapse because no one seems to be listening, we should commune as if we expect undivided attention. It is precisely because God does listen that we are encouraged to persist.

God is not to be equated with the judge in Jesus' story, though some people do so. Prayer is about persisting, not picketing or pestering. We are not breaking some rules of holy etiquette by doing so or making a nuisance of ourselves and therefore being relegated to the end of the global prayer list because we stepped out of line. Jesus invited people to ask, not argue, believe, not beg. Instead of our getting all stewed up because we do not have enough faith before we plead, he suggested that faith is expressed precisely by the fact that we do plead. Faith is a consequence of the plea, not vice versa.

Jesus' words must have fallen like spring rain on dry hearts. Everybody could give at least ten reasons why God would not hear them or consider their request as worthy of immediate attention. Jesus scythed through the jungle of methods and models that ensnare us into thinking that there is something we can do to curry favor or jump the queue. He wanted his disciples to know that verbosity was not the same as vitality, that fluency was not always a sign of faith, and that noise was not necessarily equatable with power. He wanted persistent praying to be everybody's preference, instead of its being the last reluctant resort in bad times.

This point is presented as a double feature in Jesus' picture presentation on prayer, so it must have been an important one. It is reiterated in the story about the friend who shows up at midnight wanting three loaves of bread for unexpected out-of-town guests who have just turned up. Jesus argued that if the appeal to friendship fell on deaf ears, then the persistence of the door knocker would gain an entrance into the bread basket. Jesus recommended that we ask with the expectation that we will receive; that we pray searchingly with the diligence and scrupulosity that we apply to the hunt for a hidden object, and that we knock with unashamed vigor at the larder door of provision, unthreatened by all the lights that go on in the spiritual neighborhood and all the voices that would stop us from being fed when we most need it. The world will always seek to convince us that we have restricted access or that we can only ask during daylight opening hours.

In Jesus' story, because the guy persists, he gets "as much as he needs." We're not talking numbers now, as in three loaves, but needs, as in as many loaves as it takes to satisfy everyone involved. There may be varying shades of intensity in our praying as we respond to differently weighted burdens, but one thing should remain a constant, despite the fact of human need. My certainty in God's ability to answer my prayer adequately and appropriately should never waver.

Of course, Jesus qualified our understanding of asking when he said, "You may ask me for anything in my name and I will do it. If you love me, you will obey what I command." In other words, what we ask for should be concordant with Christ's nature and his desires for us, and the one who asks should be committed to love and obey him.

On another occasion, after Jesus had given some careful instruction about how to mend broken relationships, he immediately taught on prayer. It is a logical sequence if you think about it. Individual sin that disbands is opposed by corporate supplication that binds relationships together. Having recognized that there are problems that separate people, he spoke about prayers that brought people together: "Again I tell you, that if two of you on earth agree about anything you ask for, it will be done for you by my Father in heaven. For where two or three come together in my name, there I am with them." For Jesus, prayer was a community concern. Here, he not only invited people to ask, but encouraged them to know that they have authority when they do so. This authority is vitally related to:

- His personality and presence—". . . in my name, there am I . . ."
- Our community and unity—". . . if two of you on earth agree . . ."

The most crucial element in the disciples' training in prayer had less to do with what Jesus talked about to them than it had to do with how he talked about them to his Father. It was more important to him that they were the subjects of his prayers than the objects of his teaching. They were privileged to eavesdrop on Jesus when he prayed, and a couple of those significant occasions are recorded so that we can tune in too. Jesus was described as "full of joy through the Holy Spirit" (Wow! What that must have been to observe!) when he said, "I praise you Father, Lord of heaven and earth, because you have hidden these things from the wise and learned and revealed them to little children. Yes, Father, for this was your good pleasure." Although the words hardly do justice to Jesus' pulse-racing thrill at what he was seeing happen in the lives of his followers, they do disclose some foundational convictions that Jesus had about prayer. He continually voiced his total dependence on his Father, admitting that he could do nothing of his own accord. Consequently, prayer was

- necessary for Jesus for all things
- natural for Jesus at all times

Interestingly enough, lack of prayer is therefore a sure sign of independence, the lie that we can do most things pretty well on our own. Even if we disagree that we can do anything on our own, the failure to pray will mean that we are going solo anyway, despite our protestations and sworn convictions. How Jesus addressed God is also noteworthy. When Jesus prayed to God, he always considered the kind of God he was:

- *Father*—Jesus was assured of God's compassion and companionship.
- *Lord of heaven and earth*—He was assured of his greatness and his power.

This dual understanding is so important in prayer. Jesus knew that when he came to God he had both his attention and his attentiveness. Not everyone who gives you the former necessarily gives you the latter.

Without doubt, the most intimate insight we get into Jesus' prayer life and relationship with his Father is through the prayer recorded in John's Gospel, a prayer now known as the "high priestly" prayer, for it reveals Jesus interceding on behalf of himself, his disciples, and all those who down through history would become his followers. It is probably the clearest summary of what Jesus wants for every single person. This is his prayer list for us. His request is that:

1. We accept his *word* as God's word—"I gave them the words you gave me and they accepted them."
2. We have *assurance* about who he is—"They knew with certainty that I came from you and they believed that you sent me."

3. We live under his *protection*—"Holy Father, protect them by the power of your name . . . protect them from the evil one."

4. We have *unity* in relationship with others—"I pray that all of them may be one. . . ."

5. We experience *joy*—". . . that they may have the full measure of my joy within them."

6. We undergo a change in *character*—"Sanctify them by your truth. . . ."

7. We respond to his *commission*—"As you have sent me into the world, I have sent them. . . ."

8. We be filled with his *love*—". . . that the love you have for me may be in them and that I myself may be in them."

If we don't know what to pray for ourselves, this makes a good starting point:

Dear Lord, Give me an appetite for your word and keep me in it. Help me to be assured about who you are and who you have made me to be. May I know the full blessings of your salvation, from my past, in my present, and for my future. May I be related to you and to others who know you, in unity and community. Give me a full measure of your joy, as of one who has found treasure. Help me to cooperate with your will for my life so that I become more like you in purpose, in purity and in power. Equip me to be an effective witness and a willing partner in your mission to the world. May I always be appreciative and aware of the love you have for me, and may I be a conduit for that love to flow to others. May the end result of everything that I am and that I do be that you are more clearly perceived by others as the Way, the Truth, and the Life. Amen.

Before the disciples ever heard Jesus' prayer, they did get an answer to their question: "Lord, teach us to pray. . . ." How did Jesus handle it? Typically, he avoided a long lecture and simply prayed. The result was a blueprint for prayer that has tutored all generations since. Jesus' aim was to give his disciples a pattern of prayer, and in no way was he putting it forward as a magic formula for pious parrots. It was his way of helping them to voice their needs and articulate their problems. Our familiarity with it from childhood has dulled our sensitivity to its purpose and its power, but even a cursory examination unveils both its depth of content and breadth of concern.

It has three distinctive movements. Jesus

- *Ponders* . . . he meditates on God's character
- *Petitions* . . . both for God's glory and man's need
- *Praises* . . . affirms God's greatness in a final doxology

I. PONDERS

Our Father—This establishes that it is a family prayer, only of relevance to those who know God as their Father. Jesus modeled intimacy without familiarity and is in no rush to get to his requests. Prayer was a matter of waiting on God, not God being reduced to a domestic to wait on man at the flick of his needy fingers. Jesus knew that if his followers were able to address God as Father, then most things were taken care of right there. They would know at the outset that they were loved and provided for. They in turn would be eager to express the family likeness, not only in obedience to Father, but also in relationships with brothers and sisters. They would have confidence to ask for what they needed without fear or failure. They would realize that God's fatherhood was more the issue than their faith.

They also would be convinced that he would always and only do those things that were good and right for them. The God that Jesus prayed to was not a nice uncle. The one who prayed was not an applicant for charity or a loan at the lowest possible interest, but a son or daughter seeking the love of the Father.

In heaven—Jesus draws our attention to the fact that God is not some local, parochial deity but the God of heaven—sovereign, mighty, and exalted. He is no pushover, nor will he be a party to anything that is not clean or straight. Again, we see this balance in Jesus' understanding of God's greatness yet his familial involvement. God is intimate without being intimidating. He is all-powerful without being over-powering.

II. PETITIONS

GODWARD OR FOR GOD'S SAKE

Arising from Jesus' consideration of who God is, comes a trio of petitions that essentially express the concern that God will be rightly considered by everyone.

Hallowed be your name—Here the request is that people will break through the name barrier into an intimacy that first and foremost honors and reveres who God is, applying his truth to all of life so that God's values and desires characterize every life. Strictly speaking, this should read, "Your name be honored!" For Jesus, this was a matter of some urgency, and such a request first searched the hearts and challenged the priorities of those who prayed it.

Your kingdom come—The kingdom is not a physical realm but a spiritual relationship that is entered through personal relationship with Jesus, whose arrival established the kingdom of God and whose mighty works illustrated the kingdom's presence and power. Here is a longing for God's rule and order to be triumphant over the disruption and disorder of the world that does not acknowledge any reign but that of its own systems.

Your will be done on earth as it is in heaven—Logically, this comes next, simply because the evidence of God's kingly rule is submission to his loving rule. Clearly, God's will is not the natural thing to do on earth, and Jesus is aware that there is an opposing kingdom and a dynamic and demonic will to power that are antithetical and inimical to God's intentions for men and women.

Why is heaven mentioned? Because it introduces a standard of expectation that should be normative for everybody. Jesus is expressing the desire that his Father's will be obeyed, uncomplainingly and uncompromisingly, and that it be enacted both with justice and with joy . . . as it is in heaven.

MANWARD OR FOR MAN'S SAKE

There follows a second trio of requests that have to do with human need. It is obvious by now that it is impossible to pray the Jesus style and be self-absorbed. The desire for these three prayers to be answered is related to the overall concern that God be praised, not simply that I be provided for. However, Jesus showed that are three basic areas of human need:

- for sustenance
- for salvation
- for security

Give us today our daily bread—Our bodies are gifts from God and need to be sustained and maintained. We should neither despise nor deify the physical body, but rather delight in it and discipline it. It has legitimate needs that must be satisfied, not sated. Jesus' teaching is very liberating because he assured his disciples that whereas selfish prayers were invalid, specific prayers were valid. To pray in this manner is to learn to receive what is needful, instead of laboring to retain what is needless. It involves the maturation of contentment and gratitude. It is a community prayer ("Give us . . .") that subordinates pressing personal needs to the corporate need for daily provision. This petition automatically makes us aware of our potential responsibility to others, particularly the necessity to be prepared to be the answer to their prayer for provision.

Forgive us our debts as we also have forgiven our debtors—Jesus presented sin as a debt. There are no deposits that we can make to get our personal account out of the red. We have an opportunity to deal with our guilt and confess our spiritual bankruptcy now and have our debt forgiven before we are confronted with our accounts payable. Jesus knew the teaching of the Scriptures about God's response to sin when it is confessed and renounced: God blots it out, covers it up, sinks it, forgets it, forgives it.

The consequence of canceled sin is seen in our relationship with others. Jesus taught that if we could not forgive and release another from indebtedness to us, regardless of the offense, then we understood neither the depth of our own sin nor the expansiveness of God's mercy. In dealing with others, the issue is not "How much do I like them?" but "How much has God loved me?" If we cannot forgive, then Jesus baldly states that we have not repented. In other words, we're either forgivers or Pharisees, and I think it is now fairly clear what Jesus thought about hypocrisy.

Lead us not into temptation—The world is a minefield for anyone who really wants to please God, and Jesus knew it from personal experience. God cannot tempt anyone to sin, but he does respond to our request to be shielded from unnecessary trials and testings. We can't avoid all pain and pressure, and in fact, the very circumstances that so often seem to put faith on trial or seek to destroy faith are the very ones that fortify resolve and further spiritual understanding. Jesus knew that even unavoidable and, in God's economy, desirable trials, could present temptations to sin in both attitude and action. That is precisely why he recommended that we pray against the experience, for none of us can be presumptuous about our strength. Two other things can be done:

1. We can evaluate all such trials and temptations in the light of God's rule and do what Jesus did. When he was assaulted, he affirmed what God wanted for him and therefore kept his bearings. It is easy to see now that knowing how to walk the road God's way is integrally related to our knowledge of his will, the highway code for our journey.
2. We can be encouraged and strengthened by Jesus' example, whether it be his response to temptation in the wilderness or to the opposition of the Pharisees.

Basically, Jesus suggested that we should budget for temptation. As one traveler has observed, when we're not conscious of temptation we should pray "lead us not into temptation," and when we are very much aware of its onslaught, we should pray . . .[7]

Deliver us from evil—There are dangers without as well as within. There are deceptions on the one hand and accusations on the other. Against the will of God that Jesus has already confirmed are the wiles of evil. Deliverance is not a one-time affair, but a daily appropriation of God's protection in every situation. Much bondage results not simply from catastrophic acts of disobedience but from daily neglect to pray this prayer.

III. PRAISES

It is appropriate that the prayer concludes with praise. After all, Jesus has just said that we can legitimately expect God to answer our prayers for the resources we need for ourselves, the reconciliation we need with God and others, and the resistance we need against evil. Indeed, the fitting summary of all this good news is *"Yours be the kingdom, the power and the glory!"* Whereas pride parades, humility praises; and it is the humble and contrite heart that will pray like this, or it is this kind of praying that will provoke humility and contrition. *Amen.* In other words, it's all true! Yeah! Let it be this way in me and in others, for God's sake.

 As the disciples listened to Jesus pray, who knows how much they took in? However, it was not a one-class course. Unknown to them, their learning was going to be reinforced in intensive fieldwork, and for some of them, that field would be an olive grove on a night they would never forget. This was no cute theory time. They had never seen their dear friend so agitated, so weighed down. He admitted it himself when he told them his soul was "overwhelmed with sorrow." He kneeled some, but he paced up and down more. They knew there was some kind of crisis going on but were confused.

They understood why he wanted to pray, but what could he say when he was this distressed? Is there any prayer that can effectively transmit the garbled codes of a troubled, mangled spirit? Later, they recalled some of the words that escaped through the latticed bars of the shadowy prison formed by the trees' branches: "Not as I will, but as you will. . . . Watch and pray so that you will not fall into temptation. . . . May your will be done. . . ." Although the disciples had only caught snatches and phrases, these fragments began to provoke some old memories. The more they considered them, the more they could hear their echo, except that they were no longer disjointed, compressed communiqués, but part of a single utterance that began "Our Father in heaven. . . ."

Only long after this did it occur to them that despite the

ploughing of his heart that night by the blunted blades of the world's scouring sin, it was more than likely that his final words, before he got up from the dirt and wiped the blood and sweat off his face, were "Thine be the kingdom, and the power and the glory!" spoken as by a son who was deeply in love with his Father and as by a teacher who had learned his own lesson well.

PARADISE DRIVE

MAP REFERENCE

*T*hen He said to him, "A certain man gave a great supper and invited many, and sent his servant at supper time to say to those who were invited, 'Come, for all things are now ready.' But they all with one accord began to make excuses. The first said to him, 'I have bought a piece of ground, and I must go and see it. I ask you to have me excused.' And another said, 'I have bought five yoke of oxen, and I am going to test them. I ask you to have me excused.' Still another said, 'I have married a wife, and therefore I cannot come.' So that servant came and reported these things to his master. Then the master of the house, being angry, said to his servant, 'Go out quickly into the streets and lanes of the city, and bring in here the poor and the maimed and the lame and the blind.' And the servant said, 'Master, it is done as you commanded, and still there is room.' Then the master said to the servant, 'Go out into the highways and hedges, and compel them to come in, that my house may be filled. For I say to you that none of those men who were invited shall taste my supper.'"

Luke 14:16–24

It was not one of those roads that Jesus most traveled. This was Paradise Drive where Jesus was going to attend one of those power-dinner affairs, attended by everyone who was a who's who and knew what's what. It was a far cry from The Pig and Whistle, where Jesus fraternized with all the lowbrows and thus raised the eyebrows of the highbrows!

Everything was definitely kosher here, the food having been cooked on Friday to ensure that no work was involved in its preparation on the Sabbath. Every dish smelled of sanctimony and was cooked to a legalistic turn. The eyebrows were pointing toward the rafters again on this night, for Jesus "was being carefully watched." Those who were consumed by their own theatrical self-importance would be no better than stagehands tonight. They would not make it on to the boards, let alone take center stage. It comes as no surprise that Jesus was on the invitation circuit. After all, he was in the headlines and was of increasing political interest; the combination of novelty and notoriety was irresistible to the curiosity of high society's hosts. It seems that Jesus was alone, so the disciples must have had to hang out with the limo drivers at the end of the street.

Clearly, Jesus was not there to cultivate useful relationships with influential people in case he needed a good word should he get into trouble. His eyes acknowledged greetings as he entered, and as he looked ahead of him to survey the party scene, he noticed a man suffering from dropsy, in a severely overswollen state from all the fluid retention accompanying his condition. A pulse of emotion crossed Jesus' face, and it was difficult to say whether it was a smart or a smile.

The fact was that this had all the makings of a pharasaic setup. It was going to be one of those evenings. No doubt, most of the honored guests had hoped that they would get an opportunity to sidle up to the Galilean guru and chitchat with him firsthand. As it turned out, they were all spoken to by Jesus, in a manner that was extremely personal and direct, but it certainly wasn't a party conversation style they were used to hearing.

Immediately he looked around. There was an uneasy, conspiratorial silence. Someone has to break the ice at a party, so why not Jesus? "Is it lawful to heal on the Sabbath or not?" Like a model guest, Jesus checked out what was allowed in the house! If they had replied that it was okay, then the ice breaker would have turned them into law breakers. If they said, "No way!" then they would have appeared callous and indifferent to human suffering. The silence thickened, only disturbed by some foot shuffling and weight shifting from one or two of the well-heeled lawyers and well-endowed Pharisees.

If nobody knew the answer, then presumably it was reasonable to try it. Taking hold of the man, Jesus healed him. Not a bad start to a party if you were sick, but if you were a stickler for religious etiquette, then you were not exactly entering into the spirit of the party as the ex-dropsy patient experienced it.

Jesus, annoyingly at ease and in command, pursued the matter, but this was no small talk to cover up a momentary embarrassment: "If one of you has a son or an ox that falls into a well on the Sabbath day, will you not immediately pull him out?" Now this was hitting close to home. With one incision of the butter knife, Jesus had exposed the inconsistency of their professed beliefs. It was fine to quote the law that forbade the rescue of an animal on the Sabbath, but of course, it never applied to *your* animal. When it comes to self-interest, self-righteousness has an amazing knack of converting the absolute exclusion into a situational ethic. In one sentence, Jesus examined the library of laws that they subscribed to and exposed the way they customized their customs for personal advantage and yet failed to interpret the law of Moses in a manner that brought mercy to another. No one reached for *hors d'oeuvres* and no one spoke. Paradise Drive was not rocking to good conversation and sparkling wit that night.

It was a relief when dinner was announced. Jesus was now doing the watching. The ingrained habits from years of petty pride and pathetic insecurity ensured that all the guests went onto autopilot and flew straight for the places of honor at the table. As someone has observed, these were the kind of people "who think a fun evening consists of clawing your way to the top of the social heap."[8]

 You would have thought that Jesus had done enough damage for the night. (It's incredible isn't it, that a fantastic miracle of healing should be considered by some as a disaster to the cause?) Not to be deterred, Jesus continued his controlled assault on those who lived their lives according to the "Jerusalem Top One Hundred List." As he stood back at the edge of the room, he had the marvelous audacity to provide some advice as his fellow partygoers jostled for the best seats. It reads like an excellent column from Miss Manners suggesting it was much less embarrassing to take the lowest place and be invited higher than to have to bear the humiliation of being asked to vacate the higher seating arrangements for someone more distinguished than oneself.

The sting was in Jesus' closing summary statement: "Everyone who exalts himself will be humbled, and everyone who humbles himself will be exalted." Thus far, Jesus' contribution to the meal was a bit like a cold, lumpy gravy being poured over a cooked-to-perfection filet mignon. His comments had a way of taking the bubbles out of the champagne, of making the wine goblets feel like dumbbells.

Just as well the disciples were not there to hear it. They would have stopped him right then before he opened his mouth again . . . which is precisely what he did without them.

Having addressed the general gathering, he then spoke directly to the host. Imagine it, a guest telling the host the proper way to have a dinner party. The logic was impeccable, but not obvious to those who only did this for that, or gave tit for tat. Don't invite those who are able to return the compliment. Rather, ask those who are poor, crippled, lame, and blind, those who cannot repay the favor. This is Jesus' recipe for a great party.

What's in it for the host? Jesus said, "You will be repaid at the resurrection of the righteous." In a brilliant stroke, Jesus has moved this audience's attention from the world of lobbying and power peddling to another order of reality where eternally influential evaluations take place, untainted by the nod and the wink, untempted by the golden handshake. The world of boot scraping and back scratching, eye catching and arm twisting was being seriously challenged.

While they were reeling from this sudden journey from *realpolitik* to resurrection, from first course to Last Judgment, some pious prig at the table tried to tiptoe over the bed-of-nails atmosphere with a jolly observation: "Blessed is the man who will eat at the feast in the kingdom of God." Unfortunately, he impaled himself immediately! Jesus had mentioned something eschatological, and this guy said the first thing about the end times that came in to his head. What he said is not wrong; it's just not relevant, showing that he had not understood a word that Jesus had said. Of course, the idea of heaven is great, and we can all contribute to an abstract theological conversation, but the poor at our party? The blind at our bash? The sick at our soirée? There's nothing like sanctimonious humbug for dodging the bullets and avoiding the implications of down-to-earth truth with the fancy footwork of specious spiritualizations.

Jesus responded to this skin-deep religion by telling a story that confronted their attitude with a very rude shock: "You mention the last day, the feast in the kingdom of God . . . As you sit assured of your seat at this table, what makes you so sure that your name is calligraphied at a place setting at the big, final supper that you've just referred to . . . ? How will it really be on that day that you so piously say that you look forward to . . . ?" They might as well have been in the synagogue with all the listening they were having to do. Did they carry on eating as he spoke? Did they look him in the eye? Did their breathing increase with rage? Did they tremble as they wondered how much more personal he could get? Did they wish they could stop him? Was there malice aforethought?

One small piece of background information is necessary for Jesus' tale. When you decided to throw a party, you sent an invitation to all your guests and then followed it up by sending a messenger around on the day of the celebration, to announce readiness and preparedness. The invitees in Jesus' story had already been well informed of what was happening and what was expected of them. With economy of detail, Jesus portrays the tragedy, the horror, of the way that some people respond to the most open invitation to the greatest party ever—God's invitation to feast at his table, at his expense, forever.

The fact that the guests had known about the event for a while implied a measure of acceptance. No one had declined because there was anything wrong with the invitation or the host or the provision at the party. Like many excuses, the ones that were made by the characters in Jesus' story have a certain legitimacy—if all there is to life is getting on, grabbing one dollar more, doing one's thing one's own way according to one's own schedule. However, they are still excuses and evasions, and they are all sham and flimflam, despite the talk of other necessities and priorities.

Three sets of excuses are described to illustrate the way that people delve into the past, present, and future to salvage a reason to justify their refusal of the greatest invitation on earth . . . for heaven:

1. *Future Possibilities*—"I have just bought a field and I must go and see it." What could be more exciting than a new piece of property, loaded with possibilities for planting, for building? New furrows will bring new returns. What could be more laudable than pacing it out, estimating the potential yield, using a good planning strategy?

2. *Present Necessities*—"I have just bought five yoke of oxen, and I'm on my way to try them out." You know how it is in business! Pressure of work, got to keep things moving . . . expanding the business fleet . . . new hardware. . . . more portfolios. Sometimes our business has to come before someone else's pleasure. Isn't that a praiseworthy work ethic?

3. *Past Commitments*—"I just got married." How good to hear about a thorough commitment to relationship. Usually there are enough commitments that we have already made to people we care for,

without complicating life with other demands.
Relationships can take all of our time.

On the way back to his master, there was plenty of time for the servant to sort out how he would break the bad, sad news of all these refusals. They were all plausible, even understandable. The world of labor and love is extremely demanding. However, the host in Jesus' parable would not buy it. It wasn't a last-minute invitation they had received that warranted such an insulting response. In anger, he told his servants to gather the poor and crippled, the blind and lame; when there was still room to spare, he ordered that the country lanes be scoured, "so that my house will be full." Isn't this a bit ungracious? Doesn't this kind of reaction justify the guests' response? After all, he could have said, "I understand . . . we'll miss you. . . . Hope it goes well. . . . Let me know how the meeting with your realtor went. . . . Trust the test-drive was a success. . . . Have a wonderful romantic evening together. . . ." He did not even say, "Maybe another time . . . I'll be in touch." There must have been more than one dinner-party guest who was thinking, "So what . . . did I miss something?"

Jesus' answer to that question would have been an emphatic "Yes!" They had accepted every social invitation going, but had failed to respond to the spiritual invitation that he had offered. Meanwhile, the guys and gals down at The Pig and Whistle were all ears, and what's more, all heart. For some reason, they knew a good party when they saw one. Presumably, Jesus got on with his meal at this point, leaving them to chew on the tough stuff he'd just dished out. The toothpick of their self-righteousness would have a hard time removing the traces of his cuisine, and every stab of their gums in the attempt would be paid for in kind. For every prick of their pride, there would be a puncturing and piercing retaliation . . . just wait and see.

So what is the point? Why the overkill on the host's part? Basically, just as nature abhors a vacuum, so grace abhors empty places at the table that has been prepared at great cost for the spiritually hungry soul. Jesus' host is not throwing a peevish fit because of injured pride, nor is it a display of thwarted spite or vengeful rage. It is an outburst of emotion that has its source in an unquenchable longing for good friends and good times. The invited guests, by excusing themselves, have denied the host the opportunity to bless and nourish them. The strength of feeling is that of someone who is watching the ones he loves make the most damning and disastrous decisions of their lives. The consequences are obvious to all but the beloved, who remains cavalier as far as the future implications of the denial are concerned.

The imperative that gathers human flotsam and jetsam from the highways and byways reflects not only the power of the host's affection, but also the urgency of the situation. The party is ready, and now is the time to take your place. If you fail to respond, another will take it. There is no seat that will remain empty with a "Reserved" notice attached. The invitee will be absent, not merely because of his refusal to accept, but equally because of the host's refusal to admit him. His choice will turn out to be his judgment. There are no "doggy bags" sent as consolation gifts, nor is there any facility for take-out orders so they can eat on their turf, on their terms, according to their dress code. The host's fare could be enjoyed only at his table.

We find it easier to correlate anger with judgment than with grace, but what Jesus is emphasizing here is the radically intense nature of God's grace, expressed in a commitment to save and serve whoever will come, in a way that breaches all the barricades and bastions of exclusivism. The outreach to the streets was not a second-class guest list. Power parties usually decide themselves according to who the powerful people happen to be, not according to the tastes, necessarily, of the hosts. Because you are So-and-So, you are invited. In Jesus' story, the issue is not who the guests happen to be, but what the host happens to choose to do, and his choice is to have a full house that will account for all that he has provided. No resumé is needed, just an affirmative response. Grace longs for relationship and grieves over wasted or untasted provision or over hungry people who continue to snack on their own resources when they could feast at the expense of another.

Without doubt, the host's exclusion of the original guests is meant to give us indigestion. Jesus underscored the terrible finality of refusing the invitation and missing the party. But what of those who made it? If those who were too busy to respond had passed by and peeked through the window, they would have received a severe shock to their social, political, and religious sensibilities. All their lives they had believed that only those who had made it get to the best parties. Judging by the crowd in there, it seemed that the only qualification for entry was the total lack of any qualification to be there. Those who could give reasons for being there were absent. Only those who were speechless when asked to give an account of their credit were allowed to participate in the fizzy hoopla of the banquet. They did not even have to be properly attired. There was nothing the local Chinese laundry, English tailor, or French coiffeur could do to make their appearance any more presentable or their company any more desirable. They never did have the price for the ticket. Unbelievable? Absolutely. Those who looked like seedy gate-crashers were in fact those who had been invited. Those who looked civilized and incapable of transgressing social etiquette would not be able to use their influence to gate-crash this one, not even if they offered all their land and lovers in one package deal.

As the host sent the servant, so God sent Jesus. Of course, we strut about and play the businessperson or the scholar, the romantic or the statesman—too busy, too bright, and too beautiful to be sidetracked by an invitation that interferes with the agenda. As many other invitees have testified and as we will surely find out, when the cold wind of reality begins to blow, the security wall that we build out of the bricks of our personas and possessions, our schedules and skills, is no more protective than a hedgerow. Jesus' story was right. The gospel, the good news of God's invitation to us to party with him at his place and on his terms, finds us as we really are—spiritually homeless and bereft, street urchins and alley cats, one and all. It comes to us before we've had a chance to pretty or better ourselves and seems unbothered by stubbled chins and pallid cheeks.

We always say that we "wouldn't be caught dead" in our pajamas or whatever. That is precisely how the invitation catches us . . . and by the way, admitting that we are dead, once caught in that state, is the best qualification for God's live show, simply because the price of the party ticket is our life. Of course, we are right to think that we may not be dressed right or anything-else-right, but the wedding garment is provided. To top it all, it doesn't come in large, medium, or small, but with our name handsomely monogrammed on it, tailored to perfection. Think about it. All of those who ended up at the party in Jesus' story began their day asleep over a grating, under a hedge, in a field, without any expectation that by sunset they would be hobnobbing on the croquet lawn of the lord of the manor. Every day, thousands awake without hope, accept Jesus' invitation to enter His Father's kingdom, and go to sleep assured of new coordinates for their life.

Remember, Jesus was addressing a Capitol Hill crowd. He violated their definitions of power in this world with a miracle that intimated a force that they had not accounted for in their inventory of what makes the world go round. He assaulted the citadel of their pride, with its columned concern from position and prestige, security and success—of course with lip service to deity thrown in—one nation under God and all that. He said there was another guest list more important than any power lunch or presidential banquet and that it was important to accept the invitation, even if it seemed to conflict with established appointments or anticipated liaisons. He intimated that the pursuit of a sensible, successful, decent, and dutiful life could keep you out of the party. No excuse, whether legitimate or a lie, would be accepted as valid. The key point is that anything that results in your absence from the celebration is phony and will contribute to eternal joylessness.

Yes, there is a great party for those who accept Jesus' invitation to follow him, but there is also a great pity for those who refuse. Surely, more than one of those present at that meal must have been curious to have an explanation for the story, but there is no record that it was either asked for or given.

It was a relief when Jesus excused himself. He was last seen walking down Paradise Drive with his arm around a guy who looked considerably thinner than when he first arrived at the party.

Anyone else want to leave this table and follow them?

ROUTE
FOUR

*Checking
out some
folk
he met . . .*

MAP REFERENCE

Now so it was, as the multitude pressed about Him to hear the word of God, that He stood by the Lake of Gennesaret, and saw two boats standing by the lake; but the fishermen had gone from them and were washing their nets. Then He got into one of the boats, which was Simon's, and asked him to put out a little from the land. And He sat down and taught the multitudes from the boat. Now when He had stopped speaking, He said to Simon, "Launch out into the deep and let down your nets for a catch." But Simon answered and said to Him, "Master, we have toiled all night and caught nothing; nevertheless at Your word I will let down the net." And when they had done this, they caught a great number of fish, and their net was breaking. So they signaled to their partners in the other boat to come and help them. And they came and filled both the boats, so that they began to sink. When Simon Peter saw it, he fell down at Jesus' knees, saying, "Depart from me, for I am a sinful man, O Lord!" For he and all who were with him were astonished at the catch of fish which they had taken; and so also were James and John, the sons of Zebedee, who were partners with Simon. And Jesus said to Simon, "Do not be afraid. From now on you will catch men." So when they had brought their boats to land, they forsook all and followed Him.

Luke 5:1–11

Jesus was in his element. The sun was on his back, the people were in his face, and because of that, his feet were in the water. The fact is that he was loving every minute of it. On this day, every pressure, every demand, every appeal, every inconvenience, amounted to an irresistible invitation to teach. Many years later, one of his disciples would say, "I love a commodious room, a soft cushion, and a handsome pulpit, but field preaching saves souls." Jesus felt exactly the same when it came to the choice between a synagogue bench and a lakeside beach.

A little farther down the water's edge, Simon was not quite in his element. The night before had resulted in plenty of dirty, snagged nets but no fish. He had been listening to Jesus but was frankly too disheartened to get into the spirit of the occasion. The locals could cram together and sweat it out to their heart's content as far as he was concerned. Missing every second word was a small price to pay for the safety and privacy of his boat. But his despondent seclusion and concentration were suddenly broken. The stranger was in the boat without so much as an invitation, asking him to drop his work and push out a few yards so he could have a floating platform. What could he do?

Every eye was on him, so there was no way he could be surly. Of course, the bad news was that he too would have to bob around in front of all these people, a prospect that was less than desirable. There were plenty of folk out there who had been lashed by his temper, not to mention a few who had been bruised by his fists, and they would think it a huge joke that he was stranded in his own boat, having to listen to every word that the rabbi said, especially the lines about anger being the same as murder. At least he could keep his head down and make good use of the time by repairing some nets.

The way it all happened was so effortless, really: a necessity, a quick bit of problem solving, and a push from the shore. It seemed so off-the-cuff, so spontaneous. A couple of minutes later, sitting in a boat with Jesus, staring at the net in his hand, hearing that strong but mellow voice elicit hearty laughter from people who had little to be happy about—Simon felt a bit like a fish that had been unwittingly netted, and there was absolutely nothing he could do about it.

He wasn't far off the mark. Fishing boats are for fishing, right? So what was Jesus hoping to catch?

 His net-repair kit had hardly been used. Simon had to admit to himself that the time went faster than he had anticipated and that he had enjoyed what the rabbi said more than he'd ever have cared to acknowledge. Maybe "enjoyed" was not quite the right word, for his face flushed more than once and he tried to freeze lest anyone mistake his movement for discomfort or, God forbid, conviction. All that stuff about turning the other cheek, forgiving your enemies, going the extra mile was fine for professional rabbis who'd never lived in the real world and been in a bar fight or had to compete with the other boats for a fair share of Galilee's fish market.

Whatever, the teacher had given his final blessing and wrapped things up. Simon was dreading having to make conversation once the crowd started to disperse, so he decided to look busy and get the oars ready for the pull shoreward. The stranger was staring out over the lake, as if he was looking for something, and then without turning his head to look at Simon, he said, "Put out into the deep water and let down the nets for a catch."

Oh, yeah!

Sure, by the time the preaching session was over, Simon felt flattered to have the star of the occasion on his boat and allow him to do his spiritual thing. So far, it was good advertising, high profile and all that. But this was something else. Simon was proud of his experience and expertise. He had a reputation. This guy was invading his work life and what's more, proving his ignorance by giving the dumbest command imaginable. This is exactly what you'd expect from a rabbi, even one who was an ex-carpenter. Simon was the one who gave orders on this boat, and this was one he'd never issue. You fished at night, not under the rays of the glistening sun. In any case, he'd just been out there according to all the best rules and routines, and even by doing it according to the book, he had achieved no success.

He was going to learn that Jesus does not enter someone's boat for just the religious bit. When he enters the domain of a person's life, he has more in mind than just borrowing their services or gifts or livelihoods for temporary purposes. Simon was also going to discover that the best of personal experience and know-how, the most proven of local traditions and fishlore, the most reliable of professional insights and techniques, were not in themselves all there was to it. Compared to what he was about to experience, the combined sum of every profound thing he knew about his life and work was going to appear shallow. The characteristic flashfire reaction ignited inside Simon, but somehow he managed to keep his mouth shut and not scald the stranger with his frank estimation of this suggestion.

What could he have said? This was the second time that he had been asked a question and felt hopelessly entangled. There were some possibilities, believe me. Stick with nails, carpenter. . . . You take the law, rabbi, and leave the lake to me. . . . Man, I'm dead beat because I've already tried it. . . . You can't tell me to do anything, buddy, that I don't want to do. Simon could have been too tired to go, too proud to admit that he could be told anything, too experienced to do something this off the wall, too self-satisfied because there was now no need for fish.

And yet he went. He wasn't tripping over himself to tell Jesus what a great idea it was. "Because you say so, I will. . . ." Yes, he had reason to delay, argue, refuse. The boat wasn't in full readiness, the crew was not available, the weather had not been checked out. Since when did Jesus ever find us with our act really together? What's worse, he'd be making a complete idiot of himself. In front of the entire fishing community, he'd be acting as if he knew nothing about the trade. It would be humiliating. Fidgeting next to this rabbi while he spoke for a few hours was one thing, but allowing him to order you to take him fishing in the most unfavorable of circumstances was another.

The reason Simon gave for going speaks for itself. He may well have experienced the whole emotional mix of resentment, resignation, reluctance, but his response, albeit against his better judgment, was simply obedience to Jesus against the odds. It was based not on his ability to achieve a result, but on Jesus' authority. It was going to be the best decision he ever made in his life, as a lot of intellectual tut-tutting, emotional heel-digging, spiritual pooh-poohing folk have since found out too.

For the first time in his life, Simon was being asked to go beyond himself, beyond the comfort zone, beyond the field of proven success. The best that he knew had been ineffective, and here was someone challenging him to go out deeper and try something he'd never done before. It was a matter of perception. For Simon, this was not what he was used to and he knew that it did not fit the normal pattern. It was more demanding, simply because he was no longer in control.

Jesus seemed oblivious to all these problems and was speaking like someone who not only knew there were fish out there, but knew the exact spot where he had already corralled them.

Who knows what they talked about on the way out. For all the struggle that was going on in the big fisherman, he had not realized one simple thing that we all overlook when Christ's challenge spooks us. This whole deal was a reward, not a punishment. Jesus had been blessed by Simon's kindness in letting him have the boat. As was Jesus' way, he always returned things better than he found them. What more obvious way to express gratitude than to return Simon's fishing boat to shore, loaded with fish. If it had dawned on him that Jesus' intentions were only for his blessing, then he would have spared himself needless disturbance. The fact is, even one fish by Jesus' method was more than the best boats in Galilee had managed. This couldn't turn out any worse than things already were, so why not?

In cooperation with Jesus' instruction, he let down the nets. When I say he, I mean "they," because you can be assured that Jesus was not sitting in the stern telling stories about the one that got away. It was clear to Simon that this stranger was here for business and not pleasure. He wasn't bad for a rabbi. In fact, he'd clearly been fishing before and almost looked sheepish at one point that he was appearing like an old hand.

When the nets hit the water, the fish hit the nets. Simon apologized for the oath that instinctively shot out of his mouth. It was no good. There was too much down there for two pairs of hands. Frantic signals to the shore captured the attention of Simon's partners, and while they made their way out, the only sounds in the air were the thrashing of the silvery mass in the water, Simon's incoherent, nonstop mumblings of the "I'll be . . ." school, the crackling rip of the breaking nets, and the whoops of delight from the stranger. Simon wondered at his co-worker's strength as his stretched sinews and taut muscles carried their share of the weight. He was also impressed by his hands. Clearly it would take more than this load to make them bleed.

 There was no time to do anything else but fill the two boats. The fish kept coming, and they were beauties. It seemed that this stranger knew them, their work, and their lake better than they did.

At last, when they could carry no more and the boats felt as if they would go under, Simon stood up, surveyed the scene, then crumpled at Jesus' feet in a heaving, sobbing lump. He seemed unaware that he had dangerously rocked the boat and that his face was pressed into the flailing fish. Maybe the people on the shore heard that cry: "Go away from me, Lord: I am a sinful man!"

Until then Jesus had been respectfully referred to as "Master" but Simon uttered a deep-throated, full-hearted "Lord!" He was not wowing over the fish at this point, but literally wallowing in the overwhelming sense of his own sin and failure. Herein lies one of the most profound truths. The emphasis is not the sign, but the sin. The issue never was the catch, but Christ. Simon's participation in this miracle did not convince him that he was now qualified to have more faith next time or become one of Jesus' chums. On the contrary, this revelation of divine power and love convinced him of his disqualification, of the fact that he had no right to be on the same boat as this man. There is no atom of personal prowess or self-contentedness. No one is mentioning the money they'll make or the stir that their catch will create. Simon's confession is not one of personal satisfaction but of deep need and contrition. There is always a danger of being impressed with Jesus' signs and wonders, yet impervious to our own sins and weaknesses. Simon's overpowering conviction has to do not with the kind of miracle it was, but with the kind of man that Jesus is. He is not merely the best fisherman; he is the Lord of Creation. It never was about what Simon could do, but what Jesus could do.

For all his gruff and bluff, Simon was a man acutely self-conscious of his need. While others could articulate their grievance, he could brawl. While others had their education, he had his bravado. While others maybe had the manners to succeed, he had the machismo. It is this hidden insecurity, this chronic self-doubt, and this deep fear of having to play the outsider that Jesus gently touches in his response. "Don't be afraid: from now on you will catch men." Jesus' word is always an inclusive one, after sin has been acknowledged, repented of, and forgiven.

Simon's weaknesses and failures, his lack of social graces, and his limited background may have excluded him from admission into the world's entry levels, but never from Jesus' company and team. Obedience, even when it is most resisted, creates new opportunities, a new order. The crisis of self-knowledge that Simon thought would crush him, resulted in a call to service and fulfillment beyond his imagination. Fighting for a share of Galilee's catch would be a thing of the past, since he had just been given a license to trawl the world.

The sentence that describes how this incident ended is more loaded than the boats. "They pulled their boats up on shore, left everything and followed him." By the time they got back to land, the issues had been settled, the priorities had been established. There had been no counting of fish heads, estimating of value, planning of distribution, spending of net income. The old partnership had been dissolved, and a new one had been forged. As those boats slowly were pulled onto the beach, Simon and friends leapt out like fish leaping into air. It seems that they never looked back. They left the miraculous catch, and even the miraculous nets, for they had realized the difference between a supply and the source. Cling to the miracle that is supplied, and its resources will be depleted. Follow the source of all miracle, and your life will be replete.

 Jesus continues to challenge our willingness to go deeper, where there are more dangers and fewer guarantees according to the feasibility studies of this world. However, there are some things that are assured. The effectiveness of your well-worked routines will be tested. Your insecurities, despite a brave face and good sea legs, will be exposed. What Jesus promises will come to pass. Your needs will be met. You will be made aware of who he really is, and consequently you will get a revelation of yourself, sin and all. At the moment that you will most want to jump ship, you will be invited to join Christ in a permanent shore leave doing his work rather than yours, being supplied by his hand rather than by your net. When, like Simon, you cry "Depart!" he draws near. Once you have confessed your sin and his lordship, just as Simon did, you will find that not even the best catch in the world will be a sufficient substitute for his company.

A mark of spiritual maturity is the ability to move on with Jesus, even if that means leaving some pretty impressive miracle stories behind. If we stay with the boats, we will have some good props and propaganda for a while. If we follow Jesus, we will have a daily testimony of his ability to lead and provide. As Simon was going to find out, there were plenty more fish where those came from, served with bread too!

SYCHAR STREET

MAP REFERENCE

Therefore, when the Lord knew that the Pharisees had heard that Jesus made and baptized more disciples than John (though Jesus Himself did not baptize, but His disciples), He left Judea and departed again to Galilee. But He needed to go through Samaria. So He came to a city of Samaria which is called Sychar, near the plot of ground that Jacob gave to his son Joseph. Now Jacob's well was there. Jesus therefore, being wearied from His journey, sat thus by the well. It was about the sixth hour. A woman of Samaria came to draw water. Jesus said to her, "Give Me a drink." For His disciples had gone away into the city to buy food. Then the woman of Samaria said to Him, "How is it that You, being a Jew, ask a drink from me, a Samaritan woman?" For Jews have no dealings with Samaritans. Jesus answered and said to her, "If you knew the gift of God, and who it is who says to you, 'Give Me a drink,' you would have asked Him, and He would have given you living water." The woman said to Him, "Sir, You have nothing to draw with, and the well is deep. When then do You get that living water? Are You greater than our father Jacob, who gave us the well, and drank from it himself, as well as his sons and his livestock?" Jesus answered and said to her, "Whoever drinks of this water will thirst again, but whoever drinks of the water that I shall give him will never thirst. But the water that I shall give him will become in him a fountain of water springing up into everlasting life."

John 4:1–14

The top-ranking vulture scouts among the Pharisees were in search of some more juicy bones to pick. They'd heard that Jesus was doing better than John in baptism statistics. What an ideal opening for dividing and conquering, for setting John's ministry against Jesus' mission. Refusing to be lured into a public controversy, and no doubt protective of John, Jesus slipped away from Judea to return to Galilee. His confidence was not in published results or comparisons with fellow preachers. His security was not derived from his relationship with others, but from his relationship with his Father.

For some, going back to Galilee would have been regarded as a big mistake. Fancy missing this great opportunity for publicity, for reaching a big crowd with a great message. For Jesus, doing what was right constituted an advance, even though his humble retirement from the public eye looked like a cowardly retreat. He hiked northward through Samaria. He didn't have to go that way—in fact, good Jews went the longer route and refused to take a shortcut through tainted Samaritan territory. Jesus' choice of road was not a wild impulse, nor was it self-serving. Constrained by a necessity greater than public perceptions of his own orthodoxy, he was going to end up saving more than just time.

Tired from the long trek, he found a well to sit down beside, and a little while later, a woman arrived to draw water. It was fortunate that the other guys had gone to buy food in Sychar, the local town. Sometimes, the disciples had a way of keeping people away from Jesus, and they certainly would not have introduced Jesus to this broad! Traditionally, this woman has been treated as if she had never received her high school diploma. Maybe people assumed that because she was morally loose she had to be some kind of dumb blonde. The fact is that the conversation she had with Jesus is one of the most intense and intellectually demanding in the

Gospels. Yet Jesus unashamedly engaged the woman and expressed his need of a drink.

Well, as it turned out, Jesus didn't need his tut-tutting friends there because the woman was quick to point out the obvious objection herself. "Hey, mister! You're a Jew and I'm a Samaritan. What's a nice guy like you doing here with a not-so-nice woman like me . . . and asking for a drink too?"

Both of them knew what going by the book involved, but as Jesus was going to show her, there are rules and rules. God's rules press us into blessing and when their directives are broken we are hurt. Men's traditions bring a curse, and when their despotism is broken, we are healed.

Imagine a multiple choice test for rabbis: *Check one only!*

I am excited about sharing my faith with . . .
- ☐ a woman
- ☐ a Samaritan woman
- ☐ a divorced Samaritan woman
- ☐ a divorced and currently promiscuous Samaritan woman
- ☐ none of the above, so help me God

With effortless ease, Jesus violated men's taboos by doing God's will. What he proceeded to do was a rabbi's ultimate nightmare. Jewish sources make men's rules perfectly clear:

Blessed art Thou, O Lord . . . who hast not made me a woman. . . . A man shall not talk with a woman in the street, not even with his own wife. . . . The daughters of the Samaritans are menstruants from their cradle. . . . He that eats the bread of the Samaritans is like to the one that eats the flesh of swine.

Frankly, like most legalistic nonsense, the problem had a good historical pedigree, and of course, present bitterness is directly proportional to the number of years elapsed since the original offense, multiplied by the number of offenders presently alive! It was in 720 B.C. that the Assyrians had occupied Samaria, deported the inhabitants, and replaced them with foreigners who came complete with their own false-god kits. In time, polytheism disappeared, and the locals worshiped Jehovah and accepted an abbreviated version of the Scriptures, namely the Pentateuch. But this step in the right direction could not atone for the unforgivable mixed marriages and loss of racial purity all those years before. In 128 B.C. the Jews had burned the Samaritan temple, and by the time that Jesus was enjoying his glass of water, relations between the two groups could best be described as "settled hostility."

 Yes, of course, Jesus understood the problem, the same way he seemed to understand most people's. Here, he walked eyes wide open (in fact, so open that he perceives that which is hidden!) smack into a major historical, religious, political, and personal mess. He was aware of the cold-steel separation between this woman and her community, other men, Jews, and Father God. Sure, her multiple-partners list spoke for itself. You want problems? There were enough right there at that watering-hole to irrigate the calendars of a sex therapist, a marriage counselor, an ecumenical church council, and a United Nations commission.

While we're asking the woman to draw a few more glasses of water to go on the polished table where we're going to conduct a meaningful problem-solving session, Jesus was whispering something: "If you knew the gift of God and who it is that asks you for a drink, you would have asked him and he would have given you living water." In translation, the monotone falls like the early droplets of rain that precede a deluge. This was not a cascade of counsel, yet quietly, persistently, every drop distills refreshment, spreading its moisture as it settles upon the downtrodden pavement of the woman's heart. Suddenly, the issue is not so much what he knew about the problem, but what she knew about him. He seemed to be suggesting that if she really did know him, she'd quit analyzing and start asking for what she actually needed. He was not offering another additive to maintain life or giving a navigational adjustment to get life on course—he said he was giving life itself. As we said, he didn't understand the problem.

You can imagine what was going through the woman's mind. Such a well-meaning guy but clearly not equipped to help. He was talking about getting her . . . or did he say giving her . . . some water and he didn't even have a bucket. "Are you greater than our father Jacob?" she asked rather mischievously. She reminded him that the patriarch had enough water to give to his sons, flocks, and herds—beat that! The power of the old traditions raised its head again. Hold on, honey! You're not aware that Abraham's career batting average happens to be higher than Jake's and that this stranger not only claimed to have been in the hall of fame before either of them was even born, but he even said that he invented the game!

Undeterred, Jesus passed over the opportunity to dazzle her with his "Who's Who" resumé and insistently continued to talk about the water. This exchange is a brilliant example of Jesus' consummate skill and sense of touch, for although he had said something that was taken wrongly, he was happy to try again and restate it a little more vividly. He wasn't telling and yelling but teaching and reaching. He developed the image of water, the great Old Testament sign of the messianic age, with its expectation of water gushing in the wilderness, of streams in the desert, of burning sand becoming pools, and of the thirsty ground being transformed into a bubbling spring: "Whoever drinks the water I give him will never thirst." She was thinking "drinkin'," and he was talking "dunkin'."

Here's something about Jesus you should really appreciate. Long after our ignorance and arrogance, our disdain and discourtesy have interrupted his communications, he is still on the line, hanging in there for us, not hanging up. While we bask in the jokes of our own cleverness and think of another patronizing comment, he is already planning another way of telling us what he longs to give us.

The Samaritan woman still didn't hear him! Did we the first time? She could only envision what he had to offer in the terms that ruled her life—the physical. Jesus was nothing but a salesman with a new labor-saving device. She couldn't pick up on the soul-saving gift yet. "Hey, sir! I don't understand what you're on about, but if you can get me what I want without the hassle I'm putting up with now, then count me in." But since when did salvation have to do with giving me what I want, trouble-free? It's a popular message, I know, but there seems to be a basic difference between the desires of the flesh and the demands of the Spirit. She was still in the world of the magical, wondering where this bucket was suddenly going to appear from ... or where the new instant well was going to be engineered.

Her imaginations were suddenly grounded by Jesus' request that she go back into town and get her husband. Her blunt denial that she had a husband was met by an incisive word of knowledge: "You have had five husbands ... and by the way, the guy you're sleeping with at the moment is not your husband!" It is Jesus' manner to get to the root of sadness and weariness and failure. We put the best of ourselves on display in the shop window, and Jesus goes straight for the particular fuse switch in the closet in the farthest corner of the warehouse out back that plunges our elaborate self-illuminations into darkness. He dares to leave his footprints on the newly vacuumed carpet of our tidy, mental living rooms, and he pulls back the clean bedclothes from our king-size dirty sheets. His knowledge was shocking to the woman, but it was his love that reached behind the pain barrier of her defensiveness to get to the heart of the matter. The exposure of her sin, of her moral and marital laxity, was by no means the end of the story. The worst revelations can make for the best confessions and the beginning of a journey to freedom.

 Despite that supernatural exchange, the woman did what we're all tempted to do when Christ gets too close—create a diversion. Jesus had just given a specific picture of the anarchy of her emotional life, and she veered off at a tangent to pursue a tedious religious controversy. It was a real concern and a valid subject for discussion, but it was a million miles from being the main issue of her life right then. She called Jesus a prophet—at least this was an advance on "magician"—but there was something tragic about talking religious shop with someone who had just offered her what she's longed for all her life.

Yet again we witness Jesus' extraordinary compassion for her, manifested in his patience and forbearance. He didn't chide her for dodging the issue, but treated her further questions seriously. He didn't lecture—he listened.

Of course, there may be a reason why she began to talk about temples, if she had privately been convicted of her sin and was automatically thinking about necessary sacrifice. Whatever her mental linkage, she asked about where the right place of worship was, and Jesus cut through all the divisiveness and said it's not a matter of where but of how we worship. Our place is just fine! It must be "in spirit" and "in truth." It hasn't anything to do with rituals or sanctuaries, but humble and clean hearts that are not condemned by sin. Wait a minute! What on earth has a conversation about exalted worship of a holy God got to do with a woman who lives like a whore?

HUMAN WORTH AND DIVINE WORSHIP

Jesus' wisdom had gently led her to the real problem of her life. Her sexual pursuits were but symptoms of her tragic loss of worth. However, we find no jingles here about positive thinking or self-esteem, no truisms about human potential. She had first to discover who God is before she could know who she was. When the worth of the Creator is established, the worth of the creature is assured. When the Creator is denied or denigrated, the creature will be worshiped, and the sensualist and the narcissist, the materialist and the pragmatist will rule.

Only when we truly worship God do we experience the divine appreciation and approval of our lives, for his acceptance of our praise authenticates all of our being. We do not worship to pacify a deity, but to please a Father. In the recovery of divine worship is the discovery of human worth, and should we not expect this to be so, if this happens to be the very relationship and response that we were created for?

HUMAN FATHERS AND DIVINE FATHER

In her rootless and fruitless state, the Samaritan woman had talked a lot about human fathers, about traditions and ancestors that, like her lovers, had fondled but failed her. She needed to find out who her heavenly Father was. It wasn't enough for her to believe in God; she needed to know personally the kind of God he is.

Relationship with God has nothing to do with an occasional dip into a bit of organized religion, the effects of which evaporate upon contact. No, it's more like a continual inner drenching that leaves us permanently refreshed and clean. Neither the woman's historical predecessors nor her sexual partners had given her the relational security for which she longed. In the same way that many people continue to believe in God and approve of Jesus, she confessed her general belief that the Messiah would come and sort it all out, but that was in the future and didn't really give her any hope for the present.

All the way through this dialogue, it has been painful for her to apply what Jesus is saying to her own personal life. She constantly kept Jesus at bay with abstract questions and generalized comments. However, with the mention of the Messiah, rain begins to fall again as he looks her in the eye, fixes her gaze, and says, "I who speak to you am he." Have you noticed the regularity with which down-to-earth intrusions happen at moments of spiritual revelation? This climactic announcement is picked up by the disciples who have just returned from the local fast-food franchise. Jesus' lips are dry, the woman's heart is thirsty, and they have food in their mouths! Fortunately, all that needed to be said had been said. Jesus' words do not need hushed tones, soft religious music, and extended appeals to emphasize their conviction and power. The sight of Jesus talking to a woman enforced good manners on these snackers, for they did not open their mouths nor dare ask any questions. In the silence, the woman dropped her water jar, and that strange noise was the sweet sound of breakthrough and deliverance. When she got to town, she didn't talk about the Samaritan temple on Mount Gerizim or Jacob's farming techniques. She said, "Come and meet a man who told me everything I ever did!" This news really had penetrated her heart, though she had fought hard not to admit it or show it while she was with him.

Jesus looked up to see a whole pack of hikers coming down the road. "Open your eyes and look at the fields," he said to his friends as he saw the woman returning with some of the neighbors who had relished the gossip columns of her former life. By watering a single, fragile, wilting flower, he had planted that field. The shortcut became a short stay, as he spent two further days with them. Their testimony was conclusive. "We have heard for ourselves, and we know that this man really is the Savior of the world."

 You know, it doesn't matter what your problem or controversy or how you procrastinate or evasively argue, you will hit Sychar Street on your travels and find the same patient, yet direct Christ leaning against your well, checking out your bucket. He challenges both the sources and the systems of our lives. Like this woman, we will always find he's more interested in our present relationship with him than our past record; more concerned about what we can be than what we are. A life of perpetual drawing at wells that run dry and broken cisterns that leak may be exchanged for a present supply of Christ's forgiveness and faith.

Sychar Street is where legalistic traditions can be exchanged for living truth, ritual for relationship, the grip of fear for the graces of faith, the hell of worthlessness for the heaven of worship. Here, every hiker can exchange the bucket of limited supply for a baptism of living water. The difference between dredging for your own satisfaction and being drenched by another's is the difference between death and life.

JERICHO BOULEVARD

MAP REFERENCE

*T*hen Jesus entered and passed through Jericho. Now behold, there was a man named Zacchaeus who was a chief tax collector, and he was rich. And he sought to see who Jesus was, but could not because of the crowd, for he was of short stature. So he ran ahead and climbed up into a sycamore tree to see Him, for He was going to pass that way. And when Jesus came to the place, He looked up and saw him, and said to him, "Zacchaeus, make haste and come down, for today I must stay at your house." So he made haste and came down, and received Him joyfully. But when they saw it, they all murmured, saying, "He has gone to be a guest with a man who is a sinner." Then Zacchaeus stood and said to the Lord, "Look, Lord, I give half of my goods to the poor; and if I have taken anything from anyone by false accusation, I restore fourfold." And Jesus said to him, "Today salvation has come to this house, because he also is a son of Abraham; for the Son of Man has come to seek and to save that which was lost."

Luke 19:1–10

The crowd was swelling and so were the disciples' feet. Like a gaggle of geese, the throng was awkwardly making its way into Jericho. Hopefully, the scents and aromas of the trees for which this town was famous would be strong enough to do a cosmetic job on the perspiring, plodding pilgrims. Above the general hubbub, you could still hear an exuberant but raucous shout: "Son of David! Yeah! He's the Son of David!" Bartimaeus had every reason to holler, because a few hundred yards back up the road, the lenses of his blind eyes had been divinely reground. He had heard that Jesus was coming, and from his roadside pool of darkness, he had thrust his face forward spasmodically and begun to search with his screeching voice that which his eyes could not see. Some bystanders had tried to shut him up and ship him out, but the fact is that real need knows no embarrassment and refuses to conform to the petty rules of social etiquette.

When he yelled "Jesus!" he managed to elongate the name until it spanned the distance between his mat and this rumored Messiah. Many in that crowd were following Jesus with a yet-to-be-convinced intellectual curiosity or with religious interest, but this hollow-eyed, spine-bent, sunken-chested beggar had expressed more passion and intensity, conviction and faith in a split second than many of them had done in a lifetime. Sure, Jesus heard him. There were those who knew that Jesus would have heard his need if he had been dumb as well. Caught in the middle of the human current, Jesus stopped. He probably dispatched Andrew (the resident expert in bringing people) to lead him through the masses.

Jesus' simplicity and directness were unnerving for many folk. He offered no three-point sermon, no soul-dredging, no third-degree-burn interrogation, no background check, just "What do you want me to do for you?" He always seemed to ask the obvious. The tone of his voice was relaxed, and yet he enunciated each syllable with the increasing firmness of a tightening embrace. Some people used to go into a spin-dry cycle when he asked such direct questions. They were too sophisticated or too far gone to answer simple requests, blind to their need through ignorance or arrogance.

"I wanna see, Jesus!" said Bartimaeus.

"Okay," responded Jesus. "See!" And that was that. He didn't poke his eyes, make weird signs, bring the crowd to attention, mumble special phrases, wave at the heavens, or appeal to ministering angels. He didn't even touch him! He spoke, Bartimaeus saw, and the crowd worshiped God. The blind man got what he wanted, as did God. Some in the crowd had been numbed into shame by the raw faith of this peasant, who could now not only shout louder than they could, but also see better. You would have thought that all this was enough theater for one day but not so.

Hardly had one miracle been digested than another drama unfolded. The players? Well, Jesus was the main one, not because he dominated or took center stage but because . . . well, because he was who he was. Despite the constant pressure, he always seemed calmly poised, gracious without being condescending, purposeful without ever appearing to hurry. The followers were players too, milling about like so many hens in a congested coop. Every now and again, the disciples worried when they thought they saw a shadow of concern or a wrinkle of pressure flit across his face. Maybe they were just imagining it.

There was another character, who, unnoticed, had bulldozed his way into the shade of a sycamore tree. Short in height but long on width, he gained his yardage the old-fashioned way (no feints, no fancy footwork), just head-down, headlong momentum. It turned out that he was a chief tax collector, a lucrative job in a town that happened to be an important customs post for goods entering Palestine along the trade routes from the east. In his profession, you could say he'd reached the top of the tree. That explained why he was the wiliest and wealthiest man around, and also the most despised and detested.

He had heard rumors about Jesus fraternizing with some of his buddies in other regional offices and knew that Matthew, the celebrated host of the most talked about taxman's party in years, had turned disciple and was somewhere out there. Ever since that dinner dance, the Pharisees had been popping anti-stress herbal remedies to calm their anger at Jesus' ease in eating with "tax collectors and sinners."

Meanwhile, Zacchaeus had advanced from the sycamore's shade into the safety and elevation of its branches. It was probably the best place for him to be, for he was hand in gauntlet with the Romans, though if he fell into the crowd he would have been dead meat. He was once described as a "crook, capitalist and collaborator." The joke was that his name meant "pure," which was about as appropriate as naming a harlot Chastity. At this moment, as potentially comic as the picture seems, his location up that tree is both tragic and pathetic. Separated from others by their hatred, isolated by the consequences of his own criminal activity, sentenced to alienation and exclusion from the religious community because of his business association with the Jews' enemies, Zacchaeus was the definition of exclusion from membership in anything except his own private thought-club. Yet despite all this, there was something almost admirable in the sheer determination that was exerted against gravity to hoist himself in such an ungainly manner into such a ridiculous hideout. He seemed to be peeking, more than seeking, but something must have been churning and yearning away in his troubled and lonely spirit for him to get even this far.

 What happened next is charged with humor and compassion, seriousness and firmness, all mixed up and served with concentrated grace. Jesus' timing was masterful. Of all the trees in Jericho, he decided to stop beneath the wide lateral branches of this particular one. It all seemed so spontaneous, so off-the-cuff. He didn't march up to the tree and bawl Zacchaeus down with an imperious command to take him to the local diner. While the fat tax man was on the fastest weight-loss program he'd ever experienced, Jesus was enjoying the temporary respite the tree's shade was bringing him. Clearing his dry throat and without looking up, he said in his gentle but commanding voice, "Hi, Zacchaeus! Why not come down immediately and take me to your place for something to drink?"

Typical of his touch and timing, he could deliver a lightning bolt in a jar of honey. The initial gasp of the crowd was followed by unsure laughter as a rumpled body thumped unceremonially to the ground. It was strange, but Zacchaeus had planned to get as close to Jesus as possible for his purposes, not allowing for the fact (in the way that none of us does) that Jesus was equally intent on getting close to Zacchaeus for his divine reasons. Anyway, there he was, tunic creased, face scratched, and no doubt his unhealthy joints aching.

Jesus was great with people who didn't have it together but pretended that they did. Zacchaeus was so transfixed by Jesus that he didn't even bother to dust himself down or straighten himself up. Despite the potential embarrassment of the crowd's presence, it occurred to more than one observer that he seemed strangely at home, as if this was the moment that he'd rehearsed for all his life. He was not fazed by Jesus' insistence that he be the first Jew to darken his door and illuminate his room in years. Not a bad guest to have on the first line of your unused visitor's book! Nor did Zacchaeus worry about what was in the larder, for the person at his table was somehow more important than the food on his plate. It was extraordinary! The entire pilgrimage procession to Jerusalem had come to a halt at a thief's house. Jesus' need to spend time with this little lapsed Jew was more important than anything else—almost sacrilegious wouldn't you think, with the Holy City waiting, no less? Meanwhile, Zacchaeus was waiting too . . . for the kettle to boil!

This incident occurred as Jesus was making his way to Jerusalem for the last time, to celebrate the Passover festival. In Luke's account, it was the last recorded involvement with an individual's life before Jesus' triumphal entry into the city that would crucify him. Consequently, it is charged with significance and is far more than a cute kid's story for a Sunday school flannel board. In a way, it could be considered as a crucial link between the gospel as preached by Jesus and doctrine as expounded by Paul in Romans because it deals with the question: What is it to be a true son of Abraham?

Luke has been concerned with how one becomes part of this kingdom that Jesus has been talking about, and what happens to Zacchaeus is a summary answer. Let's look even more closely at what was going on here.

We have already noted that it was Jesus who made the first move. This is characteristic of the message of the gospel throughout the New Testament. While we were lost, he looked for us. While we were sinners, he died for us. There are two features of Jesus' approach to Zacchaeus that should be noted.

HIS COMMAND

As compassionate and empathetic as Jesus is, we should not conclude that he is offering himself as an optional extra or that he is in the agony-column business. His communication is intended to be authoritative, not suggestive, and consequently when he calls someone, it is necessarily commanding and urgent. However, it is not a command in an impersonal, imperative sense. C. S. Lewis once described his difficulty in understanding God's command that we should worship him. This seemed a bit much—rather imperious and arrogant, in fact. Lewis recounted that he only understood the matter when he realized that God's command to worship him was exactly the same as His invitation to enjoy him. To misunderstand the demand was to miss the delight.[9]

Jesus' command to "come down" could be considered insensitive in the light of Zacchaeus' evident insecurity and the crowd's inevitable hostility, if it were not for the fact that he was inviting this man to leave a world of isolation for one of inclusion. Whenever he called someone to responsibility, to change—in a word, to repentance, that person had to leave where he was, who he was with, and what he was doing. Too bad if you happened to be up a tree when you got the invitation!

Maybe the account of Adam and Eve flashed through Jesus' mind, in particular the moment that they emerged somewhat startled and chastened from the bushes of Eden. He seemed to have a canny knowledge of the shrubberies and groves of human evasions, the hiding places of self-consciousness and self-indulgence. He was never more in command or more at ease than when he invited folk to leave the nooks and crannies of their isolation and fear, seclusion and loneliness; to abandon the convenient shelters of pride and politesse that allowed them to be observers but denied them the experience of being participants and followers. The command to come down or come out is equally the invitation to come over . . . to "come on in."

HIS CONCERN

The way he told Zacchaeus to move "immediately" was also typical. It was one of his favorite words, and most aptly described the way things happened when he was around. He seemed to know when it was time to get down before the limb broke; when it was time to leave the forest before the night fell. Far from being an expression of unreasonable control, it was a manifestation of reasonable concern. If what he offers is the most important gift that can be received, then "immediately" is the logical time to accept it. The entire exchange was spontaneous, and yet it was executed as if it had been scripted. Just like Bartimaeus a little while earlier and all the countless others, Zacchaeus was not an afterthought, another intruding need, another nameless face, another thin soul on a whirlwind save-the-world tour. Jesus was always there for that time, that person, that place.

The strength of Jesus' response tells us about the depth of his concern. It was directed at a man who had lost all hope, not only for acceptance by others, but for self-acceptance. Jesus approached Zacchaeus' problem by:

- accepting his *humanity* and responding to who he is;
- accepting his *hospitality* and relating to where he is.

The end of the story is presented in a series of responses.

THE CROWD'S RESPONSE

As soon as Jesus and Zacchaeus began to walk away together, the crowd "muttered," no doubt a mixture of complaint and criticism. They were probably overtaken by a flush of incipient pharasaism, disgusted at the replay of the "snack-with-sinners" routine. It was hard not to be envious or judgmental of an intimacy that was so clearly undeserved, yet so generously dished out. Crowds were generally imperceptive, unsympathetic, even downright antagonistic whenever he showed grace and mercy to someone. They protested their superior holiness and their better judgments. The truth is that the crowd was threatened and defensive whenever one of its number managed to break away from its herd instinct. Since when did it ever make it easy for an individual to take a new stand, take a new look, take a new route? Meanwhile, Zacchaeus was enjoying afternoon tea.

THE RESPONSE OF ZACCHAEUS

I don't know what he served for dessert that day, nor what transpired between him and Jesus. I've a fair idea that he didn't try to pull any deals, and I'm pretty sure that there were no cards left up his sleeve by the end of the game. If you told me he had only water to give his guest but that it tasted like the Cana vintage, I'd believe you.

No doubt, outside the house were many people who wished they'd climbed a tree, who felt like midgets themselves—short on hope, on joy, on peace.

When the time came for his public appearance, he pulled himself up to the full measure of his underpowering height, and oblivious of the crowd, he began to speak at full throttle. "Look, Lord!" Unconscious of his shape, his size, or his status, he rattled out his confession like so many coins tumbling from a miser's long-bound, leather money pouch. He even looked taller, as you'd expect a corkscrew to be, once it had the twist taken out of it. Was it the crowd's imagination or was this drip of humanity actually enjoying a conversation, enjoying himself, for the first time since whenever?

Jesus' words and ways had a knack for thawing the jagged-edged icebergs of self-hatred and of transforming the frigidity of fear into the liquid balm of forgiveness and acceptance and safety. He hadn't received a lot of heavy-duty preaching or just graduated from a lengthy "Meet the Messiah" crash course, yet his conviction, repentance, and strategy for reparation splashed out of him like water from a firefighter's bucket, spilling in all directions and soaking the consciences of all within range. He had ignited many infernos of anger and hatred that needed to be quenched by this admission of sin. The only good explanation for all this was the simple fact that Zacchaeus had met Jesus personally. The book had not been thrown at him with all its reminders of the law's demands for repayment. That law required that he repay the original sums that he had stolen, plus 20 percent. Here he was offering 400 percent! Everyone wished he'd been a victim of Zacchaeus' crimes. The challenge of the law would have demanded that he pay a fistful. The change of grace inspired him to give a cartload. Jesus had not manipulated his conscience. There were no glory-gimmicks or mind-mechanics, no faith-slogans or claim-clamors—just Jesus and Zacchaeus' arms waving all over the place.

THE RESPONSE OF JESUS

Jesus had given the first word, and now he had the last. Addressing the crowd now, but never once averting his gaze from Zacchaeus' eyes that were as big as silver shekels and that shone like golden denarii, he said: "Today, salvation has come to this house, because this man too is a son of Abraham. The Son of Man came to seek and to save that which was lost."

There had to be a mistake. What had happened thus far was different, but let's keep this thing in perspective! This guy had excluded himself from Jewish privilege and willfully betrayed the cause. He had chosen to be a friend of Caesar. What Jesus had said was indeed shocking. You're looking for the kingdom? You're looking for the new Israel? You're looking for fine examples of the new historical plan and product? Ladies and gentlemen, allow me to introduce to you the man who embodies all these long-sought-after dreams . . . a hand for . . . Zacchaeus!

To many it would have been distasteful and repugnant. However, there was no denying that his greasy fingers had become hands of grace. There had been no formal changes of ethnic or political allegiances, just a change of heart. No new Jewish membership requirements had been imposed on him, only a new relationship with God had been received. So this was what being a son of Abraham was all about? It had little to do with physical genealogies, but everything to do with spiritual regeneration.

This story illustrates the basic truth that only penitence can lead to peace. The recovery of self-worth is not related to satisfying the symbols of the world's acceptance like social status or educational success, material wealth or popular acclaim. Ironically, these are the very things that have to be denied if true acceptance is to be discovered. To be approved of God is the basis for all approval. In the acknowledgment of him is the acceptance of ourselves. The sequence that we see in this story remains as necessary today:

- Repentance
- Restitution
- Restoration

Once rejected by others, Zacchaeus had been reinstated in the community of faith, his newfound acceptance being the result of the removal of sin and a restored relationship with Jesus.

Maybe you can identify with this man. You are short on expectation and hope; long on questions and long on longing; out on a limb and unable to come out of hiding behind the foliage of your foibles and fears. Maybe you've never known Jesus as a personal savior, or perhaps you're simply in the wrong place spiritually and need to be relocated.

There is a desperate need to extricate ourselves from the branches of our own assessment of ourselves, as well as the opinions of others, that imprison and ensnare our lives. Like Zacchaeus, we must acknowledge Jesus by responding to his invitation with obedience and joy. We should not say we want to change if we are unprepared to come out of hiding. We should not pretend we are concerned about our spiritual state if our conviction is not overwhelming enough to overcome our fear of what the crowd may think. Like Zacchaeus, we need to leave the place of peeking at Christ from a distance for the place of seeking him in the open with all our hearts.

As for Zacchaeus, he was a customs man. He knew all about border controls, tariffs, and economic blockades. He knew about the process of paying dues to an evil occupying power. He had played the percentage game. His personal life was no different. He knew the separation of religious barriers and the taxing levies imposed on his spirit by the hatred in the heart of others as well as by the greed in his own soul. In a moment, though, Jesus had removed the tariffs of the law and the exclusive clause of his enemies' legislation against him. Grace had demolished the customs posts of fear and loneliness and abolished the taxes exacted by separation from God and man.

Not content with Jericho's customs posts, Jesus was going to continue his journey to Jerusalem, and in his death and resurrection he was going to destroy once and for all the control exercised by Satan's excise headquarters, so that all the tax collectors and sinners of the world could know the same transforming, forgiving, restoring power.

This same muttering crowd would turn on him. The tree he would be condemned to would not be a sycamore, but they would taunt him to "come down."

Zacchaeus woke up one morning in the pocket of Rome, met Jesus in the afternoon and went to sleep in the bosom of Abraham! Neat, eh? Christ must have felt a deep sense of encouragement as he looked at this man who had recovered his true name and nature.

JERUSALEM ALLEY

MAP REFERENCE

*T*here was a man of the Pharisees named Nicodemus, a ruler of the Jews. This man came to Jesus by night and said to Him, "Rabbi, we know that You are a teacher come from God; for no one can do these signs that You do unless God is with him." Jesus answered and said to him, "Most assuredly, I say to you, unless one is born again, he cannot see the kingdom of God." Nicodemus said to Him, "How can a man be born when he is old? Can he enter a second time into his mother's womb and be born?" Jesus answered, "Most assuredly, I say to you, unless one is born of water and the Spirit, he cannot enter the kingdom of God. That which is born of the flesh is flesh, and that which is born of the Spirit is spirit. Do not marvel that I said to you, 'You must be born again.' The wind blows where it wishes, and you hear the sound of it, but cannot tell where it comes from and where it goes. So is everyone who is born of the Spirit." Nicodemus answered and said to Him, "How can these things be?" Jesus answered and said to him, "Are you the teacher of Israel, and do not know these things? Most assuredly, I say to you, We speak what We know and testify what We have seen, and you do not receive Our witness. If I have told you earthly things and you do not believe, how will you believe if I tell you heavenly things? No one has ascended to heaven but He who came down from heaven, that is, the Son of Man who is in heaven. And as Moses lifted up the serpent in the wilderness, even so must the Son of Man be lifted up, that whoever believes in Him should not perish but have eternal life. For God so loved the world that He gave His only begotten Son, that whoever believes in Him should not perish but have everlasting life.

John 3:1–16

You could see it coming. If you had hiked with Jesus for any time at all, you knew that no sooner had he said his last word on a matter than the counterarguments would start to fly with the malevolence of stones being thrown at a heretic. "He is the Christ!" would immediately be qualified by, "How can Christ come from Galilee?" It's amazing that the most important qualification that some folk had for the Messiah was his home address. Sorry, buddy, but if your mother had been smart enough to deliver you on a different set of coordinates, you'd definitely be in the running. Right name, right power, right miracles—wrong address. Sorry.

On this particular occasion, the response was no different from the very first public reaction he received as a newborn. The dividing line between Herod and the wise men continued to be drawn down the highway of the nation's heart. Whether to assassinate or to adore—that was the question. His latest excursion into messianic territory had been a pronouncement that offered drink to anyone who was thirsty. His disciples were not in evidence manning a soft-drink stall, though no doubt they could have made a bundle with so many parched pilgrims around for the feast. Jesus had invited people to deposit their belief in him, and in return promised them a one-time, guaranteed-for-life offer of "streams of living water" within them.

Although some people tried to seize him physically, no one managed to get their hands on him, least of all the temple guards who reported later to the Pharisees that they had never heard anything like it. Instead of capturing Jesus, they had been captivated by him. It was not a "wonderful day in the neighborhood" if you were a Pharisee. Sounding the alarm of their own self-righteous horn, they exclaimed, "Have any of the rulers of the Pharisees believed in him? No!" Only one of them spoke up in reply. He was silenced by the same question that would be later hurled at Peter: "Are you from Galilee too?" He had dared to ask, "Does our law condemn anyone without first hearing him to find out what he is doing?" The speaker not only knew the law, but like a good Pharisee had practiced it. His name was Nicodemus.

It was some months earlier that he had made a special effort to get some time with Jesus. Leaving the candlelight of his luxury apartment, he dissolved into the shadows of Jerusalem to seek out this vagrant rabbi, whom he regarded with respect as a godly teacher, for apart from the explanation of God's help, how else could one account for his miracles?

It is a relief to learn that Jesus did not mind meeting with Nicodemus on his clandestine terms, "at night." The visitor was not chided because he was too fearful to converse in broad daylight.

As it turned out, the time of meeting was about the only thing that he would determine. When it came to money and power, Nicodemus was a major-leaguer, one of the elite members of the Sanhedrin. He was prestigious, principled but puzzled. Despite his social, political, and religious acclaim, he was adrift. At the time in his life when he should have felt secure by any standard, he was strangely uncertain and unsettled. As a Pharisee he knew the small print of the law, and yet he appeared bewildered by the big issues—the purpose of it all. Like most people, he began as an unlikely candidate for Jesus' message.

He was not bereft of convictions. Like so many others, he recognized that Jesus was an exceptional teacher, and his opening remarks were most courteous and respectful. But if he only came for an interesting theological discourse he was in for a surprise. Jesus was less concerned about his learning than his life. It was Nicodemus' commitment, not his compliments, that Jesus was after. Polite concessions were one thing—penitent confession was quite another. Nicodemus meant well in his expressions of approval and endorsement, but Jesus was not looking for support in a political campaign. He broke through the social etiquette with a direct spiritual pronouncement: "I tell you the truth, unless a man is born again, he cannot see the kingdom of God."

It is regrettable that the phrase "born again" has become so overworked and so undervalued in our culture. If you were an archenemy of Christianity, this is one saying of Jesus

you would seek to discredit, debunk, demean. "I'm hetero...
I'm Virgo ... I'm vegetarian ... I'm born again...." Really?
How nice for you! By making a mockery of it, or by reducing
it to a trite description, you would rob it of the impact that its
truth conveys. Jesus was not inviting Nicodemus to revise his
religious beliefs or make an on-course adjustment by accommodating a couple of neat spiritual ideas that he had overlooked. The shocker is that Jesus was presenting the notion
of a complete break with life as he knew it—so radical and so
thorough that it could only best be described as a brand new
start to life—being born again, in fact.

 You've got to feel for Nicodemus. I have no
idea what he was expecting but you can be assured that it was not this. Directness is not
something that most of us handle too well, and
we tend to cover our tracks by branding those
who speak "straight and simple" as naive and out of touch
with the real world. "How can a man be born when he is
old?" Nicodemus was at least a humble intellectual for he
asked the obvious question. His literalism had missed the
point.

There are two possible reasons for such misunderstanding:

- A genuine insufficiency of knowledge or experience
- A deliberate unwillingness to comprehend

Clearly, Nicodemus' is of the former kind. When faced with
Christ's challenge, there are several things someone can do:
ignore it, belittle it, deny it, discuss it forever, or agree to it
and act upon it. It is to Nicodemus' credit that he overcame
his fear of humiliation, the potential embarrassment of his
failure to grasp what Jesus was saying. It would have been
easy for him to have constructed any number of exclusion
clauses that rendered Jesus' message applicable and acceptable to everyone else except himself, an old, intractable
Pharisee. If Jesus had told him to follow certain rules or do
certain things or say these prayers, there would have been
no problem. Everyone is happy to do something, but the real
issue is coming to terms with what Jesus alone can do! In a
nutshell, that's exactly what he said to Nicodemus. "What's

born of the flesh is flesh, but that which is born of the Spirit is spirit." Neither the contrivance of our own efforts or the contraptions of our own self-help systems will do. All that stuff is "from below." What we need is something "from above."

Now all of us have a reflex reaction against self-examination in general and against Christ's evaluation in particular. We are tempted to assert the primacy of our own insight and experience. However, because Nicodemus listened long enough and humbly accepted that Christ had something to say that he needed to hear, we have a record of the best known, and profoundest presentation of Jesus' good news. So you have to be born again, huh?

You cannot conceive yourself. You have to receive life from another. Regeneration is God's work. Mysterious? Yes, but clearly evident—to be seen, to be savored, to be celebrated. That's the point about the wind blowing. We don't know exactly its origin or destiny, but we do know something about its present point of contact in the bending of the tree or the rustling of the leaves or the caress of wisps of hair across the face. When the Holy Spirit works, you'll know it. When new life is delivered, there will be a cry. It is only through new birth, Jesus said, that we enter a new life and become as little children. Some marvelous blessings are discovered through this new birth:

- We have a Father, God himself.
- We are assured that we are sons and daughters, secure in a present relationship.
- We have a family, spiritual siblings, the church in community.

Such a new birth is not the result of merely acknowledging the greatness of Jesus' teaching anymore than being physically born is the result of simply having a knowledge of the facts of reproduction. Spiritual conception and birth are the fruit of love, God's love, which is why Jesus says, "God so loved the world that he gave his one and only Son, that whoever believes in him shall not perish but have eternal life." Love does not barter, negotiate, lobby, bribe, or threaten—it simply gives. We are invited to receive this gift, Jesus, but with the clear knowledge that it was a costly one. This familiar statement of Jesus, memorized by every kid in Sunday school, precisely contains all the important elements of the gospel.

- Left to our own devices and desires, we are doomed to perish without understanding, hope, or fulfillment. Our sin is an inescapable fact that will reap an inescapable judgment. There is a penalty to pay.
- It was not because of any worth on the world's part that God responded to this desperate state of affairs but because he loved his creation, despite their willful refusal to be loved.
- This love was supremely expressed in a gift, Jesus, who in turn expressed his love by offering the gift of his life as payment for the penalty incurred by every human being's sin.
- Jesus thus became the focal point in God's plan to provide an escape from the inevitability of judgment. If he is made the focal point of our belief and faith, we will be delivered from an eternal death, and instead we will receive eternal life.

So important was the invitation to believe in Jesus and receive new life, that a warning is given. Jesus points out that the other side of acceptance is accountability. Having said that the purpose of his coming was not to condemn the world but save it, Jesus adds, "Whoever believes . . . is not condemned, but whoever does not believe is condemned already." In other words, if we respond to Jesus, he will save us. If we reject him, we are self-condemned and consign ourselves to judgment.

To be born is a completed action. You can't survive stuck halfway down the birth canal anymore than you can live in the womb. You can't take a lifetime to be born! To be truly born of the Spirit in Jesus' terms is to be alive and well in the kingdom of God, growing and maturing in both Christian belief and Christian behavior. What are the evidences of this new birth? Perhaps the best way to answer this is to think about a real-life baby:

It makes noises. Whether it gurgles, babbles, or screams, no one blames a baby for not being articulate.

We are just pleased that baby makes a noise, though all its noises may not necessarily be pleasing in volume or timing! Likewise, spiritually, evidence of new birth comes through the mouth—in confession, in praise, in the cry "Abba . . . Father."

It gets hungry. A baby has an amazing appetite and instinct for feeding. One of the evidences of spiritual birth is an incredible hunger to learn more about Jesus, to ask questions, to be with other Christians where the Bible is being studied and discussed.

It starts moving. Babies are in constant motion, but the process of growth is marked by increasing coordination in their movements. An evidence of new birth is the excited discovery of the various blessings of the new life in Christ, as well as of the joys of the body of Christ, the church. It is hard for a spiritual newborn to sit still. What has moved the spirit also moves the feet to go and share the good news with someone else.

It falls asleep. Just as a weaned child is calm, asleep after a contented feed, so a new babe in Christ experiences a completely new dimension of peace and rest, the result of at last being secure in whose they are, as well as in who they are.,

It needs help. Babies are not noted for their independence. Without the care of parents, life is threatened. An evidence of spiritual birth is the abandonment of the old independence and the relieved acceptance of the absolute necessity of Jesus' guidance and other Christians' encouragement.

Nicodemus was right to question that an old man could be born again. It is not a natural, but a supernatural occurrence. For a learned and worldly-wise Pharisee, the thought of becoming as a little child must have been distasteful, even shocking. If he thought it was life-threatening, he was absolutely right, for Jesus was recommending nothing less than an end to the old life. Jesus did not want Nicodemus to stroll away with another interesting religious experience for old time's sake. He wanted to impress on him the necessity of a radical new life. It's a frustrating incident, in a way, because there are no details of further discussion or of Nicodemus' reaction. Did he respond to Jesus' invitation? What happened to him?

There is a clue right at the end of John's Gospel, where we read: "Joseph of Arimathea was accompanied by Nicodemus, the man who earlier had visited Jesus by night. Nicodemus brought a mixture of myrrh and aloes, about a hundred pounds."

I like the way that he's known as the guy who saw Jesus at night. Who cares how or when or even why, so long as Jesus is actually found. Any place, any time will do!

One hundred pounds is a lot of spice, perhaps excessive, and certainly indicative of his wealth. The interesting thing to note is that such an amount would be used for the burial of a king. In the great Old Testament psalm about the King (Psalm 45), the royal robes are described as fragrant with myrrh and aloes, and this is the only New Testament reference to aloes. Without his knowing it, the silent gesture of this man was a fulfillment of a prophecy given hundreds of years before. It seems that through the love, devotion, and simplicity of a child, he had unwittingly stumbled into the joy of fulfilling God's purposes. This little reference to him can easily slip by unnoticed, and maybe that's as it should be, in keeping with this shy man. But don't miss the clue. Enough spice for a king? Had not Jesus said at their first meeting, "unless a man is born again, he cannot see *the kingdom of God*" [italics added]? I think that Nicodemus knew exactly what he was doing. He was ensuring that this was a kingly burial, an enacted testimony to the fact that he had found that kingdom, that he had been born again and renewed in his old age.

The seasoned and argument-honed intellect of this national statesman had been challenged, not in a lecture hall by a philosophic proposition, but in a maternity ward by the image of a baby. The exactitude of his knowledge and the formal dignity of his status represented a maturity that was without personal joy, without assurance of why he was created, without a vital relationship with his Creator. It was too late to teach an old dog new tricks, but not too late for an old buddy to become a new baby and to crawl and cry his way into a brand new life. Sure birth is a risk, and surely there is pain. But as every one knows, and as Nicodemus seems to have discovered, the night of labor is soon forgotten in the light of life, and the inarticulate cry of the newborn is worth a thousand physiological facts. Even so, the squeal of true faith, parented by the Holy Spirit, is worth more than all the eloquent pronouncements of an orphaned theology.

There are many "by night" inquirers, and that's good so long as the night does not remain endless. Like Nicodemus, night seekers need to become dawn treaders, identified with Jesus and unashamed to be known as his followers. Like Nicodemus, those aged by the wisdom of this world need to be reborn by the knowledge of who Jesus is. Any dark room or alley is a good place to see the light, and any old soul can be readmitted to the kingdom of God's maternity ward.

Where is it? Wherever you are right now. The Holy Spirit specializes in home delivery! You cannot deliver yourself, so acknowledge that it is Jesus alone who can save you from being spiritually stillborn. Believe in him, and confess your longing to be born again, to have his nature and to be utterly dependent on his nurture. As Nicodemus found out, it is better to be a new arrival in the kingdom of God, than to have arrived in the kingdom of men.

ROUTE
FIVE

*Checking
out how
the journey
ended . . .*

CAESAREA PHILIPPI ROAD

MAP REFERENCE

When Jesus came into the region of Caesarea Philippi, He asked His disciples, saying, "Who do men say that I, the Son of Man, am?" So they said, "Some say John the Baptist, some Elijah, and others Jeremiah or one of the prophets." He said to them, "But who do you say that I am?" And Simon Peter answered and said, "You are the Christ, the Son of the living God." Jesus answered and said to him, "Blessed are you, Simon Bar-Jonah, for flesh and blood has not revealed this to you, but My Father who is in heaven. And I also say to you that you are Peter, and on this rock I will build My church, and the gates of Hades shall not prevail against it. And I will give you the keys of the kingdom of heaven, and whatever you bind on earth will be bound in heaven, and whatever you loose on earth will be loosed in heaven." Then He commanded His disciples that they should tell no one that He was Jesus the Christ. From that time Jesus began to show to his disciples that He must go to Jerusalem, and suffer many things from the elders and chief priests and scribes, and be killed, and be raised again the third day. Then Peter took Him aside and began to rebuke Him, saying, "Far be it from You, Lord; this shall not happen to You!" But He turned and said to Peter, "Get behind Me, Satan! You are an offense to Me, for you are not mindful of the things of God, but the things of men." Then Jesus said to His disciples, "If anyone desires to come after Me, let him deny himself, and take up his cross, and follow Me. For whoever desires to save his life will lose it, and whoever loses his life for My sake will find it." For what is a man profited if he gains the whole world, and loses his own soul? Or what will a man give in exchange for his soul? For the Son of Man will come in the glory of His Father with His angels, and then He will reward each according to his works. Assuredly, I say to you, there are some standing here who shall not taste death till they see the Son of Man coming in His kingdom.

Matthew 16:13–28

They'd been hiking for days. Tyre had been the place, and tiring was the pace. There was less talk among them than usual as they headed back to the lake, whose cold water was always welcome. On arrival, Pharisees buzzed around him like so many blood-sucking mosquitoes, each one getting in his nip, mockingly demanding a sign from heaven, something spectacular to prove that he was the Messiah. Frankly, some of the disciples were hoping that he'd do something that would literally take their breath away, that would ground their harassment forever.

Of course, he would not think of such innovative signs. They did warm to his description of them as a wicked and adulterous generation, but were disappointed that all he offered them was the "sign of Jonah," the parallel between the duration of Jonah's submersion experience and Jesus' own forthcoming long weekend in Joseph of Arimathea's family vault. He was also subtly pointing out that like Jonah, he had an important message from God that demanded attention for its own sake, whether or not it was accompanied by signs and regardless of the appearance and *curriculum vitae* of the messenger.

It's a real shame that some folk have to see glitz before they'll believe in glory; that others will deny a message unless it's served up by a three-piece suit and a hundred-voice choir and topped off with a miracle. The crowd had never seen Jesus provide a miracle for entertainment or to enhance personal standings with his viewer audience. His miracles were always for needy people, not greedy publicists. They were certainly not for skeptics. (Exit Pharisees.)

As you can imagine, the fact that he didn't come up with the "miracle on demand" did not help his Messiah rating one bit. The disciples were confused and disheartened. They wanted him to be seen to be doing well, and here he was, looking like a failure in everyone's eyes and about to hit the road again. The buzzard Pharisees were bad enough, without the news that Herod was getting trigger-happy and that some of Jesus' followers were turning tail and starting to drift away. On top of it all, although they were exhausted from the long hike, they knew that it was his quietness that was really bothering them.

So there they were, straggling towards Caesarea Philippi like the remnant of a cohort that had just been given the once-over by the barbarians. It was a shame, really, because it was one of those "weekend-getaway" kind of places that should have been a joy to visit. The approach was spectacular, with the city's massive walls and towers in the foreground and Mount Hermon rising eight thousand feet to the northeast. Groves of poplars stood erect like Roman legions, and huge oak trees held their ground like the full-bellied, aproned proprietors of the local hostelries, who offered shelter and a mug that was hopefully bigger than an acorn cup. Smaller evergreens littered the area like so many burgeoning kids, full of sap and strength.

The disciples were just beginning to recover their peace, inspired by the view, when someone shuddered as if he had the creeps. The others knew exactly what he meant. Caesarea Philippi had been a center for Syrian Baal worship during old covenant days, and when the Greeks got there they built a temple to Pan, thus further fortifying this stronghold of fear and fertility worship, lust and liberation. In more recent times, a temple had been built in honor of Augustus Caesar, and of course, the town was named after this self-proclaimed god, who had long since become dissatisfied with only being ruler of the world. It's strange, isn't it, that he who takes power, demands worship. Power must have adulation to feed its aggrandizement. If it doesn't get it voluntarily, it will coerce it. Jesus suddenly stopped and turned around to look at the disciples. He must have been about fifty yards ahead. When they caught up with him, he waited until he had eye contact and suddenly asked, "Who do men say that the Son of Man is?"

Their minds had been in free-wheel for a while, so it was hard for most of them to get into mental gear suddenly. There was some stone kicking and cloud watching, some eyebrow raising, throat clearing, and shoulder shrugging. Some of them tried to recall the responses and comparisons that they'd heard. There had been many, now they came to think of it, and they were not all complimentary. Maybe they thought of some of the deeply theological but utterly incomprehensible answers that certain religious intellectuals had tried to give. "He is the ground of a renewed Israel's being." (Sometimes it's hard to discern the difference between the sound some theologians make when they speak and when they spit.) Anyway, was it a test or a trick question? His tone was direct and strong, and although they assumed he knew the answer, there was a genuinely interrogative expression in his voice.

There was nothing to suggest he was having an identity crisis. After all, he actually called himself "Son of Man" in the question! Mind you, he used this description of himself so often that they just tuned it out after a while. They heard it, but it had ceased to carry any weight. It was a bit like going around with a friend whom everyone nicknamed "Prince" and not paying attention to it until the day you found out that his father really was a king!

The disciples felt like students being examined by a teacher who thought they had received more than sufficient time to review for the exam. Although he was asking them what other people thought about him, they had an unnerving feeling that it was their personal convictions that he needed to ascertain. Had he sensed their frustration, confusion, and despondency in that last tangle with the Pharisees? Was he doubting them, or even himself? Hardly a day seemed to pass in company with this man without someone raising the question about who he really was. If you heal the sick and run rings around scribes and insist on talking about an inside track with God your Father, then you're going to provoke that question, and you're going to inspire a lot of guesses.

Now here they were, away from the crowds at last, arriving in a non-Jewish area. What could be more peaceful—yet he of all people brings up the very issue that dogged them everywhere but was least likely to be raised here! The question of his identity was the hot subject of public debate, and of course, everyone had a theory.

Their annoyance was quickly drowned by the flood of thoughts that swept through their minds. One of them remembered the time he had spoken to Jesus' mom about it. She had been amusing. She'd said that after he was born, she wondered if he'd ever be called plain "baby" or "snookums" or "little fellah," because everyone who popped into the backyard recovery room insisted upon hailing him with big titles. Mind you, although she apparently always smiled demurely when she shared such memories in her "by the by" fashion, the wistfulness in her voice suggested to the hearers that she knew a whole lot more than she would ever let on. No one ever quite had the nerve to ask her outright what she thought.

The memories kept erupting. Another disciple could hear the respectable matrons politely agreeing that he was an accomplished prophet, while another recalled the jealous indignation of those for whom it was an effort even to call him Jesus bar Joseph. Then there were those nightmares that at least one of them used to have, sequences filled with desperate voices crying "Son of David, have mercy on us!"

Who was it who had called him "Lamb of God". . . ? And as if completing that thought, one of the guys called out, "John the Baptist!"

"Elijah!" declared another.

"How about Jeremiah?" chipped in a more tentative voice.

Now, normally it would be an unbelievable honor for anyone to be mentioned in the same breath as these three men, yet, no disrespect for them intended, their names seemed to fall to the ground without even a reverberating bounce. In every case, there were some legitimate similarities with Jesus in terms of their ministry and message, but there were some begging differences. It was like the difference between people who could give you general directions how to get somewhere, and someone who could actually take you there directly and in person, immediately.

There was an uneasy pause, that was broken by his voice once again. The intonation of that next question was almost impossible to capture. It was demanding yet reassuring, blunt yet warm, confrontational yet inviting. "Who do you say that I am?" When he said "you," it was as if he looked at each of them eye to eye at the same time, searching for something that he desperately needed. The tension was like that tightly stretched anticipation you feel in the air before a storm. They were longing for thunder to break the silence, and it came. "You are the Christ, the Son of the living God!" This was no guess, no suggestion, no theory, no opinion! Peter's voice was naturally resonant, but usually it had a telltale quaver of doubt somewhere in its score, as if he feared he might be wrong and that because he was so loud, his error would be known by all. But there was no hint of uncertainty. In his confusion, thunder and lightning coexisted, fused and melded with searing certainty. The boom of prophecy and the flash of revelation pealed and streaked simultaneously and in an instant were conducted by the disciples' spirits, to be forever rooted in their consciousness.

That moment was a concentrate of history and hope, so heavy that, but for the fact that he was really standing there with them, they would have been crushed by its density. A molecule of its meaning would have been sufficient to satisfy any soul that had longed for the Messiah. Had all the centuries of covenant promise come down to this? There were no fanfares or red carpets, no histrionics or hysterics, no leaders of religion or state—just a group of guys with blistered toes, weary minds and dry breaths. Shouldn't angels attend this moment? When they stared at Jesus, he was framed by the city's ramparts, which must have braced themselves in order to protect the cultic citadels that were nurtured in their shadows.

They nervously awaited his response: "Blessed are you, Simon son of Jonah. . . ." His immediate and tender affirmation covered Peter like a comforting mantle and spread its borders to blanket the other tremulous souls.

What he said next confirmed what some of them had felt (especially knowing Peter as they did!): "This was not revealed to you by man, but by my Father in heaven." Those who had theories about who he was had not lived with him day and night as they had done. They'd seen his manner of life and his miracles. They had watched his silent humility as he had been hailed with messianic fervor by the strays and the stranded of this earth, and yet he never questioned their designations.

As on this occasion, he asked people not to tell anyone what they had just confessed. He continually did things and claimed things that decent people were brought up to believe were the preserve of God alone. Yes, they'd heard him forgive a man his sins, claim lordship over the Sabbath, and say that he would divide the sheep and the goats. They could remember the day that he said there was no need to fast while he was around. They had all breathed in deeply and chewed thankfully on the thick air. As someone once put it, "Who is this man who can suddenly tell the school they can have a holiday?" By claims direct and indirect, by the testimony of his words and works, by the too-close-for-comfort match-up of their prophetic Scriptures with the events of his life, by the evidence of their own personal experience, they had an awful lot of reasons to say what Peter had said.

But they had to admit that what he said to Peter was absolutely right. All the research in the world did not necessarily add up to the spiritual revelation that was needed to break in to a closed mental box and spring the conclusion, "You are the Christ!" The real shock was the confession itself, but his unquestioning acceptance of that momentous title produced countless reverberations as the implication of it all began to sink in. The look that had passed across his face was hardly pleasure, as if he was delighting in the recognition—it was more relief . . . spiced with a pinch of contentment.

Despite Matthew's opening presentation of Jesus' genealogy at the beginning of his Gospel, the family tree was not the end of the matter as far as Jesus' identity was concerned. Wise men asked, "Where is . . . the king of the Jews?" Shepherds declared, "He is the Christ, the Lord!" John drew attention to "the Lamb of God." A voice from heaven announced, "This is my beloved Son." After Jesus calmed a storm, his disciples asked, "What kind of man is this?" John's followers inquired, "Are you the one who was to come?" A demoniac was healed and the crowd wondered, "Could this be the Son of David?" A Canaanite woman and a blind man had no doubt and boldly declared him to be so, as did the throngs that greeted him with palms as he entered Jerusalem for the last time. Was he more than "a carpenter's son" or a "prophet from Nazareth"? He was asked by the high priest if he was "the Christ," and by Pilate if he was "the King of the Jews." At the end, it was a Roman guard, of all people, who

proclaimed, "Surely this was the Son of God!"; it was a crucified thief who asked, "Aren't you the Christ?" The pattern
that emerges from the Gospels should not really surprise us.
It's the one least likely to know who seems to know. In Jesus'
terms, his identity was understood by those who were regarded as babes by the cerebrally educated; it was wisely
discerned by those who were considered the fools of the
world.

Given Jesus' acceptance of Peter's confession, it was ludicrous to think that anyone could now treat him with mild
interest or with disinterest. A more recent hiker puts it like
this: "He produced mainly three effects—hatred—terror—
adoration. There was no trace of people expressing mild approval."[10] How could the disciples have gone a step further
with him if his claim to be Christ, the anointed one, the Messiah, was false? They knew that they had walked with neither
a clown nor a charlatan. "A man who was merely a man and
said the sort of things he said would not be a great moral
teacher. He would either be a lunatic—on a level with the
man who says he's a poached egg—or else he would be the
devil of hell. You must make your choice. Either this man
was, and is, the Son of God: or else a madman or something
worse. You can shut him up for a fool, you can spit at him and
kill him as a demon; or you can fall at his feet and call him
Lord God. But let us not come up with any nonsense about
his being a great human teacher. He has not left that open to
us. He did not intend to."[11]

In our particular map-reference, there are some important
titles used that

- *identify* who Jesus is;
- *indicate* what he could be expected to do.

You cannot separate an individual's personhood from his performance. Who someone is and what he does are inextricably linked. A title creates an expectation of that person's
character, communication, and competence. The interaction
between Jesus' words and works on the one hand and people's response to what they heard and saw on the other, is a
major concern of the Gospel writers. Let's briefly note the
titles in question.

JESUS AS CHRIST
("You are the Christ . . .")

Corresponding to the Hebrew word *Messiah*, the Greek word *Christos* means "anointed." Therefore to name Jesus "the Christ" was to declare unequivocally that he was the fulfillment of Messianic hope. Not surprisingly, it is the title for Jesus most often repeated in the New Testament.

Throughout the Old Testament we are presented with a hope for the future founded on promises that God had given in successive convenants to men like Noah, Abraham, Moses, and David. Different facets of God's plan to redeem his creation emerged with increasing focus and detail. Two significant traditions were drawn upon by the prophets in their anticipation of the Messiah: the Mosaic, with its emphasis on a lawgiver, and the Davidic with its emphasis on a king. But regulations without a ruler lead to despair, and a ruler without regulations leads to dissolution. So these were complementary expectations and represent the combined necessities of command and promise, grace and faith, obligation and reward. Clearly, King David represents the high tide of achievement, so it was inevitable that any longing for a Messiah as "Son of David" would be fed by the memories of King David's power and prowess as monarch and militarist.

This hope for a political force was tempered, however, by another crucial prophetic insight, particularly as expressed by Isaiah. He described someone who would come, not as a sovereign in splendor and pomp, but as a servant in pain and suffering. Peter's rebuttal of Jesus' prediction of death, following his confession, sufficiently illustrates the problem of acceptance. It seemed impossible that the saving king and the suffering servant could be the same man, and yet this is precisely how Jesus presented himself and how he was later perceived by many others. These two insights are brought together and summarized rather brilliantly in the last book of the Bible: "Lo, the Lion of the Tribe of Judah, the Root of David, has conquered. . . . Then I saw a Lamb. . . ." The sovereign lion and the slain lamb are one and the same.

Although Jesus did not deny he was the Christ, he was really explicit about it only after his suffering, by which time he could not easily be misunderstood. Because of the political overtones of such titles as "King of Israel" or "Son of David," Jesus avoided them. On an occasion when the crowd wanted to make him king, his prompt evasion of their enthusiasm spoke for the fact that his understanding of his mission was at variance with popular expectations.

JESUS AS SON OF GOD
("The Son of the living God . . .")

Mark begins his gospel with the words, "The beginning of the gospel of Jesus Christ, the Son of God." Mark also records that "the Son of God" is heaven's own personal description of Jesus. "You are my Son, my beloved one." Nowhere in the gospels is there a record that Jesus suddenly assumed this title or had it conferred on him. He is so designated, not only from the very beginning of his biological life, but in his preexistence. This family title is important because it presents:

- *A representation*—Jesus expressed the character and likeness of his Father;
- *A relationship*—Jesus experienced intimacy with his Father;
- *A response*—Jesus executed the will of his Father.

In his being, his feeling, and his doing, through his holiness, devotion, and obedience, Jesus the Son reveals what God the Father is like—not as an abstract proposition, but as an approachable person.

JESUS AS SON OF MAN
("Who do you say that I the Son of Man am?")

After "Christ" and "Lord," the title "Son of Man" is the most frequently used, but only because it was the most common self-designation of Jesus. Since for moral, political, and theological reasons Jesus avoided the high-octane titles, why would he apply this one to himself? It certainly sounds lower key at first hearing though the fact is that you had better pack a punch if you applied this to yourself. As the title suggests, it presents Jesus as "representative man" and draws attention to his identification with and involvement in man's domain. One fellowhiker has described this as Jesus' way of presenting himself as the spokesperson for or sponsor of humanity. (For example, Jesus knows that the Sabbath was made for man, and not man for the Sabbath. In other words, he has an inside track on the fundamental purposes for which man was made and for which created ordinances were meant to exist.) But lest we think "Son of Man" is a folksy sort of title, we must realize that it has its origins in the prophecy of Daniel, where a figure is portrayed who is both a heavenly being and also one that comes as an emissary to earth, with tremendous authority as both ruler and judge. Such a title certainly satisfies the emphasis Jesus wanted to place on his incarnate presence in the world without denying his transcendent place in heaven.

Overall, it is probably reasonable to say that because this title was not in general circulation and most people were fairly ambivalent about it, its use did not trigger an ingrained set of presuppositions and expectations. Jesus could therefore be true to his self-understanding without unnecessarily engaging the false understanding of others.

JESUS AS LORD
("Never, Lord . . .")

Peter had first addressed Jesus as Lord when he had asked him to depart from him because of his overwhelming consciousness of his sin. This title (the Greek word *kurios*) was to become the most elevated of all designations, for in its purest meaning, it signified, not a passing, polite recognition of respect and seniority, but a clear and convinced declaration that Jesus was both a sovereign of subjects and a master of servants. Of course, these images represent the exalted position of Jesus and the humble yet fulfilled attitude of his followers.

It is not an impersonal bondage or control that is presented, but a loving, loyal, and voluntary submission. It is a relationship that does not restrict, but releases; that does not chain, but cherishes; that does not negate but nurtures; that does not fetter, but fulfills. "Jesus is Lord" is the shortest creedal statement in the Bible. It declares the absolute and cosmic authority of the risen Christ.

That day outside Caesarea Philippi was a turning point for all of them, not least for Jesus. As for the disciples, they began to find out more about who he was, through his incredible names; not just Son of Man and Christ, but Lord and Savior. The titles could not make him anything that he was not. As one fourth-century saint put it, it's not names that give confidence in things, but things that give confidence in names.

As for Jesus, he now began to talk to them about things he'd never mentioned before concerning the future. He talked about going to Jerusalem and kept mentioning something to do with the third day that was completely lost on them. The reason they later remembered this so clearly was because of Peter again. He started to argue with Jesus and tell him that it was crazy to contemplate such things. They all agreed but were too timid to say anything. I guess poor Peter felt more confident to be their spokesman, given his recent triumph. After all, he was being perfectly reasonable, and the thought occurred to some of them that the Pharisees' threats might be getting to Jesus. But if he was the Christ, he could blow them away any time he wanted! If they understood anything about the Messiah, it was that his power and clout would make mincemeat out of any opposition, the Romans included. (Especially the Romans!)

What he said next to Peter was as frightening as his last communication was encouraging. "Get behind me, Satan! You're a stumbling block to me!" It came as a body blow to find out that they could be capable of incredible revelation one minute and unbelievable corruption the next. Talk about hot and cold. One true confession clearly does not make for infallibility! Just as they had all shared Peter's commendation, so they all shared his condemnation. They only wanted a Messiah who would fulfill their agendas, who would make them look good. One moment they were imagining being leaders in his triumphant clean-up operation, and the next minute, they were having to worry about their lives, for if his enemies killed him, their chances of drawing a pension were exceedingly thin. Yes, they'd heard rabbis mention that some thought the coming Messiah would have to endure some tough times, but they never could square that away with the idea that he was going to be an unstoppable ruler. How could suffering have anything to do with salvation, or death with dominion? Unless of course, he knew something they didn't. They were not able to reconcile these issues at the time, but after the big event they would!

It was most significant that it was then that he told them what was to become the very touchstone of their later preaching. "If anyone wants to come after me, he must deny himself and take up his cross and follow me." They would find out the hard way that the Messiah was not going to achieve victory without paying the ultimate price; that they could not call him Christ and Lord one minute and deny the costly implications of his battle plan the next. But I'm beginning to wander off this road and onto another. No good hiker gets ahead of himself.

Suffice it to say for now, that we must reckon with four things:

- *Revelation:* like Peter, we too can know who Jesus really is;
- *Responsibility:* such knowledge brings with it accountability;
- *Relationship:* it comes with an invitation to follow Jesus;
- *Reward:* it will cost us everything, but all sacrifice is rewarded.

The question that Jesus asked is now directed at us. What is our answer? Are we going to regurgitate our opinions, ill-considered and secondhand, religiously trite, even evangelically orthodox? Is he the Christ who both commands and inspires our worship? Is he the Son of God who has initiated us into an intimate relationship with his Father? Is he the Son of Man who has perfectly shown us how our humanity was meant to function and be fulfilled? Is he the Lord I have followed, for whom I have denied myself, and lost my life? The evidence of our understanding of who Jesus is, will be demonstrated, not in a verbal declaration but in a voluntary death—to self, to safety first, to the well-intentioned but hopelessly misguided expectations of well-wishers, to the moral and emotional junk bonds of the world's exchange systems, to every philosophy of self-discovery that denies denial of sin and exalts the exaltation of ego.

The disciples did eventually make it into town. It's strange, but after all that had happened and all that they'd heard, they found nothing either romantic or restful about that place. To walk its streets was to rub shoulders with the demons of every cult imaginable. It was while they were looking at Caesar's temple that perhaps the penny dropped. It was no coincidence that he'd asked them his questions there, where the false gods of generations had held sway, where modern blasphemies were proclaimed, where the Jordan itself had its source with all that symbolized for the Jews. In this miniature museum of the world's religions, the cry had rung out, "You, and you alone, are the Christ!" Something of that confession must have rattled the columns of the emperor's temple, swirled through the ruins of the old Baal worship sites, and gusted up the hill where Pan was said to dwell.

They had just about recovered their joy by the time they got back together at the end of the day, so when he told them that he was now heading for Jerusalem, a cloud must have begun to drift across their sun, and the accompanying shadows must have chilled their newfound warmth.

BETHANY ROAD

MAP REFERENCE

*T*hen Martha, as soon as she heard that Jesus was coming, went and met Him, but Mary was sitting in the house. Then Martha said to Jesus, "Lord, if You had been here, my brother would not have died. But even now I know that whatever You ask of God, God will give You." Jesus said to her, "Your brother will rise again." Martha said to Him, "I know that he will rise again in the resurrection at the last day." Jesus said to her, "I am the resurrection and the life. He who believes in Me, though he may die, he shall live. And whoever lives and believes in Me shall never die. Do you believe this?" She said to Him, "Yes, Lord, I believe that You are the Christ, the Son of God, who is to come into the world."

Then Jesus, again groaning in Himself, came to the tomb. It was a cave, and a stone lay against it. Jesus said, "Take away the stone." Martha, the sister of him who was dead, said to Him, "Lord, by this time there is a stench, for he has been dead four days." Jesus said to her, "Did I not say to you that if you would believe you would see the glory of God?" Then they took away the stone from the place where the dead man was lying. And Jesus lifted up His eyes and said, "Father, I thank You that You have heard me. And I know that You always hear Me, but because of the people who are standing by I said this, that they may believe that You sent Me." Now when He had said these things, He cried with a loud voice, "Lazarus, come forth!" And he who had died came out bound hand and foot with graveclothes, and his face was wrapped with a cloth. Jesus said to them, "Loose him, and let him go."

John 11:20–27, 38–44

Y
ou would not have guessed there was trouble brewing if you were to judge by the apparent ease and joy of the Sunday dinner party in Bethany, hosted as always by Martha. Well might Lazarus laugh as he reclined next to Jesus, and well might Jesus look at his friend with eyes that glinted with a strange mix of pleasure and pain. The party had been thrown in Jesus' honor, and in a way, it was a unique celebration. Until recently, most of the guests had no argument with the revered prophet who had said, "Death cannot sing your praise." Well, it was singing it that night all right, and none sang the chorus louder than Lazarus. To understand the lyrics, we have to go back a few weeks.

The pressure had been mounting. John's Gospel chronicles the rising hostility of the Judean authorities toward Jesus. All the Gospel writers record the rising temperature, but John in particular draws our attention to the fuel that was stoking the furnace. Jesus' comments about being the good shepherd who would give his life for the sheep had not won him the "Message of the Month" award. The response had been unequivocal. They said he was demon possessed, raving mad. They had interrupted one of his meditative walks in Solomon's colonnade and come straight to the point. "If you are the Christ, tell us plainly." Jesus was equally direct. "I did tell you, but you did not believe. [Read my lips.] I and my Father are one." They could justify their violent rage, and the stones that were already in their hands, on the grounds that a "mere man" had claimed to be God. At least they could no longer be accused of missing the main thesis.

Somehow, Jesus managed to evade the grasping scrap that then ensued, and he retreated to a place that had special significance for him. The section of the Jordan where he was baptized was no chance choice. He must have derived considerable assurance from the memories of that day three years before when he went public and accepted his vocation as he stood there in the water with John. "This is my beloved Son, in whom I am well pleased!" The recollection of those special words would have accounted for any encouragement he felt. Even while he was in that area, many folk came to believe on him. Somehow, despite the extremities of the conditions, whether the scorching hate of his enemies or the chilling intimations of his death, he remained faithful and fruitful.

It was late in the day when a weary messenger arrived with the news that one of his closest friends, Lazarus, was gravely ill. His response had been incredibly reassuring, almost jaunty. "This will not end in death, and through it, I will be glorified." And that was that. The conversations and conversions continued for another couple of relaxed days. Then, as if it were no big deal, he woke up one morning and said, "Hey, let's go to Judea!" They were used to him saying unusual things, but this was ridiculous. Rightly, the disciples pointed out that he was proposing to walk right back into the area of his recently attempted assassination. There had better be a good explanation.

It was not as good as they had hoped. "Lazarus is asleep and I am going to wake him up." Great, let him sleep! It's a good sign that he's on the mend. Plenty of sleep was what the physicians always said. "Lazarus is dead." Before they could gather momentum, Jesus had put another stick in their spokes by telling them that he was actually glad that he had not been there . . . something to do with their having a chance to believe in him. Clearly, there was no stopping him, and Thomas, the resident doom merchant, suggested they might as well all go and die with him. Maybe he really felt like being sarcastic, but more likely, he was genuinely coming to terms with the fact that life without Jesus was going to be intolerable, so they might as well all go down the tubes together.

All the disciples see is a problem that cannot be solved. All Jesus is thinking about is the praise that's going to go to his Father when it is resolved. They anticipate gloom, and he foresees glory. Whose perspective on your life would you rather have? That of Thomas or Jesus? Maybe Jesus appeared casual, but the fact is that Lazarus was already dead by the time the messenger arrived.

John emphasizes Jesus' friendship with Lazarus, so we know that Jesus' delay had nothing to do with lack of love or concern. The Bethany bunch would not be the last ones to accuse God of being too slow, too neglectful, or too uninvolved or to impugn his omniscience with the idea that he had overlooked something. At a time when Jesus appeared to love less, he actually demonstrated that he knew more. Saint Augustine said of this incident, "It is sufficient that Jesus knows." Interestingly enough, there are three occasions in the Gospels when Jesus was urged to do something, and in every instance it was complicated by the fact that the persuasion came from a family member or a close friend. "Are there not twelve hours of daylight?" he asked his disciples en route to Bethany. There is always time for God's will, even when the circumstances scream and it seems that no one is listening. In the face of man's pressure and persuasion, pouting and petulance, Jesus shows that he is primarily moved by God's will, not man's need, important though that is.

And when he did act according to his schedule, it was easy for the disciples to forget the enormous cost that he would pay to do so. He was walking knowingly into the inferno of hatred that was finally going to burn him to death. Likewise, as we inventory our sorrow and our sin, with all the consequences and complications, we should remember that there is hope for freedom from their entanglements only because of the price that he paid. Like Martha and Mary, when we've sent our message, we need to trust him for the miracle. Thus it was that Jesus approached Bethany the next day. Martha's cuisine was not on his mind, but he was thinking about what he liked to call his "meat"—doing the will of his Father.

What happens next is presented by John as the last of seven great events (including the water into wine at Cana; the healings of the official's son in Capernaum, the invalid at the pool of Bethesda, and the blind man at the pool of Siloam; the feeding of the five thousand and the walking on the water). These are not presented as random miracles but as signs; the emphasis is on what they tell us about Jesus and on how they glorify God. In other words, the sign points away from itself to something else (a missing element from many charismatic presentations of the miraculous).

The events in Bethany are seen as the climactic sign of Jesus' entire ministry, so this was a very significant road on Jesus' hike. After this incident, the boiler of anger and hatred was finally overloaded and consequently exploded in the plot to kill Jesus that was expedited in Passion Week. So what's all the fuss about? John describes what is nothing less than an extraordinary preview of a play that was yet to be staged. The earlier words of Jesus take on a spine-chilling resonance: "The hour is coming and now is, when the dead will hear the voice of the Son of God, and those who hear will live."

Lazarus was really dead. This is no record-breaking faint, no temporary unconsciousness, no cataleptic fit. He was not demobilized, hypnotized, or mesmerized. He was dead. What happened next is one of the clearest and most power-fully dramatized parables in the Bible. It tells us two things:

- the true nature of our problem
- the true nature of Jesus' power

The Bible speaks directly to our condition. In our natural state we are spiritually dead. The best that we achieve in our own strength is powerless to spiritually enliven us, yet we hail these dead works as the epitome of what life is all about.

Of course, we resent and resist this truth. We like to be-lieve that our problems and the consequences of our sin are passing—a touch of flu, a momentary hitch, a minor lapse, a fleeting shadow, an annoying inconvenience, or a fitful nightmare that will be gone when morning comes. However, we discover too late that all the positive thinking, stress man-agement, and die-hard determination in the world, all the psychology and technology, cannot raise the dead.

Suddenly, we find that our accolades, achievements, and statements of net worth are just so many lines in a eulogy, so many attractive bouquets for the graveside. Our increased wealth only serves to procure a finer gravestone. We can beautify the coffin but we cannot raise the corpse. Regret and sorrow, ritual wailing and remorse, could not raise Laza-rus anymore than it can raise us. Lazarus was dead. Without Christ he would have remained so. I am dead. Without Christ I remain so.

It was a fairly subdued bunch of hikers that approached Bethany. The disciples had every reason to be nervous, and no doubt they wished that Jesus would slow the pace down a bit. They'd already missed the funeral, so why the hurry? Maybe they'd be in time for theirs! Thomas smiled at his own joke, then shivered as one does when taken unawares by a bitter aftertaste. Martha was already on her way toward them, but where was Mary? So what was he going to say? "Sorry I'm late, dear?" They braced themselves for the awkward meeting.

The exchanges that followed clearly present the differences between human and divine responses to the human condition. However, there is an unnerving similarity between the reactions of the characters in this incident and the practiced reflexes of our own self-defense systems whenever we are confronted with the undeniable reality of the decomposition of our spiritual life or the decay that is consequent upon our own sin.

HUMAN RESPONSE

We have already encountered two responses from the disciples.

IT'S TOO DANGEROUS

To engage the problem now is to court disaster. It is going to cause trouble, and there are too many potentially undesirable results. Preserve the peace; maintain the status quo. You win some and you lose some.

IT'S TOO DIFFICULT

In any case, the problem is too far gone. This is not one of your straightforward spit-in-the-blind-man's-eye jobs. This is past the point of rescue or resuscitation. All hope expired with Lazarus' last breath. The very idea is so preposterous that it doesn't even make the official list of impossibilities.

As you listen to Martha's conversation with Jesus a few more characteristic responses emerge.

IT'S TOO BAD

Of course there is genuine regret, but that's the way it goes for everybody. The cup of comfort contains equal parts resignation and rationalization.

IT'S TOO LATE

Maybe something could have been done . . . if only. It could have happened back then. . . . Circumstances were better then. . . . There was a possibility of change then. If only Jesus had shown up earlier.

IT'S TOO GOOD TO BE TRUE

The disciples must have winced and wondered as they heard Jesus say, almost matter of factly, as if stating the obvious, "Your brother will rise again." How thoughtful of him to remind them of the resurrection at the last day! Martha treated it like a well-meant word of consolation, but we can sympathize with her feeling that even the best doctrines, though true, can sound hollowly trite at a time like this.

However, Jesus was not padding out the embarrassed silences with clerical-collar condolences. Martha acknowledged the possibility of change but not here in the real world, not now. It sounded great and might well be theologically viable, but of course, it was not a practical option. Concepts of change are important, but let's not confuse them with real possibilities. Hope has been suffocated enough without finally smothering it with the pillow of soft naiveté and mysticism.

Martha had the most to say. Sometimes our volubility is all we have to stop us from listening clearly enough or thinking hard enough about what that firm yet tender voice has promised. Despite her wrong interpretations of what Jesus was saying, she suddenly delivered a volley of belief that threatened the organized troops of her doubt: "I believe that you are the Christ, the Son of God, who was to come into the world."

But again, because her confession was not targeted on what Christ can do in this particular situation, her doubt was only temporarily disoriented, not dismissed. She was orthodox insofar as she stated the fact of the incarnation, but she could not grasp the relationship between that fact and the need of her own life. Yes, Christ came into the world in general, but not into her world in particular.

The logic of the incarnation is that Christ's involvement with our humanity is total and thorough. He smells both what I smell and how I smell. When Christ came into the world, he did not get hung up in a state of suspension in the general atmosphere of our lives. He was grounded in the dirt of our roads, riveted to the hull of our necessities, submerged in the sea of our experience. When he came into the world, he did not wander around with a permanently lost look on his face. Sure, he was homesick more than once, but he was the only one who was not lost. At the graveside of Lazarus, despite appearing to be in the ozone layer, he was the only one in touch with reality.

Martha was theologically sound. Her doctrine was in great shape, but it had no stamina to take her where she needed to go. Her belief was not connecting with her present need. All Jesus was doing was asking her to believe in him, rather than in a creedal statement twice removed. He was asking her to make the trip from formula to faith. Someone wryly commented that the church has only got most Christians to a place of orthodoxy where the Pharisees got Martha. Maybe resurrection, maybe renewal, maybe radical transformation—next week, next year—but not now and not for this.

No wonder Jesus wept. They thought his tears were proof of his love for his friend, but they were evidence of his heartbreak at the rampant unbelief that shrouded all hope before burying it alive. If it wasn't so tragic, it would be amusing, for we immediately read the comment: "Could not he who opened the eyes of the blind man have kept this man from dying?" What self-righteous twaddle! We should not even congratulate ourselves for our enlightened view of the miraculous, for it is no guarantee that we can trust for anything and everything. Jesus walked up to the tomb, but it was not to read the inscription. Little did the crowd expect an invitation to join him, certainly not to roll the gravestone aside.

But not even this move, this sign of his intended engagement with the horror of it all, did anything to incite expectation. His invasion of the off-limits of human despair and desolation was discouraged on the grounds that it would release a bad odor! Well might Martha place herself one last time between Jesus and that stone. It's ironic, isn't it, that when we try to resist his changes, block his advances, and thwart his loving interference, our defense of "life as it is" is in fact a desire for "death as it is."

 We may chide Martha, but we too fear the slightest millimeter of motion of that stone. We do not relish what has to be done to expose our problem as it really is, the logical outcome of our humanity without his presence. It's bad enough to name it as death, without having to realize the awful consequences of its corruption, its stench. It would be easier if Jesus dealt with such issues at a civilized distance, from the outside, without revealing the corpse, the source of the sorrow and hopelessness. That root of bitterness, that intractable bondage, that unresolved anger, that chronic sin should not be exposed to sunlight.

The stones of our deceit and hypocrisy, our suppression and denial are challenged by his command. We can't handle the problem, but we are expected to move the obstructive stone. If we do the rolling, it seems that he will take care of the resurrecting. At last, our confession surrenders access to Jesus. The crowd, even those who know us best, will draw back, but there is no record that Christ ever hid his face or held his nose.

The human response to the domain of death, to the consequences of actions long since past and long since unconfessed, as well as to situations and relationships currently marred by decay, has changed little. Is Christ's involvement too threatening, too unnerving, too embarrassing, too late? Is the enormity of our need too awful to acknowledge, or are we too far gone to believe that there is any hope?

JESUS' RESPONSE

Mourning was an extremely noisy process. Wailing and weeping were always loud, but on this occasion the racket was drowning out the offer of resurrection. Into the tangled skein of groans and moans, remorse and regret, walked Jesus. Two statements, three questions, three simple commands and a prayer, cut into the knot of grief with the incisive action of a pair of surgical scissors. Truth has a way of bowling us over with its brevity and simplicity. In Jesus' response to this problem *in extremis*, we are given a preview, not only of the travail that he will endure in the days to come, but also of the triumph that he will win for everyone who will trust in him. There are three characteristic features of his response.

A PROMISE

"Your brother will rise again! . . . He who believes in me will live . . . will never die. . . ." No science fiction, no starstruck fantasy—just straightforward fact. His promises are not about make-believe, but make-better. Basically, if we come he will not turn us away, especially if we come in a hearse. The clearer the acknowledgment of our deaths, of our inability to save ourselves, the more he likes it. In any case, we demonstrate our folly by pretending we can do mouth-to-mouth on our own lifeless corpse. The words of his mouth will breathe life. The oxygen tent of our self-created environment, the intravenous tubes of our drip-fed hopes, and all the paraphernalia of our self-help and self-survival kits have to be unplugged. All our attempts to maintain our own sterile, infection-free zones have to cease. We must be prepared to be contaminated by his presence, his breath. The terminal reality of his diagnosis must be reckoned with. But he does not come to bury with empty promises.

A PRONOUNCEMENT

"I am the resurrection and the life!" The problem has been stated. A present-tense crisis receives a present-tense response. "I AM!" It's easier to raise questions than bodies, but Jesus only indulges in the interrogative as a prelude for the imperative. It's strange, but he talks about himself, not the problem. Suddenly the issue has less to do with how much we know about death or sin or the problem or the great need for change or fulfillment. It has to do with how much we know about him. We know about death, but do we know that he is "the resurrection"? How prepared are we to trust him?

We have been morticians all our lives. We are practiced in the cosmetic arts of disguise and deception. We can garnish gravesides and pretend they're botanical gardens. We can water the blooms of our falsehood and embalm the remains of our bodies, all the time denying the stench of the reality of our need. Our volubility and vanity are expert at making what is frankly tragic look chic. Yes, we're morticians and magicians, but the black hat of neither the undertaker nor the trick maker can produce a miracle. Why do we settle for rabbits out of a hat when we need resurrection from our death? His pronouncement is no abracadabra. This is the landlord of the world serving notice on an unwanted tenant.

The sin that defeats us is an opportunity for his salvation. The problem that confounds us is an opportunity for his power. No one expected anything to happen. No one believed that such a pleasant prophet was in fact the "death killer!"

A PROOF

"Jesus wept." These words are the preface to his final action. The word used here to characterize Jesus' emotions is one of the strongest imaginable, and it is only employed in situations where it describes not only his depth of compassion for the sufferer or sinner, but also his divine anger in the confrontation with evil, with death, with the work of Satan. Devout and faithful Mary herself had fallen at his feet, not in faith and devotion this time, but in fear and despair. No wonder he was "deeply moved in spirit and troubled" when he looked out over this tempestuous sea of despondency, resignation, and helplessness, considering what he knew his Father made his creatures to be, and considering what he himself was called to do. He moved precisely and powerfully, like a lifeboat into the whitewater of capsized hopes and drowned expectations. There is an economy of communication.

"Take away the stone!" He demanded that the need be exposed. He insisted on engaging the worst reality in broad daylight.

"Did I not tell you that if you believed you'd see the glory of God?" He asked people to believe his word and simply

act upon it. He did not require them to depend on their faith, but on his Father. Sure he wanted gladness for the mourners, but he more strongly desired glory for his Father.

"Lazarus, come out!" He commands change and calls the victim by name. He does not bother with the peripheral issue of the graveclothes but gets immediately to the dead heart of the matter. You can loose all the graveclothes you like and never revive a dead circumstance. But free the spirit and the graveclothes will be loosed.

"Take off the graveclothes!" This instruction is to the community. He commits them to participate in his work, to view his power firsthand and close up and to be involved in the wider network of care and restoration that every one delivered from death needs. To sum it all up in the words of one hiker, "Jesus never met a corpse that doesn't sit up right on the spot."

 This same sequence of commands needs to be heard in every graveyard of human desolation and inertia. There must be an exposure of our sin and lifelessness. There must be an active trust in his promise to transform the cemetery of doubt and defeat into a live-show of faith and freedom. There must be a response to his command to leave the domain of our death and step into his kingdom of light. There must be a thorough shedding of the graveclothes of our former identity and a willingness to be loved and encouraged by other early risers in the community we know as the church.

There was a clear-cut response to Jesus. He does not allow much middle ground. There were two responses on this occasion.

DESTRUCTION

Of one group it says "they plotted." The fuse had been lit that would explode in Passion Week. Yes, his demands and claims are penetrating and pressing and the temptation *to eliminate* his unnerving influence is ever present.

DEVOTION

Others "put their faith in him." They set off for a memorial service for Lazarus and ended up at a welcome-home party.

Their response was to believe the words and works of Jesus, *to embrace* his message.

Nowhere in the Gospels is the nature of a proper response to Jesus more simply or powerfully demonstrated than in the episode that happened in Bethany a few weeks later, which brings us back to where we began—the dinner party in Jesus' honor. It is a well-known incident, and not surprisingly so since Jesus said it would be spoken about wherever the gospel was preached in the future. Presumably, this underlines the significance and importance of it. In an outrageously extravagant demonstration of devotion, Mary cracked open a perfume bottle (costing the equivalent of an annual salary), and poured the exquisite contents over Jesus' feet. So intense was her outpouring of soul, that she broke all polite convention and loosed her hair, as only an adulteress would do, to wipe his feet. In a single action, we are reminded of the fact that there is a place for every sinner in Jesus' inner circle, and all devotion is accepted, regardless of the responses of the tut-tutting self-righteous.

There'll always be a Judas in the crowd who can give ten good reasons why our devotion to Jesus does not accord with socially acceptable norms. He will have an arsenal of pseudo-spiritual defenses for his own emotional detachment, for his lack of affection and plain hardness of heart. For now, the issue has nothing to do with a self-oriented society's acceptance of us, but with Jesus' acceptance of self-confessed sinners. There's never any waste in true worship. Yes, it is always costly. And so it was that the ministry of Jesus reached a climax. The seals of a tomb and a perfume jar had been broken. The next day he would enter Jerusalem, but not before he had taken us from the foul stench of death to the fragrant savor of devotion.

PALM AVENUE

MAP REFERENCE

*N*ow when they drew near to Jerusalem, and came to Bethphage, at the Mount of Olives, then Jesus sent two disciples, saying to them, "Go into the village opposite you, and immediately you will find a donkey tied, and a colt with her. Loose them and bring them to Me. And if anyone says anything to you, you shall say, 'The Lord has need of them,' and immediately he will send them." All this was done that it might be fulfilled which was spoken by the prophet, saying:

> Tell the daughter of Zion,
> "Behold, your King is coming to you,
> Lowly, and sitting on a donkey,
> A colt, the foal of a donkey."

So the disciples went and did as Jesus commanded them. They brought the donkey and the colt, laid their clothes on them, and set Him on them. And a very great multitude spread their garments on the road; others cut down branches from the trees and spread them on the road. Then the multitudes who went before and those who followed cried out, saying:

> Hosanna to the Son of David!
> Blessed is He who comes in the name of the
>   LORD!
> Hosanna in the highest!

And when He had come into Jerusalem, all the city was moved, saying, "Who is this?"

Matthew 21:1–10

The mode of transport was hardly limousine service. Obviously he had planned it all, but the instructions to a couple of his disciples to go into the local village and tell the owner of the first donkey they saw that their nameless, faceless boss needed it seemed as close to daylight robbery as they could all imagine. However, they'd been around long enough to know that simple obedience was usually the best response. What was in it for him was clearly more important than what was in it for them—a good enough motivation for obedience to Jesus, if you think about it. In any case there was something in that tired yet determined tone of his voice that told them it was useless to suggest a straightforward horse rental. Here he was, at last doing what his brothers had been trying to persuade him to do for the last three years—going public in the big city. But like this?

At least they got the vehicle with no money down, no negotiations, no lease arrangements. That seemed to be the way he liked to get most things. It all appeared so low-key at the time; it was much later when the disciples realized how quietly assertive the whole event really was. It was Matthew who got the connection. Did it not say in one of the prophets, "See, your king comes to you, righteous and having salvation, gentle and riding on a donkey, on a colt, the foal of a donkey"?

There turned out to be more than one historian watching from a second-story window, who made another connection, remembering that two hundred years earlier, a certain Judas Maccabeus had entered the city in exactly the same way, when Antiochus Epiphanes had desecrated the Holy Place. The memory evoked images of swine on the altar and prostitutes in the temple—it provoked a shiver of uncertainty.

Meanwhile, it was altogether a strange sight and demanded a second look. He was usually sufficiently eye-catching without any props, but the combined effect of a sauntering donkey and colt, of coats being thrown all over the road, and of branches being lopped off trees, created a kink-in-time feeling.

The whole area was still buzzing with the stories about strange happenings in the Bethany cemetery. As for the disciples, they were frankly tickled pink that he was making himself known after all these months of slipping away here and swearing someone to secrecy there.

As crowds go, there was great diversity of response in the general racket. There was curiosity among those who asked, "Who is this?" There was contempt, expressed by the comment, "The whole world has gone after him!" But by and large, there was sheer clamor as huge numbers surged ahead of him, their chants echoed by the moving forest behind him: "Hosanna to the Son of David!" As the procession penetrated the city, it seemed that there were two predominant camps—those whose hosannas rang through the open streets and those whose hostility whispered plots behind closed doors.

If the locals thought that they were in for a festive time with lots of autographs signed and babies kissed and animals blessed, they were in for a whiplash surprise. The shouts at the opening of this drama were very different from those that would bring down the final curtain.

The euphoria of the crowd was a far cry from an incident that took place as he approached the city. In contrast to the crowd's cheers were Christ's tears as he looked at the skyline ahead of him and wept his heart out: "You did not recognize the time of God's coming to you." There is no more tragic end-of-year, end-of-life report than that. To have worked so hard, worshiped so religiously, lived so civilly, and yet completely missed the whole point of it all . . . it broke his heart. It wasn't simply a matter of temporary failure, for it was the awful finality of it all. The joy of the crowd would be short-lived, for he foresaw judgment. For all the noise in the streets upon his entry into Jerusalem, he remained wistful, nurturing his broken heart. He was the center of attention yet strangely anonymous. The spontaneity of the crowd could not quite shout out that uneasy feeling that the script and the props of this play had been rehearsed. While full-throttle throats belted out their messianic designations, Jesus delivered a dumb exegesis. Yes, he was their Messiah, but not their kind of Messiah.

Who could hear the hooves anymore? These were the

reedy clatters of a borrowed ass, not the resounding clangs of a homebred stallion. This was a strange way to "go royal" or to declare war. Surely, something was going to be purged, but it was not going to be the too-visible Romans. It would be a stronger, but invisible occupying power.

The fact is that the crowd cooled off pretty quickly. Jesus remained purely and powerfully himself, and the crowd continued to be flighty and fickle, so disappointment deepened until acrimony began to mar the welcome. The week was hardly proving to be a good PR exercise for a new politico. He had cleared the temple of traders in the most graphic confrontation of his ministry. The logic of love and truth had demanded severity, and gentleness had not excluded a show of strength as he drove the hucksters from the very center of the Jewish citadel of faith. Instead of finding communion, he had uncovered commerce, and he confronted this false exchange, this counterfeit of ransom, this commercialization of sacrifice.

He had not come to reform, but purify, and as he demonstrated, this sometimes requires a physical rearrangement of things and priorities. It would not be the last time that the gods of consumerism would be smuggled into the sanctuary, nor would it be the last time that his truth would expel them unceremonially into the world's gutter where they belong. It seems that the "ministry for merchandise" idea did not feature in his gospel. While the Pharisees were angry at the children for singing his praises, Jesus showed there was something to be justifiably angry about—the sin that had removed the motivation to pray and replaced it with the profit motive. They had enough cash to maintain the temple, but not enough spiritual currency to sustain their souls. Jesus desecrated their worship of mammon and violated the exclusivism of wealth and immediately began to heal the blind and lame. The true trade of sin for salvation, of sickness for health, of despair for praise, of alienation for incorporation, was reestablished, and the "den of thieves" was purged in order that it could be the "house of prayer for all the nations."

His answer to the question about John's baptism had left the chief priests and elders with egg on their faces. Adding insult to injury, he told a story about two sons that helped to illustrate his point that prostitutes would enter the kingdom of God ahead of Pharisees, tax-collectors before tithers. In the very next breath, he launched into another story about tenants who killed the son of the vineyard owner, thus letting his enemies know that he was fully aware of their murderous threats against him. He further fueled their hatred with a humble claim to divinity in his summary of the story's main point: "The kingdom of God will be taken away from you." You could call it the icing on the cake or mud in your eye, depending on your perspective. It seems that they got the message because they immediately looked for a way to arrest him. It would take more than waving palms to lower the temperature now and fan this thing away.

In every campaign there is a moment, often disarmingly insignificant, but nonetheless capable of propelling conflict into a "no way back" situation. Bad as the incidents already mentioned were, the moment when the escalation of the war was assured on Palm Walk happened under the guise of a well-meaning question: "Is it right to pay taxes to Caesar or not?" This was not an off-the-cuff request from a sincere seeker. This question came right out of an extra-long emergency meeting of the enemy. Their purpose was clear: to trap him in his words. What is remarkable is that the Pharisees teamed up with the Herodians, their bitter opponents. It was a clever move and showed that even adversaries will become allies in a common hatred for Jesus. Enmity with Christ is distinctly bipartisan.

THE QUESTION—SETTING THE TRAP

This was not a real enquiry but a ruse. The concern was not to investigate but to incriminate, not to discern justice but to dispense judgment. The apparent enlightenment and concern of an intellectual question can so easily hide the dark intent that seeks to dispose of Christ. Questions that belittle, entrap, denigrate, humiliate, and deny are not new, nor is the setup: "We know you are a man of integrity and that you teach the way of God in accordance with the truth. . . ." You can almost see their necks coil, their limbs slither, and their tongues dart like forked fangs. Was it not this unholy brood of vipers that Jesus had dared to suggest were sired by the devil?

So why all the fuss about a harmless matter of how we should relate to the IRS? As it turned out, Jesus knew that this question was about not civics but theology, not finances but faith, not secular politics but spiritual persuasions.

First, an explanation of the question: Basically three kinds of taxes were levied on these folk. A ground tax took a percentage of their crops, an income tax, and a poll tax, equivalent to a day's wages. The poll tax was in question here, levied by the Romans and bitterly opposed by the populace, for it reminded them of their servitude to a pagan power. Jesus was presented with the horns of a dilemma. The Pharisees and Herodians could hardly contain their smugness. Never had they hit it off so well. After all, Jesus was being hailed as the Messiah, and it was the Messiah's job to break the yoke of the Roman oppressor, right? "Gotcha," or its Aramaic equivalent, was reverberating around their heads. If he said that it was right to pay the taxes, then he would lose his supporters and enrage the Pharisees. If he said it was wrong, then he would be arrested by the Herodians for sedition. It was Herod who supervised the tax collection and owed his power to Rome. Jesus' response was immediate and unequivocal. "You hypocrites, why are you trying to trap me?" There must have been a dramatic pause as they waited for his answer. Jesus then made a brilliant move.

When Jesus asked for the coin that was used for paying the tax, he knew that they would have to go outside the temple to get one and look at it. It was not allowed in the sacred courts, for it was regarded as idolatrous. The inscriptions were hardly compatible with Jewish monotheism. "Tiberius Caesar, son of the divine Augustus . . . Pontifex Maximus." This was both a blasphemous affront and an idolatrous artifact. Suddenly, the arrogant momentum of the questioners was disrupted as they trundled outside. Of course, people would have been curious, so the crowd would be getting bigger. There was also the frustration and suspense of waiting for Jesus' answer, the one that they were convinced would condemn him any way he chose to reply.

THE ANSWER—SPRINGING THE TRAP

Have you ever heard the story about the guy who got exasperated with his rabbi and one day asked the learned gentleman, "Why do rabbis always answer a question with a question?"

The rabbi replied, "Why shouldn't we answer a question with a question?"

Like a good rabbi, Jesus had a question of his own. He took the denarius in his hand and asked, "Whose image is this? Whose inscription?" Of course he knew what he was doing. He was aware that the coin was a symbol of Roman power; that wherever the coin is good, the power is good; that ownership is settled by determining whose inscription the coin bears.

No saying of Jesus has been more debated and abused than the answer he gave on this occasion. It has been used by opposing sides in wars to defend one view and decry the other. Jesus did not establish a set of absolute laws here for governing the relationship between the church and the state. Rather, he laid down a principle that must be prayerfully and scrupulously applied in the light of Scripture and the light of prevailing political philosophy and practice. He did affirm the legitimacy of the state, but he conceded it no primacy or supremacy. He only acknowledged civil authority in the same breath that he affirmed that it is subject to higher rule. The emperor's image is one thing, but what about that which bears God's image? There is a legitimate sense in which the state can fulfill its role as God's agent, but it is not unquestioningly that agent, and of course, by the time we get to the last book in the Bible, it is quite clear that it is not.

Theistic convictions have long since ceased to influence the development of our conception of statehood. One astute hiker has rightly commented that whereas the state once governed in a manner that sought to facilitate the order of our lives, it now seeks to order life itself. That is an enlightening understanding. The state has become more centralized, and society and culture have become more politicized. This hiker went on to observe that it is utter naiveté for Christians to think that a few ready-made, well-intended religious principles and legislative reforms will ever create a social order *ab extra* when basic Christian intellectual and moral principles are discounted. In any case, "it is notorious that ecclesiastics often make the most unscrupulous politicians!" Of course, that doesn't deny vocational engagement with Caesar's systems (a euphemism for political consultancy), for we resist evil and we seek to influence with intent. But as he pointed out, "Political religion is an offense alike to religion and politics; it takes from Caesar what belongs to him of right and fills the temple with the noise and dust of the market place. The only really and specifically Christian politics are the politics of the world to come, and they transform social life not by competing with secular politics on their own ground but by altering the focus of human thought and opening the closed house of secular culture to the free light and air of a larger and more real world."[12]

Jesus' confrontation with the "Caesar question" was going to cost him his life. It is worth remembering that the early church refused the idealisms of both Judaism and Hellenism and instead offered the answer of Jesus' cross. Why? For the same reason that Jesus answered the question here in such a manner. The real enemy is not simply the state, but Satan himself and his control over men's lives. Jesus was not simply interested in winning an argument about the state but in vanquishing the enemy, Satan. Because Christ triumphed over Satan on the cross, that fundamental event was the opening statement of all apostolic apologetics. In the battle for men's allegiance and obeisance, Jesus had a clear answer: "Render to Caesar what is Caesar's and to God what is God's."

You could have heard a palm leaf drop!

Jesus carefully changed the terms of the question. They were talking *pay;* he was talking *give back*. They were asking about *options;* he was pronouncing *obligations*. The issue was not, "What should we retain?" but "What should we render?" Jesus gave them a handle on the problem in the two questions he asked about the coin. Whose image? (Who made you?) Whose inscription? (Who named you?) Rendering what is rightful is not a suggestion in Jesus' mouth, but a command. If you have something that belongs to another and you render it to that person, it is not a gift, but an indebtedness. In a sweeping stroke, Jesus scythes through the malevolent nit-picking of his opponents and gets to the main point. The issue is:

- not Caesar . . . but God
- not servitude to an emperor . . . but service to the Creator
- not a dictator's coins . . . but divinity's claims
- not temporal domination . . . but eternal dominion
- not earthly civility . . . but heavenly citizenship

Jesus' words cut through all the power lunches and power broking, the plea bargaining and the lobbying, the politicizing and compromising that characterize the way we struggle with sin and self. Here is the ultimate simplified tax form. What belongs to God? Give it all to him! He's not satisfied with a tax on our life—he wants it all. We are the ones in the taxing business, keeping him at arm's length with a 10 percent of our Sundays here and a 10 percent of our disposable income there (after the other taxes and bills have been paid). Maybe he'd be satisfied if we made baskets out of all those palm leaves out there on the street and sold them to raise money for the poor?

The basic question then arises: What belongs to God? Of course, it's easier to say "everything" than to identify specific things. It's always been easier to call him Lord than live as his bond-slave. It's important, though, not to begin to answer the question by simply concentrating on "what" belongs, but first to consider "who" it belongs to. God is presented by Jesus not as one who levies but as one who loves. Because of the lover that he is, he won't be satisfied with the floral arrangements of our church life or the chocolates of our offerings. The occasional communication does not satisfy a lover, nor by the way, does the presence of other lovers. So what should I give to God? What does he want from me? Maybe there's a better question. What did Jesus give to God? After all, he's meant to be the example.

Throughout his ministry, Jesus had a refrain that continually deferred to his Father in everything, acknowledging that God was the source for all that he was and all that he had and assuming responsibility for the stewardship of all the resources he had received: "I seek not my own will. . . . I seek not my own glory. . . ." He always recognized that everything was God's before it was ever attributable to himself. One of the clearest insights into his understanding of what belonged to God can be found in one of the most intense and intimate recorded utterances of his life when he prayed and literally took inventory of his life before he died. Anything and everything worthwhile about his life was self-described as being given to him, therefore belonging to God the giver:

- "Glorify your son": his sense of purpose and achievement
- "You granted him authority": his ability to do anything
- "The work you gave me to do": his vocation and capacity to fulfill it
- "Those whom you gave me": the fruit of his ministry, the evidence of his obedience and labor
- "The words you gave me": the meat and means of his communication
- "The name you gave me": his identity and personhood
- "The glory that you gave me": the rewards of relationship and service
- "Now glorify me in your presence": his future and his destiny

The best summary is in his statement, "All I have is yours!" He gives here the best example of what it means to "render to God what is God's."

Like all Jesus' teaching, the question raised boomerangs back, and like all boomerangs, it can't be thrown away too successfully because it just keeps returning to demand a response. Does God have what belongs to him as far as our lives are concerned? Does he have our sin, our past defeats, our present despairs, our future dreams, our relationships, our successes and rewards, our work and capacity to work, our hopes and intentions, our service and giftedness?

The issue for Jesus was never what he had obtained, which was why he retained nothing that was not his. It was not about his getting but his giving. Jesus' hearers may have taken shortcuts with their income tax and worked and milked the system for all it was worth, but they were being warned that they had better be generous to God. All that they possessed and purported to be had dulled their recognition of whose image they bore, whose name they lived under. "That coin is yours? Look again," said Jesus. "That life is yours? Think again," said Jesus. You may live with that illusion, and a convenient one it is. "It's my life" is the chorus of Everyman as he asserts his independence and his rights to uninhibited and unlimited self-expression, while absolving himself of all blame for any untoward consequences.

Jesus did not pull any punches. He once told a story about a man who was asked to give an account of his management of what did not belong to him. One may refuse in this life to render to God what belongs to him, but Jesus left us in no doubt that there will be no choice but to render an account of that decision in the life to come. If we have not given to God what belongs to him, then that day is going to be to us exactly what we have been to God—a thief. We will be robbed of the opportunity to settle accounts while there was still time to render what was rightfully his.

We've traveled a long way down Palm Avenue, and we're a long way from a happy, palm-waving crowd. The streets are quieter now, the temperature is cooler, and the stakes are a whole lot higher. Jesus had made it plain that he had come as Messiah to claim not a political kingdom, but a personal one—the kingdom of the human heart. He had come to claim it for the one to whom it rightfully belonged. His primary area of concern was not the individual's relationship with the state, but the soul's relationship to God. In the closing moments of his public ministry, there was no time for extended sermons or prolonged discourses. The urgency of the hour demanded a clear message, and he gave it.

Caesar or God? The question would be repeated to Pontius Pilate a few days later by the same enemies: "If you let Jesus go, then you are no friend of Caesar!" Amity with Caesar was enmity with Christ. Clearly, they had made their choice.

 If someone has something that belongs to you, you expect to get it when it is requested of them. If he does not surrender what is yours, then what does that make him? A robber, a thief. Herein lies the mystery of redemption. Whose place did Christ take in the public death auction? Barabbas the robber. Who was on either side of Jesus at his crucifixion? Who was the first person to receive eternal life after Christ's trial and condemnation? You guessed it—a robber. There is a direct link between the message of that reverberating public confrontation with the Pharisees and Herodians and what took place on that death row. Christ took the place of every robber who had ever denied God what was rightfully his. He paid in full for every act of spiritual larceny and grand theft. In Christ, God chose to buy back what was rightfully his anyway, thus canceling the note of my pilfering indebtedness. Those who once robbed God by forcefully withholding from him what was his could now become those who freely rendered what was never theirs to keep, but now their joy to return.

Jesus' love picked the lock of the heart of a thief that hung with him. To the robber's surprise, the doors of heaven's vaulted treasures swung open at his confession in the same way that they are oiled for anyone who will choose at last, after a life of petty thieving, to give to God what belongs to God. Forgiveness marks the end of a life dominated by hidden compartments, secret drawers, and spiritual Swiss bank accounts. As the robber found out, when you eventually say to God, "All I have is yours," you discover that what he has already prepared to give you makes the hoarding of your life and talents, the embezzlement and defrauding of his plans and purposes, seem such a pathetic and miserable investment.

God asks for the dime that belongs to him and in return seems to give you unsupervised access to his mint. But you can be trusted because you have ceased to be consumed with "my belongings" and instead have become only conscious of "my longings to be" . . . his and his alone. No more will Caesar get his thieving fingers on that which is God's. Burglars are still being changed into believers. Meanwhile, a certain coin was coffined in a tightly clinched fist. The benevolent breeze that flitted through the palms at Jesus' entry into the front door of Jerusalem changed to a brisker wind that would gust with increasing malevolence until it finally blew him out the back door that was reserved for garbage.

CALVARY WAY

Hear another parable: There was a certain landowner who planted a vineyard and set a hedge around it, dug a winepress in it and built a tower. And he leased it to vinedressers and went into a far country. Now when vintage-time drew near, he sent his servants to the vinedressers, that they might receive its fruit. And the vinedressers took his servants, beat one, killed one, and stoned another. Again he sent other servants, more than the first, and they did likewise to them. Then last of all he sent his son to them, saying, 'They will respect my son.' But when the vinedressers saw the son, they said among themselves, 'This is the heir. Come, let us kill him and seize his inheritance.' And they caught him, and cast him out of the vineyard, and killed him. Therefore, when the owner of the vineyard comes, what will he do to those vinedressers?" They said to Him, "He will destroy those wicked men miserably, and lease his vineyard to other vinedressers who will render to him the fruits in their seasons." Jesus said to them, "Did you never read in the Scriptures:

The stone which the builders rejected
Has become the chief cornerstone.
This was the Lord's doing,
And it is marvelous in our eyes?

Therefore I say to you, the kingdom of God will be taken from you and given to the nation bearing the fruits of it. And whoever falls on this stone will be broken; but on whomever it falls, it will grind him to powder."

Matthew 21:33–44

It probably ranks as his best-known story, though arguably it is the one least understood and consequently worst preached. The context in which it was first related is fairly important, though to hear it retold, you would think it was a cheerleader routine for a Pharisee convention.

Luke puts us right in the picture. "As the time approached for him to be taken up to heaven, Jesus resolutely set out for Jerusalem." He was on the last leg of a one-way trip to the capital (though as it happened, there was a return ticket but not of the usual kind). Only a few days ago he had said to his disciples, "The Son of Man must suffer many things and be rejected. . . ." As he prepared to go south, he was burdened by the anticipation of what lay in wait for him down there.

It was not without significance that it was after his prediction that he was going to be killed that he had that strange experience on the mountain with Peter, James, and John. Their description of what happened tended to concentrate on the staging of the event—the other actors (Moses and Elijah) and the incredible lightning effects. James remembered Peter's rather inane suggestion that they build three tents for the three principals. Stupid things do get said when we are overpowered by a sense of the occasion. It's a bit like going to Buckingham Palace to meet the queen and asking her if you could help her do the washing up after tea. If they'd listened to the voice more than they looked at the light, they would have realized what was going on. Jesus was the focus of attention.

Typical of his Father, an extraordinary meeting had been called where the Law and the prophets of the past met with the apostles of the future church, their worlds brought together in the person of Jesus. What did Jesus talk about with his visitors? Strategy? Maybe, but more likely, they had come to nourish and nurture him and confirm him in his calling at the very moment in his life when it was taking every ounce of energy and obedience to walk flint-faced into the mouth of hell itself. And just to make the purpose of the meeting clear, there was a voice that said, "This is my son. . . ." It throbbed with parental pride, but there was no mistaking the tremble of emotion that hinted that the Son was going to need every millebel of that loving affirmation in the days that lay ahead.

The pressure intensified immediately. First there was the case of the demonized boy that was thrown at him as he arrived at the foot of the mountain. No sooner had that been settled than the disciples got into an argument over which of them was the greatest. This was ironic considering their recent shared failure at helping the aforementioned lad!

The rejection that Jesus had predicted continued to surface like tar oozing from the ground, hampering and hindering progress. The rebuttals weren't violent, not yet, but sufficiently dogged and determined to serve notice that the worst was yet to come. The Samaritan village where he had sent an advance party to find some accommodation closed like a clam the minute they heard that Jesus was involved. Why should they aid a pilgrim to Jerusalem? Ironically, he was hated by the Jews in Jerusalem because of his association with Samaritan outcasts just like these. He was being fired on from all sides, and no-man's land was a strange place for the Creator of the universe to be. He would not survive there for too long.

The next incident was a variation on the theme, as three different individuals gulped at the cost of following Jesus and asked to be allowed to fulfill other commitments. As nice and neighborly as these actions were going to be, they still represented a rejection of Christ in that they accepted another matter as more pressing than his call to discipleship.

On this last trip south, he widened the front of his campaign. He sent out seventy-two other disciples in pairs to do some evangelistic advance work. Not surprisingly, his briefing before they left dealt principally with how they should handle rejection, with a few "woes" thrown in against the cities that had been most guilty of resisting the implications of the revelation they had received through his teaching and miracles.

So what's the story about? Have you guessed which one it is yet? No, it's not one that more obviously deals with the forthcoming events, like the parable about the tenants in the vineyard who murdered the owner's servants and finally killed the son when he was sent. The story in question was Jesus' response to a legal expert who tested Jesus by asking, "What must I do to inherit eternal life?" There's a hint of arrogance in the implicit assumption that whatever answer Jesus gave would present no problem for this guy to implement. "We have the theology—no sweat." His follow-up question, "Who is my neighbor?" was an attempt to justify himself. His involvement with laws was beyond dispute, but his involvement with lives was another matter. The story began, "A man was going down from Jerusalem to Jericho when he fell into the hands of robbers. . . ."

You know the story, but now you also know the context in which it was told, which leads us to ask what on earth Jesus was doing telling a tale that sent everyone away feeling morally uplifted and ready to be a good Samaritan to some dear soul in need. At a point in his life when the "good works" brigade was about to kill him, why did he extol such a moral? Perhaps he never did. I agree with those who would rename this story, say, The Beaten Traveler, and deflect the attention from the good deeds of the Samaritan, that are in fact very good, to the bad deeds of the robbers and the passersby, which are exceedingly bad. And what does that leave us, but a story that pointedly draws attention to the refusal of the priests and the Levites to identify with a suffering Messiah, who descended a little lower than the thirteen-hundred-foot drop from Jerusalem to Jericho. As it turned out, only the outcasts would relate to him. For days, Jesus had been teaching the cost of discipleship and the necessity to understand that he would be beaten and spat upon. Those like the priests who were consumed by the need to keep the religious services running like clockwork or like the Levites who knew the *A-Z* on specifications for sacrifice, were enemies of life, and their religious activities had blinded them to a revelation of anything that didn't fit into their pious schedule. Jesus' exhortation to the lawyer to "Go and do likewise" has less to do with helping old people across the street than it has to do with choosing to be identified with the suffering and the death of a stranger who was even now about to fall into the hands of thieves.

From the wise man's myrrh that intimated suffering to the alabaster box that was broken at his feet and presaged burial; from the blood of the massacre of the innocents to the blood of crucifixion, Jesus lived and walked on the Calvary Way. He did not stumble onto it by chance or pursue it against his better judgment. He was not dragged onto it against his will by wicked men or cajoled to stay on it by zealous friends and admirers. He walked it willingly and purposefully. Every miracle of nature and nurture, every moral restitution and righteous refutation, every exposition and exorcism, took place on this route, and all have ultimate significance because they did so. Ironically, every mighty word and work combined to add volume, not to an acclamation of worth, but to that final derisive taunt, "He saved others . . . save yourself!" Every manifestation of grace and power increased the anger of his enemies and brought him nearer to the cross. The reception of his miracles and rejection of his message only produced the response, "Crucify him!" The road of parables, of good company, of close friendships, of healings, was one of no home, no money, no welcome. Suffering and salvation, violence and victory traveled shoulder to shoulder down this road. There never was a period of thirty years carpentry and three years ministry, then a death. It was the Calvary Way from the conception of life, not the inception of ministry. The cross was not an afterthought.

From the very beginning there were clues. Joseph had one when he was told to name the baby, Jesus, "because he will save his people from their sins." Zechariah had an insight in his prophecy when he perceived the nature of Jesus' mission "to rescue us from the hands of our enemies." To the shepherds, Jesus was announced as "Savior . . . Christ the Lord." Simeon saw "salvation" when he looked into the face of the child, but warned that he would "be a sign that will be spoken against" and that Mary's soul would be pierced by a sword. The prophet Anna talked of the child "to all who were looking forward to the redemption of Jerusalem." The babe was still in arms, and the vocabulary of salvation and suffering, redemption and rejection, was already weaning the consciousness of those closest to him.

Jesus' exchange with his parents in the temple when he was twelve gives a frustratingly short insight into his developing consciousness. "Didn't you know I had to be in my Father's house?" Two observations can be made:

- Jesus had a strong sense of his unique *relationship* with his Father;
- He had a developed sense of *responsibility* to fulfill his purpose.

It is as Jesus' ministry unfolds that we learn about the nature of that relationship and the specific mission that he felt responsible to perform. In the brief but vital contact with John the Baptist, Jesus was designated "Lamb of God," and it appeared that John was not communicating anything new to Jesus, but confirming truths already established in his mind. Both in the waters of the Jordan and the wildness of the desert where he was tempted, Jesus deliberately identified with humanity, pioneering their deliverance from Satan's power and choosing to resist the opportunity to take an easier alternative route to public ministry and popular acceptance.

Jesus' mind was soaked in the Old Testament, and it is evident that his knowledge of Scripture, particularly such passages as Psalm 22 and Isaiah 53, was fundamental to his own developing understanding of his mission. In Isaiah's presentation of the suffering servant, Jesus learned how to interpret his own experience both to himself and the disciples, and it would become the crucial text of later apostolic preaching. His recorded communication about his death is full of allusions to Isaiah's prophecy.

In fact, it has been observed that apart from the second verse ("he had no beauty or majesty to attract us to him") all the verses of this chapter are specifically applied to Jesus in the New Testament. This can only be the result of Jesus' own exposition and application of this text. Although the Gospel writers were not concerned with doctrinal formulation, it is important to note that Jesus' acute consciousness of the relationship between human sin and his suffering places the atonement firmly in the Gospels and establishes the cross as the center of gravity of their presentation. Unlike most biographies, they spend most time (up to 50 percent of their accounts) dealing with their subject's death.

Even if Isaiah 53 had been the only passage of prophetic text that Jesus had access to, it would have given him an understanding of the following:

- that both messenger and message would be rejected ("Who has believed our message?");
- that despite the apparent ineffectiveness of the message to some, it was the power of God ("to whom has the arm of the Lord been revealed?");
- that the Messiah would develop without notice or fanfare ("a tender shoot") and he would not appear to have the right qualifications ("root out of a dry ground . . . no beauty . . .");
- that his life and ministry would be inextricably linked with suffering, both in absorption of personal pain as well as in the association with the pain of others ("a man of sorrows . . . familiar with suffering");
- that his suffering would not be on account of his sin ("he had done no violence, nor was any deceit in his mouth . . ."), but of the sins of others and would be the consequence of his bearing that sin for them and receiving the punishment instead of them ("he took up our infirmities . . . our transgressions . . . our iniquities. . . . He bore the sin of many . . .");
- that this suffering was not simply the plot of wicked men to silence the servant, but the plan of a righteous God to satisfy every characteristic of his personality and condition of his love that demanded punishment for sin, yet desired relationship with the sinner ("the punishment that brought us peace was upon him . . . stricken by God, smitten by him and afflicted. . . . The Lord has laid on him the iniquity of us all . . . for the transgression of my people he was stricken. . . . It was the Lord's will to crush him and cause him to suffer . . .");
- that though God initiated the suffering, the Messiah would cooperate voluntarily ("he poured out his life unto death . . .");
- that the personal cost of such sin bearing was going to be beyond comprehension in its sudden and premature separation ("By oppression and judgment he was taken away . . . cut off from the land of the living . . ."), and in its

mental, physical, emotional, and spiritual severity ("pierced . . . crushed . . . afflicted . . .");

- that he would be treated as if he was a common criminal ("assigned a grave with the wicked");

- that this suffering would fully achieve all of God's purposes insofar as it would satisfy his justice, demonstrate his love, prove his wisdom, vindicate his power, and manifest his glory ("the Lord makes his life a guilt offering. . . . I will give him a portion among the great and he will divide the spoils with the strong . . . he will see his offspring and prolong his days, and the will of the Lord will prosper in his hand . . .").

Throughout his ministry, Jesus clearly presented his understanding of the purpose of his mission. For example:

- "For God did not send his Son into the world to condemn the world, but to save the world through him." He was the one upon whom the world's salvation depended. He did not come to condemn, but to convert; not to limit but liberate.

- "I have not come to abolish the Law and the prophets but to fulfill them." He spoke with such authority that it appeared to some that he was challenging Moses' Law. However, Jesus made it clear that his was not a New Age movement but a completion of the Old Age. He was not the leader of a sect or mystery religion or personality cult or higher consciousness group. He endorsed and fulfilled the Old Testament:

    Propositions: Jesus claimed to have brought to conclusion God's covenant plan of salvation as revealed in the instructions of the Torah.

    Prophecies: Jesus claimed to be the fulfillment of the prophecies of the Messiah who was to come and therefore spoke of "Scripture witnesses."

    Precepts: Jesus subscribed to all the ethical commands of the moral law of God and fulfilled it through his obedience to it.

Jesus understood that he had come in fruition of the law, not in opposition to it. He taught that the issue was not to do with hands that were washed ritualistically, but with hearts that were cleansed redemptively. The law was all about private motives, not public manners. He came not to repeal the law but to restore it.

- "The Son of Man did not come to be ministered to, but to minister." He didn't come to seek the satisfaction of his needs, but ours. His mission was characterized not so much by legalistic demands, but loving desires. He came not to get but to give.

- "I have not come to call the righteous but sinners." He said he came, not for the up-and-aways who trusted in their own resources, but for the down-and-outs who confessed their bankruptcy. He did not come to collect nice people but to call needy ones.

- "I did not come to bring peace but a sword." He had no intention to make people feel good with the status quo or give them a coating of tranquility. He did not come to provide resolutions for troubles, but reconciliation for troublemakers. He did not market religious, iconic wallpaper to cover the cracks of our brokenness and make us feel at home with pleasant patterns of illusory serenity. He came to call people to accountability before God that would divide them from past lives and lovers and from anything that only produced an easy peace. He did not come to pacify but to purify.

All of these insights are important, but their fulfillment is premised on Jesus' fundamental understanding for his coming: "The Son of Man came . . . to give his life a ransom for many." Continually and explicitly, Jesus spoke about his death, about what it meant to God, to himself, and to the world. When he talked of it, he used the language of necessity ("The Son of Man must suffer many things . . ."), particularly because of the prophetic Scriptures ("O fools, and slow of heart to believe all that the prophets have spoken! Was it not necessary that the Christ should suffer these things . . . ?"). However, though necessary, Jesus did not see himself as a helpless product of a callous determinism. On the contrary, he saw his death as a fulfillment to embrace, not as a fate to resist. His death was a voluntary submission ("I lay down my life. . . . No one takes it from me.") His death was not about what the Pharisees killed, but what his Father willed.

Jesus described the purpose of his death as a "ransom." If something needs to be ransomed, then that means it is not presently in the place where it truly belongs, with the one to whom it rightfully belongs. For it to be returned, a high price must be paid. It cannot be stolen, and it cannot be procured by a swap or with any conditions attached. Nothing but the full price will do. Although the image describes a material transaction, Jesus employs it with all the accumulated force of its Old Testament usage to describe the cost of a moral redemption that would free men from being captive to the will of Satan in order that they may serve God. Those who need to be ransomed cannot free themselves. Their lives are forfeited until the conditions set for their release are met.

1. *The cause:* Sin has made us lawbreakers and therefore prisoners. It has resulted in an indebtedness to God that we cannot pay.
2. *The cost:* The death penalty has been incurred by sin and must be satisfied.
3. *The coin:* Christ's life was the currency for the exchange that ransomed the sinner, paying the debt by taking the full penalty of the law.

Jesus saw his death as both a sacrifice for God's satisfaction, as well as a substitute for man's salvation.

Despite the violence that Jesus knew he would have to endure, his perspective on his death was reinforced with a strong and steely conviction about the victory to be achieved. As Isaiah had prophesied and he had taught, the spoils of the strong man, Satan, were going to be plundered. Jesus' assured closing comments before his ordeal announce a verdict: "The ruler of this world is judged." When he ate bread and drank wine with his disciples at the Last Supper, he was already thinking of the triumphant future when he would drink the wine again in the kingdom of God. The cross was not a terminus of death but a through station to everlasting life.

As the events of that night unraveled, there was an uncanny echo: "He fell into the hands of robbers. They stripped him of his clothes, beat him and went away. . . ." Judas had put his hands into the purse once too often and was grateful for the opportunity to have his palms crossed with silver. His next act of thievery was to steal a kiss. Caiaphas tore his clothes in white-knuckled anger as he shouted the charge of blasphemy in the name of the law and the temple. Little did he know that in a few hours time, God would take the billowing folds of the temple veil, rip in two the material wall that barred the way to holiness, and, with a flick of the divine wrists, sweep aside the self-made custodians of truth. He would open up a new and living way, stained with blood, maybe, but uncurtained forever.

Pilate's weakness flattered Herod with its request for a considered judgment. Herod lusted for a miracle at this late hour, treating Jesus like a clown who was obliged to perform a party trick to lighten the morbid atmosphere. Little did Herod know, as he subjected Jesus to being dressed up in some of his elegant robes of temporal power, that the embroidered symbols of earthly rule would soon be taken from him. His coarse ridicule combined with the vehement accusations of the scribes, and in a common bond of tragic ignorance, the rulers of this age condemned him. Pilate did not know that it was impossible to find the right political territory of jurisdiction for the judge of the earth. However, he did know what it would be like to lose the friendship of Caesar, so with conciliatory weakness, he handed Jesus over to the people in the name of the powers of Rome, the state.

The "ruler of this world," as Jesus had characterized Satan, and the rulers of the age, combined their forces behind the faces of human institutions. The priests sentenced Jesus in deference to the temple organization. The scribes, failing to see him as the fulfillment of the law, judged him by that law. Herod and Pilate sacrificed Jesus' truth to political expediency. It all ended with a robber called Barabbas, whose ultimate "job" was to filch Jesus' innocence.

 He had held his silence while others held the floor. "He is worthy of death. . . . Crucify him. . . . His blood be on us and our children. . . . Prophesy to us, Christ! Who hit You? . . . Hail, King of the Jews! . . . Come down from the cross if you are the son of God. . . . He trusts in God, let God rescue him. . . . He saved others but he can't save himself. . . ." He chose to eventually speak when least able to do so. Each sentence, wheezed and squeezed from a frame so punctured that there was barely sufficient air left to breathe, let alone talk.

More precious than those drops of alabaster, every syllable exuded the characteristic aroma of his life. Like seeds, each bare word was a spore in the air, that planted a thick harvest disproportional to its fragile husk. "Father, forgive them, for they do not know what they are doing. . . . Dear woman, here is your son. Son, here is your mother. . . . Today you will be with me in paradise." To the last, he continued to release, to relate, to reconcile, right up to the final millisecond, when the reign of darkness itself was pierced with the sharpest cry of dereliction ever uttered: "My God, my God, why have you forsaken me?"

As crushing as the weight of alienation was, however, it did not have the last word. The remaining cubic centimeters of life gathered for the final cry, not of abandonment, but accomplishment: "It is finished!" These words of triumph that had concluded the old creation now filled heaven and earth with equal power, announcing a brand new creation. The gasping of a dying man was now gusting with the force of a holy hurricane, shaking the foundations of hell and serving notice that the contract that had been put out on humanity had been paid in full and that there would be no more negotiations for the souls of men.

In the wake of that cry came a gentle expiration, that strongly yet tenderly, briefly yet comprehensively, summed up his entire life. "Father, into your hands I commit my spirit." Truly, it was a terrible thing to fall out of the hands of the living God. His final act was to trustingly put himself right back into them and, in that redeeming movement, place into the same safe cradle the life of every person who would accept and appropriate the ransom, wherever they happened to be along the route from earthly Jericho to heavenly Jerusalem.

ROUTE SIX

Checking out how the journey began . . .

GARDEN PATH

MAP REFERENCE

*T*hen the disciples went away again to their own homes. But Mary stood outside by the tomb weeping, and as she wept she stooped down and looked into the tomb. And she saw two angels in white sitting, one at the head and the other at the feet, where the body of Jesus had lain. Then they said to her, "Woman, why are you weeping?" She said to them, "Because they have taken away my Lord, and I do not know where they have laid Him." Now when she had said this, she turned around and saw Jesus standing there, and did not know that it was Jesus. Jesus said to her, "Woman, why are you weeping? Whom are you seeking?" She, supposing Him to be the gardener, said to Him, "Sir, if You have carried Him away, tell me where You have laid Him, and I will take Him away." Jesus said to her, "Mary!" She turned and said to Him, "Rabboni!" (which is to say, Teacher). Jesus said to her, "Do not cling to Me, for I have not yet ascended to My Father; but go to My brethren and say to them, 'I am ascending to My Father and your Father, and to My God and your God.'" Mary Magdalene came and told the disciples that she had seen the Lord, and that He had spoken these things to her. Then, the same day at evening, being the first day of the week, when the doors were shut where the disciples were assembled, for fear of the Jews, Jesus came and stood in the midst, and said to them, "Peace be with you." Now when He had said this, He showed them His hands and His side. Then the disciples were glad when they saw the Lord. Then Jesus said to them again, "Peace to you! As the Father has sent Me, I also send you."

John 20:10–21

Everyone was running; everyone was breathless. Everyone was fearful; everyone was speechless. They could be forgiven for not making the right connections or coming to the right conclusions. It wasn't that they hadn't been told, but why should they have thought that resurrection was anything more than an extremely spiritual metaphor?

The Gospel narratives do not present us with a lesson in metaphysics on the one hand or a sensational, Superman-style breakout on the other. As one traveler has rightly observed, during that time of temptation in the wilderness, way back at the beginning of his ministry, Jesus had rejected the devil's attempts to sell him a pair of messianic blue tights: "He is born among us as Clark Kent; he dies as Clark Kent; and he comes forth from the tomb as Clark Kent—not as some alien hotshot in blue tights who, at the crucial moment, junks his Clark Kentness in favor of a snappier, nonhuman style of being."[13] There was no earthquake to warn them that something unusual was happening. No rocks exploded; no stars fell; no trumpets sounded; no angelic limousine service filled the sky to attend the homecoming.

In the early morning darkness, in silence, he checked out of the tomb, in the anonymous way that a stranger leaves a local motel where he had never intended to stay long. Like a good guest, he left everything in tidy order, particularly the bedclothes, which in fact looked as if they had not even been slept in. He left no forwarding address. The single most significant event in the entire history of the human race, took place without so much as a "by your leave." No wonder they did not understand. Of course, they had every reason to be disconsolate.

But had he not specifically said, "I will not leave you desolate. I will come to you"? We are not left with a yawning hole in the wall, a few scattered sightings and a bunch of disturbed people trying to sort out a scientific conundrum. Instead, we are presented with clear and articulate accounts of a risen Christ, who chooses to come to people and lead them in person into a full comprehension of what had happened and into a full communion with himself. Of course he was right. They were desolate, and their sense of loss and dereliction had different characteristics.

DESOLATION AS DESPAIR

Mary Magdalene lingered at the tomb long after Peter and John had returned home. If anyone knew Jesus' power to make a difference, it was Mary, who had exchanged her one-night stands for a lifetime of sitting at Jesus' feet. She was living proof that an ex-prostitute could be pure, that a used and abused woman could feel like a virgin again.

Suddenly, the center of her life had collapsed. Despair blurs perception, and it is not surprising that she mistook the voice that asked her who she was looking for as that of the gardener. Even as she spoke, she continued to peer into the grave's darkness, her perspective transfixed by this hopeless void. Despair abandons all expectation of change or salvation. Mary's abject posture before that tomb represents the plight of everyone who has contemplated the inevitability of death, the vulnerability of love and life, the finality of separation from this earth.

However, all intimations of mortality are suddenly, but nonetheless gently, suspended. There is no intoned sermon, not even a spiritual-sounding phrase. A single word changes everything: "Mary!" It was the mark of the shepherd that he called his sheep by name.

Not surprisingly, she clung to him, and he had to say, "Do not hold on to me!" She was not going to let him get away this time, but as it turned out, there was going to be no more need for the insecurity that grasps and grabs. The risen Christ initiated a new relationship of intimacy that was no longer dependent on physical proximity. Mary could not lose this Christ, and the very fact that she responded to his instruction to go into town and tell the others about him is evidence of her peace and his power. She was confident that he would still be accessible, though out of sight. It is precisely the despair engendered by the fact of death that the resurrection of Christ calls to account. It is a deficit that is wiped from the ledger for all who accept his new life and relationship. The risen Christ is the only explanation for the dispelling of Mary's despair.

DESOLATION AS DOUBT

Rumors and reports of the resurrection had unleashed a nervous excitement, a heady euphoria, a hold-your-breath wonder, a can-it-be-really-true amazement. Blood was coursing; adrenalin was pumping; incredulity was melting.

But amidst it all, we are given a cameo of gloom and doom. Thomas' name meant "twin," an ironic designation, given the fact that he seemed to spend most of his time in two minds. He was a realist and a pessimist, and he had predicted this disaster. Now, he was nowhere to be found. It was just his luck not to be there when all the weird stuff happened. Although he has gone into history as "doubting Thomas" and become a vernacular embodiment of double-mindedness, he was not the only doubter.

In fact, doubt emerges as the premier response in the resurrection narratives, highlighting a problem that has persisted in the face of such an extraordinary event. "They did not believe the women because their words seemed to them like nonsense. . . ." They were startled and frightened and thought they saw a ghost. "Why do doubts rise in your minds? . . . When they saw him they worshiped him but some doubted. . . ." Doubt is a common and understandable response to the resurrection. However, it is important to know that doubt is not the same as unbelief. Someone has helpfully described the relationship between faith and doubt as similar to that between courage and fear. Cowardice is the opposite of courage, not fear, in the same way that unbelief is the opposite of faith, not doubt. There is a naturalness in both fear and doubt. If handled rightly, fear can embolden courage, and doubt can enrich faith, but if allowed to fester and dominate, fear will overrule all advisable action, and doubt will undermine all reasonable explanation. Fear will surely lead to cowardice as doubt will lead to unbelief.

The Gospel writers realistically capture many of doubt's trademarks as they describe that disorienting and disconcerting state of suspension between unbelief and faith. And yet at the outset, they establish a crucial factor—Christianity invites people to an examined faith. It invites question, discussion, verification, and personal confirmation.

For many, doubt is passive, a chronic state of indifference. For others it is active, genuinely seeking what is believable and what constitutes a sufficient ground for action. Doubts arise for many reasons: no sense of need for God, inadequate knowledge of the evidence, debilitation caused by overwhelming emotional concerns, indolence in the pursuit of the issues, misinformation resulting from wrong teaching or bad examples, insufficient right understanding to encourage a right decision. There are many who fall prey to doubt because, having once begun well, they failed to pursue Christ or practice their faith. It has been rightly observed that you hardly meet anybody who has been reasoned out of faith by honest argument, but many who have simply drifted away.

Thomas was in danger of drifting. Like many doubters, he tended to hang back when he had a hang-up. Hesitancy became a mode of life. What characterized his doubt?

A LOSS OF COMPREHENSION

He allowed his understanding of who Jesus was to be shaken. His own need and suffering, his acute self-consciousness relaxed his grip on the fact that what Jesus had said was dependable, independent of circumstances or probabilities. Though tested, Jesus' word would be tried and true.

A LOSS OF COMMITMENT

It is impossible to separate our understanding and our will. When comprehension is eroded, commitment crumbles. Thomas had plenty of evidence for Jesus' trustworthiness, but he could no longer travel on Jesus' initiative alone.

A LOSS OF COMMUNITY

Sadly, Thomas compounded his problem by withdrawing from the others. Sure, they weren't Jesus, but he needed to be encouraged and loved by those who knew him for who he was, who accepted him despite his negativism, and who would encourage him to pursue legitimate questions while disallowing his retreat into solitary despondency.

What Thomas needed was a way to get back to the beginning. The making good of all these losses was dependent on one thing—a fresh encounter with Jesus. In the words of one hiker, he was no longer faced with an argument that demanded his assent, but a person who demanded his confidence. Thomas had already doused the excited testimony of others with his doubt and cynicism. There's black humor and defiance in his crude conditions that he put his finger through the nail holes in Jesus' hands.

Sure enough, Jesus picked his moment and arrived while Thomas was in attendance. He addressed him immediately, and in common with all his resurrection appearances, established a personal relationship. He was not dismissive or scolding of Thomas' doubt, but treated him almost preferentially.

HE LISTENED

All doubters need to be heard as they express their worst fears and ask their hardest questions.

HE DISCERNED

He knew exactly where Thomas was, even though he'd already said enough to be booted out of the "Eternal Order of Disciples." He'd blown his character and his judgment, but Jesus perceived his heart. Though his actions and arguments seemed to deny it, Jesus knew that inwardly he was longing to believe.

HE SPOKE

Jesus' communication was compassionate, yet direct and firm. He submitted himself to Thomas' cynical experiment and put his dignity at the mercy of Thomas' doubt. His "Stop doubting and believe!" was not a chiding reprimand but a loving appeal.

In the person of Jesus, Thomas recovered his comprehension, and his renewed commitment exploded in a confessional crescendo: "My Lord and my God!" The greatest cry of faith came from the mouth of an ex-cynic. The outsider was once again incorporated into the community of faith. Jesus confirmed Thomas, but he also confronted him with a gentle rebuke, "not because he refused to believe without enough reasons, but because he refused to believe with more than enough reasons." The risen Christ is the only explanation for the dispelling of Thomas' doubt.

DESOLATION AS DREAD

The disciples had huddled together, with the doors locked "for fear." They did not know where they stood anymore. They had withdrawn and assembled their private defenses, no doubt wondering what their fate would be at the hands of the authorities and crowds. Then "Jesus came and stood among them . . . Shalom!" They could have expected blame or chastisement, but not this. Having braced themselves for the worst, they did not know how to handle the best.

"He showed them his hands and his side." The scars of his pain and passion were medals of honor, not marks of defeat. He did not commiserate with them, but commissioned them. One moment they were holed up, and the next they were being sent out. The spirit of fear was expelled as Jesus "breathed on them and said, 'Receive the Holy Spirit.'" They had settled for a garret, and he handed them the globe. The risen Christ is the only explanation for the dispelling of the disciples' dread.

 The resurrection has been called many things: fraudulent invention; fanciful imagination; fanatical interpretation. It has been branded as myth, as metaphor, as magic. It has been described as a presence, as a potentiality, as a possibility. The disciples have been called weak, wicked, and wishful. However, one little phrase chokes all talk about concepts, images, and essences. Four words interrupt the pseudo-patter of the liberal legend-makers: "On the third day." The experiences of Mary, Thomas, and the other disciples cannot be relegated to a world of private fantasy or intuition. They were the consequences of something prior that did not take place in a world of imagination—a particular event that happened in a tomb, in time.

The series of experiences do not in themselves add up to a resurrection. Those encounters are the product of the detailed and dated physical resurrection of Jesus' body from the grave. The sequence of events that this body went through are spelled out with simple detail: dead, buried, raised, appeared. Every stage was accompanied by a body. When he appeared in one place, his physical body was not somewhere else. Something specific happened that changed the personal histories of every life that encountered it. The chorus line of every consequent gathering and every communication was unequivocal: "To this we are witnesses!"

Yes, there were other refrains: unknown tomb, wrong tomb, hallucination, Passover plot, resuscitation theory, stolen body, criminal invention. Yes, there are difficulties in explaining the empty tomb with its two-ton door, one hundred pounds of body spices, and effective Roman security guard. Yes, it was problematic to find another explanation for the circumstantial evidence of all these changed lives in the church with its sacraments of Eucharist and baptism and its celebratory worship on the first day of the week. The fact was that these disciples had seen something totally unexpected, had seen it many times over a period of seven weeks, in places as different as a cemetery, an open road, a locked room, by a lake, in the hills, in the suburbs. It removed their past desolation, empowered them to live in the present, and emboldened them to face the future, even if it included a premature death. They were convinced that the resurrection was:

- *A vindication:* The rulers and mobs had passed their verdict, but the resurrection conclusively overthrew and reversed their decision. The disapproval of men that removed Christ was overruled by the approval of God that raised him.

- *A victory:* Jesus' resurrection put a seal on all that he intended to accomplish through his death. The battle with the great enemy Satan and his dominion of sin and death had been engaged. Sin had not stained Jesus, and death had not swallowed him. He overpowered and defeated the worst powers that could assail him. The resurrection was the ultimate victory over the ultimate enemy, death.

- *A vision:* The resurrection gave the disciples a new way to think about the future. It was a pledge, a foretaste of what would be true for everyone who followed in Jesus' footsteps. Not only did it speak of a power that gave hope for this existence, but it also intimated a power that would maintain them beyond the limited boundaries of this life, simply because they too would receive a resurrection body, of which his was the prototype.

All the intentions that were represented by Jesus' life, death, and resurrection were going to be realized. The epitaph was not the final word for an individual life, any more than a disruption in nature was the end of the earth. The redemption of bodies, and indeed of the whole universe, was on the divine agenda. As surely as "the third day" arrived, even so would the predicted day of history's consummation be fulfilled. No wonder they shouted, "Even so come quickly, Lord Jesus!"

Evidentially and experientially, the Gospels present the risen Christ. Like the disciples, we huddle in our postures of defensive fear, protective of our diminishing lives, unmindful that after the last key has been turned in our emotional security system and the last rational argument has been advanced like a piece of furniture behind the door, Christ still loves to come through walls behind our backs. Like heavy window shades, our presuppositions black out the light of other possibilities, and our prejudices, like old sheets stuffed in vents and cracks, ensure that we will not breathe any air other than that which we ourselves had exhaled.

Like Thomas, we defy and deny the testimony of others and belittle and besmirch the testimony of history, unrefined in our cynicism, crude in our mockery. We throw our sarcastic and agnostic darts with the abandon of a bar game until we are unexpectedly confronted in a moment of need by an outstretched hand that looks like it was pierced by one of our missiles.

Like Mary, we are overcome by the sadness of the world in tears, distraught when life's slender thread is snapped, and we are faced with the awfulness of separation from loved ones, from laughter and life, from songs and stories, the awfulness of broken bread and half-sipped cups. At that moment, when we are most tempted to feel that our expectations have led us up the garden path, we mistake Christ's voice for that of an uninvolved stranger. The garden path that winds its way through the headstones and memorials of failed heroes and decayed dreams, lost lovers and buried hopes, is precisely the road that resurrected feet most like to travel. The chances are that you'll hear your name before you even hear the foot treads, and that is just as well, for in the moment of our deepest spiritual need, we need his resurrection power at our shoulders to deliver us from the logic of our despair and from the temptation to hide again among the tombs.

Amidst the desolation of despair and doubt and dread, Christ still comes in risen power. Through the walls of our resistance, before the barbed arrows of our cleverness, down the garden path of our unrequited hopelessness, Christ still comes.

On the third day, he came. Today he still comes . . . inviting people to attest that he is the risen Christ . . . that sin and death shall not have any more dominion over them. In a moment when you least expect him, from an angle that you would calculate as the most unlikely, in a place that seems the least conducive . . . he will come. That's the beauty of his resurrected power!

Believe him while you may, for one day he will come again, in person, and call each one of us to give an account of how we have responded to the same voice that Mary heard along that garden path.

EMMAUS ROAD

MAP REFERENCE

*N*ow behold, two of them were traveling that same day to a village called Emmaus, which was about seven miles from Jerusalem. And they talked together of all these things which had happened. So it was, while they conversed and reasoned, that Jesus Himself drew near and went with them. But their eyes were restrained, so that they did not know Him. And He said to them, "What kind of conversation is this that you have with one another as you walk and are sad?" Then the one whose name was Cleopas answered and said to Him, "Are You the only stranger in Jerusalem, and have You not known the things which happened there in these days?" And He said to them, "What things?" And they said to Him, "The things concerning Jesus of Nazareth, who was a Prophet mighty in deed and word before God and all the people. . . ."

And beginning at Moses and all the Prophets, He expounded to them in all the Scriptures the things concerning Himself. Then they drew near to the village where they were going, and He indicated that He would have gone farther. But they constrained Him, saying, "Abide with us, for it is toward evening, and the day is far spent." And He went in to stay with them. Now it came to pass, as He sat at the table with them, that He took bread, blessed and broke it, and gave it to them. Then their eyes were opened and they knew Him; and He vanished from their sight. And they said to one another, "Did not our heart burn within us while He talked with us on the road, and while He opened the Scriptures to us?"

Luke 24:13–19; 27–32

Jerusalem was reverberating with the aftershocks of Jesus' crucifixion. Everyone had an opinion and dispensed it as if it were welfare medicine, forcing it down whether you liked it or not, simply because it was free. Like all aftershocks, these spiritual seismic shudders brought some relief insofar as they signified that the main quake was over. They also brought some foreboding, for who knew when this state of affairs would settle or when the next upheaval would erupt.

Meanwhile, people were scuttling about like ants whose nests had been violated by some alien invasion. Some of Jesus' followers were among this number, especially those who had been out to the tomb and were now nervously communicating with those they bumped into on their return, telling them what they had found or, to be more precise, had not found. The bottom line was that all orders placed for graveside flower arrangements would prove to be a waste of money.

Peter had seen the strips of grave cloth lying there, like the discarded garb of an escaped convict. He had bent over to examine them, but he was out of his investigative depth, and neither Hercule Poirot nor Columbo could have done any better. So the women were right. They were still hysterical, but they were certainly not hallucinating. The problem? No body. Who knew the answers? Nobody.

The hike to Emmaus was about seven miles, a two-hour journey at an even pace. Who knows why they were on the road? Cleopas and his companion could be forgiven for an overwhelming need to leave the claustrophobic, acidic city of Jerusalem. Their animated and agitated conversation was a desperate attempt to impose some order on the chaos, conjure some sense of the confusion, replay the final, game-wrecking fumble. So intense was their discussion that it was a little while before they were aware of a third walker, half a step behind Cleopas' shoulder. Weird things were taking place, and yes, they were sure they had heard a voice. "What are you talking about as you walk along?" With startled backward glances, they froze like Lot's wife. The third man's presence was unsettling enough without the question that was almost insulting in its ignorance of recent events. The stranger's tone betrayed an unjustified innocence, and he was therefore deemed guilty.

Why is it that when the world is falling apart and one is ducking the flying debris and dodging bullets, there always seems to be some oblivious soul tiptoeing through the landmines on his way to a peaceful picnic in the country? Your battle fatigues are caked with blood and mud, and here comes a Burlington Bertie inquiring, "What's up, old chap?" The point was not lost on Cleopas, who said, "You've got to be new in these parts. Have you just arrived? Is that why you don't know what's been going on around here?" There was clearly nothing to laugh about, but a resigned can-you-beat-that-buddy kind of smile momentarily creased his otherwise passive and pensive demeanor.

Undaunted, almost cheerfully, the stranger asked the next best question, "What things?"

It had been an interminable day. Mercifully, the light was fading. Strength of will had been sapped, and physical energy seeped away. However, that simple question suddenly unhinged the sluice gate of reservoired and pent-up emotion, which volubly tumbled out, tossing facts and explanations at the stranger. It seems that he was more than able to ride these rapids, and as calmly as if he were rafting on a quiet stream, he watched and listened. "Jesus . . . of Nazareth . . . prophet . . . awesome . . . miracles . . . chief priests . . . three days ago . . . awful . . . bad dream . . . had hopes . . . amazing women . . . body gone . . . angel talk . . . alive . . . reliable guys . . . story checked out . . . tomb empty . . . nowhere to be seen . . ."

Now it was the stranger's turn to smile chidingly. Close but no cigar. Of course, he did not put it quite like that but there was a hint of schoolmasterliness in his voice, a subtle combination of admonishment and encouragement. "Excuse me, but aren't you missing something? The prophets gave us a little more info than you're accounting for. There's more to it than that. Didn't they say that it was actually necessary for

Christ to suffer all this . . . and that only then would he enter his glory? So why the surprise?" Messianic prophecy was full-flavored, double-scoop, in a sugar cone, and they were only ordering a single scoop of vanilla in a paper cup. Since the third man's arrival, they had remained anchored to the place of meeting.

With a tone that had a squeeze of enthusiasm and a slice of pedantry, the stranger said, "Let's take Moses for starters." And with that, he began to walk toward Emmaus. It was not a hurried pace, but it was steady, stately, and purposeful, like the movement of the prow of a Galilean fishing boat as it pushed off from the shore and gathered momentum in its glide out onto the lake, its crew doggedly determined to catch something. Like two fishermen, the others had a quick decision to make. Stay on the shore or jump in quickly while it was still within range. They just made it. They began that journey with wet feet and ended it with heartburn.

 This incident was consistent with other accounts of Jesus' interaction with his disciples after his resurrection, and it was also characteristic of his teaching method in his pretrial ministry. He presented the Scriptures as the basis for:

- his own self-awareness and understanding of his identity and mission;
- his personal authority for what he said and did;
- his public appeal to others to attest and accept his teaching.

This consuming concern for the Scriptures as the fundamental framework of reference is evident in Luke's last recorded communication of Jesus with his followers: "He said to them, 'These are the words which I spoke to you while I was still with you, that all things must be fulfilled which were written in the Law of Moses and the Prophets and the Psalms concerning Me.' And he opened their understanding that they might comprehend the Scriptures" (Luke 24:44–45).

I wonder how we would have advised Jesus if we had been responsible for his time management in this forty-day period. No doubt we would have suggested the venues where he could network most efficiently and impact the market most cost effectively. Would we really have let him waste his time (2.5 percent of total available) as an unrecognized hiker on a forsaken trail with a couple of forlorn, unknown has-beens? Of course not! Pack them into an all-weather stadium, for an all-age, all-day, all-inclusive seminar (spiral notebooks free with fifty-dollar entry fee). We would also have summarized his teachings and then prioritized them and repackaged them in more easily remembered and more readily available form. It is incredible to our activist natures and performance-oriented minds that he would leave no record of practical instructions for, say, the ten most likely problems to be faced after his departure. Surely some worksheets would have been helpful: Walking on Water in Three Dry Steps, Five or Six Possible Suggestions to Overcome Spiritual Indecision, Macro-Management of a Micro-Church, How to Lobby Caesar Nonviolently, Demanding Your Miracle, Financing Your Faith. How much easier it would have been if he had taken the time to reduce the entire message of his kingdom to a single overhead projector sheet. He did not rush around giving "last words" performances, nor did he take the disciples on a farewell road tour of all the old gig sites. He did not write any last-minute "When I'm gone, whatever you do, don't forget to . . ." memos. When he wall-crashed various gatherings, the thing he loved to do most, apart from watching their faces as he swallowed fish, was lead a small group study of the Scriptures and show his followers how to understand the teachings themselves and how to explain their importance and meaning to others.

It has been observed that there is a logical progression in the development of many people's spiritual knowledge. They begin with a general but sincere belief in God and then increasingly discover the many ways that he seems to have left his signature on various astounding works that help them to discern his possible personality, perspective, and purposes. They then find out that God has revealed himself fully and finally, supremely and superbly in Jesus Christ, who, upon closer examination, spends most of his time teaching the truth of Scripture and speaking personally and authoritatively about what makes for life as God originally planned it to be. These teachings then become the indispensable source of their learning—instructing, warning, feeding, nurturing, directing. Cleopas was finding out what we all need to know—that it is impossible to know who Jesus is without knowing him in and through the Scriptures.

What is amazing is the fact that it was more important to Jesus to teach the Scriptures dutifully and show how they related to him than to perform sensational (and no doubt potentially more faith-building and decision-clinching) aerial and ethereal displays of his newly acquired resurrection physics. Jesus did not say, "Hey! My recent resurrection will be sufficient to make them take the Scriptures seriously and treat my teachings with respect." On the contrary, he remarked, "If they do not listen to Moses and the prophets, they will not be convinced even if someone rises from the dead."

Jesus insisted that there was an inviolable relationship between himself and the Scriptures, so much so that if you really believed them, you would certainly believe him and if you refused him, then you would with equal certainty reject the Scriptures.

But Cleopas and friend had a problem. They were bitterly disappointed and disheartened. The nails driven through Jesus' hands and feet had punctured their belief and their hopes were leaking out. Just when they thought that they were making $1+1=2$ and concluding that Jesus was the Messiah, they were staring at $1-1=0$, computing that nothing had been what it seemed. They could make no sense of the available data. There could be no explanation plausible or powerful enough to lift their heavy despondency.

Could Jesus have approached them differently? Surely! He could have done a fly-by or materialized in front of them, instead of using the somewhat low-key "catch-up-from-behind" routine. Having chosen that method, he could at least have shown them his hands immediately or convinced them with a feat of supernatural knowledge like "Hi there, Cleopas! Why are you going to Emmaus and talking about me as if I were dead and gone?" Why this long-winded tour of the Old Testament when a new trick would bring in the verdict? Why catechize with Moses when you could mesmerize with miracles?

Isn't it significant that despite his new mode of being and his access to the Father, he did not appear with any new formula? He gave them more of the old, with ever increasing fervency and with an illuminating articulateness. True, the Gospels don't give us a lot of details of these sessions, but listen to the preaching of the apostles in Acts, part 2 of Luke's history, and you will hear it. Our response to Scripture will inform our understanding of Christ, and our response to Christ will determine our attitude to Scripture.

But what should influence our view of both Christ and Scripture? We should take our cue from Jesus' own response to himself and to his textbook, implicit in this chat with Cleopas. Let's take a closer look, and turn over a couple of roadside rocks.[14]

CHRIST AND THE OLD TESTAMENT

Clearly, Jesus' extended discourse on the Emmaus Road is a good example of his intimate knowledge of the Old Testament. He was soaked in its truths and thought patterns. He never neglected it or disparaged it. On the contrary, he continually drew from the full vault of its history and quoted from the entire range of its literature, by both direct reference and allusion, to illustrate his instruction, advance his argument, or reinforce his prophecy. His use of it was natural and effortless, as if it was the native language of his intellect and imagination.

He heartily endorsed a study of Scripture that produced the fruit of obedience; he commended the appropriate use of reason and diligence in the pursuit of practical ways to know God and please him, but he qualified such a quest with the reminder that spiritual understanding was not self-derived, but a product of the Holy Spirit's illumination and education. However, he roundly condemned the kind of scribal learning that claimed to understand the microbes of religion, yet could not recognize and diagnose a leper if he was standing on the other side of the desk. Academic endeavors that produced no spiritual understanding were abhorrent to him, as was a preaching of Scripture that elicited no response toward God. In the crises of his temptations and his sufferings, the Scriptures were the means of his rebuttal of Satan's assault and of his communication with his Father. In his ethical teaching, he reiterated the need for obedience of the law in letter but, more crucially, in spirit. He recovered the necessary relationship between God's commands and man's conduct.

For Jesus, the Scriptures were true and inspired. Because he acknowledged their authorship as God's, he unquestioningly and wholeheartedly accepted their authority with the same vigor he denounced those who abused them. He was uncompromising in his condemnation of scriptural knowledge that produced self-congratulatory elitism and sectarianism. He denounced willful ignorance of the Scripture, and the failure to take it at face value. He opposed human traditions that bent Scripture to the shape of their agenda, that denied or deleted certain truths, that falsified the facts or reinterpreted them to suit taste or temperament. He spoke out against hard, unyielding hearts that would not heed Scripture or receive it.

Essentially, Jesus gave Scripture back its voice. The personality of the Creator, the sovereign Lord of history, was unveiled, and the law was once again presented as a heartfelt expression of love rather than a heartless exercise in peevish limitations. Jesus' use of the Old Testament was:

- *Positive* . . . he affirmed it, accepted it, employed it;
- *Pointed* . . . he emphasized the specificity of its demands and implications;
- *Persuasive* . . . he applied its truths to convince of the need for repentance and right relationship with God.

CHRIST IN THE OLD TESTAMENT

It is said that the material used to make British naval uniforms has a red thread running through its weave. No matter where you cut into it, you will find a red strand. A cursory glance won't reveal it, but penetration of the exterior will yield the secret. So it is with the Old Testament. No matter which way you slice it, no matter where you begin to scrutinize it, you will find evidence of the continuous thread of the history of redemption as it inexorably unfolds its drama. Whether it be the ark of Genesis (salvation from wrath), the Passover of Exodus (blood sacrifice of a substitute), the atonement and Jubilee of Leviticus (the removal of guilt and the release of those in bondage), the uplifted serpent of Numbers (the deliverance conditioned by believing faith), or the refuge cities of Deuteronomy (escape from judgment); whether it be the direct prophecies of the Mosaic period (seed of woman, descendant of Abraham) or of the Davidic dynasty (a royal leader whose spiritual kingdom would know no bounds or end); whether it be the rich veins of three hundred years of prophecy (from the nerve center of Isaiah 53 to Micah's election of Bethlehem); whether it be the witness of the Psalms, the historic expectations of the chroniclers, the symbolism and typology of the ceremonies and ordinances—whether it be any or all of these, the fact is that to read the Scriptures is to discover infallible proofs and great news about Jesus.

For him to talk to Cleopas and the others as he did meant that he understood and believed the exactitude of the correlation between past prophecy and present history—between him whom the prophets had said would come in time, and who he knew he was at that very moment. It has been reckoned that 333 of the references to Christ in the New Testament have their origin in the Old. This is sufficient testimony to the importance of paying serious attention to the prophetic in the same way that Jesus and the apostles did. It speaks volumes about the rootedness of Jesus' teaching in Scripture, and about his self-consciousness as it was shaped and developed by his own reading of it. Above all, it confirms the supremacy of Jesus as the climactic fulfillment of God's brilliantly conceived and executed plan for the rescue and redemption of his creation. Frankly, it's a tale for detective buffs—the most compelling "whodunit" of all time. (But, Miss Marple, where is the body?)

CHRIST AND HIS OWN TEACHING

Yes, the Gospels record events and collect facts, but as we have seen, they are more than mere histories. Written from different perspectives for different audiences, they share a common concern to convince us of the uniqueness of Christ and to show us how he was the fulfillment of prophecy, not only according to the witness of others but also according to Christ himself.

Jesus' direct claims to messiahship and deity cannot be

tucked away in a closet to keep the religious world tidy. Try hiding an elephant in a washing machine! The magnitude of his view of himself leaves no room for a quiet and polite accommodation of Jesus in the Hall of Fame for Democratically Elected Saints.

Taken at face value, this apparent megalomania has been described as "rampant" and "imperial," but of course, the nature of his character subverts the charge of egotism. You have it all here on the Emmaus Road. Jesus was not suggesting some possible interpretations of Scripture to help them put a brave face on their sorrow and recover an outside chance of hope. No, he was teaching methodically, definitely, and conclusively that he is the subject predicted and praised in these writings. Yet all the time, he was in disguise and refused to disclose himself! He believed that the evidence, when related to the text, would speak for itself.

Without apology, hesitancy, or embarrassment, yet with humility, dignity, and assurance, Jesus:

- presented himself as the authoritative teacher (not "Thus says the Lord" but "I say to you");
- used the personal pronoun with consistent conviction ("I am the way, the truth and the life. . . . I am the light of the world.");
- commanded people to hear and obey what he said ("He who hears my word and obeys it . . . teaching what I have commanded.");
- called men and women to follow him ("Come unto me. . . . Take up your crosses and follow me.");
- testified to an intimacy with God his Father that was his inevitable portion as God's Son ("I and the Father are one.");
- claimed divinity ("Before Abraham was I am.");
- identified himself so closely with God that response to him was equatable with response to God ("Anyone who has seen me has seen the Father. . . . He who hates me, hates my Father.");
- accepted as applicable to himself both the descriptions of the Messiah in Scripture as well as the designations he received in his ministry ("You are the Christ . . . My Lord and my God.");
- received confession, forgave sins, bestowed life, healed

as a sign of his moral and spiritual authority ("Your sins are forgiven you. . . . Rise up and walk. . . . Today you will be with me in paradise.");

• declared that he would judge people by their attitudes and allegiance to him because eternal life depended on a response to his words ("Whoever does not believe stands condemned.").

For Jesus, what Scripture said, God said. Equally, his teaching was God's teaching. Therefore his exposition of Scripture and his explanation of the kingdom of God ("my kingdom") are communicated with an authority and an imperative equal, not to the voice of the great prophets, but more radically to the voice of God himself.

CHRIST AND THE NEW TESTAMENT

The acceptance of the revelation that God was incarnate in Christ and that he was the author of the Old Testament prepares the way for our understanding of the nature and necessity of the New Testament. Like Cleopas, we have the pleasure of discovering Christ in the Old Testament, but we also have the added privilege of learning about him in the New. Just as our attitude to and affection for the Old Testament was modeled by Jesus himself, so does his intrinsic involvement with the New Testament guide our acceptance of its authority and therefore our response to its instruction.

Jesus' endorsement of it is understood through the many ways that he anticipated and consciously prepared for its formation:

• he foresaw that beyond his own ministry there would be a continuing witness by the disciples to what they had seen and heard;

• he taught that the Holy Spirit would talk through them, teach them further, remind them of the things forgotten, guide them into all truth, equip them to teach others;

• he commissioned them personally to communicate unashamedly and boldly the gospel that had been directly revealed to them;

• he authorized them as apostles and empowered them to fulfill their mission to make disciples and authenticated their teaching with his blessing.

Like the Old Testament, the New presents Christ, and in particular, it shows how he continues to speak and act by his Holy Spirit, through the church, in the world. The various writers understood their inspiration and the significance of their endeavor to be consistent with that of the Old Testament. Their continual use of the Scriptures as a basis for assuring, warning, expounding, and proving establishes the continuity of the "prophetic word" with apostolic teaching. Their teaching, including the use of typology, was learned from Jesus, and the influence of his touch and tone, method and manner, is patent throughout.

This brilliant interweaving of the message of Jesus with the message of the Old Testament is perhaps best illustrated by the climactic book of Revelation that deals so emphatically and exaltedly with the risen, glorified Christ, yet 278 of the 404 verses contain allusions to the Jewish Scriptures.

In the New and in the Old, Christ is clearly the central figure, the fulfillment of God's plan for the world's salvation. It is not surprising therefore that the quest to determine his identity will lead us to Scripture, just as Cleopas was led there by Jesus himself.

 When Scripture speaks, Christ speaks. A personal knowledge of Jesus in the Scriptures is important for making sense of things. Why? Because he is God's answer to man's questions; because he is the keystone to the bridge that God has spanned between himself and his creation; because he is the cornerstone of the church that God has built for our community and of the city that God has designed for our eternity. Good theology begins with some good archaeology! We must dig with the right tools. (Get a good Bible translation, a concordance, a Bible dictionary, and to begin with, a good one-volume Bible commentary.) Effective archaeologists don't just scrape the surface with their heels!

Some people would rather be beachcombers and just pick up an interesting tidbit here and there. Others like the metal-detector approach and like to take shortcuts, only choosing to dig for the things of particular interest to them. Neither of these methods will yield the whole picture. Consistent, planned, methodical study will reveal the general outline of the foundations, and then, like all archaeologists, you will marvel at the smaller treasures that you will discover, whose significance will be understood in relation to the bigger picture. What Jesus gave his disciples, he can give to you as you pursue him through the Scriptures:

- *Panorama*—you will get a view of the extent of God's love as it is mirrored in his brilliant rescue plan down through the centuries;
- *Pattern*—you will begin to understand some of the fundamental principles of God's character and actions in recurring situations;
- *Purpose*—you will discover that there is nothing haphazard or arbitrary about anything that God has done because it is all related to his great purpose to redeem men and women and have a personal relationship with them.

Meanwhile, Cleopas was shocked when he looked up and saw the familiar outline of the village. Before the stranger had joined them, their perplexity had been hardening around two questions. Why had their own religious leaders disowned Jesus and handed him over to the Romans? Why would God appear to endorse his ministry one minute and abandon him the next? But right now, while twilight was dimming his physical vision, Cleopas' spiritual understanding was experiencing a power surge of light. Thoughts were sunrising over silent suburbs of mental darkness. In retrospect, the stranger had been generous and gentle. They were bigger fools and duller students than he had let on. Of course, he could see it now.

There was no contradiction between the Messiah's grief and glory. They'd completely missed the point. Without the violence, there was no victory; without the suffering there was no salvation; without the death there was no deliverance. Cleopas felt as if he had just mastered the unexpurgated version of the meaning of the universe. He was feeling as relaxed and unwound as if he were sunning on a Mediterranean beach. However, just as he was tanning in the heat of his new revelation, a momentary gust caught his breath. Like an irritating grain of sand in the eye, a simple question aggravated his peace—then where is he?

He came to as the stranger was referring once again to the

fifty-third chapter of Isaiah. He seemed to have a love affair with this passage, for he continually referred to it, not only as if it put his whole theological integrity on the line, but as if his very life depended on it. Darkness had fallen now, which gave the stranger's words a particular iridescence as he quoted: "He will see the light of life and be satisfied."

Cleopas slipped out of the overdrive of spiritual vision and double-clutched to a grinding halt. Far from satisfied, he was starving, and he could have done with a miraculous five-loaves-two-fish pack. He realized that the stranger had not stopped and was intending to pass through Emmaus, but his friend cajoled him to stay till morning. Once in the house, they decided to dispense with the foot wash in the interest of other priorities. Cleopas sat down to eat and was still sighing with a mixture of contentment and hunger when the stranger reached out and took the bread, gave thanks to God for it, and broke it. The fluidity of that action was a *deja-vu*. There was never time to bow the head. Cleopas felt the crust being pressed into his hand as those eyes pierced his soul. The stranger offered the bread to his friend and it was then, in an instant, that he noticed the hands. Before the exclamation mark could punctuate his cry of "Lord," the stranger was gone. A flash of heat suffused their bodies as they competed with one another to say that they knew something was up . . . and that they guessed it was . . . and that they thought they'd heard that phrase before . . . and that. . . .

They had begun their journey with hearts like empty grates. As they walked with him, they felt as if he was filling the fireplace of their souls, first with small kindlings of encouragement and then with the logs of heavier explanations. And now, their sudden recognition of him ignited it all. He had set the fire with his discourse, but his presence gave it flame. They were already on their feet, celebrating on each other's shoulder.

When you've seen the Lord, you've got to tell somebody. They were still arranging their outer garments to protect them from the night air as they hurriedly scampered out of Emmaus to retrace their steps to Jerusalem. Cleopas was like a detective who'd just broken the case after a long investigation, and he was repeating what appeared to be a vital clue: "This is my body broken for you." Back at the house, two broken pieces of a loaf lay on a rough-hewn table. Also left behind, forever, were two broken hearts. The old had passed away, and the new had come. The simple fact is that the knowledge and presence of Jesus make sense of everything.

BEACH WALK

MAP REFERENCE

*A*fter these things Jesus showed Himself again to the disciples at the Sea of Tiberias, and in this way He showed Himself: Simon Peter, Thomas called Didymus, Nathanael of Cana in Galilee, the sons of Zebedee, and two others of His disciples were together. Simon Peter said to them, "I am going fishing." They said to him, "We are going with you also." They went out and immediately got into the boat, and that night they caught nothing. But when the morning had now come, Jesus stood on the shore; yet the disciples did not know that it was Jesus. Then Jesus said to them, "Children, have you any food?" They answered Him, "No." And He said to them, "Cast the net on the right side of the boat, and you will find some." So they cast, and now they were not able to draw it in because of the multitude of fish. Therefore that disciple whom Jesus loved said to Peter, "It is the Lord!" Now when Simon Peter heard that it was the Lord, he put on his outer garment (for he had removed it), and plunged into the sea. But the other disciples came in the little boat (for they were not far from land, but about two hundred cubits), dragging the net with fish. Then, as soon as they had come to land, they saw a fire of coals there, and fish laid on it, and bread. Jesus said to them, "Bring some of the fish which you have just caught." Simon Peter went up and dragged the net to land, full of large fish, one hundred and fifty-three; and although there were so many, the net was not broken. Jesus said to them, "Come and eat breakfast." Yet none of the disciples dared ask Him, "Who are You?"—knowing that it was the Lord. Jesus then came and took the bread and gave it to them, and likewise the fish. This is now the third time Jesus showed Himself to His disciples after He was raised from the dead.

John 21:1–14

It was a tale of two fires. One fire burned amidst the tense, taut atmosphere of the high priest's house in Jerusalem where a police investigation was being conducted. The other was glowing on the Galilee beach where the water lapped listlessly against the shore. The first fire burned in the heat of the night, where heightened emotions were being held in check by the tight rein of law and order. The second one burned in the cool of the morning, as a group of disconsolate fishermen languidly drifted on the lake's current. But despite the differences that they represented in circumstances, convictions and company, there were similarities: charcoal, embers, and Peter.

It was amazing that Peter had even got that far. His presence in the inner courtyard was a tribute to his courage, for the others had long since fled. His perspiring muscularity would have convinced any observer that he was strong and confident, were it not for the dark and darting eyes that betrayed a confused and troubled spirit. But had he not drawn his sword in the garden—and even drawn blood? Had he not vehemently protested, "Even if all fall away, I will not!" When Jesus had predicted that he would be disowned three times within the next twelve hours by this sincere protester, had he not insisted emphatically "Even if I have to die with you, I will never disown you!"

In that last extended exchange in the Upper Room, Jesus had responded to a question of Peter's by saying, "You cannot now follow me where I am going, but you will follow me later." Was it not Peter who had aggressively replied, "Why can I not follow you now Lord? I will lay down my life for you!" His boisterous belligerence was in character, well-meaning but ill-considered. Silence and cogitation had never been his forte, and as always he had an immediate proposal to "go over the top." So although Jesus had said that he could not follow him, Peter had reason to believe, as he warmed his calloused hands by that fire, that he had already come farther than anyone might have supposed possible.

However, the intimacy of that last meal together was a far cry from the intimidation of that courtyard. The hostile public world has a way of testing confessions uttered in private. What is promised behind closed doors will surely be demanded in the open courtyards. Peter was learning what we all discover at some time or another: all the good will and good intentions in the world, all the protestations of concern and professions of commitment, do not in themselves guarantee our trustworthiness, underwrite our belief, or secure our salvation. If Peter had been challenged by a three-hundred-pound Roman guard, he might have toughed it out, but it was the indirect question of a slave girl that subverted his resolutions. "You are not one of the disciples, are you?"

It was several days later, though it seemed an eternity, that Peter's attention was directed to the flames of another fire. Throughout Christian history, the mystery, awe, and haunting beauty of the last chapter of John's Gospel have captivated and stirred imaginations. Dawning light rises throughout the sequence, but the scene fittingly begins in predawn, muffled darkness that fairly represents the smothered hopes and dreams of the disciples who, with no expectation of a future, have reverted to the past, to what they knew best in the good old days—fishing.

The hopeless return to the familiar was pivotal and potentially dangerous. The half-light and their half-hearted labors captured the frustration and aimlessness of life without Jesus. One commentator remarks that this incident was written, "to demonstrate once and for all, the reality of the resurrection." There was no ghost here, no hallucination, no flight of fancy, no figment of the imagination, no ethereal spirit. There was a distinct voice belonging to someone who was cooking breakfast on the beach. Again, Peter's mental reverie is shattered by an inquiry that has continued to challenge men and women who try to kick-start their own lives: "Do you have what you're looking for?" Another fire, another question.

For Peter, the first fire was a place of denial.

A DENIAL OF REVELATION

 Jesus came to reveal who God his Father was, and what he was like. Jesus' own testimony was, "I have revealed you to those who you gave me." Was it not Peter himself who had said, "You are the Christ, the Son of the living God!" His later denial erased the truth of who Jesus was, what he said, and what he did. He denied Christ despite the evidence and despite his experience—not once or twice but three times. The warmth of that fire could bring no solace to the cold denial of revelation. Like Peter, we may plead that we have not seen, but we cannot plead that it has not been revealed.

A DENIAL OF RELATIONSHIP

The denial of revelational light was one thing, but the denial of relational love was another. Jesus was not a proposition or a principle but a person. To deny relationship was to discount the very reason that he came—to restore broken relationship with God, to be the mediator, the reconciler. The heat of that charcoal could not melt the frigid denial of relationship. Like Peter, we may plead that we do not know him, but we cannot plead that we are not known.

It is a large company that huddles at denial's fireside. There are many disguises and many forms that it takes. Sometimes it is a shameless assassin, sometimes a polite public relations agent. In particular, there are two common forms of denial, one that works by avoiding Christ, the other by accommodating him. These are:

- *Forms of rejection:* practiced evasion, neglect, the suppression of conscience, the silencing of conviction, ignoring the truth, compromise, hearing without doing, lip service without heart sacrifice, willful wrong choices.
- *Forms of religion:* a creed without Christ, a form of godliness that denies the power of salvation, religious rites without spiritual righteousness, songs without worship, liturgy without life, congregational order without spiritual unity, confessions without conviction.

Any attempt to take Christ on our terms only is tantamount to denial. We'll let him in but not let him speak. We'll tell him what he meant without letting him reveal what he means. We'll tolerate Christ as icon, Christ as institution, but not Christ incarnate. We'll accommodate Christ patronized, Christ politicized, Christ fraternized; we can handle Christ in rubrics, Christ in aesthetics, Christ in myths and symbols. Acceptable as a Galilean teacher, he is shunned as the exalted Lord. Maybe he's a martyr, but not the Messiah. Perhaps he was a radical, but never the Redeemer. The sound of the cockcrow continues to echo with every denial, with the sorrow of every failure, with the shame of every unforgiven sin.

There could be no more hopeless picture than the one of Peter in this courtyard—a deepening night, a dying fire, and a denied Christ. In Luke's account, the final moments of this scene read as follows: "The rooster crowed. The Lord turned and looked straight at Peter. Then Peter remembered the word the Lord had spoken to him." As the lights go out, the desolate shout continues to echo in the darkness: "I do not know the man. . . ." And there the history of Peter and every person would end, were it not for one inescapable, incontrovertible fact: "On the third day, he, Christ, rose again from the dead."

AFFIRMATION

Which brings us back to that second fire. The voice from the shore told the hapless fishermen to cast the net to starboard. It seemed he had a perspective that they lacked. As the immediate heavy catch began to strain muscle and sinew, a sudden memory flashed through the mind of the quiet, anonymous disciple who was as thoughtful as Peter was impetuous. "It is the Lord!" he whispered. All who have struggled and wallowed in the upheaval of their denials of Christ, and who have suddenly heard this voice for themselves, will know what snapped in Peter's heart and what energized his tired body and wasted mind.

Many moons ago he had experienced a similar miraculous catch of fish, and he had fallen at Jesus' feet and said, "Depart from me Lord, for I am a sinful man." He knew from experience now that the best thing a sinful man could do was get to Jesus as quickly as possible. He was out of the boat with the speed and desire of a fish that has managed to escape back into its true environment. For all he knew, he was walking on water, and when he hit the shore, he saw the flickering flames of another charcoal fire, and his toes dug into the dirt, as if gripping the earth for fear of falling off it. For the millionth time, he heard those questions: "Aren't you one of them? . . . Weren't you with him? . . . Don't you know him?" Going, going, gone.

 The last time he looked into those eyes, it had been heartbreak. He dared not raise his head. He wanted to slam his hands to his ears to block out any unbearable word of justifiable rebuke. What happened next, in its deftness and softness of touch and tone, is nothing less than brilliant: "Come and have breakfast." The last decent thing that had occurred in Peter's life had been a meal with Jesus. Silently, he ate as the other disciples joined them, none of them daring to ask, "Who are you?" They all knew. They had just counted 153 fish in their net. They had just watched the characteristic flick of the wrist as it broke the bread and divided the fish. There was always food left over when he did that.

Who knows how the conversation eventually started? Maybe they just couldn't eat anymore. Once again, history uncannily repeated itself, and sitting by a fireside, Peter became the target for a question that was asked three times. "Simon, son of John, do you love me?"

"Yes Lord, you know that I love you!" Three times Peter made his confession by that fire as he affirmed his love for Jesus and had his soul restored. If he'd denied ten times, there would have been sufficient affirmations, for Jesus' redeeming love cancels the power of every sin. The risen Christ continues to confront the denials of our lives with his call to repentance and responsibility. His reconciling love does not condone our sin but convicts us of it; the penitent is not condemned but confirmed. His affirmation has two distinct elements:

ACCEPTANCE

Despite Peter's denials, despite his sin, despite his track record, Peter ran right into Jesus' acceptance. Christ's first words to him were, "Bring some of your fish . . ." Inclusion, not exclusion, marked his initiative to everyone. The invitation is his; the response is mine.

> Just as I am without one plea,
> But that Thy blood was shed for me,
> And that Thou bidd'st me come to Thee,
> O lamb of God, I come! I come![15]

ASSURANCE

The knowledge of his denials had riddled Peter with chronic doubt as to his standing with his Lord. Would he ever know the security of being sure about where he stood? The repeated affirmations insistently and tenderly convinced him of the assurance of forgiveness, of restoration, of renewed relationship.

> I know not why God's wondrous grace
> To me he hath made known,
> Nor why, unworthy, Christ in love
> Redeemed me for his own.
> But I know whom I have believed
> And am persuaded that he is able
> To keep that which I've committed
> Unto him against that day.[16]

 Nothing has changed. Jesus is not after our respect or our institutional allegiance, our church attendance, or our good works, but after our affection and love. No doubt Peter felt like the prodigal son in the story that Jesus told so well, the son who wanted to become a hired servant. Of course, forgiveness refuses to allow the son to live as a slave. The party that the father in the story throws celebrates the end of slavery and the triumph of sonship in the same way that Jesus' brunch celebrates the end of denial and the triumph of devotion. Sure, Peter wanted to do something to prove his sorrow, to warrant his forgiveness, to atone for his sin. Jesus does give him something to do, but the commission only comes after the confession, simply because Peter's security can not be wrapped up in his labors for Christ, but only in his love for Christ and Christ's love for him.

Once we have grasped that our atonement is Christ's achievement, then we are forever delivered from the foolish idea that we can do anything to make us more worthy of his acceptance and assurance. Out work for Christ becomes the evidence of our worship, not our worthiness.

Jesus and Peter are last seen strolling down the beach together. Consistent with his earlier teaching, Jesus reminded Peter that all obedience comes with a price tag. Peter's confession of love will be tested yet again in the public square. It will demand both service and sacrifice. Jesus sifted Peter's desires and motives for following him as he does ours. Is it for religious satisfaction or social obligation or humanitarian conviction? All motives are insufficient that are not rooted in a love for Jesus. Otherwise, the temptation to deny him will present itself at the first flush of suffering and deprivation.

Just when we think everything is settled, a shadow momentarily passes over the scene. Peter heard some shuffling footsteps, and looking over his shoulder, he spotted that quiet, thoughtful disciple following them—the one who had already managed to get pole position next to Jesus the entire time they had been together. He was the one who had raced him to the tomb—and won. As long as he was in the class, Peter felt doomed to second place. "What about him?" he suddenly asked Jesus, half nervously, half defiantly.

His question revealed a hidden insecurity, a residual jockeying for position in the acceptance stakes. He had to trust that Jesus' love for him was full-blooded and unconditional and that there was no business class or economy class on this pilgrimage—only first class. Peter had to learn that his decision to follow Jesus could not be contingent on any other circumstances or on anyone else's response. To worry about John's status or calling or abilities would only result in further denial of Jesus' will for him.

As it turned out, honors were shared as Peter's influence was primary in the beginning of the story (see the book of Acts) and John got the last word (see the book of Revelation).

It is always a tragedy when the influence of others denies God's will for our lives. When we ask, "What about my parents or my wife, my children or my friends, my career or my future, my this and my that . . . ?" we are told, "What is that to you! You must follow me!"

That first fireside had proven conclusively that Peter could not follow Jesus in his own strength, under his own steam, according to his plans and agenda. He could not go all the way then. But now he could! Jesus Christ's message and ministry have not changed. His acceptance of the denier and his gift of the assurance of forgiveness remain the trademarks of his love, the fingerprints of his nail-pierced hands. If he had not risen, we would all have remained silent and guilty around a dying fire, in the company of a world that had denied and crucified the only hope of salvation. Because he is risen, there is another fire. It is a place where life is redeemed and renewed, where the laughter of friends and the smell of breakfast are hallowed evidences of Jesus' presence. That fire still burns for all of us wherever hope has been beached. All of us who have said, "I do not know the man!" can yet cry, "It is the Lord!" We can leave the embers of denial for the hearth of devotion—today.

MAP REFERENCE

*T*o whom He also presented Himself alive after His suffering by many infallible proofs, being seen by them during forty days and speaking of the things pertaining to the kingdom of God. And being assembled together with them, He commanded them not to depart from Jerusalem, but to wait for the Promise of the Father, "which," He said, "you have heard from Me; for John truly baptized with water, but you shall be baptized with the Holy Spirit not many days from now." Therefore, when they had come together, they asked Him, saying, "Lord, will You at this time restore the kingdom to Israel?" And He said to them, "It is not for you to know times or seasons which the Father has put in His own authority. But you shall receive power when the Holy Spirit has come upon you; and you shall be witnesses to Me in Jerusalem, and in all Judea and Samaria, and to the end of the earth." Now when He had spoken these things, while they watched, He was taken up, and a cloud received Him out of their sight. And while they looked steadfastly toward heaven as He went up, behold, two men stood by them in white apparel, who also said, "Men of Galilee, why do you stand gazing up into heaven? This same Jesus, who was taken up from you into heaven, will so come in like manner as you saw Him go into heaven."

Acts 1:3–11

The pains and pressures of this world have played their tune across the entire keyboard of his human experience. He had always been dogged by the scandalmonger's gossip about his dubious beginnings, and those whispers of bastardy had been breathed wherever he went. He had experienced the hurt that originated in the misunderstanding of loved ones and the rejection of friends and hometown folk. He knew the discomfort of homelessness and the fatigue that came from being on demand all the time, not to mention the weakness that came from expending himself in ministering to others and the weariness that accompanied the unrelenting assault of the demonic. He knew the mental strain that came from a continual onslaught of intellectual criticism. He knew what it felt like to be deserted by those closest to him and betrayed by one of them. The horrors of mental torture that cankered the minds of those subjected to the cruelty of crucifixion were bad enough, without the ultimate spiritual desolation that he endured, alienation from His Father.

But underlying all this was homesickness, that gnawing ache that longed for his native country and his seat by his Father's fire. When he had originally left his home, he had not been issued a diplomatic passport. There was no heavenly embassy wherein he could seek safety, and he was granted no special immunity from the vices and vicissitudes of earthly life. But that was all behind him now as he entered the home stretch. Had he not taught that where your treasure is there your heart would be and that treasure should be stored in heaven? There was no doubt where his was kept, and he was moving closer by the minute.

It was no surprise that he was particularly adept at describing the emotions of going home, whether those of the returning, repentant sinner or those of the welcoming angels who were having a holy knees-up and exchanging extremely elevated high-fives. Whether it was a story about a lost sheep being found by the shepherd, or about a missing coin found by its mistress, he was able to illustrate the joys of reunion, with its sense of relief and recovery. His intense understanding of what it felt like to be parted from home is nowhere better seen than in the dynamics of his story about the lost son. There are no similarities between Jesus and the son, but the emotions of separation and reunion are authentic to Jesus' own experience and expectation.

If there is any prodigality in the tale, it is that of the father's love, spring-loaded on the veranda, ready to be released the moment the hinges of the gate began to swing. As it turned out, he hurdled the fence, for when he saw his son "a long way off" his compassion catapulted him toward the runaway. There is no record of moral drubbing or financial frisking, just a lot of hugging and kissing. How did he know that the son had not returned to wangle some more money? He didn't. He could afford to be separated from his substance but not his son. There is no more vivid a picture of heaven in the Gospels than the no-holds-barred, no-expense-spared party that exploded on the farm that night. There had never been a barn dance like it in the county, and never had the fiddle and the bow sounded so sweet or the barbecued beef tasted so tender.

However, there were some who never heard the band, for the music was only loud enough to wake the dead. If you did not know the loss of all things, you did not feel the joy of restoration. If you did not know what it was to be dead, then there was nothing alive about this carnival. The elder brother was unable to enter into the spirit of the occasion. Despite the availability of caviar, there's always someone who prefers dill pickles with extra vinegar on the side.

The father would not countenance the request of the son to be a hired servant. At those wages, a lifetime was too short to pay back what was squandered or atone for wastefulness and dereliction of duty. He was made to be a son, and a son he would ever be. If his sinful departure was at the father's expense, how much more shall his penitent return be underwritten by the same account? This was no paper-tablecloths-to-save-on-the-laundry affair. The one in whose honor the party was thrown could not slink into the corner or merge with the shadows, for he was the one who stood out a mile—the one who looked like a wealthy farmer, with his jewelry from Alexandria, suit from Damascus, and shoes from . . . where else but Rome? But why? "For this son of mine was dead and is alive again; he was lost and is found!" So they began to celebrate. How much more the joy of heaven at the homecoming of another son, otherwise known as Son of Man and Son of God, once dead but now very much alive again.

As it happened, earth got in on that party too. It was another day, typical of the others, but you could hardly describe it as ordinary if it was spent in the company of the resurrected body of Jesus. Mind you, the disciples had ceased to be shaken with surprise when he showed up now. They'd had six weeks of this coming and going. If there was any amazement, it was when he actually used the door!

What a time that was, for it seemed that at last they had him all to themselves. They hung on his every word as he ranged throughout the Scriptures, with his usual good wit and colorful stories thrown in, explaining his favorite topics of conversation: the kingdom of God and the Spirit of God. They concentrated the best they could, but they figured there'd be plenty of time to go through it all again and ask further questions. When they looked back on these days, they would remember them as a time of:

- *Convincing proofs:* "He *appeared* to them over a period of forty days and *spoke* about the kingdom of God. . . . He was *eating* with them. . . ."
- *Comforting promises:* "Wait for the gift my father promised. . . . You will be baptized with the Holy Spirit. . . ."

 There was no reason to expect anything untoward when Jesus suggested that they walk out to the Mount of Olives. None of them was complaining about either the peace they were feeling or the pace they were walking. However, although it seemed that time had stood still, it was obvious to some of them that this could not go on forever. Something incredible had happened, and it was not just going to be business as usual. What was he up to? (A prophetic question if you think about it!) It was time to pin him down, get the plan, begin to organize—scope and sequence and all that.

They put on their most intelligent voice and their most discerning look and asked what turned out to be the dumbest question. "Lord, are you at this time going to restore the kingdom to Israel?" Who knows what went through Jesus' mind. Should he laugh or cry? Three years of teaching, followed by a six-week refresher course, and this was it? Jesus could have been forgiven for disappearing there and then . . . forever.

In retrospect, his answer was extremely controlled and gracious. "It is not for you to know the times or dates the Father has set by his own authority." Of course, we'd have added, "Nor know anything else, even though you've been told it a hundred times!" They were still thinking the kingdom was going to be national, when it was going to be global. They suggested its establishment would be now, instead of gradual as Jesus had taught. They were thinking in temporal rather than spiritual terms. On the three main issues, they had scored zero.

Jesus continued, "You will be my witnesses in Jerusalem, and in all Judea and Samaria and to the ends of the earth." If they thought that he was going to unroll a map at this point and talk detailed strategy or even answer the original question, which he seemed to have avoided, they were very much mistaken.

No sooner had he said the word "earth" than he began to leave it, literally rising before their very eyes before melting, as it were, into a passing cloud. They knew instinctively that this was different to his other recent "good-byes." This was a distinctive exit, and they knew that he had made an entrance into a realm of being that would be his domicile for a long time.

The teacher did not even correct their recent error. He seemed to have left the classroom without finishing the curriculum. These guys were clearly not ready to graduate. He certainly hadn't left because they were a hopeless cause. On the contrary, he'd just commissioned them to be his witnesses. While they were sky-gazing, Luke described the appearance of two men who simply told them that he'd be back and they believed them and set off for home. Talk about extremes! One moment they had been concentrating so much on the earthly with its temporal and territorial concerns, and the next they were completely transfixed by the heavenly dimensions of Jesus' departure. They were about to discover that the link between earth and heaven was their obedience to get on with the mission they'd been given.

Let's face it. This is not how we would have organized the final hours. If we'd had anything to do with it, there would have been no final hours at all. We would have calculated the unbelievable potential that we had in a resurrected Christ, and, excuse the phrase, worked him to death. The itinerary for the next twenty years would have been settled, and the advance party organized. Jesus could drop in whenever he liked, so long as he appeared on time for the opening meeting. Just beginning a service with one of his "through the wall" appearances would surely convince folk. At the end of the message, he could literally fade out. It would be spectacular, especially after a miracle rally. But to have come so far and gone through so much and be in possession of such an amazing power now, with the world as your oyster, and to just leave it at the very moment the deal could have been clinched? Why miss such an opportunity? Have we traveled this road all these miles to finish "not with a bang but a whimper?"[17] Maybe the ascension was a high point if we're talking altitude, but what if we're talking plain achievement or business acumen?

These are all understandable responses until we stop and consider how Jesus had characteristically acted throughout his ministry. The conclusion that should be reached is that this event was utterly consistent with the pattern of behavior he had established.

When Mary reached out to snatch the cloak of the resurrected Jesus, she was unconsciously expressing the natural reaction that wants to localize Jesus and secure his presence on our terms, for our purposes. However, what is particularly noteworthy about the ascension is that forty days after Mary's desperate grab, there is no attempt to hang on to Christ. No one begs, whines, or pleads for him to stay. Nobody reacts as if he's been abandoned or betrayed. Even if they were too stupefied to respond then, there is no subsequent questioning or doubt about this event. On the contrary, their response was not to worry, but worship. It must have been an instinctive reaction, beyond their understanding of all the issues. There was a rightness and appropriateness that was praiseworthy, even if it flew in the face of all expectation. Though often neglected, or deliberately bypassed, the ascension is of a piece with the resurrection. You cannot have one without the other.

But how does it provide a fitting and logical epilogue to Jesus' earthly ministry and a perfect preface to the ministry of the church? In a word, it all had to do with trust.

 No one was securer than Jesus. As we've seen, he knew who he was and why he came, and he never overreached himself. He always deferred to his Father, whom he trusted with his life, even when he had no guarantees other than his Father's word that it would all work out.

JESUS TRUSTED THE POWER OF THE KINGDOM

Not only did Jesus not hang around to ensure the disciples' theology was all squared away, but he departed without even leaving a rudimentary organization, not even trustees. As it turned out, his confidence was not in systems but in seeds. In a strange way, he had become the farmer in his own parable, who had planted a seed and could now do nothing better than leave it alone while it turned out to be everything the packet said it would be. Then, of course, he would come back and reap it.

The message appeared to be that they could all get on perfectly well without it having to be seen that he was doing everything. Mind you, the temptation was going to be for the disciples to get in on the act as if the success of the kingdom only depended on what they were perceived to do. Such was Jesus' humility that he not only said they would have the joy of doing things, but that they would do even greater things than he had done.

Their actions did not create or construct the kingdom, however. Rather, they confirmed its presence and power, as established by Jesus. Far from creating a distance or an absence, his departure had the opposite effect. He was now continually present and close to them. All he had taught about heaven suddenly became a reality because the real Jesus was clearly now in its sphere of influence. Those strange explanations of their resurrection were now making sense too. Who he was at this moment was exactly what they were going to become. So instead of their faith vaporizing when Jesus disappeared into the cloud, it was substantiated. So many penciled promises now became etched in indelible ink, not least of which was the one about a place that was being prepared for them. Roll on the countdown for that lift-off.

JESUS TRUSTED HIS DISCIPLES

In a way, they'd received a backhanded compliment. It wasn't that Jesus had faith in their ability, but he certainly had a conviction about the power of that kingdom to be expressed through them, regardless of their imperfections. It would have been scary if he had not been so serene about it all. Of course, he loved them, and despite his intimate knowledge of their weaknesses and failures, he saw their strengths and potential. Before they had time to ask the coach for a time out to take inventory of the opposition and plan a new formation, the coach had left the field, and the ball was in their hands. To go home at this point in the game could only mean that the coach was assured about the outcome. He definitely knew something that they didn't, about themselves, their adversary, his own training techniques, and the ability of his assistant, who was already sending in the next play.

THE DISCIPLES TRUSTED THE PROMISE OF THE HOLY SPIRIT

The disciples' need for a schedule that they could bank on, that would give them an idea of what they could expect and when, was blatantly ignored. Dates and times were strictly for God's eyes only. Just as Jesus had to take his hands off all guarantees save the Father's promise, so they had to be content with no contractual agreements except the promise of Jesus that he would return one day. In the meantime, he would ensure that they received such power that they would conclude that it was as good as having Jesus around, maybe even better, because they could all have all of him, all at once and all at the same time.

THE DISCIPLES TRUSTED JESUS

The only possible explanation for their immediate acceptance of the ascension and for their resolute peace and patience in the years of persecution that lay ahead is the fact that they believed Jesus' promises. In submitting to Jesus they accepted the mystery of his plan and refused the temptation to demand a managerial flow chart or any tool that would mislead them into thinking that they could control the means of this kingdom's production or that they could incorporate its interests under their direction. An almost effortless sequence of events conveys the strength of their trust: they watched Jesus go, they worshiped Jesus, they waited for Jesus' promise, and when they received it, they witnessed about Jesus to everyone. The transition from a frightened lock-in to a fearless outreach is certainly explicable by the empowering of the Holy Spirit, but it is fundamentally premised on a simple trust that took Jesus at his word and that received without question everything that Jesus offered.

It all turned out just as he'd said. In that last gathering in the Upper Room, he had predicted that while the world rejoiced, they would mourn. True enough, the crude jeers of the crowd had coincided with their hot tears at the foot of the cross. But he had also said that their grief would turn to joy and that from then on, no one would be able to rob them of it. They remembered the illustration he had used: "A woman giving birth to a child has pain because her time has come; but when her baby is born she forgets the anguish because of her joy that a child is born into the world."

We seem to have come full circle. Our travels began on the Bethlehem Road, where we heard good news of great joy because a child was born into the world. We end our journey with a joy that Jesus likened to the news of another birth. Is there any way that the party being rapturously celebrated on the occasion of Jesus' homecoming could be equaled, that the joy could be matched? As a matter of fact, there is. It can only be described as two parties in one. You must take the unrestrained laughter and the smothering physical hugs of the father that welcomed the prodigal home and combine them with the unashamed tears of wrinkled joy and the tender embraces of the father who has just welcomed his newborn baby into the world. And what have you got? You have the joy of heaven that explodes when young prodigals come home to Father God and old men are born again.

Once home, it seems that Jesus left the front door open. A narrow road leads to that door. It winds through the hills and valleys of our human experience and traverses the world oblivious of creed and culture. Sometimes it seems to end at a lakeside, a river bank or an ocean shore, fooling the traveler into thinking that there is no way ahead until he discerns footsteps on the water.

Sadly, there are too many who have never traveled this road. Some did pull on their hiking boots once upon a time and began the journey, but never quite lasted long enough to get their first blister or see their first vista. Their squeaky new footgear has since gathered dust in an insulated attic. The good news of Jesus is that you can follow in his footsteps, regardless of your present evaluation of your spiritual mobility.

"I'M LOST"

Perhaps you have tried one route after another, seeking the end of the road, pondering the purpose of the journey, and one thing has led to another until here you are at another intersection of your life, lost and in need of spiritual guidance. Jesus specialized in helping those who knew they were lost. What you have read in this book is another example of his concern to find you and be found by you.

"I'M SIDETRACKED"

A while back you were traveling well, it seemed, but you were lured off the main road and ended up in unfamiliar back streets. Maybe you remember traveling Jesus' road many years ago, together with family and friends, but you now feel as if you are experiencing the nightmare of the modern motorist who has left the highway but can't find a way back on. Jesus puts people back on track in a way that makes up for lost miles and years.

"I'M IN A DEAD END"

Maybe the direction that you chose for your life has become a "No Through Road." The gold of the yellow brick road turned out to be a desert track. The open road that promised so much freedom has become a claustrophobic cul-de-sac, and there's no energy left to retrace your steps. Jesus said that he is the way that leads not only to a future in this life, but on and on for the life to come.

"I'M TOO TIRED"

Lethargy and disinterest will certainly keep you bound to the couch of isolation and introversion, of boredom and escape. You may have lost heart, feeling it's too much like hard work to hit this road and find out where it leads. It's frightening to be overtaken by exhaustion on the road. You begin to ignore the road signs, and eventually you succumb to wayside disaster. Jesus invited the weary to follow him, promising not only strength for the trip, but also rest.

"I'M WALKING IN THE DARK"

You are not antitravel, or antiwalking—it's just that you can't see where you are going amidst the gloom of your present circumstances and the fading light of your own insight. Jesus said that he was the full-beam light of the world and that whoever traveled with him would never have to walk in darkness.

"THE ROAD'S TOO DANGEROUS"

Maybe you've watched others who have joined this road and followed Jesus, and you have observed the changes that this commitment brought to their lives and the things that they left behind. You may have concluded that you cannot afford to take the risk. In a way, you're right. There is a cost, there are hazards, and travelers do suffer wear and tear; but it's better to finish the trek to heaven with a limp than the bus ride to hell with sound limbs.

"I'VE SEEN IT ALL BEFORE"

You say that you joined this expedition once before and that you've examined the flora and fauna of Christian experience, and you have no need to take a second look. If you did not find Christ on your travels, then there is a road that you left unchartered. Your stay in the hostelries of churches or in cathedral hotels may well have convinced you that you have seen it all, but did you find him?

"I'M TOO FAR BEHIND TO CATCH UP"

Perhaps you once walked this road with enthusiasm and joy, and you realize that you have been dragging your feet for years. Your commitment has dwindled, leaving you feeling that you are too far behind where you should be and could be. Jesus did not demand that you catch up, but he said that he would come alongside wherever you are and accompany you personally for the rest of the trip.

"I PREFER FLYING"

Apparently statistics prove that there is less risk in flying than in walking the road. No doubt the apparent speed and ease of emotional jet-setting and the stimulation of cross-cultural, cross-faith interests makes the invitation to travel some Middle Eastern byways somewhat of an insult. Flying a religious space shuttle may be more fun in this life and may appear to save time, but it will never get free of the gravitational field of human sin. While some argue that astral planing and aquarian channeling are the pleasant ways to travel, Jesus said that we should choose the down-to-earth road of his instruction, rather than the high altitude of our intuition.

"I WANT A LIMOUSINE"

Many religious transport systems promise to get you to your destination with class and clout. Their limousine services allow you to do what you like behind shaded glass and invite you to give your own directions to the driver and go where you want to go, so long as you keep paying the tariff with its hidden extras, including the nonrefundable deposit of your soul.

Regardless of where you are on the spiritual road map, you can get back on track. The coordinates that have been presented in this travel guide have led you directly to Jesus, where you have been given an opportunity to:

- Admit your disorientation . . . that your life is off track
- Come to a decision . . . that you will get on course and follow Jesus
- Accept his direction . . . for your daily life and its safe passage
- Commit for the duration . . . to pursue him to the end of the road

Jesus made it clear that there are routes which seem to be good ways to go but end in irrevocable disaster. However, we have also seen there is another road that bears his name. Jesus said only a few find it, but it leads to life. Therefore, though it may be the road least traveled, it is still the road best traveled.

NOTES

1. Michael Green, "Preface," *The Truth of God Incarnate*, ed. by Michael Green (London: Hodder and Stoughton, 1977).

2. C. S. Lewis, *A Preface to Paradise Lost* (Oxford: Oxford University Press, 1967), chap. 13.

3. Graham Kendrick, *Footsteps on the Sea* (Key Records, 1972).

4. Christopher Nugent, *Masks of Satan* (London: Sheed and Ward, 1983), 11.

5. Robert Farrar Capon, *Parables of the Kingdom* (Zondervan, 1988), chap. 3.

6. A. M. Hunter, *Introduction to New Testament Theology* (London: SCM, 1957), 17.

7. J. I. Packer, *I Want to Be a Christian* (London: Tyndale Press, 1983), 220.

8. Robert Farrar Capon, *The Parables of Grace* (Grand Rapids: Wm. B. Eerdmans, 1988), 125. Anything by Capon on the parables will illuminate your understanding as it has mine.

9. C. S. Lewis, *Reflections on the Psalms* (London: Bles, 1958), 97. It would be well worth your while to read the entire chapter called "A Word about Praising."

10. C. S. Lewis, *God in the Dock* (Collins, 1981), 81.

11. C. S. Lewis, *Mere Christianity* (Bles, 1969), 42.

12. Christopher Dawson, *Religion and the Modern State* (London: Sheed and Ward, 1936), chaps. 3 and 6.

13. Robert Farrar Capon, *Parables of the Kingdom* (Grand Rapids: Zondervan, 1988), 41.

14. John Wenham, *Christ and the Bible* (Tyndale Press, 1972).

15. Charlotte Elliot, "Just As I Am," 1836.

16. Daniel Whittle, "I Know Not Why God's Wondrous Grace," 1883.

17. T. S. Eliot, "The Hollow Men," in *Complete Poems and Plays of T. S. Eliot* (London: Faber and Faber, 1978), 86.